Marika Cobbold was born in Gothenburg, Sweden, where her father was Editor and Publisher for the daily newspaper of western Sweden. She was educated in Gothenburg but in her teens spent some time in England and France in order to learn the languages.

She met her English sailor husband when his Naval helicopter squadron was visiting Gothenburg. They were married in 1975. She now lives in Hampshire with her family. GUPPIES FOR TEA was her first novel and was selected for the W.H. Smith First Novels Promotion and was subsequently shortlisted for The Sunday Express Book of the Year Award 1993. Her second novel, A RIVAL CREATION is in preparation.

Guppies For Tea

Marika Cobbold

BLACK SWAN

GUPPIES FOR TEA
A BLACK SWAN BOOK 0 552 99537 1

First publication in Great Britain

PRINTING HISTORY
Black Swan edition published 1993
Black Swan edition reprinted 1993 (five times)

Set in 11/13pt Linotype Melior by
County Typesetters, Margate, Kent.

Black Swan Books are published by Transworld Publishers Ltd,
61–63 Uxbridge Road, Ealing, London W5 5SA, in Australia by
Transworld Publishers (Australia) Pty Ltd, 15–25 Helles Avenue,
Moorebank, NSW 2170, and in New Zealand by Transworld
Publishers (NZ) Ltd, 3 William Pickering Drive, Albany, Auckland.

Printed and bound in Great Britain by
Cox & Wyman Ltd, Reading, Berkshire

Do not go gentle into that good night,
Old age should burn and rave at close of day;
Rage, rage against the dying of the light.

Dylan Thomas, 1914–53

For Richard
with love

Acknowledgements

I would like to thank Elizabeth Buchan and Hilary Johnson for their invaluable help. Warmest thanks too, to Diane Pearson, my editor, for her belief in this book and to Sarah Molloy, my agent, for her support.

Special thanks to Richard Cobbold, Lars Hjorne, Anne Hjorne, Liz Bebb and Ann Drake for their help and support and to Jeremy and Harriet Cobbold for their constant encouragement.

Chapter One

'And there's the Admiral.' Sister Morris gave a cheery wave into the gloom of the Residents' Lounge. 'We like to sit him by the aquarium; reminds him of his seafaring days, I always think.'

Standing behind Sister Morris, a firm grip on the handles of his mother's wheelchair, Robert Merryman looked around him approvingly. Had it not been for the smell of disinfectant one could almost believe one was in a private house.

Sister Morris led the way upstairs. The walls of the first-floor landing were painted soft grey-green and on each white glossed door hung a ceramic tile, a number painted on it, garlanded with pastel flowers. She stopped at the third door on the right where a five tangled with a blue clematis.

'And here it is!' Sister Morris sounded as if she was about to announce the winning ticket in a raffle, 'Number Five.'

She lowered her voice and added, 'If you knew how many enquiries we've had about this room since it became vacant . . .' She flung open the door.

Robert leant over the wheelchair and peered inside.

'It's a very well-appointed little room, Mother, you'll see,' Robert said heartily, feeling like a Ford car salesman who knew that at the end of a day he'd be driving home in a Jaguar.

Selma Merryman, hunched in her wheelchair, tried to turn her head to look at her son. 'Robert, I don't wish to see. I have a perfectly comfortable room at home.' Her voice trembled, 'There really is no need for me to be here, my toe is healing very well.' But the protests by now had become mechanical, hammered too feebly into the wall of family decisions surrounding her. She was wheeled inside.

Number Five was a small room, the shape of a shoe box, and the smell of disinfectant was stronger in spite of the open window at the far end. The walls were off-white and there was a narrow bed with an orange nylon bedspread. High above the dressing-table, with its easy-to-clean melamine top, hung a bright water-colour landscape adorned by an ice-cream-pink sunset. Under the window with its moss-green curtains stood a chair, its seat striped beige and brown. It was the kind of chair, Robert could not help thinking, that you would never find in anyone's home.

'We've had new curtains put up, and there's a new floor. Well we had to, with the floor.' Sister Morris pursed her thin, cyclamen-pink lips. 'Even with the toilet just round the corner.'

'It's not a bad room,' Peggy Merryman whispered to her husband as Sister Morris busied herself around the place closing the window and fluffing up a cushion. 'Very clean.' Peggy, looking unhappy, pulled the collar of her green husky closer around her thin neck.

'You'll be much more comfortable here, Ma, you'll see,' Robert said, his voice like that of Sister Morris, a little raised.

'I'm in a wheelchair Robert, it does not automatically follow that I'm deaf.'

'Of course not, Mother, of course not.' Robert smiled nervously at Sister Morris, whose sandy eyebrows had jerked upwards at Selma's words. He walked around and squatted down, level with his mother. 'We'd better be off, I'm afraid. Time and tide wait for no man and

12

we've got a long drive home.' He took Selma's hands.

At the word home, Selma looked up, fixing him with eyes like pebbles, dulled by sand. She snatched his right hand back against her chest and held it there. Robert tried to ease himself free. 'Dagmar will visit while we're away, and Amelia of course; it's a good thing she's back in the country.' Still, Selma would not let go of his hand, her grip was surprisingly strong.

'Well, off we must go.' And with a yank Robert finally managed to pull his hand away. He kissed Selma on both cheeks, then gave her an awkward little pat on the head before leaving the room, his shoulders a little hunched as if he was avoiding a low beam. Peggy embraced her mother-in-law, tears in her eyes, and then they were gone, followed out by Sister Morris.

'Don't go yet, dear,' Selma called out, sitting where they had parked her, unable to turn around even to see them leave. 'Don't go.' But as she sat listening to the silence, she knew it was no good. Just as it had been no good when she had stood on the large stone steps at school calling after her parents; just as when, later, she had pleaded with Daniel at the quayside not to sail for Germany. If they wanted to go, there was nothing, nothing at all, she could do to stop them.

Sometime later, she was not sure how much – she got confused over time – there was a yank at the back of the wheelchair and she felt herself being moved.

'I'm Nurse Williams, Mrs Merryman. You come along with me and I'll introduce you to our other residents. You'll soon make friends, you'll see.'

'I'd rather not.' Selma raised her voice. 'If you don't mind, I'd rather stay in my room.'

'Nonsense,' answered Nurse Williams cheerfully. 'You don't want to sit here all by yourself.'

'I hated boarding school as a child,' Selma said as she was wheeled out of the room.

13

'Did you dear?' All the staff were told to use the residents' names, not 'dear' or 'love', but Nurse Williams tended to forget.

'Hated it!'

'Well, this isn't a boarding school, it's Cherryfield.' Nurse Williams sounded as if a problem had been solved.

They passed the kitchen, its swinging door allowing the smell of boiled fish to mix with that of the ever present disinfectant. 'That will be your cod for tea,' Nurse Williams said.

Selma straightened in her chair. 'Cod for tea?'

'Fish is food for the brain,' Nurse Williams chanted briskly.

'I don't have cod for tea. A sliver of smoked salmon on thin brown bread, yes; a small sardine sandwich maybe; but not cod, not for tea.' Selma's voice, with its breath of a Swedish accent, was firm.

'Call it supper then if you prefer.' A note of irritation crept in amongst Nurse Williams' determinedly cheerful tones. 'Here we are anyway, this is the lounge.' She pushed Selma's wheelchair into the centre of the room.

Wine-red Dralon curtains were half drawn against the spring afternoon and, from a huge television set, *Blue Peter* blared into every corner. Two upholstered armchairs flanked the French windows at the far end of the room, and opposite the television, lined up against the wall, stood a row of beige, imitation leather chairs, each occupied by an elderly resident.

Selma looked with mounting panic at the row of old people, some returning her gaze with little nods and smiles, the others continuing to stare ahead at the television.

'. . . and then you fold it like so.' The *Blue Peter* presenter, a purple tinge to her long hair, flipped back the corners of an empty box of cornflakes. 'And here you have it.' Her young face beamed out across the room. 'Your own stables!'

'If you don't mind, I'd like to go to my room now. I can't read with all this noise.'

'Funny how the old dears will get on their high horses all of a sudden,' Nurse Williams would say later to Sister Morris, over a cup of tea.

'Who are all these people?' Selma fretted. 'What is this place?'

In the still, auntly drawing room of the Old Rectory, Abbotslea, Gerald Forbes looked up from the file on his knee. 'A café! No, I don't think that's a very good idea, Amelia. You very sweetly gave up a perfectly good career to come and look after me, and to be free, you said, to write on your own terms. Not to become a café owner.' He looked down again at his file.

He's going bald, Amelia thought. His hair is all black and silky, and just at the top of his head there's a little pink patch. She said, 'Don't say café in that way.'

'In what way? How should one say it?' Gerald looked irritated.

'You say café meaning, "Nasty little place where you stop reluctantly for a greasy sausage because the pubs are shut." What I'm going to have is a haven. A place where writers write, artists sketch, shoppers rest and aspidistras grow.' Amelia was smiling again as she perched on the arm of Gerald's chair.

'If you expended a tenth of that imagination and energy on your articles, you'd be appearing in every magazine in the country,' Gerald said.

Amelia appeared not to have heard. 'And I must have a trio. You know, an old boy at the piano and two large, grey-haired ladies playing the cello and the violin. They have to be large so that one can see them above the aspidistras.'

15

She kissed Gerald absent-mindedly on the bald patch on his head. 'In the old days in Gothenburg, Selma would meet her friends in a place just like that, twice a week on a Monday and Friday, and sometimes in between.' Amelia leant back against Gerald's shoulder and looked dreamily ahead.

'Of course they wore hats. I'm not sure I could enforce a hat rule. What do you think, Gerald?'

Gerald sprang up from the chair, giving her a little shove on the way. 'I think you're waffling. I thought you said supper would be ready at a decent time tonight.'

Amelia sat down in the vacant chair and looked at him, hurt. 'Two years ago you were a struggling artist looking for a muse, your head full of pre-Raphaelites and artists' communes. Now you're back to being a country solicitor, the rules are changing.' She added, 'If at least we had children,' managing to seem longing and encouraging both at once.

'I can't see the rush. Lots of women have their first baby in their thirties. One of the girls at the office was reading this article the other day which actually said that older women make better mothers.' Gerald had walked over to the drinks tray and was pouring himself another gin and tonic, 'Top up?' He held the whisky bottle up to Amelia who shook her head.

'Poor Aunt Edith only left you the house in the hope that we'd fill it with the children she could never have,' she said.

'Aunt Edith was a dyke.'

'That's what I said, she couldn't have children. Anyway, you can't be a country solicitor without having a big family. Watch any television series and you'll see.'

'You watch too much television. Clarissa Edwards, our new clerk, gave her set to Oxfam the other day.'

'That's kind of her,' Amelia said. 'But she'll regret it in a day or two, people who get rid of their sets nearly always do. They have a honeymoon with themselves, reading all the books they always meant to read but never found as engrossing as *Dallas*. They play patience and discover silence, and after two weeks you'll find them next door, watching their neighbour's set.'

'When did you say supper was?'

Amelia sighed and got up from the chair. 'In two minutes.'

'Is this wise, my darling?' Selma had said when Amelia had told her she was moving in with Gerald. Sitting in the bay of her Devon drawing room pouring strong coffee into two tiny, gold-encrusted cups, Selma looked at her granddaughter over the spiralling steam.

As she moved, Amelia sniffed the air, drawing in the comforting scent of tea-rose, as much part of Selma as if she had been the rose itself. 'I'm doing it for love,' she had answered simply.

She reminded herself of that now, as she stood in the kitchen of the Old Rectory taking a casserole out of the combination micro-oven that had been Aunt Edith's last purchase. Amelia hated it and wished it was an Aga.

'Anyway, is it wise do you think . . .' She turned as she heard Gerald's voice uttering Selma's lines. '. . . For you to have children, with your family history, I mean?' Gerald stood leaning against the kitchen door, drink in hand, his eyes carefully avoiding hers.

Amelia looked at him appalled. 'What do you mean, "my family history"?'

'You know. Your mother, she's bonkers after all.'

Amelia continued to stare at him. She felt like someone who had shared her innermost secret with a friend only to find the same friend busy pinning it up on the school notice-board.

Then the telephone rang and Amelia hurried from the room. There were tears in her eyes, Gerald could see. With a mournful look at his near-empty glass, he drained what was left of the gin and tonic and thought of Stewart.

Stewart, his boyhood friend, had owned a pretty red setter and one day he beat it. It had been a careless beating, delivered with scant vigour, the cause of it soon forgotten. But before long Stewart was giving the dog regular whippings harder and harder, his face red with guilt and pleasure.

Until the first beating Stewart had been fond of the dog, but soon he hated it.

Gerald got up and put the casserole dish back in the oven. I could never hate Amelia, he thought, any more than I could hit her, but she irritates the shit out of me.

When he first met Amelia, at an art exhibition preview a little over two years earlier, she had just come back to England after three years away. 'Why Sweden?' he had asked, thinking that a long absence abroad would explain the air she had of looking at, rather than participating in, the scenes around her: an air of being permanently surprised.

'My mother's Swedish. Also, I fell in love with the son of her oldest friend,' she had said almost in passing, as they admired a large, gouache nude. 'He was married,' she had added. 'And one day I bumped into his wife and three children. Three children, all small and golden haired.' She had turned and looked at him directly now, her almond-shaped eyes opened wide at the unfairness of it all. 'They were feeding the seals at Slottskogen and that was it; I left him and came back here.' Then she had wandered across the room to study a seascape.

As he got to know Amelia better, Gerald found that her air of being a little at odds with her surroundings was constant and a source of regret to her. It seemed she had spent most of her childhood curled up in a chair reading and dreaming, feeling more at home in the world of her books (where children came in fives, mothers smiled serenely and fathers, stern but loving, steered their children through a life of mild adventures and cosy morality) than in her progressive boarding school or the immaculate flat where she lived alone with her mother.

'My father buggered off and left us when I was two,' she told Gerald on their second meeting, her soft voice enunciating the swear-word in clear, precise syllables. 'Then he died.'

When they made love for the first time it was her turn to surprise him, first by her passion, then afterwards by her obvious distress, as she dressed hurriedly and refused to speak of their lovemaking.

Weeks later he had said to her accusingly, 'Each time after we've been in bed together you behave like a deflowered virgin.'

She had thought a while before saying wistfully, 'I always hoped to be a virgin when I married, but it didn't work. Actually,' she went on, answering his question thoroughly, as usual, 'I was only sixteen when I first slept with my boyfriend. It was very odd,' she sighed. 'At school all my friends were desperate to lose their virginity but few of them actually did. I, who had a drawer full of white lace cotton nighties, fell practically into the first pair of outstretched arms. I didn't seem to be able to help myself.' She looked intently in to his eyes, as if she hoped he might be able to explain her life to her.

'I just wasn't prepared for it. I mean look at them; Pollyanna, Anne of Green Gables, the lot of them, cruising from girlhood to mother of multitudes with a purity that would have impressed the Virgin Mary.

'I ran off to my grandparents and locked myself away with Winnie the Pooh for a week. I lay on my bed there, crying for hours on end, banished by every upstanding, God-fearing character in every decent novel I had ever read. Banished to the world of *Kitty, a Teenager in Love*, and *Sister Barton Gets a New Doctor*.' Amelia had smiled weakly and shrugged her narrow shoulders.

Gerald could hear the soft, slow voice speaking, could remember everything it had told him, but now the words only annoyed him. He got up from the table and slammed the glass down on the sink. 'Why does everything always have to be so bloody complicated?' he shouted. 'Why the hell can't you just be normal?'

Out in the hall where the last shafts of evening sun were still coming through the leaded window, Amelia stood with the phone in her hand. 'Miss Lindsay? Miss Amelia Lindsay?' The voice on at the other end did not wait for confirmation of this before continuing in an aggrieved voice, 'Miss Lindsay this is Sister Morris from Cherryfield Residential Home for the Elderly. I know we are expecting you at the weekend but I'm afraid that won't do.'

As the voice paused for breath, Amelia asked, 'You don't want me to visit my grandmother?'

'Oh, but we do. We most certainly do. But at once. It has to be at once I'm afraid,' Sister Morris said with the grim satisfaction of the bringer of bad news.

'She's not ill?'

'She might well have a sick mind after what she said to that young nurse, but physically your grandmother is as well as can be hoped. I can expect you tomorrow then.' And Sister Morris hung up.

Chapter Two

All that evening Amelia fretted. What could be wrong with her grandmother? What made Uncle Robert think he had the right to scuttle off to Brazil, leaving Amelia and a useless Dagmar to cope? On and on she worried until Gerald snapped, 'Why don't you just call up and find out exactly what is wrong, not that you know anything is, instead of sitting round whinging at me?' Then he strode up to bed.

'I can't call now, it's too late, I'll wake them all up.' Amelia called feebly after him, remembering the days when he would have put his arms round her and told her gently not to be such a worrier.

The next morning she drove to the station in Basingstoke, having first fed the hens and watered the tomato and aubergine seedlings in the green-house.

Rich, black soil clung to the heels of her red court shoes and she had forgotten to put on the belt that, Gerald said, really made the skirt and jumper she was wearing. Amelia well knew the value of the right accessories but she often had her mind on other things. Not always more important ones, just different.

She arrived at the station in good time, she always did at railway stations and airports, and found a seat in a no-smoking carriage.

As the Plymouth train pulled away from the platform, Amelia picked up a novel from her large black velvet bag. Finding the right page, she gazed over the top of it, out at nothing in particular.

She thought of Willoughby, Selma's husband, dying in the Kingsmouth Cottage Hospital, the curtains drawn round his bed, separating his dying from the supper-time chatter on the ward. It was the night before Willoughby died that Uncle Robert first brought up the idea of a Nice Home. Amelia had been trying to sleep, lying in the high, mahogany bed where great-grandfather Jocelyn had died forty years earlier: peacefully, Amelia had been told. But she had always hated the bed; she knew that Jocelyn had lain tied to that bed by his own withered limbs, silently screaming, unable to fight off death's unsolicited advances. Now, she had thought, it was Willoughby's turn to lie fighting the Grim Rapist.

She had switched on the light and looked at her watch, it was three-fifteen. She had been about to switch it off again, when she saw her grandmother in the doorway, the two cats, Tigger and Tim, circling her feet.

'There you are darling,' Selma said 'I don't seem to be able to get this damned thing open. Here, you try.' She held out a tin of Whiskas. 'There's the opener; it's terribly stiff.'

'Mother, what are you doing up.' Robert, his hair ruffled but his tartan dressing-gown tightly belted, had appeared on the landing. He looked into the room and saw Amelia sitting on the bed, a tin of cat food in her hand. 'What's going on, Amelia?'

'The cats dear,' Selma said in a patient voice. 'They haven't had their dinner.' Robert had stared after her as she took the open tin and disappeared out on to the landing, the mewling cats in her wake. It was then that he had mentioned the idea of a Nice Home.

The next day, Willoughby died. The family, Robert

and Peggy, Amelia's mother Dagmar and Amelia herself, had stayed on for the funeral and Selma was grateful to them all.

She shouldn't have been, Amelia thought as she turned back from the train window and flicked over yet another unread page of the novel, because that week she had been on trial. The fridge filled with out-of-date yoghurt and small, carefully wrapped remnants of long-ago meals, the endlessly repeated questions, the fruitless shopping expeditions that turned into hours of aimless wandering, everything was taken down and used in evidence against her. Taken down by the loving, spying eyes of her family.

Peggy had stood speechless, peering into a grease-proof-paper parcel.

'Lamb chops,' Selma, who had just appeared in the kitchen, said helpfully. 'I wondered where they had got to.' She picked up a fork and stabbed one of the chops. Lifting it out of the paper she had looked thoughtfully at the mould that clung to it with spindly tentacles. 'I think they might be a little off. I really wouldn't eat them if I were you, dear.'

Then there had been Dagmar, wandering backwards and forwards to the bathroom to wash her hands and carefully spreading Kleenex tissues over the seats of the comfortable, shabby armchairs, before sitting down.

Robert, who didn't see much of his half-sister, had taken it all as further proof that their mother's days as a housekeeper were over. Amelia wondered at how her mother's obsession could once again spread like an ugly stain across other people's lives.

'I miss him, I miss him so terribly.' Selma's tears, her eruption into grief after days of stoical control, had interrupted *The Nine O'Clock News* and embarrassed them all.

Robert turned the sound of the television down, before turning to his mother with an air of infinite patience. 'You know, we all feel you would be so much happier at a Nice Residential Home, rather than wandering around this great barn of a place all on your own and with constant reminders of Pa.'

'I'm not likely to forget your father,' Selma had looked at her son with a small smile. 'Whether I'm here or somewhere else; I was married to him for nearly fifty years.'

Then Peggy found out that Selma had not had a bath since the day of Willoughby's stroke, since the day he had not been there to lift her into the tub. 'You must see that you need looking after,' Robert had said more sternly this time.

Amelia had turned to Selma. 'What do *you* think?' she had asked.

Slowly Selma had lowered the coffee cup towards the saucer, concentrating on her shaking hand, willing it to still. Her movement accelerated and the cup clattered on to the saucer. She looked up at Amelia with eyes that seemed to have faded, as if all the tears had finally washed the colour away. 'I want to stay here. This is my home.'

A month later, five days ago, Selma's house had been sold and Selma herself moved to Cherryfield. Amelia's objections had been strongly felt but weakly supported by word or action.

So, sitting on the Plymouth train, Amelia worried as much about herself, about her lack of loyalty and strength of purpose.

The taxi ride through the small town of Kingsmouth took Amelia past Ashcombe, once Selma's and Willoughby's house, now soon to be the residence of Mr and Mrs Desmond Hamilton, a local builder and his wife. Amelia looked up at the whitewashed house on the hill above the creek, its green lawns sloping down towards the water, yellow with the hundreds of daffodils that Willoughby had planted. The car turned a corner and Ashcombe disappeared from view.

Cherryfield stood square in its own grounds at the other end of the small town. It too was on a hill, it too was white painted with green windows, and Robert had debated whether the proximity and likeness to her old home would pain or please his mother. Would it comfort her to see across the river her home of fifty years? Would the view over the water from the green windows of Cherryfield make her feel secure? Or would it be to her, gentle, well-meaning torture?

'I think a move right away from here would be worse,' Robert had declared finally. And Selma, with the ill-fitting deference of an old woman to her son, had said to him, 'I know I'm a nuisance dear, but can't I just stay here, at Ashcombe? I promise I won't be any trouble.' She had given a little laugh that meant, 'As if I ever would be,' but her eyes were fixed intently on Robert's.

Robert had exchanged glances with his wife who, when Selma rose laboriously from her chair, nodded towards the spreading dark patch on the seat.

At Cherryfield a pretty, blonde nurse opened the door. As she stepped out to greet Amelia, a white petal from the cherry tree at the side of the porch drifted across on a gust of wind and settled in her curls. The nurse looked charming and very young. 'If you'd like to wait here,' she indicated a chair in the hall, 'Sister Morris will be with you in a second.'

Amelia sat down, feeling all at once quite calm. Nothing seemed to be seriously wrong and Cherryfield was at first glance as nice as Robert had described it.

She looked approvingly at the large vase filled with

blossoming cherry branches that were reflected in the highly polished mahogany table, and at the Redoute prints on the whitewashed walls. The sun shone through the coloured glass at the top of the door creating a drifting pattern across the brown carpet. There was a certain tranquillity about the place, Amelia felt, as she leafed through last month's copy of *The Field*.

'Leave me alone you bloody woman! I'm not sitting on that thing.' Amelia scrambled to her feet as she recognized Selma's voice, accented and furious.

'I'm telling you for the last time, I'll sit where I want and I'll pee where I want and that's all there is to it. I pay you enough.'

The inner door of the hall opened and a round woman in her fifties entered. 'Miss Lindsay, I'm Sister Morris.' She held her hand out, then withdrew it the moment it touched Amelia's. 'I assume you heard our little outburst. We have them all the time.' Sister Morris's sandy eyebrows jerked upwards and she clamped her lips together, as if to say that although far harsher words were queuing up to leave her mouth, she was manfully stopping them.

When Amelia said nothing, Sister Morris drew her breath in between her teeth and said 'I'm afraid it's all having a very disruptive effect on our other residents, not to mention the staff. Only yesterday one of our girls actually went home in tears.'

'I'm sorry,' Amelia said at last. She could think of nothing better. Then, as Sister Morris looked expectantly at her, pale green eyes protruding, she added, 'What can I do?' clinging a little longer to a world where grandparents disciplined their grandchildren, not the other way around.

'It's quite simple,' Sister Morris assured Amelia. 'Your grandmother must, I emphasize must, be made to understand that as a guest with us here at Cherry-field she has a duty to behave according to our rules and regulations . . .'

Amelia had a vision of Selma manacled to the wall of an immaculate torture chamber with Amelia herself standing beneath, shouting out the rules of Cherryfield Residential Home for the Elderly.

'. . . and that includes sitting on an inco pad on the chair especially allotted to her.' Sister Morris's voice quietened and her cheeks ceased to vibrate. Almost confidentially now she added, 'It's very strange how upset she got at my suggestion that she discuss her little problem with her family. I fear you can't be very close.'

Amelia was about to object that feeling close to someone didn't automatically mean you cared to have little chats about your urinary tracts with them, when Sister Morris spoke again. 'You know, I'm sure this refusal to look her incontinence in the eye and face up to it is half the problem. Now if it was me,' her face took on an expression of awe-inspiring jollity, 'I would say, "I'm afraid I'm incontinent so where would you like me to sit?"'

Sister Morris tore herself back to a less amiable reality. 'It's all about facing up to things, you know. You'll find your grandmother in the conservatory, she seems to like it out there. Have a heart to heart.'

'About peeing?' Amelia asked, but Sister Morris had already disappeared through the double doors.

In the conservatory, where scarlet begonias trailed from white plastic pots along the sills, Sister Morris stopped to point an accusing finger at the far end of the room. 'There she is, still in her wheelchair I see. Her toe was in a frightful state, I don't know what her doctor can have been thinking of.' And she bustled back into the lounge.

Amelia looked past the row of Cherryfield residents,

most of them connected like electrical appliances to bottles and stands, towards the far corner where Selma sat like a baby elephant, her bent, chubby back half turned to the room.

She did not look up as Amelia walked towards her along the row of chairs. A couple of the old people, 'Old Folk' she felt sure Sister Morris would call them when in a better mood, responded to her 'Good afternoon', the others continued to stare wordlessly out at the garden or inwards, to their own vaguely remembered, subsiding pasts.

Gently, Amelia put her hand on Selma's shoulder. Like an old-fashioned computer, slow to load the new information, Selma took her time reacting. Her head turned and as her matt-brown eyes focused, the expression of angry confusion gave way to a wide smile. She straightened a little in her wheelchair and put a small hand to her hair. It had lost its blue-toned smoothness and was set in the little scalp tightening curls she had always despised.

'Amelia darling, how lovely to see you.' She turned her face up to be kissed and Amelia flinched at the sight of the hair on Selma's upper lip and chin normally smooth and petal-pink powdered. Embarrassed for them both, and attempting to disguise the gesture, Amelia swatted at a non-existent insect that disturbed her with its imaginary buzzing.

'When was it we saw you, last week was it not?' Selma added with studied nonchalance as she looked intently at Amelia. 'You'll think I've gone dotty but I can't seem to remember.'

Amelia paused before answering. It was tempting to say in the same casual tone, 'That's right, last week,' instead of the truth, that she had not seen her grandmother since the funeral four weeks earlier. That same evening, Selma had sat at the head of the table,

28

still pretty in a black velvet dress, dignified in her laced-up sorrow. She had adored her husband but there she had sat, making conversation, facing her balding middle-aged son across the table in his father's chair.

But she was still the mistress of her own house then, and senility could be called forgetfulness as she moved around her own, comfortably arranged, household.

'It's been a little longer than that I'm afraid,' Amelia said finally, 'I seem to have been terribly busy.'

'Haven't we all?' Selma on autocue agreed as she was flung back to the days where she had indeed been busy.

'Jane Austen again.' Amelia picked up the thick paperback omnibus edition that perched on top of Selma's handbag.

'Have a sweet?' Selma bent down over the bag with a movement as if filmed in slow motion. Her hand shaking, she fished for the handles. Amelia was wondering if it would be tactless to help, when Selma caught the bag, only to lose it halfway in the air. As it fell, a bunch of keys dropped out followed by three boiled sweets, unwrapped and covered in fluff, a selection of copper coins, a flurry of credit card receipts and a Chanel lipstick. Last, a white lace handkerchief floated down, settling on the coins like a shroud.

'Silly me,' Selma said with a little laugh, then, 'You take the keys to the house darling, make sure the heating is put back on.'

Amelia was about to reply when she heard the sound of crying, snuffling, abandoned weeping. She turned to see a big-boned woman wedged into a dainty chintz-lined basket chair, like a large child in a doll's seat, tears rolling down her smooth cheeks.

A nurse appeared with a watering-can and began

watering the begonias. After a couple of minutes Amelia went up to her, tapping her softly on the shoulder to catch her attention. 'She seems distressed,' she said pointing to the weeping woman.

The nurse turned round and smiled soothingly at her. 'Oh that's all right, that's Mrs Wells.' And that apparently explained all. She continued to water the plants, and after waiting a moment, Amelia went back to Selma, looking surreptitiously as she passed at the still weeping Mrs Wells.

'I'll take you outside.' Amelia picked up Selma's things and began pushing the chair, careful to avoid the rubber tubes and thin legs stretched out under crocheted blankets.

Selma looked around her with distaste. 'Who are these people?' she asked in a carrying whisper. 'I can't remember asking them here.'

Amelia brought Selma into the dappled shadow of a large cherry tree. She secured the brakes and sat down herself on the wooden bench splattered with bird-droppings.

'Ghastly lot of old people in there,' Selma said conversationally. Then, 'How's the poetry?'

'Oh that,' Amelia said, surprised that her grandmother should remember. 'They say it's difficult being a genius. I would say not half as hard as not being one.'

'Don't I know, don't I know.' Selma rocked in her wheelchair, laughing quietly. 'When I was a girl, how I longed to hear people say, not, "Doesn't Selma play well," but, "Listen to Selma, she plays like an angel."'

And Amelia felt happier; her grandmother was not so much changed after all.

A cherry blossom fell from the branch above, landing at Selma's feet, then another. Like a snowflake, Selma thought. How long since she had seen snow.

As she closed her eyes she could almost feel the

crunch under her soles of the crisp, early morning snow as she ran through the streets back home, late for school as always, her breath ahead of her like a smoky standard. That piercing scream from above, a sound, she had thought, like that of the peacocks at home being chased across the lawn. When she looked up, she had seen Mrs Hollander, all dressed in white, standing on the roof of the great apartment house. Another piercing scream and Mrs Hollander lifted her shrouded arms and leapt. In front of Selma's eyes she fell through the air like a giant snowflake, down, down, spinning, before hitting the pavement, turning the fresh snow red. 'Poor flying Dutchman,' Selma said out loud.

'What was that, Grandma?' Amelia leant forward on the bench. But before Selma had time to answer, they heard a voice calling.

'There you are.' Sister Morris stepped determinedly towards them through the daisies in the damp grass. 'Had our little chat?'

'Mrs . . . ? Oh you must think I'm dotty but I can't remember your name,' Selma laughed merrily.

'Sister Morris, Mrs Merryman, I'm Sister Morris.'

'Of course you are. I don't believe you know my granddaughter.'

'Oh yes, we have met. In fact we've only just had a little talk. About our problem.' Sister Morris bent down to come face to face with Selma, her expression one of jollity. She's going to pinch her cheeks, I know it, Amelia thought, but Sister Morris straightened up, contenting herself with a conspiratorial little nod in Amelia's direction. Selma looked uncomprehendingly at her.

'Our toilet difficulties,' Sister Morris explained helpfully.

Selma couldn't turn away, but for a moment she

closed her eyes. Then she said slowly, 'I'm afraid I don't know what you're talking about. Now if you'd excuse us, I'd like to give Amelia some tea. Amelia darling, could you help me into the drawing room?'

Inside, Selma hailed an auxiliary. 'Would you be so kind as to bring us some tea.'

'Tea's not until half six Mrs Merryman, you know that.'

'I was not referring to supper.' Selma, crumpled in her wheelchair, hand shaking, attempted haughtiness. 'If it's not too much trouble we'd like a cup of tea please and a slice of cake and a biscuit or two.'

'You'll have your biscuit with your cocoa, Mrs Merryman.' The young nurse spoke firmly now, but she turned to Amelia with a friendly grin. 'They get ever so greedy you know,' she said in a stage whisper.

'I'm so sorry,' Selma said to Amelia, 'I don't seem to be able to offer you tea.'

'It doesn't matter,' Amelia said quickly. 'I had an enormous lunch on the train.'

By the fish-tank something stirred. 'Nonsense, damned cheek. If you want a cup of tea, you should have one.' And the Admiral sank back in his chair.

'Good afternoon everyone.' A small figure being wheeled into the lounge, raised an emaciated arm and gave a cheery wave.

Selma looked up with distaste. 'There's that tiresome woman. She never stops talking.' Ignoring her furious shaking of the head, the nurse transferred, first the inco pad, then the woman herself, to the chair next to Selma. 'Here's Miss White for you.' She sounded congratulatory.

Miss White was aptly named, Amelia thought, as the tiny woman continued to beam at her. Her large eyes were of such a watered-down blue that they seemed almost colourless, and the face, its complexion the texture of crumpled tissue paper, was framed by white curls tumbling over her tiny shoulders. She sat upright in the chair, the edges of the inco pad showing at the sides of her baby-blue polyester dress.

'I'm Phyllis White.' The little woman reached out a surprisingly large hand for Amelia to grasp. 'I'm a new girl like your nan. It's lovely here, don't you think? Always someone to chat with. Of course some of the old things are a bit quiet, but even a quiet one is better than no-one, that's what I say.' She laughed uproariously and Amelia looked across at Selma who sat scowling and jealous at Miss White's hijacking of her visitor.

An hour later, Nurse Williams came in with a young auxiliary in tow. 'Tea-time,' she announced cheerfully, as they began helping the residents back in their wheelchairs. The Admiral and some others needed help only to get out from their chairs, then with the aid of walking frames they proceeded with surprising speed towards the dining room.

The evening meal, any meal, Amelia thought, must be a break from the monotony of the Cherryfield day, a Geriatric Happening, even when it consisted of three pilchards and half an egg on a lettuce leaf.

'Darling, don't go yet.' Selma's voice was light but her podgy hand gripped Amelia's wrist like a trap.

'I'll walk you to the dining room,' Amelia said. 'And I'll be here again tomorrow morning before I go back.'

Once at the table though, seated between the Admiral and Miss White, Selma seemed not to mind Amelia going. She obediently turned her face up to be kissed then, as Amelia walked off, she lifted a piece of hard-boiled egg carefully to her mouth. Pale yellow crumbs settled on her lips and chin as she chewed and picked at her food.

'Now then Mr Hurst!' Amelia turned in the doorway

to see a nurse hurrying over to the table next to Selma's, where Mr Hurst, a fit looking elderly man with a mild, faraway expression stuck his fork purposefully into his neighbour's pilchard. The nurse directed his hand back over his own plate before hurrying over to another table, where some milk had been upset. As Amelia left she saw Mr Hurst calmly attacking his neighbour's plate once more.

Chapter Three

Amelia lay on the bed in her room at The Anchor Inn, a picture of sloth.

It was ten o'clock at night. She had had dinner in the small dining room: roast shoulder of lamb with potatoes and two vegetables. She had called home. Gerald had sounded in a hurry but said he was staying in watching television. He had used that voice too, his Star Wars voice, able to destroy any attempted intimacies before they hit him. These days everything she did seemed to irritate him. Take the other evening. She had run herself a hot bath, scenting it with half a bottle of gardenia oil. Then she had waited for his car to turn up the road before running to the bathroom and jumping into the tub, only to leap out again as she heard the front door slam. All so she could greet him in the hall, wrapped only in a towel, her body warm and scented from the water. Of course it had been a bloody silly idea, she thought now, wiping a tear from her eye, but still, there had been no need for him to be so unpleasant. She winced at the memory: 'Have you got nothing better to do with your day than lounging around in the bath. I would have thought the least I could expect after a hard day is to find you dressed.' So embarrassing. And so unfair: on that particular day she had started and all but finished a major article on the Hampshire watercress beds she was doing for a Swedish magazine.

She sighed, Gerald was right though, generally she

was disorganized, completely lacking in any sense of urgency. She lay on the hotel bed, weighed down by the heap of things she ought to be doing: about Selma, about the collection of poems Gerald had rightly predicted would never be completed, and about the unanswered correspondence that piled up with the unread books on her bedside table back at the Old Rectory.

This lack of self-discipline was what Amelia most disliked about herself, the way she had of floating away from tasks, of knowing exactly what needed to be done, and then doing nothing.

Sighing, she sat up on one elbow, staring out of the window and at Ashcombe across the harbour. The house was in darkness. Had Selma still been living there, lights would have come on in room after room like bright beads threaded on a dull string, as she pottered through the house in her emerald green, velvet dressing-gown.

She would feed the cats, dust a little if the urge took her, chatter to her husband, her voice sometimes within hearing distance, sometimes not. Neither of them minded, it was the comfortable knowledge of the other being there that mattered.

Soon she would pour hot milk into two mugs, hers, twice mended and decorated with a marmalade cat, and Willoughby's owl with the hairline crack running through. Both mugs had been Christmas presents from Amelia over twenty years earlier.

Willoughby had been good at mending china. The restoring of an object to usefulness always gave him great satisfaction.

Amelia had always loved the oldness of the things in her grandparents' house, the familiarity of them. In the bright flat she shared with her mother things never grew familiar, they were thrown out before there was time. As Dagmar's obsession with cleanliness grew stronger, the life expectancy of possessions, clothes, shoes, ornaments, kitchen utensils, became shorter. Once when Amelia was nine she had asked her mother, half jokingly, half apprehensively, if she, Amelia, got really dirty, would her mother throw her out too?

Dagmar had looked at her and laughed for such a long time that Amelia had got bored waiting for an answer. Then, suddenly, the laughter had turned to crying and Dagmar had fled the room.

'You must be patient with your mother,' Selma had said later when the child told her what had happened. She took Amelia's hand. 'She's frightened you see.'

Amelia liked the feel of her grandmother's hand, soft like the chamois leather she used to polish the windows in the flat. Her mother's hand felt more like a nutmeg grater. 'Frightened of what?' she had asked.

Selma had shrugged her shoulders and looked sad. 'Life, I think. And that is too big a fear for anyone to cope with. So what does your mother do?'

Amelia, her slanted eyes fixed intently on Selma's face, shook her head.

'She carves the fear up, like you've just cut that big piece of chocolate cake I gave you, into manageable pieces. She creates little fears, bite-sized ones and concentrates on them. So many times I've talked to her, tried to winkle the problem from her like meat from a crab claw.' She shook her head.

'I wish she was more like you,' Amelia had said, looking adoringly at her grandmother.

Selma had been a child's, or a man's, idea of beauty. There were no edges to her, everything was rounded, arms, chin, even the tip of her nose. She wore soft, flowing dresses and Amelia had never seen her in trousers. Her hair, black, then slowly turning bluey-grey, was brushed smoothly from her forehead and behind the ears, cut in softly at the nape of the neck.

Amelia always saw her visits to Ashcombe as a boat ride in the sunshine down a smooth lazy river. With her mother the boat was out at sea and you never knew when the next storm would gather. Maybe it was because Ashcombe had for so long been a refuge from the newness and brightness of the flat that Amelia had not noticed when it slid from cosy disorder into squalor. Dagmar, of course, had stopped visiting after Tigger the tom had been sick in her suitcase as it lay open on the spare room bed, waiting to be unpacked. But as silent dust settled layer upon layer on every surface, dulling the colour of the china ornaments as passing centuries muted Old Masters, Peggy had said something would have to be done.

Then Willoughby died and the thin mask of competence had been torn from Selma, revealing a frightened and confused old woman who did not always remember to grieve for the husband she had adored.

Reluctantly, yawning, Amelia heaved herself off the bed and walked into the bathroom to remove her make-up. She slapped a large clot of expensive night cream on her clean skin and wondered why people said 'as natural as brushing your teeth'. Brushing teeth was a bore, particularly when there was no-one next to you in bed to repel with your bad breath.

Alone or not, Selma would never have gone to bed without brushing her teeth, Amelia thought. Dagmar, strangely enough, would. Amelia's mother was selective in her quest for cleanliness, she had to be. When you have disinfected all the hangers in your wardrobe twice in a day, there is so little time and energy left for normality.

Amelia pottered back to bed feeling angry. Gerald was right; her mother was bonkers. Selma, therefore, had no right to abscond into old age; Amelia needed her. Drifting down a stream of self-pity, she fell asleep.

'I've brought you some clotted cream fudge from the Dairy.' The next morning back at Cherryfield Amelia kissed Selma and handed her the small, wrapped box.

'What a sweet girl.' Selma smiled, then began to untie the string. It seemed impossible that, with her shaking right hand, she would ever succeed, but Amelia knew better than to offer her scissors; her grandparents had never been mean, but string was untied and carefully rolled and stored.

'I haven't got my glasses on,' Selma said. 'You try.'

The box was opened and placed on the teak-veneered coffee table. Selma was silent as she bent over the fudge, carefully choosing the largest piece. While she chewed it, slowly at the front of her mouth, her fingers were already searching for another one.

Amelia looked away, out over the garden where the wind strewed the cherry blossom across the grass. She could not bear to watch Selma, frowning, rapt with concentration as if a box of fudge was an event.

'You have one, darling,' Selma said finally, putting yet another sweet in her mouth before giving the box a little push in Amelia's direction. Then she looked at her hard and added with studied nonchalance, 'Of course Robert promised I would be back home by my birthday.'

Amelia, about to have a piece, stopped, her hand halfway to her mouth. 'Robert said that?'

'I don't see why you should be so surprised. You weren't surely expecting me to stay in this place for ever.' Selma laughed a little at the absurdity of the idea. 'My toe is healing very well as a matter of fact.' She stretched her bandaged left foot in its Scholl sandal out for inspection, wincing as it touched the leg of the chair.

'They are trying their best here, I can see that,' she conceded. 'The staff on the whole are very nice, but I couldn't live here. Those dreadful old people.' Selma paused meaningfully, rolling her eyes in the direction of a couple of her fellow residents propped up in chairs along the conservatory wall. 'The only one worth talking to is Admiral . . . Oh dear, I can't seem to think of his name.'

Amelia sat quietly, feeling as if she was talking to a robot who'd had a small but essential part from its control panel removed, making its behaviour just one step to the side of normal. 'So Robert said you would be home for your birthday?' she repeated.

'I just told you so, darling. Are you not paying attention? Oh look, there's the Admiral now.' Selma raised herself up a little in her chair and gave a small wave.

Admiral Mallett was steered through the conservatory doorway by a large young man in his mid-twenties, with untidy brown hair and a strong-featured, but amiable face.

'I don't believe you know my son, Henry.' The Admiral looked on proudly as Henry shook hands first with Selma and then Amelia. As if he was doing something outstandingly clever, Amelia thought, amused.

'Sailor, like his old man,' the Admiral said, as Henry helped him into the chair next to Selma. 'I married late you know. Henry here came along when I was practically in my dotage.'

'I was just telling my granddaughter that I'm not expecting to stay here for very long,' Selma said rather grandly.

'Good for you,' said the Admiral. 'Jolly good for you.' He cleared his throat noisily. 'Of course I've sold my house. Voluntary confinement this. The old place became much too large once my sister kicked the bucket, bless her soul. And of course Henry isn't around very much.' He shrugged his shoulders and grinned. 'Well that's the Service for you.'

'The Navy could stand on its head and blow raspberries at my father and he would smile indulgently and say, "Well that's the Service for you,"' Henry said, smiling indulgently himself. He had a surprisingly boyish, light voice coming from such a large frame, Amelia noticed.

'Well this isn't a bad place, food's all right, what there is of it. The nurses are nice enough gals.' Admiral Mallett spoke with all the determination of a man persuading himself. 'Of course the place advertises itself as "For the Active Elderly". Can't say that I've seen much of the active so far, present company excepted of course.' He indicated Selma with a little bow.

'It's my wretched toe,' Selma said.

'And then there's Death Row,' the Admiral continued.

'Death Row?' Amelia shot Selma an anxious glance.

'That's the other part of Cherryfield, the Annexe,' Henry explained with a little smile, choosing his words carefully. 'For the less active residents, the ones needing a little more care.'

'For the chronically dying, shall we say,' the Admiral intercepted with a hoarse laugh that ended in a loud cough.

Selma stirred uneasily in her chair. 'Of course I haven't played tennis for months,' she said. The Admiral and Henry looked a little surprised.

'Look, coffee.' Amelia pointed to the door where Nurse Williams came in, carrying a huge tray of blue, plastic cups and saucers. Behind her followed a

41

procession of wheelchair-bound residents in various stages of awareness, a kind of geriatric pageant, Amelia thought.

'I said to Sister Morris, why don't we have our coffee in the conservatory, it's such a lovely morning!' Nurse Williams exclaimed to anyone who cared to listen.

'Over here, Orderly,' Miss White commanded with some authority, 'with my new friends.' She was placed between Selma and the Admiral. 'And who is this?' She twinkled at Henry who had stood up as she arrived. 'Navy like your father, I say. Have you been to Crete? You must have been to Crete. I had such a wonderful trip there. We went by bus, the whole way.'

Henry smiled encouragingly at her and Amelia wished he hadn't. 'Of course there was the ferry . . . But we were still on the bus, if you see what I mean. Lovely people they were on that trip. Then I've always been lucky that way. Some were not as nice as they could have been though, I must say, a bit offhand. That courier girl. She wasn't what I would call nice. No . . . I told her I liked a seat at the front, but after the first day she changed me right to the very back of the bus. I felt the motion of the vehicle very badly. But people are ever so nice.' Miss White paused at last, to help herself to a biscuit from the plate Henry held out to her.

Selma's cup clattered as she placed it back on the saucer, Miss White dunked her biscuit and sucked noisily on it before munching it between thin lips. 'I wrote travel features for the *Hereford and Worcester Gazette*,' she said, having finished her biscuit and established there were no more to come. ' "A Spinster's Journey: Europe Through My Bus Window". Very popular they were. Until the fashion changed.'

'Amelia dear,' Selma said, 'take me out in the garden, there's a sweet girl.'

Amelia stood up with an apologetic smile.

Outside, Selma lifted her face to the sun, closing her eyes and sighing contentedly. The warmth of the sun on your skin, Amelia thought, was one of life's few enduring pleasures.

Until Willoughby died Amelia had never worried about what happened to a corpse once inside the grave; she only knew she didn't like the thought of being cremated. But, since the funeral, she had been unable to ward off images of Willoughby's kind face and short-sighted blue eyes at various stages of decomposition that haunted her with no warning.

Not so many weeks ago, on a day like this one, he would have been gardening, she thought. His square hands, like a mole's paws, digging away at weeds, planting out seedlings for a summer he would not see.

'Amelia,' Selma's hand gripped her shoulder, the long nails digging in hard. 'How did grandpa die? I know you must think I've gone completely mad, but it's all so confused.' Selma's eyes pleaded with her to understand.

Amelia thought of Willoughby lying in the narrow hospital bed, as breath by laboured breath he approached death. She thought of Selma visiting and of her calm as she sat stroking his hand, talking all the while. At times something close to irritation had crept into her voice; for so long he had been the strong one, the trellis round which she had entwined the branches of her contented existence. 'So what are you doing,' she seemed to ask, 'lying here broken?'

'He had a stroke, he died in hospital a week later.' Amelia's voice was gentle but, as she looked at her grandmother's pinched face and anxious eyes, she felt as if she was shooting her in the heart with arrows dipped in cotton wool. 'He went into a coma and he just never came round. It was pneumonia that actually

43

killed him.' 'The old man's friend,' the young doctor had called it.

'He was never uncomfortable, one of us was always there.' Amelia took Selma's hand, forcing the constant shaking to cease for the moment.

'Thank you darling,' Selma sighed. 'I miss him so much, you know. It's worst at night. I dream about him all the time, and when I wake up I believe he's still there. Then I remember.' She stared out over the garden, in silence. Amelia sat feeling useless, aware that the one thing her grandmother wanted, her husband, she could not give her.

Selma's eyelids fluttered and closed, her chin falling against her chest, then she snorted loudly and, with a little shiver, opened her eyes again. She stared at Amelia for a second – she's wondering who the hell I am, Amelia thought – before saying, 'I know it's very kind of these people to have me to stay, but I'd much rather be home. I'm sure once I'm back with my own things I'll be as right as rain.'

Amelia smiled weakly, thinking that it might be worth the air fare to Brazil just to go and throw something hard at Robert. Selma fell asleep again, her grey-toned cheek resting against the back of the wheelchair.

'My father's asleep too, in there.' Amelia turned round to find Henry looking down at them, smiling.

'It strikes me,' Amelia said fiercely, 'that there will have to be an awful lot of good things in one's life before it compensates for this.' And she gesticulated at Selma who gave a loud snore before closing her mouth and making little chewing movements with her lips. 'I wonder if being born is at all a good idea if, at the end, there's got to be Cherryfield.'

'Luckily one's not asked,' Henry said briskly.

'The worst time of all,' said Amelia, not listening,

rubbing her eyes with the back of her hand and getting it streaked with mascara, 'is when there's no-one left who loves you best. Selma has been lucky; at the peak of her existence, she was loved by her parents, husband, children, she was the centre of their world. But look at her now, what is left of all that love, where is the security? At the end of the day, you're just an old teddy that everyone's grown out of.'

'There's always God, He never stops loving you.' Henry said, somewhat startlingly.

'Ah, you're born again.' Amelia nodded.

'Certainly not,' Henry said. 'I'm a Naval Chaplain.' And he sat down on the grass by the bench.

'Goodness,' Amelia said looking at him properly now, 'how comforting for you.'

'Actually, it's meant to be sort of comforting for others.' He smiled mildly at her.

Well, comfort Selma then, Amelia thought, irritated by the smile. But she said, 'Is your father happy here?'

Henry lay back resting on his elbows, staring up at the sky. 'Not happy exactly, but he's used to community life, institutions if you like; Dartmouth, ships, Naval bases. It's not really Cherryfield he minds, it's being old.'

'My grandmother is very unhappy.' Amelia looked at Selma whose mouth had fallen open again as she snored gently. 'She thinks she's going back home. Would you believe,' she turned to Henry, willing her outrage on him, 'my uncle didn't tell her the house had been sold. And now he's buggered off to Brazil, leaving me to tell her.' Then she blushed, remembering the invisible dog collar that should shield Henry Mallett from that sort of language. 'Sorry,' she said.

'That's all right, I have been down the odd sailor's mess deck you know.'

'I think this is a dreadful place,' Amelia sighed.

'Everything about it upsets me. It's unfair I know, they seem to try their best. Couldn't you just see the headlines? I'm a journalist by the way; I even think in bold, "**Ill-treatment at Retirement Home**: Nurse wipes old woman's bottom." Not much of a story in that!'

A snore turned into a hiccup and Selma awoke. Her eyes flickered between Amelia and Henry, uncertain and unfocused, then her gaze fixed on Amelia. 'Darling, how lovely to see you. When did you arrive? And who's your young man? You must introduce us.' Selma stretched out a chubby arm and smiled coquettishly.

Henry stood up and took her hand. 'I'm Henry Mallett. I think you know my father already – Admiral Mallett.'

Amelia smiled at him gratefully. She did not go to church much herself, but had inherited from Selma a respect for men of religion, were they Chaplains or Rabbis: an expectation of goodness. She approved of Henry.

'Grandma,' she said, 'Henry's a Naval chaplain.'

'Now isn't that interesting.' Selma beamed at them both. 'And tell me, how did you come to meet my granddaughter?'

Chapter Four

'That's what's so disconcerting.' Amelia stirred the earthenware pan filled with vegetable soup. 'One moment she's the old Selma; with it, sensible, the sort of person you feel you can go to with your problems. Next thing you know, whoosh, she's gone, replaced by this large, malfunctioning child.' She looked across the kitchen at Gerald. 'It's really very upsetting.'

'Well there you are, it was obviously right to put her in a home,' Gerald said, picking up the *Independent* and turning to the sports pages.

Amelia slammed the spoon down by the side of the cooker making Gerald wince. 'It wasn't all that long ago that she enthralled people with her piano recitals. You know, back in Sweden a young man actually shot himself underneath her balcony because her parents wouldn't let her marry him. And now, now she's someone who's "put" places. What the hell help is it knowing that "it was obviously right"?'

'A lot I should think,' Gerald said sourly.

How her vagueness irritated him, he thought, her habit of making illogical remarks in that rather slow, deliberate voice of hers, a voice that, just like her grandmother's playing, had once enthralled. Even her prettiness annoyed him these days. Her grey, slanted eyes, the soft wavy hair that framed the oval face, all reminded him of how much in love he had been with her once.

Oh Amelia, he thought, looking at her moving about

the kitchen, wiping down the cooker, using three matches to light the candle on the kitchen table, you're altogether too languid, too useless. Suddenly angry he snapped, 'Why don't you do something about the situation if you think it's so terrible.' And he slammed down the paper and strode from the room.

Amelia cried as she kept the soup warm on the stove, stirring it slowly. She cried bitterly, because now she really feared that Gerald had stopped loving her, but she also cried carefully, so as not to smudge her make-up, because he was not lost to her yet, and he could come back in to the kitchen any moment.

'There's a sweetness about you,' Gerald had said soon after their first meeting, and he had shaken his head with a bemused air as if to say, I might seem strong, but against you I'm helpless. He was so good natured too, like over that silly business with the modelling. He had been as hard-working and serious a painter as he was a solicitor now. Yet he had shown no irritation when, after having promised to sit for an important canvas, she had turned up in his studio only to end up wasting his day. She hadn't intended to, of course. She had watched him set up his easel, she had undressed and sat down where he wanted her to, and then she had panicked like a fool when he asked her to part her legs for the pose. But Gerald had been only kind and understanding. She had sat crying in his huge blue armchair, her knees pressed together as if they had been welded that way, and he, kneeling by her side, had just smiled and said, 'You're a sweet, fragile, dreamy girl, and I should never have asked you to do this.'

'Sweet, dreamy, fragile,' Amelia hissed, splashing the wooden spoon round the soup. 'Try wet, gullible and inconsistent.'

The soup had simmered so long she knew there

would be no flavour left. She took it off the stove and went to look for Gerald. She found him in the bedroom, speaking on the phone. As he looked up to see her in the doorway, he said a loud and hurried goodbye and hung up.

Amelia took a deep breath and walked over to the bed. She sat down next to him and, giving him a little smile, she put her hand out, running her fingers through his hair. Ignoring his irritated flinching, she kissed him lightly on the cheek. 'Gerald, I love you.'

Gerald looked at a point somewhere over her left shoulder. 'And I love you too,' he mumbled.

Grateful, she hugged him and, after a few moments, she felt his arms round her back.

In a small but beautifully furnished flat not far from the Cathedral in Exeter, Dagmar Lindsay shone a torch into the back of her wardrobe, making sure it really was clean, that it was just a shadow she'd seen earlier, not dirt. Again she rubbed her finger against the back wall of the cupboard, checking. Her long-fingered hands – pianist hands Selma always said delightedly – were raw, the skin chapped and rough, not fitting the creamy complexion of her face and the soft skin on her slim arms.

'I just haven't got the time to go off to Kingsmouth,' she muttered to herself, as she removed hanger after hanger from the rail, wiping them with a J-cloth drenched in Dettol. 'I can't see why Robert should get away scot-free, I really can't.' She went over to the basin and rinsed the cloth carefully, turning it under the hot tap, then she washed her hands. She pushed a strand of pale, blond hair from her forehead and, taking a deep breath, smoothed down her cornflower-blue, silk skirt before returning smiling to the sitting room where her guests were having coffee.

'So sorry,' Dagmar said, 'I had to call to see how mother was.'

'Miss Lindsay, Miss Amelia Lindsay? I hope we didn't wake you up.' The voice on the phone was nasal and apologetic. 'I told your grandmother it was much too late to call anyone up, but she would not listen I'm afraid. Miss Lindsay, are you there?'

'Yes. No you didn't wake me up, it's quite all right. Are you calling from Cherryfield?'

'I'm sorry, didn't I say. It's Nurse Kelly, I'm duty tonight. Your grandmother has quite a temper when she wants.' The voice laughed uncertainly. 'Here's your gran now.'

'Amelia darling.' Selma's voice sounded faint, there was a crashing noise, nothing, then, 'Oh bugger!'

'Miss Lindsay, Mrs Merryman dropped the phone but here she is again now.'

'Amelia,' Selma's voice was small and frightened. 'I wanted to make sure I had your number.' There was a pause and Amelia could hear Selma breathing heavily into the phone. 'It's 0962 3628 . . . Bother, I can't read the last number. Is it nine . . . Or one?'

'But grandma, you've just called the right number, you're talking to me now.'

'Yes of course, silly of me. What did you say the number was? 0962 . . .'

Gerald, however irritated he got with Amelia, found it impossible not to continue giving her advice, attempting to sort her life out for her. The next evening he looked up from his brief and explained that it was a form of arrogance believing that no-one but she could look after Selma. 'You just can't go running off to Devon every other week. You have your own life to lead, responsibilities here, a home to run. Then there's the question of the cost of all these trips, hotel rooms . . .' He turned a page in the brief. 'You're not your grandmother's keeper you know.'

Still Amelia couldn't stop thinking of Selma alone and confused at Cherryfield. Friends with new babies had said that suddenly the world seemed populated almost exclusively by infants in prams. A member of the family, not recently arrived in the world, but on the way out, tottering into certified old age, had the same effect, Amelia felt. Old people, harassed by a blinking green man turning all too fast into angry red, crossed in front of her car at pedestrian crossings. They were found in their own cars at every roundabout, sitting paralysed by the stream of traffic pouring from every direction. There they were again, fumbling for the right change in the check-out queue at the supermarket, apologizing for their outmoded habit of carrying real money.

Two weeks after her first visit to Cherryfield, Amelia was again boarding the train to Plymouth. She wondered, as she looked for a seat, what had made Gerald suddenly quite happy with her decision to go. Could it just be that she had sold another couple of articles and was able to pay for the weekend herself?

An old man settled like a large shabby bird on the seat opposite, his dark brown mac flapping round his scrawny limbs. 'All right, all right, I don't need any more reminders, I'm going down, aren't I?' Amelia muttered in an inaudible voice.

When the train passed a large and heavily populated graveyard the old man and Amelia both stared out at it.

The stones, mostly marble, rose from the ground, new and shining like giant teeth, or old crumbling white, streaked by years of rain like powdered cheeks by tears. Amelia looked over her book at the old man and wondered if he felt the pull of the graves, or if death, even at his age, was something that only happened to others?

'Nice day,' smiled the old man, showing a perfect set of white dentures.

'Lovely day,' said the nurse who opened the door for Amelia at Cherryfield.

Selma sat in a chair in front of the television, her face half turned from the programme on learning difficulties in adult life. On her lap lay her copy of the Omnibus Jane Austen. Amelia had to go right up and put her hand on Selma's arm before she looked up, a frown on her face. Resting the back of her head against the chair she gazed at Amelia, then, with a sudden delighted smile, she put out her hand. 'Darling, what a lovely surprise.'

'I phoned and told them I was coming, they should have told you.'

'The maid's been in and out of my room all morning, but she never said a word.' Selma frowned, 'I do wish I'd known, I haven't been to the shops at all this week.'

'We'll go out for lunch,' Amelia said quickly. 'Is your toe better? Are you able to walk a little?'

'It is a bit sore, but of course I can walk on it. Just give me a hand up darling.'

Amelia braced herself and began to pull. For a moment Selma stood tottering on both feet, her dress riding up at the back showing the edge of her flesh-coloured knickers, then with a shriek of pain, she toppled back into the chair.

'Why don't I get the wheelchair, just for today, give the foot a bit of a rest?'

'This is quite ridiculous,' Selma muttered. 'There's absolutely nothing wrong with my foot, a small cut that's all.'

As Amelia came through the door a few minutes later, pushing the wheelchair, she heard Selma's laugh, soft and flirtatious like a girl's. At her side, chatting, stood the Admiral and his son. Henry, looking relaxed, was leaning lightly against the half-empty bookcase behind him, his father, on the other hand, attempting the same easy pose, looked strained; his elbow resting on top of the bookcase the only thing preventing him from collapsing.

'I'm going to sit down, won't you join me?' Amelia hurried forward. The Admiral shot her a grateful glance and said he'd love to.

'I get very tired standing,' she added, wondering if she might be overdoing it.

'Amelia darling, you didn't tell me your young man was here.' Selma smiled graciously at Henry.

'Grandma, that's Henry Mallett, Admiral Mallett's son.'

'What a coincidence!' Selma looked gratified. 'I believe the Admiral is staying here too.'

'Well, seeing we're all here,' Henry said, 'why don't we have lunch together?'

Amelia didn't notice the make of Henry's car, but it was burgundy coloured and they all fitted inside quite comfortably. Selma, fresh lipstick and scent applied, was hauled from the wheelchair into the front seat of the car and Amelia sat in the back with the Admiral.

Henry suggested they went to a hotel he knew on the edge of Dartmoor. They drove for half an hour, through nearby Totnes and out again on to narrow winding lanes flanked by tall hedgerows. Selma wound the window down and sighed happily as the air blew through her washed-out curls. The Admiral looked out at the passing landscape.

'You almost forget there are such creatures as children.' He smiled at three small girls on bikes.

As they parked in front of the hotel, there was a slight fracas when Selma could not release the seat belt. 'The stupid thing,' she fumed pink faced. 'It's completely stuck. No,' she said to Henry as he leant across to try, 'it doesn't matter what you . . . Oh, thank you.' And she was helped out and back into the collapsible wheelchair. 'I can't wait to be back on my feet again,' she said over her shoulder to the Admiral, as Henry wheeled her towards the hotel entrance.

At the table in the restaurant, the Admiral was in expansive mood. 'I'll do the wine shall I, dear boy?' he said as he peered short-sightedly at the wine list.

They had stilton soup to start with, and a glass of dry sherry. This was followed by lamb chops and new potatoes and what the Admiral called 'a robust claret'. Selma and he then ordered trifle. 'None of this nouvelle stuff,' the Admiral sniffed, 'a fellow could starve to death.' He hailed the waiter, 'Be liberal with the cream.' And he winked at Selma who giggled happily.

'You are a dreadful man.' Her chubby shoulders heaved with laughter.

It was, Amelia thought, as if the atmosphere at Cherryfield was too thin to sustain real life and that now, back in the world, Selma and the Admiral filled out and coloured in, ceasing to be old people, and becoming just people.

She looked up to see Henry smiling at her. 'How long are you home for?' she asked him.

'Most of the summer, then we deploy to the Gulf for six months. At least my father will have had a chance to settle in at Cherryfield first.'

'I wish I wasn't so far away,' Amelia sighed. 'My mother lives in Exeter but without a car it's no good staying with her.' Amelia didn't say that the thought of spending time alone with her mother in the flat made her feel like an escaped convict hauled back to prison.

'. . . and of course they couldn't believe their eyes at

the High Commission when I dived into the pool in tropical mess dress.' The Admiral laughed loudly at the memory as he raised a spoonful of cherry-topped trifle to his lips. Suddenly there was silence and the Admiral's long face turned pink, then purple. Amelia stared as he gave a strangled cough, his pale blue eyes bulging, tears rising. Henry leapt from his chair.

At the table opposite, a young girl stared and nudged her mother, and the lunching family at another, carried on their conversation in carefully loud voices, as if to show that they at least were minding their own business.

The Admiral sat rigid in his chair as Henry prised his lips apart. He had stopped coughing and was making rasping, staccato noises, his face turning a bluish hue.

Selma didn't move but sat silent, gripping the table edge with both hands.

'An ambulance, quick!' Amelia called to the waiter.

Beads of sweat appeared on Henry's face as he pushed his fingers inside his father's mouth. Suddenly the Admiral yanked free and, with a loud belch, disgorged his dentures on the plate of trifle.

Henry dabbed his father's face with a napkin dipped in mineral water. 'It's all right Pa,' he whispered, 'I'm here.'

The guests at the next table left, gingerly carrying their cups of coffee, and, opposite, the teenage girl dissolved in giggles.

'It's not funny,' Amelia whispered near to tears, 'it's not funny.'

'He'll be fine now,' Henry said, looking up at her. 'I don't think we need the ambulance. Don't worry he'll be fine.'

Chapter Five

The Admiral had rested a while on a chaise-longue in the Ladies powder room, a pink towel, with 'For Our Guests' embroidered in gold thread, dampened and placed across his forehead. Now he sat in the front seat of the car, next to Henry. His head was resting against the seatback and the sun, shining though the car window, showed up little patches of colourless stubble on his chin, where he had not seen to shave.

To make room for Selma's bad foot, Henry had pushed the driver's seat forward, almost as far as it would go, and, as he was driving, his knees were pressed right up against the wheel.

Amelia was chatting, thinking it the best thing to do. 'Oh look,' she exclaimed, 'just look at those lambs. Aren't they adorable? Spring really is wonderful, so full of promise, a new beginning . . .' She stopped. I'm being tactless she thought.

'I mean whatever one's age,' she tried again, 'spring is . . . well sort of promising.' She caught Henry's face in the rearview mirror. A smile flickered in his eyes.

Back at Cherryfield, the Admiral was put to bed. Downstairs, Selma said, 'Don't go,' and she took Amelia's hand. As Amelia said nothing, she added as if she had just thought of it, 'Why don't I come and stay with you for a few days?'

If Selma had been ten years old, Amelia thought, she would have had her fingers crossed behind her back.

'I do feel I need a holiday,' Selma continued, in the

same pretend-nonchalant voice. 'I can't remember when I last had one.'

'Grandma, I'd love you to come, but,' she paused, 'well just at the moment, things are a bit difficult at home.'

'Oh, I shouldn't worry,' Selma said cheerfully, 'I'm sure Henry wouldn't mind, he seems such a nice boy.'

Amelia breathed in deeply. She was tired, it had been a difficult day. Then she remembered how all through her life, Selma's door had always been open to her. If it had ever been inconvenient to have Amelia to stay at Ashcombe, Selma and Willoughby had never said so.

'We'd love you to come, of course we would,' she said, firmly. 'I'll arrange a day as soon as I get back home. I'll see you tomorrow before I go, anyway. Mummy's coming too.' And she freed her hand and walked quickly to the door, feeling Selma's gaze on her every step.

The next morning at ten, Amelia met Dagmar outside the hotel. 'You're looking well.' Dagmar held Amelia at arms length for a moment, studying her face, then, with a pleased smile, pulled her towards her and gave her a kiss.

'So do you,' Amelia said, smiling back, surprised to find her mother's presence comforting. Dagmar did look well too; tall, blonde and elegant in her grey slacks and navy blazer, it was hard to think she was well over fifty. Constant obsessive worrying must agree with her, Amelia thought.

'It's such a nice day,' she said, 'I don't think we need a taxi.' On the walk, she told Dagmar of the disastrous lunch party and about how confused and unhappy Selma seemed.

'I agree, I agree,' mumbled Dagmar.

'And,' Amelia said, thinking, this will get a reaction from her, 'Robert lied to get her to agree to move to Cherryfield. She still thinks she's got Ashcombe to go back to. He must have used his power of attorney.'

'Dear, oh dear. That's too bad.' She heard her mother's voice suddenly a little way off. When she turned, she found that Dagmar had stopped a couple of yards further down the hill and was busy checking the soles of her shoes, balancing precariously first on one foot, then on the other.

'What's the matter?' Amelia snapped. 'You haven't walked in anything, if that's what you are worried about. I would have smelt it.' And all the irritation accumulated over years of being her mother's daughter rose up in her, making her cruel. 'Concentrate on something other than yourself for once, will you. You have not stood, walked or sat in dogshit, no passing seagull has relieved himself in your hair . . .'

'Please darling,' Dagmar interrupted her, 'don't speak to me like that. I just can't help myself, you know that.'

Amelia felt like hitting her. Slap! Right across the cheek. Slap! An angry red mark across that pale, smooth skin. She could not remember a single time when she had had her mother's undivided attention, not had to compete for it with dog's mess, germs, worms and things that need wiping down in the night.

'I'm sorry, tell me again.' Dagmar's reddened hand touched Amelia's arm. And, as always after unpleasantness of any kind, whether with Dagmar, or Gerald, a friend, or the man in the shop who tells her fourteen months is a good innings these days for a washing machine, there lurked, deep under layers of righteous anger, a voice that whispered, 'It's really all your fault Amelia.' It was a triumphant little voice and Amelia constantly feared it was the voice of reason.

'No, I'm sorry,' she said, and she went on telling her mother of the lunch with Admiral Mallett and Henry.

As the door was opened for them at Cherryfield, Dagmar stood aside to let Amelia pass, then she wiped her feet on the doormat, six times for each foot.

Selma was in the lounge. 'Do sit down, Mrs Lindsay,' Nurse Williams said to Dagmar before breezing out to answer a bell.

Dagmar said no thanks, she felt like stretching her legs, then she bent down low, kissing Selma on the cheek, careful not to touch the armrest of the chair. Dagmar always said that she wasn't worried about germs on her own account, what filled her with panic was the thought of passing them on to others. Amelia thought it might be psychologically sound to point out to her mother that by worrying about getting her hands contaminated by the chair, she risked toppling over and crushing her fragile, old mother. She put her hand under Dagmar's elbow and said, indicating the chair next to Selma, 'Why don't you sit down?'

'Yes darling, do,' Selma insisted. 'You make me feel you are about to go any moment and I do so love having you here.'

Dagmar, looking pained, perched on the armrest. 'You sit,' she said to Amelia. Her voice was light but her look implored Amelia not to argue.

'Has the Admiral been down today?' Amelia asked, doing what she was told.

'What's that darling?' Selma looked politely alert.

'Admiral Mallett, how is he this morning?'

'He wasn't down for breakfast. But of course neither was I.' Selma smiled expansively. 'Oh look, there's your young man,' she nodded towards Henry who had stopped in the doorway. 'Why don't you ask him? He seems to know Admiral Mallett better than any of us.'

'Gerald, is Gerald here?' Dagmar looked pleased. 'That's very sweet of him, coming all this way to see Mummy. Quite unlike him too.'

'Good morning everyone.' Henry joined them.

'That's not Gerald,' Dagmar hissed in Amelia's ear.

Amelia leant her head in her hands.

'Let me get you a chair, Mrs Lindsay.' She heard Henry's voice. 'You can't be very comfortable perched like that.' She looked up to see Henry carting a small chintz-covered armchair across from the other side of the room. Dagmar kept smiling as her eyes homed in on the uneven stain that spread across the rose-patterned seat. Henry too was smiling as he held the chair out, waiting. Slowly, Dagmar sank down on to the seat.

'I saw such a lovely wedding dress in *Vogue* the other day.' Selma looked meaningfully at Amelia. 'Just your sort of thing too, darling. Simple, but beautifully cut.'

'You're about as subtle as a tank,' Amelia said.

'I wonder where the bathroom is,' Dagmar mumbled.

'When are you getting married?' Henry looked at Amelia with interest.

'That's a funny question coming from you?' Selma gave a disapproving little laugh.

Amelia turned to Henry, who was beginning to look confused, and said firmly, 'Not at all as far as I know,' and she felt like shaking her grandmother. Alzheimer's will only protect you so far, she thought furiously. Then her eyes fell on Selma's right hand which, even when resting in the grip of the other, kept on shaking. Like dancing feet on lame legs, she thought. What a swine I am to get angry.

She smiled across at Selma. 'It's my fault, Grandma, I keep changing my mind.'

Dagmar shot up from her chair, rather like someone who had sat with her hosts' farting dog at her feet for about as long as she could stand it. 'Where did you say the loo was, Amelia?' she demanʇed.

Amelia told her. And her mother would go there, she knew, not because she needed a pee, but to check her slacks, make sure there was no stain from the chair seat and no smell. Then she would soap her hands, scrubbing right up the wrists, before rinsing them in scalding water, careful all the while not to touch the edges of the basin.

Amelia had seen it all often enough. Dagmar would utter little phrases like 'Oh that bun was sticky,' or 'I don't know why they can't make newsprint that doesn't come off the pages.' People on the whole did not think her behaviour odd. If you were good looking and well dressed, Amelia had come to realize, it took stranger acts than Dagmar's for the world to see that you were mad as a hatter.

Dagmar returned relaxed and smiling, all the tension gone from her body. 'Why don't I take Mummy for a stroll, it's so lovely out there? Coming darling?' She asked Amelia.

Amelia said she'd catch them up. 'I'll just finish my coffee.' A nurse came and helped transfer Selma into her wheelchair. Whilst they shifted and hauled, Amelia chatted all the time with her grandmother, trying to take her mind off the undignified procedure, just like a gynaecologist, she thought.

At last Selma was ready and Dagmar pushed her outside in the wheelchair, gripping the tips of the handlebars gingerly.

Henry leant closer to Amelia. 'Just go ahead and yell.' He smiled encouragingly at her.

'Is your father better today?' she asked instead, but she thought Henry very perceptive.

'He's not too bad, thanks, but he's spending today in bed. I left him asleep.'

'Amelia! AMELIA!' Selma was calling from the terrace where she had been parked. 'Darling, I've just had a lovely idea.' She leant forward in her wheelchair, peering at them through the open French windows. Across the path, Dagmar stared dreamily at the blossoming cherry tree. 'I shall give a party for my birthday, like we always used to.' Selma held out her hands for Amelia to come over.

'I'll be home well in time for August. I know it won't be the same without darling Willoughby,' for a moment the pleasure was gone from her face, then she made an effort to smile, 'but life must go on, we have to make an effort.'

Amelia took the handlebars and began slowly pushing the wheelchair along the terrace, and down a wooden ramp on to the lawn. She waved at Henry, who sat flicking through a magazine.

'I'll ask Admiral Mallett. You've met the Admiral, haven't you?' It's the repetitions that get you down in the end, Amelia thought, as Selma went on, 'And we mustn't forget little Mrs Finch, and Sheila and Mark, of course, and Tony Bellamy . . .' Dagmar joined them as they rounded the corner back towards the terrace.

'. . . and then there's Violet. We'd never hear the end of it if we left her out.' Selma was smiling happily.

Through the French doors, Amelia noticed that Henry had disappeared.

Later, as lunch was being served, she said goodbye to Selma and, turning to Dagmar, she said sternly, 'You're staying the day, aren't you Mummy?'

Dagmar nodded, a glint of martyrdom in her eyes.

'I have to get back to Devenport,' Henry came down from his father's room. 'I can give you a lift to the station.'

They drove for a while in silence. It took time always, Amelia thought, to shake off Cherryfield. Then as they turned on to the Plymouth road, she said to Henry, 'Would you mind if I raged against God, just for a minute or two?'

'Dig out.' Henry smiled. He was driving rather fast on the outside lane.

'Seriously though,' Amelia said, feeling hot and pushing her hair from her face, 'it's the way God seems to have of giving with one hand, whilst taking with the other. Just look at life. We're given it, great, hurrah! But there's always a sad ending. I mean, who's ever heard of a happy death?'

Henry said nothing but seemed to be listening as he overtook a stream of heavy lorries swaying along the inside lane.

'You would think that birth, at least, would be a completely happy affair, but oh no. Even these days when it's fairly safe, it's still painful and essentially, humiliating. It makes a mockery of what every nice girl since Eve has been taught. "Keep your fanny to yourself, dear," the cry has echoed through the ages, and then the poor girl has half the world staring at her . . .' Amelia stopped. 'I'm doing it again,' she said. 'I'm sorry. I'm just hopelessly coarse.'

'Don't worry. Really.' Henry turned a sharp left where it was signposted, 'Station'. 'You carry on.'

'It's just a small example of course,' she suggested meekly, 'but I feel it would have been helpful if the things we like to keep private and the things that have to be public had been more equally divided between the organs. Not concentrated higgledy-piggledy in one area,' Amelia finished lamely.

'I think,' Henry said, 'that you're a little bit unfair to God. He gave most of us perfectly good, effective, reproductive organs that also happen to take care of other, equally important functions. That's all. So you can hardly blame him for us losing our innocence and getting all coy and refined, can you now?' He drove up in front of the entrance. 'Anyway,' he said, 'you'd need awfully big ears.' And he walked round and opened the car door for her.

Chapter Six

The neck of a champagne bottle periscoped through the ice that was melting inside a red, plastic bucket. It stood in the middle of the kitchen table and was the first thing Gerald saw as he came in, two hours late from the office. 'What's this in aid of?' He threw his briefcase on a chair and loosened his tie.

'In aid of? Oh, nothing in particular.' Then Amelia smiled and threw her arms round his neck. 'I just felt like celebrating, that's all.'

'I don't expect you've noticed, but there is a recession on. Anyway,' he made his voice patient, 'felt like celebrating what?'

'That we're not old and incontinent – all right so I go to the loo four times a night, but at least I get there – that we've got our own place where we can please ourselves, sit with our feet on the table drinking wine and reading, stay up all night, sleep all day, throw a party.' She flung her arms out. 'Anything.' She put a tall-stemmed glass in front of him.

'Do you realize what a luxury it is just to be able to go into your own kitchen and cook whatever *you* want to eat, maybe bring it into the sitting room in front of the television.'

'You know I hate TV dinners,' Gerald said, sitting down with a sigh.

Amelia tried again. Looking quite serious now, she said, 'Most importantly of all, we've got each other.'

She hauled the bottle from the bucket, dripping

water all over the front of her khaki skirt and white cotton shirt. One of his shirts, Gerald noticed. And he wondered, how does she do it? How does someone as vague, as fragile as Amelia, cling on to an illusion with such strength? Wearily he accepted the glass she handed him, she had over-filled it of course. He sipped the champagne and thought how much he preferred a really first class Chablis.

Earlier in the day, Gerald's father had come into his son's office for a chat. 'Gerald, old chap,' he had begun, touching Gerald's shoulder rather in the manner of someone being told to caress a pet snake, 'I know things have changed since my day, we're in the nineties after all. I mean to say, you can hardly put on the television these days without being reminded of the fact.'

At this Gerald couldn't help enquiring, 'Is that the only reason you know what decade it is, because you've seen it on the box?'

'Oh never mind that.' Norman Forbes slid his middle finger along the inside of his collar. 'What I'm trying to say is; it's time you and Amelia got married, time you had a family too for that matter, although that of course is none of my business. With Amelia having passed the thirty mark though . . .' He caught Gerald's eye and clearing his throat, went on, 'This bohemian bit, it's a phase you go through, like having a crush on a chum, that sort of thing.' For a moment, Norman looked wistful.

Gerald was drumming a little tune on the desk with his fingers.

'Living in sin,' Norman said, 'people expect that sort of thing from an artist, positively good for business I shouldn't wonder. But let's face it, you're a solicitor now, and that makes it all different, well in Hampshire it does, anyway.'

Gerald sighed, 'That's exactly what Amelia keeps saying.'

'Well she's a sensible girl. Now I've told you my opinion, as your father and senior partner in the firm. But of course it's your life and your decision entirely.' And Norman had coughed in an encouraging manner and, looking well pleased with himself, strode from the room.

Gerald had banged his fist against the frame round the closed door, very hard, several times, then he had gone in to Clarissa's small office next door and given her some extra work to keep her late.

Back in his own office, he had sat in the brown leather wingchair he'd inherited from his grandfather and thought of how he agreed with his father and Amelia. It really was time he got married and had a family.

There was one point, however, on which he differed from them; it was not Amelia, but Clarissa he wanted to share this new life with. It was Clarissa he wanted to marry, and to be the mother of his children. Clarissa with her solid good sense and her working girl independence, tempered so nicely, he couldn't help thinking, with a good deal of respect for Gerald himself. Amelia, he thought, is a constant reminder of all those past dreams that crash-landed on impact with reality.

'You're not exactly sparkling company.' Amelia, careful not to sound whining, leant across the kitchen table, smiling at Gerald who sat staring morosely into the huge vase of daffodils. She sniffed the air and sat up straight. 'Your scent clashes with mine.'

'What? Oh.' Gerald cleared his throat. Here was his chance. The moment, handed to him on a plate, to come clean. 'Sorry old girl,' he would say, 'there's someone else. It's her scent, Diorissimo, you can smell on my lapel.'

He drained the almost full glass of champagne. 'Oh that,' he said. 'One of the girls, temp as a matter of fact, spilt a whole bottle of the stuff over a brief I was handling.' And that was that. He'd blown it. 'Quite a nice scent really,' he added pathetically.

Later that evening, Gerald lay, unable to sleep, on his side of the wide brass bed. What kept him awake was the unfairness of everything. How could he rest when the world around him was so utterly unreasonable? After all, here he was, an increasingly popular and successful solicitor of thirty-five, unable to marry the nice, perfectly respectable and above all, reasonable, helpmate that was Clarissa. Unable to marry her because of his mistress.

He threw his part of the duvet aside and sat up, noisily splashing Evian water into a glass from the bottle on the bedside table. 'Mistress' was a dated concept, he knew that. He drank down the water in great gulps. But his mistress was what Amelia was. It would have been nice to add 'kept woman', to 'mistress', but he knew that would not be fair. After all she earned quite a bit from her freelancing and there was the money from the sale of her flat.

But she had the mentality of a kept woman then, he decided angrily as he threw himself back down on to his pillow. Come to think of it, he was surprised that she was as successful as she actually was at her work.

He remembered the first time he'd met her, at the exhibition. 'Will you model for me?' he had asked pretty soon after first being introduced. 'I'm planning a nude,' he'd said, looking deep into her slanted grey eyes. 'A sort of eighties Rubensesque effect; the lusciousness of the past, with the new, more angular woman of today.' He had drained his wine glass, expecting her to either laugh or be offended.

But she'd just smiled and said, 'I'd love to. When?'

All so typical of Amelia, he thought bitterly. That immediate and surprising yes, her turning up all smiles in his studio the next afternoon, as agreed. And then panicking, flatly refusing to place her slender, naked right leg across the arm of the chair in the pose he required.

'I'm sorry, I really am,' she had sobbed, 'but I can only model with my legs together.'

Raising himself on one elbow, Gerald looked down at Amelia sleeping at his side, her wavy, auburn hair spread across the white pillow-case, her cheek with its sprinkling of pale freckles, resting on her hand. For a moment, quite against his will, tenderness replaced anger. He bent down and brushed her cheeks with his lips then, sighing deeply, he rolled on to his back and closed his eyes.

Hitler had been a handwasher, Stalin too, Dagmar had read somewhere.

I'm not keeping very nice company, she thought, and she couldn't help smiling, a sad flash of a smile. She was sitting in bed, wrapped in misery as if it was a second blanket. She was in no doubt that the misery was self inflicted and wholly unnecessary, but that, she thought, was about as much help as knowing that you should never have walked under that bus.

I drove away my husband, worried him away. And I've lost Amelia's respect for ever. Dagmar wiped tears from her eyes and, taking a fresh Kleenex from the box at her side, blew her nose noisily. How could a child ever respect a mother like Dagmar? One who, while all normal mothers fretted over the Cold War and what Mick Jagger's lips might do to their daughter's innocence, spent precious hours and days worrying whether or not a door handle could pass on a deadly disease.

And now I'm fifty-five, she thought, and still worrying about the wrong things. All over the world, women were voicing their concern over nuclear power and Aids, and the safety of hormone replacement therapy. But Dagmar was not amongst them. Her thoughts would often drift towards these topics, hover anxiously, touch down briefly. On the whole the resulting conclusions were sensible, robust even. 'Make him use a condom if you are at all unsure,' she would say to Amelia. 'And cold hearted as it might seem, I would think twice before giving mouth to mouth, especially if there are bleeding gums involved.'

But then these were normal concerns and when you've spent the day disinfecting clothes pegs, there was so little time left for normality.

And now, sitting in the king-sized marital bed she never could make herself throw out, she thought for a moment of all the squandered years, of all the planes that had flown overhead, whilst she was stuck on the ground with her unnecessary luggage. She could only dwell on it for a moment though, any more and the thought of all that waste became unbearable.

She reached for the books on the bedside table. She'd read some Wodehouse, she decided, he never failed to cheer her up. It was a new trade paperback of collected novels, her own copy. She had stopped borrowing from the library after discovering that people really did pick their noses whilst they read.

She opened the book at the start of the second story. She read a few lines but she couldn't concentrate. Her hands needed washing. She told herself there was no reason to wash them. 'Look,' she said to herself, 'look, they're clean, perfectly clean.' But she couldn't enjoy Madeleine Basset's soppy speeches or laugh at Bertie's struggles with his aunts, not whilst her stomach felt as if it was filling up with performing fleas.

Again she stretched her raw hands out in front of her. 'Look you stupid woman, there's nothing on them, can't you see?' She was pleading with herself now, but it didn't work, the fleas were performing a clog dance round her guts by now. Near to tears once more, she put the book down carefully on a pristine part of the bed cover and padded across to the bathroom.

That was the trouble with germs, she sniffed to herself as she soaped and scrubbed her hands under the scalding water, they could not be seen. She wished the little buggers could be. They should wear scarlet sweat-shirts with 'I'm a Harmful Germ' blazoned across the chest.

She got back into bed, stretching her legs out, the fleas were gone for now. Next time, she promised herself as she picked up the book, she really would not give in.

At Cherryfield, Selma too was in bed. She'd been there since nine o'clock. She had slept a while, now she dozed. Her bed was warm and soft, the room dark. Her toe wasn't hurting. When Willoughby came to bed she would tell him. He was worried about her, she knew from the way he looked at her when he thought she didn't notice, half affectionate, half exasperated.

'Go and see Dr Scott, there's a good girl,' he had said as her toe got steadily more painful, as the dark shadow on the skin grew in diameter.

But Selma never visited the doctor and Willoughby, bless him, knew that.

She smiled to herself in the darkness of the room. 'Dear, dear Willoughby,' she mumbled sleepily. How lucky she was to have found him. He had married her when she had felt she had nothing to share but grief. He had been as loving and patient a father to Dagmar as he had been to his own son.

'I came to Sweden to look for iron ore and what did I mine but pure gold,' he would tell anyone who'd listen, anyone who'd ask how he went to Sweden to return with a beautiful, Jewish wife and a small, blonde daughter.

Selma drifted along on her good memories. Then, as her gaze fell on unfamiliar objects, she tried to sit up. Where was the large painted mirror that lived on her dressing-table? And her mother's chaise-longue? Where was Willoughby?

She felt the side of the narrow bed. 'Willoughby!' she screamed.

There were footsteps outside the room, then slowly the door opened, letting in a sliver of light. Shuffling steps approached the bed. Out of the darkness, a hand appeared, groping round the top of the bedside table. Muttering to himself, the Admiral reached into the glass where Selma's teeth lay. Drying them in a perfunctory manner against the silk lapel of his dressing-gown he dropped them into a sponge bag where they clattered on top of the five other sets already gathered up.

'Who's that?' Selma's voice trembled as she searched for the light, her blanket pulled up to her neck. 'Who *is* that? What's going on?'

But the Admiral had retreated.

Chapter Seven

The next morning Amelia woke feeling hungover and miserable. It was Gerald's fault. She'd been forced to drink almost the whole bottle of champagne herself last night, he'd refused even a second glass. She rested her throbbing temples against the cool palms of her hands. With all his talk of a recession, she thought angrily, how could he expect her not to feel she had to finish the bottle. And now he'd gone off without waking her.

Brushing her teeth, thirty seconds on each one as her dentist had told her (it seemed less of a bother than having to decide what next to do) she looked at her face in the mirror. Not too bad, she thought, wiping the toothpaste from her mouth, considering how rotten she was feeling. She didn't think Gerald really looked at her any more; it was a shame. Soon all those little plump cells would become desiccated and the skin would support her flesh no better than a washed out bra or one of those net shopping bags that expanded downwards with every new pound in weight added.

Arching her back, she wondered idly whether a pencil would still drop to the floor if placed under her breasts. She thought she'd better not put it to the test.

It was not that thirty-one was old, she thought, more that nowadays the streets seemed full of people younger.

She pulled the nightdress over her head and,

stepping over it as it lay crumpled on the floor, wandered in under the shower.

Even forty wasn't old, it was just that much nearer to fifty. She tried unsuccessfully to rub up some lather with the Strawberry Body Shampoo. Life, she thought, was just a rush from one birthday to another. You were born, had a quick dance round the flame, then Cherryfield.

Maybe, she thought as she dried herself with Gerald's towel – hers was still in a heap in the bedroom – maybe he was suffering from the male menopause? Her married friends used the phrase frequently on the subject of their husbands. It was a useful blanket explanation of course, as it covered as many sins as the husbands themselves. Anything from unprovoked bursts of fury, bad tempered remarks like, 'So what, grilled lamb-chops have always been my favourite, they damn well aren't now!' to erratic behaviour in bed.

She dressed and slapped some sun-block on her face while she waited for two aspirin to dissolve in a glass of Gerald's fizzy water. She felt she could understand what these men were going through, not excuse them, but understand. She could see them young and confident, so sure they would matter, believing the world to be a mess just waiting for them to clear up. Then all too soon there they were, knocking on the door to middle-age, powerless to change anything much but their wives.

But Gerald was still young. She looked at his photograph taken the summer before, as she sprayed herself liberally with Shalimar. She liked to wear Shalimar when she gardened, it was so unsuitable. There was still time for him to appear on breakfast television as their legal eagle, or to fight to save the rain forests.

Why was Gerald so discontented? Amelia stabbed at the heavy, black soil with a massive garden fork, attempting to dislodge the last of the season's leeks.

It had rained during the night and the sun refracted through the drops of water collected in the pale green foliage. The fruity scent of the slowly warming soil mixed with the sour smell of the leeks, and a few steps away at the edge of the vegetable garden, the cypress was flowering with tiny pink tips at the end of its coniferous leaves.

Amelia straightened up, holding the trug heavy with soil-laden leeks. Looking around her, she listened to the comforting counterpoint of rumbling traffic and bird song; I love this place, she thought.

On her way inside, the phone rang and, not bothering to take off her boots, she hurried through the kitchen and into the hall.

'It's Henry Mallett.' His voice sounded lighter than she remembered. 'They gave me your number at Cherryfield, I hope you don't mind.'

'Not at all,' Amelia said as she perched on the edge of the hall table, idly watching the mud slide off the sole of her boots and on to the fawn-coloured carpet.

'Sister Morris said she was sure you wouldn't. "You are a man of the cloth, after all, Mr Mallett."' Henry managed a passable imitation of Sister Morris. 'Actually I wondered if you were planning to come down again soon. We might have dinner together?' There was a slight pause. 'It would cheer me up.'

'I'm afraid Gerald takes a pretty dim view of me going down too often,' Amelia said. 'I wasn't planning to go for another week or so.' She paused. 'Is anything wrong that you need cheering up?'

'No, not really. There's been a bit of trouble over my father, nothing much, something to do with dentures.

I'll see you next time you're down.' And he said goodbye.

Amelia replaced the handset with the uneasy feeling of having let someone down.

At just that time, Sister Morris was sitting in the kitchen at Cherryfield, gazing in despair at the heap of dentures that lay before her on the formica-topped table. In the dining room, the residents were getting restless.

'I just don't know how we'll ever work out which belongs to whom.'

'Be Prince Charming.' Nurse Williams breezed in with a couple of empty jugs in her hands.

'I beg your pardon.' Sister Morris glared at her.

'You'll just have to go round all the kingdom trying them on.' And Nurse Williams was gone.

'Very droll.' Sister Morris returned her disapproving gaze to the dentures. Shaking her head she said to the cook, 'They'll have to have tapioca, Ruth, there's nothing else for it.'

'No tapioca,' said Ruth, who rationed her words as if they were taken from her own meagre salary. 'Wednesday's All Bran.'

'But what are we to do?' Sister Morris wailed. 'Just think what All Bran will do to their gums.'

'Rather not,' said Ruth.

When Gerald returned from the office that evening, making Amelia run to her typewriter in the bay of the sitting room pretending she had been working all along, he announced, 'I'm taking a week off, to go fishing with Nick and Tom.' He said it rather angrily. As if, Amelia thought studying his face, he was reacting to a fuss not yet made. 'Oh,' was all she said.

'All right, out with it, you're upset.' Glowering,

Gerald threw his jacket on the armchair. 'You don't own me you know.'

'I never . . .'

'You really have to develop some independence.'

'. . . said I did.'

'Learn to be on your own a bit.' Gerald picked up the magazine on Amelia's desk, looked at the open page and slammed it down again.

Amelia looked at the page too, it was a perfectly harmless one, she thought, unhappily, on the subject of religious festivals.

There was a fizzing noise as Gerald opened a tonic bottle. Then he swore as the tonic overflowed on to Aunt Edith's rosewood card-table. 'Someone's been shaking the bloody bottle,' Gerald said slowly.

Amelia had had enough. 'That was me,' she said, 'I ran out of maracas. As for you going fishing, you are perfectly entitled to go where ever you like, after all, we're not even married.'

'That's right,' Gerald turned, looking almost pleased, 'bring that up, I knew you would, sooner or later.'

Close to tears, Amelia said, 'It's like speaking to the Red Queen in Alice. I only meant that I agree, I don't own you. And if I do mind you going it's only because I would not want to go on holiday without *you* so maybe I'm just a little disappointed that you don't feel the same.' She wiped her eyes angrily with the sleeve of her sweat-shirt. 'That's all,' she added lamely.

On Sunday, Gerald left for his trip. He had spent most of the two previous days noisily carting rods and tins and boots from various parts of the house into the hall. They hadn't spoken much, other than for the purpose of getting on with daily life. Amelia had nursed the hope that her uncharacteristic silence would come to worry Gerald, but in the end she thought that he either liked it or hadn't noticed. She carried on searching the housing pages of local papers for premises suitable for a tea-shop, and worked on the article on the introduction of multi-cultural assemblies in the local schools. 'I'm particularly well qualified for that one,' she muttered to herself as she watched Gerald search for his copy of *Fly-fishing: Poetry in Motion*. 'Seeing as I'm a half-Swedish, half-English, Anglican Jew, living in an unorthodox relationship with a pig.'

'What was that?' Gerald turned to her with a really friendly smile and Amelia, feeling instantly ashamed, smiled back. 'Nothing, nothing at all.' Possessiveness really is an ugly trait, she thought. So she added, 'I hope the fish bite.'

'Where?' Gerald asked, making her laugh.

His goodbye kiss was surprisingly warm, especially considering he had a suitcase in one hand and two fishing rods in the other. 'Was it Friday you were going down to Cherryfield?' he asked. 'I like to know where I can reach you.'

'You take care,' he called from the open car window, raising his arm in a salute as he drove off. And it seemed to Amelia, as she stood waving by the front door, that the car leapt out of the drive like a spring lamb sighting green pasture.

Chapter Eight

Amelia closed the front door behind Gerald, straightened her shoulders and decided to make good use of the time he was away. In fact, she thought as she walked briskly through to her desk, it was no bad thing having a week to herself; she could finish the article, clear out her wardrobe, have lunch with a friend, even visit Selma.

But each evening, as the shadows lengthened in the garden, like ghosts dragging their cloaks across the rose-beds, she felt lonely. It was as if she needed another living body around to assure her that she existed outside her own imagination.

When she first moved with Gerald to Abbotslea she had dreamt of concerned vicars on the prowl for dry sherry and converts, of gossipy post-mistresses and nosy neighbours. She had always had a soft spot for nosy neighbours; they cared, she thought, but the village had turned out a disappointment. Pretty as a chocolate-box cover it may be, but there was a constant display of For Sale signs, standing like flag-poles, in front of the rose-covered cottages as the younger residents climbed up the housing ladder and the older ones, the nosy, gossipy, church-going ones, died off.

True collectivism, Amelia thought, was to be found, not on a farm in Bulgaria, but amongst the older inhabitants of an English country village; 'I've got a glut of broadbeans this season, you have some and I wouldn't say no to a trug of that tasty looking beetroot.'

Signs in the village shop-window saying, 'I'm off to town the first Thursday of every month and will have three spare seats in the car. Any one wanting a lift, stand at the disused bus stop on Main Street at eight-thirty.'

But that was all going. It lay interred in the pretty churchyard on top of Vicarage Hill with the bones of old Mrs Craig, bossy Miss Payne and Major Stapleton, lately of the Royal Fusiliers. Behind them came the new-age villagers, blaming each other for the lack of village life as they boarded the seven-fifteen for London or, to be fair Amelia thought, stayed behind locked doors writing articles for the national press about the dissolution of the village spirit.

As she sat on Wednesday evening watching six recorded episodes of *Neighbours*, her supper on a tray in front of her, Amelia thought she really was a true parasite. Without another human to feed off she began to function badly, becoming shrivelled of thought and pale of mind.

She looked at the video, pushing forkfuls of the glutinous, cooling pasta around her plate. There was Cherryfield, beckoning in the distance like an old, painted tart: 'Give me your cash and I'll soon make you comfortable.'

'And this,' she said out loud, 'is how I choose to spend the precious time until her arms close round me.' As she spoke, she saw her words fanning out into the room, beetling along the skirting-board, across the sofa and chairs, searching for a listener, before returning to her in ribbon formation.

That's it, she thought, I'm going to bed.

The next morning she opened her curtains to a sky that looked as if it had been painted by an artist with only one shade of dull, mid-grey at his disposal. After dressing, Amelia put the now-finished article in a brown, A4 envelope and, grabbing her handbag, went off to the village shop.

It had stopped raining but a chill breeze made her button up her washed-out green puffa. She always wore the puffa in Abbotslea, it was a statement: I might live in sin with your family solicitor, it said, but at heart I'm a harmless and conventional creature. It was impossible, Amelia hoped, to be a threat and wear a puffa, both at the same time.

As she reached The Stores, she heard her name called. Approaching from the opposite direction, pushing a pram, came Rosalind Hall, Amelia's closest friend in the village. She was wearing a canary yellow sou'wester and round the huge wheels of the old carriage pram, the water splashed, throwing little glistening spears in every direction.

Amelia waited for her, glad to find someone to chat to, although since the birth of little Ronald, Rosalind's son, their friendship had lost its comfortable quality. Rosalind spent a good deal of the time apologizing for having a baby, whilst Amelia apologized for not having one.

'Lucky you,' Rosalind said now, not meaning it, 'you can just put on your coat and march off. If you knew the time it took to get ready with a tiny.'

Amelia refrained from asking, 'Tiny what?' Instead she told Rosalind sincerely that she longed to have someone holding her up.

'Gerald seems very pleased with himself these days, what are you doing to him?' Rosalind asked for something to say, as she smiled down at Ronald who showed his naked gums in an irresistible grin. 'Who's Mummy's little man then?' she cooed to him as she gently rocked the pram with her gumbooted foot.

Amelia looked pleasantly surprised. 'I didn't think I was doing anything right as far as Gerald's concerned.

He's not home at the moment, actually.' Amelia sighed. 'It's ridiculous, he's only away for a week, but I really miss him.' As she spoke she bobbed up and down, trying to keep at eye-level with Rosalind whose head kept disappearing under the hood of the pram.

Rosalind looked up with an indulgent smile. 'If that's what not being married does to a relationship, maybe Chris and I should go for divorce. I mean, London is only an hour away.'

'What do you mean London is only an hour away?'

Rosalind's sou'wester appeared again. 'I mean London is not a long distance away from Abbotslea.' She spoke with the same practised patience she employed when speaking to little Ronald. 'As I saw Gerald across the street from the Royal Academy – and you told me he was away for the week – and as childbirth has not completely addled my razor sharp brain, I put two and two together and assumed London was where Gerald was. 'We wanted to see the Monet exhibition.' Rosalind's head darted back under the hood and Amelia heard a muffled, 'Didn't we Ronnikins?'

'Gerald was in London yesterday?' Amelia's main feeling was of stupidity. She saw Rosalind's lips move, she heard the words they spoke, but she was damned if she understood. 'Did you speak to him?'

Rosalind was beginning to look impatient. 'No, as a matter of fact, I didn't. We just waved across the street. Yes, Mummy's sausage waved to Mr Forbes, didn't he?'

'You're sure it was Gerald?'

Ronald let out a sudden, anguished wail. Rosalind looked at her watch as she loosened the break on the pram with a kick of the foot. 'I didn't go up to him and ask for his driving licence or genetically fingerprint him or anything, but it looked like Gerald to me. Now I really must get home and give Ronnie his elevenses, the poor little mite is starving.'

For once, as she stepped inside the village shop, Amelia was pleased that it was no longer run by Wing Commander Stephens OBE AFC. He'd been a source of endless amusement to Amelia as he plied his trade, always fearful that in so doing he had come down in the world. His manner was chill towards anyone with a small child, an ice-cream or an address in the wrong part of the village and jovially officious to others. It was a manner that had sent most of the villagers into the anonymous comfort of the supermarket in nearby Alresford. Sometimes, Mrs Stephens would appear in check polyester overalls, and tell Amelia of their days attached to the Embassy in Peru, the glittering parties they gave, and the people they met. In the end though even the weekly Saturday sell-off of out-of-date stock couldn't save the Wing Commander from the realities of supply and demand. When he finally sold up, the view of the village was that it had been only a matter of time until he was closed down by the health inspector anyway.

The Stores had been taken over by a big-thinking young couple from a nearby village who were planning a chain of Mini-Marts. Whilst continuing to carry the usual stock: sweets and biscuits, tinned soups and rice-puddings, speciality cheeses and teas, they added frozen Weight-watcher meals, videos for hire and a sub-Post Office, and employed a girl for the newly installed check-out who displayed much the same attitude to her customers as a gardener to worms; as a breed they were necessary but on a one to one basis they had little to offer.

In the old days, Amelia, who had won favour with the Wing Commander due to her pretty face and connections with the Forbeses and in spite of her short skirts and unorthodox relationship with the Forbes' son, would have had to explain both Gerald's business in being absent and her own glum face. As it was, she posted her envelope and bought her cheese and bread with the minimum communication needed for the transactions.

'First class is it? That'll be thirty-one pence,' at the Post Office counter, and 'Two pounds exactly, thank you,' at the check-out.

The rest of the morning, Amelia tried to make sense of what Rosalind had told her. She hated mysteries and uncertainties. They sent her into frenzied, ineffective action, like someone with a ceiling leaking in five places but only one bucket. First she called Gerald's office to ask his father where Gerald was. She liked Norman and he was fond of her. She wouldn't mind admitting to him that she had mislaid his son. But Norman was at a meeting and the secretary didn't know where Mr Gerald Forbes could be reached, either. 'Is this Miss Lindsay?'

'No, no it isn't,' Amelia answered, suddenly talking at the front of her mouth, in a feeble attempt to disguise her voice.

Next she telephoned Gerald's friend Tom, who was meant to be on the trip. Only the answering machine was at home and, in the manner of those machines, gave little away other than that, 'Tom can't come to the phone right now . . .'

She couldn't call Nick, she didn't have his number or address. She sat by the phone, trying to calm herself down. Gerald would be in touch. There was bound to be a reasonable explanation of why he'd been seen in the centre of London whilst on a fishing trip to Scotland. Gerald was nice. He didn't lie. Any moment now he'd come through the door explaining that the trip had been cut short.

He didn't come home and there was no word from him that day, nor the next. Furious, fretting, with a feeling in her stomach as if her guts were being twisted like spaghetti round a fork, she sat at the kitchen table breathing deeply: in, out, in and out. She visualized herself as a giant boiling kettle with a cork stuffed down its spout, making it impossible for the steam to escape as the pressure was building (she had once attended relaxation classes with Dagmar). 'Now remove that cork,' she said to herself, her voice taking on a faint American accent. 'Feel the steam just pouring out.'

'Sod it!' she screamed, as the vision was taking on a life of its own, with Amelia straddling the huge kettle, desperately wrestling with the cork. 'Bloody hell, bloody, fucking hell!' She stood up, yelling so her throat hurt, her fists pounding the air.

That did help. Pacing the room, she stopped at the open window and leant out, breathing in the damp air.

'Amelia, is that you?' Mrs Jenkins from next door stood by the low stone wall. She was smiling, but it was rather a tight-lipped smile. 'I thought I heard your voice.'

'Mrs Jenkins, ah, yes . . . I was just rehearsing my lines for . . . for the Cherryfield Home for the Elderly's summer play. They're a pretty modern lot at Cherry-field.' She gave a quick wave and dived out of sight.

Twenty-four hours later, Amelia packed an over-night bag and, leaving a note for Gerald to contact her in case he arrived home before her, set off for Kingsmouth.

Chapter Nine

Selma loved plants. At Ashcombe they had surrounded her; green bodyguards in the drawing room, a scented, multi-coloured fence outside. When she had first arrived, holding her small, white-faced daughter by the hand, she had walked outside on to the terrace in the moonlight. The camomile crushed under their feet had filled the air around them with its soporific scent, as she looked across the garden to a glimpse of the sea beyond.

'Get away from me you bloody fool!' As Amelia approached Cherryfield in the late afternoon, Selma's voice reached her from the open first-floor window. Amelia, shocked at hearing her grandmother yell obscenities in much the same manner as she herself had done earlier that day, ducked to avoid a beige Scholl sandal flying straight at her.

A potted begonia, tracing the path of the sandal, crashed at her feet, having narrowly missed her right temple. She could see no-one at the window until a uniformed arm appeared slamming it shut. Bending down again, she picked up the shoe from amid the soil and bits of shattered clay and brushed it off, before resuming her walk to the front door. She rang the bell, her cheeks reddening in anticipation of the telling off from Sister Morris. 'I'm sure she didn't mean to,' she rehearsed. 'She probably didn't realize the window was open.'

'Cooee! Amelia darling!'

She took a step back to find that Selma had managed to open the window again and was leaning out, pink-cheeked and smiling. 'What a lovely surprise. I'll be right down, if ...' Her voice became laden with reproach as she turned into the room. 'If I'm allowed to.'

As Selma descended sideways in the chairlift, her chubby back straight, Amelia wondered if she should mention at least in passing that she had been almost knocked out by a potted plant, maybe even get Selma to give some kind of explanation that might satisfy the still absent Sister Morris. But her grandmother looked so normal, so happy to see her, that she said nothing.

'If you could pass me that wretched thing,' Selma said, pointing at the walking frame standing at the bottom of the stairs. Slowly, her hands, then her weight, were transferred to the frame, and Amelia followed her grandmother's hesitant shuffling towards the conservatory. Now and then Selma would halt, forgetting to move one foot in front of the other, like a sick baby forgetting to breathe. Then with a little start, the shuffle would continue.

'We're doing ever so well on the frame now.' Nurse Williams smiled approvingly at them as they passed in the lounge. There was no mention of the scene upstairs. 'I told you Mrs M, didn't I tell you, there's no harm in trying, I said.'

Amelia got Selma settled in a wicker armchair. She looked at her grandmother's face, it looked such a small face all of a sudden, unsure, all fury spent. 'Are you eating properly?' she asked.

'I get terribly bored with the food here,' Selma said. 'I much preferred it in the other place.'

Amelia couldn't bring herself to ask, 'What other place?' So she said nothing.

'Of course I can't wait until I'm back in my own kitchen.' From having fussed with her handbag and the position of her sore foot, Selma suddenly looked directly at Amelia, 'Play the game with me, please,' her eyes seemed to say.

'I'm sure you're getting better every day,' Amelia said sidling round the truth.

'I won't get better whilst I'm here,' Selma insisted. She leant over as far as she could towards Amelia. 'It's a funny place. You can't make any plans. You know, I don't think I've had a swim in weeks.' She leant back again, closing her eyes for a moment. 'There are no animals here either.'

Each visit, Amelia had dreaded Selma asking after the cats, but she never did, and it struck Amelia that Selma didn't ask about lots of things because she was too frightened of the answers.

'I only live for the moment when I can go back,' Selma said matter of factly.

Amelia felt her cheeks going hot. It was her turn to lean forward and she took Selma's shaking hand between her own two and forced it still. 'It won't be long, I'm sure it won't.'

'Promise?' Selma smiled.

'Promise,' said Amelia, feeling sick.

Selma closed her eyes, and soon she was asleep, leaving Amelia pondering impossible schemes of how to fulfil that promise. Maybe, she thought tiredly, Selma would forget, like she forgot so much else.

Amelia relaxed. Time, in the overheated room, seemed to float. There had been so many times when she'd sat watching Selma doze off in her chair after lunch. Selma had always been a great one for naps. 'You stay here by me, darling,' she'd say, sitting in the bay of the drawing room at Ashcombe, her chair turned towards the window and the view of the sea.

'I'll just close my eyes for a moment,' and she would lean back and go to sleep in just this way. Selma loved the sea, the constantly changing scene from the window. She seemed to bear it no resentment for taking her first husband, Amelia's real grandfather, away from her.

'I stood on the quayside in Gothenburg, waiting each morning for the ferry that would bring him and his parents and sister back from Germany,' Selma had told Amelia.

'I was like the statue of the Seaman's Wife, looking out over the harbour entrance, hoping, watching. The ferries came and ships too, and there were refugees onboard, but never Daniel or his family. Your grandfather was a brave man; he went back to Germany knowing what might happen.'

Selma never wanted to talk about what followed, but there was the postcard, in a hand quite unlike that in the old love letters from Daniel that Amelia had found in a silk-lined box at the back of Selma's huge walnut closet. The uncertain writing on the card said in German, 'I've been taken to a detention camp for my own safety, and am well and healthy.' But Daniel had died in Belsen, and in a drawer in Selma's desk was the letter from Daniel's mother before she too was taken. Only Selma could read the spindly writing, but they all knew the letter, Tante Magda's last letter in its yellowing envelope. There were some photographs too, snapshots of a long-ago summer holiday. In one, Daniel, tall, auburn-haired like Amelia, smiled into the camera, his arm round Selma's shoulder. In another, Tante Magda sat in the shade of a parasol with Ella, Daniel's little sister, at her side. Some letters, a few photographs, were all that remained of a family.

Amelia sat at Cherryfield, thinking of her grandfather Daniel who had died when he was younger than she was now, and she knew that against his suffering the mislaying of Gerald weighed less than a feather.

When she was small and feeling sorry for herself, Amelia, like most children, had been told to think of those who were worse off. It had always worried her, this summoning up of images of suffering just so that her infinitely lighter burdens would seem even slighter. What was it other than the exploitation of tragedy? Who was there to ask? Selma, more often that not, averted her eyes and mind from that which disturbed her, homing in instead on what was pleasant, a flower, a pretty face, a swath of material just right for the dining-room chairs. Dagmar, on the other hand, seemed convinced that suffering lay in wait behind every poor dupe engaged in carefree pleasure, so rather than be taken unawares, she would seek trouble out, take it by the hand and invite it into her life. Then of course, she could sit back, relax for a moment even, and say, 'There, I told you, we're none of us safe.'

Amelia turned her chair away from the sun that shone low and straight through the window, making her eyes ache.

'What was that darling?' Selma jerked awake in her chair, gazing sleepy-eyed at Amelia.

'I ought to go soon,' Amelia said. 'It's nearly your supper-time. I'll be here most of tomorrow, maybe we could go down to town.'

'Don't leave yet,' Selma said as she always did. 'There,' she pointed at the glass doors leading in to the lounge. 'There's Admiral Mallett, you must stay and meet him.' She raised herself a little in the chair and waved. Smiling at the Admiral who had spotted them, she mouthed, the smile still in place, 'Poor old Admiral Mallett, he's a dear, sweet man, but, between you and me, I think he's just the slightest bit potty.'

The Admiral, leaning heavily on two sticks, turned

to speak to someone and Henry stepped into view, guiding his father through the doors.

Her voice, carrying, gracious, Selma called out, 'Admiral, how are you today? Do come and join us.' She indicated an empty chair with her good hand and, as she moved, Amelia noticed for the first time that the bandage which used to reach Selma's ankle bone was now spiralling its way up the leg like a pale serpent. Amelia shuddered and searched Selma's face for signs of pain, but Selma looked relaxed, smiling at the Admiral.

'I've just promised my grandmother that she'll be back home soon.' Amelia bent close to Henry, speaking in a low voice that could not be heard over Selma's conversation with the Admiral.

'That's nice,' Henry said. 'Why didn't you tell me you were coming?'

'I don't know your telephone number, or your address.'

'Nor you do.' Henry smiled at her.

'The point is,' Amelia paused, irritated by the intense way he was looking at her, as if, she thought, he's expecting me any moment to perform a particularly stunning card trick. 'The point is,' she tried again, 'there *is* no house. It's been sold. Now do you see?'

Henry stopped smiling. 'Yes, I do see.'

'Just don't start preaching to me about the sin of dishonesty,' Amelia snapped. 'I couldn't take it.'

'Now you're being unfair,' Henry corrected her mildly. 'I only preach on Sundays and Wednesdays, anything else would have to be considered overtime. What I was going to say,' he stretched his rather heavy legs out in front of him, 'is that you'd better start working on a plan of action.'

Amelia frowned. 'What do you mean, "Plan of Action"?'

'I mean that you need to work out how you are going to get your grandmother back home.' And he turned to his father who was trying to attract his attention with a series of 'I say old chap'.

Amelia stared for a moment at Henry's serene profile, the firm, short chin, the slightly stubby nose, and thought he must be very thick.

Selma put her chubby hand on Henry's arm, she'd always needed to touch, to hold on and caress. 'Your father has just promised to come to my little party. You must come too. Amelia will bring you. Now don't you forget, sixteenth of August. You put that in your diary.'

Amelia had to listen to Selma chirruping about her plans interrupted only by the twittering of Miss White, who, on joining them, had immediately secured an invitation by demanding one. 'You get nothing in life if you don't ask.'

'Will you have dinner with me tonight?' Henry's voice was casual, but his eyes, squirrel brown Amelia thought, were fixed on hers.

She was starved of admiration. She felt she was a little like one of her own neglected potplants. That's right, she thought, I'm like that poor African Violet who should be fed with tomato fertilizer once a fortnight but is lucky if it gets a drop or so every other month, its blooms growing fewer and fewer until there's just dense, dull-green foliage.

She smiled and said she'd love to have dinner with him and was rewarded with a huge grin of pleasure and relief.

Amelia too felt grateful. She was saved from an evening waiting for a call from Gerald that would not come, saved from yet another dinner on her own in the small dining room of the hotel. Those lonely meal-times always reminded her of awful teenage dances she was forced to attend, when cropped red hair and a flat chest had very little appeal when compared to long blond tresses and a size 36D bust. Once, at a party in a village hall, a left behind brochure on woodworm infestation had provided relief. She had sat gazing earnestly at its pages, able to pretend, at least to herself, that the last thing she wanted to do at a dance was dance and that, seeing she was so busy with her brochure, it would be a miracle if one could be fitted in, should anyone ask. She had reached 'The Woodworm and your Heirlooms', when a boy with spreading wet stains under his arms finally asked, by the way of an elegant lead in, what it was she was reading.

'Proust,' Amelia had answered, and she hadn't danced that dance either.

Now at each lonely meal, as she sat engrossed in the wine list and the bit at the bottom of the menu about Cromwell having been there first, she felt she could discern a whiff of pesticide in the air.

With a warm smile, she said to Henry, 'I had planned to wear a sign round my neck tonight, with "I'm eating on my own because I've got leprosy", written on it, and now I won't have to.'

Then it was six o'clock and there was tea or, as Selma insisted, supper-served-far-too-early, in the dining room.

'We're abandoning them to that.' Amelia standing with Henry in the doorway, pointed at the plates of corned beef and limp lettuce being handed round.

Henry said nothing but, as he turned his face away, she saw his cheeks redden.

Looking out over the tables of old people raising forks to their mouths, stabbing at the food, drinking water from thick, cloudy glasses, she felt as if she was watching a programme with the sound turned off, the room was so quiet. The strain of staying alive another day had taken its toll on the residents of Cherryfield; there was no energy left for conversation.

Amelia and Henry walked through the empty Residents' Lounge and into the hall, guilt padding behind them like a big-eyed mongrel refused a walk.

'I'm afraid I'm crying,' Amelia apologized to Henry as an auxiliary locked the front door behind them. 'But today in particular, I feel life's very sad. "Often sad, but never serious." Who was it who said that?' She dabbed at her eyes with a Swiss, embroidered handkerchief that Selma had given her.

'Winston Churchill, Bernard Shaw, Oscar Wilde?' Henry reeled the names out with a smile, but his voice sounded thick, as if he too was crying.

Amelia tried to say something that would cheer him up. 'What about Jesus, what would he say?'

'Don't make fun of me please,' Henry said quietly as he opened the car door for her. 'Not just now.' And he slammed her door shut and walked round to his side before she had time to answer.

They left the car by the ferry and went for a drink at a pub nearby, before wandering the cobbled streets looking for somewhere to eat.

'Not Wimpy,' Henry said as they passed one, 'or Kentucky Fried Chicken. What we need is something French and pretentious, or Italian and lingering. Italian, I think, with dripping candles stuffed into green bottles.'

But Kingsmouth these days was short on anything lingering and long on anything to do with fast food. '"Tato n'topping",' Henry read on the sign. 'I don't think so.' But as they turned up the hill from the harbour they heard faint piano music coming from further up the dark street.

'That used to be rather a shabby boarding house.' Amelia looked at the floodlit façade of the building, where baskets of geraniums were suspended from wrought-iron hooks. The music had stopped, but inside Henry pointed triumphantly to the round tables, each with a lit candle in a wine bottle placed on the check cloth.

'Perfect,' he sighed happily.

As they sat sipping their wine, a tiny dapper man with unnaturally black hair entered through a back door. Stooping slightly, he made his way across the restaurant with quick steps, past a trolley laden with cakes and puddings, and over to the upright piano in the far corner. He lifted his right hand high in the air, before striking the first chord of 'The Blue Danube'.

'Can one ask for more?' Henry said, sitting back in his chair.

The little man played on as the restaurant filled with people. He played waltzes and polkas and marches while Amelia and Henry ate their whitebait and the Roman pork ('We find there is a certain resistance to veal amongst our British diners,' the head waiter had explained) and, after the final medley, he lifted his hands high in the air once more for a final onslaught on the keys. Then he leapt from the stool with surprising speed and, as Amelia and Henry applauded, acknowledged them with a graceful bow before disappearing out the way he had come.

'Selma would love him,' Amelia said. She paused for a moment, thinking. 'It's funny really that classical music or poetry or pictures are regarded as luxuries when they are actually tremendous equalizers. I mean . . .' Finding Henry looking as if he was actually listening to her, she stopped for a moment, giving him a quick smile before continuing, 'You don't need to be able-bodied or employed or even sane to get the same kick out of those things as the rest of us. My grandmother can't produce or nurture, she can't explore.

She has no say even in her own life and I very much doubt she would survive on her own for more than a week. But Mozart and Strauss, a poem read aloud, a beautiful painting, can still open the same doors to her as they do to us, give the same peace or elation, the same peek at immortality.' Amelia, feeling she was talking too much, drained her glass of red wine, her cheeks a little pinker than usual.

'Maybe that's why so many men at the front write poetry,' Henry said. 'I hate to talk shop but, as the Bible says, "Consider the lilies of the field, how they grow; they toil not, neither do they spin."' He spoke the words softly, but with an intensity that made Amelia feel sorry when he stopped with an 'etc etc'.

She wished too that he wouldn't assume she knew the rest of the quote; she didn't, not exactly, and she would be too lazy to look it up later. 'All right, so I'm not an original thinker,' she laughed.

The little man returned to the piano and, settling again on the round stool, began to play 'A Rhapsody in Blue'.

Whilst she listened, Amelia looked around her at the other diners. At the table behind Henry, five women were chatting and laughing, constantly and easily. At the other tables sat mostly couples, eating their food in near silence, scattering a word here, a comment there, like Amelia chucking corn at her bantams.

Maybe a good gauge of the dynamism of a love affair was not how often you made love, she thought, but how much you talked to each other in restaurants. It was not so long ago that she had been smugly aware of the wealth of things that Gerald and she would find to talk about when they were out. They'd sit, heads close together, forgetting even to eat at times, but lately, lately they had been more like the silently chewing couples she used to despise.

Sighing, she said suddenly to Henry, 'Gerald, that's who my grandmother thinks you are, Gerald might be having an affair.' And she looked up, astonished at her own words, admitting to him what she hadn't even admitted to herself until then.

Henry did not seem surprised, but just looked thoughtfully at her, his head a little to one side, like an overlarge bird, listening for the song of another.

Amelia smiled weakly, 'It's a bit upsetting actually as I love him with all my heart and that sort of thing.' She looked thoughtful, 'I suppose that to you, to most people, I'm an affair already, so where that leaves his new relationship I don't know. Tell me, Henry, what would the church say? Has a deceived mistress got any rights? Can she in fact ever be deceived or just punished?'

'Never mind that for the moment,' Henry said unexpectedly. 'You must ask him straight out if he's playing around. If he is, leave him.'

Amelia looked at him. 'How old are you?'

'Twenty-six.'

'You're very young.' Amelia touched his cheek. 'Funny how having something strategically placed round your neck, a stethoscope, microphone, dog-collar, makes people expect great wisdom from you.'

'I'm sorry.' Henry looked embarrassed.

Amelia smiled and shook her head. 'No I'm sorry, I was rude. It's very kind of you to listen to me. I feel quite alone sometimes. My mother is fine until something really interesting, like a dog's mess, catches her attention. I adored Willoughby but he's dead. I sometimes feel Selma might as well be.' She looked at Henry. 'What's your view on euthanasia?'

'No,' Henry said.

'But why?'

'Because only God has the right to take a life.'

'God giveth and God taketh away,' Amelia mumbled. Then she said, 'But he doesn't decide on giving life, we do, the man and the woman. It's we who decide whether to have a child or not.'

'God gave you that ability.'

'He's given me the ability to take life too.'

'The ability, yes, but not the right.' Henry's amiable face had taken on a stern look. 'What you can do, what you are doing, is to ease the pain, make what's left of someone's life as bearable as possible.'

'But what you are saying is that you can condone the killing of perfectly healthy young men in a war, or I presume you do as you're in the Navy, but you can't accept the easing of the dying of very old ladies?'

Henry poured what was left of the wine into their glasses. 'You have to stand up to evil. Sometimes, in doing that, you might need to use force. There's St Augustine's Doctrine of the Just War; it may have been conceived to justify Rome's colonial wars, but the idea itself is sound. Humans are imperfect.' He smiled. 'Some are a lot less perfect than others. When Hitler rampaged through Europe, should chaps like me have stood back and said to the men and women risking their lives to put an end to some of the worst suffering in the history of mankind, "Thou shalt not kill"?' Henry shook his head. 'I don't think so. You have to build your life on certain principles but, for mere mortals, I do believe it's a mistake to etch them in stone.'

'Wasn't it George Bernard Shaw who said to a lady sitting next to him at dinner, "Now all we're doing is arguing about the price"?'

Henry looked at her, his face serious. 'No, not at all. What we are arguing about is right or wrong as we perceive it, honestly and in our hearts. I believe and so, I'm sure, do you that it is right to defend a child from a brutal killer, even if that means using force, the minimum force necessary to save the child. But who is your grandmother threatening? Your peace of mind?' Henry leant closer to Amelia, putting his hand over Amelia's. 'If you asked her if she wanted to die, what do you think she'd answer?'

Amelia, looking flushed, snatched her hand away, glaring at Henry as if he was personally responsible for the injustices of the universe. 'And that', she said, 'is just the final little nasty thrown in, the ultimate trap, this absurd instinct of survival that we've got. This pathetic desire to cling on long after we know the party is over. Not that it's often much of a party anyway.'

'Tut, tut,' Henry said. 'What a cynic you are.'

'Not a cynic,' but Amelia couldn't help smiling. He is like a sponge, she thought; any anger thrown at him gets soaked up and dissipated. 'No, not a cynic at all. I'm just possessed of what Selma calls "a black bottom". I think what she means is a melancholy disposition.'

'I prefer black bottom,' said Henry. 'It sounds much more dashing. Don't let it take over though.'

'I won't. I keep it decorously covered most of the time. And I won't kill Selma, however much I love her. In my case, conviction is never matched by courage.'

'Thank God for that,' Henry said simply.

There was no message for Miss Lindsay. 'No, no call from a Mr Gerald Forbes,' the night porter answered, looking up from the sports page of the *Evening Herald*. 'Yes,' he was quite sure.

Chapter Ten

Dagmar felt pleased with herself as she parked her car in front of Cherryfield. She had woken that morning feeling strong and positive, ready to fight. She had wasted too much of her life already, but no more. She smiled as she thought of the interesting conversation she'd had with the new visiting professor from the States about the relevance of fiction in society. She had surprised herself as much as him with how much she had to say on the subject.

'No risk, no fun.' She mumbled the phrase her husband had used on the ski-slopes where they first met. 'No risk, no fun.' And she refused to give in to the impulse to wrap the car keys in tissue paper before letting them fall into her handbag.

As she rang the doorbell, Amelia caught up with her. They kissed hello, but before they had a chance to speak the door opened and Selma's voice, carrying her outrage through the rooms, reached them from the Residents' Lounge, 'Murderer, brute, Nazi!'

Dagmar and Amelia looked at each other, then ran towards the commotion, Amelia narrowly avoiding knocking into a nurse carrying a bedpan.

'Stay away from me, do you hear?' They heard Selma's voice again, but it sounded smaller now, trembling. 'How do I know you're not planning to boil me too? I'm old, I'm ill.'

They reached the Lounge to find Selma sitting

ashen-faced, as far back in her chair as she could, her fingers gripping the armrest.

'Steady on, Selma my dear, steady on.' Admiral Mallett tried to control his voice, as unreliable as a fourteen-year-old boy's, as he rose with difficulty from his seat by the empty aquarium. 'I must say though, Matron.' He stood facing Sister Morris, leaning heavily on his crutches. 'Boiling the little chaps does seem a bit excessive.'

'What on earth is going on here, Sister Morris?' Dagmar demanded as Amelia knelt by Selma, hugging her.

Sister Morris turned, purple-cheeked and panting with fury. 'A ridiculous fuss over nothing, that's what's going on! And may I tell you, Mrs Lindsay, that it's your mother who's the ringleader as usual.'

'Now I say,' the Admiral tottered on his sticks, but his voice was steady, 'you can't call the little fellows nothing. I liked 'em. So did Mrs Merryman here. It's not a question of any ringleader.'

Amelia, still with her arms protectively around Selma, asked gently, 'What is it that has upset you so? Try to explain.'

Selma managed to heave herself half out of the chair and now she pointed an accusing finger at Sister Morris. 'I called into the kitchen to see what foul repast they were preparing, the smell coming from there was disgusting. And I find her,' Selma had fallen back into the chair but she was still pointing, 'her, standing like a witch from *Macbeth* over a steaming pan, lowering the Admiral's little guppies into the fiercely boiling water, one by one. She wasn't actually chanting, but it was a near thing; her lips were moving.'

'That's it. I'm going to my quarters,' Sister Morris spoke with hysterical calm. 'If anyone should feel the need to hear what actually happened, I'll be waiting.'

And she marched out, head held high, her wooden slip-ons sucking and letting go of the heels of her feet with every angry step.

'I suppose I should feel guilty,' Clarissa tossed the green salad with vigour, 'being here in Amelia's kitchen, using her things.' She gave Gerald a coy glance underneath her thick eyelashes, 'Sleeping with you in her bed.'

'My little Goldilocks.' Gerald ruffled her hair affectionately.

For a second, Clarissa stared blankly at him, then her wide brow cleared and she gave an appreciative little laugh. 'Somehow I don't feel bad about it,' she said, 'that's the thing. It's like I'm in my rightful place, and she is the interloper, you know what I mean?' She licked some oil from her fingers. 'Well, she will be soon anyway. It's not even as if I'm breaking up a marriage.'

A whisper of guilt passed through Gerald's mind, but like a solitary cloud on an otherwise perfect blue sky, it cast no lasting shadow. 'You're so sensible, I like that,' he said.

Placing the salad bowl on the table, Clarissa said, 'You are sure though, aren't you, that she's not coming back until Monday? I mean, why did you make such a thing about putting the car away?' She looked earnestly at him. 'It's just that it's so important to do this right.'

Gerald had a vision of Amelia on an operating table, with him expertly removing her heart with the able assistance of Clarissa. He shook himself, Amelia's fancifulness seemed to be infectious. 'I'm quite sure,' he said firmly. 'She really is very good about her grandmother, I must give her that. Too good,' he added hastily, at the sight of Clarissa's already firm chin, jutting. 'I suppose,' he said, 'that the old girl always was more of a mother to her than poor Dagmar.'

'Is she really mad, the mother I mean?' Clarissa picked a Little Gem lettuce leaf from the bowl and nibbled it.

Gerald considered for a moment, as he uncorked the bottle of Chablis. 'Not actually and certifiably, no; neurotic as hell though. She was quite a promising pianist apparently, as was Selma. But, according to Amelia, she spent so much time disinfecting the piano keys, there was no time left to practise.' He felt a little guilty as he spoke, about betraying Amelia's confidence, but then he reminded himself what a pain Amelia could be. 'Amelia is a bit like that.'

'What? Disinfecting things?'

'Good heavens no, look around you. No, I mean unable to follow anything through. Great ideas, a fair amount of talent, but nothing ever comes to anything.'

'Well as long as she doesn't come here.' Clarissa, delighted with her joke, wound her strong arms round Gerald's neck.

Gerald laughed a little uneasily, remembering Amelia's remark that one could always tell a man in love by the way he laughed at even the most feeble of his loved one's jokes.

At the same time, Henry arrived at Cherryfield. He was worried about his father, he hadn't been himself since that disastrous lunch with Amelia and Mrs Merryman. All the fight seemed to have gone out of him. And then there had been the business with the stolen dentures. Henry sighed, raking his fingers through his hair. He had been told by a past girlfriend that she could always tell when he was upset because of his habit of doing just that. Of course months later when he broke off the relationship, she told him how it had always irritated her. There, he did it again: his fingers pushing through his hair as if they could push his problems away with them, but it was a bad time to go off on exercise, now, when his father needed him most.

He found the Admiral in the Residents' Lounge, sitting miserably by the fish-tank, whilst next to him Selma rocked backwards and forwards in her chair, weeping like a child, tears running unstemmed down her pinched cheeks. Amelia was kneeling by her side, crying herself at her grandmother's distress. The television in the corner by the window added to the confusion with an Australian soap being played out at high volume.

Amelia looked up at Henry, her slanted eyes wide and tearful. 'I'm taking her home to Abbotslea. No-one else cares.'

'But what on earth has happened?' Henry asked gently. He put his hand on his father's shoulder.

The Admiral just shook his head and pointed his stick at the empty fish-tank. Henry turned to Amelia.

'Ask that awful Morris,' she said, standing up.

Henry gave her a long look. 'Right,' he said finally. 'I'll go and find her,' and he stalked off.

'She's in her flat,' Amelia called after him, 'but if I were you, I wouldn't bother.'

Henry found Sister Morris in her quarters on the second floor. As she opened the door to him, the heat from an open coalfire hit him in the face like steam from an engine. Above his head, a bell-rope tinkled.

Sister Morris maintained a dignified silence as she indicated a seat for him on the plump sofa covered in differently shaped and patterned cushions. He sat down, moving a pink heart-shaped one embroidered with 'Home Is Where The Heart Is', to avoid it being crushed.

On the mantelpiece stood a collection of china pigs dressed in the manner of different professions: one wore a tie and bowler, another a nurse's uniform, one was a fireman, and there was even a pig with a dog-collar Henry noticed, amused. Sister Morris herself shared her armchair with a large teddy, a calico cat and a giant, stuffed hedgehog, and on the coffee table stood an open Paddington Bear biscuit tin. She seemed determined to keep at bay the ever-present spectre of old age by cramming her tiny sitting room with childish whimsy. Like a medicine-man, Henry thought, decorating his hut with totems and charms to ward off the evil eye.

He cleared his throat and began, choosing his words carefully. 'There seems to be some sort of problem downstairs. I wondered if you could possibly fill me in.'

Sister Morris's chins quivered with emotion and her cheeks reddened. 'I'm glad that someone sees fit to ask me. Of course you are a man of the cloth,' her voice softened, but just for a moment. 'This whole thing has been blown out of all proportion . . .'

Five minutes later, Henry returned to the Residents' Lounge. 'Right,' he said, sitting down in the empty chair between his father and Selma, 'there's a perfectly good explanation, nothing to get too concerned about. You see the fish were ill,' he continued, feeling like some grotesque version of *Listen with Mother*, as more residents gathered round like ancient vultures, determined not to miss any morsel of scandal.

'Well, boiling them can't have helped,' Miss White said firmly as she manoeuvred herself into an armchair. 'And if that's Sister's little remedy for the ailing, none of us can sleep soundly in our beds. Not that I'm ever blessed with sound sleep.' Her expression suggested suffering bravely born. 'I toss and I turn, I toss . . .'

'The vet told Sister Morris that there was nothing he could do for them.' Henry spoke firmly. 'I'm afraid putting them out of their misery was the only option.' He smiled encouragingly at Selma who slumped in her rose-patterned armchair. 'Apparently, immersing the fish in boiling water is the quickest and least painful way of doing it.'

'I had lobster once,' Miss White said. 'Highly overrated I thought.'

A large woman, whom Henry hadn't seen before, leant across, her cheeks pink with excitement, her eyes opened wide, 'I don't care *what* that Sister Morris says, I'm not having those poor little fish for my tea.'

'I'm not either,' a cacophony of voices agreed. 'I won't eat a scrap.'

Henry clenched his teeth, worried and ashamed of his sudden urge to shake them, scream at them all to shut up. He looked into the old faces, sagging, whiskery, toothless, confused, and he saw the humiliation in his father's eyes, how straight he sat in the chair by the empty fish-tank. God forgive me, he thought. Getting up from his chair, he walked across and put his hand on the old man's shoulder. 'What do you say we go for a drive, have a drink at the Anchor?'

Then Amelia came downstairs with a small suitcase, badly packed by the look of the corner of blue material that hung out from the side. She was about to help Selma from the chair when she stopped, looking round for the walking-frame.

'I think you're overreacting.' Henry spoke quietly, but he went over to the television which was still on, bleating out some incidental music from a motionless screen, and brought out the walking-frame that stood in the corner behind. He placed it by Selma's chair, then he turned and said quietly to Amelia, 'You should never make decisions when you're in a state. Get your grandmother upstairs for a rest, sit down yourself and think this over.' He looked from Selma's grey expressionless face to Amelia's bright pink cheeks and moist eyes. 'How will you get her back? How will you cope when you get her home? You're not strong enough to lift her?'

'We'll manage,' Amelia said. She smiled mechanically in his direction. 'It won't be for long, she just needs a break from this place.'

Henry didn't argue further but helped Selma up. 'At least let me drive you to the station,' he said as he held the door for them.

Amelia turned. 'That's very kind of you, but my mother should be arriving back any minute, she'll take us.'

Selma too had stopped in the doorway, and for a moment Henry thought he saw a look of triumph in her eyes. He sighed and went back across the room, sitting down, next to his father, on Selma's empty chair.

'What about you, Pa, do you want to get away from here too?'

The Admiral turned and attempted a smile but his hands, black-bruised and wrinkled, gripped the handles of the sticks at his side. 'I'm fine, dear boy, don't worry about me. It's not this place, it's being old. It's no fun.' He put one hand on Henry's. 'But that's life in a blue suit, and even a chap with your connections can't change it.'

Dagmar drove Selma and Amelia to Plymouth Station.

'It's jolly good of you to have Mummy,' she hissed over her shoulder to Amelia. 'I would have liked to have had her myself of course, but they'd never give me the time off.' She added in her normal voice, 'Well, at least I managed to find you a decent dress, Mummy, rather than that permanent-press monstrosity the woman at Cherryfield picked up for you.'

Amelia had calmed down during the trip. She could feel the heat going out of her cheeks and her pulse rate slowing but, as Dagmar pulled up in front of the station, she began to worry again, but for different reasons. Henry had been right, how would she cope? Then again, hadn't Rosalind felt the same mixture of panic and inadequacy when bringing little Ronnie home from hospital in his flower-sprigged Moses basket? Amelia went through her duties in her head: bathing and dressing, food to prepare that was both nourishing and suitable for dentures. How on earth did one clean dentures? At least she had had the forethought to ask one of the nurses at Cherryfield for Selma's medication. Then there was Gerald. Amelia looked helplessly at her mother, but it was too late to change her mind now.

Dagmar wrote, 'Transporting Invalid', in large letters on a piece of paper and fixed it to the windscreen. Then they walked Selma across the platform to the waiting train. Amelia got on first and, taking Selma's wrists, she began to pull her up. Dagmar, careful not to rub her trouser-leg against the dirty bottom step, heaved at Selma's polycotton-clad bottom. 'Just like Pooh getting stuck in Rabbit's hole,' she called cheerfully. Selma, facing Amelia, pretended not to hear.

A guard strode purposefully past the beached Selma, on his way to help a young mother with a twin push-chair on to the next carriage. The babies smiled their toothless thanks. Little blond cherubs, Amelia thought bitterly, as with a final heave, Selma stood tottering on board the train. She too smiled, out of relief and embarrassment, she too showed her gums. Oh my God, Amelia thought, she's left her teeth behind.

Waving at Dagmar from the window, Amelia thought how unfairly arranged it all was. Babies' toothlessness was sweet, their chubbiness, cuddly. They dribble their food, they burp and sick up, lacking all control over their bodily functions, but the package came wrapped in such irresistible cuteness that few people failed to coddle and assist. After all, Amelia thought, how may Residential Homes for the Active Infant did you see dotted along leafy, small-town streets?

She turned away from the window and sat down opposite Selma. So what about old people, why was it made so easy for us to want to abandon them? Amelia felt a pity that was almost painful when she looked across at her grandmother slumped in her seat, unlovely, her dress riding up over her thick knees, an uncertain smile on her pinched, grey face. No, it wasn't fair.

She handed Selma a copy of *Good Housekeeping*. Selma said, 'How lovely,' and leafed through it happily. She had always had *Good Housekeeping* reserved for her at the newsagent in Kingsmouth, even after Willoughby's retirement when economies had to be made.

Does she know, really know, Amelia wondered, as she sits avidly reading those recipes that she will never again prepare a meal?

'I need to spend a penny.' Selma put the magazine down.

Amelia's back hurt as she pulled Selma up from her seat. For a moment, they stood facing each other, Amelia bent, Selma tottering, their hands clasped together. Amelia wondered what to do next. Dagmar had helped tow Selma to her seat, as the aisle was too narrow for the walking-frame.

'We have to turn,' Amelia said finally. 'The loo is

that way.' She pointed over Selma's shoulder. Still holding hands, they circled slowly round, an unmatched pair in a bizarre dance.

At Ashcombe, Dagmar had played the piano with the sun pouring through the half drawn blinds, as Selma grasped Amelia's small hands in hers. '*Dansa min docka*,' she had sung in Swedish, 'Dance my doll, dance whilst you're young, soon you'll be old and heavy.' Round and round they had danced, across the pattern of sunbeams on the oak floor.

The train jolted to a stop. Selma lurched towards Amelia who managed to stay upright, stopping them both from collapsing on the floor. 'I can't go now,' Selma whispered, 'we're at a station.'

'I'll just take you through now. It's easier to move when the train is standing still.'

Walking backwards, step after careful step, Amelia lead Selma through the carriage. People looked up at them only to immediately avert their eyes in embarrassment, a couple of children giggled. Selma's eyes were blank as she stared ahead.

'You sit here.' Amelia placed Selma on an empty seat at the end of the carriage whilst she pulled at the heavy, sliding doors. She pushed her bottom against one, to hold it open; at the same time she leant forward to help Selma up and through. My vertebrae are going to crack, I'm going to spend the rest of my life a helpless cripple, Amelia thought, biting her bottom lip. As the train was about to pull out, she jerked Selma from her seat and helped her out into the corridor. Sideways like crabs they manoeuvred themselves in front of the door marked WC and Amelia began propelling her grandmother inside.

Selma stalled. There had been an English setter at Ashcombe who used to dig his paws in, just like that, when asked to go for a walk in the rain.

'Don't you want to go?' Amelia asked her gently.

Selma looked helplessly at her. 'I don't need to now.'

Amelia stared somewhere in the direction of Selma's good leg. She thought, I'd rather be dead, if I was her, I'd rather be dead. But making her voice matter of fact, Sister Morris-like, she said, 'No problem,' and, with a smile fixed determinedly on her face, she began helping Selma back to her seat.

On the taxi-ride from Basingstoke, Selma brightened, chatting happily, enjoying the drive through the rain-washed streets of Alresford. She knew the town from childhood visits to an aunt, and her memories were all of those visits long ago. When the car stopped at a red light, an old woman, her thick legs disappearing inside dumpy suede boots, a plastic rain cover tied round her whispy grey hair, hastened across.

'Goodness me, some people are hideous,' Selma remarked cheerfully. She sat there, whiskery-chinned, and missing her teeth, her cardigan spotted with stains, and yet she looked at the woman at the crossing with gleeful disapproval. Selma had been beautiful. Thank God, Amelia thought, that in her mind she still is.

The taxi pulled up in front of the Old Rectory and the driver got out to help extract Selma from the passenger seat. As she was hauled from the car, Selma farted loudly. For a second no-one moved. It was as if the driver's eyes and Amelia's were fencing in embarrassed attempts to avoid a meeting, darting here and there, up, down, right, left. Finally, they both spoke at once, the driver inspecting his fingernails, Amelia investigating the contents of her purse. 'How much do I owe you?'

'That'll be nine pounds eighty, love.'

'No dear, let me.' Selma, looking as if the little

incident had nothing to do with her, leant heavily against the car as her hand scrabbled round the inside of her handbag. She handed a five pound note to the driver before bringing out some loose change which she counted out carefully, her hand shaking, 'One, two, three, four pound coins,' she smiled at the driver, 'and two fifties. Keep the change,' she added graciously.

Amelia hadn't cancelled the papers and she picked out the bulky bundle from the box on the gate. She frowned at the study window. 'I must have left the light on,' she said.

She helped Selma inside the house and left her in the armchair in the sitting room before getting the bags from outside. 'I'll bring you a cup of tea.' She smiled encouragingly.

The room seemed to Selma, as she waited, like a half-remembered face. There was something familiar about its square shape and regular features, but to whom did it belong? She sat miserably searching her mind, which seemed to her increasingly like a treasure chest to which she had lost the key.

As she heard murmurings from the room next door she grew restless. She had arrived here with Amelia, but where was here?

The sounds from next door grew louder, worrying sounds: muffled, agonized, oddly familiar. Where was Amelia? Selma tried to get up from the deep chair, but, like a woman drowning, each time she managed painfully to rise to the surface, the soft hold of the chair reclaimed her.

At last Amelia returned. She appeared smiling in the doorway, a tray in her hands, just as from the other room a name was called, then repeated over and over again. 'Gerry, oh Gerry, Gerry, Gerry!'

Amelia stood motionless, listening, then, with the smile still on her face like a hand held in a wave to

112

someone already gone, she walked across the room. Her cheeks were bright pink as she carefully placed the tray on the table in front of Selma.

A few more steps, quicker now, and she reached the study door and flung it open.

The tall back of Gerald's swivel chair rocked, two thick legs hung over the arm-rests, the toes of the small feet curling and straightening in ecstasy.

The chair swivelled round and she saw Gerald, his face contorted, a girl straddling him, her skirt hitched up over her naked buttocks.

'Hello, Gerald,' Amelia said, 'I didn't realize you were home.'

Chapter Eleven

Watching Gerald's attempt to leap from the chair with Clarissa still straddling his waist, gave Amelia a few seconds of intense enjoyment. Slapping her hand across her mouth, she bent over laughing until the sound of Gerald's voice stopped her.

'Get off darling,' he hissed. It was the 'darling', that alerted Amelia's attention.

'I'm doing my best,' Clarissa groaned as, swinging herself round on her bare bottom, she managed to stand up. Her skirt slid down over her hips and covered her as she balanced on one foot, threading the other through the leg of her knickers.

Amelia stood silent, looking at the heavily built young woman whose fine blond hair hung in damp tendrils over a square-shaped face that was turning ice-cream pink as she wriggled and tugged at her pants through the fine floral skirt. Amelia looked away.

Gerald stood by the desk. He had pulled his trousers on, but through the half-open fly peeked a corner of his blue-and-white-striped shirt. The one that took absolutely ages to iron; the thought flew through Amelia's mind, as appropriate as a paper aeroplane at a funeral. 'Who is this girl? It's Clarissa isn't it?' Amelia answered her own question in a quiet, level voice. Stay calm, she told herself, and any moment now he'll cross the floor to me. He'll say how very sorry he is, how it should never have happened. Soon that solid girl with her unremarkably pretty face, will be escorted to the front door and I can begin to deal with all of this. At least now she knew who it was that had squirted lemon into the cream of her existence. Figments of the imagination were notoriously difficult to fight; young women with lank hair and pink-flushed bottoms, should be easier.

'Of course it's Clarissa,' Gerald snapped. 'I'm sorry,' his voice softened, 'I forgot you haven't met.'

He's behaving as if we're at some slightly awkward drinks party, Amelia thought. Next, this Clarissa will be telling me she feels as if she's known me for absolutely ages. She bit her lip, waiting for Gerald to revert to script.

'Look, old thing.' Now Gerald did take a step towards her, but what followed was all wrong. 'I'm really sorry you had to find out like this, it's the last thing we wanted to happen. But you see I've been meaning to tell you for weeks. You're so bloody unsuspecting.' He flung his arms out helplessly, glancing over to Clarissa for support.

'I feel absolutely awful.' Clarissa, in control again now that she had her knickers on, spoke with a Perspex-voice, clear and brittle. Gerald moved closer to her and put his arms round her shoulders.

The quiet gesture of realignment hit Amelia like a punch in the solar plexus. Sitting down in the hard chair by the door she doubled over, trying to stop herself from being sick.

'Amelia darling, won't you introduce me to our hosts?' Selma stood in the doorway, having got herself across the sitting room by walking sideways, transferring her hands and weight from one piece of furniture to the next. 'Amelia, are you all right?'

Amelia sat up slowly. 'Yes, of course. Fine, absolutely fine.' She gazed helplessly at Gerald who looked away.

Amelia stood up. 'Grandma, you remember Gerald. And this is Gerald's . . . friend, Clarissa.'

Selma looked pleased with the introduction, saying in a rather grand voice, 'How very nice to meet you both. It's most kind of you to have my granddaughter and me to stay.' She wobbled on her feet and clung on to the moving door. She looked as if she was about to fall but Amelia grabbed the chair and pushed it under her just in time. Selma collapsed on to it with a little thud.

Gerald shot her a worried glance. 'I think we'd better go.'

'You can come back later, Gerald, when we've all had a chance to calm down,' Clarissa said with quiet authority.

'Let her go Gerald, but *you* can't, surely you must see that. You can't just leave like this.' Amelia's voice rose and then, bang! Her fist slammed into the shelf of the bookcase.

The colour rose again on Clarissa's cheeks, like bright pink dye washing over shiny paper. 'Gerald, you are not sending me home like some . . . some trollop!'

At the familiar old-fashioned word, Selma grew alert. 'Now don't you fight children,' she said from her chair.

'Oh can't you see this is hopeless, trying to talk like this?' Gerald said. 'You can stay here for the present Amelia. Your grandmother too, of course.' He gave a little nod in Selma's direction. 'And I'll be over in the next day or two.'

Before Amelia could think of anything to stop him, he was at the front door. 'Really, I mean it. There's no hurry for you to move out, I can stay at Clarissa's for now.' He looked at her and raised his arm, touching her cheek with his index finger in a quick caress. Then he hurried off, following Clarissa down the short path to the gate. As she stood watching after them, Amelia imagined a shadowy image of herself separating like a film from her body and popping up between Gerald and Clarissa, slipping its wafer-thin arms into theirs. Shuddering, she slowly closed the front door behind them and wandered into the sitting room. Her gaze fell on Selma sitting crumpled in the armchair. She felt utterly alone.

'You have to keep going, for the children's sake.' How many times had she read that phrase in a magazine, or heard it spoken by an acquaintance or some sad, faded figure in a television interview? By that evening Amelia knew just what these people meant. She couldn't throw herself on the bed and weep, she couldn't rant and rave or shred Gerald's cashmere sweater. She couldn't even get drunk on his most expensive wine, not now she had Selma. So, two hours after Gerald had walked out she was cooking onions and carrots which she blended into a thick, smooth soup: easy to swallow, teeth not essential. Then there was the broken china to clear up, after Selma had dropped the plates she was trying to bring over to the sink. Selma had looked down surprised at the blue and white chips scattered at her feet. 'I seem to be all fingers and thumbs these days. Mind you I've never liked working in someone else's kitchen.'

By nine o'clock, Selma was asleep in the armchair. Amelia woke her an hour later. 'Bedtime don't you think?' she said, working a smile across her lips.

The walking-frame had to be abandoned at the bottom of the stairs. Amelia began the climb backwards pulling Selma along by both hands, coaxing her up step by step. Halfway up they stopped for a rest and Amelia burst into tears.

Selma stared at her and her face crumpled. 'Don't cry Amelia. Please stop it. I can't bear it when you cry.'

Amelia took a deep breath and tried another bright smile. 'I'm sorry. I'm just a bit tired. Silly me.'

She helped Selma undress, peeling off layers of foundation garments that lent shape to the sagging, grey-toned flesh. Arching her aching back she said, 'Let's not bother with a bath tonight.'

At last Selma was in bed. Propped up against two pillows she looked expectantly at Amelia. After a moment she said, 'You know I think I might just go downstairs and make myself a mug of warm milk.'

'I'll do it.' Amelia came downstairs slamming each foot down so hard on the wooden steps that it hurt. She heated the milk, muttering all the while into the saucepan. When she thought she heard Selma calling, she hurried to the door only to come back to find the milk rising above the rim of the saucepan, flooding down on to the hob. When finally she got back upstairs, Selma was fast asleep on her back.

Three days after Gerald walked out with Clarissa, he returned on his own. He had telephoned to see if Amelia would be in, and now he sat in his usual place at the large kitchen table. Amelia sat opposite him, elbows on the table, her chin resting on the upturned palms of her hands.

'You all right?' he asked as if he didn't know the answer was no.

Amelia looked into the face she knew so well, the long chin and the large grey eyes, not unlike her own in colour, the small white scar on the upper lip. She knew now, she thought, how people in those science-fiction films felt when their loved-ones' minds were taken over by aliens. The man sitting opposite her at the table looked like Gerald, rubbed his eyes with his knuckles like Gerald, had a voice like Gerald's, but inside she had no doubt, the little green men had taken over.

'I miss you,' she said.

Gerald looked mildly irritated. 'Well, there we are.' He cleared his throat, drumming his fingers surreptitiously against the edge of the table.

I wonder what he would do if I walked over to him and put my hand down his trousers? Amelia tilted her head a little to one side as she continued to gaze across at him. This man, she thought, has lain naked and vulnerable in my arms several times a week for two years. Suddenly, he is a prohibited area; if I put out my hand and touch his cheek, I'm trespassing.

Trying to sound business-like, rather than pleading, she asked, 'There is really nothing I can do or say to make you come back?'

'No Amelia, there isn't.' Gerald's voice was patient, commiserating even, in an impersonal way. It was the voice he used, she thought, when telling Mrs Smith that all avenues had been exhausted in the firm's attempts to stop Mrs Smith's neighbour blocking her access with his lawnmower.

Gerald leant across the table towards her. 'I really am sorry you had to find out the way you did. It's the last thing Clarissa and I wanted. But it can't have come as a complete shock. If you were honest with yourself you must have known that things weren't right between us.'

'I wasn't.'

'What?' Gerald pulled back in his chair. 'What do you mean?' Again that awful irritation crept in, making Amelia blink hard to stop embarrassing tears.

'I mean that I wasn't honest.'

Gerald sighed. 'Can't you see we're too different? It's no-one's fault, but to be truthful . . .'

'Truthful and Honest,' Amelia thought, two paragons often used to prop up the most cruel constructions.

' . . . I don't understand you. Everything you do seems like a game, something to occupy you whilst you drift around waiting for life to start. I take you one way and you come meekly enough, but all the time I have the feeling that you're floating off in the opposite direction looking for goodness knows what.' Gerald spoke with sudden passion. 'I needed someone . . . someone substantial.' He looked at Amelia, pleading for understanding.

Amelia stared back at him, horrified. She had given him her love, shared his life for two years, and that was how he saw her: insubstantial, floating, not quite normal. She blinked and swallowed, reeling from his latest punch, seeing Gerald before her again in the chair with Clarissa. Looking helplessly at him, shrugging her shoulders, she said, 'Clarissa is certainly substantial.' It was all she could find to say.

'For Christ's sake! You're just hopelessly immature.' Gerald, his cheeks reddening, slammed his fist on the table. 'Faced with a serious situation, the best you can do is come up with a juvenile crack like that.'

'I'm sorry,' Amelia said but she felt a curious sense of relief; after all she was hopeless, shiftless, nothing was expected of her now.

'Would you like a drink?' She stood up from the table.

'Thanks,' he nodded, mollified.

Amelia brought a bottle of Chablis from the fridge. The cork fragmented as she drove in the corkscrew just off centre.

'Here, let me do it,' Gerald said, as he always did, taking the bottle from her. Then, as if he had only just then remembered Selma's existence, he asked, 'Where is your grandmother?'

Amelia pointed to the lawn where Selma sat, her back turned, an emerald green, gold-tassled shawl wrapped around her shoulders. 'I brought her walking-frame back inside with me.' She gave a little smile. 'It was the only way we could get some privacy.'

Leaving Cherryfield had shaken what was left of Selma's sense of place. Like a young child who had moved too often, she kept close to her granddaughter, the one constant in her life. So now, wherever Amelia went, she would hear behind her the sound of the wooden legs of the walking-frame, bashing against doors and furniture as Selma, swearing and muttering, shuffled in her wake.

Gerald turned the bottle round in his hand. 'A bit excessive, a 1983 Chablis?'

'No,' Amelia said simply.

Gerald sighed and changed the subject. 'You might not think you have any reason to like Clarissa, but she suggested I let you stay on here until the end of the summer, to give you plenty of time to sort out a place of your own.'

He really needs to bring her into his conversation, Amelia thought. Like a speaker in a television debate taking sips from the glass of water by his side, Gerald refreshes himself with little gulps of her name.

'She's a real brick, is Clarissa,' she said. 'I don't know where I'd be without her. Have some more wine.'

'No thanks, I'm driving.'

'You could always stay the night,' Amelia offered, watching Gerald make up his mind whether she was being helpful or provocative. He settled on the fence and said in a neutral voice, 'It's only half past six.'

Amelia glanced unnecessarily at her watch. 'So it is.' She smiled brightly across the table at him. 'What a lot of time we've got to chat.'

Ten minutes later Gerald stood up to leave. 'I'll come over again,' he said. 'There's still the matter of how to divide up all the stuff.' He patted her cheek with the quick, embarrassed gesture she had begun to hate. 'I'll always be your friend, Amelia. If there's anything you need you only have to ask.'

'Actually,' Amelia said, 'there is something.'

Gerald turned on the doorstep. 'Yes?'

'I could do with a good solicitor.'

'Very funny.' Gerald's mouth turned up at the corners in something that could pass for a smile, Amelia thought, if one wasn't very fussy.

She went round the house to the lawn where Selma was asleep in the soft-cushioned chair under the apple tree. Quietly she sat down on the dry grass, leaning back against the tree trunk. The evening sun spread a golden tint through the air and, by the shrubbery, rabbits were appearing, cautiously at first, then as nothing moved they got braver, grazing on the uncut grass.

God! I love this garden, she thought, then she buried her face in the crook of her arm. Until Gerald's visit she had found it impossible to extinguish completely a belief in her power over him. Now he pranced before her closed eyes like a pied piper, taking her life with him; home, garden, her hopes of children. She lifted her head and in front of her, hedging the terrace, were the beds of Bourbon roses she had planted when they first moved in. Souvenir De La Malmaison, Honorine de Brabant, Mme Isaac Pereire, Louise Odier: now all those richly scented, extravagantly painted grand-dames would give their autumn encore to Clarissa.

Amelia flinched as she felt a hand on her shoulder.

'Are you all right, darling? You're looking a bit peeky.' Selma was peering down at her, concerned.

Selma, with Amelia's Indian shawl draped round

her shoulders and her hair brushed smooth, looked so much like her old pre-Cherryfield self that Amelia was aching to tell her all about Gerald and Clarissa. For years she had come to her grandmother with her problems, confided in her and no-one else, and Selma had listened, plucking out the troubles as if they were thorns, advised and made better.

Oh no, Amelia thought, straightened up against the warm tree trunk. Don't even try it now. It's a mirage, this familiar Selma, tempting your words towards her into nothing.

'Come on, darling something's up, I can tell.'

She'll look at me, Amelia thought, and she'll tell me none of it would have happened if I'd stopped sucking my thumb or she'll ask me to go to fetch her game of ludo. But Selma's gaze was on her, steady and alert.

'It's Gerald, he's left me. I still love him and this place,' she gesticulated out at the garden. 'Now I'll have to leave here too, start again somewhere else.' It wasn't until she was halfway through the sentence that she realized how that might sound to Selma, whose only option was Cherryfield.

'I am sorry darling, this, this . . . what did you say his name was?'

'Gerald.'

'Gerald, yes of course. I don't know why, but I keep on thinking his name is Henry. I'm sorry you and he aren't friends any more.' She put her hand out to Amelia who took it, keeping it still. 'I know it's not much comfort now, but you'll find someone else. You forget about him and concentrate on finding yourself a nice place to live; your own home is the most important thing.'

Amelia looked up at her with tears in her eyes. If her grandmother had leapt from the deck-chair and torn a rubber mask from her face revealing her old self, wise, serene, and beautiful, she could not have surprised Amelia any more than she had just done by speaking perfect sense. With a deep sigh of contentment Amelia edged closer to her.

'Anyway,' Selma pursed her lips. 'It really was very naughty of him to leave so early when you'd gone through all that trouble.'

Chapter Twelve

'I felt rather hurt,' Amelia said and, as she said it, she wondered why she always seemed to oscillate between understatement and exaggeration without ever settling comfortably in between.

'Yes?' Rosalind, sitting at the kitchen table, stopped gazing adoringly at Ronald and looked instead, in a waiting way, at Amelia.

'Oh sorry.' Amelia started again. 'It was him saying I was vague and drifting. It was so unfair. I mean I might not be a constantly focused mapper-out of every detail of my life, but I did have plans. Not very fashionable plans maybe. I admit that articles in *Cosmopolitan* about young women attempting to emulate Maria in *The Sound of Music* are rare . . .'

Rosalind looked faintly surprised. 'I didn't know you sang.'

'. . . better her in fact; I was going to have all the children myself.' She looked up from her coffee mug at Rosalind. 'Sang? No I don't.' She frowned. 'It was the big happy warm family bit I was after. I dreamt of being an inspirational mother. Jam making, huge teas, animals and homework jumbled up all over the kitchen, picnics in the garden. I even thought of turning Aunt Edith's sitting-room curtains into children's clothes.'

Rosalind leant across the table saying in a quiet concerned voice, 'Are you very short of cash?'

It was Amelia's turn to look surprised. 'No, not

really. I mean I've still got most of the money from the flat invested and the freelancing brings in quite a bit. Of course I lived rent free, there was no mortgage. The deal was that I should look after everything here, grow our own vegetables, keep the hens, all that. He would support us with his painting.' With what she felt was unusual clear-sightedness she said, 'It was a kind of reversed trendiness, it made him feel original, a bit of a rebel. There I'd be, floating around in long frocks, the very model of a good old-fashioned artist's muse.' She rubbed her eyes. 'I suppose that, to him, I was just a phase, like his painting, but he was my whole life.'

'But isn't this Clarissa woman a clerk at his office?' Rosalind asked. 'I mean she's a career girl.'

Amelia sighed. 'I know. I think giving people what they want is a very dangerous thing.' She bent down and stroked Ronald's satin cheek. He jumbled up his features and produced a beaming smile.

'So what are you going to do? Are you moving back to London?'

'I really don't know. I can't think yet. And London is so . . .' She shrugged her shoulders helplessly. 'Well, so big.'

Rosalind picked Ronald up from his rug on the floor and stood up. Draped across his mother's shoulder he looked sideways at Amelia, attempting another smile, his large head bobbing like a peony on a weak stem.

'Well, come for coffee next week anyway,' Rosalind said. 'That'll be something planned. I have to dash, Ronnie needs his bottle and a rest.'

'I better start Grandma's lunch too,' Amelia said seeing Rosalind and Ronnie out. 'She's having a nap but she's always ravenous when she wakes up.'

Flushed from the heat of the stove, Amelia flung open

the kitchen windows to let in a breeze. She stayed for a moment, enjoying the air on her face and the sound of the housemartins nesting under the eaves.

'Lentils?' Selma, already seated at the table, said in an affronted voice. 'Lentils in June?'

Reluctantly, Amelia turned round. 'I'm sorry, but I felt you needed the protein, and I couldn't think of anything else to make; for soup I mean. I do wish those teeth would hurry up and come. I bet Sister Morris is being deliberately slow in sending them.' She sat down opposite Selma and smiled encouragingly as she put the spoon into her own bowl. 'Mmmm,' she said, 'I make quite a good lentil soup.'

'If you say so, darling,' Selma said, both eyebrows raised. She lifted the spoon to her mouth, snatching at it as her shaking hand kept pulling it away from her lips. Splashing it back down into the bowl she said, 'You know, I haven't been for a swim for ages. I'm sure that's why I'm feeling so stiff.'

Amelia swallowed a mouthful of soup, wondering how to respond. 'Rosalind's parents have a pool,' she said finally. 'They live just outside the village.' She smiled suddenly. 'I'm sure they wouldn't mind us having a dip.'

Rosalind's mother was delighted for Amelia and her grandmother to use the pool. 'She even offered you the loan of a costume,' Amelia told Selma as they waited for a taxi. Luckily, she thought, Mrs Rowlands was a large woman.

The pool was separated from the main garden by a crumbling brick wall covered in clematis and pink roses. The walking-frame did not move well on crazy-paving, but slowly Amelia managed to get Selma across to the small gate that was kept locked in case of visiting grandchildren. Mrs Rowlands arrived, all smiles and easy chatter, clutching a monstrous bathing-costume in shocking pink. Amelia took Selma in to the changing hut.

'Here,' she pulled out a plastic freezer bag and a rubber-band from her bag. 'For your foot.'

The water was warm and Selma lay on her back, holding the stair-rail with one hand, letting the water carry her weight. Her eyes were closed and she was smiling. Amelia swam up and down the widths of the pool, careful not to take her eyes off Selma for long. 'Lovely water, doesn't make my eyes sting or anything,' she called up to Mrs Rowlands who sat knitting in a candy-striped deck-chair.

'It's because we use hardly any chlorine, thanks to the dye,' Mrs Rowlands called back.

Amelia swam to the edge and heaved herself up on her elbows. 'The dye?'

'We won't pour in masses of chemicals, Ambrose can't stand it, so we've got this completely harmless dye you see. If any of the grandchildren do a wee, the water turns bright purple all around them. They don't do it again I can tell you.' Mrs Rowlands laughed uproariously.

'Excuse me.' Amelia dropped back into the pool and swam over to Selma. 'I'm getting cold, shall we get up?'

Selma, still floating on her back, her hand on the rail, opened her eyes. 'You get out darling. I'm not in the least bit cold.' And she closed her eyes and continued to float pleasurably on the sweet clear water.

'What about your toe?' Amelia tried again.

This time Selma opened just one eye, it looked displeased. 'My toe is fine.'

Amelia swam around in little fretful circles, her neck craned, watching for any signs of bright purple dye. It isn't fair, she thought, it just isn't fair. She stopped and trod water.

'It's getting pretty late. I asked the taxi to pick us up at half past three, it's ten minutes past now.'

From the poolside, Mrs Rowlands gave a little wave. 'There's no need for you to feel you have to keep us company,' Amelia called. 'I'm sure you're terribly busy.'

'Never too busy for you Amelia. We haven't seen enough of you since little Ronnie was born. Rosalind never seems to have time for anyone else any more.' Mrs Rowlands finished a row and put the knitting down. 'Ronnie is much too young to swim, of course, we don't hold with this water-baby thing you know. Ambrose thinks it's terribly unhygienic.' She had come up to the edge of the pool, and now she stood looking down at Amelia, a dimply smile on her large moon face. 'I said to him, "They don't understand shame at two months."'

Amelia grabbed Selma under both arms. 'I'm getting you out now,' she hissed, hauling her up on to the first step. A whirling snake of purple dye uncoiled in the water round Selma's knees. As she looked up, Amelia's eyes met Mrs Rowland's across the width of the pool. Pushing her dripping hair from her forehead, she smiled nervously. 'Well well, time to get up.'

'I'm sure you're right Amelia.' Mrs Rowlands didn't smile back as she picked up her knitting from the chair. 'Don't put the cover back on please. There are things . . .' Here she paused, looking pointedly at Selma's plump and crumpled figure on the steps and at the whirl of purple fading to pale pink at its outer edge. 'Things we have to do.' And she turned and hurried back up towards the house with outraged little steps that seemed to tap out against the paving, 'Wait till Ambrose sees, wait till Ambrose sees.'

When Amelia came in with a mug of hot milk to

Selma's room later that night, she found her already asleep, flat on her back, snoring. Amelia stood looking down at her, a reluctant mother gazing at her monstrous child. Then she turned and walked down to her desk in the sitting-room alcove. Half an hour later she switched off the light and went to bed; it was as she had always suspected, suffering did not necessarily make you a better poet.

Two sets of square white sheets and pillow-cases from Selma's double bed flapped on the washing-line, adding to Amelia's sensation of being a Lilliputian nanny landed with a Brobdingnagian baby. As she added a pair of panelled knickers to the line, the telephone rang. It was Dagmar again, wanting to know how Selma was.

'All right,' Amelia said, listening for the slamming and clanking that would herald Selma's appearance. 'No real problems,' she added.

'And you?' Dagmar sounded concerned.

Amelia wanted to tell Dagmar about Gerald, but she knew that the instant she did, she would regret it. Confiding in Dagmar was as comforting as putting your head in a lion's mouth; she would tear at your problem, worry it and gnaw it, leaving you with the chewed over remains. Then again on other days, bloated with her own worries, she would have no energy left for Amelia at all.

'We're all fine,' Amelia said mechanically.

'That's good. Amelia, you won't believe this but I've met this wonderful man. He's a visiting professor of North American literature, about my age, divorced. Oh darling, I really think something may come of this.'

'That's lovely,' Amelia said and meant it.

'You must make the effort to come over to Exeter to

meet him, when you bring Mummy back.' There was a pause. 'When is she coming back?'

Amelia leapt backwards to avoid the passage door being smashed in her face by Selma's sudden entrance. Selma found the push-open doors of the Old Rectory very helpful as she could shove them open with the legs of the walking-frame whilst steadying herself against the door-frame.

'Here's Grandma now,' Amelia said pointedly. 'Do you want a word?' She handed the phone to Selma. As she left the room she heard her say, 'I'm very well, thank you, apart from this wretched toe playing up. I haven't been able to play tennis once. I had a lovely swim though. No, not this morning, last week I think,' she said guessing wildly.

Last week, Amelia thought as she wandered back into the garden, was when I still believed I could have a future here. Gerald used to accuse her of being negative. She knew that was not true. She was in fact as rosy-edged, as reality-bashing an optimist ever to protect her most precious visions of heaven under a cloak of pessimism. Too much happiness had always made her feel insecure though, like a trapeze artist reaching the highest platform, the one nearest the ceiling of the circus tent. Too much happiness might tempt God, the God who felt that Job needed to be taught a lesson.

Nothing to be frightened of now, she thought, and looking heavenwards through the garnet-red leaves of the copper beech she called, 'You didn't surprise me, you know that God!' Then she continued to peg out the washing.

On her way back to the house she stopped at the vegetable garden and pulled out a large weed from the soil in one satisfactory movement, leaving no roots behind. Why do I bother? she sighed. I should hire a

131

plane to fly over the garden showering it with Weedol.

Back inside, there was a smell of burning. She ran through the passage and into the kitchen. A saucepan stood on the ceramic hob, boiling dry as spirals of stinking smoke rose from the black puddles on the side of the hot-plate. Amelia grabbed the saucepan handle only to pull her hand away, swearing. She grabbed an oven cloth and removed the pan before putting her burnt palm under running cold water.

'What a dreadful smell.' Selma's walking-frame bashed into the kitchen door, causing her to stop abruptly, doubling over the top of the frame. Recovering her balance she added helpfully, 'Something burning I wouldn't be surprised.'

'I think you left a saucepan of milk on the stove,' Amelia said, shoving her irritation to the pit of her stomach where it was left to fester. 'I'm going in to town for some shopping, do you want to come? We have to take the bus I'm afraid, but I'll book a taxi for coming back.'

Selma got through the main doors of the supermarket, but got stuck in the trolley turnstile. A small queue of shoppers formed behind whilst Amelia unwedged her. They manoeuvred themselves through the crowded aisles, Selma catching ankles with the legs of the frame and Amelia smiling nervously as apologies rolled off her tongue like sweets off a conveyor belt. Near to tears, she looked enviously at the young mothers whose babies fitted so conveniently into the trolley-seats. Then she looked at Selma who stood gazing expectantly at her, a packet of smoked kippers in her hand. All those years, she thought as she gently removed the package from Selma's grip and replaced them in the chill cabinet, dreaming of children and family life and this is what I got. It was as if God had read her heart's desire, but through a mirror, and given her Selma.

'Let's carry on shall we.' She smiled encouragingly whilst before her eyes was a vision of her grandmother stuffed into the child-seat of the trolley, her cone-shaped legs sticking out through the gap in the bars.

Wandering round the shelves like a robot programmed at random, Amelia picked a packet of peas here, some butter there, lentils, tins of tuna. It was probably silly to expect something as easy as a child to love and nurture, she thought. History after all was full of women whose youth had been spent in tandem with age and decline. She returned a leaking Mr Muscle bottle to the shelf, then thinking it anti-social to leave it for the next shopper, she promptly removed it again, giving it to a passing supervisor.

'All right?' she asked Selma who looked small and tired from the halting progress through an hostile environment.

I will campaign for especially designed old people's trolleys in every supermarket, she thought, demand large plastic-covered chairs in every restaurant. Why not old people's crèches at the workplace? Why not, why bloody not? All those mothers had chosen to have babies, or at least acquired them through a careless act of pleasure. But Amelia had not sat down one day, misty-eyed, saying, 'What about it darling, shall we have our own, our very own shaking, muddled, incontinent human remnant?' Nor was Selma the product of a moment of abandoned pleasure, well not Amelia's anyhow.

She parked Selma in a chair by the Ten Pence a Ride plastic camel and queued up at the check-out. Looking at her watch she saw that the taxi would already be waiting, so when it was her turn she didn't bother to pack her shopping but threw the tins and packages willy nilly back into the trolley. Picking up Selma again on the way out she had to push herself forward to stop the automatic doors clamping the walking-frame. The taxi was waiting outside, its meter running, and the driver stood by impatiently while Amelia loaded her shopping into the boot.

'You know, I'd love some chocolates. Did we get any?' Selma asked from her seat in the front.

'No.'

'Would you be so good as to help me out?' Selma asked the driver. Then she tried to turn round towards Amelia. 'I won't be a moment darling.' She grabbed on to the walking-frame parked by the car door, and began shuffling towards the store entrance.

'I've got another pick-up in twenty minutes,' the driver grumbled.

'There isn't time!' Amelia called, her head appearing from the boot.

Selma turned and looked at her incensed. 'Really darling, don't fuss. I'm just getting some sweets. I'll get you some too.' And helped through the doors by another shopper who shot Amelia a disapproving look, Selma disappeared inside.

Ten minutes later the taxi driver invited Amelia to unload her shopping from his car. He drove off revving his engine, leaving Amelia to find another trolley before going off in search of Selma.

She did not find her at 'Pick'n Mix' nor by 'Chilled Produce, Dairy or Household Goods'. Surely no-one kidnapped old ladies? Was there a back entrance through which she could have wandered? Amelia hurried through the aisles finally reaching 'Tobacco and Spirits' at the back.

'There you are, darling. We wondered where you could have got to.' Selma was sitting at the tobacco counter attended by a young man in the red uniform of the supermarket staff, in her left hand was an unlit cigarette. She waved it in Amelia's direction.

'Yes, madam.' The young man with a sparse moustache nestling amongst his spots, made the 'madam' sound like an insult. 'To leave Granny like this. She was in quite a state when I found her I can tell you.'

Selma took a poor view normally of people other than Amelia calling her Granny, but today she joined the young man in looking reproachfully at Amelia.

Then with a pointed 'You take care now' to Selma, the assistant was off.

Selma smiled fondly after him. 'What a dear little man,' she said.

'You don't smoke,' Amelia said coldly.

'Of course I smoke.' Selma looked at Amelia as if she thought she had gone quite mad. 'But not in here, apparently you're not allowed to. Cullen's never had silly rules like that.'

Amelia narrowed her eyes at her grandmother but felt it would be unsporting to point out that Selma hadn't smoked since 1959, the year Amelia was born in fact. Instead, she helped Selma up and again manoeuvred her back out on to the pavement.

'Excuse me Madam, do you possess a receipt for these goods?'

Amelia looked up to meet the pebble stare of a middle-aged man in a black leather jacket. He flashed an ID in front of her face.

'What do you mean?' Then her brow cleared and she smiled. 'Oh I see, you think that because I walked out from the shop without going through the check-out . . .' The man crossed arms shaped like legs of lamb, heavy at the top, narrow little tubes at the bottom, and pushed his chin out. Amelia stopped smiling. 'What I'm trying to say is that I paid once but then I lost my grandmother who had gone back in to buy some sweets . . .'

'Where is the car, darling? I'm feeling rather tired,' Selma said in a small voice.

'Just show me the receipt, madam, would you? Then you'll be free to go.'

'The receipt.' Amelia riffled through her handbag.

'A credit card receipt or check stub will do,' the man said, scenting blood.

Amelia knelt down and tipped the contents of her bag on the pavement: house-keys, tampax, lipstick, brush, a photo of Gerald.

'It isn't there, is it madam?'

'You don't have to sound so bloody pleased about it,' Amelia snapped, as she caught sight of Selma's white face. She began emptying the trolley hoping the receipt would be hiding somewhere amongst the mound of groceries. In the end her shopping was all around her on the pavement but there was still no sign of the receipt.

'If you would be so good as to come with me now, madam.' It seemed hard for the man to hide his satisfaction and Amelia wondered when she was last called 'madam' by someone not intent on crushing her.

I definitely shouldn't have sworn at him, Amelia thought as he remained with his arms folded across his chest while she re-loaded the trolley. When she had finished, he grabbed the handle and began pushing it towards the shop with one hand, the other he kept at Amelia's elbow.

'I assure you, I have paid.' Amelia stopped by the doors. 'Just ask the check-out girl.'

'Which check-out would that be?'

'How the he . . . How should I know?' Amelia said resignedly.

The man gave her a little nudge through the door,

then kept it open for Selma who stopped halfway inside, blocking the entrance. 'Why are we going in here?' she asked.

'It seems your . . . granddaughter is it, left the shop without paying.'

'Amelia? Nonsense.'

The man ignored her and marched Amelia to the supervisor's desk, pulpit-like in front of the vast picture windows of the store. Picking up the intercom he announced, 'If any member of staff remembers taking money from this lady, could he or she proceed to the manager's office.'

'Can someone please tell me what's happening.' Selma, her face grey and pinched, wobbled on her feet.

'I'm sorry but I really must get my grandmother home,' Amelia said.

The man looked from Selma to Amelia. 'I'll get the police to drive her. She can wait in the office with you until they come, there's a seat there.'

As she was marched through the shop, at a pace slow enough for Selma to keep up with, Amelia felt the looks of the other shoppers: hostile, embarrassed, amused. She didn't look away but returned their gaze, stony-faced. Suddenly overcome with loathing for every one of her fellow men, she felt sure it was moments like these that made people fire machine-guns into crowded places.

'Now I've seen it all,' an outraged voice declared. It was Selma's friend from the tobacco counter. 'That woman is not fit to look after a cat.'

The police arrived at the small upstairs office and Selma was taken home by a sympathetic police-woman. No-one turned up to say that they had taken Amelia's money. The policeman perched on the manager's desk.

'Now are you sure you didn't just think you had

paid? It can't be easy with the old lady to keep an eye on as well.'

'I didn't, and it isn't,' Amelia said tiredly.

She took the bus home. The girl at check-out number five remembered Amelia paying, but she had been at lunch when the store detective made his announcement. 'Lucky the supervisor asked me,' the girl said with a pleased smile, helping to pack Amelia's groceries in plastic carriers.

'Keep the receipt next time,' the policeman called cheerfully.

Amelia had wandered out from the shop, slouching, leaving a trail of multicoloured ice-cream dripping from the air-hole of one of the bags. As she hurled it into the Victorian reproduction rubbish-bin by the bus-stop, she wanted to sit down on the cobbled pavement and scream, give all the shoppers something worth gawping at as she was carried off to a nice, peaceful asylum. She stood there, fists clenched, mouth open and ready to howl. Nothing happened. A nervous breakdown, she thought, obviously didn't come cheap. Then the bus arrived.

Back home, Selma was watching the World Cup. She sat leaning back in the armchair, her bad foot stretched out in front of her. In her hand was a lit cigarette tipped with a long snout of ashes. As she turned to greet Amelia, the ashes crumbled on to the floor.

'Listen,' she said, taking Amelia's hand when Luciano Pavarotti began to sing at the end of the transmission. As the last notes of 'Nessun Dorma' faded she sighed, and there were tears in her eyes. 'Rugby might be the game for gentlemen, but the music isn't half as good.'

In the night, Amelia woke from a dream where

Gerald had insisted they light a fire although it was a hot summer's day. She forced heavy eyelids open and sat up, sniffing the stale bedroom air into which flowed the raw smell of burning. She threw off the duvet and ran from the room. On the landing the smell got stronger and as she hurried along, her bare feet thudding against the worn, green carpet, a broken vale of smoke floated towards her from Selma's room.

Chapter Thirteen

'I won't keep you a moment Alan,' Dagmar called anxiously from the bathroom. He was taking her to the best restaurant in Devon and now she was making them late. Alan abhorred unpunctuality. Dagmar did not know him well, but she did know that, so she had been sitting waiting in the armchair by the window a good ten minutes before he was due.

She had dressed with even more care than usual: was there not a flavour of 'mutton dressed as lamb' about the black lace dress? It would look lovely on Amelia, she thought with an irritated sigh as she slipped it off. She brought out a blue check suit. The sort of suit that turned her into just another middle-aged woman, a background person past whom the indifferent eyes of shop assistants and waiters swept on the way to something worth while. She chucked it on the bed.

Finally she had appeared in the sitting room wearing a translucent cornflower-blue skirt that billowed round her ankles when she walked, and a bright yellow blouse. Alan was fond of Matisse. Lounging in the emerald-green armchair, she thought she'd remind him of one of the painter's languid ladies reclining.

While she had waited, craning her neck to see if his car had arrived in the street below, she felt a smell. Not a strong smell, more a faint discord mingling with the rose and lily of the valley of her scent. Tilting her head, sniffing the air like a setter scenting a bird, she decided it must be her shirt. She wasn't absolutely sure it had been to the cleaners. Even if it had been they seemed to throw everything in together these days, bundles of stained trousers, dirty macs and fine silk blouses, all into those great troughs by the counter. She looked at her watch and hurried off to her bedroom, tearing off the shirt and pulling one she didn't like quite as much off its hanger. Nothing was going to be allowed to spoil her evening. She was going to be as pristine as a library book, just unboxed.

The door bell rang as she buttoned the last button. 'Come in.' She had flung the door open. 'Nervous pee.' She flashed Alan an apologetic smile as she dashed off to the bathroom.

'I won't keep you a moment Alan,' she called again as she washed her hands and straightened her skirt, checking her face in the mirror. Parting her lips in a fake smile to check there were no pink lipstick smears on her teeth, she picked a comb off the shelf. It slipped from her fingers, landing on the floor behind the basin. 'Bugger,' she murmured softly to herself as she bent down groping for the comb.

'I'm coming,' she called again, but her hands had begun to shake and her heart thumped hard; she feared the undersides of things, the unseen surfaces, like others feared a dark cellar. Her fingers touched the plastic of the comb and she pulled it out between her forefinger and thumb and put it under the tap, rinsing, soaping, and rinsing again. Then it was the turn of her hands. She washed them like a surgeon would before an operation, scrubbing between the fingers and high up on the wrists. The soap foamed round the shirt cuffs leaving transparent patches on the silk. Last she washed her yellow and white metal watch in case it too had rubbed against the back of the basin. When she dried it the strap left little grey oxidization marks on the pale-yellow towel.

'There you are. I sure hope they'll keep that table.' Alan, amiable normally to the point of placidity, frowned at Dagmar as she draped a flowery chiffon shawl round her shoulders.

Dagmar hurried down the stairs behind him, her chafed hands stinging from the hot water. She really would have to stop all this nonsense she told herself sternly. She smiled up at Alan as he held the car door open. I won't waste you, she thought. Not you.

As they drove out of town, she chatted ceaselessly, drowning her lurking fears in great rivers of words. Now and then she glanced sideways at Alan to make sure she still amused him.

The restaurant was small and the crowded tables so close that, to sit down, Dagmar had to slide her bottom along the top of the next door table. The smell of cooking food, grilled and sautéed, steeped in garlic mingled with tobacco fumes in a warm haze above the rustic oak furniture. On each table stood a vase of pinks and lavender and a Dartington glass candle stick with a pink candle.

'Hey, not bad.' Alan reached across the table for Dagmar's hand. 'I'm sorry I snapped at you back there. I suppose I've got something of an obsession with punctuality.'

I wish people wouldn't use that word 'obsession' so lightly, Dagmar thought as she smiled back, giving Alan's hand a little squeeze. When her friend Claudia didn't care to leave her warm bed on a raw Monday morning, she suffered from exhaustion. When Penny had a weeping attack after three weeks of building works at her house, she suffered depression. What did Alan know about obsession, the tiger that gripped Dagmar between its claws day and night even in her dreams.

'I do understand,' she lied easily. 'There's nothing more irritating than being kept waiting.' She warmed to the subject. 'I mean it's a kind of arrogance, assuming that other people's time is less precious than one's own.'

'Now that's exactly it!' Alan emphasized his agreement, banging his fist on the table. 'And Imogen, my ex-wife, she never saw that, she was just late all the time.' He scanned the menu. 'The snails here come recommended.'

Dagmar, who disliked snails, said she'd love to try some. Her cheeks glowed and her laugh, as she arched her long white neck, was a little loud.

'If you prefer,' the waitress said at her elbow, 'we do a mock escargot.'

'I don't think I like the sound of that.' Dagmar laughed again. 'How is your mock turtle?'

The waitress registered polite confusion.

'Now don't tell me you're a fan of Alice too?' Alan leant across the table.

'But of course,' Dagmar lied. She had always been uncomfortable with *Alice in Wonderland.*

Alan talked about his favourite writers and Dagmar followed like a practised dancing partner. He thinks I'm wonderful, she thought jubilantly. Her next thought, snapping at the heels of the first, was: Dear God, let it last, let me stay in control.

'You'd love the Cape.' Alan pushed his plate away, and leant back in his chair contentedly. 'My home is pretty small, but it's in a real nice part of town, all clapboard and wisteria.'

Dagmar had made sure to place her handbag on a shiny, stain-free part of the floor and now the waitress coming to clear the plates caught her foot on the strap. Losing her balance for a moment she put her other foot flat on to Dagmar's bag. As Alan spoke of his home

143

town Dagmar stared at the brown mark on the toe-cap of the waitress's sturdy shoe.

'I've always wanted to go to the States, especially New England.' Dagmar dragged her gaze from the floor, looking up at Alan with an uneven smile.

'Christmas back home is glorious,' Alan said. 'Snowdrifts like candy floss, coloured lights on the trees in the yard . . .'

The girl could have stepped in something. There was enough dogmess on the quaint streets outside the restaurant to render it a faeces minefield. Dagmar nodded and smiled across the table as her thoughts rampaged. It was like the test of coordination Robert had set her when they were children, rubbing your tummy with one hand while you patted your head with the other. She would smile and talk while all the time her mind was engaged in a quite different dialogue.

'I've always loved a white Christmas,' she said, but the constant performing of the trick made her weary. She could almost feel her mind being drained of sparkle and enthusiasm, leaving her conversation stale. She tried hard to plug the leak.

'One year when I was a little girl in Sweden during the war, we had what we call a real Wolves' Winter . . .' Her voice trailed off as she kept sneaking glances at the floor, checking the bag for marks. She thought she could see a tiny smear by the clasp. 'It was Christmas . . .' she began again but the gloss had worn off her story like glitter off an old bauble. She had wanted to tell Alan about the huge Christmas tree her Jewish grandparents insisted on decorating so that she would not feel left out from the fun of her friends. She wanted to tell him of the night when she had crept up on the deep window-sill and peeked through a gap in the black-out curtain at the snowdrifts glistening in the starlight. By the time Selma came and led her away, she had decided that God must be rather careless to let all that light through the black sky.

But she said nothing of this to Alan. Instead she picked up the bag from the floor, searching the tan leather for dirt whilst pretending to have difficulties with the clasp. 'Got something in my eye.' She brought a powder compact out and pulled at her eyelid.

Alan chatted on but after a while his conversation too grew less animated. They finished their pears in port wine sauce with the odd routine sentence interrupting their eating.

'You're tired, aren't you?' Alan put his hand over hers. 'I'll take you straight home.'

Back in her flat, Dagmar tilted her face up for a good night peck on the cheek, and closed the door behind him. She stood for a moment, her back against the door, thinking of how the charm had been squeezed from their evening by that great, spreading tumour of anxiety. With a little moan of distress she held the handbag up to her face. Then she shook it hard, tipping its contents on the floor, before running white-faced into the kitchen, smashing the bag into the bin, kicking the bin-lid shut.

Later she sat in bed with a mug of tea and a plate of chocolate biscuits trying to repaint the evening in more pleasing shades. The telephone rang. She grabbed the receiver hoping for a miracle, for it to be Alan saying what a truly lovely evening it had been.

It was Amelia. 'I'm at the hospital,' she told Dagmar. 'It's Selma. I'm afraid she set fire to herself.'

Chapter Fourteen

Amelia spent most of the night staring at Selma who slept sedated at the hospital in Basingstoke. Rasping breaths were forced from her smoke-damaged lungs, a curtain had been drawn round her as it had been round Willoughby. Amelia felt she was in a capsule floating through space. Now and then sounds would reach them from faraway earth, muted clatter of heels on vinyl, whispers.

The curtains opened and a nurse told her to go home and get some rest.

At the Old Rectory, Gerald slept in the wing-chair in front of a flickering television screen. Gingerly Amelia picked the remote control from his lap and pressed 'Off'. She stood for a while just looking at him. She felt like a cannibal feasting on his youth and wholesomeness, listening to his breath that pulsed lightly and easily from his parted lips. She knelt by him, putting her cheek close to his face, feeling the warm breath against her skin. Gerald stirred and she got up quickly.

'You looked so, so . . . unsinged.' She smiled, embarrassed.

'I heard about the fire.' Gerald sat up straight, brushing the hair from his eyes. 'When Mrs Jenkins called, I came immediately. I've checked the damage upstairs.' To her surprise he smiled. 'It could be worse.' Crossing one long leg over the other he asked, 'What about your grandmother, how is she?'

'I don't really know.' Out of habit Amelia perched on the arm of his chair. 'She was smoking in bed; I should have thought of that one. But she's hanging on, and the hospital doesn't think she's in any immediate danger. Whether she will recover fully or not is another matter.' She spoke calmly, then suddenly she bashed her forehead against the palms of her clenched fists. When she looked up again, there were tears in her eyes. 'God help me Gerald, I don't even know if I want her to.'

Gerald pulled her down on to his knee and put his arm round her shoulders. He made little comforting noises to stop her crying. 'It's the shock,' he mumbled, 'it's the shock.'

The worry and guilt that had been like a grinding fist in her stomach began to ease and she was almost asleep when she felt Gerald's arm pull away from behind her back.

'Blast! It's five o'clock, I have to get home.' Nudging her off his knee, he sprang from the chair.

Amelia looked at him sleepily. 'I thought you'd come back.'

Gerald sighed. 'You have to accept it's over between us.' He took a step back towards her. 'God Amelia, I didn't mean to give you the wrong idea.' He looked pityingly at her. 'I'm sorry, I really am.' He patted her cheek.

She shied away, drawing in a long, shivering breath. She could see him back at Clarissa's place. 'Poor old Amelia,' he'd say. 'It's pathetic really the way she clings on.'

If my head split open this moment she thought, hot anger would spew out and drown us like the great flood. She clenched her fists, staring after Gerald who was walking towards the door, stiff-backed, eyes ahead as if he believed one backward glance would turn him into salt. I'll give Selma a blow torch next time, she thought. But before I die, I'll hang that big-assed Sloane by her thick ankles and choke her with her own Laura Ashley skirt.

'No, no I'm sorry,' she called after him. 'I can't think what got over me. It's the shock as you said.' She forced a smile to her lips and left it to fight with the expression in her eyes.

Selma surprised everyone but Amelia by remaining alive. A week after setting fire to her continental quilt she was still coughing painfully from the smoke and her legs were covered in weeping burns, but she was alive and her heart stayed strong; it seemed to have marched to a different tune from the rest of her used-up body.

The hospital needed her bed.

Amelia phoned Cherryfield and asked to be put through to Sister Morris.

'And who shall I say is calling?'

'Judas,' Amelia mumbled. 'I mean to say, it's Miss Lindsay.'

'Sister Morris here.'

Amelia had sprung Selma from Cherryfield and now, on the eve of recapture, she was actually finding the voice of the Chief Warden comforting. Sister Morris told her that there would be no problem having Mrs Merryman back as the payments had been kept up.

'I feel so responsible.' Amelia humbled herself. 'She had taken up smoking again, I think she'd forgotten she ever gave it up. But I never thought ... It was awful. There she was like one of those toadstools, you know they look like an upside-down skittle and give out puffs of smoke. She wore her hairnet too.' The picture was vivid before Amelia's eyes and somehow the hairnet added to the horror, she wasn't quite sure why. 'There's no doubt she needs better care than I can give her. It's all my fault, I should never have taken her away.'

In victory, Sister Morris was magnanimous. 'Don't be too hard on yourself Miss Lindsay, you did what you thought best. Although, as we professionals know only too well, with our elderly that's seldom enough. Now if you could give me the name of the doctor in charge of your grandmother.'

'I can't wait to get out of here. I do so detest hospitals.' Selma greeted the news on Saturday morning that she was being discharged, with a self-congratulatory little smile. 'I've had far worse burns than these,' she gesticulated in the direction of her bandaged legs, 'so I really don't see what all the fuss is about.'

She raised her arms out obediently for the nurse to dress her, and Amelia stared at the bones that seemed like a giant clothes hanger holding up the sagging flesh. She glanced at her own arms, bare in a short-sleeved T-shirt, as if making sure of their firm round-ness and the honey-tone of the skin before turning away guiltily.

Gerald's Citroën was parked outside the hospital. When he came around to measure up the spare room for wallpaper, Amelia had asked to borrow it for the trip down to Cherryfield.

'I'm sure Clarissa has a Fiat Uno or something to take you around in, and I bet she calls it Algie,' she had added ungratefully.

'Hughie actually.' Gerald had smiled briefly before remembering where his loyalties lay.

Now Selma was installed in the front seat of his car, padded legs stretched out in front of her, the seat pushed back as far as it would go. Amelia waved her thanks to the orderly as she drove out of the hospital car park.

'I hate hospitals,' Selma said again, then she coughed, a racking cough that wrenched mucus from her nose and eyes, a cough that doubled her over and sucked the energy from her so that when it finished she sat back, grey faced, moist eyes staring, and said nothing for a long time.

Amelia suffered with her, driving along on the motorway, unable to stop the car and put her arms round her to comfort. Chopin had died playing his 'Polonaise', coughing blood until there seemed to be more over the ivory of the piano than inside his own frail body, or so Selma had told her once. Maybe, Amelia thought, that was a better death; a great fountain of agony in the midst of life and beauty? It had to be better than what Selma was going through; having life sucked from her in little painful spurts.

They were on the A303 driving west, when Selma spoke again. 'I thought I was going home with you. We seem to have been driving for an awfully long time.'

'Do you need the loo?'

'No, darling, I said we seem to have been . . .'

'Cherryfield,' Amelia interrupted, pity and shame making her brusque. 'We're going to Cherryfield. You need looking after properly and it's a lot better than a hospital. You're lucky to be alive.' The phrase slipped out and they both considered it in silence.

'I suppose I am,' Selma said finally to Amelia's astonishment. Was it an automatic response, or did she actually mean it? Amelia glanced at Selma's profile. Did she really feel lucky to be alive? Did she even remember Cherryfield?

'Admiral Mallett will be pleased to see you,' Amelia tried. Selma didn't seem to have heard.

Gerald's mother had said once that she wanted

150

Gerald to put her down if she ever got senile. 'Put her down,' that was the phrase she had used and she had spoken in earnest. Amelia had asked Gerald later, 'Why are people so scared of becoming senile? After all you yourself, are the one person who won't know. There you'll be making everyone else's life a misery, but *you* won't know or care.' A senile mind, she had imagined, was like a wiped-clean video, all gone, blank. She had been so wrong. The film was still there, but with scenes cut out at randon, replaced out of sequence, rendering the whole senseless. Familiar faces turned up in strange places, flashbacks made more sense than the dislocated present. No, senility offered no escape. She put her foot down on the accelerator, watching the speedometer rise to eighty. You were condemned to stay snatching at bits of reality as tantalizing as sunbeams and as hard to hold.

'I know Admiral Mallett, nice man,' Selma said, answering suddenly.

Amelia looked out at the rape fields and the rich green meadows, bright as a flea-market picture, as if it was her journeys through the English summer landscape that were numbered, not Selma's.

'You do remember Cherryfield?' she asked quietly.

Again there was a pause, as if they were communicating by satellite.

'Of course I remember it, awful place. Robert tried to persuade me to move there for good.' Selma turned to look at Amelia. 'Where is Robert? I don't seem to have seen him for ages.'

'Brazil, he lives there now . . .' She was about to add, remember? But she said instead, 'He knows about the accident. He'll phone as soon as you're back.'

'I must go over and visit him,' Selma declared.

*　　*　　*

At Cherryfield, Sister Morris greeted them in front of the house, a large, ginger-haired man in tow.

'Welcome back, Mrs Merryman,' Sister Morris smiled, her lips moving not up, but horizontally before springing back to their usual defensive position clamped across her teeth. 'This is Mr Jones, he's joined us in your absence to help behind the scenes: fetching, carrying, that sort of thing.'

Amelia looked at the hefty, grinning Mr Jones and imagined him bounding up and down the passages and stairs of Cherryfield on all fours, old people dangling like wounded birds from his jaws. But he was gentle as he eased Selma from her seat, transferring her to the wheelchair parked on the grass verge.

Amelia hauled a small case from the car boot. 'I left most of her clothes here. They should all be in her room still.' She started to walk towards the house.

'She's not in her old room.' Sister Morris, to Amelia's surprise, coloured, lowering her gaze like a guilty child. Any moment now, Amelia thought, she'll be scuffing her white lace-ups against the gravel.

'Is there a good reason for moving her?' Amelia asked.

Sister Morris looked up as Selma was wheeled past by Mr Jones. 'At this present moment in time,' the round-about phrase gave Sister Morris time to recover her breezy confidence, 'we feel Mrs Merryman would benefit from a higher degree of care. So we put her in Honeysuckle.' She added the last sentence speedily as if to race through any objections Amelia might have.

'But that's the Annexe.' Amelia was horrified. She felt like a mother who having persuaded her child to have a verruca removed finds the surgeon poised for an amputation. 'You can't do that, she couldn't take it.' And as Sister Morris started towards the door she called after her, 'She calls it Death Row you know!'

Sister Morris continued inside. 'And that's not a helpful attitude, not at all.' She chucked the words over her shoulder at Amelia. 'We are only doing what we think best for our residents. If I may remind you, it's that kind of emotional response which got your grandmother into this sorry state in the first place.'

It was Amelia's turn to hang her head. Sister Morris was right. It had been a panic withdrawal, removing Selma from Cherryfield. It had done only harm.

'My room is upstairs.' Selma tried to look over her shoulder at Mr Jones. 'I'm sure of it. Amelia are you there? Could you please tell this man that my room is upstairs.'

Again, Amelia thought how easy it would be to cruise along on Selma's senility, to say with absolute conviction that she was mistaken yet again, that her room was, and always had been, in the Annexe; as easy as pulling the lifebelt from a drowning man.

Mr Jones had stopped at the bottom of the stairs with a helpless glance at Sister Morris. Amelia hurried up to Selma and knelt at her side.

'It's all right Grandma, it's just for a little while.'

'What is?' Selma's voice rose to a squeak.

Amelia looked up reproachfully at Sister Morris, then she put her hand on Selma's. 'They're moving you into the Annexe just while your burns heal. It's not an age thing, nothing like that. It's only because of this nasty accident. I mean, if it was I who had got burnt, I'd be in a hospital ward now.'

'So why am I not? Why am I not in hospital?'

Amelia had tears in her eyes when she looked at Selma. 'Please,' she whispered, 'I'm trying.'

'I want to go home.' Selma snatched her hand away. 'I want to go to Ashcombe. I miss the cats.' She looked hard at Amelia. 'Where are the cats?'

Amelia stood up. And what do I say now? Do I look

her in the eyes and say: Ashcombe is sold. Your things are in storage waiting for you to die so they can be divided up between your children. And the cats? They were put down. We tried to find a new home for them but they were too old and smelly, no-one wanted them. Was that what she was meant to say? She sighed. 'Let's get you settled in your room shall we?'

'Amelia.' Selma grabbed her elbow, looking at her as if there was no-one else in the world. 'I know I won't get home for my birthday, not now I've had this stupid accident.'

She's giving up, Amelia thought, distressed, relinquishing hope.

'But Christmas, darling,' Selma continued, 'that's altogether different. I'll be one hundred per cent by then.' She put her hand on Amelia's arm and whispered, 'I couldn't bear not having Christmas at home.'

Amelia just stared after her as Mr Jones began to push the wheelchair towards the Annexe.

'Amelia!' Selma sounded terrified now.

'Yes, of course,' Amelia said quickly, 'of course you'll be home for Christmas.' And merry little devils danced through her mind chanting, 'Liar, liar, pants on fire.'

She followed Mr Jones through the double swing doors at the end of the long passage. A stocky young nurse, her starched cap perched on spiky black hair, hurried towards them with a big smile. 'We haven't met,' she said to Amelia, putting out her hand. 'I'm Nurse Scott.' Then she bent down over the wheelchair, putting her face close to Selma's. 'We'll look after you, Mrs Merryman. There's nothing for you to worry about.'

'Oh bugger off,' Selma said.

The nurse pretended not to hear. She took the wheelchair from the silent Mr Jones and pushed it inside a brightly lit, sparsely furnished room. As she took Selma past the first bed, she said, pointing, 'That's Mrs Ambrose. Her husband's over in the main house. They're new this week, in fact.' She parked Selma at the foot of the second bed by the small window.

The table by Mrs Ambrose's bed was cluttered; there were several photographs, unframed ones, leaning against the carafe of water and against the small vase of roses, and two in silver frames of the same young man in an RAF cap. A Bible lay nearest the bed and a rosary of milky beads rippled across the leather cover. Over the bed was pinned a drawing of a matchstick boy with an enormous head, playing on a beach, and written across the bottom was 'To deerest Grany, from Joe'.

Amelia took a step closer, peering down at the bed. But where was Mrs Ambrose? She had an image of a skeleton in a frilly nightie jumping up from under the smooth pink counterpane crying, surprise, surprise!

'I don't think she's here.' Amelia turned to Nurse Scott. 'Mrs Ambrose, she seems to have disappeared.'

Nurse Scott turned briefly from undressing Selma, who seemed for the moment to have stopped protesting. 'She's in the Lounge, visiting Mr Ambrose. Now, while I do Mrs Merryman's legs, why don't you have a nice walk round the garden. Come back in fifteen minutes or so.'

From the open door of his room, Admiral Mallett watched the girl in her pale blue and white uniform collect Mrs Merryman's clothes. The bundle, three patterned summer dresses, a couple of cardigans, a gabardine mac that had ceased to be beige in favour of motley grey, hung over the girl's sturdy freckled arm as she clip-clopped along the landing.

'What's going on, Nurse? Mrs Merryman is coming back, isn't she?' In his mind his voice was firm, the

155

words casual. What he heard was an old man's croak pleading for assurance. People kept leaving, dying, and he could do nothing to stop it.

The nurse didn't answer so he called out again, 'Nurse!'

Now she turned. 'Admiral Mallett, I didn't see you there. Yes Mrs Merryman is back, we're moving her across to Honeysuckle.' And she was off, brisk heels across polished boards.

Poor little Mrs Merryman. An old man's tears, quick to appear, welled up in his eyes. How she will hate it. He turned and stuttered across to the huge mahogany chest of drawers brought from home. The keys to the Rover lay in the top right drawer. He slipped them into his trouser pocket and, refusing the chair-lift, laboured downstairs holding the banister tight with both hands, moving crab-like down the steps.

In the hall, Sister Morris stood by the large vase on the refectory table, subjugating a bunch of gladioli.

'I'm off for a drive,' the Admiral said airily as he passed.

Sister Morris turned, a rebellious bloom in hand. 'Really Admiral, is that wise?'

'Entirely,' he replied. 'I possess a valid licence.'

'But Admiral . . .'

'Now I mustn't keep you, Sister. Good day.'

He hadn't driven the car himself since he moved to the wretched place, when was that now? Late April, three months already. Silly not to have done so, he thought, as he reversed the car from the Cherryfield parking lot. His reactions might not be as quick as they were, but he made up for that with experience. Experience did still count for something, he told himself as he drove out from the drive and on to a clear road. At the next junction a tractor pulled out in front. Admiral Mallett didn't mind, he was in no hurry. It was good to have a reason to slow down in fact. Henry had been clever persuading him to get an automatic, saved the hip. Leaning forward a little in his seat, he flicked his eyes over to the left, enjoying the sight of the three large oak trees that stood in the centre of the vast field, defying the farmer's wish for uncluttered progress.

A flash of red screeched past the Admiral's Rover, swaying back to the left side of the road ahead of the tractor before disappearing round the twist in the road. 'Bloody fool,' the Admiral muttered to himself.

A few hundred yards down the road the tractor turned left. The Admiral slammed on the brakes. The man hadn't indicated, he could have sworn it. Behind him the Volvo Estate stopped inches from the back of the Rover. The front of a white Audi, nosing the rear of the Volvo, folded like a fan as it clanked into the metallic-blue boot.

The Admiral saw the crash in his rear-view mirror and pulled on to the verge. Pushing the door open, he heaved his legs on to the ground. He grabbed his stick and got to his feet. Peering at a passing car he stepped across to the site of the accident. By the side of the Volvo a woman stood crying, clutching a small girl by the hand. The Audi driver, a young man, the sleeves of his white shirt rolled up, stared red-faced at the folded front of his car.

Wobbling on his feet, the Admiral shook his head and tut-tutted sympathetically. Turning to the weeping woman, he cooed, 'There, there, young lady, it's not so bad, no-one's hurt. Worse things happen at sea eh?' He smiled at the little girl who smiled back, a small smile.

The young man glared. 'You know,' the Admiral jabbed the stick at him, 'this is what comes of not keeping your distance.' He turned back to the woman. 'Are you sure you're all right, madam? Would you not

like me to drive you to a doctor. And the little girl?'
Taking a couple of steps towards them he smiled
again, competent, in charge; that was service training
for you.

'You silly old fart.' The words came slowly, steeped
in contempt, making him turn around, stooping over
his stick, cheeks colouring. 'Stupid old sod, you
shouldn't be allowed on the road.' The young man
with his heavy arms crossed over his chest was
shouting at him. Somehow this all appeared to be his
fault; the crying woman and white-faced child, the
concertinaed car, were all his fault. The Admiral
blinked and swallowed hard.

'Don't speak to him like that.' The woman had
stopped crying and now she glared at the Audi driver.
She took a step towards the Admiral and said soothingly, 'There's no great harm done as you said, no-
one's hurt.'

'No harm done, you silly cow, what do you think
this is?' The young man aimed a kick at the smashed-in
front of his car. 'It's all right for you in that bloody tank
but what about this? "No harm done."' He mimicked
her voice.

That young man should not be allowed to speak to
her like that. I should stop him, the Admiral fretted.
But he was frightened, just a frightened old man who
was no use to anyone. For the second time that day he
felt close to tears.

'Don't you worry.' It was the woman comforting him
once again. 'It's difficult sometimes to see the indicator
in this bright light.' She turned to the young man who
had sat down in the passenger seat of his car, his feet
on the road, his head in his hands. Now he looked up
miserably.

'It's a new car. My own too, not the firm's.' He
sighed, not even bothering to look at the Admiral. 'Tell

the old fart to piss off and let us get on with it. You are insured, aren't you?' he asked the woman.

She nodded, then took the Admiral by the arm. 'You just drive on home,' she said, escorting him back to the Rover. 'We'll be fine.'

'We'll be fine,' the child echoed, speaking for the first time. 'But you should go home. My daddy says old people shouldn't be on the roads.'

The Admiral drove off. He could still hear the level-toned insults spouted at him by the Audi driver, wounding words lobbed at him with the indifference of a kick aimed at a stray dog. And the little girl, 'Daddy says old people shouldn't be on the roads.' In the eyes of those young people he, Rear-Admiral John Mallett DSO, DSC, was an alien life form. As if on entering his eighth decade he had simultaneously exited the human race. Could they really not see that he was just like them, only a few years on? After all, he had not entered this earth a scraggy, trembling old man.

He passed two teenage boys on their bicycles, rucksacks slung over one shoulder. They were calling to each other, laughing. I'm your future don't you see! he wanted to cry out after them. You're my past. That's all it is.

He turned off the main Totnes road on to the quiet lane leading to Harbertonford. There was no-one behind him, no-one in front. He dared take his eyes off the road to feast them on the lush greens and bright yellows of the fields. He took a double bend expertly.

'Not so fast, Johnnie.' He heard a soft voice, half scared, half excited, in his ear. Lydia, the girl who had become Henry's mother, had clung to him like a soft baby vine on that first drive together. A London child, dressed for the country in a cotton shift dress and with a white floppy hat on her long, straight hair, she had found the Devon lanes wild, she told him.

'Wild,' he had repeated smiling down at her. 'I never thought of them as that.'

He was forty-nine and an Admiral already. She was twenty-four and liked the Beatles.

'You must have been in the war?' she had asked at the London drinks party where they met.

'Which one, the big one or Korea?'

'You mean you were in both?' Her huge, black-fringed eyes had gazed blue at him. 'Crikey!'

She had chatted and laughed on that drive to Devonport, and he, quiet as always, hadn't tired of hearing her voice, small and breathless, fluttering in his ears like puffs of dandelion seeds. She had touched the dark hair on his forearm with her pink-frosted nails. 'I love your arms. They're so reassuring. Boys my age are all such weeds.' Her skinny shoulders heaved in a sigh. He could feel her look on him. 'You're sexy.'

The car had jerked to the right.

'You don't mind me being honest, do you? I think if one feels something positive about another person, one might as well tell them. Don't you?'

Heart beating faster, mouth twitching into a smile, he had said, 'I think I do.'

The lorry looming in the rearview mirror brought him back to now with angry hooting. He glanced at the speedometer and saw the needle at twenty. Putting his hand out of the open window he gave a little wave as if to say, 'Sorry, old chap, I'll get on with it.' He put his foot down. The lorry stayed close up. He pressed his foot harder on the accelerator, went faster than was comfortable, but the lorry was always there, its cab in the rear-view mirror almost on top of the Rover.

Round the next bend was the crossroads. He had to turn right on to the main road to get back to

Kingsmouth. The light was fading. He edged the car out to get a better view past the tall hedges. The cars ran in a steady stream from both directions. Opposite, somebody was waiting too. The chap wasn't signalling so he'd be wanting to cross straight over: his right of way. The Admiral leant far over the wheel, eyes right, eyes left, right again as if he was watching a tennis match. There was a gap. He stood back for the other car to cross. The lorry hooted. 'All right, all right,' the Admiral muttered, but he was fretting. The car had crossed but there was another one now. No more gaps in the traffic either, just a road like a conveyor belt, pushing out car after car. The lorry driver put his fingers on the horn and kept them there. The Admiral glanced in the rear-view mirror, then stretched further over the wheel, heart pumping, eyes flicking from side to side and across. His mouth tasted sour. He ran his tongue across his cracked lips. He needed a pee too.

The lorry driver had stopped sounding his horn. The Admiral sat back a little and some of the tension left his neck and shoulders.

'No need to panic old boy,' he told himself. Bound to get across eventually. The blighter will just have to wait.

'Beeeep!' It started up again, and now others joined in, a chorus straight from hell. The shock sent tears to his eyes. His eyes darted from side to side as he jerked the car out on to the main road. Another horn made him look right. He saw the open mouth of the driver of the van. This is it, he thought, and everything was sound: crashing, splitting, shattering. Then silence.

Chapter Fifteen

Henry Mallett stood in the garden at Cherryfield, his back to the French windows. He stood quite still under the cherry tree, his head slightly raised. Talking to God maybe, Amelia thought as she came up quietly behind him. He turned and, when he saw her, a slow smile of pleasure softened his face. Amelia thought it must have taken a lot of effort to find a shirt as awful as the one he was wearing – turquoise with an asymmetric pattern in black and lime-green.

Henry looked as if he was about to kiss her cheek, then thinking the better of it, he took her hand instead in a firm handshake.

'Pleased to meet you I'm sure,' Amelia simpered but he ignored her and said, 'I heard about the fire. Thank God you're both OK.'

Amelia stopped simpering. 'I'm OK, Selma is in Death Row.'

'I heard that too. I'm sorry. How is she taking it?' He waited for her answer in that way he had of cocking his head slightly towards you as if he couldn't bear to miss a word you said. It always made her feel she ought to reward his attentiveness with a comment of earth-shattering profundity.

'Badly,' she said.

Still, Henry's attentive silence, as they wandered across the lawn, seemed to suck thoughts from her she hadn't even admitted to herself.

'I wish she was dead.' She looked up at him, half

expecting him to raise a condemnatory finger with a flash of Old Testament fire. But he didn't. He just kept listening, so she went on talking.

'Selma's the only person left whom I really love and who loves me back, and still I wish her dead. That's how badly she's taking it.' She flung herself down on the dry grass. 'I might be wrong of course.' She turned to him as he sat down next to her. 'Of course she might have taken one look at the Annexe and thought, "This is the place for me, I'm happy," but somehow when a person sits slumped in a wheelchair, tears trickling down their face, their poor, useless hand jerking and dancing on the end of the arm like a badly managed puppet, I reckon they're not so happy after all.' She glared at him. He smiled back at her. She stopped glaring and asked, 'Is your father well?'

'Not too bad. He's out for a drive apparently. It's good news that, I think. He's not been out on his own since coming here.' Henry changed tack seamlessly. 'Your mother, don't you love her?'

As she thought about it, Amelia pulled a tuft of grass from the lawn and scattered it over her legs. 'Maybe, I suppose so. But it's like sunlight trying to penetrate so many layers of atmosphere that, when it finally arrives, it's weak. Selma was life enhancing. My mother is life denying. I worry that I might be like her.'

'Your poor mother, she must be very unhappy,' Henry said.

Amelia gave him a dirty look. 'And this time I promised Selma she'd be home for Christmas.' She made it sound like a challenge to him: so what does someone like you, with your faith and your energy, do with someone like me, so shiftless and feeble?

'How long are you going to go on lying to her?'

Amelia had no fight left in her. 'Oh Henry, I don't

163

know. It's like paying off one credit card with another; sooner or later it will end in tears.'

'But what are you going to do about it?' Henry insisted.

'I don't know what I'm going to do,' she whined. 'You always say, "What are you going to do about it?" in that revoltingly energetic way. But I'm tired.' Her voice rose in pitch. 'I'm tired of worrying about Selma, tired of feeling sorry for her. It's not fair.' She finished pulling the petals off a daisy and looked up at him. 'Isn't it the Bible that says, "For everything there is a time"? Well, this is the time for me to be concerned with three months colic and the aluminium content in baby formula. Or at least to be left in peace to get on with being a self-centred thirtysomething minding my brilliant career. Instead, pity for Selma rides my back like a witch whose claws dig deeper into my shoulders each time I try to shake her off.'

Henry cleared his throat and Amelia added quickly, 'And please don't tell me to get my pleasures from helping others and to look forward to an absolutely stunning afterlife. I couldn't take it just at the moment. I've got a dreadful headache.' The face she raised to him was pallid in the strong light, each gold-brown freckle showing against the white skin.

'It's obvious you haven't been to church for some time if that's your idea of preaching,' Henry said dryly, but he looked concerned.

I could cover his nice, firm mouth with passionate kisses, Amelia thought. That would make him run off and leave me alone.

'I was actually about to offer some constructive advice,' he continued.

'I don't want that either. I just want to be left alone to get on with my life.'

'Get on with dreaming about how to get on with

your life, you mean. Waiting for Gerald to marry you. Waiting for children to be born who can do everything you never had the guts and energy to do yourself.'

Amelia didn't even bother to look offended. 'Gerald's left me for an independent career woman, the sort, in fact, that I was before I gave it all up for him.' She added thoughtfully, 'Of course I was better looking.'

'Are better looking,' Henry surprisingly corrected her. Then he mumbled dutifully, 'I'm sorry to hear it though,' before allowing his normal expression of barely harnessed eagerness to return. 'But now it's happened, take the opportunity to do something positive with your life. Take charge. See that witch on your back as a jockey spurring you on. Cherryfield is not that far away from any of us, so get on with life. Grab it by the neck, wrestle it to the ground and say "I'm on top".' Henry's bright brown eyes were round as he looked intently at her.

'That's the Naval part of the Chaplain speaking, is it?' Amelia couldn't help smiling. She scratched her right knee thoughtfully; her tights were itching in the heat but she refused to go barelegged. When Gerald had asked her why she seemed to be the only female still wearing tights in the summer she had said, 'Blue-tinged, freckled legs just aren't nice.' Of course stockings were cooler, she thought now as she scratched on absent-mindedly, but the suspender belt kept slipping down over her hips, making the stockings wrinkle. Hold-ups were positively dangerous, she was sure of it, the way they gripped the flesh part of your thighs like a tourniquet.

'Penny for them?' Amelia looked up to find Henry gazing at her.

She stopped scratching and smiled suddenly. 'Would you believe: stockings and suspenders?'

He grinned back. 'As it's you, yes.'

'I do have something planned you know,' she said, serious now. 'I want to open a café. The old-fashioned continental kind. Somewhere where elderly matrons can catch their breath after a hard day's shopping for darning needles and corn plasters. Somewhere where they can slam down their copious shopping baskets on the table with a sigh of contentment as they order fattening pastries. I picture them wearing hats,' she said. 'I find the hats important you see, because it takes a person in control of their life to wear one regularly.' She looked at Henry with a little smile. 'I don't suppose that's the sort of thing you mean.'

Henry looked a little taken aback. Amused, Amelia noticed that he was trying hard not to look at her legs.

'What about your journalism?' he asked.

She shrugged her shoulders. 'I should never have left the paper. It's not easy to break back in, particularly in the present climate. It's almost all dead men's shoes. I could try the provincials of course, but it would be a step back.' Hoping to impress him a little she added, 'About the café; I thought of arranging poetry recitals, that sort of thing, and there'll be the antiquarian books. I want people to be able to look at them while they eat. I'd have to be careful about stains, of course.'

Whilst she spoke, Henry was looking intently at her and she paused, as always a little disconcerted to find herself listened to. 'I can't see my matrons buying many books really, they prefer the library, but younger people, the kind who think old ladies are trendy . . .' She fell silent, looking out over the garden. It was only July but the soft mist that rolled in from the sea, settling across the beech hedges, belonged to autumn. She liked autumn; no hot days demanding you made the most of them.

'Why don't you open your café down here?' Henry asked. 'You'd be near your mother and grandmother. And me.'

'Maybe.' She smiled up at him. 'I like London, but I didn't enjoy living there much. I prefer little nosy places.'

'Well get on with it then. Go down to the estate agents in town and see what they've got.'

I'm so weak, Amelia thought, that I will even turn decisive on someone else's say so. She looked him in the eyes. 'OK, I will. I'll check on Selma and then I'll go.' She stood up and brushed the grass from her skirt.

Henry got up too. 'I wonder where my father is?' Glancing at his watch, he frowned. 'He should have come back by now.'

While Amelia wandered around the estate agents by the harbour being shown details of houses with shop-fronts, houses with sub-Post Offices and houses with permission to erect twenty-five dog kennels, Henry was told of his father's death.

A woman police constable came to Cherryfield to inform Sister Morris of the accident. 'I was told I might find the son, the Reverend Mallett, here,' she said.

Out in the garden the mist had cleared, giving way to evening sunlight. 'Did he die instantly?' Henry asked, bending double as if he was going to be sick.

Everyone asked that, the policewoman thought. 'Not instantly, no,' she said softly, adding quickly what she knew he wanted to hear, 'but he didn't suffer. He died in the ambulance, put up a real fight they told me, but he didn't suffer. He's in the hospital now if you'd like to see him.'

'I don't think he fought to stay alive. I think he fought to die,' Henry said, his fingers raking through his hair.

The policewoman thought it a funny thing for a Reverend to say. From the shadow of the cherry tree Sister Morris cleared her throat.

'Now why should you think that, Mr Mallett? Your father was quite happy here you know.'

'I'm sure he was,' the policewoman mumbled soothingly as she prepared to leave. She thought the Reverend Mallett had an almost wild look in his eyes as he got up to follow her. 'I'm sure he didn't suffer,' she said again, trying to comfort.

It was the unexpectedness of his death that made Amelia burst into tears when Sister Morris told her of the Admiral's accident. She had returned from town with a bundle of prospectuses to show Henry, finding Selma still asleep and the Residents' Lounge a nest of lustily growing rumours. The Admiral had had a stroke. He'd been run down by a lorry. He'd collided with a tractor.

But Miss White felt sure she had the real answer to what had happened. 'It's the KGB.' She shook her head. 'That Blake has a lot to answer for.'

Then Sister Morris came in and explained to everyone what had happened.

Miss White nodded wisely. 'That's right dear. It's always known as a car crash when the KGB have done their dirty work.' She added thoughtfully, 'One would have thought they'd have come up with something new by now.'

'The Russians are our friends now, Miss White,' the old man in the next door armchair corrected her mildly.

'They might be your friends Mr Ambrose,' Miss White snapped, 'but they're certainly not mine.'

Amelia fled.

*   *   *

168

She called the Naval Barracks at Devonport from the hotel, asking to speak to Henry. While she waited, she practised little suitable phrases of commiseration and comfort. I'm thinking of you at this difficult time: too formal. It was all for the best: too cold hearted. Anything, anything at all I can do: so bland. Then before she had a chance to stop it, the worst thought of all broke loose from its harness of decency and bolted through her mind: You're free. Henry you're free. She shuddered and blushed, changing the receiver from her left to her right ear. Finally the exchange came back, informing her that Henry was nowhere to be found.

She called Dagmar, but something in her mother's voice, a kind of honeyed impatience, took Amelia back instantly to her childhood when it was never quite the right moment or there wasn't enough time. Her desire to tell was replaced by a sullen desire to withhold, and, in the end, all she said was, 'We're back.'

'Alan and I are planning to come over tomorrow,' Dagmar said. 'I'll bring the puppy. Did I tell you I've bought a puppy. Alan adores dogs.'

Amelia went for a walk after dinner. Away from the harbour, the narrow streets were empty. There was a full moon in the dark-blue sky and the evening breeze was Mediterranean in its warmth. A little out of breath she stopped at the top of the hill and looked towards Ashcombe. A light came on in the sitting room, then the curtains were drawn.

In Selma's childhood home, at the Jewish New Year, glasses would be raised in the toast of the Diaspora: Next Year in Jerusalem! Ashcombe had become Selma's Jerusalem now. It had held everything she wanted in life: husband, children, calm, flower-filled rooms and a sitting room with a grand piano and windows looking out at the sea.

At Cherryfield there was Sister Morris and Miss White, nourishing pilchards for tea, music from the television and a vista of ornamental cherries. Selma never did like ornamental cherries. 'Next Year in Jerusalem,' Amelia sing-songed to herself before turning around and walking back to the hotel. And how on earth am I meant to achieve that?

It was two in the morning when Amelia was woken by a knock on her hotel-room door. At first the noise seemed part of her dream where she pushed Selma in a supermarket trolley round a small town full of glass-fronted houses. But Selma kept shaking her head and saying, 'No darling, that's not Jerusalem either.' Amelia knocked on yet another door, louder and louder, and then she woke up. She rolled over in bed and, half asleep still, put her feet on the floor. She padded across to the door and asked, without opening, 'Who is it?'

'Night porter, Miss Lindsay. Sorry to disturb you at such an hour but I've got a priest for you downstairs. He won't go away. Says his name's Mallett.'

Amelia opened the door. 'Send him up, would you please?'

The night porter had obviously been in as deep a sleep as Amelia. His sparse sandy hair rose in a coxcomb and his eyes were bloodshot. Now he opened them wide, taking in Amelia's short nightshirt and the amount of naked leg appearing below it. 'Up here Miss?'

'He is a priest. A priest in need of comfort.'

'I thought they were the ones meant to give comfort,' the porter muttered.

'Well this one operates both ways.' Impatiently, Amelia took a step past him out on to the landing.

'I'll get him,' the porter said quickly, obviously deciding his boss would prefer sin to be contained within four walls rather than wandering the hotel at will.

Amelia stayed in the open doorway listening. She heard mumbled voices, then heavy steps hurrying up the wooden stairs.

'Amelia, I'm sorry about this.' Henry almost fell into her arms and she backed inside the room, still holding him. He was crying, she could feel it. She moved her hand up carefully, stroking his hair, patting him, mumbling small phrases of comfort. She felt him shivering and, just as she was beginning to think her back would break, he released her.

'I'm sorry,' he said again, throwing himself down on the pink boudoir chair by the window.

'I'm glad you came. I've tried to reach you all evening.'

'I know. Thank you.' He wasn't looking at her. 'He's better off where he is now. Grief is just selfish.' He sobbed and tried to pass it off as a cough.

Amelia knelt by the chair and took his hands. 'And none the worse for that,' she whispered. 'You're a chaplain, not a saint. You loved him.'

Henry looked up at her with a small smile. 'It was always just him and I, and Winter of course. My mother died when I was one. I don't remember her at all.'

'I don't remember much about my father, other than that he had bright blue eyes and no interest in his daughter. "Irish eyes," my mother has a tendency to mutter and that's all the answer I get.' Amelia fell silent, trying to weigh up how much idle chit-chat was appropriate.

Henry seemed calmer now as he sat gazing intently at her. Squeezed into the small, pink-upholstered chair, he reminded her of Willoughby's boxer who all his life had nurtured a hopeless ambition to fit on to

171

the plate-size silk cushion belonging to Selma's Siamese. 'Who is Winter?' she asked gently.

'Winter.' Again that quick smile. 'He was my father's PO steward. When he retired from the Navy he stayed on working for us. He helped bring me up until I went away to school. Then he went off to run a pub in Modbury. We kept in touch until he died five years ago. I loved him.'

Amelia sighed. 'There are times,' she said, 'when there seems to be more death than life in life, if you see what I mean.'

Henry laughed miserably. 'At least Winter died a happy man. His doctor told him he'd have to cut out beer or at least switch to the low alcohol stuff. He died of a ruptured bladder while trying to get the old kick from Kaliber.' Henry laughed again, unsuitably and loudly and for so long that Amelia got worried. Then he sobbed, a snorting embarrassed kind of sob.

'I just miss my father so much already. You see I never mourned my mother; I was too young. Of course I missed the idea of a mother, all that soft indulgence . . .' He looked wide eyed at Amelia. 'What other children had and took for granted. But losing my father; it's a bit as if all your life you've been in this warm, cosy room and suddenly the walls collapse around you and you're standing there exposed to the world.'

He gripped Amelia's hand. 'I just hope he wasn't scared. He was one of the bravest men I knew and the thought of him being scared and alone . . .'

He just wants his father back, Amelia thought. How can you ever hope to help a person who is grieving when the one person really able to comfort them is the one they've lost? A phrase appeared in her head, one she'd heard Selma use. 'Say not in grief that he is no more, but in thankfulness that he was,' she mumbled more to herself than to Henry.

Henry smiled at her and she sat back, leaning her shoulder against his knees. 'Tell me about your father.' She had always found it strange how there seemed to exist a conspiracy of silence around someone grieving, as if his friends were attempting, out of sheer embarrassment, to kill even the memory of the dead.

They talked about the Admiral for a long time and then Amelia stood up and put her hand out to Henry. 'Shall we go to bed?' The moment she spoke she regretted it. Tasteless, that's what it was. She felt her face go hot as Henry sat back and looked at her. Like a guilty child she said quickly, 'I didn't really mean it.'

'I wish you had,' he smiled and pulled her down on his knee. 'Although I would have had to say no, I'm not a chaplain just for the pretty uniform.' He kissed her hand lightly. 'It was a very nice thought. Thank you.'

It was five o'clock when he left. Amelia stood at the window watching him walk off towards the car park as the sun rose over the sea beyond.

Chapter Sixteen

'Mrs Merryman has had a good night,' Nurse Williams said as she opened the door for Amelia later that morning. 'She insisted on waiting for you in the Lounge. We really felt it would be better for her to rest in her room, but she can be quite determined when she wants to, your gran.'

'I know,' Amelia said. 'It's excellent that she knows what she wants, isn't it?'

Sister Morris busied past them with an anxious looking middle-aged couple in tow. 'And this is our Residents' Lounge.' There was a pause. 'Normally, of course, we have a waiting list but what with the cold spell in March and Number Two suddenly becoming available . . .' They disappeared upstairs.

Before Amelia had got out of the hall the bell rang and Dagmar stood in the doorway together with a tall man who was holding the lead to a struggling black puppy that looked like a labrador.

'Darling.' Dagmar's lips brushed against Amelia's cheek, Dagmar's smile radiated across the hall. 'And this is Alan.' Her eyes darted between Amelia and Alan, the words rushed from her lips. Alan took a step inside and almost fell over as the puppy entwined its lead round his legs.

'Admiral Mallett died yesterday,' Amelia whispered as they approached the Lounge. 'I expect Grandma will be pretty upset.'

'There'll be wailing and gnashing of dentures,'

Dagmar said and laughed out loud. She stopped suddenly. 'Oh I'm sorry, darling, he was a dear old boy. It's just that it's all so awful.' Her voice rose shrilly and Amelia stiffened and glanced at Alan. She couldn't bear her mother making a fool of herself.

'He looked so fit, I always thought,' Dagmar said in a normal voice now. 'How old was he?'

When you're old and you die, no-one thinks to ask how it happened, Amelia thought. It's just assumed that you expired by the rules, quietly, without fuss.

'He was a bit of a devil in the car. He crashed,' she said, hoping she'd done right by the Admiral.

'He was a dear friend of yours?' Alan stood back to let her go through the door first. He had a nice voice; quiet with a soft New England accent.

'I was fond of him, and I've got to know his son quite well,' Amelia said, raising her arm to wave at Selma who was slumped in a chair by the television. The seat by the fish-tank was empty. A sad son and an empty space by a fish-tank, were those all the traces left from the Admiral's moment on earth? Amelia wondered, shuddering.

Selma stared blankly at them as they approached. Her tightly bandaged legs rested on a small stool and she was dressed in a shapeless, yellow dress that accentuated the greyness of her skin. When Dagmar bent down and kissed her she smiled suddenly. 'Hello, darling.' She snatched at Dagmar's hand. 'You know for a moment there I didn't recognize you. Have you changed your hair?'

Dagmar had worn her hair in the same glossy bob for twenty years. 'No, Mummy.' Dagmar winked at Alan as she straightened up. 'Mummy this is Professor Blake, he insisted on meeting you,' she announced, smiling proudly.

Amelia thought she might as well have thrown her

arms out wide, announcing, 'And now for my next trick and without a safety-net, I will introduce my mother.'

Alan extended his free hand to Selma, who received it suspiciously. 'A great pleasure to meet you, ma'am.' Selma looked stonily at him; she had never been keen on conspicuously good manners.

The puppy had been licking his scrotum absorbedly, but now he lifted his face, alert, ears pricked. He got up and took a little leap at Dagmar before settling down to licking her legs in their shiny tights, with the same rapt attention.

Alan offered a chair to Dagmar who refused, saying she needed to stretch her legs after the journey.

With a 'May I?' to Selma, Alan sat down himself. 'Cute little fellow isn't he?' He pointed at the puppy. 'You know I never would have guessed the country-woman in your daughter. Of course, I've always loved animals, nature, feeling the dirt under my fingers, that kind of thing. Now Dagmar here comes and tells me that's the life for her as well.' He brought a pipe from his pocket and crossed one long leg over the other. 'Of course that comes as no surprise to her mother.'

Selma opened her mouth to speak.

'That's enough now.' Dagmar, speaking between clenched teeth, was doing a little dance to avoid the long pink tongue of the puppy.

'Simon, you little rascal . . . That's enough. Simon! Do you hear me? That's enough I said.' Dagmar's eyes darted across to Alan to make sure he wasn't looking, then she gave the puppy a shove with the point of her shoe. 'Get him off me, will you, Amelia?' she hissed. 'Did you see where he had his tongue just now? All over his you know what.'

Amelia squatted down on the carpet and put her hands out. Simon, stubby tail wagging, threw himself towards her to investigate.

'Why don't you sit down, dear?' Alan asked again.

Dagmar smiled nervously at him and rushed a tissue from her pocket, dropping it across the seat of the chair before sitting down.

Leaning down towards Amelia she hissed, 'Puppies are worm-infested. It doesn't matter what you do about it.' Then she forgot to whisper. 'How am I supposed to enjoy the rest of the day with these filthy tights on?'

Alan turned around and looked at her, one bushy eyebrow raised.

'There are no worms on your legs,' Amelia said. She hadn't meant to sound so sharp.

'Shuss.' Dagmar glanced nervously at Alan who was once more in conversation with Selma. 'Anyway,' she whispered, 'it's the eggs that are dangerous. They get stuck everywhere. You can't see them, and even the strongest disinfectant can't get rid of them.' It almost sounded, Amelia thought, as if she was making a commercial on behalf of the wretched worms.

She whispered back to Dagmar, 'I don't know how to break it to Grandma about Admiral Mallett. It doesn't seem as if she's been told.'

'Oh, don't you think so?' Dagmar stretched her right leg out in front of her, twisting it to check the back of the glossy tights. 'Did you know a child could go blind if he ingested those eggs?'

'I hardly think some little cherub will dive out of the woodwork and begin to lick your legs. Not here. Not at Cherryfield.' Incensed by Dagmar's inability to think of anyone but herself even for a minute, Amelia ignored Dagmar's hurt look and moved her chair closer to Selma's.

Alan was saying how he too loved Jane Austen, and when there was a pause, a long one waiting for Selma to fill it with a reply, Amelia broke in.

'Any news? All well around here?' She made her

voice light but she looked intently at her grandmother. She was aware that Miss White, sitting by herself a few yards away, was listening, an expectant smile on her lips, head cocked as if waiting for an opportunity to pounce on the conversation. Now she seized her chance with the ease of a trained hijacker.

'I hear you're one of our American cousins.' She leant so far towards Alan that Amelia feared she might topple from her chair any moment. Alan turned with a polite smile. Selma looked furious and did not introduce them.

'You will agree with me that it would almost certainly be the KGB?'

'Pardon me, ma'am.' Alan looking confused, turned in vain to Dagmar for help, but she was staring out across the room with the faraway look that intrigued strangers but Amelia knew meant she was wondering how to remove her tights without seeming odd.

'Admiral Mallett.' Miss White sounded impatient.

Amelia sat up in her chair, ready with a comforting hand for Selma.

'They're burying him tomorrow I'm told. Bury 'em quickly if you want to stop tongues wagging, they say.'

Well they failed miserably with you, you old crow. Amelia glared at Miss White. She turned to Selma with soothing words ready to fire and found that her grandmother's expression of sullen confusion had not changed by a flicker. She still hasn't taken it in, Amelia thought, taking Selma's hand. As she prepared her speech she could feel the hand trembling in hers like a frightened heart.

'I meant to tell you yesterday but you were asleep.' She spoke softly. 'The Admiral was involved in a car crash. They say he didn't . . .'

'I know,' Selma interrupted. 'Poor old boy. Awful shame. We shall miss him.' But she directed her next

178

remark at Alan, eager to snatch back the conversation from Miss White. 'Of course it's her endings I find a little disappointing.'

Amelia had let go of Selma's hand and now she stared at her open-mouthed.

'Shut your mouth, darling,' Dagmar said unnecessarily, as she moved her shoe away from Simon who lay prostrate on the carpet, his adoring gaze following her every move.

Amelia kept looking at Selma. Was this another display of dignity and a stiff upper lip from a member of the generation that lived through a world war, or had senility blanked out compassion and affection too? Maybe Selma spoke so little of her grief for Willoughby not because she was brave, but because she didn't really feel any? Had age blunted love and loss like waves blunting bits of glass on the shore, until they were smooth and round, unable to hurt you?

Selma was taking a lot of trouble to ignore Miss White, arranging her lips into a supercilious half smile every time the little woman spoke.

Maybe you can't love me any more either, Amelia thought, and she sniffed and blinked away a tear. Oh my grandmother, what have you become?

'My God he stinks!' Dagmar leapt from the chair and pointed at Simon who placed his plump behind on her shoe, looking up adoringly, the tip of his tail wagging slowly, expectantly, like a snake sizing up its prey. The two old women stopped glaring at each other and stared instead at Dagmar, loose-mouthed. As the room fell silent, Dagmar's cheeks turned slowly pink.

'What's the matter, dear?' Alan asked, his voice chilly.

Amelia couldn't smell a thing but she chipped in hurriedly, 'He does stink a bit.' Dagmar's addiction was to fear rather than drugs or alcohol but Amelia was, all the same, an addict's child; her mother might drive her to despair, irritate her more than a sackful of red ants, but it was Amelia's job to make sure no-one else got to share those feelings. 'It sort of hits you in wafts,' she added for good measure.

Alan bent down and, putting his hand out, called Simon over. 'Hi there fellow. What's all this about you making smells?' He sniffed the puppy's neck. Simon, snout lifted, black gums stretched back, grinned at him. Then Alan slid his hand under Simon's collar before smelling his fingers. 'I'd say he's had a bit of a roll. Must have been when he ran loose from the car,' he said to Dagmar. 'You, little fellow, will get into the tub when we get home.'

'By car?' Dagmar looked near to tears.

'Well, you don't expect the little fellow to walk to Exeter do you?' Alan laughed up at her.

'I'm sure there's a tap outside,' Selma said. 'Why don't you wash him off there?' Dagmar and Amelia looked at Selma, shocked by the sense of her suggestion.

Alan said, 'It's OK, thanks but we'll . . .'

'I'll do it straight away.' Dagmar was up from the chair already, a too bright smile on her lips. She grabbed the lead from Alan giving it a little jerk. 'Come on, Simon darling.' Her voice was so tense, Amelia thought, you could shoot arrows from it.

Simon remained sitting.

'He doesn't want to come,' Miss White said.

'Oh do shut up.' Selma frowned.

'Mrs Merryman really!' Miss White looked around her with relish as if to say, 'There did I not tell you she's a naughty girl.'

'Dagmar for God's sake, can't we just forget about Simon for a minute. We're upsetting the good folks here.' Alan glared under thick eyebrows.

Dagmar ignored him, but regretfully, as if she wished she didn't have to. 'Come on Simon, we're off.' Dagmar gave the lead such a tug that Simon, still sitting, slid on his bottom across several yards of high-gloss floor, the collar riding up over the folds in his fat little neck and up across his ears. Then suddenly he got up and trotted out of the room behind Dagmar as if that's what he'd intended all along.

'Temper, temper,' chirruped Miss White.

Old age makes you evil, Amelia thought.

They sat in silence as a nurse brought a middle-aged woman to see Mr Ambrose, who had melted chameleon-like into the taupe cover of his armchair, a little away from their group.

'I'll go and give my mother a hand with Simon.' Amelia got up.

'Stand still! Stand still I tell you.' Dagmar stood, feet wide apart, clutching a gushing hose in one hand and the puppy's lead in the other. Simon was making little leaps in all directions to avoid the sharp jet of cold water. The whites of his eyes were showing but his tail was attempting a wag.

'If you move away once more . . .'

With a squeal of terror the puppy hid from the jet behind Dagmar's legs. 'Go away! You little bastard, go away, do you hear me!' Dagmar grabbed the end of the lead, lashing the puppy over and over across his chubby back. Simon screamed and, pulling loose, tore past Amelia on her way out.

Dagmar, red-faced and panting, looked up to see Alan staring at her from the terrace. 'You beat that little dog,' he said and strode off after Simon.

Chapter Seventeen

For a child, the unpredictability of a neurotic parent was terror in an apron. Even now, at thirty-one, Amelia was shaking as she led her sobbing mother to the bathroom. Her heart was still racing, her windpipe still felt as if it had shrunk two sizes, as she sat on the edge of the bath, watching Dagmar wipe the smudges of mascara from her cheeks.

Dabbing at the paper-thin skin under her eyes with the corner of a rough towel Dagmar turned her streaky face to Amelia. 'I didn't mean to hit Simon. I just don't know what came over me.' Sobbing, she leant against the wall, burying her face in the crook of her arm.

The usual I expect, Amelia thought. She felt only a little pity for Dagmar, little and highly diluted by pity for Simon and for herself. One day, she thought as she waited for Dagmar to stop crying, I'll tell Henry what it's been like. 'How would you feel,' I'll say to him, 'if your God suddenly started hurling bricks at you as you stood chatting to him by the altar? What would it do to your confidence if he returned your prayers with a string of four letter words? Because that's how it feels for a child having the grown-up in her life go mad.'

With a deep sigh she got up and walked across to Dagmar. 'It's all right,' she said, putting her arm round her mother's thin shoulders that were so like her own. 'It's all right.'

Alan waited unsmiling in the hall with the puppy, wet and shiny, curled up at his feet. As Dagmar came down the stairs he said nothing, but looked pointedly at his watch. Simon unscrambled himself and padded up towards Dagmar, a questioning little wag to his tail. Looking up at Alan, she kneeled and put her hand out and Simon stretched out his fat neck towards it, sniffing it as if it was hot.

'Let's go shall we?' Alan's voice was cold. 'I've said goodbye to your ma.'

'I haven't yet. I won't keep you a moment.' She almost ran from the hall, knees a little bent.

'Well it was nice meeting you.' Alan put his hand out to Amelia with a smile big enough to be polite but too tight to be warm.

'I'll see you again soon I expect.' Amelia poked at his anger, testing it.

Alan shrugged his shoulders and said, 'Maybe.'

Dagmar returned to the hall so flattened by what she had done that she might have been her own shadow slinking through the doorway. When she kissed Amelia goodbye she held her cold cheek against hers for a long moment.

'We had planned for you to join us for lunch in town, but I think under the circumstances maybe not,' she whispered. In the doorway she turned and shrugged her shoulders with a little smile before going off after Alan.

Alan held the door of the estate car open for Dagmar, before lifting Simon into the back and walking round to the driver's seat. She's done it again, Amelia thought sadly, she's seen an opportunity for happiness, grasped it with both hands . . . and throttled it. She gave a little wave to the departing car and closed the door.

Back in the Residents' Lounge a tiny woman sat in a wheelchair next to Mr Ambrose, head flopping as if it was too great a burden for the thin neck. Now she got a kiss from her visitor. 'You take care, Mother. See you next month as usual.' The Ambroses' daughter-in-law nodded and smiled at Miss White who sat engrossed in a holiday programme on television, then she made for the door with such hurried little steps that she almost bumped in to Amelia.

'So sorry,' the woman mumbled but there was no hiding the relief in her face: it was over for this time.

What could one do when old, Amelia wondered, to avoid putting such an expression on a loved one's face? Tell jokes, tap-dance, hand out large sums of money?

Slumped in her wheelchair, Mrs Ambrose's lips moved ceaselessly, churning out mumbled, jumbled phrases; words without end, Amen, Amelia thought as she stepped over the woman's twig-like legs to get across to Selma who slept in the chair by the French windows.

'Don't trample me.' The voice was strong and firm. 'What I'm saying is: you don't pay all this money to sit here being trampled on.'

Startled, Amelia turned to look into Mrs Ambrose's lifted face. Her eyes, large and sky-blue, were smiling.

'I'm so sorry,' Amelia mumbled.

Mr Ambrose looked up from his crossword puzzle. Taking his wife's hand he said, 'It's all right Dorothy, you're quite safe,' and once more Mrs Ambrose's head dropped down on to her chest, like a wind-up doll who had sprung alive, done its turn, then fallen still.

Would Gerald have become her comforter when she got old and made no sense? Amelia wondered as she sat down next to Selma. She didn't think so. He had often said, with the air of one confessing to an endearing quirk in their personality, 'I know it's silly but I'm just no use at a sick bed.' Not many men were, she had noticed. He'd probably be safe with Clarissa though, it was difficult not to feel she would be as crisply put together at ninety as she was now.

Selma slept on. Amelia wondered if Dagmar had been forgiven. Maybe this very moment they were making up in bed. Amelia, though pleased at the thought, blushed. Teenagers refused to contemplate that their parents' sexual organs were there for anything other than show, rather like a false pocket or a button without a button hole, once they themselves had been achieved. At thirty-one you knew better, but that didn't mean you had to like it. Amelia looked surreptitiously at the Ambroses. And when did it stop anyway? Was it sudden or gradual? A situation reached multilaterally or unilaterally?

Just then Mrs Ambrose raised her head, giving Amelia the uncomfortable feeling she might have spoken the question aloud, but Dorothy Ambrose just gazed at her husband with huge, clear eyes. Mr Ambrose seemed to feel his wife's eyes on him and, looking up from his paper, he took her hand once more, giving it a little squeeze.

Amelia, feeling moved by the little scene, smiled, just as Mrs Ambrose, her eyes fixed on her husband's face, bared her teeth, good teeth still, and sunk them into the fleshy part of his palm.

Miss White was bored with the television. Mr Ambrose's small cry of pain and Amelia's sharp intake of breath provided a welcome break. She prodded Amelia with her stick as Mr Ambrose, quite composed again, gently released his hand from his wife's teeth. 'Mrs Ambrose bites I'm afraid,' she explained in a loud whisper. 'I don't know why.'

Mrs Ambrose smiled cheerfully at her husband. 'Silly old fart,' she said.

Selma had woken up and now Miss White turned to

185

her with a self-important air. 'I said, I don't know why Mrs Ambrose bites.'

Amelia made herself small, avoiding looking at Mr Ambrose, but Selma didn't seem surprised. She nodded, her faded eyes grave. 'They're the worst,' she said. 'Human bites are the worst.'

For the first few miles of their journey back to Exeter, Dagmar thought there was a chance that Alan might forgive her. He chatted amiably enough, complimenting her on Selma and Amelia as if, Dagmar thought, I could take credit for either. But she smiled modestly and said she had tried her best.

'It hasn't been easy, being a single parent.' Growing in confidence she carried on, 'I used to read these books about beautiful women hurling themselves off cliffs and under trains rather than living with their lover's betrayal. At the time it seemed rather a good option, but then I looked at this chubby red-haired little thing, my daughter, and thought it would be the worst betrayal of all.' She laughed as she always did when talking about what was serious.

When Alan neither looked at her nor spoke, Dagmar knew she had lost him. For the rest of the journey she might as well have been appearing on a television set with the sound turned off; her lips moved, she sang her heart out, but not a sound reached through to her audience.

They drove up in front of Dagmar's block of flats and Alan, as always, dashed around to open the car door for her. 'Here we are.'

He makes the little phrase seem so final, Dagmar thought, like a coach driver in a Hammer horror pulling up outside the Castle of Doom. 'Here we are Miss.' Dagmar burst into loud giggles.

Alan didn't bother to ask why, but walked around

the back to let Simon out from the boot, handing her the lead.

Dagmar pulled her hand away and shook her head. 'You take him, please.' Simon tried to lift his leg against the porch and lost his balance.

Alan nodded but he was looking pityingly into her eyes as if he had already broken the bad news. 'Goodbye Dagmar.' He pronounced her name as he always did, with the emphasis on the 'r'. 'You take care now.'

Shall I scream, she thought, throw myself at his feet and beg, cling to his legs as he walks away? 'Goodbye then,' she said.

Alan walked off to the car and started the engine.

Dagmar looked around her at the sitting room: tables shining with beeswax, spotless carpet, clear-surfaced ornaments, dust-free picture frames. Lots of people chose the colours for their home according to how easily they showed the dirt. Dagmar knew she was different in as much as she picked the ones, dove greys, pinks and yellows, that showed it most. That way she could identify the enemy. At the furniture store she had shuddered at the golden-brown carpet – God only knows what could be lurking in there – and shaken her head at the practical chintzes.

She wandered through into the kitchen where the kitchen cupboards dazzled white. She made herself a pot of tea and sat down at the high-gloss table. 'There,' she said out loud, clanking the teaspoon down on the saucer. 'I've managed to drive away everyone I've ever cared for, but through it all I've kept my flat clean.' Then she threw the cup across the room.

As soon as Amelia entered the lobby she heard the playing.

The more she had thought, as she sat in the Lounge at Cherryfield, the surer she had become that Alan would be giving Dagmar a hard time. 'If he even bothered to do that,' she muttered as she dialled her mother's number. Someone the other end had lifted the receiver and then hung up immediately. Amelia had worried some more and then got into Gerald's car and driven off to Exeter.

Now she hurried up the stairs, wondering briefly why steps always seemed constructed for someone with a natural one-and-a-half-step stride, when she noticed the difference in the playing from upstairs. Dagmar's music tended towards the ladylike; there was no excess in the playing. But the notes now echoing down the stairwell seemed to be hounded from the instrument, fleeing, stumbling.

Out of breath, she reached the second floor and rang the bell but the playing continued. She rang again, but as there was still no answer she tried the door and finding it unlocked, stepped inside. At the entrance to the sitting room she stopped dead.

Dagmar sat crouched over the piano keyboard like a bird of prey. Mould seemed to be growing from her head and shoulders, the blue-grey spores covering her hair and hanging in furry threads from her arms as she lifted them before letting her hands crash down for the final crescendo.

'Oh my God.' Amelia rushed over to Dagmar who merely swivelled around slowly, a sweet smile on her lips.

'There you see,' she said, opening her eyes wide. 'It really doesn't matter being dirty.'

Chapter Eighteen

It was a remark in the Kingsmouth Post Office a week later that had caused Amelia to sit as she did now, crouched in the shrubbery that sheltered Ashcombe from the lane running past the front of the house.

'Those Hamiltons, no sooner have they got that house than they are off on holiday. "And while I'm about it," she says, "cancel the papers for the Christmas period too, we're off to our little place in Antigua."' Mrs Hodges, the newsagent, made a passable imitation of Doreen Hamilton for the benefit of her customers.

'They're away over Christmas too, are they?' Amelia paid for Selma's *Good Housekeeping*.

Mrs Hodges nodded and pursed her lips. 'Three whole weeks. They're always moving house those Hamiltons but they never seem to take much pleasure in what they get. Not like your grandmother. She loved that place, she did.'

'She loved that place, she did,' Amelia repeated to herself as, knees aching, she watched Doreen Hamilton lock the front door on her way out. By the look of the large, old-fashioned key in her hand the locks hadn't been changed.

As Doreen click-clacked down the hill in her high-heeled sandals, a wicker basket dangling from the crook of her arm, Amelia emerged from behind an oleander shrub and ran through the heavy wooden portal that led into the main garden. Looking around to make sure she was on her own, she walked up to

189

the French windows and pressed her nose against the glass, framing her face with her spread-out fingers. She stood for a while peering into the sitting room before stepping back and pulling a small black notebook and a pencil from the back pocket of her jeans. She wrote intently in the book for a minute or two, looked into the room again before checking her notes, then, putting the book and pencil back in her pocket, she hurried back on to the road.

After five minutes she reached the start of a footpath. She turned left on to it and, when she found a large flat rock, she sat down, stretching her legs out in front of her. Looking across town to the green terraced hill and Cherryfield, she thought how soft the light was in Devon, as if the rain never quite left but only hung back a little distance, filtering the sunlight, ready for its next appearance. She rested her elbows against the warm rock and closed her eyes; it had been a bad week and she was tired.

Dagmar, sitting at the piano, had seemed surprised at Amelia's distress but she had allowed herself to be led into the bathroom. Amelia had found the ripped and empty hoover bag behind the sofa and the fluff and dust had insinuated itself into every cranny of the room so that with each step they took it rose on the air like a fountain.

'Being clean causes so much misery,' Dagmar said reasonably as Amelia stripped her down to bra and pants and pushed her towards the bath-tub.

Amelia tipped half a bottle of Apricot bubble-bath into the hot water and, having watched the foam rise, she turned the taps off. 'I'll leave you to it then,' she said in a small voice.

She had found the number of Dagmar's GP. 'There's no chance of an appointment today I'm afraid, none at all.' The receptionist spoke with quiet satisfaction at an obstacle well placed.

'But this is an emergency. My mother is insane.'

'Could you hold please, there's a call on the other line.'

Amelia listened for sounds from the bathroom and as there were none she had visions of Dagmar floating in the bath like an elderly Ophelia, grey tentacles of fluff instead of flowers trailing from her hair. 'Come on, come on,' she muttered into the phone.

'Yes?' the receptionist had returned, and sounded as if she had hoped Amelia would have given up.

'My mother; she's gone mad.' Some people lied in times of stress, Amelia always got an urge to be truthful, flawlessly exact. She added, 'More accurately; she's gone madder.' She paused again. 'A lot more mad.'

The doctor came. By then Dagmar was sleeping, warm and clean, in her bed. 'In there.' Amelia opened the bedroom door gently to let him in. Outside she paced the sitting room like an expectant father in a fifties comedy.

'What do you think?' She pounced as Dr Norland reappeared.

'She's quite calm now.' The doctor, young and tweed-clad, perched on the arm of the nearest chair.

'Quite calm now.' Amelia had visions of a raging ape, bellowing and rattling the bars of its cage before sinking to its haunches, silent, hands still clinging on to the bars. 'Quite calm now.'

'I'll admit her to the psychiatric unit overnight, for observation. I don't hold with doling out pills willy-nilly but see she takes these for the next month, just to help her over the acute stage of her problem.' Dr Norland held out a prescription.

Amelia remained standing. If she settled down in a

chair it might scare him off, make him think she was going to keep him there talking for a long time.

'There's a question I've wanted answered all my life,' she said. 'What exactly is my mother's problem?'

Dr Norland closed his bag and stood up. 'Not all that much. She's an obsessive of course. Today's incident was an extreme reaction to stress. I doubt it will recur.' He moved towards the front door.

'But Dr Norland.'

He stopped and turned. 'Yes.'

'This whatever it is, this obsessiveness has blighted her life, and mine. Today she tipped the contents of a hoover bag over her head whilst playing the "Warsaw Concerto". How can you say it's nothing much?'

'Because in a way it isn't.' He smiled and shrugged his shoulders. 'Anxiety is natural. We need it to survive. Our forefathers were busy doing just that, surviving, but increasingly the every-day threats, the ones we could see and hear and identify, have been removed from our lives, leaving us free to worry about remoter and vaguer issues that are almost always beyond our control. The anxiety increases, but its focus is blurred. That in itself induces stress. Your mother is a naturally anxious person, probably with low self-esteem, and her unfocused anxieties have been allowed to take over. In due course some sessions with a therapist would not be a bad idea.' He opened the door but turned on the threshold. 'You've heard of rebels without a cause. Well, my surgery is full of worriers without a worry.' With a quick smile he was off, running down the stairs.

Amelia had expected some cataclysmic change in her mother, whether for better or for worse she didn't know, but surely no-one could go through such turmoil and come out the same? But Dagmar, returning from hospital, was quiet but otherwise how she had always been; a little distracted, a little irritable, busy worrying away at her worries.

Amelia stayed on though, just in case. In case of precisely what she didn't know but, when she set off for the Admiral's funeral on the Wednesday, she kept thinking of those films where people clear away ropes and sharp instruments from the suicidal and she wondered briefly if maybe she should hide the hoover.

Henry had assisted the vicar of Kingsmouth at the funeral service. He had looked pale but he had smiled at Amelia when she entered the church and he had read the lesson with a steady voice. It was only when he had stood up again to speak those lines by Tennyson, that his voice had faltered.

Lying on the warm rock, looking at the clouds appearing over the hills, Amelia said them to herself: '"Sunset and evening star, And one clear call for me! And may there be no moaning of the bar When I put out to sea."'

Then the vicar had led the mourners into the churchyard, and a high wind had driven the rain into their faces like a shower of tacks. At Willoughby's funeral the sun had been shining from a high February sky. Amelia remembered thinking it almost an insult, like giving a painting as a birthday present to a blind man No, Amelia had approved of the rain and the wind as she followed the vicar, watching his huge black cloak dance round his ankles with the prematurely fallen leaves. There it goes, she had thought as the coffin was lowered into the ground, the universe according to John Mallett.

It was Sunday now, a week exactly since Dagmar's breakdown. 'Breakdown,' Amelia mouthed the word to herself as she got up from the rock, it makes her sound like a beat-up old mini. She checked her back

193

pocket for the notebook and began the walk down to the ferry where Gerald's car was parked. Dagmar was as able to cope now as she had ever been, so there was no reason not to go back to the Old Rectory: it was still her home for another two weeks.

'Five Warden-Assisted Bungalows – Buy Now, Pay later.' Was that really what it said? Driving into Abbotslea, she turned and looked over her shoulder, 'Five Warden-Assisted Bungalows, For Sale,' she read on the large sign by the new development she had just passed. Then, as she slowed down for the blind corner at the crossroads, she thought quite calmly, I'm going mad. She found herself relax at the thought. After all Selma was going mad slowly, through old age. Dagmar had simply gone mad. If some Biblical curse or, if that was being pretentious, maybe a more ordinary gypsy one, had been lobbed in the direction of her family why not just give in? No more responsibilities; now there was a nice thought.

She slammed on the brakes, narrowly avoiding Old Mike Aylard wandering round in the middle of the street with his deer-stalker and his wife's fox collar to keep him warm in the July sunshine. Far from getting a sense of fellow feeling, she had a sudden urge to run him down. Maybe it's the competition, she thought. She could stay in Abbotslea, buy herself a little place, but would there be room for two afflicted in the village? Could she hope to oust Old Mike from his position as village fool?

She saw Rosalind and Ronnie coming out of the stores and gave them a cheery wave.

Now Mrs Wetherburn-Pryce, for example, had never invited Amelia to one of her coffee mornings. Amelia had never wanted to go to one, but she resented not being asked. There were no real gentry in Abbotslea so the Wetherburn-Pryces, residing at The Poplars, the largest house in the village, and possessing a double-barrelled name, were commonly agreed to be the next best thing. Rosalind had explained as tactfully as she could to Amelia, when she had first moved in with Gerald, that it wasn't that dear old Janet didn't like her, more that Amelia confused her, refusing to be placed.

'She feels you are People Like Us, really,' Rosalind had mumbled the phrase a little shamefacedly, 'but she can't cope with the thought of you living with Gerald and not being married. She was very fond of his aunt.'

Now, on the other hand, Amelia thought cheerfully as she drove up outside the Old Rectory, I might well get her racing over with an invitation, just by strewing ashes in my hair and ambling through the village dressed in a dustbin liner; thereby qualifying as A Worthy Cause. In fact, by the simple task of going completely mad, I might achieve the social acceptance that has so far eluded me. She yanked the hand-brake tight and got out of the car.

There was a note for her on the hall table: 'Please return car immediately. Love, Gerald'.

She crumpled the white paper and left it on the table. It was nice to be in possession again of something he desired. She sniffed the air, scenting the prickly smell of wet paint. Had Gerald had the spare room redecorated already? She passed the sitting-room door and the smell got suddenly stronger. Opening the door carefully, as if expecting to see a rotting corpse on the hearth rug, she stopped, looking in amazement at the strange room she had entered. Gone was the slightly shabby creamy-yellow of the walls. Instead they had been ragged or dragged, she wasn't sure which, with a vivid shade of coral that seemed to prise her eyes open as she looked at them. And the books, where were they? And the bookcases on either side of the fireplace? Amelia took quick steps into the room, looking around, bending over and peering down as if she hoped to find them hiding behind the sofa. Then she saw the second note, written on the same thick paper as the one in the hall and placed on a green china plate in the shape of a flattened cabbage. Clarissa's plate she thought as she picked the paper up and read: 'Thought that as you weren't coming back for a while we might as well do the sitting room too. Books in the garage. Love, Gerald'.

She stared at the note as she sank down into the old armchair that was as vast as a two-seater sofa and blessedly familiar. 'Books in the garage. Love, Gerald.'

That was it. It really was all over. Deep down in the small, steel-enforced compartment of her mind where the really big dreams were stored, she had kept the hope of Gerald returning. Those words blew it open as if they were gelignite, and out hope hobbled, gasped and died.

'It's your loss Gerald Forbes,' she said out loud. 'You're stuck for ever now with a woman who came into this world wearing a calf-length pleated skirt.' Then she cried.

After a while, when her crying had made the sides of her face ache, and the light outside was going, she pressed her mind gingerly for a beautiful phrase; surely all this sadness could result in one decent line of poetry. She wiped her nose on the back of her hand and got up to find a notepad and pen. At least they had left her desk untouched.

In Swedish, she thought, heart and pain obligingly rhymed, a God-send for bad poets. But no lines, bad or good, came to her, only the memory of the evening shortly after they had moved into the Old Rectory when Gerald and she had unpacked the tea-chests with their respective books, comparing taste and showing off with heavy titles.

'I enjoy Proust tremendously,' she remembered saying as Gerald picked up her unbroken copy of *Swann's Way*, 'it's just that once I put him down, I find it rather difficult to pick him up again.'

She thought of the evenings they had sat a little self-consciously in front of the fire reading aloud to each other from novels as dense as German bread and finding they actually enjoyed them. Amelia sighed and scribbled on her pad.

'Heart . . . ? Fart. Although you are a great big fart, your name is engraved all over my heart.'

The telephone rang. It was Henry.

'Thank you again for coming to the funeral, it meant a lot.' He was silent for a moment. 'Anyway, how are things?'

'Gerald and Clarissa have just turned my home into a bookless mixture of Laura Ashley and a tart's boudoir.'

'That's bad luck,' Henry said. 'Actually I called to say I've seen this place for sale in Kingsmouth that might do for your café. It used to be a dairy.'

'Is it the one by the harbour?'

'That's it.'

'I don't know,' Amelia said unsatisfactorily, waiting for Henry to say, 'What do you mean you don't know?' Instead, he said, 'At my father's funeral, in the middle of all the sadness, the thought went through my mind that you look really good in black. I feel pretty awful about that.'

'Well, you shouldn't, and you know that. Anyway, your father liked me, why would he mind that you thought I looked nice at his funeral?' There was no answer so she asked, 'Henry, how are you coping?'

She could hear him swallow hard. 'When someone you love, dies,' he said, 'it's as if they leave you with half shares of your life together. The person you were in their eyes dies with them.' He paused, and just as Amelia was trying hard to think of something to say that was comforting and not commonplace, Henry went on, 'I just miss him. Anyway, I thought I'd let you know about the dairy.' He hung up so quickly Amelia hardly had time to say goodbye.

Amelia spent the evening packing. She put her clothes in three suitcases and two dustbin liners. She put the bin liners and one of the suitcases in the garage where the books lay in neat stacks. Then she fixed little stick-on labels, marked with a large red A, on everything in the Old Rectory that belonged to her: two Swedish oil paintings given to her by Selma, three English watercolours she had bought herself, a couple of small tables, some chairs, ornaments, kitchen utensils. On things they had bought together or been given as a couple, she stuck labels with a question mark. By ten o'clock it was all ready and she wandered up to the bedroom wondering how many times Clarissa and Gerald had made love in the bed.

'They can't always want to use the chair,' she said trying to cheer herself up. Before turning off the light, she phoned Dagmar who answered in a polite, detached little voice and said that all was well.

How nice it would be, Amelia thought after ringing off, if she had had a mother to whom she could say 'I've arrived back at my home to find it in the process of metamorphosing into someone else's. In the sitting room and in the spare room the transformation is almost complete, and I daren't go to sleep for fear of waking up in a mock-virginal chamber with frilly dressing-table and ruched blinds at the windows.'

She lay for a long time flat on her back staring at the shadows on the ceiling, then she threw off the duvet and ran downstairs. She switched the light on in the sitting room and went across to the French windows, unlocking them and flinging them open so that they hit right back against the wall of the house. She stood for a moment breathing in the cool night air before hurrying out on to the terrace in the path made by the beam of light from inside. Shivering in her short nightshirt, she ran round to the front of the house and got in to the car, starting the engine. With the headlights full on she mounted the lawn and continued through the opening between the yew-hedge and the house, back towards the terrace, scratching the paint of the car as she forced it through the narrow gap. The wheels ran smoothly across the lawn and she lined the Citroën up opposite the wide-open French windows. For a second the wheels lost their grip and slithered as she forced them up the low verge, then she was up and edging through into the sitting room, stopping neatly in front of the fireplace. She tightened the hand-brake and switched off the engine before letting herself out.

She was shivering as she got back into bed but she pulled the duvet up close and within minutes she was asleep.

The next morning she called a taxi and walked out of the Old Rectory for the last time. On the hall table was a note. 'Car's in the sitting room. Love, Amelia.'

Chapter Nineteen

Amelia went to stay with an old colleague in London. Her friendship with Kate had been a mostly apologetic affair over the telephone since she moved away to the country, but when you're fleeing, Amelia thought, there's no time for pride. She stayed with Kate for two weeks, helping her with some research and writing a feature on 'The New English Novel' for a Swedish magazine. She had posed the question, 'What is the New English Novel?' in the article and counted herself lucky that no-one seemed to expect an answer. It had brought her a cheque for two hundred and fifty pounds. Then she had gone to Dagmar, home to mother, telling herself she was doing Dagmar a favour.

Dagmar told her the burns on Selma's legs were healing. They had stopped weeping and had kept dry for a whole week, enough of an improvement for Amelia to ask Sister Morris if it wasn't possible to move her back to her old room in the main part of Cherryfield.

'She hates being sidelined,' Amelia explained, keeping up with Sister Morris's brisk step along the glossy corridor. 'It's important for her to feel the pulse of life. However weak. Sister Morris, please, I hate talking to a moving object.'

Sister Morris stopped and turned, her hand on the kitchen door.

'Sister Morris, my grandmother doesn't feel she belongs in a nursing home at all . . .'

'Few people do Miss Lindsay.'

'. . . let alone in Honeysuckle. She thinks she only gave up tennis because of her injuries in the fire.'

Nurse Williams came bustling out from a Staff Only room, wanting to know if Sister Morris knew where Thursday's clean sheets had got to.

'Maybe someone is trying to escape,' Amelia suggested.

'Very droll,' Sister Morris said. 'If you'll excuse me for just one moment.' She started down the corridor.

'You'll have her back in a sec,' Nurse Williams called as she followed behind.

Amelia was staying at The Anchor. She was meeting Henry for dinner and the next morning she had an appointment to look over the dairy. She sighed. She didn't want the dairy, she wanted her home. All those things she had wrongly thought of as hers, my home, my car, my Gerald, my stuff all!

It was getting expensive too, this staying in hotels. She had taken on writing verses for a greetings cards company to eke out her income, but she took so long over each one that she never earned much. Every week it seemed she was writing out a cheque for forty pounds or more to the indifferent receptionist who was so at odds with the old world charm of the oak-panelled reception of the inn. The thought of the money had even kept her awake at night. Cheque after cheque floated past her inner eye. It was worse even than counting sheep, something she had always hated.

'Count sheep, darling,' Dagmar used to say when some particularly virulent childhood monster had kept sleep at bay. Obediently, because Amelia had been an obedient child, she had closed her eyes and soon become entangled in the problems of sheep. Sheep that crowded over the fence, shoving each other out of the way in their fight to reach the greener pasture at the other side. And always there had been the lamb. A little white lamb with a black patch who got left behind, bleating pathetically, leaving Amelia to try and retrieve its errant mother who had been amongst the first to jump the fence.

Amelia was deep in her own thoughts when Sister Morris returned with a throwaway apology before picking up the conversation where they had dropped it.

'. . . Gangrene,' she said. 'We fear the foot is gangrenous. So you see, moving her in that condition . . .'

Amelia stared at her. 'But that's not possible. Gangrene I mean. It's the sort of thing people got in *Gone with the Wind*, in that dreadful field hospital. You know the bit where Scarlett goes looking for Ashley?'

Take a grip on yourself, she thought explaining, 'What I mean is, I didn't think it was something that was allowed to happen these days.'

'It's not a question of allowing it to happen Miss Lindsay, I assure you. I'm afraid that even with the best care in the world,' Sister Morris emphasized best, 'it does still occur, especially in our elderly. Her foot was quite bad already when she came here you know.'

'But what are you doing about it?'

'Everything that can be done, I assure you. But you can see that it's quite out of the question moving your grandmother. Now you must excuse me.' Sister Morris hurried off.

Selma was sleeping in her wheelchair. Have wheelchair, won't travel, Amelia thought sadly as she bent over and kissed Selma's forehead. Selma's skin felt clammy and it took longer than usual for her to wake. When she did open her eyes, she looked at Amelia as if she had seen her only moments earlier.

'I'm sorry, darling, I must have dozed off. You should have woken me.'

The curl had gradually gone from Selma's hair and it was the flat grey of wire wool, an unfamiliar shade on Selma, but of course her natural one. She was wearing a haphazardly-patterned polyester dress that rode up over her knees, straining round the thighs. Amelia began to understand the sense of having no mirrors in the rooms in Honeysuckle, other than a tiny one above the basin. When Sister Morris had asked Amelia to buy some more easy-care dresses for Selma, Amelia wanted to know what was wrong with the clothes her grandmother had brought with her to Cherryfield. 'My grandmother hates man-made fibres,' she had explained, 'and I do think it's important to let her keep some dislikes.'

Just listening to Sister Morris's explanation of why precisely Selma should wear easy-care dresses seemed a betrayal though, an unacceptable intrusion into her privacy, so Amelia had nodded agreement halfway through and rushed down to the town to find what little there was to choose from in Wash'n Dry, size eighteen.

As she wheeled Selma through into the conservatory, Selma said, 'There's a woman here who keeps a rabbit in a box. Very strange.'

'A real rabbit?' Amelia asked, feeling stupid.

'Must be, she keeps taking it greens, or tries to.'

Amelia parked the chair at the far end of the room. 'I've brought you something.' She bent down and picked a package from her bag. 'A Disc-man.'

'A what, dear?'

'A Disc-man. It's like a record player only better and you have little earphones so you won't disturb anyone else. It will stop you hearing that blasted television too. I've got you some discs as well: Bach's "Concerto for Two Violins", Lars-Erik Larsson's "Pastoral", "Finlandia" and . . .'

'There's that Hudd woman, the one with the rabbit.' Selma pointed to a tall woman entering the conservatory with the aid of two sticks. Her limbs were long and bony and her large face was crowned by a thick white plait wound round the top of her head. As she searched for a chair she liked the look of, she spotted Amelia and hastened across the tiled floor.

'I wonder, would you mind getting some oats? Porridge oats will do.' Her voice was deep and her eyes flickered nervously from Amelia to the door as she spoke. 'Some carrots too.' And, groping round the pocket of her long cardigan, she pulled out a pound coin.

Poor old soul, Amelia thought but she took the coin and nodded, 'Of course, no problem.' She wondered if she should collude in the madness and ask after the rabbit's health and happiness.

'I've never had much truck with pets,' the woman said. 'Cats huh, vicious smelly things. But rabbits, they're different. There's no malice in a rabbit.' She shuffled off.

'Silly fool,' Selma hissed.

China that matched, Henry thought: cups, saucers, plates, all matching in some cheerful pattern and no chipped edges, was one of the things his children would grow up with. He fingered the ashtray as he waited for Amelia in the bar of The Anchor Inn.

Would she be upset, he wondered, when he told her they were sailing soon? He took a deep gulp from his vodka and tonic. Lately he had felt something dangerously close to excitement at the thought of war; so he had prayed with more fervour than ever for peace and the other night he had stayed in the chapel until morning. He had thought of the people in the squadron, his people, and had wanted to beg their forgiveness.

He kept asking God's. It was the thought of being needed that caused that shameful excitement. In a war, people would be faced with the most basic reality; you stay alive or you don't, and he would be able to help. All the years of work and preparation would be put to use as never before. He sighed, his thoughts were as ill-disciplined as a street full of urchins, racing through his mind unbidden and unwanted, upturning ideas and scattering the contents all over his mind. He rubbed his eyes with his knuckles, hard, relishing the pain as the bones pressed against the eyeballs; he could almost hear the veins popping.

When he looked up again, he saw Amelia coming through the doors. As he stood up to greet her he wondered at how pale she still was after a whole hot summer. *She* needed him, she might not know it yet, but she did, he thought, as he watched her cross the floor. It was always a surprise to him to see how straight backed she walked; he suspected that mentally she wandered through life with an apologetic stoop. He smiled to himself; at heart he was just a frustrated big brother. There had been no little sisters or brothers at home, not even a dog or a cat, just two large, well-meaning, preoccupied men.

Amelia looked hard at him before kissing him hello. 'Your eyes look a bit red. Are you all right?'

'Me?' He smiled. 'I'm absolutely fine.' He went over to the bar to get her whisky and water, and when he got back he asked, 'Have you looked at the dairy yet?'

'Not yet,' Amelia said, feeling her glance crawling around shiftily somewhere at floor level. 'I'm not really so sure now about this café idea, or rather I'm worried that Kingsmouth isn't quite the place for it.' She sipped her drink and felt irritated by her own habit of adding little unnecessary 'actuallys', 'not sos' and 'quites' to any unpopular statement she made, as if trying to dilute what she was saying to an acceptable blandness.

'You're not giving up already, are you?' Henry looked expectantly at her. She wished she had the guts to look expectantly back instead of wittering on obligingly. It was the same at dinner parties, she thought. Ten people fell into simultaneous silence and Amelia felt wholly responsible for filling it.

'Or maybe it will work,' she added lamely. 'Oh I don't know.'

Henry smiled at her. 'What don't you know?'

Amelia laughed. 'Where do I start? I don't have any faith in my ability to carry anything through. You know when you're little and say, "I want to play the guitar", or "learn to ride" or "build a matchstick model of the Eiffel Tower" and some grown-up comes along and says "That's all fine and well, dear, but will you finish it?" Well I'm doing it all myself now. I've cut out the middleman. Each time I decide to do something, each time I get swept away with a new plan, I say, "That's fine and dandy Amelia dear but will you ever carry it through?" Serves me right too; I'm a project nymphomaniac, always looking over the heaving shoulder of one idea at the newer and better one beckoning in the distance.' She stopped. There he was again, fixing her with that keen round-eyed gaze as if what she said actually mattered. Disconcerted, she fiddled with the pearls round her neck. They had come out of a Christmas cracker and Gerald had said she couldn't possibly wear them. Amelia thought they were very pretty.

'I still think it's quite an interesting idea,' Henry said now. 'Just make up your mind to do it. Lots of retired people round here, holiday-makers too. All you need is to stock the book section with Hardy, Dick Francis and Jackie Collins, and you're away.'

Amelia finished her whisky with a little grimace; she was training herself to drink the stuff because she thought the world was too full already of women ordering dry white wine.

'The newsagent across from here sells books of course,' she said, 'but they hide them under such a mountain of speciality interest magazines and Ninja Turtle stationery that you'd need a sniffer dog to find them. I might stock the odd voucher or Talking Classic, but otherwise it'll be strictly books. I'd be liberal in my selection though: Sex and Shopping, Sex and Suffering, Sex and your Intellect, No Sex but a lot of Intellect; it'll all be there. I can see myself on top of some rickety old library steps reaching for a dusty volume on the top shelf, captivating my customers with my intellectual air and spectacular legs.'

'What about the pastries?'

'Oh don't you worry, I'll fit them in. That's if I decide to go ahead of course.' She sighed. 'I don't suppose I will.'

'You sound as if you have no control in the matter.' Henry looked annoyed.

'Some of us are blessed with self-control,' Amelia said primly, 'and some of us are not. So don't mock the unafflicted.'

'Rubbish,' Henry said. 'Shall we eat?'

Every time Amelia came into the hotel restaurant she was struck by the determined brownness of it: brown beams bore down from the ceiling, brown tables and chairs were placed at nudging distance around the brown wooden floor, even the curtains and the seat cushions had a brown pattern. She wondered who the little devil was who had slipped in red napkins.

They sat down and were given the large menu covered in improbable suggestions: 'Butter fried Dover Sole and Banana, Breast of Wild Duckling with Kiwi sauce, Fillet Mignon with a garnish of lobster claws.'

'It will have to be Dover sole and banana,' Amelia smiled across the table at Henry. He was fiddling with his napkin, smoothing it down and folding it, smoothing it down again.

She put her hand over his. 'Having you as a friend through everything, potty grannies, errant lovers, it's been marvellous. I'm just so sorry about your father. I don't feel I was a great comfort there.'

For once Henry didn't seem to be listening. Taking a deep breath as if he was about to launch himself off a ten foot rock in to the sea, he said, 'We sail Monday week. We'll be away for about six months. Longer maybe if there's a war.' He looked guilty, as if he felt he had let her down.

When Amelia didn't answer he asked, 'Are you all right?'

'Fine.' She smiled. 'I think I'm getting immune to men leaving, or at least I've come to expect it.' And she realized that what she had begun to say for effect was actually true. Daniel, her father, Willoughby and Gerald; they had all left. Pulling a face, she said, 'It's as if it's in the Trade Descriptions Act, Man: non-child-bearing member of the species, lots of body hair, one willie, leaves a lot.'

There was a bit of indulgence, she thought, in Henry's laugh as he reached across the table for her hand. Pulling it to his lips, he began kissing her fingertips each in turn.

While she enjoyed the sensation of his warm dry lips against her skin, she tried hard to think of something to say, ready for the awkward silence she guessed would follow when he'd run out of fingers.

'Every radio and television priest worth his collar is telling us to pray for peace. I'm all for it of course, but . . .'

Henry stopped kissing and gave her her hand back. 'But what?'

'I don't understand it. I never have. We're told God is almighty. So we all ask the same questions: why does He allow children to be tortured and murdered? Why does He allow mass starvation, wars, the holocaust? And we're all given the same answer give or take a hallelujah: God gave us free will. We're not puppets. If we are not free to choose evil, we will never be able to understand the meaning of goodness. He suffers with us but He does not interfere. That's fine we say nodding wisely. That is, until someone comes along and tells us to pray. Why, I ask myself, why pray in the face of this determined policy of non-interference?'

'Oh that. Easy peasy Japanesey.' Henry lifted his hands to make room for the plate of stilton and apple soup.

Amelia put her spoon into the rubbery flesh of her avocado Mary Rose. 'I'm waiting. And "God knows" won't do as an answer either.'

All of a sudden Henry looked serious. 'I can't give you an all-enveloping, iron-cast, bullet-proof answer, but then you knew that. But first of all, you have to look at prayer not as a shopping list: long life, happiness, a plague on Aunt Caroline, etc but a way of keeping in touch, of keeping the lines of communication open. Both ways too.' He tasted the soup and quickly drank some wine.

'The Bible describes prayer as something like a torchbeam through the darkness.' He sat quiet for a moment. 'This might seem like a cop out,' he said at last, 'but I was given a book once by a master when I was at prep school. It said that we shouldn't always want a reason for everything. Why should we expect to understand everything about God? In the last resort to be a Christian you must be a bit like a trapeze artist, prepared to take a leap across the gulf between what you know and what you believe, reject the safety net of certain knowledge and just go for it. Once you've done that you hang on to those beliefs and, as time goes by, little by little God's purpose will be revealed to you.' He looked up at her and smiled, touching her forehead with his fingertip and drawing it down the bridge of her nose to her lips. 'I've taken that leap,' he said.

Later, when they had finished their dinner and were walking along the quayside with a tepid breeze coming off the water, Amelia asked, 'If there is a war, will you be frightened?'

He thought for a moment. 'Probably.' He slipped his arm round her shoulders and said, with all his usual energy, 'Fear can be a very useful emotion.'

Amelia stopped abruptly. 'You wouldn't say that if you knew my mother. Fear has ruined her life. It hasn't exactly added reams of jollity to mine either.'

Henry pulled her along. A seagull squawked over head, circled and glided off over the water. 'Fear has to be husbanded, harnessed, then it becomes useful. Your mother, from what you've told me, fights ghosts, spending her fear wildly in every direction, achieving nothing.'

Amelia shrugged off his arm. 'You make it sound as if she had a choice in the matter. As if she blighted her life through sheer carelessness.'

'I'm sorry,' Henry said quietly. He stopped her and pulled her close. Framing her face with his hands he bent down and kissed her.

In the circle of light thrown by the street lamp, Amelia was smiling.

'What are you grinning about?' Henry dropped his hands.

'You don't want to know,' Amelia said matter of factly.

'Yes I do.'

She sighed and put her hands on his shoulders. 'I smiled because I enjoyed your kiss. You're the nicest man I think I've ever known. And . . .' She looked down at the tip of her blue shoes.

'And . . . ?'

'And I enjoy feeling a strong man weaken in my arms, and that feeling is enhanced when the man is a priest,' she said quickly. 'There, I told you you wouldn't like it.' She turned pink. It had been a mistake being honest. It nearly always was.

Henry looked at her unsmiling. 'Us chaplains do a good line in bondage too if you think it would give you a kick.'

'See, now you're offended.'

'No I'm not.' They had walked round the block and were back at the hotel entrance. 'How long will you be down here?'

'I go back to my mother's tomorrow. I'll stay for a couple of weeks and then . . .' She shrugged her shoulders as if life really was too much of an effort.

Henry took the telephone number of the flat and, after a moment's hesitation, kissed her again before walking her inside.

I'm like the Princess of Wales, he thought as he drove back to Devonport, making himself smile at the unlikely comparison. I would marry knowing that what ever the rest of the world gets up to, I could never get a divorce.

211

Chapter Twenty

The next morning Amelia got the keys to the dairy from the estate agent and wandered round the empty shop playing Bach on her Walkman. She liked Bach, the orderliness that would erupt into passion. She hadn't got Selma's and Dagmar's ability to play music but she had got their love of it: Mozart, Chopin, Beethoven, Bach, their music played like drums of war whenever she wanted to attack a new idea, because if mere humans had created beauty like that surely everything was possible. Or so she thought as long as the music lasted.

She pulled her right index finger lazily across the dusty wooden shelves and thought of Henry returning from sea, surprising her as she served a customer or arranged books along the shelves. And what then, she thought sourly to herself? What do I do then? Rape him? Do I confess to needing love like a stomach needs lining, a base before anything else can be successfully added.

She climbed the creaking oak staircase and, as her favourite passage of the concerto played, she thought of Selma whose decline had been gentle until Willoughby died, then it became a free-fall.

She remembered coming with Selma to the dairy to restock their empty egg boxes. Selma would let her pick out the large, white eggs one by one, making sure she checked them for cracks. Amelia could almost feel the shell between her fingers now, cool and grainy as if covered in goose-pimples. Then they'd buy the cream, thick yellow cream, like soft butter. She sighed. Maybe it should stay a dairy. Remain as a stubborn unprofitable memorial to the days when people still found minutes in the day to queue up at more than one counter. God knows how they did she thought when, thanks to all the cholesterol-ridden dairy products, their days must have been fewer anyway.

As she walked upstairs to the flat, she thought that, to her, maybe to all the customers, Mrs Philips, owner of the dairy for more than thirty years, round and apron-clad, began and ended with the handing out of cream and butter and eggs, only to vanish like Brigadoon to the place where all the people in the service industry go when their customers have done their business. So standing there in Mrs Philips's flat, peeking through into the tiny kitchen, inspecting the narrow bedroom where the multi-coloured roses on the wallpaper waged war against the peonies on the curtains, was a little like glimpsing suddenly an actor's legs sticking out from underneath the television set.

Before she left, she stood for a moment by the sitting-room window looking out at the grey, foam-tipped waves. It was a good view for a poet.

Later that afternoon she told Selma, 'I'm thinking of buying the old dairy. Mrs Philips is selling up and moving to Portugal. I'd like to turn it into a bookshop with a café part. Or maybe it's a café with a book-shop part?'

'That's very nice, darling.' Selma paused and thought for a moment. 'But why don't you keep it as a dairy. People need good cream and eggs. Mrs Philips always had the best, fresh from the farm.'

Amelia laughed. It made her happy when Selma said something like that, something perfectly normal and quite logical. Rosalind smiled in much the same way when Ronnie waved his fat little hand in a goodbye or held his own bottle.

'I thought about that. But it was making a terrific loss. No-one uses the little shops any more, the speciality ones. It's simpler to go to the supermarket and get everything from one place.'

'Young woman today are very lazy,' Selma said. 'They can't even be bothered to push a pram. They dress their poor little babies in boiler suits and strap them into these striped deck-chair things you trip over.' She lifted her coffee cup and saucer to her lips, her hand trembling so it seemed impossible that her lips and the rattling cup would ever meet.

After a small wait, Amelia took the cup and saucer gently from her and held the cup steady for Selma to drink. It was a simple enough movement but, as Selma sucked at the coffee, Amelia felt that at Cherryfield it was showing off the most precious commodity of all, youth and an obedient body.

'I've still got your old pram. It's in the garage I think,' Selma said. 'It should clean up beautifully.'

Miss White had been craning her neck in their direction for some time, her lips moving in sympathy with every sentence they spoke. Seeing an opening, she moved in. 'Expecting a little one, are we?' she twinkled at Amelia.

Selma gave her an evil look which Miss White studiously ignored.

Miss Hudd sat in the high-backed chair in the Admiral's old place by the replenished fish-tank. 'I like babies,' she said in her deep voice. 'Babies and rabbits, no bad in 'em.'

Amelia suddenly wished, as much for the two childless old ladies as for herself, that she could conjure up an infant to match the excitement in their eyes and their softening gaze. 'No baby just at the

214

moment,' she said, not wanting to close the door on the idea completely.

'Don't worry about it, that's what I say.' Miss Hudd nodded knowingly. 'These things take time.'

'Particularly,' Selma said, 'when there's no father involved.'

'I absolutely must get some greens for the rabbit.' Miss Hudd made a show of ignoring Selma's scorn. 'You did get the oats, didn't you?' She leant towards Amelia, staring expectantly at her.

Amelia blushed. 'I'm terribly sorry, I forgot.'

Miss Hudd moved agitatedly in her chair. 'But that won't do. It won't do at all.'

'Oh shut up, you silly old woman,' Selma cried.

Miss Hudd opened her eyes wide, then burst into tears. Like boys, large girls don't cry, or so they are told. Miss Hudd, like someone having their first taste of a forbidden luxury, wept diffidently, carefully at first. Then, as seconds passed and no thunderbolt struck, she abandoned herself to the experience, crying in great snuffling sobs until Sister Morris appeared in the doorway. Taking one look at the scene in front of her, she hailed a nurse, much in the way of a head waiter directing the attention of his staff towards a soiled ashtray, and Miss Hudd was removed.

Amelia was shocked at the pleasure that lit up Selma's eyes at Miss Hudd's humiliation. Miss White sat very quiet, her back pressed hard against the chair.

The evening sun was autumnal, its light paler than only a week before. Selma dozed: the enlivening effect of spite, like that of most pick-me-ups, was short-lived. Nurses clip-clopped in and out of the room, checking on the residents, sometimes removing one, as if they were dead-heading a plant, Amelia thought, and now and then they would check on Selma to see if she too was ready for plucking. The room was hot, they must

215

have turned the heating on already, and the television droned away, not quiet enough to be ignored, yet not loud enough to make sense. Amelia wondered what had become of the Rosenthal coffee cups that Selma liked to drink her morning coffee from at home. Selma stirred uneasily in her chair as her stomach thundered. Amelia sighed, the price of life was high, that was for sure.

Back in Dagmar's flat she asked, 'Have you got the Rosenthal cups?'

Dagmar shook her head. 'They must be in store with the rest of the things. Why? Do you want them?'

'No, no it's OK, only asking.' Amelia turned over the page of her book, *How to Set up your own Business – Beat Recession at its own Game.*

'Play something please,' she said after a while, nodding towards the piano. Obediently, Dagmar got up from the sofa where she had sat leafing through *Vogue.*

Amelia listened to 'Traumerie' and thought that nothing, nothing at all, had changed in the neat little flat. Since her collapse, Dagmar had slowly returned to her old shape like a tired piece of elastic. She had lost what was probably her last chance of love and companionship and she had scattered her nerves all over her life, yet nothing at all had changed. What a waste of suffering.

When Dagmar had finished playing Amelia asked her, as she had asked Selma, 'Why did you not make a career of your music?'

Dagmar did not get up from the piano, but swivelled round slowly on the stool. She shrugged her shoulders with a little smile, poised for an excuse as always, Amelia thought.

'I like music too much,' Dagmar said. 'I have too

much respect for the great composers. They deserve to be performed only by the best. I was never going to be more than adequate.'

Amelia felt the old irritation spread like a rash inside her. 'How can you possibly know? You never tried hard enough. I read Dylan Thomas but I still dream of becoming a poet.'

Dagmar got up from the stool, scanning the seat cover, smoothing down her skirt. 'Well, then you're very brave, darling,' she said.

Amelia was crushed. After a short pause she said, 'Have you got the address of the storage people? I promised Granny to check that everything was in good order.' Telling Dagmar a blatant lie made her feel better.

Three days later she was rummaging through the tea-chests full of china and silver and books, measuring the length and breadth of furniture that had once combined to create a home and were now just listed items in the store room of Grant & Son, Removals and Storage. The gilded lion's paw of Selma's empire chaise-longue peeked out from under a dust sheet, making Amelia think of those mortuary scenes from American films where all you could see of poor Mr X was his pallid, labelled toe sticking out from under a shroud on the trolley.

She found the ring-binders where Selma had pasted in magazine cuttings with pictures and information of all manner of beautiful and useful things: hand-painted chairs, Victorian tiles, shoe-tidies, cut-price linen sheets, Edwardian storage jars, china tooth-brush mugs. There were ticks against the things she needed straight away, crosses against the things she hoped one day to acquire, and at the back of each binder was a section marked 'Babylon' after the Hanging Gardens.

On those pages were pictures of the unattainable: a painting by Monet, a Chippendale chair or Flora Danica china. Yet Selma had never seemed materialistic, more an artist perfecting an ever-changing picture. 'Come in, come in,' she would say like a benevolent spider inviting a visitor into her enchanted web.

Wrapped in plastic and stacked behind a large sideboard were Selma's hatboxes. She had collected them for years; extravagant, inessential, striped and spotted, they had paraded along the shelves in the hall. 'Just a bit of fun, my dears,' Selma would say showing them off.

Amelia lifted the boxes from their plastic wrappings and stacked them on the chaise-longue. She pulled the whole lazy-looking, sumptuously gilded piece over to the only open space in the store-room and, looking around her, picked up her black notebook from her pocket and checked the list. She moved Selma's favourite armchair across to the chaise-longue, together with two small coffee tables, a display cabinet, two smaller chairs and a foot stool. She pushed it all close together then measured the space it all took up. Ticking items off the list, she unpacked several tea-chests, picking some things out and adding them to the court around the chaise-longue, putting others back in the chests. Finally, before leaving, she brought out two large blankets to cover the collection of bits.

That night she telephoned Henry onboard his ship. She launched her question with little prelude. 'I know you're not a Jesuit, but in your view does the end ever justify the means?'

Henry did not seem surprised by her question nor did he ask why she wanted to know. Amelia liked him more than ever for that. 'It depends, I think, on the end you're trying to achieve and the means by which you intend to achieve it. Boring answer I know.'

Amelia paused before saying, 'That's all I'm going to get?'

'I'm afraid so.' Henry sounded amused. 'If you'd like to tell me more I'd be very happy to listen.'

'Oh Henry, I don't know. My first instinct in any situation is to confess, shift my great dripping burden on to someone else, but this time I think I'll wait.'

'If you're sure,' he said. 'We sail on Monday, first thing. I was going to ask if you'd like to spend the weekend with me. I've got a friend's cottage in Cornwall for a couple of days while he and his family are away. It would be great just spending some time with you.'

Amelia said she thought it was a lovely idea, and they arranged to meet at the flat on Saturday morning.

Maybe it's a mistake to think too hard about these things, Henry thought as he stepped into his car and started off towards Exeter. Maybe with Amelia too, it's just a question of faith, of taking the leap. He had been in love before, of course, with glowing cheerful girls who studied, or cooked or cared for little children, but most of all cared for him: Alice, Arabella, Olivia and Jane, nice girls with even teeth and even tempers who didn't complicate life unduly. And now there was Amelia. He had began to see that one of the reasons he was falling in love with her was the way she made him feel about himself; like an engine on permanent boost. She made him feel, well . . . He searched his mind for a word . . . Essential, that was it. And she was so pretty. He sighed and pushed his hair back from his forehead with a hand that was becoming embarrass- ingly damp.

*   *   *

Amelia was finishing her packing. She looked at the small suitcase lying open on the floor. A moment ago it had been on the bed, but Dagmar had come in and shuddered and asked if she realized the amount of dirt a suitcase accumulated on its travels in the boots of cars and holds of aircraft, let alone on those filthy conveyor belts. And did she not see that all those germs and disgusting bits were transferring on to Dagmar's bedspread that had to be drycleaned. Amelia had pulled the case off on to the floor without protest and now she looked at it, shaking her head. It really wasn't very small at all. She always aimed to go away with just a holdall or, best of all, a rucksack with some clever mix and match in uncrumpable cotton that would take her everywhere. But she never did. There was the midnight-blue silk jacket; it just didn't roll up well. And the linen shorts and the chiffon skirt in a pattern of faded flowers, and shoes and make-up. She knew she looked good in the soft straw hat with the upturned brim. She glanced at her watch; it was eleven o'clock and she was expecting Henry to arrive at any moment.

He really was so nice. She knew that, to many of her friends, nice was not an adjective that made them adjust their clothes and put on fresh lipstick but, to her, it was about the best compliment she could give anyone. Henry was the nicest man she had ever met. His smile lit up his face and he laughed a lot. He listened to her. He was so . . . so positive. She had needed a friend and he had been there.

As she got her sponge-bag, she glanced at her folder with poems lying next to it on top of the chest of drawers. Some of the work in there was good, some of it, and not necessarily the best either, had been published in magazines, but there just wasn't enough there to send off to a publisher. On the cover of the folder she had quoted Elizabeth Smart: 'I must satisfy Nature before I invite God.'

That, Amelia had thought, is a slightly pompous way of saying what I've always felt: I have to get my love life sorted out before I can write; pompous but clever. But now, now she felt she knew the quotation across the folder for what it was; an excuse to put life on hold. It might in all fairness, she thought, have worked for Elizabeth Smart, but it's done nothing for me. What good anyway could come from inviting anyone, Nature or God, into a shaky building? She sighed as she packed her nightdress, smoothing out the folds of peach-coloured silk with the back of her hand; a shaky building, not a nice image to have of oneself, not an image she would ever want to see mirrored in Henry's eyes.

Then she thought of the trip ahead and, slamming the case shut, she said out loud, 'Bugger it! What harm can a weekend do?'

Henry took her for lunch at a small pub in Modbury, and not once did they mention Selma or the nursing home. It was, Amelia thought, as if they were testing each other out, making sure that they had somewhere to go beyond Cherryfield. She remembered Rosalind sitting in Amelia's kitchen with Ronnie on her lap saying sadly, 'All Chris and I can talk about is the baby. These days we seem to be rushing through life on different tracks, converging only on Ronnie, and when we run out of chat about him, we just sit there in polite silence, waiting for his next step, or tooth, or word, to rescue us.'

She thought suddenly of Gerald dressed in prickly silence as if it was a cactus skin. Henry would never be like that. He threw himself into every conversation like a puppy attacking a new friend. And all that energy:

in a midday heat that made even the buzzing of the bees sound like a tired gesture, he made sitting down seem like freeze-framed action rather than a rest.

During lunch he had wanted to hear all about her plans for the dairy: was she serious about opening the café, was she continuing with her journalism?

Amelia began to feel like one of those middle-aged mothers with a miraculous first baby, exhausted, a little frustrated but charmed.

'I'd love to see some of your poems,' Henry said.

Amelia gave him a lazy smile. 'Little Bo-Peep has lost her sense and doesn't know where to find it.'

'Ha, ha,' Henry said.

'You shouldn't ha ha,' Amelia said reproachfully. 'I've had to take on writing jingles for Happy Thoughts Greetings Cards, to support my granny habit.'

'Really?' Henry looked interested.

'Really,' Amelia said. 'They rejected my last lot though.'

'You must try again,' Henry said.

He kept humming as, later on, they drove towards Cornwall, happy little hummings from no particular song that Amelia knew. He didn't have a bad voice, deeper than his speaking voice. He would sound good in church, she thought. She pulled her fingers along the naked skin in the crook of his arm. It was a hot day and his skin was damp.

'You've got nice arms,' she said.

Henry turned pink. 'Apparently,' he smiled suddenly, 'my mother used to say that to my father. He couldn't work out why she had married him, he was almost fifty, twice her age, quite staid and boring he said. I remember him laughing about it. "It must have been my arms; she thought my arms were sexy."'

'All right, all right.' Now Amelia was laughing. 'Your arms are sexy too.'

She looked at her watch. It would be tea-time when they arrived. She wondered what the cottage was like. Henry had said that the Cowans would be leaving them some food, but she had still brought some cheese and grapes, a few scones and a pot of home-made jam. The jam was made in someone else's home admittedly, and it had probably done the rounds backwards and forwards between different bring-and-buy sales in Abbotslea, but it looked like nice jam: strawberry, and the pot had such a pretty cloth-cover over its lid. Amelia kept trying to ward off thoughts of Henry leaving, leaving so soon and maybe even going to war in the Gulf. The idea seemed quite absurd in the midst of all that sunshine and normality, the way, she thought suddenly with a little shudder, it must have seemed eight years earlier to the people waving off the men sailing for the Falklands.

She shook herself. 'Twenty-four hours,' she said, 'just think, twenty-four hours all to ourselves.' She smiled as he put his hand on hers.

Chapter Twenty-one

As they got out of the car by the grey stone cottage with its garden all jumbled up with roses and fox-gloves and cabbages, the front door opened and a small boy ran down the path and out of the gate, flinging his arms round Henry's neck.

'Uncle Henry, Uncle Henry! Mummy said you wouldn't be pleased to see us but you are, aren't you?' The boy was five years old and quite convinced that his mother was being very silly.

'Elvira was sick all night.' He jumped up and down with excitement, stirring up little puffs of grey dusty soil from the road side. 'First she was sick in her bed. And then she got into mine because hers was all icky and then she was sick in mine.' His voice rose to a high pitched squeal, 'And then . . .'

Henry gave a pleading look over the child's blond head. 'This is Freddie, my godson.'

Amelia smiled back helplessly.

'Are you Amelia? Mummy said that you wanted to be on your own with Uncle Henry. You can come into my playroom, it's quite big. Come.' Freddie put his hand in hers.

Freddie's mother appeared at the door and, giving an embarrassed little wave, she called, 'I'm terribly sorry, really I am, but you can imagine . . . camping with Elvira at the moment.'

Henry hurried towards Jenny Cowan and kissed her on both cheeks. 'Mark's inside watching the athletics,'

Jenny said, before turning to Amelia, shaking hands. 'Come through, I'll show you your room.'

The trick is, Amelia thought, not to burst into tears on the Cowans' doorstep.

'I'll get the bags,' Henry said and disappeared off towards the car.

'We know how things are with Henry's "calling" and all that, so we've got you in the spare room,' Jenny explained as she took Amelia through the house. 'But I'm afraid Henry will have to share with Freddie. Actually,' she smiled conspiratorially, 'the little chap can't believe his luck. He was so upset when he heard you were coming and he wasn't going to be allowed to be here.'

She opened the door into a small, sunny room dominated by a double bed that stood like an insult at the centre of the wall. 'I hope you'll be comfortable. I'll just go and check on Elvira. I'll have a cup of tea ready in a sec.'

Think positive, Amelia told herself as she hung up her clothes. It could be worse. How? She thought for a moment: at least the children make a change from Cherryfield, she tried. And Jenny does seem very nice. She brushed her teeth and tried out a smile before joining the others in the sitting room.

Mark asked her if she wanted a large gin and tonic rather than tea. 'To get over the shock.' He grinned at her, as if they were all sharing in a really good joke.

'Tea will be fine.'

She went over to Henry who sat smiling with a look in his eyes as if he'd been struck by someone he trusted. She took his hand and said, trying to sound cheerful, 'It's lovely to have a chance to meet you both.' She smiled at her hosts. 'And the children of course.' She was rewarded with a grateful glance from Henry.

After tea Henry suggested Amelia came with him for a walk. 'Can I come, can I come?' Freddie, who had been busy building a Lego zoo, jumped up and began looking for his boots.

'You don't need boots, Freddie,' Jenny called after him, 'it's dry as a bone outside.'

Henry took her hand again as soon as they got out of the house. 'I'm so very sorry,' he whispered. 'Do you want to leave? We could go to a hotel.'

Freddie circled them like a cheerful vulture. 'There are planes on Uncle Henry's ship.'

'Helicopters,' Henry corrected automatically.

Freddie circled closer. 'Amelia, there are helicopters on Uncle Henry's ship. Hundreds and hundreds of helicopters.'

Amelia smiled at him. 'Isn't that wonderful?' And she whispered to Henry, 'We couldn't do that, could we? They'd be terribly hurt. It would be very rude.' She half hoped that Henry would contradict her but of course he didn't.

'And this business with the rooms too,' Henry put his arm round her shoulders. 'You see, Jenny knows how I feel, how I normally feel about . . .'

'Uncle Henry, does God love everybody?' Freddie interrupted him. He had stopped circling and settled into their steps. His cheeks were bright pink and his hair was damp from the running.

'Yes Freddie. God loves everyone.' Henry looked unhappily at Amelia. 'It's all getting to be such a mess. If at least we'd had this one night . . .'

'Did God love the dinosaurs?' Freddie squeezed in between them and took both their hands.

'Yes!' Henry almost shouted. 'Yes, the dinosaurs too.'

Freddie frowned. 'But if he loved them, why did he let them get extinct?'

Freddie and Elvira were asleep and Amelia had helped
tidy their toys away from the kitchen. She wandered
into the garden to pick some flowers for the table and
coming back with a bunch of foxgloves in her arms,
she bumped into Henry on his way to get some wood.

'Digitalis,' she smiled at him. 'For the children.'

Henry let go of the woodbasket and put his arms
round her, squashing the flowers. 'I adore you, do you
know that?' he mumbled the words so quickly that
they came out almost on top of each other. Then he let
her go and hurried outside.

Amelia stood looking after him, the crushed flowers
in her arms. She had been told she was loved quite a
few times by quite a few men, but never before had she
been adored. She smiled as she arranged the flowers in
Jenny's vase.

Henry opened the bottle of wine and Jenny served
lasagne with a corner missing that had gone to the
children's supper. There were caramelized oranges to
follow, and Amelia's cheese. As Mark spoke of the
possibilities of war, probing every angle, pulling out
morsels of information from press and television,
chewing over the options, Amelia kept hacking off
little wedges of the cheese and popping them into her
mouth absent-mindedly. Throughout their lives, she
thought, at any particular time a war was being fought
somewhere. Yet they could as well be sitting there
talking of witches or dragons or a haunted house, as of
war, because somehow, deep down amongst the fear
and the excitement, none of them really believed in
it.

'Now Mark's on to the Gulf he'll go on for hours,'
Jenny grimaced at Amelia. 'He used to be in the Navy
too, that's how we all met.' She pushed her plate away
and, putting her hand on Henry's shoulder, she said,

'You boys can do the washing-up. Come on Amelia, I'm dying for a chat.'

Amelia stood up obediently, thinking it was like a sticky spider's web, this kind hospitality, choking the life out of their weekend.

Henry got up too. 'Let's get on with the clearing up,' he said to Mark.

'Oh, there's no hurry,' Jenny smiled at him. 'You two hardly ever get a chance to have a really good talk. We'll be all right, won't we?' She turned to Amelia. As there was no reply she tried again, 'Won't we, Amelia?'

Amelia felt there was no more fight in her. She allowed herself to be seated on the sofa next to Jenny, allowed herself to be plied with coffee and mint-flavoured matchsticks, the extra long variety.

'Don't you just love these?' Jenny giggled as she put a third chocolate in her mouth.

No, Amelia wanted to say. I hate them. I only like the orange ones. But she muttered and smiled agreement.

'You must be worried sick with all this talk of war.' Jenny reached for the box again. Then, before Amelia had time to answer, she went on, 'He's totally wrapped up in you, you know. We've seen him with quite a few girls, but nothing ever seemed this serious.' She added kindly, 'He's obviously been waiting for someone special and now it looks as if he's found her.'

'We don't know each other all that well,' Amelia said gracelessly, annoyed at having their tentative affections all tied up and despatched by Jenny. 'I mean most of our meetings have been in a nursing home. I'm older than him too,' she added for good measure.

'And now you've got us around to spoil your last weekend,' Jenny said. 'Poor you.'

Amelia blushed and apologized, but Jenny just laughed.

Feeling hot, Amelia excused herself and hurried into

the bathroom to put on fresh lipstick and some scent. When she returned, Jenny looked up at her and said, 'Gosh, I remember making all that effort before we were married. I give you two months, and you'll be as slack as the rest of us.'

She hadn't been listening at all, Amelia thought, but when Henry joined them at last, a tea towel slung over one shoulder, she felt as if the door to home had opened.

Eventually, Henry had thought, Jenny would suggest that he would be much more comfortable sharing the spare room with Amelia, but she hadn't. During dinner he had almost heard the clock ticking away their last night together as Amelia grew quieter and quieter. She had a way, he thought, of hunching her already narrow shoulders when she was unhappy or worried, which made her seem smaller than she really was. Next to her, Jenny had seemed indecently robust, dark-haired, pink-cheeked and so sturdily married that she seemed to have all but forgotten about people needing to be alone together. And Mark, Mark was his best friend, but he had been no better, going on and on about the Gulf. Henry thought of the young sailors and Wrens in his care sailing off with him that Monday, none of them knowing whether war was at the end of their journey. He felt suddenly furious with Mark and all the men like him who sat pontificating in the safety of their homes, wishing they were 'out there'.

On the bottom bunk below him, Freddie snuffled and snored, twisted and turned, legs and arms flailing; he was fast asleep though. Carefully, so as not to make a sound, Henry swung his legs over the side of the bunk, dropping down on to the soft carpet below.

'Uncle Henry.' Freddie sat bolt upright in the lower bunk. 'Where are you going? Mummy says big boys should last the night.'

'Go back to sleep, Freddie, please.'

'I can't.'

'Go back to sleep, Freddie, I mean it,' Henry hissed.

'You're being horrid.' Freddie began to cry. 'Mummy says that because you're a Chaplain you're extra nice, but you're not and I'm feeling sick. I want Mummy.'

Henry sighed and knelt down by the boy, stroking the damp cheek. 'I'm sorry, Freddie. I'll get Mummy. Come with me to the bathroom first though.'

Freddie gave a small smile and crawled out of bed, putting his hand in Henry's.

'Did you sleep well?' Jenny enquired brightly of Amelia the next morning. 'I'm afraid Henry might have had enough of his godson for a while. The poor little chap was awake most of the night.' She smiled lovingly at Elvira who sat, looking interested, in a bright red plastic high-chair. 'Did my naughty girl give Freddie her bugs?'

Amelia and Henry went to church on their own, no-one followed them there. Seated in the pew she looked sideways at Henry. Although this was not his parish, here in church he ceased being Henry and turned into a chaplain, public property. The thought of their kisses and mumbled endearments suddenly seemed nicely improper, like sitting in court and being the only one knowing that, under his gown, the judge was naked. Amongst all the dubious wisdom handed down to women, Amelia thought, there must be one about not lusting after officials.

Next to her, Henry was deep in prayer so she stopped looking at him and mumbled Our Father, lest her unworthy thoughts should somehow vibrate across into his contemplation.

After lunch with the Cowans they said their goodbyes and set off back to Exeter. 'I'll write with my new address,' Amelia called through the open window of the car. 'Promise you'll come and see me.'

Henry grinned at her. 'Such warm farewells could be caused only by a bad conscience. Actually,' he said, serious now, 'you were marvellous, and I'm very grateful.'

'I'll come and wave you off tomorrow.' Amelia stroked his hair, smoothing it behind his ear. 'Isn't your hair too long? Won't you be ticked off?'

'Probably,' he smiled. 'I'll be very busy, you won't mind?'

She shook her head.

They stayed for a while in the car outside Dagmar's flat. Henry sat with his arm round Amelia's shoulders, looking out across the park. Suddenly he took his arm away and, putting his hand in his pocket, pulled out a heart-shaped locket on a chain. Holding it out to her he said, 'This belonged to my mother. I would like to think of you wearing it.'

Amelia touched the matt gold of the heart gingerly with the tip of her finger. 'It's a beautiful locket.'

'Please take it.'

Relaxing a bit, she took the necklace, making a fist around it.

Henry touched her cheek lightly, tracing her jaw-line round to her lips. 'You've got what is known in the trade as an expressive face, so what's wrong? Am I going too fast?'

As Amelia looked away, he said softly, 'You're a very nice person, Amelia, and you don't want to do anything to upset me because I'm going away and there might be a war, is that not right? But you see that's why it's especially important that you're honest with me.' He took her hand. 'I suppose what I'm saying is, that I'd like to know how you feel about me.'

'It's funny,' Amelia said, 'you're five years younger than me, but compared to you I feel unformed. And . . . What's the opposite of self-possessed?' she smiled. 'Unpossessed? That too.'

She lifted his hand to her face, pressing it against her cheek. 'I don't know how I would have coped the last few months without you. And as you have probably guessed,' she let go of his hand, 'I would have loved going to bed with you. But you see, it wasn't very long ago that I thought I was going to spend the rest of my life with Gerald.' She paused.

'I've only just finished driving him away. I ought to have a break before I start on someone else.'

'If that last bit was an attempt to lighten the atmosphere,' Henry said, 'it wasn't very successful.' But he was smiling again.

'Henry, that locket belonged to your mother.'

'I know, I told you.'

Then he looked at her with such understanding sympathy that she wished that there was nothing for him to try to understand. She unfolded her fingers and picked the necklace up, about to put it on.

Henry stopped her. 'Truth, remember?' he said.

Amelia looked unhappily at him. 'Why do you want truth at a time like this? I've been nicely brought up, I'm not used to it.'

Henry began to laugh. 'Take it and keep it safe for me anyway.' He slipped the locket into her handbag.

'I had always planned to meet the ship when you all return, if you wanted me to that is; we're friends,' Amelia said. 'And I listen to you. It was you who told me that I drifted around expecting others to bring me the things I wanted from life. Like one of those women who sits around in middle-age thinking bitterly: I should have been a managing director's wife, or I should have been the mother of a doctor.'

'Did I say that?'

She grinned at him. 'Maybe not exactly, but something like it anyway, and you were right. And it won't do any more. I'm thirty-one years old and most of those years I've been flapping round like a homing pigeon whose loft has been demolished, trying to edge on to someone else's perch. It hasn't proved a great success. I'm not very proud of myself, in fact I come pretty low down the list of people I'd choose to spend an evening with.'

She leant forward and kissed him lightly on the cheek. 'And the thing is, soon you'd feel the same.'

As Henry was about to protest, she put her finger softly across his mouth.

'No, I mean it. I will have to like myself a little before I start all over again asking someone else to.' She pressed her finger harder against his lips. 'Please, Henry.'

'You make me sound like some medieval princess,' Henry said at last, 'waiting for her sodding knight errant.'

Amelia leant her head on his shoulder. 'Some princess,' she said.

Henry twisted free and looking her straight in the eyes, he cupped her face in his hands and kissed her. 'So I'll wait,' he said.

233

Chapter Twenty-two

The lines of the large grey frigate seemed fluid in the mist of the September morning, making it seem to Amelia, standing at the brow, as if at any moment it would dematerialize, leaving the small crowd of women and children isolated in the drizzle. But the leaving was slow; the brow was removed, the riggers let go wires and ropes leaving a single wire attaching the ship's fo'c's'le to the jetty: a rush of water as the engines eased the stern out. Three short blasts of the siren, the final wire detached from the bollard and the Union Flag was lowered. Now the ship was off, disappearing through the Narrows, past Devil's Point and out into the Sound. Everyone was waving, the goodbye kind; no throwing up of the arm with the hand whisking the air in excitement but a slow salute held for a long while as if, while they waved, the ship had not yet really gone.

'Henry has left. Admiral Mallett's son, he's sailed for the Gulf,' Amelia said to Selma. 'I watched them leave this morning.' She was hoping for a miracle, for Selma to understand and say wise and comforting words.

Selma said nothing but watched Amelia intently, her hand trembling in her lap.

Amelia felt angry again, she couldn't help it. What right did Selma have to look so enticingly herself? On Amelia's own instruction the visiting hairdresser had carefully blue-toned Selma's hair, and set it in loose waves. Her nails had been cut and she was wearing the nicer of the two polyester dresses. She was a Huldra, the Swedish fairy-tale creature who, in the guise of a lovely young girl, would appear in the woods before a lost traveller, beckoning him to follow, leading him further and further from the track, deep into the forest where the massed crowns of the pine trees obliterated the sky. Then, only then would she turn her back on him and in that moment the traveller knew he was doomed, knew that it was the Huldra, because where her back should be, there was just a hollow.

The Huldra at Cherryfield looked so much like Amelia's wise and loving grandmother that Amelia was beckoned further into her confidence. 'He gave me his mother's locket to keep for him, it's all very confusing. And so soon after Gerald too.' She looked up at Selma who was looking intently at her. 'You know, Grandma, I can't just keep dropping in and out of relationships. I'm beginning to feel like a baton in a relay race, always the baton but never the runner. Then again, I was beginning to get very fond of Henry, and now there might be a war and I might never see him again.' She sighed. 'He would insist on me being honest too and you know how wretched that can make one feel.'

Selma blinked as if she'd just woken up. 'Oh darling, let's not talk about the war, you know how I hate it. All these films and television programmes, making it out to be exciting and romantic when it was all so horrible.'

Be gone with you Huldra, Amelia thought resignedly.

Selma made an effort; 'And how are you anyway darling? Been to any nice parties lately?' as if she was racking her brains for suitable topics of conversation with a dull guest.

Amelia sighed, then she covered up quickly with a smile. 'I'm fine, absolutely fine.' Physical contact, she thought, that's the thing, that's the way of getting through. She looked surreptitiously at Selma's hands, the one that trembled and the one that was still, like a visitor picking a child from the line of abandoned urchins in an orphanage. If she picked the pathetic one, the most helpless, she would show up all the clearer the weakness of the whole and embarrass Selma. She took the good hand.

Selma's eyelids kept drooping, she seemed content. It occurred to Amelia that at Cherryfield the only touching you got, the only time you felt someone's arms around you or their skin against yours, was in the course of maintenance; when hands lifted you on to the loo or from your bed, washed you, wiped you. But no-one touched you just because they wanted to.

A while later, Nurse Williams popped her head through the door, and when she saw Selma and Amelia she smiled and called, 'Ah, there you are Mrs Merryman, I was looking for you.' She sounded as if she thought Selma had been playing Hide and Seek and she stepped briskly towards them with an empty wheelchair. 'It's time for your bandages to be seen to.'

Selma shrank back in her chair. 'I can't come with you now, I'm afraid. I've got my granddaughter here.' She relaxed a little. 'I don't believe you've met.'

'Of course we've met, dear, haven't we Miss Lindsay.' Nurse Williams winked at Amelia. 'We won't take a moment, Mrs Merryman, I'm sure your granddaughter will wait.' She began to haul Selma up from the chair.

Suddenly Amelia felt Selma's nails digging into her arm. 'You must take me away from here. I want to go home,' and she began to cry.

With an expertly executed pull and twist, Nurse

Williams plonked her in the wheelchair. 'There we are,' she sing-songed. 'Nothing to it, is there Mrs Merryman?'

Amelia thought the nurses must develop the same selective deafness as mothers of young children. 'Just wait a moment could you Nurse Williams?' she said. 'My grandmother seems distressed.'

The nurse leant closer to Amelia. 'I know dear, it's upsetting, but she'll soon forget all about it and be back bright as a button and as sweet smelling.' And as Amelia gaped at her she released the brake of the wheelchair with a little kick of her sturdy white lace-ups.

Amelia put her hand on Selma's shoulder.

'She's fine, you know,' Nurse Williams said, and her large brown eyes had a hurt look in them. They were the same eyes, Amelia thought, as those of Mrs King, the kindly neighbour Dagmar sometimes left her with as a child. Amelia hated going to Mrs King, having taken an instant, virulent and completely unfounded dislike to her, and each time as Dagmar prepared to leave, she'd begin to howl. That same confused hurt look would fill poor Mrs King's eyes as she tried to defend herself against the accusations of ill-treatment that were never made. And Dagmar had been embarrassed in the same way as Amelia was now; right in the middle of feeling sorry for Selma she felt embarrassed at the tactlessness of her tears.

Amelia patted Selma's shoulder awkwardly and said to Nurse Williams, 'I know you all look after her, it's not that.' She patted Selma some more. 'It's all right,' she mumbled, 'it's all right.'

Selma lifted her head. 'It's not bloody well all right!' Then she began to cry again. 'I don't understand anything any more. Robert said it would only be for a short while, but no-one takes any notice of what I say,

237

no-one seems to listen when they see it's me talking.' She pulled a soiled pink tissue from the sleeve of her cardigan and wiped her nose.

It was the small, slightly upturned nose of a pretty young girl, Amelia thought sadly: noses just didn't age. She knelt down and put her arms round her grandmother. 'I'm listening,' she said, then she looked up at Nurse Williams. 'I'll bring her to you in a moment, if I may?'

Nurse Williams still looked hurt, but she did leave them.

'I'm frightened, Amelia.' Selma hung her head like a small child. When she looked up again she was pleading. 'I'm frightened I'm going to die in this place.'

It was the first time Selma had mentioned death. Some old people never stopped talking about it, their own and others', in a busy possessive way as if dying was an exclusive hobby. Selma, though, had avoided the subject as if it was a bad smell. 'Ignore it dear, and it'll soon go away.'

Her uneven nails dug deep into the fleshy part of Amelia's arm, her eyes were locked on Amelia's face, anxiously following every flicker of her eyes, every twitch; as if the conclusion of her life is written in my features, Amelia thought, looking helplessly back at her. And what was she to say? 'Nonsense, you're not going to die. You've got years left in you.' Was that what she was meant to say? She had planned and schemed for weeks, enjoyed what was nothing but a state of madness or an over active day-dream. And now Selma, who not so long ago had been the serene and loving centre of her life, was begging like no-one should have to beg, for her help.

Amelia closed her eyes for a moment then she leant across and took both Selma's hands in hers. 'You'll be home for Christmas, I promise you that.'

Selma sighed a deep shuddering sigh as she relaxed back in her chair. 'Thank you, darling.' She added almost nonchalantly, 'I don't know what I'd do without you.'

Amelia felt as if she had just risked life and limb rescuing someone from an approaching steamroller only to find out when it rolled past that it was a *Potemkin* cut-out. Her heart still thumping, she wheeled Selma out to Nurse Williams who was waiting in the corridor outside Honeysuckle. Selma greeted the nurse with a gracious little smile and went off as if she hadn't a care in the world.

She's put them all on me, Amelia thought as she wandered out into the garden. At Cherryfield you grabbed your fresh air when you could. There was a moment, as she stepped out on to the lawn, when she expected to see Henry standing under the cherry tree in one of his awful shirts. With his head a little to one side, he'd look at her with those keen brown eyes, so different from Selma's, where age, confusion, sadness, had each, drop by drop, diluted the colour. As for Nurse Williams, Amelia thought, kicking a stone across the lawn and indulging her desire to be ten again, she had the large mournful eyes of a cow who had just been shooed off her favourite patch of grass.

'There's just no right way with old people,' Amelia wanted to complain, basking in Henry's warm interest. She sat down under the tree and thought how right she was. You put them in a Cherryfield and you break their hearts. You take them to live with you and they break your spirit and make you fellow prisoners in their decline. 'No thank you Rosalind I can't go to London with you, Granny doesn't fit in the train,' and, 'Dear Editor, I hope you like my article on Japanese businessmen in Milton Keynes. I had to guess what Milton

Keynes is like because there's only me at home with granny.'

How long would Selma have lasted, Amelia wondered, if they had all left her at home at Ashcombe, if they had never interfered?

She sat under the tree trying to think of all the reasons why she should not fulfil her promise to Selma and she remembered Henry saying once that doing nothing could be a grave sin too. The worst maybe, she thought, because you're so seldom brought to justice. She looked at her watch and got up, feeling her skirt all damp at the back. I'm one of life's hand-wringers she thought. You can see people like me at every bad happening through history, be it big or small. 'Oh dear, oh dear,' is our motto, as we stand at the foot of the cradle, squashed between the bad and the good fairy, peering down anxiously, 'Oh dear, oh dear.'

'Your gran is having a little snooze,' Nurse Williams told Amelia who came looking for her in the hall. 'It always takes a lot out of her I'm afraid, seeing those legs when the bandages are changed.' Then with surprising speed she dived after Miss Hudd who was arranging herself in the chairlift, and wrenched a small paper parcel from her fingers.

'Boiled carrots from the kitchen,' she mouthed at Amelia.

'You'll rot, you murderer,' Miss Hudd said calmly and clearly before propelling herself around and starting to walk back to the lounge. She looked straight past Amelia as she met her in the doorway and settled herself in a chair a little removed from the others.

Amelia waited a moment, then she walked up to her and asked, 'The carrots, were they for the rabbit?'

Miss Hudd turned slowly to face Amelia with an expression of such raw pain that Amelia flinched as if slapped by Miss Hudd's large, blue veined hand.

'I'm so very sorry about forgetting the food the other day. Would you please let me run down and get some now?' I'm taking the easy way out, she thought, joining in her disillusions: buy a smile now, pay later.

'It's too late.' Miss Hudd wasn't looking at her any more and she spoke more to herself than to Amelia. 'The carrots wouldn't have been any use either, but I felt I owed it to him to try.'

Amelia was wondering what to say when Miss Hudd looked directly at her. 'Come and see for yourself, it doesn't matter now.' She heaved herself up from the chair.

Upstairs in her room Miss Hudd walked over to the chest of drawers on the bare wall opposite the narrow bed. Letting go of one stick, supporting herself on the other, she pulled out the top drawer. She looked up at Amelia. 'Here,' was all she said.

Thinking hard of fluffy toys, Amelia took a step closer and looked down. On a piece of thick green velvet lay what seemed at first to be an untidy mesh of pale grey wool. Then she saw the silky ear and the small front paws. 'Oh my God!' Amelia slapped her hand across her mouth and took a step back.

Miss Hudd dropped the second stick and, leaning her side against the wall, put her large hands into the drawer. Gently she lifted the little creature out and, shifting so that her back was supported by the wall, she stood, holding the rabbit tight against her flat chest. Amelia turned away for a moment, the expression in Miss Hudd's eyes was hard to bear. Then, coming up closer, she whispered, 'Is he dead?'

Miss Hudd bent her neck and kissed the rabbit's head. For a moment his sparse lashes fluttered as he struggled to open his eyes. Then he lay still.

'I didn't really mind coming here,' Miss Hudd said, in an even voice. 'I know I was becoming a nuisance;

always scalding myself, falling over. I had agreed to go when my nephew told me pets weren't allowed.' She buried her nose in the tousled fur, and when she looked up again there were tears in her eyes. 'I couldn't go without him, you understand that, don't you?' She looked as if she was going to sink to the floor.

Amelia reached out and steadied her, guiding her across to the chair. Still clutching the rabbit to her chest, Miss Hudd collapsed on to it. She sat, silently stroking the rabbit, her big hand covering the animal like a heavy blanket. Then suddenly she cried out.

'Look how big I am! Look at me. "Let Hudd do it," the teacher at school said, "she's a big strong girl." And my mother, "Trust Elizabeth, Elizabeth will cope, she's so sensible, so capable," she said. Look at me!' Miss Hudd cried again, stretching her long arms out, showing the emaciated rabbit laying motionless on her large palms. 'I'm no use,' she whispered, 'no use at all.' She began to cry, tears falling down her cheeks, dropping one by one on to the rabbit's face.

Amelia knelt by the chair and put her hand gently on Miss Hudd's shoulder. 'I'm so sorry I didn't believe you. I'm so very sorry. Let me take him to the vet, please.'

Miss Hudd shook her large head violently like a distraught child and her plaits uncoiled and dropped down her back. 'It's too late. He's gone.' She rubbed her wet cheeks against him, kissing him over and over, then with a shudder she held him out to Amelia. 'You take him. Bury him for me, would you? Please. Under the cherry tree.'

'I'd like you to use my car while I'm away,' Henry had said as he sailed that morning. 'It will actually be a help for me. I would have to sell it otherwise or pay for garaging.' So Amelia placed the dead rabbit on the floor of Henry's car and, as Selma was still sleeping, drove off to pass the time until dark fell. She took tea down by the harbour and had another look round the dairy. Then she drove back to Cherryfield and sat at Selma's side until the cherry tree at the centre of the lawn grew fainter and disappeared in the darkening evening.

She had taken the gardener's shovel from the shed before it was locked up and now she brought it from its hiding place under the rhododendrons. She carried the rabbit from the car wrapped in a white Cherryfield towel, and she could feel its bones under the cloth, as fragile as a feather pen. Glancing up at the dull, starless sky she pushed the shovel into the hard soil and, as the crust broke, the sickly-sweet smell of mud and rotting leaves rose from the ground.

She placed the rabbit in the shallow hole she'd dug, still in his towelling shroud. The small theft gave her some pleasure. The wind rustled the branches of the tree and fresh leaves floated to the ground, some settling on the small white bundle in its shallow grave. Amelia had a sudden image of Sister Morris, black-cloaked and wild, toiling away over a much bigger grave. She shook herself. Sister Morris was nothing if not orderly. Every body that passed through Cherry-field was sure to be properly accounted for.

'Everyone but you,' she whispered to the rabbit. She covered him with black soil, shovelful after shovelful, until it was impossible to see that someone was buried under the cherry tree.

Chapter Twenty-three

'Doreen? Amelia Lindsay here. Yes, we're all well thank you.' Amelia held the receiver a little away from her ear as Doreen Hamilton seemed not to trust the telephone to carry her voice all the way to Exeter. 'I'm calling on behalf of my uncle,' she lied. 'He's living out in Brazil at the moment but he's asked me to make sure that everything is satisfactory.'

She fiddled with her key-ring, gazing out through the open window at the street. The dry autumn leaves rattled along the pavement like a plague of brightly coloured cockroaches, while Doreen, her voice stiff with complaints, told her about cracks, damp patches, loose tiles and funny smells in the cellar.

'Well that's excellent then,' Amelia said breezily, 'I can tell him everything is fine.' Ignoring any complaints with cheerful resolution was a trick she'd learnt from the builders that had worked on the Old Rectory.

'Oh, by the way,' she said quickly, as Doreen, sounding confused, was preparing to hang up, 'I hear you're spending Christmas in the sun this year. Over the actual holiday is it?' She tucked the question in with her goodbyes. 'Until the sixth, lovely.' She put the phone down and went to find her diary.

The red ribbon marker running along the inside spine of the blue leather diary (she always bought the best in diaries ever since reading Mrs Miniver when she was fourteen) was placed to make it fall open on the twenty-third of December. The red-ringed date made her jump as if it had announced itself in a ringing baritone; only two months away. Time, these days, was money in more than the obvious sense, she thought, as she sat down on her bed with the open diary in her lap. Ever larger amounts of it disappeared faster and faster. Two hot summer weeks when you were seventeen were time to be reckoned with; you got a lot for fourteen days when you were very young. Now, it was nothing but small change, and she squandered it, as if she still had riches of years ahead of her, when instead she should be making the minutes go a long way, like a pensioner counting coins at a check-out counter.

She sighed and got up, putting the diary on her desk with the letters from Henry. For him, time seemed suspended as he sailed in the ship, closer and closer maybe to war. There was already a small pile of his letters to her. Funny, clever, sometimes beautiful letters, each written with that last weekend like an unanswered question between them.

Later that day, Amelia stood by the window in Selma's room looking out at the gentle dying of the leaves that were at their loveliest just before dropping to the ground. Then she looked at Selma.

There was no more talk now of her moving back to her old room. The darkening evenings and the cold winds were kept at bay by electric light and central heating but, like wolves howling at the door, they still seemed to threaten the residents of Cherryfield.

'We always lose a few more in winter,' Nurse Williams said.

A week later Mrs Ambrose died. They had brought her husband in to sit with her and Selma spent the day in the Residents' Lounge before being allowed back to the room with its empty second bed. She didn't ask about Mrs Ambrose, so no-one told her.

245

The new vicar went his rounds though, and he even mentioned a rabbi friend to Amelia. 'When the devil gets old he becomes religious,' Selma used to say. But she was in no more mood for religion now in her dying days than she had been before. Amelia thought it was because she didn't know she was old.

'Your grandmother seems much more settled these days, don't you think?' Sister Morris moved her lips in the direction of a smile as she passed Amelia in the passage.

'I was thinking of taking her over to my mother's flat for the day,' Amelia said.

Sister Morris had only paused briefly on her clip-clop along the glossy floor, but now she stopped again. 'I don't know Miss Lindsay. We normally encourage outings, but with those burns only just beginning to heal . . . The skin is as fragile as tissue paper.'

Back at the flat, Dagmar washed her hands three times at the news. 'I feel guilty. You don't know how many snide little remarks I get from people. Some of mother's old cronies have even called up to tell me they think I'm a bad daughter for not having her to live with me.' She rubbed some handcream into the cracking skin on her hands. 'Not one of them, other than old Evelyn, of course, has bothered to visit her but they all know that I should have mother here with me.'

Amelia had written an article for the local paper on the importance of helping old people to keep their pets. She had since been asked to do another on the topic of old age. The editor had suggested 'The Care of Our Elderly: Shame or Shambles?'

'Shame and Shambles,' Amelia had corrected him mildly. But she had admitted she could think of no clever alternatives to that particular mess.

'How to care for Selma?' she asked now, more to

herself than to Dagmar, as she followed her into the sitting room. She knew it was one of life's unanswerables.

'I love William Hurt, don't you?' Dagmar put a tape in the video and settled into the sofa, her long legs tucked under her. As the credits were running she asked Amelia, 'Are you sure you want to settle in a little hole like Kingsmouth? Isn't London really the place?'

About to answer, Amelia felt all wrong, like a pink button on an orange cardigan. She knew she should love London for its galleries and theatres, its shops and restaurants. And she did love it, as a visitor. But she had tried living there and the loneliness froze her, slowing her down until just getting out of bed was an effort.

'I only like the rich extravagant bits I can't afford,' she said, portioning out the truth to her mother in bite-sized chunks because who wanted, at thirty-one, to admit to their mother that living in a big city frightened them? 'I've tried to like the squalid bits. Tried calling them cosmopolitan and full of flavour, real and alive.' She threw herself down on the small sofa. 'Anyway, why is it that what's scruffy is described as real as if anything else is not? Why are quiet leafy terraces and tea at the Ritz not deserving of the label? It is the reality for some. Lucky sods.'

'Hush.' Dagmar turned the sound up on the video.

In her bed, Selma rolled about uneasily and when her arm hit the hard edge of the bedside table she woke. For a few moments her thoughts floated round pleasurably as if in a warm lagoon, then unease seeped through. This was not just another day, pleasantly filled with family routines, about to begin.

Bang! It hit her like a tidal wave of misery and she

struggled to sit up. Daniel, Daniel was dead, that letter had said so. She opened her mouth and screamed, 'Daniel!'

Footsteps hurried towards her and a bright striplight was switched on. 'Mrs Merryman, Mrs Merryman! What's the matter? Are you all right?'

There was much shaking of heads that afternoon when Dagmar and Amelia visited. Nurse Williams sucked in air through the gaps in her teeth and said, 'She was totally confused. Going on and on in some foreign language . . .'

'Swedish,' Amelia said.

'. . . then she switched to English but we were hardly any the wiser because she kept on talking about her husband having just died and calling him Daniel but we all know her husband was called Willoughby.'

After that, Selma's decline seemed to Amelia like one of those speeded-up sequences in a nature film; almost before her eyes she folded and wizened. She always recognized Dagmar and Amelia but the smile now seemed joyless, accusing almost, and each time Amelia stood up to leave she felt the barrier come down between the visitor free to go and the prisoner who was not. Sometimes she wondered if Selma hated her.

She bought the dairy. She had to call in a removal firm to bring her things down from Abbotslea. The day she was there packing it all up, Gerald took a couple of hours off work to be there too. He made her sad by the charm and kindness he exuded so carelessly in her direction, smiling at her with a warmth he had not shown since he stopped loving her. By showing his pleasure with her for disappearing from his life with comparatively little fuss (as he so rightly pointed out, you could hardly see the scratches on the car from when she had parked it in the sitting room and the carpet cleaned up beautifully) he came close to rekindling her love for him.

When, a day later, she shopped in the supermarket next to her new home, she looked enviously at the tired looking young woman in front of her stacking the conveyor high with food, her two small children squabbling somewhere at hip level. Amelia looked at her own basket, she didn't even merit a trolley, and thought, I'm turning into that awful cliché: the one-chop woman.

Soon, though, she got into a soothing routine and she found, as always, that inactivity had one busy trait; it begot more of the same. She got up no earlier than eight and padded down the bare-board stairs to the front door where the papers waited on the mat. She took three papers, two national and one local, and she read them all while she ate slices of toasted whole-meal bread with butter and Devon honey. At around ten she was dressed and ready to work on her articles before going for a long walk along the cliffs. She had forgotten how much she enjoyed the sight and smell of the sea. The walk was the time for some fairly vigorous day-dreaming of poetry readings in the café, and of bus loads of London critics squeezed in around the little tables downstairs. She hadn't yet found furniture that she both liked and could afford, so the tables and chairs these phantom poets and journalists were offered varied: sometimes the chairs were bentwood, placed round cloth-covered tables and sometimes the tables were oak and the chairs became pews.

After lunch she would work some more on her articles and she studied her correspondence course in accountancy, and around tea-time most days she wandered up the hill to Cherryfield.

No, for me, all is for the best, in this the most static of all possible worlds, she sighed, as she sat by Selma in the Residents' Lounge; and what would Henry think of me now, after all my bold words when we parted?

All through the autumn, Amelia had gathered the brightest autumn leaves off the ground and pressed them between the pages of Strindberg's *Collected Plays*, and by the time the Christmas lights had replaced the last leaves on the oaks in the little park by the harbour, she had put them in a huge padded envelope and sent them to Henry. He loved autumn in England, he'd said, just before the ship sailed, and now he wrote to her of the heat that lay like cling-film across the ship, suppressing all spare energy, and of how instead of dolphins playing on the pressure waves at the bow, there were the bloated bodies of dead sheep tossed overboard from some livestock trans-porter bound for Daman.

When Amelia walked in the garden at Cherryfield she found little pieces of boiled carrot in the grass under the Cherry tree where Miss Hudd's rabbit lay buried.

'I'm taking my grandmother home for Christmas,' she said to Sister Morris.

Sister Morris puckered her lips. 'We do encourage Christmas visits with friends and family but Mrs Merryman really isn't in a fit state to be moved. She's such a weight for a start, I doubt you'll even get her out of the car and as you know she's quite unable to help herself in the smallest way now.'

'She sort of dresses herself. A bit.'

Sister Morris didn't answer.

'The burns are healed now. I really can't see why nothing is being done about the foot. It's been getting steadily worse since she came here.' Amelia felt that for once she had Sister Morris on the run.

'Come into my office would you, Miss Lindsay?' Sister Morris said.

She offered one of the two hard chairs in the closet-sized room to Amelia and sat down herself. No fees had been siphoned off in the direction of the office, Amelia thought, handing a sour little portion of approval to Sister Morris as she waited for her to speak.

'The gangrene is spreading.' Sister Morris looked straight at Amelia, a business-like tone in her voice. 'We could amputate but that would almost certainly kill her. Her blood pressure is very high, she's got early signs of Parkinson's. I'm sorry but there really is very little we can do. We are managing the pain very successfully and, quite honestly, all we can do now is continue to make her comfortable and hope the infection doesn't spread above the knee.'

'How long has she got?' Amelia asked and she blushed as she realized that a part of her felt it would be easier if it, death, happened before Christmas. Then she remembered Selma's face when she had begged her not to let her die at Cherryfield.

Sister Morris sighed and shrugged her shoulders. 'It could be a few weeks, it could be months. Who's to say?'

'There seems to be a general assumption that it's God,' Amelia snapped. 'And by what right, I sometimes ask myself.' She enjoyed Sister Morris's look of horror before getting up to leave.

She walked past the Residents' Lounge with its smell of stale urine, its grunts and murmurings, through the corridor to Selma's room. Hell, she thought, was most probably not fire and brimstone, but acres of passages with super-polished floors where each poor sinner's footsteps showed against the high gloss, and the air was heavy with disinfectant.

Chapter Twenty-four

On the twenty-third of December Amelia stood in the hall at Ashcombe for the first time since the house had been sold back in the spring. She had put her old key in the lock, turned it easily, and here she was inside, running her hand along the familiar ochre walls that were lit by milky winter sunlight. She wandered round the house, amazed at how little seemed to have changed. There was less dust around than in Selma's latter days and the smell of cats had gone, allowing the pot-pourris that Doreen, like Selma, kept in bowls around the rooms, to exude their scent unchallenged. It was a blessing that Doreen had always admired what she called, the Country-House style. The rooms themselves: the study with its bookshelves and carved pine fire-place, the sitting room with its deep bay looking out over the garden, the sunny passages, they all had character of their own so that any change of furnishings altered them only slightly, like discreet make-up on a strong featured face. Only the dining room was really different, not golden yellow any more as if it had its own sun in residence, but dark green and hunting-print adorned.

Having toured the house, Amelia went outside again and, as she unloaded the hired van she had parked in front of the garage, she felt thankful for the tall yew hedges that shielded the house and drive from the lane, and the neighbouring gardens.

She worked hard, singing as she went, 'The bells of

hell go ding-a-ling-a-ling,' returned for a second armchair, 'for you but not for me.' She dragged the chaise-longue along the gravel path and into the study. 'Ding-a-ling-a-ling,' put the tea-chests in the hall and dumped the pile of sheets and blankets on the old card table. When she stopped for a moment to wipe the damp hair from her forehead she decided that if she did go to hell as a result of what she was doing, she'd at least go there a better person.

By the time the light was going, she stood in the sitting room, a bunch of holly twigs in her arms, surveying her work. Unfamiliar tables had become Selma's again because Amelia had draped them with the Christmas cloths Willoughby's mother had embroidered. The two Swedish oils of Gothenburg and the west coast archipelago flanked the fire-place and Selma's armchair was in its place by the bay window.

Once, long ago, Amelia had asked Selma if she wasn't offending her Jewish faith by celebrating Christmas with such enthusiasm. Selma had been decorating the tall tree, standing on top of the library steps, a box of baubles in her hand. Amelia could see her now, looking down at her, smiling. 'Jesus was a great Jewish man, why should I not join in the celebrations?' and she had fixed the final decoration, a gold star Amelia had helped her make, at the top of the tree.

The last thing Amelia had brought from the van outside was a six-foot Christmas tree. She had decorated it with the contents of four cardboard boxes that she'd found amongst Selma's stored belongings. The star, a simple shape cut in cardboard and covered with gold paper, caught the light from the electric candles and Amelia saw now that it was remarkably like a Star of David.

'Tasteful Christmas trees are an aberration,' Selma had always said. She would like Amelia's tree. It stood in the bay so laden with tinsel, lights and baubles that it had become one solid glittering pyramid. Amelia took one final look around before slipping out of the front door and locking it behind her.

In the Residents' Lounge at Cherryfield, a plastic tree twinkled in the gloom. The traffic-light colours of the fairy lights flashed, throwing their colour across the magnolia walls and the grey faces of the residents, and jazzed-up carols played from a cassette recorder on the coffee table.

'You shouldn't worry about your gran,' Nurse Williams said. 'We do a lovely Christmas here: turkey with all the trimmings, it has to be carved the day before of course on account of the kitchen staff but they always do us proud, Christmas pud, no charms because of our teeth, but everyone gets a pressie.' She dazzled off a smile at Amelia.

'You think of everything.'

'Oh yes, I almost forgot, there's the crackers: green and gold this year.'

'With paper hats?' Amelia asked in a voice as if a lead weight had been attached to her vocal chords.

'Of course with hats.' A wailing noise came from a small woman hunched in a chair by the French windows and, hurrying away, Nurse Williams said, 'Your gran is having a little rest in bed today, so you'll find her in her room.'

Amelia turned in the doorway. 'What if they don't like paper hats?'

Nurse Williams looked puzzled for a moment then her face cleared. 'Everyone likes a hat for Christmas, don't they?'

Amelia had not slept well. She had kept on waking with her mouth dry and her heart going so fast it seemed it was trying to run right out of her chest and

254

she was sure she had acquired at least one extra arm expressly to get squashed under her body as she tried to ease herself into a comfortable position.

As she went to find Selma, she tried to calm herself. Nothing had been done yet that couldn't easily be undone. When it came to it, maybe Selma didn't really want to leave. After all, she was used to Cherryfield now. It was warm and quite comfortable and . . . there was always someone about.

I shall tell her that I'll spend the whole of Christmas Day here with her, she decided. I can bring chocolates, dried fruit, cake, champagne even. She opened the door to Selma's room.

'There you are at last, Amelia. I've been waiting.' Selma sat in bed, a shabby Gucci headscarf tied under her chin, an accusing look on her face. She seemed to be wearing the entire contents of her jewellery case; two gold chains hung round her neck and three sizeable brooches were pinned any how across the chest of her purple cardigan, the gem-stones twinkling amongst the spills and stains.

'I'm all packed,' she said, pointing.

Amelia looked at the small suitcase lying on the chair, bits of material sticking out from under the soft bulging lid, a stocking foot peeking out at one side, then she looked back at Selma. She took a deep breath and, moulding her voice into something cheerful, sensible sounding, she asked, 'Are you sure you wouldn't rather stay here where you are all snug and comfortable?'

Selma's laugh was scathing. 'Of course not. I want to go home.'

'Ah.' Amelia nodded emphatically as if the rhythmic movement could calm her. 'Right.' She picked up the suitcase and a bead necklace dropped out, falling rattling to the floor.

Amelia pushed the wheelchair out from Honeysuckle. She stopped outside the Residents' Lounge. 'Do you want to say goodbye to anyone. I can see Miss White and Mr Ambrose there.'

Sister Morris too was in the Lounge. She looked at the suitcase in Amelia's hand and said, 'Mrs Merryman is going off for the festivities then.' She opened her eyes wide making them round and incensed looking and the loose flesh under her chin trembled.

Christmas time, Amelia thought, and even Sister Morris makes me think of turkey.

'You'll miss all the fun,' chirruped Miss White. 'We've been promised a party.'

Sister Morris's expression softened as if she was hearing the words of a favourite child. 'Indeed you have Miss White, and a very jolly party it will be too.'

Selma had been looking from one speaker to another, her fingers gripping tighter round the arm of her wheelchair. She opened her mouth and a shriek came out. 'I'm not staying here, do you understand? I'm not staying!' Her arms flayed about her as she tried to twist round to see Amelia behind her. 'I'm going home.'

Apart from Miss White who looked up at Sister Morris as if to say, Now there's a naughty girl for you, no-one took any notice but continued to stare at the walls or the turned off television. The carols played on from the tinny sounding tape recorder.

It's like the New York subway here, Amelia thought as she moved in front of the wheelchair; nobody dares to care. She took Selma's hands. 'It's you who decide,' she said in a clear slow voice and, as she spoke, she felt those words were about as important as anything she'd ever said.

'Would you be so good as to stop by my office on your way out.' Sister Morris spoke in the dangerously perky voice of a teacher who has finally given up on a pupil.

'Wait here,' Amelia said unnecessarily to Selma before hurrying off.

Sister Morris handed Amelia a form. 'Sign here please.' She indicated a gap in the print towards the bottom of the page. 'It's to say you accept that Cherryfield carries no responsibility whatsoever for your grandmother whilst she is in your care. Have a nice Christmas, Miss Lindsay.'

Chapter Twenty-five

Many years before, Willoughby's old boxer had come home after a journey to the vet's from which no-one had expected he would return. Lifted out from the back seat of the car, he had limped inside with all the speed he could muster, making straight for his favourite spot on the hearth rug. He had circled it once before lying down and then, with a little wag of his stumpy tail and a sigh of contentment so deep it sent a shudder through his whole body, he closed his eyes and fell asleep.

Some things were the same for people as they were for dogs; coming home after you've had a bad time, when you thought you might never make it, was one of them, Amelia thought as she put another log on the fire. Selma, dozing in her old armchair, stirred and mumbled and, even as she slept, the smile was there at the corners of her mouth together with the froth from the milk she'd been drinking. By her side on the three-tier cake-stand stood her mug with Willoughby's mend running like a black thread through the marmalade fur of the painted cat. Amelia thought Willoughby would be amused to think that his repair had lasted longer than him.

On the drive back to Ashcombe, Amelia had explained to Selma by way of cunning little lies that seemed to spawn ever more intricate deceptions, why she would find her home changed. 'Someone has been living at the house whilst you've been away. Sort of house-sitting. They moved quite a lot of their own things in with them. Their own house got flooded so that seemed the sensible thing to do. Of course the woman is allergic to cats . . . and we haven't quite got it all back to normal yet . . .' Hearing the thinness of her explanation stretched to breaking point, Amelia shot Selma a worried glance as she parked the car by the front door. But Selma just smiled and nodded and said she understood perfectly and Amelia wondered at the need for self-delusion, every bit as strong as the will to live.

'I've made up the chaise-longue for you in the study,' she said now as Selma woke in her chair and smiled hazily at her. 'Just until your leg gets better.'

It was a large room, the study, but it had never been heavily furnished; books, the chaise-longue with an old Chinese screen to partition it off from the rest of the room, Willoughby's old desk by the window, and the room belonged to the Merrymans once more.

Selma was undressed and resting between her own patched and thinning linen sheets. Amelia was about to leave the room when she noticed Selma's lower lip wobbling and the pale brown eyes brimming with tears. Amelia stood, looking at her horrified, like a mother who's carefully picked, beautifully wrapped gift has just been kicked across the room by her darling's sandalled foot.

'What's wrong? Oh dear, whatever is wrong now?' she pleaded, scratching at the small chapped patch on her hand until a tiny, almost transparent, drop of blood appeared.

Selma sniffed and smiled, holding her good left hand out to Amelia. 'Nothing is wrong, darling. I'm just so happy to be back.' She gave Amelia's hand a trembling squeeze and said with a little laugh, 'I know it was silly of me, darling, but I was beginning to think I was never going to come back home.' The tears ran down her cheeks, making snail-trails in the thick powder and her hand shook so hard it was as if she was trying to shake it right off the arm. 'Darling, I was so frightened.'

And I was about to tell her that she'd have to go back to Cherryfield after Christmas; Amelia looked helplessly at Selma who was smiling again. 'Well you're home now, that's all that matters.' Amelia stood up, tucking the sheet in tighter round Selma, raising the pillow a touch. 'Comfortable?'

'Mmm,' Selma's smile glowed. 'Thank you, darling.'

Dagmar thought the call from Amelia strange. 'What do you mean, come and spend Christmas at Ashcombe instead of your place? All right I won't ask questions. I'll be there tomorrow. Twelve o'clock.' Dagmar put the phone down and went to fill the kettle. She was intensely curious as to what Amelia was up to. Who wouldn't be under the circumstances, she thought. The whole thing sounded like an adventure. Dagmar had always felt that she was meant to be quite a different person from how she'd turned out: bright, exciting, like a Renaissance painting before the grime of centuries distorted the intentions of its creator. Someone who would love adventure, that is, if she'd allow herself five consecutive care-free minutes to do so.

So what could Amelia be doing? Dagmar poured herself a cup of tea and curled up in the large armchair by the window, ready for pleasurable contemplation, but her thoughts wouldn't play ball. Since her Little Turn, as she referred to her breakdown, her fear of germs and worms had faded a little, turned soft at the edges. But there had been no respite, because a new enemy had formed out of the anxiety that lurked in the layer just beneath reason: I'm sure there was something I was meant to remember, she would fret, what was it now? She felt she had to catch and hold every thought: amongst the flotsam and jetsam of the mind something of importance might be hiding. Something that, if not dealt with, could cause harm, but the thoughts would drift off, just out of reach, like thoughts will, leaving her scrabbling in the dark.

Now she packed her bag with clothes and parcels, called her neighbour to say she'd be at a different address if anything should happen, wrote the note to cancel the milk, all while she scratched round inside her mind: the bank, maybe that was it? Or was it to do with work? Anyway, how had Amelia got the Hamiltons to let them spend Christmas at Ashcombe? Long red skirt for Christmas Day, red blouse, pine-needle green velvet jacket. She loved Christmas and every year she hoped she might enjoy it.

Christmas Eve morning was mild and misty. Dagmar rang the doorbell at Ashcombe and Amelia opened, snatching her inside. 'Did anyone see you?'

Dagmar looked offended. 'Happy Christmas, Amelia. What do you mean, "Did anyone see me?"?'

Amelia took her into the kitchen and Dagmar wrinkled her nose at the newly installed, leaded, dark oak cupboards that had replaced Selma's white and blue painted ones. 'Ye Olde Yuk,' she said, sitting down.

When Amelia had finished explaining, Dagmar burst out laughing. Then she said, 'How will you get her to go back?'

Amelia was pouring water into Selma's silver coffee pot. 'I don't know.' She put the kettle at the side of the old beige Aga, left from Selma's days, and sat down. She smiled at Dagmar but she kept rubbing her forehead hard with her fingers. 'I don't know,' she said finally. 'I just don't know.'

'But that's no good,' Dagmar said getting up and pouring herself a cup of coffee.

'All right!' Amelia shouted. 'I'll tell more lies, that's how I'll do it. I'll tell lies until I can't tell any more and then I'll have to drag her back and that'll destroy her and Sister Morris will tell me she always knew it would end like that, and you'll say something helpful like "Amelia, that's no good", and bloody Uncle Robert will make a miraculous return to England just in time to tell me I should never have interfered. Of course the only person who won't come back is Henry because he really would be of some use and we can't have anything nice happen now, can we?'

'Now you're being silly,' Dagmar said.

Amelia buried her head in her arms for a short comforting while, inhaling the faint traces of her favourite jasmine scent.

'Sorry,' she said, lifting her head again and smiling across at her mother. 'But at least something Selma wanted to happen is happening. She wanted to spend Christmas at home and now that's what she'll do. That must count for something. It will show her she's not entirely without say in her own life. When you have no control you have no hope. When you have no hope you're better off dead.' She stood up looking at her watch. 'Come and say hello. It's time for her pills anyway.'

It was Christmas Day, and the mist from the day before lay frozen across the lawn, and the sun shone pale and wintry as it should.

'Thank you, God,' Amelia said as she stood by the open window in her old bedroom. 'Can we please go on this way?'

Selma drank her cup of tea in bed, with Amelia and Dagmar sitting at the foot of the chaise-longue. 'I'm afraid I haven't made you up a stocking this year, darling,' Selma said, lifting the cup to her lips and snatching a drink before it came clattering back down on the saucer. 'I don't seem to have had as much time as usual.' She caught an irritated glance from Dagmar and put her hand over her mouth. 'I didn't say something I shouldn't?' Then she laughed. 'Of course I didn't. You've known for ages it was granny.'

Amelia wondered why Lewis Carroll felt he had to use a white rabbit to take Alice into Wonderland; a white-haired grandmother would have been quite sufficient.

At twelve o'clock the doorbell rang. Amelia, kneeling by the oven, basting the turkey, kept down. The bell kept ringing, drilling through the voice of the boy soprano carolling on the radio. Amelia stayed kneeling, knees aching, praying her mother would stay out of sight. There was a pause, then another ring. Amelia reached up with one hand, searching the worktop above her head for her glass of champagne. Feeling her fingers touch the cold crystal she pulled the glass along the surface, lifting it down. She sat back against the cupboard and sipped the wine. Selma never cooked a Christmas lunch without several glasses of champagne to spur her on. 'It's a good way of getting through the less exciting bits of the day,' she used to say. By the time Amelia had finished the glass, the door bell had stopped ringing.

Moments later Dagmar hurried into the kitchen glancing over her shoulder several times. Checking for wolves, Amelia thought.

'Fill up?' Still on the floor she reached up for the bottle.

Dagmar shook her head. 'I've still got some. So has Mummy. I'm sure she shouldn't really have any.' She opened the oven door and glanced absent-mindedly at the sizzling turkey. 'Maybe we should have answered the door. If whoever it was asked, we could have said we'd just popped in on our way from church to make sure everything was all right. Or something.' Her voice rose a little. 'Maybe whoever it was had already seen us and is ringing the police this very moment.'

Amelia looked at her mother and took a long gulp from her glass. Actually, she thought, at this precise moment, Gerald and Clarissa are celebrating Christmas together in my home. My Gerald, my home; all gone.

'You'll get tipsy.' Dagmar raised a pencilled eyebrow.

'I hope so.' Amelia got up from the floor and put the water on for the sprouts.

In the sitting room the white Christmas lights sent a shimmering haze through the baubled branches of the tree, holly twigs rested on the gilded picture frames and a fire burnt in the grate. Amelia had covered the Hamiltons' table with a red cloth embroidered with cross-stitch holly leaves and snowflakes, and set it for three with Selma's blue and gold china.

'I hope you don't mind eating in here,' Amelia had said to Selma. 'But the heating doesn't seem to be working in the dining room.' It was another lie of course.

Selma didn't mind at all. Amelia and Dagmar had helped her dress in a loose-fitting peacock-blue cashmere dress that they had given her that morning, and now she sat, a smile on her face like someone three lines behind in the telling of an amusing anecdote.

'No pad?' Dagmar had hissed after Amelia had placed Selma in the chair.

'No pad,' Amelia had whisped back. 'I want the seat of her dress to touch the seat of her chair with no go-between.'

'Why?' Dagmar had signalled back. Amelia wasn't sure. 'Just a feeling.' She shrugged her shoulders.

When Amelia put a plate of smoked salmon in front of her, Selma looked up with that puzzled look in her eyes again, although she was smiling. 'I've been away you know.' The smile turned shaky. 'I didn't enjoy myself very much at all.' After that she ate with quiet concentration, crumbs of turkey, rivulets of gravy and flakes of sprouts settling in the soft folds of her dress. Dagmar had cut the food in neat little squares on her plate and Selma had made no objections. She had come to accept her reliance on others, that much Cherryfield had done for her.

Amelia had lit candles all across the room: on the coffee table and the card table, in the window-seats of the bay and on top of the chimney-piece. They sat circled by candles while outside the light slowly died.

'Though I say it myself,' Selma said, her cheeks a little pink from the wine and the warmth of the fire, 'it really is a lovely turkey.'

She's happy, Amelia thought. She sits there, an old woman with a rotting leg, dying of at least three separate complaints, and she's happy. And it's all thanks to me. She got up to fetch the Christmas pudding and returned, holding it high over her head to show off the blue-burning flame.

'Bravo the cook!' Selma laughed and clapped as Amelia put the pudding in front of her and they watched as the blue flames sank and drowned in the sugary liquid.

'Don't throw the left-overs away now, will you?' Selma said, nodding at the sticky heap left on the serving plate. 'It will be delicious fried tomorrow.'

Laughing and thinking about tomorrow, Amelia continued saying to herself as she cleared the plates: And it's all my doing.

When they had finished eating, Selma asked Amelia to get her jewellery box. 'It's still in my case I think.' She looked up, explaining, 'I've been away you see.'

Amelia remembered unpacking the small leather case and she fetched it in from the study.

Selma bent low over the box, riffling through its contents. 'I've got some little things for you.'

'But you've already given us some lovely presents.' Amelia gesticulated towards the little heap of things; a couple of books, a scarf, a bottle of scent, lying on the seat by the fire. Gifts from Selma to her and Dagmar that Amelia herself had carefully chosen and wrapped.

'Oh those, that's nothing.' Selma waved her hand dismissively. 'I don't seem to have had much time to do my shopping this Christmas,' she turned to Dagmar, 'but I'd like you to have this, it's from your father's family, from Germany.'

The brooch was shaped like a basket of flowers and set with diamonds and rubies and Dagmar fastened it on to her red blouse. 'It's beautiful. I've always loved it,' and she got up to kiss her mother.

Selma gave Amelia a jade bracelet and lastly she brought out a large signet ring. 'It was Willoughby's. You remember it don't you, darling? Robert has got his grandfather's, so I'd like your young man to have this. It should be worn. It's no use lying here in this box.'

Amelia glanced across the table at Dagmar. They both wondered which young man it was that Selma was thinking of.

'Come on darling, take it,' Selma prompted. So Amelia took it and thanked her. 'That's wonderful, he'll be thrilled.'

Selma looked pleased. 'You didn't think I had forgotten your presents now, did you?' she said and then she added, 'I don't think I've had a proper look at my cards.'

Amelia tried to avoid her eyes. 'No,' she said weakly, 'nor you have.'

Selma turned her head to the chimney-piece, then back to Amelia. 'In fact I can't even remember opening them. Aren't I silly?'

Not really, Amelia thought, seeing that I put them there straight from the packets just before you came.

'So darling, could you take them down for me?' A touch of impatience had crept into Selma's voice. 'I don't seem to be able to get up as easily as I normally do. Too much good food I expect.'

'Shall I crack a nut for you?' Dagmar asked, reaching for the bowl that she had made in woodwork when she was nine.

Selma ignored her and kept on looking keenly at the row of cards. With a deep sigh she couldn't help, Amelia got up from the table and picked out a winter scene in a Dickensian Trafalgar Square. She had thought carefully before buying it as it had cost over a pound just for the one.

'I'll read it, shall I?' she said. 'It's rather dim in here and I don't know where you put your glasses.' Selma didn't object, so she began, reeling off polite, Christmassy phrases of good cheer and well wishes, recalling the names of Selma and Willoughby's friends, as she went along. '. . . all the best, Gordon and Sheila.'

Selma had smiled and nodded at each familiar name but now she looked up with a frown. 'Gordon's dead.'

Amelia felt like a captain of a ship illicitly slipping anchor under the protection of fog only to find beams of sunlight breaking through, scattering the mist and making his deception clear to the world.

'Sheila, she must have signed automatically for both of them, it happens, I hear,' she added weakly.

'Not from the grave it doesn't,' Selma said. 'Poor Gordon was a widower for years.'

Amelia was tired. And why, she thought viciously, is it that your memory gets busy only when it's not wanted?

'Are you sure you don't want me to prepare a pecan for you? They're lovely.' Dagmar insisted.

'And here's one from the Hammonds,' Amelia exclaimed, waving a glossy, gold-edged card at Selma. The Hammonds were definitely not dead, she'd seen them in the supermarket only the other morning. But Selma had lost interest by now. The colour had gone from her cheeks, turning them the shade of unbleached writing paper, and her eyelids kept closing. Dagmar got up and began clearing the discarded wrappings from the floor. She was about to drop a shiny green sheet into the fire when Selma put out her hand and said, 'Don't darling. It'll do for next year,' and she took the paper and placed it across her chubby knees, carefully smoothing the creases with trembling fingers.

By eight o'clock she lay in bed smiling at Amelia like a contented child. 'I've had a lovely day.' Then she frowned. 'But where did your young man get to? I'm sure you said he was coming.'

Amelia kissed her lightly on the cheek. 'He had to work over Christmas,' she said. 'He was terribly disappointed.' But Selma had gone to sleep.

Amelia looked down at her for a long time, then with a shudder she turned away. I was willing her to die, she thought. I was standing here thinking it would be just perfect if she never woke up.

She looked up to see her mother in the doorway. As they walked from the room Dagmar whispered, 'It would be kinder all round if she just died.'

Amelia looked at her with a small smile. Then she said, 'I can't help wondering why what is right and what is kind so often seem to be quite different things?'

Chapter Twenty-six

Of course Selma did wake the next morning, and the morning after and each day she seemed to grow stronger. It was as if with every touch of a familiar surface, every feel of her lips round the rim of her own china cups, each sight of the trees and shrubs outside, life seeped back into her.

'We'll have to ask these people to move their things out now I'm back,' she said as Amelia brought her breakfast on the fourth day. 'I still don't quite see why they had it all moved here in the first place.'

When Amelia told Dagmar she rolled her eyes and sighed, 'I told you you hadn't thought this through. We're meant to take her back tomorrow and she still believes the place is hers and that she's back for keeps.'

'You go back to Exeter as planned,' Amelia said. 'We might stay on a day or two. The Hamiltons aren't back for another ten days.'

'It's not going to get any easier telling her,' Dagmar warned.

'I don't expect it will, but each good day when you have only a hundred or so left, is a gift.' Amelia improvised the answer and ended up quite pleased with it.

So Dagmar left and Amelia was alone at Ashcombe with Selma. That was the problem, she was alone. Selma's new lease of life had been as brief as a Swedish summer, and now, once more, the dark and muddled moments of her mind grew longer. She slept so much that Amelia became worried. Was it good for her to doze away large chunks of the day? Should she be stimulated like an overdoser, kept awake and aware? There was no-one to ask. She telephoned Dagmar every day but Dagmar's only advice was 'Take her back.'

She wrote to Henry. She imagined herself talking to him, she asked his opinion and got so carried away at times, sitting in the window-seat chatting to him, that she felt quite let down when she paused and there was no answer.

Sometimes, when she walked through the silent house, she imagined it floating in space, as whole and separate as a planet. She ventured out into the garden only after dark and she realized that if no-one knew about you, you had only your own word that you actually existed. Other times though, in the early morning or when evening fell so depressingly early at four o'clock, her thoughts would race like crazy horses through her mind; discovery, newspaper reporters, prison. She wished she hadn't left Willoughby's law books in storage, they would have told her if trespassing was a tort or a criminal offence. Surely she couldn't be charged with theft; even the brandy on the Christmas pudding had been her own. But what about electricity and gas? One early morning she lay in bed wriggling and sighing until she thought her chest would split open, releasing this great putrid stream of worries.

There was a poverty of light too over the days between Christmas and New Year. Each morning Amelia pulled the curtains back as far as they would go but still there was an air of evening about the house any hour of the day.

'Those hedges need clipping,' Selma said one morning when Amelia brought her breakfast. 'I'll have a word with Mr Edwards in the New Year.' Amelia thought her grandmother's voice sounded faint, as if the words were spoken from a much greater distance than halfway across a small room.

'I'm not doing as good a job of looking after you as they do at Cherryfield,' she said, 'and I'm late with your pills again.'

'I hate pills. My father died because of the wretched things. Too many and none of them agreeing with the others.' She smiled weakly and held her hand out to Amelia who had to grab it quickly before it fell back on to the sheets. 'There's nothing much wrong with me you know. Nothing a few days' rest here in my own home, with my little granddaughter to look after me, won't cure.' She shifted in the bed, trying to reach the tray at her side.

'Anyway,' she said dropping a piece of buttered toast on to her chest, 'wild horses wouldn't drag me back to that awful place. You know I hated boarding school as a girl.' She closed her eyes and mumbled, 'Hated it.'

Amelia heaved herself up from the foot of the chaise-longue as if she was fighting her way up from under a mountain of rubble. I'll tell her tomorrow. She sighed. I'll get everything packed and ready and then just tell her and go, leave her no time to argue or worry.

The next morning was New Year's Eve and Amelia had to shake Selma gently by the shoulder to wake her. Even then, she opened her eyes only to smile and close them again, and her breathing was quick and shallow. Amelia stood looking at her and as she looked she grew more and more scared. She was like a whist player from the village hall caught up in a game of poker in Las Vegas: out of her league. Pale faced, she turned and ran to the phone, dialling the number of the health centre.

Putting her stethoscope away, Dr Donaldson turned

a grave face to Amelia, beckoning her away from the chaise-longue where Selma lay drifting between sleep and waking.

'She's very poorly I'm afraid, not really responding to the medication. Her blood pressure is right up, as for her leg ...' Again she shook her head. 'I'd like to consult with her own doctor but he's not on again until the second.' She looked up from her notes. 'We've got her registered as living at Cherryfield Nursing Home though.' She glanced at Selma. 'I really think she would be better off there now. When were you planning to take her back?'

'A week ago, but she fears and dreads that place.' Amelia felt the lump in her throat swelling. 'How long has she got?'

Dr Donaldson, like Sister Morris, shrugged her shoulders. 'It's impossible to say, days, weeks, maybe more.'

Well, we've only got five days, Amelia thought, close to tears. Five days for Selma to die in peace. She gave her grandmother a long look, then she turned away and followed Dr Donaldson into the sitting room.

'Which are the vital pills, the ones she couldn't do without? I mean maybe she's taking too many.'

Dr Donaldson looked at her. 'They're all vital in keeping her alive, all but the painkillers of course.' Then she looked around her. 'I thought the Hamiltons lived here.'

'They do,' Amelia assured her. 'But they're completely neurotic about burglars, so I'm house-sitting. I had to bring my grandmother with me.'

Dr Donaldson seemed satisfied with the answer. 'How long before the Hamiltons come back?'

'A couple of days or so,' Amelia was deliberately evasive. 'You couldn't spare a commode, could you? It's my back.'

'If you're quite sure your grandmother prefers staying with you here, I'll send the community nurse along twice a day and I'll try to come myself at the end of each morning surgery. We won't be able to keep it up for ever though. I'll see about the commode, they might be able to lend us one from the Cottage Hospital.'

The nurse came that evening. She helped wash Selma, checked her blood pressure and changed the dressing on her leg.

'I'd like to get up today,' Selma said on the second day of the nurse's visits. 'I'm feeling much better.'

They dressed her in a warm, emerald-green housecoat and lifted her into the wheelchair. She winced as her leg touched the side of the chaise-longue but she didn't complain, instead she said, 'I'm afraid I haven't been able to do as much of the cooking as I usually do this Christmas. My little granddaughter has managed beautifully though.' She tried to turn to give Amelia an encouraging smile.

When she left, the nurse said to Amelia, 'You soldier on if you can, dear. Allow them to die in their own place, that's what I always say.'

'When do you think it will be, this dying?' Amelia caught the nurse's surprised look and gave a little apologetic shrug. 'What I mean is, I'd like to be prepared.'

The nurse's brow cleared. 'Of course you do. But who's to say? But you'll find the strength when the time comes, don't you worry.'

Amelia didn't want her to go; all that cheerful competence, all that approval, the whiff of the real world where young women of thirty-one did not break into people's houses to spend Christmas with their dying grandmother. She lingered in the doorway, watching the nurse stride off towards her car and, as the little red mini drove off, she felt as if her own sanity had gone with the nurse, riding away cheerfully in the passenger seat. 'Wear a seat-belt,' she murmured. 'I might need you again.'

She was in the kitchen the next morning, preparing Selma's milky coffee when she heard the front door slam shut. It was too early for the nurse and anyway she didn't have a key. Automatically Amelia had sunk her knuckle into the milk to test the temperature and now as she heard footsteps in the passage she stayed that way, staring at the door. The steps hesitated then stopped, the door was pushed open and a long pale face peered round. 'Oh my Gawd,' it said as it caught sight of Amelia. 'Who would you be?'

Amelia remembered that attack was the smartest way of defence and said, 'May I ask who you are?' Adding truthfully, 'We weren't expecting anyone.'

The woman had obviously decided that if Amelia was dangerous she would by now have put down the coffee cup and picked up a knife, so she stepped inside but remained close to the open door just in case. 'I'm Mrs Clover. I do for Mrs Hamilton every Tuesday and Thursday.' She crossed her thin arms over the smooth tongue of her flower-sprigged apron. 'This is Tuesday.'

'Well don't let me stop you,' Amelia said. 'With the Hamiltons returning Sunday, I'm sure you've got lots to do. I've hoovered the sitting room by the way.' And she made for the door, her heart thumping so hard she felt sure Mrs Clover could hear it.

Mrs Clover barred her way, braver now. 'Mrs Hamilton said nothing to me about someone staying in her house.'

'That was remiss of her.' Amelia shook her head. 'One likes to be told about these things I know. I'm Mr and Mrs Merryman's granddaughter, Amelia Lindsay. My grandparents used to live here and the Hamiltons asked me to house-sit. Are you sure they didn't tell you?' she asked sympathetically.

'They most certainly did not.' Mrs Clover looked aggrieved, then her thin face softened. 'I remember Mr and Mrs Merryman. I used to do for friends of theirs, the Franklins. I thought the old couple passed away.'

'Not quite,' Amelia said bitterly. 'Now I mustn't keep you from your work. By the way, the study is best left for now I think.' She slid past and out of the door.

Selma had gone to sleep again in her chair in the sitting room, so Amelia went upstairs to the bedroom to fetch her writing case. 'I need you Henry Mallett,' she said to herself as she hurried back down to Selma. 'A chaplain would do wonders for my credibility just now.'

She sat down in the window-seat and began to write: 'My Dear Henry, Wish you were here.'

She paused, chewing the cap of her pen, listening to the sound of the vacuum cleaner coming closer.

'There's something going on here.' Mrs Clover appeared dragging the hoover behind her. 'Look at this place. It's different.'

'My grandmother is asleep.'

Mrs Clover glanced in Selma's direction, then lowered her voice to a hiss. 'I'm calling the Hamiltons. I've got their number in case of burglary or fire.'

'Well this is neither,' Amelia said in a tired voice, 'so why worry them?'

Selma snored and shuddered, her head lolling against the wing of the chair, her mouth hanging open. Her face looked so small and her skin was grey. The grey of a corpse on a mortuary slab before the undertaker had got to work with colour and brushes, Amelia thought with a shiver.

'Please don't call.' She looked intently at Mrs Clover, as if she hoped pity was catching. 'Please. We'll be gone by Saturday.'

Mrs Clover's eyes narrowed. 'You're squatters, that's what you are. I should call the police, really I should.' And as Amelia stood up and moved towards her she fled from the room.

Amelia sat down again and buried her head in her hands. Soon they'd come and take Selma from her beloved Ashcombe, drag her from her chair, away from the view over the garden and the sea. Drag her back to Cherryfield to die with all her hopes gone and her illusions shattered.

'They know who you are.' Mrs Clover was back, speaking to Amelia from the doorway ready to retreat again. 'They said to tell you to leave immediately and they'll deal with you when they return. Lucky for you they don't want the police. Not at the moment they don't.'

Amelia lifted her head and looked at her. 'We're staying.' There, she thought, I've done it. As she got up from the seat, Mrs Clover took a step backwards and when she saw Amelia come towards her she turned and ran. Amelia heard a clanging noise, then a yell and as she hurried out into the hall she almost tripped over Mrs Clover lying prostrate on the floor her right foot tangled in the flex of the hoover.

'Here.' Amelia put her hand out.

Looking as if she knew she was going to regret it any moment, Mrs Clover allowed herself to be helped up.

'I'm quite harmless really.' Amelia smiled at her. 'But we're not leaving.' It all seemed quite simple now, simpler by far than taking Selma back to Cherryfield.

Mrs Clover shrugged her shoulders. 'Suit yourself, but I'm not stopping here a minute longer, not with a criminal in the house.'

'That's fine,' Amelia said tiredly. 'I'll finish the vacuuming.'

Chapter Twenty-seven

Outside, the sky was an unbroken dome of grey, allowing night to creep up with such stealth, Amelia thought. Selma had drunk some broth and now she sat in bed propped up against the pillows. She held on to Amelia's hand and didn't want to let go, so Amelia stayed and talked, their conversation weaving in and out of Selma's memories like a needle and thread.

'Of course you never knew your grandfather,' Selma said suddenly and in a clear strong voice. 'He died in Germany you know, before the war.'

'I'd love to know more about him,' Amelia said, realizing that for the first time she meant it. But Selma had gone back to sleep.

The nurse, her name was Mary she told Amelia, stood looking at Selma. She was smiling. 'I wish all my old people could go like her, in their own place with a relative to care for them.'

Amelia was smiling too. It doesn't matter a bit that it's all an illusion, she thought. Selma believed she was in her own home, the lady of the house with tomorrow to plan for, and not a helpless inmate of a nursing home where tomorrow seemed more like a surcharge than a bonus. Mary certainly didn't know any different, so perhaps illusion had turned into reality. Amelia waited as the nurse took Selma's blood pressure and checked the dressing on her leg. Wasn't a well-maintained, oiled and running illusion a must for a happy life? If we all saw ourselves and others and life itself for what it truly was, would any of us have the heart to carry on?

She realized that Mary was speaking to her.

'Her heart is remarkably strong, she could go on for weeks you know. Will you be able to cope? Isn't there someone else who could come and stay with you for a bit?'

Amelia shook her head. 'Weeks did you say?'

'It could be, then again she could go at any time. But she's not suffering. She's quite contented, isn't she?' Mary looked up at Amelia, her round face all smiles and approval, but Amelia returned to the study near to tears.

'If you're going to die, do it now please,' she whispered between clenched teeth. 'I'm like a juggler adding the last plate to an impossible number already spinning over my head, I've peaked. Any more and it'll all come tumbling down, crash, crash, crash,' she mumbled, banging her fist against her forehead. Selma snorted and turned over in her sleep, a small smile passing her lips.

Amelia telephoned her mother.

'You're still there,' Dagmar said. 'I was just about to call Cherryfield to see how Mummy's settled back in. You really must take her back immediately. I can't take any more of this worrying.' She sounded affronted, as if Selma's continued stay at Ashcombe was a deliberate attack on her nervous system. 'You know I'm sure there was something absolutely vital I had to tell you but I just can't remember . . . Anyway, I've said what I think, now I wash my hands of you, Amelia, I really do.'

'Ho, ho, ho,' Amelia said and Dagmar hung up.

A neighbour came to the door; Mr Squire who knew Amelia from the Merrymans' days at the house. 'Mrs Clover's told us you're squatting or something.' Mr

Squire, tall and stooping, scratched his bald patch. 'It's not really the sort of thing we go in for around here you know.' He looked unhappily at a point to the left of Amelia's ear.

Amelia stood in the doorway saying nothing. I'll smile him away, she thought.

Mr Squire looked disturbed. 'Ah well, I suppose it's between you and the Hamiltons,' and he left. Amelia went back to the study and continued reading *Emma* to Selma who knew the book so well she could drift off comfortably at any point in the story and come back as if she'd never been away.

The night before the Hamiltons' return, Amelia stayed all night in a chair in the study watching over Selma, listening to her breaths that came as quick and light as a runner's steps. She had opened the window, letting in an icy wind from the sea, but Selma was warm, covered up with several blankets. Amelia felt she knew somehow that when you were dying you didn't want silence and sterility but air and movement, smells of flowers and of cooking, voices and music; all the sounds and sights of life as long as you were still a part of it.

Earlier in the day, when Dr Donaldson had told Amelia it was unlikely that Selma would get up again, she had tidied away the Christmas decorations and loaded the van with Selma's furniture. She had taken the sheets off the bed in her old room and put them on the chair in the study. All the china except a cup and saucer and plate was boxed up and back in the van. Only the study she left as it was.

Now she stretched and yawned in her chair and, leaning across the chaise-longue, pulled the covers up higher across Selma's shoulders. She was about to open the writing case to continue her letter to Henry, when she paused and got her handbag instead. In the small zipped compartment was Henry's locket; she picked it up and, looking at it for a moment, hung it round her neck. With a little sigh she sat back and started to write:

'Selma is dying and, loving her as I do, I wish you'd tell me what the purpose is of making it such a drawn-out affair. Soon I'll find out if the Hamiltons are prepared to drag a dying woman from her bed. Life that once seemed quite a decent length now appears pitifully short. She lies there, her breathing is so quick and shallow, her time here almost up. I bet it didn't seem much more than a moment to her. I don't suppose it ever does.

'If I escape the consequences of my actions, which I very much hope I will, I don't think I shall stay in Kingsmouth, not once Selma is gone. I don't expect I'd be very welcome either. I'll probably go back to London and find a job. I suppose down here I have actually done something at last. I've taken action. I've lied and cheated and broken into a house, and do you know, for the first time in my life I feel proud of myself. I remember saying to you once that there was no such thing as a happy ending in life, no such thing as a happy death. Well maybe I was wrong. Maybe Selma is having a happy death, or as near to it as one can get, and I've had something to do with it.

'. . . I enclose my grandfather's signet ring; I would like to think of you wearing it, and so would Selma. It's really a present from her.

'. . . As I write, I can feel your locket against my skin. Keep safe Henry, I pray each night that there will not be a war . . .'

Selma stirred and mumbled. Amelia put her pen down and went up to the window, parting the curtains to let in the morning light. Then she went in to the kitchen and made a pot of tea and buttered some white bread. There was no more of their food left in the freezer now and only one pint of long-life milk. She carried the tray back into the study and put it down on the table by the chaise-longue. A little later Selma opened her eyes and tried to sit up. As her head fell back against the pillow she whispered, 'Could you do meals on wheels for me today, darling? I don't think I'm feeling terribly well.'

It was eight o'clock and Amelia wandered out into the garden. Two camelias, one red, one pink, grew against the south-facing wall at the back. The pink one was already flowering; un-English, un-blushing pink against lush green leaves. She picked a few blooms and brought them inside for Selma, placing them close to her.

At ten, Selma woke and drank a little warm milk from the flask Amelia had made up. 'I must tell Willoughby the camelias are out already,' she said.

Soon after that the front door opened and slammed shut.

'And what, Miss Lindsay, is your grandmother still doing on my settee?' Doreen Hamilton, wrapped in a white mohair coat, stood in the study doorway framed by light from the sitting-room bay, her bleached hair streaked further by a tropical sun, her turquoise eyes, fringed by mascara'd lashes stiff and furry as flies' legs.

Amelia got up from Selma's bedside and pulled the screen closer. Then she walked across the room to Doreen. 'She's still dying,' she said in a quiet voice, 'and the chaise-longue is hers. If you make her leave you'll most probably speed up the process: I believe lost hope and a broken heart are tried and tested killers.' She forced herself to stay calm in the face of

281

the image of Selma being taken back, confused and terrified, to Cherryfield, of her whispering, 'My mother died in a place like this.'

'She's dying, did you say?' Doreen hissed. Nudged by Amelia she backed out of the room and turned to her husband who had appeared behind her, only his round sleek head visible above the huge collar of his sheepskin coat.

'Desmond, Mrs Merryman is dying in our study and it's not even acute.'

'I'll phone the nursing home.' Desmond Hamilton glared at Amelia. 'And the police.'

'No!' Amelia ran past him and yanked the phone from its socket.

'What the hell do you think you are doing?' He strode out to the hall where the second telephone stood.

'It wouldn't look good in the paper,' Amelia called out after him. '"Local property developer hurls dying woman on to street".'

Desmond Hamilton's head appeared around the door.

'I'm not hurling your grandmother anywhere. I'm getting her back to the nursing home where she belongs.'

For a moment Amelia did nothing, feeling her will to fight dissolve; what Desmond had just said was so reasonable. Then she thought of Selma, dying so contentedly in the study of her beloved Ashcombe. Would she cry and beg? She'd be so frightened. With a little sob, Amelia rushed past Doreen and into the study, locking the door behind her. Panting she ran up to the window and shut it, sliding the double-glazing pane across. She stood there for a moment looking out at the garden where the mist was breaking up reveal- ing the familiar shapes of shrubs and trees. Her heartbeat slowed down and she began to breath normally.

'Hello darling.' Selma had opened her eyes and was smiling at her. 'Is it morning already?' She put her hand out, tipping over one of the medicine bottles on the small table by her side.

Amelia automatically checked the time on her watch; it was about time for the first lot of pills of the day. She stayed sitting down, resting her head against the back of the chair, closing her eyes. The pills could wait a minute or two. When she opened her eyes a short while later, Selma was sleeping again, and she could hear murmuring voices from the other room. There was a knock on the door making her jump. With a glance at Selma she hurried across the room up to the door.

'Yes?'

'Miss Lindsay, Amelia,' the voice was coaxing. 'It's Doreen here. We've called the nursing home and spoken to the Matron and they're sending transport, so you might as well open the door.'

Amelia began to cry, fat salty tears rolled down her cheeks. What could she do now? What could she do to stop Selma's poor old body, barely able to contain her soul, from being stretchered off to Cherryfield where a suitable dying, a well-ordered, well-mannered and, above all else, legal dying was being arranged?

'Just give us a moment, will you Doreen?' Her voice broke. 'Please.'

There was silence, then Doreen's voice again, measured and reasonable. 'Very well then, Amelia, five more minutes but then you'll have to open the door.'

Five minutes passed and then five more. Amelia stopped crying and put some music on. She sat down by Selma, watching her, listening to the two violins making love to each other. She put her hand in her pocket and traced the outline of the signet ring that lay with the letter, waiting to be sent to Henry. There was another knock on the door.

'Desmond says they'll be here any minute now.'

Amelia didn't answer and miraculously, so that Amelia began to believe miracles really happened, nothing was heard for a good half hour other than the music and the wind blowing through the chimney.

Then: 'Miss Lindsay, there's someone to see you.' Doreen, on the other side of the door, sounded inviting.

'Leave us alone, please.'

'Miss Lindsay, this is Sister Morris. I think you're not quite yourself. You'd better let us in, your grandmother needs professional care.'

Exhausted, Amelia went up close to the door. In a quiet, even voice she said, 'You're right, I'm not myself and I'm all the better for it and if you don't stop bothering us I will kill her. Now, will you please GO AWAY?'

As she waited, Amelia was pleased that she had made a store of sandwiches and drinks. She ate some at lunchtime, but she cried when she couldn't get Selma even to drink.

'Miss Lindsay,' again a voice beckoned her to the door. 'It's Dr Donaldson here. Sister Morris from Cherryfield has left now. I told her that there was no overwhelming medical reason for your grandmother to go back.'

'Desmond will call the police, I'm warning you.' That was Doreen.

'So I'm afraid you've got to sort out your differences with the Hamiltons, Miss Lindsay.' Dr Donaldson spoke again. 'I'll be back in a little while, if you're still here. In the meantime please check your grandmother's dressing and make sure she's not in pain.'

Again, Amelia heard nothing from the Hamiltons for a while and she managed to put clean dry sheets on Selma's chaise-longue. Changing the sheet with Selma on top wasn't easy, but Selma woke for a moment and helped by easing up her legs and shoulders. She smiled weakly at Amelia. 'I'll be better tomorrow, you'll see, darling.' Then she closed her eyes and fell back into a deep sleep.

Amelia needed a pee and, checking to see there was no-one in the garden, she opened the window, climbed out and hurried along the wall of the house to the shrubbery on the corner. Coming back again, locking the window behind her, she heard Doreen calling.

'Amelia, have you come to your senses yet? We don't want a scene.'

'Can't you think of us as guests?' Amelia pleaded, pressing her face to the small crack in the door. 'You've got the whole rest of the house and it's not as if we're complete strangers.'

'You're not guests, you're squatters or house-breakers, or whatever. Anyway, my guests don't come here to die.'

Amelia started to laugh. She laughed so much that Doreen had to shout at her to stop. Selma mumbled something Amelia couldn't make out, but she didn't wake.

Then it wasn't long before she saw Desmond Hamilton's face at the window. He looked grey and unfocused in the dusk and he mouthed something, holding up a piece of paper for her to read: 'You have until 7.00 a.m. to think things over. Then we call the police.' His sleek head nodded emphatically and disappeared into the darkness. Amelia settled down to wait.

'Has she eaten?' Dr Donaldson asked through the door some hours later. 'And what about you? Have you had anything?'

'She had a teaspoon of broth a little while ago.' Amelia's voice broke. 'I can't get any more down her. She sleeps the whole time, it's such a deep sleep.'

'It's all right.' Dr Donaldson's voice was calm, soothing like calamine lotion. 'Try her with some water and make sure you have some of that broth yourself. Has she had her pills?'

'I missed this morning's lot . . . I tried a while ago but I could only get her to take the white one, you know the one for her blood pressure, and the black and yellow capsule. She doesn't seem to be in any pain.'

'That's not so bad then. Try to sleep. And Miss Lindsay, they do intend to get you out tomorrow, one way or the other. I'm sorry.'

Amelia sat on the floor, her back against the side of the chaise-longue and her fingers clasping the locket round her neck. Now and then she would doze off only to wake with a start, her mouth dry and her heart pounding.

It was six o'clock when she got up, stiff-legged and aching, to open the window. She leant out, feeling the cold morning air on her face. As she turned around her gaze fell on the soft pillow supporting Selma's head; already Selma's breath was as fragile as a glass thread, it wouldn't take much, a quick movement, the slightest of pressure and the flow would be cut. Amelia walked across the room with little quick steps, up to the chaise-longue, putting her hands on the pillow. She stayed there looking at her grandmother, then she closed her eyes as if she was standing at the edge of a cliff, preparing to leap into the cold clear sea below. When she opened her eyes again she found Selma looking back at her.

'Is that you, darling?' Selma's voice sounded as if it came from a long way away. 'Darling, are you there?' Her voice was a little anxious now and Amelia knew she could be addressing any number of her darlings: Daniel, Dagmar, Willoughby, Robert, or Amelia herself, it didn't matter whom really, as long as one of them, one of those people that belonged to her, was there.

With a little sigh she bent down and kissed Selma's cheek, it felt papery and hot against her lips.

'It's time for your pills,' she said, 'time for your pills.' She stretched across the pillow and reached for the first of the bottles, shaking out two small red capsules into her sticky palm.

Selma opened her eyes wide. Raising herself from the pillow she looked straight at Amelia and whispered, 'Bugger the pills.' She slumped back and, with a little frown, she died.

Slowly a tear appeared in Amelia's eyes, then another. She kneeled by the bed and put her arms round Selma, holding her for a while then, when she heard the sound of a car on the gravel, she got up and unlocked the door.

THE END

A SELECTION OF FINE WRITING
FROM BLACK SWAN

☐	99198 8	THE HOUSE OF THE SPIRITS	Isabel Allende	£6.99
☐	99313 1	OF LOVE AND SHADOWS	Isabel Allende	£6.99
☐	99248 8	THE DONE THING	Patricia Angadi	£4.99
☐	99201 1	THE GOVERNESS	Patricia Angadi	£3.99
☐	99322 0	THE HIGHLY FLAVOURED LADIES	Patricia Angadi	£3.99
☐	92464 2	PLAYING FOR REAL	Patricia Angadi	£4.99
☐	99385 9	SINS OF THE MOTHERS	Patricia Angadi	£3.99
☐	99489 8	TURNING THE TURTLE	Patricia Angadi	£5.99
☐	99459 6	SHINING AGNES	Sara Banerji	£4.99
☐	99498 7	ABSOLUTE HUSH	Sara Banerji	£4.99
☐	99467 7	MONSIEUR DE BRILLANCOURT	Clare Harkness	£4.99
☐	99387 5	TIME OF GRACE	Clare Harkness	£5.99
☐	99483 9	ZIG ZAG	Lucy Robertson	£4.99
☐	99460 X	THE FIFTH SUMMER	Titia Sutherland	£4.99
☐	99529 0	OUT OF THE SHADOWS	Titia Sutherland	£5.99
☐	99056 6	BROTHER OF THE MORE FAMOUS JACK	Barbara Trapido	£5.99
☐	99130 9	NOAH'S ARK	Barbara Trapido	£5.99
☐	99494 4	THE CHOIR	Joanna Trollope	£5.99
☐	99442 1	A PASSIONATE MAN	Joanna Trollope	£5.99
☐	99470 7	THE RECTOR'S WIFE	Joanna Trollope	£5.99
☐	99410 3	A VILLAGE AFFAIR	Joanna Trollope	£5.99
☐	99126 0	THE CAMOMILE LAWN	Mary Wesley	£5.99
☐	99495 2	A DUBIOUS LEGACY	Mary Wesley	£5.99
☐	99548 7	HARNESSING PEACOCKS	Mary Wesley	£5.99
☐	99082 5	JUMPING THE QUEUE	Mary Wesley	£5.99
☐	09304 2	NOT THAT SORT OF GIRL	Mary Wesley	£5.99
☐	99355 7	SECOND FIDDLE	Mary Wesley	£5.99
☐	99393 X	A SENSIBLE LIFE	Mary Wesley	£5.99
☐	99258 5	THE VACILLATIONS OF POPPY CAREW	Mary Wesley	£5.99

HOME

HOME

Manju Kapur

ff

faber and faber

First published in 2006
by Faber and Faber Limited
Bloomsbury House 74–77 Great Russell Street,
London WC1B 3DA
This paperback edition first published in 2010

Typeset by Faber and Faber Limited
Printed in England by CPI Bookmarque, Croydon

A CIP record for this book
is available from the British Library

ISBN 978–0–571–6065–2

2 4 6 8 10 9 7 5 3

Manju Kapur lives in New Delhi, where she is a teacher of English Literature at Miranda House College, Delhi University.

Her first novel, *Difficult Daughters* (1998), received tremendous international acclaim, won the Commonwealth Prize for First Novels (Eurasia Section) and was a number one bestseller in India. *A Married Woman* (2003), her second book, was praised as 'fluent and witty' by the *Independent*. Writing about her fourth novel, *The Immigrant*, the *Guardian* praised Kapur's 'non-commonplace gift for writing about commonplace people.' Her latest novel is *Custody*.

Further praise for *Home*

Number One Bestseller in India

'Manju Kapur creates a novel full of bright spaces and dark corners; her telling is brisk, unsentimental, and capable of turning domestic drama into suspense . . . Darkness underlies the chatty brightness of this very enjoyable novel's surface.' Aamer Hussein, *Independent*

'As its title suggests, *Home* is partly about where you live, but also about where you belong. Its detailed evocation of the quotidian is skilfully balanced with the faint glimpses it provides of another sort of life altogether.' Peter Parker, *Times Literary Supplement*

For

Amba

Maya, Katyayani, Agastya

&

Nidhi

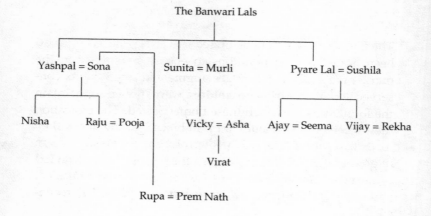

Joint family

The Banwari Lal family belonged to a class whose skills had been honed over generations to ensure prosperity in the market-place. Their marriages augmented, their habits conserved. From an early age children were trained to maintain the foundation on which these homes rested. The education they received, the values they imbibed, the alliances they made had everything to do with protecting the steady stream of gold and silver that burnished their lives. Those who fell against the grain found in their homes knives that wounded, and once the damage had been done, gestures that reconciled.

I

Sisters

Mrs Sona Lal and Mrs Rupa Gupta, sisters both, were child-less. One was rich, the other poor, one the eldest daughter-in-law of a cloth-shop owner, the other the wife of an educated, badly paid government servant.

They lived with their in-laws in the same neighbourhood in Karol Bagh. They met frequently, allowing each husband ample opportunity to justify his secret contempt for his wife's relatives, while each sister reinforced her belief that the other's problem was light in comparison to her own.

Rupa, the younger one, had difficulties that are easily nar-rated. She was fortunate in that she only had a father-in-law to look after; in her case, the thorn in her life came from the wicked tenant upstairs, a man skilled in making the couple's life miserable. He was a lawyer, who refused to pay his mea-gre rent on time, and who was protected against eviction by unfair, tenant-favouring laws. The family was fighting him in court, but instead of getting justice, the lawyer, who repre-sented himself, was successful in using legal tactics to delay hearings and continue the status quo. They knew his goal was to torture them into believing the only way they could achieve peace was to sell him their home at distress rates.

The educated, badly paid government servant had to spend much time and money, blood and sweat, on this case. Rupa frequently remarked to her sister, while spending the day, 'We are cursed, Didi, what to do? It is our fate. Perhaps it is just as well we don't have children, that man will trouble us life after life.'

It was all very well for Rupa to be complacent, thought Sona bitterly. She had her own cross to bear, and she thought Rupa's troubles insignificant. What was some nuisancemongering tenant, who ultimately would be got rid of, compared to relatives, attached for life? Rupa was supremely lucky, she only had her husband and father-in-law to deal with. She was not subjected to sneers and taunts, she was not the only barren woman amongst myriad sisters-in-law whose wombs were bursting with perpetual pride. She didn't have to dandle a thousand babies on her lap, coo over them, pretend to love them, while the ache in her empty heart and belly increased day by day.

Unlike Rupa, whose marriage had been arranged, the history of Sona's courtship did much to intensify her misery.

Sona first entered the Banwari Lal Cloth Shop on a hot morning during the marriage season in May 1965. She was seventeen, in her last year of school, and had come from Meerut with her mother and sister to attend an uncle's wedding. It was necessary for marriageable girls to blossom during such occasions, it being likely that among the guests a boy, or better still his parent, would cast a glance and hold it steadily upon her person. Then it was hoped subsequent enquiries would yield results.

With this in mind, the mother was shopping in Karol Bagh, determined that her daughters should look their best for every function. The Banwari Lal Cloth Shop, they were told, provided tailors who could stitch blouses in a day, with free dyeing thrown in. Sona's mother was at that moment trying to stretch the free service to its limits. Her own old blouses she had already altered for her daughters, now for the price of one little cloth piece, she wished them dyed to match the saris she was showing the young attendant.

He was patiently explaining the service, one free dyeing per blouse material bought, when Sona, blushing, looked up and smiled appealingly. The shade card the young man was holding persuasively against the mother's saris drooped. Confusion overtook him as he fell in love, and contemplated a future with this beauty by his side.

3

He flung the card away, and picked up the old blouses. Yes, of course, he could get them dyed and sent to her house in one day, and in order to secure a client's good will, dyeing, delivery, all would be free. The shop was theirs, they only had to let him know how else he could serve them. All the while his eyes sought to convey that such sales talk would be, in this instance, the literal truth for the rest of his life.

He found out that the girl was from Meerut (he had to move fast, she might return before he could secure her), here for a wedding and wearing a sari for the first time (still unattached, obviously meant for him).

Alone, he held her Delhi address in hot sweaty hands and stared at her handwriting. The girl was reflected in the tidy round curves and careful lettering – now all it needed was a proposal.

Yashpal spent the night in the throes of love, and next morning presented the address to his father. At this place for a few days resided the girl on whom his happiness depended. His father should go and talk to the family without delay. If he could not marry her he would leave the shop and spend the rest of his life celibate, by the banks of the Ganges.

His parents did not take kindly to this threat. They were traditional business people. In order to remain financially secure, and ensure the family harmony that underpinned that security, marriages were arranged with great care. The bride had to bring a dowry, come from the same background, and understand the value of togetherness. Falling in love was detrimental to these interests. How was it that their son, so sensible, had forgotten this?

'The girl must have done black magic to ensnare him,' wailed the boy's mother. 'Otherwise would he go against his own family after seeing her face for a second? Tell him not to bother leaving the house. I myself will disappear to make way for the wretch he prefers before us all.'

Her husband recognised the shock that made her talk such rubbish. He himself was disturbed. He had hoped for an alliance from one of the better cloth shops in Karol Bagh, Sadar Bazar or Chandni Chowk. Perhaps he should not have waited so long to marry his son, already past twenty-five. At that age he had been a father. But circumstances had stepped in, shaken the family, along with a continent, and irrevocably altered the life he had known.

∽

Lala Banwari Lal, the family head, had a deep belief in fate. Before Partition, his had been one of the largest cloth shops in Anarkalli, the famous commercial district of Lahore. However, fate had seen fit to teach him that in this world nothing is permanent. His shop had been one of the first to be destroyed, but amid the slaughter that raged, his family survived, and grief for material loss assumed a less significant place in his scheme of life.

With his seven-year-old son, two-year-old daughter, pregnant wife, and wife's jewellery, they crossed the border into their new, wizened nation. First they were sent to a camp in Amritsar, then Delhi, to finally arrive in Karol Bagh. The jewellery was sold, a house bought, and a shop rented within walking distance on Ajmal Khan Road.

Which was a good thing because Banwari Lal was not about to waste money on even a cycle in the early days. All his profits were poured back into the shop. The family never took holidays. Their main entertainments were eating and an occasional trip to the local cinema. The clothes they wore had everything to do with shop leftovers and wholesale prices.

Lala Banwari Lal allowed no regret to weigh down his attempt at rebuilding their lives. At thirty-two he felt great rage at being forced to start again, but that made it all the more necessary to bury his feelings in the determination to recreate every brick, every shelf, every thread of that which had formed the substance of his life from the age of fourteen.

Once settled in Karol Bagh, Lala Banwari Lal became a devotee of a holy man, a Baba, who lived near the house. His faith needed an anchor, and the holy man combined astrology, palmistry, spiritual guidance, and reassuring predictions about the future. Pray to the Devi, everything will be all right, feed the cows, feed the Brahmins, everything will be all right.

When she turned eighteen, Lala Banwari Lal married his daughter Sunita to someone Babaji knew in Bareilly. The dowry asked for had been negligible, and the boy, when Banwari Lal went to visit him, had seemed decent enough. There was no mother-in-law to trouble Sunita, no sisters to share the house with, the family business was a small retail one in hosiery with every prospect of growth.

That these facts proved inadequate to ensure Sunita's happiness, that the boy drank and became abusive was something the daughter did her best to hide from her parents. This shame was now her own.

The Banwari Lal Cloth Shop continued on a small level for fifteen years, while the father waited for his sons to grow. Yashpal finished school at sixteen and joined the trade. The younger brother Pyare Lal followed rapidly in his brother's entrepreneurial footsteps by refusing to graduate. The shop was his future; he saw no reason to postpone its realisation for the dreary memorising that passed for studies. The father saw his point: the boy kept on failing, and at forty-six, he felt the need for the active presence of both his sons. A year after Sunita's marriage, the fourteen-year-old Pyare Lal started travelling with his father and was in the interesting process of being introduced to all the ins and outs of purchasing. Every month or so, depending on the season, father and son journeyed to large retailers in Madras, Varanasi, Bombay and

Calcutta, besides investigating new ranges at annual summer and winter garment fairs.

The two sons had been brought up to consider their interests synonymous with those of the family. The patriarch was keenly aware of any disagreement between them. Neither must feel exploited, but the eldest had to have the final say. This was not a democracy, in which freewheeling individualism could be allowed to wreck what was being so carefully built. United we stand, divided energy, time and money are squandered.

In Lala Banwari Lal's mind, the business was still struggling to reach the heights of the Lahore days, and he had chosen to wait in order to get the best possible match for his son. Though the boy's mother sometimes complained of his advancing age, he knew how obedient the boy was, and thought he had nothing to fear. He had not seen the dangers of celibacy in his pliant son till his falling in love spread terror and confusion in the home.

Even he had noticed the girl, but then dealing with cloth and colours, appearance and apparel, one became adept at observing people. The girl was pretty, very pretty – but to want to marry a customer? Where was his son's professional objectivity?

She had been dressed in the latest fashion. Churidars, kurta tight around the knees, two large flowers appliquéd across the front. Her fringe swept her eyebrows, highlighting her long brown eyes. She had a little bouffant, and down her back hung a long, glossy, thick plait with reddish tints. Did all this portend simplicity? Homeliness? Dutiful service to elders? Was this girl destined to make his son happy, while at the same time understanding that the interests of a business family came before personal concerns?

Ah, the fires of youth, he sighed, thinking of his slightly pot-bellied son, so careless of the larger picture, so heedless of where the collective good might lie.

His wife was not so tolerant of the fires of youth. The boy had to see sense. She would rather eat poison than negotiate for a girl like that. With their status and position, why should they have to ask anybody for anything?

Babaji was consulted. The son's horoscope was as good as his father's. Their stars were in the ascendant, anything they touched would turn to gold.

Gold. Sona. It was the girl's name, and from Babaji's mouth, the word took on the hue of a good omen. His wife should make the required visit to the address his son had given.

The wife repeated her threat. She would rather eat poison.

'It is our son's happiness we have to think about,' said her husband severely. 'If he wants a love marriage, he shall have it. He has worked sincerely all these years. He has never had a holiday, never taken one paisa. His younger brother travels with me, spends what he can, while the elder one is simple and retiring. Who knows what he might do if he is thwarted in the only thing he asks for?'

'Better he had asked all his life than stab us in the back like this,' muttered the mother. The thought of her favourite son entrapped by a clever, manipulative, dowryless creature made it barely possible for her to look pleasant during the visit her husband forced her to make. She looked at the blushing girl and found nothing remarkable. If it was beauty the boy wanted, she could have found a dozen such, accompanied by similar backgrounds and suitable dowries. Adamant though he might be about Yashpal's happiness, she knew her husband had planned to aim high with his son's marriage. Those hopes were now ruined. She could tear the girl's eyes out, mischief-makers, tear them out with her bare hands.

Meanwhile the girl's side was apprehensive. They were small people. In marriage they could offer nothing but their daughter, whose heart was golden like her name. They did not wish any regret to follow this alliance. The boy's side should think

8

carefully and contact them in Meerut if they wished to pursue the matter. Sona's father said he understood young people to behave irrationally; wisdom lay in greater introspection.

Yashpal wanted nothing to do with greater introspection. If the girl's parents did not agree, he would devote himself to the life of an ascetic. His parents made a trip to Meerut to finalise the marriage.

Perhaps her relative poverty would ensure the necessary amount of gratitude needed to be an ideal daughter-in-law.

The news spread through Sona's community in Meerut. The girl was going to marry the Banwari Lal Cloth Shop in Karol Bagh! How adroitly had her looks been used! It is all the mother's doing, cunningly she has been pushing her daughter forward since the girl turned sixteen. She must have known there was a marriageable son in that shop, or why did she pick that particular place to go with her blouses? As though you can't dye blouses in Meerut. Now she will think she can do the same with Rupa, but let us see if she has the same luck with the sister, who is so much darker.

And did you hear what the father said to the boy's side? We have nothing but our daughter – we are small people. And the cloth shop was forced to say their only interest was the girl. Will Sona, from an educated family, be happy with shopkeepers? The boy is only high-school pass, but Sona now says she does not want to study any more, she wants to remain on the same level as her husband.

Babaji was consulted about the wedding date, which was fixed for six months later. The marriage took place with the ceremony due to the eldest son of the Banwari Lal Cloth and Sari Shop. The barat travelled to Meerut, the shop closed for one day, and by the following evening Sona shifted to her new home.

∽

Why, this house is smaller than mine, thought the young bride, as she surveyed the small paved area between front door and gate, the angan at the back, with its toilet and kitchen on opposite ends, and the four rooms in between.

'Who lives upstairs?' she asked her husband a few weeks later, when some of the timidity had worn off.

'Tenants,' he replied, caressing the peach-like skin and tracing the red lips with his fingers.

Playfully she held the finger between her teeth. 'Shall I bite you?' she asked.

'Just try,' he invited.

She giggled. He was her husband. How could she bite him? Her thoughts wandered. 'I didn't know the whole house was yours.'

He put his hand over her mouth.

'Whose?'

'Yours,' she mumbled.

'Naughty. Married a whole month, and still saying yours. Say ours.'

'Ours,' she repeated, flushing with the pleasure of togetherness.

'Maybe, when the children come,' said the husband, caressing the wife's still-flat belly, 'we can move upstairs. Or Pyare Lal can use it after he gets married. We can't bring his wife to the dining room.' For that is where the younger brother-in-law had been shifted after Yashpal's marriage.

'I don't want to leave Baoji and Maji,' said Sona, trained from an early age to love, serve, and obey her in-laws.

Her husband looked at her with approval. 'You are my everything,' he murmured into her ear. His parents in the next room were sleeping, he could now lock his door, now undress his wife, still shy. With the lights off, he at last got what he had longed for all day.

Yashpal's love was so overwhelming that he was driven to demonstrate it endlessly. In the way his eyes kept seeking her face, in the small gifts he secretly gave, in the way he waited for her to finish eating before leaving the dining area, in the way he hung around the kitchen when she was cooking, in the way he demanded her presence even when he was talking to his mother.

The mother's eagle eye noted these variations in her son's behaviour. Truly you never knew your boy till he married, she thought bitterly. All her years of silent suffering after fleeing Lahore, the years of sacrifice for her children, were now to be rewarded by the obvious preference for a wife. She had known nobody else would matter from the moment he fell in love. Her overwrought feelings made this knowledge public.

Yashpal knew his mother was distressed; since childhood he had been attuned to her moods. He turned to his wife, giver of so much joy, and expected her to bring the same joy to his mother.

'She can't help herself, she spent nights and nights in camps wondering how we would survive, and then my father had to sell her jewellery when they came to Delhi, and when Pyare Lal was born there was no one to help her. She was all alone.'

'So were thousands of others,' pointed out Sona, possessor of the husband's history, bound by love to try and make him feel better. 'Besides, you supported her in every way. You cooked, you shopped, you cleaned, you looked after the baby.'

'She feels things deeply,' sighed the son.

Even the eighteen-year-old Sona knew the difference between feeling things deeply and voicing them loudly, but she was in no position to destroy her husband's illusions. 'I want to be a daughter to her,' she sighed, 'but sometimes I feel Maji does not like me.'

'Never mind,' said Yashpal, pulling her close for the second time that night, 'once we have children, she will melt. Sometimes she gets into moods.'

11

By now Sona knew this. When the two of them were alone, she could see how her mother-in-law had to struggle to even talk to her. Every gesture suggested the daughter-in-law had no right to exist, and if she had to live, why was she doing it in their house? Only when the men came home at night was there the semblance of a caring family.

So between day and night Sona seesawed between love and something more unnameable. Had it been outside the family it would have been called hatred.

Sometimes she cried and told her husband she wanted to go home, nobody had asked him to marry her, her self-respect did not allow her to be subject to such treatment.

'She's not threatening or beating you,' reasoned Yashpal.

'No,' sniffed Sona.

'Then patience, my life, patience.Once we have children, you will see how she changes. Inside she is all love.'

At this Sona allowed her tears to flow copiously, which drove her husband to take her for a little outing to cheer her up, without making sure it was convenient for everyone else to accompany them, thus adding to the black marks against his wife.

Two years passed. Sona still wasn't pregnant, though twenty and old enough. 'Enjoying, enjoying,' muttered the mother darkly, imagining the use of birth control. Sona said nothing. Her husband's steady love helped inure her to these taunts.

By this time the younger brother's marriage was arranged. One love match was all any family could sustain, and Pyare Lal had turned twenty-one when his father told him he was going to wed the daughter of one of the wholesale cloth dealers in Chandni Chowk.

'Whatever my elders decide,' said Pyare Lal, showing that model sons could not be judged by daily behaviour. His father was pleased with him. He had a head for figures, he managed the bank work and his separate bookkeeping for the number-one number-two money was meticulous.

The girl was in her first year of college, but marriage provided enough reason to discontinue her education. She was reasonably pretty, reasonably fair – to be too extreme in the looks department could be deceptive, look at the eldest daughter-in-law, still without issue.

Once the engagement was decided, the tenants upstairs were asked to move. A bride of this quality could not be asked to share a dining room. Silently Sona watched as Pyare Lal's father-in-law gifted a scooter to his future son-in-law and furnished the four rooms of the second storey with a fully stocked kitchen, fridge, cooler, double bed, dining table, chairs, and an upholstered sofa set in red velvet. She realised as she had not realised three years ago, how poor in gifts her own marriage had been.

The upstairs kitchen would not be used for regular cooking, just tea, snacks, and special meals should someone fall ill. Otherwise, everybody would take their meals downstairs, the new daughter-in-law sweating in the small, hot kitchen along with the older one. Listeners to these explanations nodded, yes, wisdom lay in this only. Separate kitchens led to a sense of mine and yours, dissatisfaction, emotional division, and an eventual parting of the ways.

If families did not even eat together, what was the point of living as a unit? You might as well emigrate, pursuing your autonomy in lonely isolation.

Meanwhile in Sona's heart festered the bitter knowledge that had she had children she would have been the one upstairs, with or without a kitchen, while Sushila, Pyare Lal's bride, would have been the one moving into their old bedroom, next to the parents-in-law.

She indulged in one wild fantasy, maybe Sushila will not have children, then sadly got rid of it. Her sister's condition led her to believe hers was the fault, but this knowledge was too frightening to contemplate, let alone discuss openly.

Pyare Lal's prospective sons lay upon her consciousness like a stone. How their mother would shine, how little by comparison would there be to recommend her in the family's eyes! What had she given them? So far as wealth was concerned, they had chosen with their eyes open, it was not expected she provide gifts like Sushila. But no children? How could anyone justify that? To blame nature was a poor excuse, she did not even try. She trembled at her future, and lay awake for hours with her adoring husband snoring gently beside her.

But how gaily she participated in the plans for the coming wedding, how completely she agreed with all who described the joy she would feel as a new sister entered the house, how pleasantly she acquiesced in the insinuation that the barren spell would be broken with babies to gladden the grandparents' hearts.

During the wedding, none looked happier than she, none more loving and tender to the bride, none more delighted about upstairs being done up so nicely, none more willing to show every curious visitor how much the bride's family had given.

And over the three-day festivities none so beautiful as she. She shone, she glowed, her husband looked at her and thought he would never wish to exchange places with his brother, despite all the obvious advantages of an arranged marriage. He was continually attracted to Sona, and though he knew Pyare Lal would fall in love within a few months, his own method of doing things was vindicated every time he looked at his wife, more beautiful than when they had first married.

Sona's fears were realised sooner than she had anticipated. Sushila exhibited no difficulty in conceiving; within a year she gave birth to a baby boy.

Great was the jubilation at this first grandchild. (Sunita's son Vicky, born six years earlier, did not count.) The male line was augmented, courtesy of Sushila and Pyare Lal. A boy brought up within the nurturing ambit of the shop would in turn ensure its continuing prosperity when he grew up.

The new aunt was secretive about her feelings. Yashpal was not to know how jealousy raced up and down her veins like sharp-pointed needles when he came home and called for the baby to play with. He actually thought she would be happy when he proffered the child to her, and said, look, now our house is full, actually thought she would be happy. Was it men, or the exceptional large-heartedness of her husband?

Covertly Sona became even stricter in the rituals she observed. Where could she turn except to God? Her face was already in that direction; now she did not allow herself even a sideways glance.

Every Tuesday she fasted. Previously she would eat fruit and drink milk once during this day, now she converted to a nirjal fast. No water from sun-up to sundown. She slept on the floor, abstained from sex, woke early in the morning, bathed before sunrise. For her puja she collected fresh white flowers, jasmine or chameli, unfallen, untrodden, from the park outside the house.

In the evening she went to the local temple, buying fruit on the way to distribute to as many Brahmins as she could.

By the time Pyare Lal was twenty-six he was the father of two sons, and Sona thought it was not possible to be more miserable. There must be some deficiency in her prayers or a very bad past karma that made her suffer so in this life – and that too when she had the appearance of every joy a woman could have. Beauty, a fair skin, an attentive husband, a well-to-do family. She had tried to make sure her in-laws never regretted her husband's transgressive love, proving her suitability every day, year after year. She was humble, easy to mould, and ready to please. Sona was gold, like her name. But what use was all this if the Banwari Lal blood did not pass on in its expected quantity?

The fruits of Sushila's womb delivered with so much promptness caused the gold in Sona's nature to bend under their weight. As she lay in bed, she could feel the fecundity of life upstairs, falling through the floor and pressing upon her heavily, so heavily, that for nights and nights she could not sleep.

In the day small things drove her into a frenzy of irritation. Everyone, she felt, found her defective goods, despite her pale colour, large hazel eyes, small neat nose, red lips, even teeth, and perfect skin. How she wished she did not have to live in a joint family! If she and her husband lived separately, she too could be happy, like her sister Rupa.

∾

Sona's marriage had not in fact led to a brilliant future for Rupa. No proposal had forced her to give up her education. She finished her BA, after which her father arranged her marriage to the son of a retired colleague, based in Karol Bagh. The location of the groom in the sister's neighbourhood was one of the reasons the alliance was deemed suitable.

Given Rupa's dark skin, she was considered to have married as advantageously as her circumstances allowed. The family was very small: one father, one married daughter, and one son. Their eligibility came from the ownership of a house in Karol Bagh, their security from the boy's government job as a minor employee in the Defence Ministry.

It turned out that Rupa too failed to conceive. Sona hid this fact as long as she could from her in-laws, she knew exactly the kind of comment it would elicit. Bad stock, tainted bloodlines. But concealment was useless, eventually these things were said.

'Why don't you ask Babaji for a remedy?' Rupa asked Sona occasionally. 'Your father-in-law has so much faith in him. He might be able to help.'

'It is up to them to suggest it,' said Sona proudly.

'You can give them the idea, no?'

'Look at what happened to Sunita. That was Babaji's doing.' Sona lowered her voice. Disrespect of Babaji was not allowed in the house.

'But he also encouraged your marriage,' pointed out Rupa.

Sona sighed. How could she make her sister understand? Looking at Rupa, it was possible to envy a woman in the same situation as herself, and with less money too. Rupa was childless, but free from torment. She accepted her fate, she didn't spend every Tuesday fasting, she had no one to envy, no one to rub salt in her wounds, no one to keep those wounds bleeding by persistent hurting comments.

Without children, Rupa had the time to start a little pickle business. Her husband encouraged her, her father-in-law helped her paste on the labels with a trembling hand, her brother-in-law (Sona's husband) helped her with his contacts among the shopkeepers of Karol Bagh. As long as her products were good, orders were plentiful. Rupa worked hard at her recipes, experimenting with new ones and expanding her repertoire.

∽

Sunita seldom visited her parents. If money was sent to spend on a trip home, she usually made some excuse: the husband is not well, the father-in-law is not well, I am needed to look after them. They thought maybe her postal order was snatched away, they sent tickets instead. But the visits were still infrequent.

Lala Banwari Lal insisted the brothers take time off from the business to see their sister once a year. Though she was married, her unhappy situation made her their responsibility, now and after his death. The brothers went, though reluctantly; their sister's life was the result of bad karma and there was nothing anyone could do. Still, they made allowances for a father's love.

Once Sona accompanied Yashpal to Bareilly to meet her sister-in-law. The plan was to take Sunita and Vicky for a holiday to Rishikesh, forcibly if necessary.

Force was not required. The brother-in-law, Murli, whatever his treatment of his wife, was always exceedingly hospitable towards his in-laws. Their superior status meant his politeness and warmth never ceased.

During the trip Sona and Sunita exchanged confidences. Why she would never come home, why the tickets were returned instead of used. Murli wanted her family to invest in Bareilly, to either open an outlet that he would manage, or failing that, to help upgrade his shop. Her dowry had been small, he demanded redress. They are cheating you, they palmed you off like a poor girl, now they are rich, they should share. Should she visit Delhi, it would have to be with him, and her life would be hell afterwards. But she would not exploit her father, no matter what her husband's demands were.

She shared the general belief in her bad karma. Let her present miseries expiate the sins of her past lives. All she wished was to leave this world, it was only her son who kept her back. Here she clutched Vicky to her bosom, her face contorting with tears and tenderness. The boy remained there passively, while Sona looked on. See, how children were recompense for everything.

Fourteen years after her marriage, Sunita's hopes were answered. The Banwari Lal family got the news by telegram. There had been an accident in the kitchen, and Sunita had died of burns in the hospital. The cremation would take place the next day. She was only thirty-two.

Banwari Lal and Yashpal prepared to leave for Bareilly by the night train. Pyare Lal would man the shop. The women stayed home, as was appropriate.

At home the mother cried non-stop. 'Why not me? Why not

me? What crime have I committed that my child has to go first?' she wailed. She hit her head repeatedly with her hands while her daughters-in-law looked on, their faces serious and solemn, tears in their own eyes. It could have been them, but for their own more fortunate destinies.

The night meal was sombre. Sushila's maternal responsibilities allowed her to retreat upstairs afterwards. Sona was left to continue the comforting.

'Sleep now, Maji, sleep – you will make yourself ill if you cry like this, and it will not bring her back.'

And then for no reason, no reason but that they were alone and nobody else could see her true colours, the old woman glared at Sona and spat out, 'You think sleep is possible? What can you know of a mother's feelings? All you do is enjoy life, no children, no sorrow, only a husband to dance around you.'

It took all of Sona's training in daughter-in-lawhood to continue her attentions as though this had not been said. Then, as she had so often, she lay awake at night, going over her mother-in-law's words, gnawing at them, teasing out of them the last shred of bitterness.

All the suffering in the world was not enough to make that woman human. Though grieving, she could still find energy to taunt. She talked of love, but did she know the meaning of the word? If she had cared for her daughter, would she have allowed her to be murdered? Could she believe the lie that her clothes caught fire while cooking? They knew how badly off she was, still they neglected her. If she had a daughter in a bad marriage, she would insist she come home, she had so much love to give.

Here Sona pressed her hands to her breasts: they felt good, large and full, but their weight only increased her wretchedness. How could she accept they would never be used for more than one purpose? She tried to calm herself by praying, closing her eyes to concentrate on her favourite image of God, the little Krishna, looking so naughty, so mischievous, so adorable – please, I am growing old, bless us with a child, girl or boy, I do not care, but I cannot bear the emptiness in my heart.

The adopted son

Sona did not realise her prayers would be answered in two days. Her father-in-law came back with Vicky, ten years old, skin the splotchy brown of mud, large staring eyes, bony knees, neatly oiled hair, spindly legs, and snot that continually ran into his shirt sleeve.

The boy was pushed towards her. With a presentiment of what was going to happen she drew back in revulsion before a word had been exchanged.

'Maybe it was meant to be like this,' sighed the patriarch, as the men sat around sipping tea, looking grave, relating the story of their trip. How Murli had received them at the station, weeping steadily, how they had been pushed into the role of consolers rather than accusers, how Murli had said wildly he was going to give up his life, there was no meaning in it any more. How the boy, sobbing hysterically, had begged his grandfather to take him with them. Murli encouraged this. What could he do with a child, alone as he was, poor and distraught?

Perhaps he had already found someone to marry, they speculated darkly, he was always on the lookout for money. And that was the real reason for Sunita's death.

The two sisters-in-law were able to be more dispassionate. Sushila – mother of sons, her concern about their future claims still too remote to be considered insensitive – could say: might not Murli exploit the child to get money out of the family?

Sona added her weaker voice to Sushila's suspicion. With a full heart, her eyes red with distress, she hinted that Murli would use the boy to gain entry into the business. She recounted again Sunita's confidences in Rishikesh. Murli had been bent on using his wife to extort money from the family. She had resisted, and now in deference to Sunita's wishes, such intentions should be thwarted by returning the boy.

Lala Banwari Lal was unable to bear even the suggestion. They had a moral responsibility to Sunita's child. His head was bent, his tears were falling. He would carry the curse of his daughter's death till the day he died. Had he remained in Lahore, this never would have happened. She would have married into a family of equal status.

His grief further shook the family. What else could they do but cluster around him, soothe him, tell him they would do whatever he wanted?

His wife wept in turn; this child was all that was left of her daughter. The boy, who had been hunched silently over his tea, was now grabbed, clasped to his grandmother's chest, and rocked violently back and forth till he started crying.

It was decided that at the first hint of financial pressure Murli would have his son back, but till then he would remain with them. Where duty to one's own was concerned, the heart should always be big.

∾

In the days to come it became clear that Vicky fell to Sona's lot by default. Sushila's two sons were still small; she had her hands full. Sona's were palpably empty.

Sona did struggle at this fresh arrangement by the fates for her certain misery.

'I do not think I will be able to look after him,' she said to her husband a few days later. The emotional levels of the house were lower, she could now speak her mind. 'At least send him back to finish the school year. Right now he sits around all day, doing nothing.'

Yashpal smiled lovingly at his wife. 'Yes, we must see about a school here. In the meantime if he does miss a year, how does it matter? It is not as though he is going to be a scholar.'

'Maybe not, but it will add to his discomfort. No child likes to fail.'

'Poor boy, I doubt he will think of it as failure. A new school, a new city, a new home. He has to get used to all this, though only ten. Poor boy,' he repeated, 'he was so glad to come with us.'

'Making use of the goodness of his grandfather and uncle.'

'Sunita's soul will be at peace if we take care of her son; it is all we can do for her. You heard how upset Baoji was. I have only seen him like this when I was very young.'

Lahore again.

'Only daughter, bound to feel it,' was the answer dragged out of Sona. Everything was stacked against her, she could see that. Her husband never reproached her for not having a child, and she was grateful, but did that mean she could be saddled with some dirty boy, and be expected to dance with joy? 'He will miss his mother, he will never accept me. It is better if he is returned to his father. Like this, instead of losing one parent he will lose both.'

'You will make it up to him, I know,' said Yashpal. 'You have such a tender heart.'

She went on trying. 'Isn't it better if he goes upstairs? He will fit in nicely with the children there. As it is, looking after Maji takes all my time. You don't know how it was when you were away. I thought she was going to fall sick, she cried so much.'

Yashpal sighed. 'The boy is orphaned. He needs a mother's special attention. Let him be your child.'

'A borrowed child? Ten years old? From another woman's womb? Tell me, is this what you really want?'

'It is the will of God, what can we do? This is what has been given us.'

Sona felt her chest would burst with pain. Tears gathered on her face. Her husband touched her cheek, and said, 'Sona,

23

you will get used to it. We cannot decide how our prayers will be answered.'

So he had prayed too. She looked at him, her heart melting with anguish. It was for his sake she wanted a child. He was such a good man, why should he be deprived of issue?

For the moment there was nothing more she could say or do. Maybe Rupa, her mind unfettered by Banwari Lal blood ties, would be able to suggest something.

Rupa was no help. 'What can you do, Didi?' she asked. 'You are the one without children.'

Sona glared at her. 'Is that my fault?'

Rupa quickly covered her mistake with her sister's favourite topic. 'That witch upstairs will not take him, instead she will say all kinds of things against you.'

'Ever since that woman has come, my life has been a misery,' responded Sona eagerly.

'Why give her more opportunity to rub salt in your wounds? It may do you good in the long run, Didi. With the family.'

Sona's eyes filled with tears, as she murmured hopelessly, 'I want my own child.'

Rupa stroked her back and murmured, 'Bas, bas, in the end it will be all right. Your time will also come.'

'Never. Your Jijaji says we must acknowledge we will not have our own children. Now he looks on others as his own, first his brother's, then his sister's. I do not understand him.'

'He has accepted the situation, that is all. At least he is not blaming you.'

Sona remained silent.

Rupa said, 'Didi, why have you never considered going to a doctor? You can afford the best medical care. Even God needs to be helped sometimes.'

Sona side-stepped the question, not wanting to reveal how humiliating it would be to be seen as a flawed creature, whose body needed expensive medical aid to perform its natural functions. If her family had wanted it, how willingly she would have put herself in the hands of modern medicine, suffered a thousand tests. But strangely her in-laws had never suggested this. Perhaps they wanted to punish her, perhaps they felt she was not worth the money.

Suppose she did manage to go, secretly with Rupa, and there turned out to be something really wrong with her, she would be doomed to live with this weight on her hopeless heart.

'I don't understand you, Didi,' went on her sister, irritated by the way Sona was staring at her perfect white feet, encircled with silver anklets, studded with tiny blue and red meena hearts. 'If I wanted something as badly as you do, I would try everything, not just rely on puja and fasts, which you have been doing for years, with nothing to show.'

'If you are so keen on doctors, why don't you go?' flashed Sona.

'I have accepted my condition, my husband does not hanker after children, he says his sister has enough, he helps with their education, his heart is as big as the sky,' said Rupa, with a pride her sister thought totally unbecoming.

'It is easy to accept when you have no in-laws always making you feel bad.'

'But we have other things to make us feel bad. The tenant upstairs sits on our head, with his schemes and his plans. From before our marriage they are fighting. My father-in-law worries he will die with it unresolved, and *he* feels it is just as well we don't have children who will inherit our problems. At least your house is properly your own.'

Depends on what you mean by properly, thought Sona sourly.

'And,' went on Rupa, still inappropriately exaggerating the difficulties of her life, 'I have to work very hard with the pickles, just to make a little extra money. The case costs a lot, he sends his sister an allowance every month, we even buy the cheapest tickets at the cinema in order to save. If I didn't have this extra income, we would never go anywhere, never go to India Gate, restaurants or films, always sit at home.'

'You are lucky your Jijaji helps you so much with the pickles, making sure they are sold. He takes so much personal interest in grocery shops only to help you, otherwise it is not really his line of business,' pointed out Sona, annoyed that her sister should be talking about the money she made without due reference to her husband.

'We live in your shadow, you know that, Didi,' said Rupa guilelessly.

'He was even saying the other day that later you can supply the local eating-places. Your Jijaji always has very good ideas.'

At this news, Rupa's mind began to race, as many fantasies filling it as might have been justified by the news of a pregnancy. She felt a little ashamed, and said modestly, 'I am so stupid, on my own I can do nothing.'

Sona gave her a sharp look, and said, 'Because you are a woman, with no business background, he feels he should help you.'

'Your husband is so generous, always thinking of others. One day your time will come, Didi, I am sure of it.'

Sona's childless situation continued to make her vulnerable. She was considered to have a fund of motherly emotion waiting to pour itself into the orphaned Vicky.

'Bechaara,' said her mother-in-law to Sona, 'he has only us now. We have to make up for his sorrow in life. It was your kismet not to have children so you could be a true mother to your nephew.'

Sona's position forced her to bear these remarks in silence, but her internal repartee was fierce and pointed: How can I be his mother? Or make up for anything? If it is in my fate not to have children, it is in his not to have parents. I have to accept that as much as he. How can some dirty little street boy be forced on to me as my child? I would rather die.

Oblivious of her thoughts, they reiterated night and day, 'Beti, now you are his mother. God has rewarded your devotion. Sometimes our wishes are fulfilled in strange ways.'

She was the instrument of their care, and like most instruments she writhed in the hands that wielded her. Dark and vicious thoughts crept up in Sona as she looked at Vicky, the answer to her prayers.

It turned out that his Bareilly education did not equip him for the school his cousins went to. He had to be accommodated somewhere, so he was sent to the poor-quality English medium school around the corner, where learning was crammed into the upper storey of a house, with no playground and certainly no status. If the boy showed aptitude he would be shifted to a better place. Meanwhile Sona could help develop his potential.

The whole family rejoiced that there was something so tangible by which Sona could express her thwarted maternal longings.

With Vicky, Sona had to be on her guard all the time. The house had many eyes quick to detect neglect, and many people quick to attack with their conclusions. As God was her witness, she had nothing against Vicky. But was this dark, ungainly, silent, sullen child any substitute for the baby that was to still the yearning in her heart, that was to suckle from her breasts, and use her ample flesh to its satisfaction? Her blood burned, and though her blood was used to burning, it now raged so fiercely that nothing but her own blood could staunch the flames.

'Didi,' said Rupa one weekend, as she was over with a new lot of mango chutney for her brother-in-law to supply to the grocer he knew, 'how is it with Vicky?'

'All right,' said Sona tonelessly.

27

'Isn't the Ganesh Chaturthi fast coming up?' It was winter, and she was well aware of Sona's fasting schedule.

'I'm not keeping it this year. What is the use?'

Rupa clicked her tongue disapprovingly. 'Don't be like this, Didi. God is watching; you should be afraid.'

'I don't care. I am tired of praying, tired of hoping,' said Sona bitterly.

Look at me, thought Rupa. I also don't have a child, or half the other things she has. From the time we were children, she was the special one, always noticed for her fairness, her prettiness, and every day I had to hear how well she would marry, while I would be lucky to find anybody, dark and ugly as I was. For nine years now, I have seen her become more and more depressed. For a condition she shares with me, I have to console her all the time. Beauty is not everything; just as well, or some of us would be left with nothing. 'Won't your mother-in-law notice?' she asked at last.

'What will she notice? According to them my prayers are answered. Now they are busy making sure that child is a noose around my neck. Why didn't he die with his mother?'

Rupa examined Sona. She was thinner, her flawless skin had a dull, pallid tone. 'Didi, you shouldn't say such things, you are forgetting we cannot always see the purpose of what happens in our lives, maybe this is a test,' she reasoned, while Sona let tears testify to her state of mind. Rupa started the caressing that was now automatic with her. Poor Sona, if only she could get rid of certain notions her life would be easier. Having Vicky was not such a bad thing, all the boy needed was a little love, he was still a child, and from the same family.

'Do you want me to keep him sometimes?' observed Rupa to her sister's back. 'He can come when he doesn't have school, *he* can also help him with his studies.'

Sona shuddered and shook her head. 'Can you see what they would say?' she demanded. 'No, I have thought and thought. I am going to tell your Jijaji that if he doesn't move to a separate house, I am going to fall ill – you can see how thin I am.' She held out her arm – the sleeve of the blouse hung from it.

Didi has gone mad, thought Rupa, that is why she is so out of touch with reality. How else can she even suppose that an old-established joint family with a growing business would deflect its time, money, and resources to cater to the whims of a daughter-in-law? 'Try this mango chutney,' she said nervously. 'It is a new recipe, sweet, sharp and salty, you can have it with Chinese also. It will bring back your appetite.'

'Nothing will bring back my appetite,' declared Sona firmly, 'and I know what I am doing. That woman upstairs keeps talking of how the children are growing and need more space, and how we should all move.'

'*All* move,' pointed out her sister.

'I am sure your Jijaji can be made to see reason,' said Sona, setting her mouth in a pretty red-lipped pout. Rupa wondered how far her beauty would take her. Would it take her out of the house?

Rupa waited in vain for any change in the Banwari Lal household. Sona continued as Vicky's reluctant mother in her marital home. Obviously she had thought better of a plan that would result in suspicion, resentment, opposition, and further opprobrium.

A few months later a supplier came to the shop with a box of the finest almond sweets Karol Bagh had to offer. The occasion? A baby son, after years. The man was fervent in seeking the blessings of everyone in his life. He talked, and in what he said Lala Banwari Lal found much to ponder.

A few days later he revealed an unprecedented plan for the summer. They were going on a holiday. For one week Pyare Lal would look after the shop, Sushila would look after him, while Yashpal, Sona, the three boys, and the grandparents went to the hills. Among the places they were going to visit was a shrine at Chitai, near Almora. Though the shrine was small it was famous, the Devi of those hills was said to have miraculous powers.

Yashpal added to his wife's joy by telling her they could include Rupa and her brother-in-law on the trip. A childless couple, they might benefit too.

Sona looked at him, put her hand on his knee and smiled. Yashpal was a man of few words, but she understood everything without his having to open his mouth. In his silent way he was doing what he could for her: he had seen her pain, he had registered her trauma, he too wanted a child of his own. He had found out where to go – the very fact that he was taking Rupa too was a sign of the faith he placed on their journey. And best of all, he was making sure Sushila was left behind. There would be no evil eye to negate the blessings bestowed by the Devi.

'I am sure Rupa will be very happy to join us,' she murmured. 'She is always talking about how good you are, helping so much with her pickles and chutneys.'

'Poor woman, she is your sister after all,' said Yashpal.

'There is no man like you,' said Sona, gazing at him, love in her eyes, the desire Vicky had driven away palpably swelling back.

Yashpal drew her soft and yielding mass to himself. His arms around her, he tugged at her lower lip, sucking it. In the morning he knew it would look even redder, and only he would know the reason. This secret made him increase the pressure. Sona's hand crept to his pyjama tape, the darkness allowed her to do things she never would have if they could see each other. She opened the buttons of her blouse, slithered down, kissing him all the way to finally press her breasts on either side of his erection. Yashpal moaned. Sona took him in her mouth, teasing him with her tongue. The man arched into her, and thought no one on earth could ever be a wife to him but Sona, and he would give his life to please her.

This thought remained with him next morning as they made plans for the trip, and made him insist once again they take Rupa and her husband with them.

Chitai, near Almora.

A little mandir, painted white, in the bend of a road. Pine trees tremble nervously around it. The ground is covered with dry yellow needles. Busloads stop here. The temple is on a raised platform, a tattered red flag waves from its top. All around are bells, innumerable bells, hung on ropes strung between poles criss-crossing the temple courtyard. Big ones, little ones, jammed together till they are silenced.

The door to the mandir is so small that pilgrims have to bend double to enter. Inside, a decrepit old man squats beside the small marble sacred figure. Smoke from a thousand incense sticks colours the dim interior grey. A few diyas flicker, glowing in the haze. Motes of light filter through the cracks in the bodies plastering the entrance.

The stone platform is hot, bare feet burn, the rush to fit inside the shrine is desperate.

Sona, Rupa and Maji come dressed in bridal clothes, red and gold dupattas around them, new glass bangles on their wrists, sindhoor bright in their hair, bindis large on their foreheads. In their hands are trays of offerings for the hill goddess, the goddess with miraculous powers. Ask and she shall give.

Sona asked, as she had been asking for ten years. Rupa must also have asked – certainly her little business continued to thrive, while other things remained the same.

During the trip, Sona felt closer to her husband. It was their first holiday, and with a cunning she could only admire, he arranged two large rooms in the hotel for his parents, Rupa, and Prem Nath, farming out the children between them. They themselves had a small room on another floor – nothing else available, he explained.

Nightly, away from home, family, and shop, Yashpal gave himself over to the pleasures of his wife's body. Sona had not realised how much difference leisure and a change of location could make to a man's sex drive.

The three boys also grew friendlier during the one week. Six years older than Ajay, and eight years older than Vijay, Vicky was looked up to by the two boys when given a chance.

Back in Delhi it was easier for Sona to send him to play with them. Vicky's skill with a cricket bat, his dexterity at gulli danda and pithoo, established his reputation, and by implication raised Ajay and Vijay's stock in the neighbourhood.

Shortly afterwards Lala Banwari Lal decided they could at last afford a car. Once a week in the evening, all nine would get into the Ambassador that Yashpal or Pyare Lal drove, and go to India Gate. There the children and the two uncles played badminton, the women took out tiffin carriers, spread food on durries, and bought strings of jasmine buds to put in their hair. After they had eaten they bought ice-cream, and because the shop was doing well, they bought the most expensive, cassata – slabs of pink, green and white ice-cream, topped with cream and chopped nuts, on thin paper plates, eaten with little wooden spoons.

A few months and Sona could look at Vicky and see a child. Perhaps her luck was going to change (maybe this was a practice run?), she thought superstitiously as she tried to be a mother to the poor orphaned boy.

With three boys in the house Banwari Lal felt the need to cater to their futures by expanding into shawls. Pyare Lal's travelling time increased as he journeyed to the Punjab and Kashmir commissioning shawls from weavers in all varieties: men and women's shawls, plain, fully embroidered, or just with borders; woven in wool, pashmina, or mixes.

Birth

Two months later Sona discovered she had conceived.

'Maybe it will be your turn next,' was how she broke the news to her sister.

Rupa received the information stoically. Her mind leaped to the little baby in her sister's arms, to the loneliness that would be hers as the only childless woman in the family. But then Rupa was also fair. She had not suffered like her sister, nor had she fasted and done penance. With only initial difficulty, she smiled and hugged Sona, whispering that not for nothing had she prayed, and looked after Vicky so selflessly. God was rewarding her.

'I feel it is because of the Devi,' went on Sona, not wanting to take credit for her pregnancy. 'I felt a change after we went, didn't you?'

Yes, Rupa had. She was now supplying pickles and sweet chutneys to local restaurants as well as shops, and had hired a woman to help her. She wished to purchase a car, she wished to go on more holidays, above all she wished she had enough money to buy out the tenant who was causing her husband and father-in-law so much tension. More than an elusive baby, Rupa focused her attention on financial success.

'We must go again, our trip has been very auspicious,' she now said.

'Your Jijaji can't be travelling all the time,' said Sona tartly. Really, her sister must learn to be a little more independent, and not be taking her brother-in-law's generosity for granted.

A storm rose in Rupa's heart. This was the kind of woman her sister was: cry on her shoulder incessantly, and the minute things improved, she turned her back. Always she had been like that, getting her way in everything because she was pretty. If Sona wasn't her only relative in the city, she would never bother with her again.

'See what *he* gave me, when I told him,' said Sona now, going to her Godrej almirah, unhooking the keys that hung from her waist. 'Even though I said I didn't want – *he* insisted,' and flushing with pleasure, she handed her sister a long, red velvet box.

'He is so good to you, Didi,' sighed Rupa, removing the hostility from her mind when she saw her sister take out in addition an almost new silk sari, divining it to be for herself. In the general happiness she too must have her share.

She opened the velvet box carefully. There lay not only a gold filigree necklace but matching dangling earrings. How had Yashpal managed to buy a necklace for his wife, and that too for no recognised occasion, without having to buy one for every other woman in the family? Was Sona's pregnancy going to divide them? Had Yashpal Bhai Sahib gone mad for love of his wife?

'Don't be silly,' giggled Sona when she asked. 'It's just one little necklace.'

'Not so little,' said Rupa, taking it out of the box to calculate its heaviness. 'Must be thirty grams at least.'

'Thirty-five.'

Worse and worse, thought Rupa, while Sona held the necklace against her sister's neck in order to admire it more.

'Does your father-in-law know?' she persisted.

'How do I know?' pouted Sona. 'Really, Roop, how can you grudge me a bit of jewellery after all these years?'

Rupa gasped and shut up. If the Banwari Lals were going to be divided over one necklace, it would not be for lack of warning.

But she noticed that Sona never wore the necklace publicly. It remained a private thing hidden by husband and wife.

A pregnancy after ten years in a woman almost thirty had to

be guarded, protected, and encouraged. The elders decreed that Sona should not be allowed to deliver at her mother's, as was the custom. God knew what facilities those people would provide – they were not well off, it's better to do everything here.

The next seven months were momentous ones. Sona's diet, her rest, her activities were treated with the greatest of care. Vitamins, minerals, iron supplements, almonds, butter, and milk were showered on her. Her body grew heavy with the weight of two; her round face became rounder and shone like the moon.

She was never allowed to go alone and friendless for her check-ups. Always there was Sushila and the mother-in-law, asking questions, carefully holding Sona's medical file, meticulously inserting the test reports.

'What does Maji say to you now?' asked Rupa once.

'Oh, she has completely changed. She doesn't even let me bend to pick up anything,' giggled Sona.

'That's very convenient,' remarked Rupa, 'to change from poison to honey just like that.'

'Oh, she wanted a grandchild. It is understandable,' replied Sona, taking two glasses of tea from the boy who had been recently hired to help in the house.

'But that is hardly fair to *you*,' flashed Rupa, who after all had been the repository of everything Maji had said through the years, and could neither forgive nor forget so easily.

'It is the way of the world,' said Sona, speaking across a divide Rupa had never felt before.

One day, two days overdue, waters burst but no contractions, and Sona was rushed to the hospital. She was put on the drip to induce labour, while the family waited patiently, knowing this would take time.

How often had Sona waited in similar situations. Now it was her turn to be waited for. Let her take her time, let it be as long and as difficult as possible, Sushila, Maji, Rupa, their husbands, all were prepared.

Morally, mentally, emotionally, financially, domestically. One amongst them was dispatched when it was time for the children to come home from school. One received the men in the evening when they came home from the shop. Yashpal himself was shadowed constantly, he could not be left unsupported for even a second.

The waiting period grew tense as it became clear that Sona was not responding to the drip. Even after fifteen hours she had not dilated beyond six centimetres. Rupa sat with Sona throughout, holding her hand, pressing her cold feet, giving her little sips of iced water, wiping her forehead, and listening to her groans.

Finally the doctor said what everybody had suspected all along, but nature had to be given a chance. 'The baby's heartbeat is recording stress. Sign here for a Caesarean.'

Yashpal signed.

A girl was born.

Commented the doctor as she finished with her injection, polio drops, and silver nitrate: 'Nowadays what's the difference, boy or girl?'

The nurse added, 'She will bring great wealth to her family, be its goddess Lakshmi.' Nurses know which way the wind is blowing. In a birthing room longings and disappointments are palpable, and dealt with in a routine way.

'Such a sweet little baby,' said Rupa dutifully, while Sushila was making sure that the new-born was wrapped in the soft old clothes that had been kept ready.

'It is good to have a girl in the house,' replied Sushila as Sona dozed. 'The brothers will have a sister.'

'Indeed,' said Rupa guardedly. Sushila was the enemy, she was well aware of that, but her experience of Sushila had been drawn from the thousands of words expended on her, hour after hour, year after year. Alone with her, she felt uneasy and unprepared.

'Now I can tell you how worried we were that something would go wrong. With Sona's history, you know.'

Rupa bridled. 'I believe there were no serious complications. She may have taken a long time conceiving, but in the end it was all right.'

'Such care we took, of course it would be all right. We protected your sister from every possible shock.'

'What shock?'

'We knew. We asked the doctor after the ultrasound – girl or boy? She told us confidentially. She's my old doctor, and she knows we are not the type to abort a female foetus. That is why we kept telling Sona the main thing is the child should be healthy. Isn't that so?' she cooed at the baby, before the nurse took her away.

'Lakshmi will follow her into the house,' rallied Rupa, disconcerted by this information.

'Of course,' agreed Sushila.

'And now the womb has opened,' continued Rupa, 'a baby brother will come.'

'It is all in the hands of God. Our house is blessed with sons, do not worry about that,' remarked Sushila.

Rupa was uncertain of what to say, wanting to assert her sister's right to her own son, but not wanting to imply that one son was not as good as another in the Banwari Lal eye. She remained silent.

~

Births and deaths bring their own pollution. For ten days no god figure could be touched, no meals cooked, no fire lit. Food was provided by the relatives of the daughters-in-law, unaffected by the increase or decrease in the members of the Banwari Lal household.

'Will you be able to feed so many?' whispered the new mother to her sister. 'Take the keys to my cupboard, there is some money there.'

'Didi, why do you worry so much? Your milk will dry up. I keep telling you I will manage. This is my business, have you forgotten?'

'Still, they are used to nice things.'

'I am quite able to produce nice things for the Banwari Lal family. It is not as though their diet has been holy nectar.'

Why did Sona always think that her own side would be found wanting? For years they had steadily consumed and praised the pickles, chutneys, and packaged savouries she freely supplied them. Now when she had to turn out a few meals, Sona was pushing the cupboard keys at her. She had seen enough of the in-laws over the past few days to know they did not expect a five-star banquet. Maybe it was the birth of a girl that pumped the insecurity in her sister's nature into the food she was going to provide.

Rupa returned to her house thoughtful. There was more to Sona's life than she had previously realised. There had been so much family feeling at the nursing home, everybody pitching in to take care of things. What did she have in her home besides one husband and one old father-in-law? Nothing, and with a dry and barren womb there would continue to be nothing. She sighed, and gave her karma a gloomy thought before concentrating on the provisions that needed to be bought for tomorrow.

'Maybe I too will now get,' she remarked at random to her husband the next day, as they were packing the food in tiffin carriers and cardboard boxes. 'After ten years is quite something. Anything can happen.'

'Maybe,' he said slowly. 'But things are all right the way they are.'

'If we have children, they will look after us in our old age.'

'Who knows how children will turn out?'

'Still, it is nice. Didi has so many people to care for her. Always someone there, never lonely.'

'With more people there is more tension also. In your sister's family, remarks travel from down to up, up to down all day. And then she cries to you.'

'That could be Didi, you know, used to feeling bad. Perhaps they mean well. See how nice they were about the baby.'

'With three boys in the house, you think they are being especially nice if they have a girl? We are better the way we are – no giving, no taking, everything neat and clean.'

He was trying to console her. Her husband was a decent man, never throwing her barrenness in her face. Maybe she should also fast and pray like her sister. But she had always loved eating, and her husband loved to eat with her.

'Now only I will be left,' she remarked sadly, as she poured some chutney into a steel container.

'What can one do?' asked her husband, this time also sounding sad. It must have been difficult for him to see Sona getting a baby, and nothing from her, thought Rupa.

Now everything was going to change. Sona would be swallowed into that family, she could see it already. There would be no more hints of barrenness. If they were really keen about a son, with their money they could go on producing till they finally got one. Her own role in her sister's life would become limited. She hoped Yashpal would go on helping her, neither she nor her husband had the contacts to do outside liaising. And Vicky, what was going to happen to Vicky?

After a week Sona and her daughter came home. Relatives and friends, having done the hospital round, now did the home round. Among women, details of the Caesarean were canvassed, the drip, the labour, the baby's heartbeat, the decision, the operation, the pain, the stitches, the necessity of care, healing, and prolonged rest.

And the baby, they cooed, tea in one hand, plates of sweet and savoury in the other – look at the baby, look at her colour, she looks like her father, her mother, her grandmother, grandfather, aunt, uncle, even the odd cousin (from which side depended on the speaker). And again her colour so clean, ah yes, so necessary these black threads around her wrist and ankle, the kaajal smudged on her forehead to make her ugly and keep away the evil eye.

The baby's horoscope was cast: the configuration of the planets at her birth made her a mangli. This was not good news, manglis were horribly difficult to marry off. Unless they found a man with similarly unfortunate stars unhappiness or death was the sure result.

Yashpal said he did not believe in such nonsense, there were manglis in this world who led perfectly decent lives. He had to be reminded that Sunita had been a mangli. Though she had been married off with Babaji himself matching the horoscopes, look what happened to her.

Lala Banwari Lal felt so protective towards his baby granddaughter that he actually declared it was not necessary for girls to marry. Sona silently hoped the family would not blame her too much for a mangli girl. Rupa thought that maybe her sister might still have problems she could share with no one but her. Sushila smiled and dandled the baby lovingly, such a pretty little thing, it took her back to when her children were born.

They did the naming ceremony on the fortieth day. The auspicious letter taken out was 'a'. For the horoscope the pundit chose the long and old-fashioned Anandalakshmi, which no one would use, the name that would confuse the evil eye and deflect ill from the person. Her everyday name would be Nisha, short, sweet, with a modern ring to it.

The grandfather decided to celebrate on the scale reserved for sons. Yashpal should not feel that more money was being spent on Pyare Lal's children than on his own. Everybody remotely related was called. All a baby could need was displayed in the drawing room. There was a pram, cotton sets for summer, little sweater sets in pastel colours for winter,

sets of silver glasses, cups, spoons, and rattles, little brush
and comb sets, dolls, a doll's house, gold bangles for baby
wrists, gold chains that hung around her neck and reached
her knees.

With this gold Nisha's dowry was begun.

Vicky

Vicky hovered at the edge of the relatives milling around the baby. He remembered how in Bareilly, as the only child of his parents, he had longed for someone to play with.

A few times he had pleaded, 'Amma, get me a brother.'

Her reply: 'So your father has someone else to beat, and I have someone else to suck my blood.'

'I'll protect him.' Thus the child urged, begging his mother for something no one else could give him.

'Before you can protect anybody I'll be dead.'

'No, you won't. You can't be dead before I have a chance to beat him for beating you.'

'Shush, don't say such things. There will be sin upon your head. He is your father. Better I die, then they will come to take you.'

'Who?'

'Your uncles, grandmother, and grandfather. They love you like anything. Only he doesn't let us go and see. Never mind. After I die.'

And now she was dead, and he was here, like she had said. The baby drew him back to his own mother and he wept and wept, shedding every tear accumulated over the past year and a half.

Nisha's birth meant a certain neglect of Vicky, now nobody's particular responsibility. Vicky made up for this lack by crying, first in bewilderment, then as a means of communication. In his old home he had cried seldom – he was silent with his father, and with his mother there had been no need for tears.

Here his crying was a weapon, but in whose hands it was not yet clear.

Sona lay tranquilly on her bed. For forty days the pollution of birth was upon her, she could do nothing, not even be with her husband who during this time joined Vicky in the dining room. Yashpal tried to pay Vicky attention, asking school all right, homework all right, eating all right. When the boy stared at him silently, Yashpal gathered him to his chest, never mind, his aunt would soon be better, and in the meantime here, here was his baby sister, his to love and protect, his own sister.

Nisha was lain next to the dark gangly boy, her kaajal-smudged face, closed eyes, pale skin, and little pink mouth folded inwards, still and sleeping. Vicky looked at her – she was so small, he couldn't help but be distracted.

Yashpal noticed the boy's absorption, and in the evenings when he had his daughter, he would allow the boy to hold her. He was very cautious with the little bundle, balancing her carefully over legs stiffly clenched together. In addition to the wonder of something so tiny was the full attention of his uncle hovering over him.

'What a caring nature the boy has, just like his mother,' remarked Vicky's grandmother. 'She always looked after other people, slaving for them day and night.'

Vicky looked solemn, glad of the comparatively rare mention of his mother. It reminded him that it was through her that he had a rightful place in this house, a place that often seemed doubtful. With Nisha, he could pretend she was his real sister and there was no distinction between them. He thought all these things between coming home from school, playing cricket in the evenings, and labouring over his homework upstairs.

Sushila was quite anxious that her sister-in-law recover soon from her birthing ordeal – three children were too much for her to manage.

'Perhaps there is no space in her heart,' remarked Sona to Yashpal. Motherhood increased the things she could openly say.

'Poor Vicky,' sighed Yashpal. 'You are now his mother, it is natural he should want you.'

'I feel tired all the time. My stitches keep hurting. Even lifting such a small baby, I feel the strain,' responded Sona.

'It is difficult, I know. But it is our duty not to let the boy suffer more than he has.'

From these pious generalities Sona concluded it was now considered beyond her capacities to soothe Vicky's sorrow from his heart. Family equations had changed, his welfare was no longer solely her responsibility.

Ajay and Vijay were completely bored by the baby – they did not understand how a cricketer like their cousin could even want to hold her. The only thing she was good for were the presents and sweets given on her behalf when rakhi and bhai duj came along.

Sona began to wish Vicky shared his cousins' unconcern. 'He keeps wanting to hold her,' she complained to her sister, 'but he is so dirty and sweaty, I don't like it.'

'He does a lot for the baby,' pointed out Rupa, who during her visits had seen how Vicky was used. Bring this or that for baby, watch baby for a while, make sure baby doesn't fall off the bed, take her out in the pram, bring a hundred things from the fridge, run to the Udipi restaurant and get dosas and idlis, baby is ill, it will be difficult to cook.

'There he is, dark and ugly, leering like a crow over her, that's why I try and keep him occupied,' explained Sona.

Rupa said nothing. Sona went on, 'With no one to look after him, he is running wild. For hours he disappears into the galli. If only he weren't so young he could help in the shop.'

A few months of do this and do that and Vicky took to running out of the house and not returning till after dark.

Sona took to thrashing him, her head heavy with rage, using his studies as a further excuse for wielding her mighty chappal. 'If anything happens, my name will be mud. Where do you roam about all day? Don't you care about the money spent on your school, failing every year?' she shouted.

Within anybody's earshot she complained vociferously. 'The boy is growing wild. If he turns out like his father, don't blame me. I have done all I can,' she would say, virtue trembling through her body.

Vicky, hunched on his bed, pretended to study. Last year the Principal had passed him in tacit recognition of the liberal discounts given him by the cloth shop. His aunts reminded him of this daily.

'Let him be, bahu,' observed the grandmother. 'It is not as though he is going to be a teacher. Your father-in-law also didn't finish school.'

'In this day and age society expects you to be high-school pass,' Sona pointed out righteously. 'When he fails I am blamed. His uncle thinks I can put brains into his head.'

Vicky hated school, hated studying. The pattern had been set for failure, and he saw no point in struggling against it. When forced to stay inside he roamed restlessly through the four rooms, driving Sona mad. No one else seemed to mind him, but he crept under her skin, irritating her to the point where she wished him dead or at the very least out of the house.

Years in a joint family had given her appropriate communication training and she approached the matter indirectly, when she was serving the men their meals. This was a good and public time and she used it to show how distracted she was by the baby. Things had changed, and it behoved the family to notice.

Lala Banwari Lal did notice. When Sona remarked for the umpteenth time that poor Vicky was performing miserably in school, and it was time his own father showed interest, he decided that some changes in the boy's routine were necessary.

He knew women could make things difficult. Besides, God had blessed Sona with a second pregnancy, and tranquillity in the house was essential. He knew he had to look after Vicky till he stood on his feet; if those feet could only stand in the shop, so be it. Early in life he would learn you had to work for everything you got. This was not a bad thing for someone in Vicky's circumstances. His wife concurred.

Vicky would come straight to the shop from school, have lunch, and make himself useful. He would start him with a full day on Sundays and two till five on weekdays.

∾

That Sunday Vicky left the house with the men to start his career. It was the end of July and the lane leading to Ajmal Khan Road was churned with mud wet from yesterday's rain. The sabzi wallahs sat on either side under awnings of plastic, vegetables arranged on sacking. The vivid pale greens and bright red of cabbages, tomatoes, lauki, tinda, tori shone against the dull pavement. Vicky stepped through the mud carefully in imitation of his grandfather and uncles. Now he was part of the earning section of the family. His status would change: he would be looked up to, and given the respect that was given them. His meagre chest swelled at the thought of his future power. He would show everybody.

Two assistants were already waiting when they arrived. Yashpal took out the key, and motioned one of the boys to open the heavy padlock and crank the shutter up.

Inside, Yashpal and Banwari Lal took off their shoes, and arranged themselves on the white sheet-covered mattresses. Pyare Lal disappeared into the downstairs section, built after his marriage, gesturing Vicky to follow.

If Vicky had any fantasies of unfolding saris at a leisurely pace and draping them around himself to display to customers, he had to get rid of them with each step into the narrow, brightly lit, stuffy basement. He had to stand behind the counter all day, taking out rolls of cloth the assistant gestured to, serving the assistant, not even his uncle. The latter was remote, sitting on a comfortable swivel chair behind a glass-encased cash register, a modern version of the primitive cash box still used upstairs.

'Vicky – it is your first day here,' said Pyare Lal after a few hours. 'Do you want something cold?'

'There is still the whole day,' replied Vicky bashfully.

Yashpal slapped him on the back, told him not to be shy and gave him five rupees.

Vicky had never had five rupees to himself before. He fingered the green note, disappeared into the market, but nothing seemed worth the pang of parting with the money. Back in the shop, caressing the note in his pocket, he stood silently next to the entrance, before the pictures of Babaji and the Devi circled with sandalwood garlands. He folded his hands and prayed, may this be the beginning of my fortune.

'Beta,' said his grandfather, beaming at him. 'Believe in the Devi and Babaji. They will always keep your hands full. You must work, work, work, and leave the result to them. I lost everything, but today I have a shop of two floors.'

'Ji Baoji,' murmured Vicky.

Six days a week Vicky had his lunch in the shop. Banwari Lal and Yashpal would call him upstairs, move to the corner of the mattress, turn their backs, open up the four containers of their tiffin carrier, spread out the food on little steel plates, and begin to eat quickly, so that Pyare Lal could have his turn soon.

The meal over, Vicky was allowed to lie down behind the counter in the basement. He loved these moments. He dreamed of the day he would be big and earn lots of money. His father would be afraid of him. Maybe he would go back to Bareilly, but only after he accumulated wealth.

His mother had told him many times that he would be a big

man some day. To this end she remarked hungrily over every centimetre he grew, and fed him secretly on things that she never fed his father or herself. Growing boy, you are a growing boy, you need to eat well.

In Delhi his tallness, smallness, fatness, thinness gave nobody a minute's anxiety. Sometimes he heard his aunt remark, how much the boy eats, but this never resulted in more love, or more food. The hollow feeling in his stomach grew as he did. In the shop sometimes they exclaimed indulgently at his appetite, but they took pleasure in feeding him the samosas and kachoris that went with their tea.

Now, with more access to food and attention, he felt this was just the beginning. Money would follow. Lying on the floor in the afternoons, next to the assistant's feet, hidden by the counter, he saw the writing on the wall.

At home Vicky lorded it over his cousins, making Ajay and Vijay clamour to be taken to the shop. Sona watched this grimly. Now they will know what kind of troublemaker the boy is, they will see he is not to be trusted. She wondered how one child could produce so much evil in the house. The day she saw his face first thing in the morning was bound to be a bad day. Either Nisha would cry a lot, or she herself would get a headache, invariably compounded by irritability in her normally attentive husband on his return home.

Besides which, she had to slave in the kitchen for Vicky, who ate enough for six children. Maybe the birth of the second baby would push that unwanted child back to his proper home. By which time the register of black marks against Vicky would be full.

Raju, Vicky, and Nisha

Five months later Sona delivered her son. That moment on the hospital bed she experienced as the most blessed of her life. The mother of a son, she could join Sushila as a woman who had done her duty to the family, in the way the family understood it. Gone was the disgrace, the resentment, gone with the appearance of little Raju, as dark and plain-featured as his father, but a boy, a boy.

'Nisha has opened the luck of this family, I tell you,' exclaimed Rupa. 'Two children in two years after a decade of drought.'

'God has rewarded you,' cried the mother-in-law, clutching the day-old boy to her withered chest. 'At last the name of his father and grandfather will continue.'

'What are you talking about, Maji?' said Rupa, pretending to scold the old woman. 'When you have enough grandsons upstairs to carry on the family name.'

'What is that? Both sons should be able to hold their head high, not only one,' retorted the grandmother. 'Now the older one has a complete family I can die in peace.'

Sona listened, an IV attached to her wrist, dazed with the pain of her second Caesarean; the complications had been severe. But nothing mattered. She too had produced, produced a baby boy, who at this moment was being positioned against her burgeoning chest. Confidence began its steady journey, pumped into her veins along with the fluids of the drip.

The family was unanimous that Raju should be welcomed in a way suited to the first son of an eldest son. The room that had been filled at Nisha's birth was now filled with things essential to a little boy, down to cricket bat, ball, and tricycle. There were silver things from which this baby must eat and drink, gold chains to wear around his neck, little gold pendants for his forehead, and small gold bangles for his wrists. Many envelopes of money passed back and forth.

The grandparents gave ten thousand and one rupees, his uncle five thousand and one, his aunt Rupa one thousand and one, family friends, distributors, suppliers, and fellow shopkeepers five hundred and one, more distant connections a hundred and one.

All the children got new clothes and money. Even Vicky received a four-hundred-rupee watch.

Banwari Lal was a bit uncomfortable about the money spent. Whether five thousand and one came to little Raju from the upstairs uncle, or Ajay and Vijay received one thousand and one each, or Nisha was given a gold necklace she would not wear for another fifteen years, all this had only one source.

On the other hand, for too long there had been an unequal distribution of children, and therefore of expenditure. For once he would have to let family politics govern spending instead of market considerations.

As the children grew, Vicky hovered uneasily between shop and home, between upstairs and downstairs, between his grandparents and his aunts. By the time he was fifteen he was moody and gangly. He looked as though he had worms.

Sona alternated between using him to help with Nisha and Raju, and trying to get rid of him.

When he came home from the shop she and her children had napped, consumed their milk and tea, and now it was time for Vicky to amuse the younger children. Since he was their elder brother, Sona was convinced it was a pleasure for him to take Raju out to the park, push him on his tricycle, put him on the swings, and ensure he did not hurt himself on the jungle gym. Vicky resisted this under the guise of his homework. It was humiliating appearing as a boy servant in the park where he had impressed with his cricket bat.

One evening.

'Vickeeee,' screamed Sona in the angan.

No answer.

'Vickeee, Vickeeeee, Vickeeeeeeee.'

'Must be upstairs,' said Nisha, and waited for her mother's reaction.

'Always upstairs. Why doesn't he live upstairs? But no, it is my kismet that he should be a noose around my neck.'

Upstairs Sushila was telling Vicky, 'Go na. She is calling you.' Vicky shrugged his shoulders. He was watching TV with his cousins, eating the fried potatoes their mother had provided, and sipping a glass of tea.

'She must be wanting you to do some work,' said Sushila, sowing seeds in fertile ground.

'She always wants that,' tittered Ajay, faithfully following his mother's lead.

'Han, Mummy,' added Vijay, 'she doesn't like it when he comes up here and sits with us.'

'Don't talk about your tai like this,' said the aunt, approval dripping from her voice, touching the corners of her tender smile. 'She is the eldest in the house. She has looked after Vicky ever since he came here. It is a mother's right to scold, it goes with a mother's love.'

Vicky remained where he was, closed face and moving mouth. Finally Nisha arrived. 'You have to come quickly. Mummy says it is very important.'

Sushila looked knowing. Vicky left, and Sona had to get angry in a low voice, because she knew that prying woman upstairs was listening, and this irritated her even more. 'For this I clothe you and feed you? So somebody has to dance attendance on you? Why can't you come when called, two, three times? Deaf, are you? Especially when you know it is time for Raju to go out.'

Raju started to fuss. 'Out, out, out,' he shouted.

'But no, you are too busy enjoying yourself upstairs.'

The boy sullenly grabbed his cousin and tricycle and left. Nisha set up a wail. 'I want to go too.'

'You can't,' said her mother shortly.

'Why? Why can't I?'

'It is better for girls to remain inside.'

'Why?'

'You will get black and dirty.'

'So what? Raju is black. Blacker than Vicky.'

The mother's face twisted. The boy's darkness was a pain in her heart, all the more noticeable next to Nisha's fairness and Vicky's nondescript yellow. 'Raju is the colour of Krishna,' she now said.

'He is not. Krishna is blue,' retorted Nisha.

The mother was momentarily diverted. 'He is shown blue because no human hand can paint what He is. He is the colour of the darkest clouds on a monsoon day. The blackness people long to see because it means an end to their suffering.'

The girl looked at her mother. Her eyes were dreamy, she seemed to have forgotten her anger. 'I also want to be the colour of Krishna. I am going to play cricket in the sun.'

'Krishna is a god. You, you will look like the sweeper woman who comes to the house. You want to look like a kali bhainsi?'

What kind of question was that? Who would want to look like a black buffalo?

Sona drew her daughter on to her knee, and pinched her round white cheeks.

'You take after me. When I was young people used to say I was like the moon, the champa flower, the lotus. And when your father saw me,' she stopped and giggled, 'he said he would become a monk if he couldn't marry me. Even so, my father was not keen.'

52

'Why?'

'We are service people, not traders, more like Rupa Masi's husband. My father thought I would have to adjust too much. But then your father threatened to run away, and your grandfather begged my parents to agree.'

Nisha couldn't imagine her grandfather begging anybody.

'Now how can you be like me if you get dirty and black playing in the sun?' continued the mother. 'Who will want to marry you?'

Another step taken to make sure Nisha grew into the family princess.

Every evening Nisha was dressed in beaded, sequinned, lacy, frilled frocks of nylon, polyester, and cotton mixes. On her feet she wore shiny pointed shoes with little heels, and socks with bows to match the dresses. Her hair was combed into ponytails secured with elastic bands dangling with plastic birds, fish, and multicoloured flowers.

Unfortunately her outfits did not match her inclinations. 'I want to play in the park,' she whined periodically, as she saw the boys rush out accompanied by bat, ball, wickets, purpose, and excitement. Soon, however, she became reconciled to preserving her clothes and complexion by playing board games with her grandmother. Occasionally she wished she had a sister. Of her four brothers, Vicky was the only one who paid her any attention, touching and stroking her when he could. When he came home it was usually with something small for her, aam papar or sour churan sweets twisted in a paper cone.

೧

Vicky was by now seventeen. If he could only pass his tenth boards he would be free of school for ever. Free of his aunt's hectoring, free to sit in the shop all day – one of the men, displaying cloth, running errands, hoping to prove his worth. His grandfather was by now sixty-six; the travelling was all done by his uncles. He could easily go along with them to Bombay, Madras, or Ahmedabad, easily accompany them to the garment fairs they talked about.

But first he needed to shake the dust of school off his feet.

'Vicky?'

'Hoon?'

'Where are you going?'

'To the roof.'

'Why?'

'To study.'

'Why?'

'Why? Because my exams are coming, and I have to pass. Why else? Because I love to read?'

Nisha giggled.

Because Vicky was fond of Nisha he did not add that on the roof he would not be at the constant beck and call of her mother.

'Will you pass this time?' asked Nisha with interest.

'How do I know? They fail me to get bribes from us.'

'That's very unfair,' said Nisha indignantly.

'That's the way they all are. Otherwise I know as much as the other boys.'

'When can you play with me?'

'Not now.'

'I'm also coming. See, I've got this.' She showed him the snakes and ladders board she was carrying.

'Go find somebody else. I can't be playing with you all the time.'

Nisha caught him by the arm, 'Please, na, please.'

'I've told you I have to study. If I don't pass they'll cut my throat.' Vicky drew his long finger across his thin and bony neck. His Adam's apple stuck out as he flung his head back.

'You yourself say you know everything. I'll tell Papaji to talk to your teachers,' persisted Nisha, with the confidence of a petted child. 'It's mean to go on failing you.'

'I don't care. As soon as I can, I shall open my own shop. Baoji didn't finish school, look at him.'

They reached the roof, and Vicky spread his durrie in the shelter of the water tank. Around them jars of pickles and kanji were fermenting. Nisha rolled the pickle around, so that the top pieces would get soaked with the sour juices. She peeked into the black carrot kanji, dipped her finger in, and sucked it, but the rye hadn't permeated the liquid, and it lacked body. She was disappointed. 'Look,' she said to Vicky, 'the colour hasn't taken yet.'

'Hoon.'

'Do you want a carrot?' She dropped her fingers experimentally into the jar once more.

'Mamiji will beat me.'

That her mother would react strongly to any tampering with the jars on the roof was undeniable. Especially if she thought Vicky had a hand in it.

'Arre, how will she know?' said Nisha. 'I will tell her I have taken.'

'And she will believe you?'

'Yes.' The little girl pried open his mouth and shoved the carrot in. Vicky looked at her for a moment and then flung himself on the durrie and moodily opened his books. Nisha arranged the snakes and ladders board, the dice, and the coloured pieces next to him and waited. Vicky started chanting passages from his book. She began to fidget. 'Why are you always studying so hard? No one else does.'

'No one else has the same problems passing.'

'Then why do you?'

'I don't know,' said Vicky gloomily. 'School is good for nothing. You can't make money with it, I don't know why I even have to go. Maybe because all of you do, but my school is bad, and yours is good.'

'Your mother would have wanted it,' said Nisha, repeating something she had heard her father tell his nephew often.

Vicky did not reply. Nothing in his mother's life had hap-

pened the way she wanted it, and this argument always
· struck him as convenient rather than true.

'This time you won't fail – I say you won't.'

'Oh – you are the teacher now, are you? And the Principal
– Nisha says don't fail, and I don't.'

Nisha tittered.

'I want to leave school, I want to manage a shop,' said
Vicky, straining towards visions of independence, money,
and recognition that would come when allowed to handle
customers. Till now he was only an onlooker in the games of
persuasion and seduction, could only hear rather than par-
ticipate in talk of prices, fashion, how well the material would
wear, wash, stitch, fall, how many metres of this needed, how
many metres of that matching. One day, one day, he dreamt,
one day he would be the one showing, he would be the one
seducing, he would be the one looking sideways at pretty
girls. 'Meanwhile I live like a poor boy in this house.'

Nisha stared at him while Vicky continued, 'I know they
only keep me because I am useful. It is my fate that no one
wants me. How many times has your mother said, even your
own father doesn't want you – so what can I expect from
other people?'

They were alone on the roof, there was no one to see or
scold, and Vicky allowed himself the luxury of some tears.
Nisha, whose tears had always been immediately attended to,
couldn't bear it. She threw herself on his back, and put her
arms around his neck. 'You have me, Vicky, you have me,' she
said, rocking against his back, while Vicky snivelled into his
sleeve. 'And everybody else too,' Nisha went on. 'Raju,
Mummy, Papaji, Dadu, Dadi, Chacha, Chachi, Ajay and Vijay,
all your own blood, Vicky, your own blood,' parroted Nisha.

'Don't talk to me of my own blood. In this world you can
trust nobody,' said Vicky, in turn parroting phrases that
suited his vision of the world. 'One day I will run away from
their house and shop. I will show them,' he continued, flapping the books he loathed.

Pretty, precocious and petted, there was not a lap in the house Nisha was not familiar with. And in those laps, as she was fed, cuddled, and bounced, words flowed around her, and into her, informing her of the ways of her house before she could even think.

And in the ways of the house, the shop was central: travelling for it, buying for it, fighting for it, working and planning for it, collecting its outstanding dues from the market, dealing with its defaulters, being vigilant about shoddy goods, being let down by wholesalers not as scrupulous as they, being worried by weavers and mills, striving to keep their reputation pristine. What else was there for any man of this family but the shop?

Now she dug her puzzled chin into Vicky's back. How could one show anybody in her home? There were too many. They were not paying attention.

'Bas. Now get off my back. You are getting heavy.' He put his hands around the plump legs, stroked them up and down, while trying to pull her off.

Nisha wound her feet around his stomach. Vicky pulled her legs again and she slid around him into his lap, laughing. Vicky looked at her. She was so sweet. If only she was his real sister he wouldn't have to leave her one day.

Nisha started resetting the upset snakes and ladders. 'Now you have to play with me. Before you run away.'

'You will have forgotten me,' said Vicky. He stretched himself beside Nisha, moodily rolling the dice. Gradually he curled himself around her, his head propped on one hand. She leant against him, her mind on the game. Her dress rose higher as she fidgeted, her legs banging up and down on the durrie, next to Vicky's nose. Entranced, he put his hand on the inside of her beckoning thigh and whispered, 'How soft you are, Nisha.'

An intent look came on his face, his gentle fingers kept up a steady stroking. He began to trace the elastic of her panties all around the leg. 'What are you doing? Chee, that's dirty,

57

take your hand away,' she cried, but Vicky was in no state to hear her. Panting slightly, he pushed his hand inside, touching the place where she did su-su, tracing the slit that divided her. Nisha wriggled even more frantically – 'I'll tell everybody how dirty you are' – but his grip tightened, and his arm pressed her thigh down so that both her legs were parted, and the slit was looser. A little su-su she could not help came out and wet his hand. She tried to draw her legs up and away from him, but he forced himself closer.

'We are not going to tell anybody about this,' he whispered, holding her. 'This is our secret. See, you have done su-su. Ajay, Vijay, and I are always doing su-su in front of each other.'

He put those fingers against his mouth. 'Give me your hand,' he went on. 'I want to show you something.'

'I don't want to see.' Nisha was crying.

'Of course you do.'

'No, I want to go to Mummy. Leave me.'

'See, another secret.' And quickly, so quickly that she didn't know how it happened, he introduced it to her. Terror-stricken, she looked at the black thing sticking up, and then quickly looked away.

'Feel it.' He grabbed her hand. She pulled back, and felt the stiff, straight thing knock against her fist. It felt dry and hard and hot.

'See.' Vicky's voice was hoarse. Once she started looking she couldn't look away. It appeared weird, repulsive, and fascinating. 'Hold it, go on.'

'No, no, I don't want to.'

Vicky gripped her wrist so hard and painfully that her fingers opened around the big dark thing. There it was, the small, pudgy, fair little hand against the much darker skin, with the boy's larger hand clamped over the girl's.

He started moving their hands up and down. Quickly the tempo increased, as the fear grew in her. When she tried to struggle, he increased the pressure of his hand.

He gasped, and out spurted white liquid on to the snakes and ladders, then trickled down her fist. The thing shrank, his face shrivelled. 'It's our secret. If you tell anyone, they will beat you and me.' He gripped her arm. 'No one must ever know. No one. You understand.'

Nisha nodded wordlessly. Vicky wiped her hand, then the snakes and ladders, with a corner of his shirt, and gave the game to her. She took it gingerly. They started down, Vicky clutching the durrie and his books, his hair flying over his forehead, his blue Bata rubber chappals going clutter-futter loudly down the stairs. Nisha followed.

They reached downstairs and Vicky disappeared into the corner of the dining room to his cupboard. Nisha stood silently, staring at the game in her hand. She crossed the angan to the outer wall of the house, and as high and hard as she was able, threw first the board, then the small cardboard box of counters, over the wall, waiting to hear them thud on the other side before going in.

Nisha

In the days that followed, Nisha grew silent. For the first time she felt divided from the family she had so unthinkingly been part of. Her mother was always so particular about her being clean, now she had done something dirty. Her hand had touched that filthy black thing. She tried to block it from her mind, but it proliferated, grew large and terrifying.

Meanwhile Vicky's preoccupation with Nisha increased, his eyes fixed on the small white hand that had caressed him, the hand that had made him come all over the durrie. Just thinking of the excitement and the release made him long for it again.

He started making excuses for coming home early. 'I can't study in the shop,' he said. 'I need to stay home and concentrate.' This was accepted as a sign of mature behaviour.

With the small change he wheedled out of his uncles, he bought more gifts for her, little chocolates, sticks of chewing gum, packets of sour mango, sugar-coated fennel seed.

Vicky was always on the lookout for opportunities to get Nisha alone. Then bliss would follow. She was too young to understand what was happening, and then he really wasn't doing anything bad to her. Certainly she showed no signs of remembering anything.

He bought kites. 'Come, Nishu, I'll teach you to fly them.'

Nisha didn't look up from her colouring book, and Raju came instead. Sona watched in approval while Vicky made himself useful with her son.

It was evening, the time children drink their milk and go to play. When adults move out of bedrooms darkened against the glare by heavy curtains, sip their tea, and contemplate the heat receding against lengthening shadows.

The little servant boy had left the hosepipe on in the angan to cool it, and was now sweeping the water into a hole in the corner connected to the drain outside. Raju was getting in his way, squirting water at the swept areas, flooding them all over again, grabbing the broom, insisting on sweeping himself.

Nisha was staring at the glass of milk in her hand.

'Drink, beti, drink,' urged the grandmother. She took the glass and held it against the resisting lips. 'One for Papaji, come on, one sip.'

Nisha took the smallest possible sip.

'One for Mummy.'

Another infinitesimal swallow.

'One for Bhaiyya.'

Sip. The grandmother looked into the steel glass. 'Beti, your sips must be larger. Otherwise how will you grow into a big girl? Bhaiyya will race ahead of you.'

Nisha said nothing. 'Now finish, finish,' coaxed the grandmother. 'One for Bhaiyya.'

'You said that.'

'Achcha achcha, sorry. One for Vijay – one for Chacha – one for Chachi – one for Dadi – one for Dada – one for Vicky –'

'I don't want to drink to Vicky.'

'Arre, why? He is your Bhaiyya, just like Raju –'

'No, still.'

'O-ho, poor Vicky, what has he done to you?'

Nisha pushed the glass away.

'Whatever it is, forgive him. He has no one else, poor boy. Now, one for Rupa Masi – one for Uncle –'

The names of the family slowly recited took almost twenty minutes, as the level of the milk sluggishly dropped. The grandmother kept her eyes firmly on the little girl. She knew that if no one was looking she would pour her milk down the angan sink.

The milk finished at last, Nisha got up, put her glass next to the tap on the floor of the kitchen for the utensil washer-woman, and disappeared into her grandparent's room, where she had been placed after Raju's birth.

She lugged her school bag over to the bed, and took out her English book to learn the names of the months for tomorrow's dictation. Twelve names, five sums in addition, an eight-line poem in Hindi, and then she could go out to play. Back and forth on the bed she swayed, her hand covering the words she was trying to memorise, chanting the spellings softly to herself.

She had reached August when she heard Vicky settle himself on the bed behind her. He too had dragged his bag in, and was making a great show of opening his books. Nisha kept the letters of August firmly running through her mind.

'What are you doing?' Vicky asked after five minutes.

Nisha bent her head further over her book.

There was silence for a while. Then Vicky murmured, 'Nishu?'

'I'll tell Mummy you are not letting me study.'

'Mummy has gone upstairs with Raju.'

'Dadi then.'

'She is talking to the neighbour.'

'Go away.'

He shifted a little closer. Instantly her skin began to prickle.

' Nishu,' he whispered, 'are you angry with me?'

The smallest shake of the head.

'Then why aren't you talking to me?'

'I'm talking to you.'

'Here,' he coaxed, drawing her stiff, resisting body nearer him, 'show me that you are not angry with me.' His hands reached under her dress. She pressed her thighs tightly together, but his fingers forced themselves between her legs. A little su-su she could not help came out and wet her panties. She wanted to die of shame.

'What have you done, naughty? So big, and wetting your

panties?' he said hoarsely, his lips against her ear. He started stroking her, the wet panty resting on the knobbly knuckle. 'See, I am drying you,' he rasped. 'You must thank me, dirty girl.'

She tried shaking her head, bumping it against his shoulder, but he was concentrating on what he was doing and his grip grew harder. She winced in pain, his deep, uneven breaths burnt against her cheek.

In a daze she struggled against the body that was pressing itself so completely into her. Her book fell from her hand. She could feel him tugging at something behind her back. Then he reached around, took her hand, and clasped it on that hot monstrous thing. She turned away her head, he gripped the hand in his, and began the fast movement up and down, but not for long – the liquid came, his clutch loosened, he sighed, moaned, and wiped her hand.

'If you say anything to anybody,' muttered Vicky unnecessarily into her ear, 'they will beat you. They will lock you up, and never let you go to school.'

Nisha freed herself, got up unsteadily, and went into the angan. Her grandmother was still outside with the neighbour, her mother still upstairs with Raju. She sat alone in the kitchen, till her mother scolded her for being a lazy girl, and not attending to her schoolwork – did she want to end up like Vicky, failing all the time?

That evening Nisha could not eat. Her mouth felt dry, her head heavy, her hands clammy. When her Dadi coaxed a morsel down, she coughed and threw up.

'Look at this girl,' scolded her mother in routine exasperation. 'Why can't she ever eat? Fussing even when it is her favourite black dal with butter.'

Nisha broke her roti into bits, hid some under her bowl of curd, dropped some on the floor, and scattered the rest around her steel plate, so that it would look as though she had eaten.

'Why have you left so much?' demanded her mother.

'Poor thing, she couldn't be feeling hungry. She is looking pale,' interposed the grandmother.

'Is she ever hungry?' asked the mother. 'The whole day is spent feeding her. Still she is so thin. And upstairs of course they fill her with rubbish so that at dinner she eats nothing again.'

'I wasn't upstairs,' Nisha replied, stung, tears filling her eyes. 'I was here only. Vicky also.' She choked on the word.

No one understood what that meant. She threw herself into her grandmother's lap, and pulled the palla over her head, like she had seen Raju do countless times when given his bottle. Once in that safe, filtered world she wept and wept.

∾

Ever since Raju's birth, Nisha had been sleeping with her grandmother. The ancient woman, after the required amount of grumbling, tried to keep secret how much she doted on this gift from heaven. For the first time in thirty years she had a young one in her bed, a young arm thrown around her neck. Her nights were now tinged with care and wakefulness; feeling useful, she clung to the sleeping child.

Now she felt something was not right with Nisha. From being a child who went to sleep the minute her head hit the pillow, she refused to lie down or close her eyes.

'I will stay up all night,' she declared.

'Why, baby, why?' they coaxed.

'I want to,' was all she said. When she dropped off in exhaustion, she awoke crying, 'Why did you let me sleep? I had bad dreams, I had bad dreams.' But she couldn't say what they were.

'It was nothing,' they soothed. 'It was nothing, just a dream – you are in your own home, safe and sound, with Mummy-Papaji, Dadi-Dadu, Chacha-Chachi, Ajay-Vijay, Vicky-Raju, who all love you.'

*

In the nights to follow the child's screaming became worse. As a result it was often impossible to wake her in the morning. Her father began to say, 'Let her be, do not send her to school today.'

How long can a child not go to school?

'Maybe she should see a doctor?' suggested her Sushila chachi. 'Such crying and screaming is not normal.'

'There is nothing wrong with Nisha,' retorted Sona coldly. 'All children have bad dreams from time to time.'

'Send her upstairs to sleep with us,' said Pyare Lal.

'Yes, yes,' echoed his wife. 'She will be all right there.'

'No need. She will settle down in a few days.'

The uncle and the aunt said nothing more. Who could teach Sona to put the interests of her children above her jealousy? No one.

But they were wrong. Sona was bothered enough by the child's obvious distress to ask her later whether she wanted to sleep upstairs. Nisha mutely refused.

The nights continued the same. In the day she looked pale and sick. When her sister came over, Sona discussed the problem. 'Put her to sleep in your bed,' advised the aunt.

'Impossible. Raju will never be able to sleep with so much disturbance,' said Sona. 'As it is he is a light sleeper.'

Rupa nodded. All the other children in the house were heavy sleepers, the consequence of restricted space and unrestricted noise, but Raju's sleep was guarded fiercely by his mother.

'Send her to my house,' suggested Rupa. 'Maybe something has frightened her. You cannot always tell.'

Sona was torn between objecting to the idea that anything in the house could frighten her daughter and agreeing because there seemed no other solution. Besides, it would show the people upstairs that she had her own resources, she needn't depend on them, thank you very much.

Nisha departed and the grandmother was left to an empty bed and long, restful nights. Through those nights she wondered about the little girl. What had happened? When she asked the mother how she was in the aunt's house, Sona said she was just fine, her sleep was peaceful, and her aunt was looking after her very well. Perhaps something in this house had scared her?

A mulish look came over the grandmother's face. Sona was envious of the child's attachment to her, that was it, and was making up things to take her away. What could frighten her when she was never alone?

Vicky also doted on the child – poor boy, so much affection in him, just like his mother. Soon he would finish school, and then he would be old enough to get married. Maybe his wife would bring with her a destiny that would better his.

She now insisted that for the Class X Boards a tutor be hired to make sure Vicky passed. They had to be careful, results could not be arranged for Board exams.

Sona protested for form's sake that Vicky was being spoiled, in her time nobody had heard of tutors. She didn't raise too many objections though, because in her heart she was grateful to him for her children. That she couldn't bear to see him was another matter. Her womb had opened when he came.

A neighbourhood tutor was found. Every evening Vicky walked to his place, to join five others also cramming for the exams. Like him, these were sons of traders living in Karol Bagh, seized of the necessity to be at least tenth-class pass. The lessons were two hours each, and Vicky's time out of the house was by now considerable. School, shop, tuition.

During evening classes, Vicky frequently boasted of his family's business. 'Lala Banwari Lal & Sons, Saris, Shawls, Suitings, Shirtings' was a prominent board on Ajmal Khan Road, and easily noticed.

~

The childless Rupa was now partially blessed. Her sister's prayers had benefited her as well, and the day Nisha moved in with her aunt, she felt she had not valued their efficacy enough.

The first night the child was there, three adults hung about her, watching every bite of puri aloo she put into her mouth. After she had eaten, Rupa changed her clothes, made her brush her teeth and wash her feet, put a little cream on her face, and replaited her oiled hair.

Nisha slept between her uncle and aunt in the middle of a big double bed, the tips of her soft feet and hands shining with the nail polish her aunt had applied to amuse her.

Her mouth was slightly open, her little cheeks round and white. 'Just look at her,' murmured her uncle, taken, as everyone must be, by the picture of sleeping innocence. 'What gave her those nightmares? Something must have happened in your sister's house.'

Rupa's heart caught in a beat of sorrow. What a father the man would have made! Yet he never made her feel inadequate, nor had she experienced the hell her sister had.

'They say nothing happened,' she slowly replied. 'Someone is always around.'

'That is not the same as paying attention.'

As so often, Rupa was struck by her husband's wisdom. Of course something had happened, the child's sudden nightmares were sufficient testimony. But what? She never went outside, it had to be something within the house. Sexual suspicion, never far away where a girl was concerned, hovered in egalitarian fashion over Banwari Lal, Pyare Lal, Yashpal – no, no, no, too improbable – Ajay, Vijay – no, no, too young – and Vicky . . . yes, Vicky was just right. As she reached her conclusion, waves of hatred for the boy submerged her. Sona was right, he was a black crow, a vulture, pecking at whomever he could. When would he finally leave? Till that moment she was determined to keep the girl. If it meant presenting uncertainty as fact to her sister, so be it. The child's life was at stake.

Nisha now found herself in an atmosphere very different from the one she had lived in. As the only child she was the centre of interest, concern, and attention.

She came back from school to the smell of pickles maturing, the fragrance of frying savouries, the sight of slices of mango, cubes of lemon, slivers of chilli, and mottled dates soaked in lemon juice all drying in the sun.

'You and Uncle eat so much pickle!' she remarked, such abundance demanding comment.

Rupa laughed. 'Who can eat so much? I sell it. It is my business.'

Nisha stared at her. Rupa laughed again. 'You know that shop in Karol Bagh? The one near your father's? Roopams? Some of the pickles, chutneys, and sherbets there are mine.' She laughed again – indeed, she couldn't stop laughing. At home Nisha's father, grandfather and uncle were never amused about business. Maybe it had to do with pickles.

'Your Papaji helps me,' went on Rupa. 'Now come, take off your uniform, wash up, then we will eat,' she said, extending a hand that smelt strongly of mustard oil and chillies.

Gradually the girl's bad dreams grew infrequent. In their cessation Rupa found proof that the demon lay in her home – otherwise, would such a small child willingly leave her mother? She could only marvel at the spirit that made her scream till she was rescued.

∽

Rupa's husband Prem Nath was small, thin, and dark, with clever eyes, a neat moustache, and sparse hair combed smoothly back. His pastel-coloured bush shirts hung straight and limp over his pants. He was a mechanical draughtsman

68

with the Air Headquarters under the Defence Ministry. His job was to draw detailed parts of Russian and American planes when something went wrong. This enabled local imitation and removed the need for importing expensive components.

Like so many men in government positions he felt undervalued and underpaid. His salary and his privileges were on a par with those of men who did nothing, knew nothing, and cared nothing.

That was the trouble with government jobs. Security of employment was guaranteed democratically for able, unable, deserving, undeserving, conscientious and unconscientious. It was unjust and frustrating.

He had sat for the IAS exam once, knowing he would never be able to pass. But what was the harm in trying? When he was disqualified at the interview stage his detachment deserted him. He knew it was his clothes, his small-time air, that went against him. Bitterly he registered with the Employment Exchange and took the first job that was offered. It guaranteed security till retirement, a phone, and a minuscule flat in a high-rise. The flat he rented out illegally – with the pittance he was paid, he was entitled to make whatever money he could on the side. Most of his energy was spent in fighting his case.

He did not regret not having children. Part of his capacity to think, felt his admiring wife, was reflected in his stoicism. To want children was another word for I, me, mine. It was easier to be free without such attachments. Besides, India had enough children.

Such thoughts earned him the reputation of the philosopher in the family.

Prem Nath despised the fuss that had been made over Sona's so-called barrenness. Vicky was not considered child enough. No, they had to have their own flesh and blood. Such a merchant-like quality. Traders, shopkeepers, with not an idea in their heads, not a book in their past. If he thought like this, he would not send a paisa to his sister to help with her children. Rupa may say what she liked, but his assistance was far more generous than the charity doled out to Vicky. Thank God his family knew how to share. Though poor, their hearts were large.

Two sisters more different than Sona and Rupa he could not imagine. One self-obsessed, complaining, and dissatisfied, the other a well of sweet water from which everyone drank. Maybe it was thwarted maternal instinct, but the latest example was the niece that his wife was treating like a daughter. He hoped Rupa would remember this was a borrowed child and would one day have to be returned.

Shortly after Nisha's arrival, Prem Nath came home from work carrying two books.

'Here, beti, see.'

Nisha looked. *Stories from the Ramayana* and *Jatka Tales.*

'Arre, how can she read such big fat books?' scolded Rupa. 'Why didn't you get her the k, kh, ga?'

'I know the k, kh, ga,' said Nisha indignantly.

'Of course you do,' said Prem Nath. 'These I am going to read to you. I am sure nobody bothers with such things in that house of yours.'

While Rupa wondered whether the aspersions cast on Sona's family should gratify or annoy, Prem Nath put Nisha on his lap and started showing her the pictures.

And so Nisha's greater education began. Prem Nath became a regular visitor to the second-hand bookshops of Daryaganj. Often pencil-marked, dog-eared, sometimes torn, yellowed, and smelling of wet paper, they were still books, and her uncle made sure Nisha treated them with respect.

Months passed, Nisha close to six, and was about to exhaust the possibilities of play school. Weren't her parents going to see about a proper educational institution, thought the uncle irritably. In most schools applications had to be submitted by the end of December. He could make enquiries, but he was afraid this might be overstepping avuncular boundaries.

'Isn't that family of yours going to do something?' he demanded of his wife. 'Fine way to abdicate responsibility, dump the girl here and forget her.'

'How can you say that? They are always sending us things so she is more comfortable.'

'I hope they realise children are not brought up on things,' said Prem Nath, ignoring the reference to the heater and geyser that had been the most recent offering. 'They need thought, attention, timely action.'

'Why don't you take the initiative about her school?' demanded Rupa in turn. 'Bhai Sahib is in the shop all day.'

'Yes, making money is more important than his daughter,' flashed Prem Nath. He knew the family had suffered during Partition, over Sunita's death, over Vicky's upbringing, but they were making money, and therefore their suffering was held to be of a dubious nature. They were not involved in a long and useless lawsuit to claim what was rightfully theirs. In fact, what was rightfully theirs went on multiplying.

His wife did not take his taunts seriously. It's only his manner of speaking, she would laugh, his heart is so large, just see him with the child.

'I am sure Didi will approve any school you chose. Poor thing, how can she know where to go, or who to talk to? Bhai Sahib is always busy, she needs you,' flattered Rupa now.

First Prem Nath approached his brother-in-law. He wanted no allegations of meddling. A matter of unnecessary precaution, perhaps, but in his position he had to be careful. The balance between crude money and intellectual superiority should have made everything equal, but to his sorrow he often found this was not so.

He decided to talk to Yashpal at his work place. He didn't feel like getting Sona's uninformed opinion on Nisha's schooling, nor did he feel like acknowledging indirect references to various gifts. He dropped in at the shop, noticed the small garland of winking red lights that adorned the pictures of the Devi and Babaji, greeted Lala Banwari Lal in front of the cash box, nodded at his brother-in-law, who was unfolding gorgeous Kanjeevaram sari after sari before three choosy women, and seated himself at the far end.

Prem Nath hadn't been to the shop in a long time. Gilt-splashed mirrors covered the wall next to him. There were glass doors at the entrance, and the atmosphere was air-cooled. The benches were crowded with customers, more were making their way to the basement. Prem Nath tried to calculate the amount of profit the Banwari Lals must be making in a month, then gave up. There was too much he didn't know.

A boy brought him a cup of tea and a plate of Dalima coconut cookies. Prem Nath had not seen the gesture that resulted in this, but gratefully sipped, nibbled, and waited.

Yashpal looked at the man sitting next to the mirror-covered wall. It was unusual to see his brother-in-law in the shop, they always met at home, and during the past months, always with Nisha. He sighed.

When he came home every evening, he missed her, but there had been one casual reference of Rupa's to Vicky that prevented him from demanding her return.

'How well Nisha is settling down, of course she misses everybody at home, but between you and me, Bhai Sahib, I think it well if she stays away until some other arrangement is made about Vicky. In a family matter one cannot say more.'

'Has Nisha said anything?' was all Yashpal could manage.

'She is just a child, what can she say?' said Rupa, 'But notice how she avoids him. I have been observing, only then am I saying.'

'Does your sister know?'

Rupa shook her head.

'You cannot be sure – besides, she was never left alone.'

'It is my duty to warn you,' replied Rupa stiffly. Really, her husband was right about these people. 'Otherwise, she is your child, you can do what you like.'

'I will see,' said Yashpal, hating his sister-in-law. Who was she to make these allegations? After all he had done for her.

Every time his daughter came home clutching some dog-eared books, resisting Raju's attempts to snatch them, he noticed how happy she looked. He saw how the uncle and aunt doted on her, heard the many stories told of her, watched her climb into Rupa's lap when Vicky was there, and observed his own wife preoccupied with her son – the fruit of years of sacrifice and, as with such fruit, demanding of cease-less attention. With an aching heart he realised wisdom lay in doing nothing.

'They are spoiling her,' Sona sometimes complained in front of the grandparents – to let them know there were oth-ers in the family who could spoil her children.

'Nisha will bring raunaq to that household,' said Lala Banwari Lal comfortably. 'Rupa is someone who takes care.'

Sona looked proprietary, while Yashpal told himself that children were meant to be shared. If Nisha was flourishing in her aunt's house, and the childless couple experienced joy as a result, he should not stand in the way. As daughters, sisters, and wives, women lit up their households, and it was Nisha's good fortune that, despite being a mangli, she could start so early. Besides, one should not be too attached.

Now Prem Nath was asking about schools. He knew he was also asking how much part they could expect to play in Nisha's life. Did he share Rupa's suspicions?

'You are doing so much for her, too much I think. Perhaps she would be better off at home with her brothers,' he probed.

'She is a very good girl,' Prem Nath responded, 'but it is better if she is brought up away from boys. They are very rough. All her screaming has stopped now.'

A pause, and then Prem Nath could not help a small display of the little one's power. 'My father loves her. Every night he tells her a story from our scriptures. And how she remembers everything!'

'She is yours. I rely completely on you, Bhai Sahib, to send her to a good girls' school. That she reads so much at her age is due to you.'

'She picks up things very easily. Just have to tell her once,' said the uncle, trying to be modest.

∾

Distance was a consideration in choosing a school. Prem Nath didn't want the child travelling long hours in a bus. And of course gender was a consideration, he didn't need the father to tell him that. A girls' school would provide a traditional upbringing, and after her probable experience it was best there be no exposure to boys. The school had to have labs, the girl should be able to do science if she wanted.

He visited all the suitable institutions in the area and filled in every form. If the child passed the entrance examinations, and she was so bright there was no reason why she shouldn't, then his final choice would be the New Horizon Public School. He liked the compound, the facilities were modern, the Principal caring. Nisha would do well there.

Both he and Rupa appeared for the parent-teacher interview. She lives with us, we are her guardians. They had decided to say this to avoid bothersome requests for the signatures of the parents.

Nisha was tested for Class I: English, Hindi, and Maths. She passed with flying colours.

'It is all due to you, Bhai Sahib,' said Yashpal.

'She is your daughter,' said Rupa, not wanting to seem possessive of the girl. Sona might get jealous.

Sona looked complacent, while Sushila from upstairs

74

pointed out that with her uncle caring so much, the girl was bound to do well. She would be a dunce if she did not.

Rupa knew the subject of the next week's conversation was being created right there. So that she should be able to repeat her own remarks as a counterpoint, and win her sister's approval, she added, 'Her uncle does take a lot of pains, it is true, but Nisha is so intelligent it is clear she comes from this family.'

The pattern of Nisha's next ten years was now set. She spent all week with her aunt and uncle. A rickshaw picked her up, took her to school, dropped her back. When she spent weekends with her parents, her father made sure that Vicky was never close to her.

Vicky

To everybody's delight Vicky passed Class X with a third division. Sweets were distributed. Done with education, Vicky left school, never to open a book again.

There was now the question of his future.

He should go back to his father, argued Yashpal.

Pyare Lal concurred. We have done our duty, if we keep him he will be a noose around our necks.

But Lala Banwari Lal looked upon Vicky as the agent through whom he could redress the wrongs that had been inflicted on his daughter. Such a tender sentiment was not to be tampered with easily.

Suggestively, persuasively, insinuatingly, persistently, hoping that reason and common sense would prevail, the family kept at it. Send him back, we have Ajay, Vijay, and Raju to establish, as well as Nisha to marry. The father should be given a chance to settle the boy, they were being unfair in keeping him away. An only son, he would shine in his parental home, here he was lost among cousins. Finally the grandfather agreed.

Vicky was used to Karol Bagh, and remembered his father with loathing. He wept, he asked what had he done to displease them, why were they casting him off. If he was sent back, he would kill himself.

Uncles and aunts were united in their opinion of Vicky's behaviour. Deceitful, cunning, his father's son, not poor Sunita's. Vicky was told that if he disturbed Lala Banwari Lal by tears or threats, future connection with his mother's relatives would be severed.

Lala Banwari Lal was now approaching seventy, but such was his heart, exclaimed the family, that he insisted on taking the boy to Bareilly himself. They would travel by the night train, spend the day there, and return the next morning.

A week later, Vicky, with his possessions in an aluminium trunk, was escorted to the station along with his grandfather and younger uncle. He was silent. The men tried to persuade him once again that he was embarking on the future his mother would have desired. His grandfather had cared for him all these years, his father now wanted a chance. There would of course always be visits.

Vicky saw very little visiting when his mother was alive and preferred to express his feelings through stubborn silence.

The journey was not a pleasant one.

Bareilly. Was it always like this? Dirty, crowded, everything small and mean, the buildings indistinguishable from one another? Lanes so narrow that for a car to pass, rickshaws, cyclists, and pedestrians had to squeeze against the side of the road next to open drains?

And the house? True, with two angans it had a sense of space. The one in front led to a veranda, with a latrine next to the entrance. The central angan had a charpai in the middle with some aluminium folding chairs. The kitchen and the bathing area were to one side, sleeping rooms bordered the other two. But its dingy, slovenly air shrieked negligence from every one of its bricks. Paint was peeling from the walls, the ceilings were lined with patches of damp, flies and mosquitoes rivalled Murli's hospitality. It was perpetual night in the bathroom, a forty-watt bulb shone on the green slime that lined the walls. There was no running water, a hand pump in the middle had to be worked over the bather.

For the moment Vicky was treated on a par with the visitors, seated with them, given sherbet with them.

Almond sherbet, commented Lala Banwari Lal appreciatively. You made?

Murli only smiled.

After breakfast, the men bathed while Vicky brooded in a

small dark room next to his trunk. He was now in the house his mother's death had made hateful to him. Tears came to his eyes, he let them fall.

If the boy's happiness lay in Delhi, remarked the father, drawing attention to the boy's long face, he would not stand in the way. He put his welfare above everything, no sacrifice was too great where he was concerned.

This was exactly the attitude the uncle had come prepared to deal with.

In the journey of life, he pointed out, the mother's family had brought Vicky this far. Now it was the father's turn to settle the boy, use his help in the shop, train him for his future role as owner.

'I do not need any help,' remarked Murli sullenly.

They looked at him. Dark, weedy, paan-stained lips, alcohol-stained eyes, gaps in his mouth where the teeth had fallen; Vicky's features. He wore a white pyjama, and a brown, long-sleeved, striped polyester shirt over it. From time to time he hawked and spat into the little gutter running along the angan edges.

However unprepossessing the person or the place, Vicky's home was here, with his father.

It took a month for Vicky to escape to Delhi. He tries to beat me, he is abusive, he has a woman, I will kill myself if you send me back.

His stories were so wild, no one believed him. But he was still young enough for his elders to feel responsible for his welfare. Lala Banwari Lal refused to force him back.

They wrote to the father. Get him married. Once he settles down he will be happier.

Vicky declared he would only marry if he could live with them. Otherwise what would he do with a wife in Bareilly?

After much discussion they agreed to build him a small room plus bathroom on the barsati. In this way they would fulfil an obligation, without having to see him all the time.

Once he stood on his feet, he could set up independently somewhere.

Murli found a girl in three months flat. She was high-school pass, suited to Vicky's own level of education. Her father was dead, her background impoverished. Such a girl had all the makings of a good wife, she would have no expectations and would create no fuss.

There was no question of anybody from Delhi travelling down to see her. The father had chosen, if they interfered he would be only too glad to leave the whole thing to them.

Vicky went with Pyare Lal to Bareilly for the engagement, along with moderately expensive saris to give as presents plus a gold set for the bride.

Murli found an opportunity to inform his son that his future lay with his mother's family. He should guard against letting them get rid of him cheap, they had short-changed his mother and now they were trying to do the same to him.

'Do you like the bride?' demanded Ajay, Vijay, and Raju when their cousin came back an engaged man.

Vicky scowled and said nothing.

'Bhabhi will think her husband has gone dumb if you never say anything,' they teased.

The wedding was fixed for the end of May. The date was auspicious. The children would be on holiday, and as it was a slack period the shop could shut for a day. For a wedding everyone, far and near, must come, must come.

A tailor was installed, cloth brought home from the shop. Day and night he stitched, to make way for an embroiderer who in turn embroidered day and night.

Rupa moved in to help. Her husband was invaluable in getting things organised. Reliable, decent, honest, he saved them money on the vegetables and food he bought, on the bus he booked, on the pundit he hired, seeking the best for the least. It was a blessing that his job with the Government was undemanding and secure enough to allow absences to go unnoticed. The Banwari Lals were loudly appreciative of his services, and frequently pressed him to spend the night. But Prem Nath put a limit on the time he would devote to his wife's family. Pleading his father's ill health, he left his wife and Nisha, to return as early as he could the next day.

∾

At last, the night before the wedding. The hired bus stands outside the Karol Bagh house, while inside the last rites of puja, packing, and mehndi application are simultaneously taking place.

'Lock the rooms.'

'Have you got the keys?'

In an undertone, 'Have you got the money?'

More undertone, 'Have you got the jewellery?'

This is repeated with variations as each adult settles into the bus that is taking the nineteen-year-old Vicky to his bride. As they start, Banwari Lal is filled with a sense of satisfaction. The family has seen to an orphaned child's welfare, and is transmitting him with a sure hand into the future, equipped with the responsibilities of adulthood (employment) and the rites of manhood (marriage).

The bus speeds across the city in the dark, still heat of May. The lights are put off. The barat tries to make itself comfortable in the hard, cramped space. Children stretch across laps. Vicky sits in front, a starched pink turban on, a firm red tikka blazoned across his forehead. He smells of cheap hair pomade, sweat, and nervousness. He is not sure of what the coming days will bring, but he is the centre of attention, and he likes that. This bus with all its passengers is going to Bareilly because of him, the shop is shut for one day because of him, everybody has got new clothes because of him. And it has been made quite clear he is going to live in Delhi, that is a battle he has won. He slumps down until his knees are level with his head and tries to sleep.

The grandmother sits behind him, her heart full of strong feelings. Her grandson's marriage is the completion of the final duty left by her daughter's tragic death. It had been difficult with Vicky: failing continuously, Sona perpetually angry with him, but now everything is going to be all right.

Nisha lies on the hump of her grandmother's stomach. Her gaze flickers across the shapes of her family in the bus. Three years have passed since her removal to her aunt's house, and the dark thing inside her is deeply buried.

She thinks of the wedding, and all the clothes that have been made for her to wear. Slowly she drifts off to sleep, the jolts of the bus cushioned by the stomach she has her head on.

The driver stops for tea at five a.m. at a roadside stall in Rampur, an hour away from Bareilly. A few step out into the dark, torpid air on to a pavement lined with benches. A kerosene stove hisses under a huge saucepan of steaming, red-brown liquid. Next to somnolent flies on piles of filth lining the gutter, hawkers are busy tying together bundles of morning newspapers.

The wedding party sips hot tea in sticky glasses. 'How sweet it is, bap re! Bhai Sahib, less sugar in the next round, if you please. We are Dilliwallahs.'

In the darkness of the bus, Sona yawns and stretches. She takes a peek at Raju, slumped against Vicky, his mouth open, saliva staining the bridegroom's new kurta. Satisfied, she rummages under her seat for the snacks packed in Delhi. Forty little packets of biscuits, barfi, mathri, gulab jamun. Sweet, spicy, salty, and bland. Her husband distributes them to everybody, driver and tea maker included.

'The boy is getting married,' he explains.

'Wedding party,' says the tea maker understandingly, and throws some extra leaves and milk into the boiling cauldron.

81

The sky lightens. The flies begin to rise. Some more in the bus yawn, stretch, and stagger out for a second round of tea.

The tea does its job. 'Nature calls,' whisper some wives to their spouses. Rupa's husband goes to look for a suitable place.

He comes back much excited. 'There is a gurudwara round the corner. Neat and clean. Everybody can do their business there.' A wave of ladies descend, murmuring 'latrine'. Seduced by the promise of neat and clean, they drag along half-asleep children.

Minutes pass. The bus driver sleeps. From time to time 'Let's go, let's go' is heard. 'Murli Bhai Sahib will be at the bus depot in Bareilly at six-thirty' is also heard.

By now the sun can be seen. The women stagger back, affirming that the gurudwara is indeed neat and clean. They settle to the breakfast packages. The men are inspired. They slyly disappear around the corner. More tea is boiled up.

And finished. Restlessness grows. 'Are we going or not?'

'I will take Vicky and go. You people can join us for the wedding dinner,' cackles the grandmother.

'Where is Vicky, that you will take him and go? He too is sitting on his throne in the gurudwara,' points out Sushila. The bus giggles. Sushila looks pleased.

'How will there be a marriage if we are here all day?' points out another Banwari Lal.

'Arre, barats are never on time. It is all right.'

'At least phone Murli and tell him we shall be late. Poor man standing in the sun at the bus stop.'

A group of young men troops to the nearest phone booth to phone the boy's father.

'Is Murli himself ever punctual that we should waste money phoning him STD?' demands Sona as they go.

'Arre, he is the boy's father. Let him feel important. It is still not full rates.'

'What has he done that he should be made to feel important?' asks an older aunt known for her frankness.

82

'He is making all the arrangements for dinner,' replies Sona, in a way that suggests Murli had never done enough, nor ever would.

'Well, it is his son who is getting married. If he doesn't make the arrangements even for this, when will he do anything? When Vicky is dead?' opines the frank aunt.

'Hai, hai, don't talk like this at Vicky's wedding,' comes a sleepy mutter from the back of the bus.

The speaker looks abashed, and silence spreads in the bus. A newspaper vendor clambers on and shrieks the name of the local paper. A few are bought and used as fans.

Finally the men come strolling out from behind the corner. They look fresh, washed, and combed. As they get in and settle down, the barat realises that the bridegroom is missing.

'Where's Vicky?'

There is no Vicky.

'Vicky has run away on his wedding day,' declares Vijay. 'He is frightened of his bride.'

Ajay is sent to find Vicky. 'Now hurry up,' the barat shouts after him. 'Or should we tell this chai wallah to start our lunch?'

Five minutes later Vicky and Ajay appear. 'He was having his bath,' says an indignant Ajay.

His bath. Amazement ripples through the bus. Vicky has outdone them all.

'Couldn't wait to get ready for his wedding,' chortles the frank aunt.

'Now let us go,' says the grandmother, whose legs are cramped and swollen from being dangled over the seat all night long. 'The bridegroom may be ready but no one else is.'

The driver is woken up, and the bus sets off in a swirl of dust into the increasing heat. The stop at Rampur has taken two hours.

❧

Murli is waiting, sweat pouring off him, a wet hanky wrapped around his head. The many Banwari Lals descend, shake out their clothes, and stretch. Yashpal asks him whether he got the STD call. Murli's gratitude at their thoughtfulness knows no bounds. Neither does his hospitality. He has made arrangements at the Gupta Ashram. It is neat and clean, he avers, neat and clean. The barat begin to walk through the gullies of Bareilly. The luggage follows on rickshaws. From time to time they almost collide with a scooterist. The lanes grow increasingly narrow.

The large central hall of the ashram has two long rows of mattresses covered with white sheets. Quickly the baratis stuff their luggage in the alcoves above, and settle down to the serious business of getting ready. Murli hangs around the halwais in the back angan, supervising the breakfast, puri aloo and lassi.

In a corner of a smaller room, a pundit sits under a whirring fan, slowly putting out puja things. By the time breakfast is finished and the first puja starts it is 12 o'clock. Father and son have to be invested with the sacred thread. Murli sits, eyes glazed, his turn first.

Next Vicky is called. He is found, bathed yet again, lying on the mattress in the next room, talking to his younger cousins, the centre of attention.

'Vickeee, hurry.'

Vicky's shirt is whipped off, and the thread slung around his chest. The havan fire is lit in an old aluminium cooking pot. Water and cold drinks are passed around. Polish boys creep from guest to guest, urging their shoes off.

The puja goes on and on, as does the lunch. Smoke fills the room, the elderly sit on cots, the younger ones hand them plates of food. Guests exhort each other to eat. Flies rise and fall with each passing step. Trays of sweets give off a heavy, sugary smell.

The groom has a fresh red tilak on his forehead, conferred by the pundit and he looks self-conscious.

'It's just a few more hours, Vicky.'

'How much can you delay now, Vicky?'

Vicky scowls, and his audience titters.

By four, tables are being cleared to make way for the six
o'clock chaat. The press-wallah is ironing, guests retire to
mattresses, children run around, Vicky plays cards, while
some men think of bottles hidden in suitcases.

The ladies are getting ready to go to the bride's house. On two
large decorated trays they carry a sari, petticoat, blouse,
underwear, chappals, perfume, oil, hairpins, powder, jewellery, make-up and trinkets. From head to foot the bride has
to be made over in things belonging to the groom's side.

And there is the bride, a small, thin girl hovered over by
her female relatives. They watch as her future in-laws paint
her nails, undo and redo her hair, apply lipstick, brush powder over the sallow complexion, stroke eyeliner on to the
hopeful eyes.

'Be careful, don't smudge, otherwise Vicky Bhaiyya will
get very angry,' snigger the younger ones.

Now it is the turn of the sari, blouse and petticoat. At this
point the bride's side declare there is no need to go through
all this disrobing and robing. The bride will wear the sari in
due course.

We have to put it on her. We. This minute. She is ours.

At this, the pundit from the bride's side comes alive and
asserts his authority.

'No,' he says.

'No,' replies the boy's side.

They confer.

It was put on me.

Me too.

The bride looks down. A younger cousin is dispatched to
demand of the elders in the Gupta Ashram: bride's side says
no – are we to listen?

The cousin runs through the gullies of Bareilly, while the

85

rest politely sip cold drinks, pick at chips, sweet and salty biscuits.

As they wait the bride's side clarify their links to the girl, the groom's side specify their connections to the boy. From time to time the girl's relatives ask, 'How is she?' The groom's side swear she is the nicest thing they have seen. The bride flushes.

The message comes back

She has to change.

A sheet is held against the corner of the wall. With her back to them the bride changes. Her blouse is tight. She mutters something, struggling to get the hooks together, the silk quickly revealing rings of perspiration.

'These are your measurements,' say the groom's side tartly. 'How can it be tight?'

But the bride is wearing a bra padded with much cotton. Her cousin whispers, 'You should have given your measurements with this one on.'

'It's all right,' murmurs the bride.

In a corner the bride's sister begins to cry. Ladies cluster around her – do not think your sister is gone, think you have another family to call your own.

She doesn't stop.

Then she is scolded: how can you cry on such an auspicious day?

She does not listen. Her mother joins her. The bride's side looks pleased. To lose their girl is a sacrifice they hope the other side will register.

Finally the bride is dressed. With a final dusting of powder and spraying of perfume, the ladies of the groom's side disappear.

Back at the ashram everybody is consuming vast amounts of chaat. It is close to eight o'clock.

The two bathrooms are full. The baratis are running around, clothes under their arms. The press-wallah looks harassed as suddenly a mountain of garments materialises on his table for him to iron without a second's delay.

Tempers rise.

'Get out, get out, get out of the bathroom.'

Bang, bang, bang. The chain hanging from the old wooden doors shudders with each bang. If the person inside is lower in status – that is, woman or child – the banger gets abusive.

'You think no one else has to have a bath?'

The splashes get louder. The water flowing into the drain outside gets a soapy scum. The waiting person screams, 'You are still soaping yourself? You think the whole world is going to hang around for you?'

The world has no choice. There are only two bathrooms in the ashram.

Meanwhile the men are drinking. The women look the other way: it is a wedding, what can you expect?

The children are tired, some whimper, others droop with exhaustion – the non-drinking men dandle them while the ladies get ready, peeping surreptitiously into secret mirrors to indulge the vanity of believing that how you look matters.

At last the barat sets off in the glare of portable tube lights, the band screeches in the background, and people line the gullies to watch.

The wedding is to take place in an empty lot near the bride's house. The bride is inside, dressed and patient. 'Where are they now?' the women ask from time to time.

'In the Kapur walli gully.'

'Still two hours for them to come.'

'Now where are they . . . now . . . now?'

'Bank gully, chowk, Agarwal Dharamsala gully, temple gully.'

'Oh, still another hour and a half . . . another hour . . . another half-hour.'

The older family members stretch comfortably and yawn.

It is eleven-thirty. The sound of the band can be heard as the barat circles the house, taking the longest possible route.

The more adventurous of the barat dance in the streets, others clap and egg them on. Children are whirled about on shoulders. The band plays in a frenzy, the men carrying the rods of fluorescent light are drenched in sweat. Vicky, high on his horse, watches through the tinsel strings that dangle from his light-pink turban.

Nisha is following the procession in her father's arms. Sushila chucks her under the chin, tells her what a pretty girl she is, and that one day it will be her turn.

The gullies are crowded, the men's dancing gets wilder, and the women are unable to keep up with their alcohol-aided abandon. They stop to watch, absorbed, half-smiles playing on their lips. Their feet are trampled on, some get pushed towards the drains; just as they are about to slip into the sewage, they are pulled back.

Finally they reach the bride's house, with its glittering, blinking welcome sign in huge coloured lights. But the young men refuse to stop. The bride's mother, waiting with garlands stretched between her hands, gazes with tears in her eyes, her shrunken, widowed lips twitching. The drums beat, minutes pass, then quarter-hours, before the baratis decide to be welcomed at the entrance of a pink tunnel. White gathered bands drape its length, chandeliers hang above.

The bride is hiding in the depths of the house.

'He has come, he has come, he has come,' they shout at her. The bride rises, balancing herself on her extremely high heels.

Her shortness has already been canvassed extensively.

'How do you like her?' This inevitable question is now the property of Murli's side, the people associated with the engagement.

'We like her very much, very much, very much.'

'She is short,' remark a few.

This truth hangs accusingly in the air. The bride in her high heels comes up to Vicky's shoulder. The listeners look shifty. The chooser of the bride looks aggressive.

The topic is changed.

Dinner is served at one in the morning. Puris, kachoris, naan, tandoori parantha, aloo sabzi, channa, fried potato, grilled paneer and mixed vegetables, paneer in tomato gravy, dahi pakori, soft pink ice-cream, gulab jamun, spiced sweet milk served in kulhars, then paan, sweet and plain, and lots and lots of bottled drinks, enthusiastically swung around by children, drunk, spilt, finished, drunk, spilt, finished again.

The guests have all eaten. It is now the bride and groom's turn; they descend from their gilt red velvet thrones, and are led to chairs in front of the still-laden tables. Excited young ones surround them. A single plate is piled high with food and thrust at Vicky. He is to feed himself and his bride. The romance has begun. Someone pulls the sari covering the bride's head back, so that Vicky's hand can make its way unhindered to her red-painted mouth, to lips that open to receive the food, to a heart that is ready to receive a husband's love.

It is two a.m., the auspicious time for the union has started. The bride and groom are escorted towards the pandal, where the priest is setting out in a leisurely fashion the paraphernalia necessary for the three-hour ritual that is to follow.

At six in the morning Vicky returns to the Gupta Dharamsala a married man. The newly weds touch the elders' feet, ask for blessings, have money pressed on to them. The bride cries continuously. She is patted and soothed continuously. Young sisters-in-law clutching babies look sympathetic. The older ones look indifferent, their attention taken by collecting wedding presents, distributing saris and suit pieces brought from Delhi, ensuring everyone has a box of sweets.

One last meal at the Gupta Dharamsala – breakfast, which is sevar with aloo, puri with aloo, kulcha with chola, chutney, lassi, and rooafzah.

The bridegroom is again handed a plate for his bride and himself.

Everybody watches.

The question goes around once more: 'How do you like her?'

She is nice, she is good, sweet, and docile. All this was pre-determined by the mechanics of choice. There is no room for anything but hopeful, fervent liking.

A meal is packed for the journey back. 'Packed lunch, there is packed lunch for everybody,' shouts Pyare Lal. At the term packed lunch, Murli looks important – it is he who has arranged it on instruction.

The barat, along with bride and luggage, pile into rick-shaws that will take them to the bus on the main road. There is no space in these gullies for buses.

The whole wedding procession is the standard two hours late.

The bride continues to weep as she is escorted inside the bus by her mother and sister, both crying as much as she. Her aunts and cousins look covertly at her new relatives jammed on the seats– who is what relation to their girl is remembered, noted, and filed away, to be brushed up later. The local men-folk stand around waiting. Vicky scuttles in, anxious to avoid his father. He is seated next to his wife, Lala Banwari Lal sits next to them. At eleven o'clock the bus sets off, travelling to Delhi during the hottest part of the day.

The bride stops crying. She can feel her husband's arm down the length of her own, each lurch momentarily increases the pressure. Love is going to begin. Fated, ordained love, unquestioned, unexamined love.

Vicky looks down at his wife's head. It is covered by a sequinned magenta sari palla; its smooth material slips and is pulled up, slips and is pulled up again and again. The hands that do this are dark with mehndi, gold glitters on the wrists. That gold is his, he realises, as is the gold around her neck, the rings on her fingers, and the body underneath it all.

Satisfaction pervades the bus. Vicky is married, another job done, another responsibility over. The men dance in the aisles.

'Vicky, come dance.' They pull him by the arm.

'No, I am not in the mood,' he mumbles.

'Just married, and won't leave his wife.'

'So soon, and hanging on to her. Arre, Bhabhi, leave him. You have a whole lifetime with your husband. Then you will say, take him away.'

'Take him away now,' responds Asha, the new wife, her lipstick creasing with her smile.

Vicky violently shrugs off their pulling hands, the men laugh and shout at the bus driver to put on another cassette.

Bale, bale scream the loudspeakers into the bus, bale, bale echo the wedding guests, long into the journey.

Growing children

The following years were among the sisters' most fulfilling. They each had a child small enough for them to feel the centre of that child's world. Since both children were Sona's, Rupa knew more anxiety than her sister, but still, hers was a complete home and a happy heart. Her business continued to prosper, with Yashpal redoubling his efforts to help the relatives who were looking after his daughter.

As Nisha grew, Rupa bestowed careful love on her, mentally standing before the tribunal composed of her sister and brother-in-law, defending herself against neglect on the one hand and stealing the child's heart on the other. The business that had occupied her attention so successfully seemed more meaningful when she saw Nisha peering into the pickle jars, or tasting the sweet and salty aam papar drying in the sun under an old muslin sari. She sometimes found herself fantasising about adopting the child. She had heard of such cases.

When she treated her husband to these thoughts, Prem Nath demanded irritably, 'Why do you make yourself miserable thinking of the impossible?'

'It is hard when she leaves every weekend.'

'A child belongs to her mother.'

'Don't you like having her here?'

'What does it matter what I like or do not like?' asked the clerk fatalistically, settling down to his dinner in a Nisha-less household. 'We have what God has given us. Nobody has everything.'

From time to time Nisha's mother insisted her daughter come home to be groomed in the traditions of the Banwari Lal household.

The first time Nisha was told she had to fast for her future husband she protested. 'Why should I? That's for older women.' She didn't want to spend the day without food or water.

Sona rolled her eyes. Only ten and the girl was beginning to argue. She had never questioned anything her mother asked her to do.

'How are you going to get married, madam, if you do not make sacrifices?'

'In school nobody does it.'

'They are not manglis.'

There could be no answer to this, but Nisha tried: 'So?'

'So? What do you mean, so? What kind of wife are you going to make if you can't bear to fast one day a year for your husband?'

'I don't want to marry,' mumbled Nisha.

'Who will look after you if you don't marry?'

'Rupa Masi,' declared the girl, to the aunt's horror. Hastily she intervened: of course the child would come. To herself she thought that Sona was determined to make being a mangli a bigger deal than it was. Pay some pundit five thousand rupees and see if they didn't find a way out. The girl would be married off to a tree, or a plant, or the sun, anything that would absorb the evil of the planets, and everything would be all right. It was just like Sona to worry even when there were well-known solutions.

So Nisha stayed home from school to learn how to be a good wife. The next morning she rose with the other women before dawn. It was late October and while she huddled under a shawl next to her grandmother, Asha prepared tea, Sona heated the halwa, and Sushila started frying puris. Nisha was not used to breakfast at four in the morning, and could not bring herself to eat.

'Have, have, beti,' cajoled Sushila.

'No, Chachi, I don't want.'

93

'Arre, come, come, after this you can't eat anything till the moon comes up.'

She wrapped a bit of puri around some halwa and, holding Nisha's chin up, coaxed it in. 'Good you are starting so young. It's never too early to fast for your husband – there now, open your mouth, good girl, a little more, little more, a little . . .' The puri finished, Nisha was allowed to rest her mouth.

Later in the morning Pyare Lal took the fasting females to Hanuman Mandir where they bought bangles and had mehndi traced on to their palms. Once home, they settled down to watch a rented video, palms outstretched, the dried, flaking mehndi smeared with a sugar-lemon mixture to darken the colour.

The boys went straight to the shop after school to have their lunch there. In the evening the men came home with kulcha-cholla, dahi bhalla, and rasmalai; their women must not labour over dinner.

Sona, Sushila, and Asha dressed in bridal colours, gathered to perform the puja and listen to a story underlining its significance:

The Karva Chauth Katha

There was once a fourteen-year-old girl, recently married. She was at her mother's house for her first Karva Chauth. She fasted along with her sisters-in-law, but by the time it was evening she had become crazy with hunger. Her brothers, unable to see her plight, climbed the nearest tree and shone a torch through a sieve. The moon has risen, now eat, they said. And she did.

Her husband, far away in his own home, died immediately, killed by his wife's unwillingness to examine the moon that was shown to her so ambiguously, through multiple layers of shadow and doubt, hunger and desire.

The girl returned home to a husband embalmed in a

tub of oil. Now began her initiation into the true meaning of wifehood. She fasted for one whole year. She
prayed to the Devi every chauth. On the fourth day of
the waxing moon, she waited to see it climb the sky
slowly, slowly, and when she did see it, she completed
her puja slowly, slowly. Her mother-in-law watched her
like a hawk. She took her pliable daughter-in-law
through every ritual in the book, reminding her every
second of the day of what she had done, and how near
widowhood was upon her.

It was the last fast of that year. The girl's tongue felt
thick and swollen with thirst, but her mind was now
trained to repress the demands of her body. That they
were a source of trouble was as plain for all to see as
that body blanketed by strong-smelling mustard oil,
glistening through its deep yellow.

She was rewarded. Her husband came back to life.
Great was the joy and firm was the girl's resolve to follow for ever the path laid down by her elders.

The story concludes and the power of a wife lingers seductively before the listeners, inviting identification, so that the
girl who was so foolish could be them, the woman who was
so self-disciplined could be them.

But Nisha was young and protested. 'It was not the girl's
fault, it is the brothers who should be punished. They made
her a widow.'

'It is nothing to do with the brothers,' scolded the mother in
turn. 'That girl should have followed her elders and not eaten
by herself. After all, no one else was eating, were they? She
was trying to be independent, and you can see the consequences.'

Asha laughed ingratiatingly. 'When you are older you will
understand.'

Meanwhile at nine-fourteen Raju and Vijay announce the
arrival of the moon, visible from the roof, and the women

proceed there to offer water, grain, and fruit. Last of all, the daughters-in-law touch the feet of their mother-in-law. 'Stay a wife for ever, be the mother of sons,' she blesses them. Nisha's unmarried years do not involve feet touching, there will be enough of that in her husband's home.

Finally they eat with the waiting men.

The next day Nisha returned to her aunt's house.

'Why don't you do Karva Chauth, masi?' she wondered aloud while her aunt was making dinner.

Rupa dreaded explanations that might antagonise her sister, but neither did she like appearing in a bad light. She resorted to emphatic slicing of potatoes.

'Huh, masi? Why don't you do Karva Chauth?' Nisha persevered.

'You think the whole world fasts for their husbands?' Really, that sister of hers needed her head examined. There was an age for everything, and when the child should be thinking of studies, she was forcing her to think of husbands.

'But still,' persisted Nisha, 'Mummy does.'

'Your mother has to follow the traditions of her family. Besides, your uncle does not believe in fasting. If I don't eat, he won't either.'

'Oh,' said Nisha.

'Now finish your homework quickly. See, we are going to have potato fry for dinner.'

Nisha's favourite. Her mouth started watering.

It turned out Nisha had a flair for studies. She was quick to memorise, her written work was neat, she had nothing to fear from the printed page. It always offered, never asked.

The aunt and uncle were determined their niece should perform brilliantly in school. Tests and exams were tests and exams for the whole family. Afterwards her uncle went over every question in detail, then calculated her marks. He was always right.

Sometimes Nisha writhed under this tyranny. 'Raju doesn't study so much,' she complained, though with a touch of superiority. Her marks were always better than Raju's.

'Raju has the shop,' replied her aunt.

'So?'

'You must be able to look after yourself,' said the aunt delicately, not wanting to spell out the possibility of death and disaster to a child so young.

'Do you look after yourself?'

'You see that I do my business. Not that I need to, but with no children, one has to have a time pass,' said Rupa, faltering in the quagmire of simultaneously rearing a modern and a traditional girl. 'A lot depends on one's in-laws,' she added.

'When did Mummy marry?'

'After school.'

'And you?'

'After college.'

'Why?'

'Not so pretty,' snorted her aunt into the dal she was stirring. 'Or so fair.'

Silence.

Rupa glanced at the girl anxiously. Her niece was undeniably good looking, but her horoscope was also undeniably bad, and in the long run stars had greater staying power than beauty.

In the five years she had had her, Rupa had loved dressing her niece in satin, nylon, net, and sequins, loved putting lipstick, kaajal, and bindis on her, and making ringlets in her hair. Sometimes her husband got irritated – 'She is just your plaything' – but in another couple of years Nisha would begin to menstruate and her childhood would be over.

At Sona's a woman could not cook, worship, or serve anybody food during her monthlies. But thankfully Nisha need

97

not be acquainted with all this yet; besides, in her own house taboos were not so strict.

∽

Sona had spent years exhibiting hysterical anger over Vicky's education. Now, alas for her, those exercises in recrimination would serve as a practice run for Raju's similar failings.

Raju was following in Vicky's footsteps. Not that doing poorly in school particularly mattered in this shop-owning family, but between upstairs and downstairs there existed a rivalry that flourished or languished depending on the material it could feed upon. Unfortunately for Sona, during the children's school-going years it peaked around report card time.

The misery Sona felt at Raju's performance was exacerbated on parent-teacher day. Every year he did a little worse, belying his promises and her hopes and expectations. This perpetual disappointment drove her to violence.

Ineffectually she shook him by the ear, wrathfully reminding him of his primary obligations. 'For this I gave birth to you? To bring such shame on me? To hear teachers complain that you are noisy, inattentive, and don't study?'

'Boys will be like that,' remarked the grandmother complacently. 'Leave him.'

What did the old woman know of fields of competition in contemporary family life? Sona knew her son was bright, sharp, and intelligent, it was obvious from his face, and it was galling to feel he had to appear small in front of the world.

'These teachers don't like me,' whined Raju. 'On purpose they give me less marks.'

'Why don't you make this excuse to your aunt when she comes downstairs to find out how you have done?' said Sona bitterly. 'See if she will believe you.'

Raju looked resentful. 'It's true. They are always comparing me to Ajay. Can I help it if I am not clever like him?'

'I knew it was not a good idea putting him in the same school as his cousins,' fumed Sona. 'Now see how the poor boy has to suffer – but who listens to me in this house?'

'Just because your son cannot work, you want to separate the children of this family?' rebuked the grandmother.

Anger, resentment, and the struggle to keep silent drove Sona to the kitchen, where Asha's sympathy was readily available.

That evening, Sushila came down to pry. 'How did you do, beta?' she asked, giving Raju a playful shove.

'Arre, who can remember so many marks?' declared Sona. 'It is enough to remember Nisha's: 89 in Maths, Science 82, Hindi 86, Social Studies 90, English 87, Sanskrit 88. But why attract the evil eye by boasting?'

'I believe your brother-in-law gives a lot of attention to Nisha's studies. A pity a girl should benefit and the boy be neglected, but each family has its kismet,' sighed the solicitous aunt.

Two things occurred to Sona at this point. That the base nature of the woman upstairs made her rub chillies into the wounds of innocents, and that all Sushila's uncharitable deeds, thoughts, and words would eventually add to her bad karma. Still, it was beneath her to retaliate by mentioning Ajay's and Vijay's weak points.

Sona communicated her lofty position to her sister, trembling with rage. Rupa listened silently. Sushila periodically got under her sister's skin and this would work itself out without her intervention. But she had never thought of getting Raju the full benefit of her husband's attention. She must rectify that now.

'Send Raju to study with his uncle, Didi. In this house the poor boy, otherwise so smart, gets distracted.'

Instead of responding to this offer, Sona turned on her daughter. 'What is the use of doing brilliantly if you cannot help your brother? You are older, you should teach him.'

'How is it my fault if he doesn't do well?' demanded Nisha sullenly.

'Didi, what are you saying? You know Nisha will do anything for her brother,' interjected Rupa, wishing her husband hadn't worked quite so hard with his niece; it was not having all the desired effects.

That evening, having dropped Nisha off at her mother's, Rupa returned home, had her bath, and served her husband tea. 'Having children in a joint family is not easy,' she remarked.

Prem Nath looked at her. The days his wife visited her sister's house, she would return either depressed and withdrawn, or with an air of tenderness that told him things were going badly with Sona. He now pulled her towards him and put his hands under her petticoat.

'Oho, what are you doing?'

'Why? There is no one here.'

'How can you be so shameless?'

'How can a man be shameless with his own wife? You want me to be shameless with some other woman?' he demanded.

'Chut,' scolded Rupa, playfully pushing away his hand, but sitting close so she was within arm's reach. She pulled the tray towards herself and started pouring tea.

Her husband looked admiringly at her. There she was, hair still thick and black, skin still smooth and young, dressing gown carelessly tied so he could see the large, heavy breasts swaying against the soft material with every movement she made. As she bent down to put the tea on the little table next to him, his eye followed the way they swung out and down, and then his hand followed his eye.

Rupa went on with her routine struggle. 'You are not listening about Raju, ji,' she complained.

'I am,' said her husband, as he increased his caresses. He caught his wife's pouting lip between his own and sucked it. He massaged her heavy buttocks towards him. Let's try it on

100

a chair, he suggested, increasing the pressure and spreading open her legs.

'I don't know where you get your ideas from,' said Rupa. 'Thank God no one knows what all you make me do.'

'Who else do I have in the world but you? God intended it like this.'

'Still.'

'No still. Why else did he not give us children? Otherwise you too would be dancing attendance on some Raju, day and night. Where would be the time or place to do anything?' asked the husband as he got up to lock the door.

As the rhythms between them became faster on the chair, her husband pressed her straining body towards himself, and whispered, 'Tell me, does your sister get this, and this, and this?' while she cried and told him to stop, she didn't know, and why should she care. But he went on, because it excited him, and he wanted her to know that her sister was not rich in everything, there were other things to be had. 'Ask her,' he moaned, and she moaned back that he was a shameless man.

Later Prem Nath suggested, 'Why don't you invite Raju to spend a few days with us? Then I can see to his studies in the evening.'

Rupa looked at her husband lovingly; really, the man was too good to be true. How he shared all her concerns!

She passed that concern on to her sister the very next day. Having Prem Nath teach Raju was so much better than putting the burden on Nisha. But Sona was not interested in handing over her other child, even for a day.

'It will be good for Raju,' persuaded the sister, expansive from last night. 'He will learn from Nisha's example.'

'He is very sensitive, if I send him away he will feel I am punishing him. He can learn from her example right here,' said Sona heavily, looking at the dark, dusky glow of her sister, the diamond she had given her when Raju was born, glinting in her nose.

Strange were the ways of Fate. She had been the one with the good looks, the lucky marriage, and now she was the one feeling sad all the time.

Rupa caught Sona looking at her. Was the act of sex apparent? She blushed, quickly frowned, and began talking of her troubles. She suspected the woman working with her was stealing. Really, these people had no loyalty; who can supervise all the time?

Sona did not reply. If Rupa wanted to grumble about a business where she was earning almost as much as Prem Nath Bhai Sahib, she would have to do it alone.

Asha and Vicky

Five years have passed since Asha, Vicky's wife, was installed as a bride in the barsati. When it became appropriate for her to unbend her head, and take stock of her situation, she could not but notice the general meanness of her own quarters compared to the rest of the house. Her husband, on questioning, demanded tartly who was she to complain, did she come from a palace?

But her intention was not to complain. She was talking about differences. As her husband never tired of pointing out, she did not come from a palace. The barsati was enough for her needs, but it was too separate. How could the strange, lonely feelings of a bride be alleviated if there was no con-vivial sharing of space, nobody coming up with knitting or stitching to settle on her bed prepared for talk?

She did not know how to convey her uneasiness to her husband. How to ask him, where do you belong, tell me so I can place myself there. With whom to share the responsibility of a husband? Vicky got angry with her questions, behaving as though she was betraying him by a desire for information.

As they ate downstairs, she directed her allegiance towards Sona's kitchen, and laid the duty of a daughter-in-law at her feet. Her link with this woman would make her place in the house stronger, and in establishing her usefulness Asha was planning her future.

She cooed over Raju, she pressed her grandmother-in-law's feet, she ran with the grandfather-in-law's tea when he came home, she practically lived with Sona next to the stove. She had no airs, no graces, she was humble, obedient and helpful. From time to time Sona couldn't help thinking that Murli had chosen well.

*

A month into the marriage Asha became pregnant. She threw up, looked pale, and went off her food. Vicky had no idea of what to do with her. He was only twenty, it had not been his idea to get married, and he could not be held responsible for any consequences. Asha knew this as clearly as if it had been spelt out.

It was through her own treatment that Asha fully realised her husband's marginal status. She was careful to be especially sick in front of Sona and the grandmother, but their responses were slow. Days passed before they asked her if something was wrong, and when her pregnancy was confirmed they talked of sending her to Bareilly for her confinement. Asha didn't care if this was tradition, she could only feel the indifference of a plan that involved going home to a mother who could not afford modern treatment for her delivery. She got around this by saying she could not leave Sona Maji for even a day, her heart would break.

Eventually they did arrange for a nursing home, did insist she work less. But when her son Virat was born, she didn't feel the importance that should have been hers. She had borne the first grandchild, still there was no appreciable increase in her status. They didn't send her family presents, they didn't have an elaborate naming ceremony, she got nothing beyond a silk sari. Would they behave the same if one of those other sons produced a (male) grandchild?

When she shared her thoughts with her husband, he asked curtly, 'Where do you get your ideas from? Your mother was supposed to send gold sets for everybody, plus money for Virat – did she, huh? I even heard Sona Maji say how can one extract anything from the gullies of Bareilly?'

Mortification struck Asha. 'Who do they think they are?' she retaliated weakly.

'Quite,' responded her husband, adding, 'What is it to us what they think or do?'

These pronouns. Them, they, not us, we. It was a little

daunting, and not what Asha had expected from marriage. As long as they were in the barsati she would have to exhibit devotion to her husband's family, but there were times when that devotion was saturated with poison.

Above all, she was determined not to have another child, ensuring this through a quiet visit to a local lady doctor. Not for her more humiliation. Proper in-laws would have appreciated Virat, given him due importance, made her feel she was adding to the family, not depleting its resources. Maybe one day . . . if they had their own place . . .

This was Asha's dream. An independent place. Her mother and sister could visit her, something inconceivable at her in-laws. To this end she nagged:

'Why can't they pay you a decent salary?'

'They don't own you.'

'You can still work with them and live elsewhere. Are you listening?'

Vicky tried to explain to his wife the reasons why they were already so beholden to his uncles. Despite their practice of investing all profits back into the shop, they had built him a small room on the terrace with an added toilet for his own use, a luxury none of the others had. Due to them she was living in Delhi instead of Bareilly. But his wife's discomfort in that tiny room had eroded her sense of obligation.

'Why should we be so grateful for this hot, hot room?' she demanded. 'You don't know what it is like running up and down with a baby. There is no place for me to rest downstairs, nor can I leave the baby sleeping and come up – they will say, what kind of mother are you? If I lie there on the floor, I feel I am in the way, not that I am complaining, but you only tell me how am I to manage?' She felt so sorry for herself her eyes filled with tears.

Vicky finally installed a little stand-up desert cooler in their room. If you put your face next to it, you felt some cool, moist air, but it made no difference to the child's prickly heat.

When her complaining got too much, Vicky threatened to

send her back home. Where did she think she came from to exhibit such airs and graces?

'I think you deserve better, that is all.'

'I am fine here, I wasn't born in a palace like you.' He had not yet learned to hate his living quarters. They ate their meals downstairs and he liked sleeping on the terrace even during the heat of summer. After midnight the air grew gentle and they had privacy.

∾

Vicky yearned for more children. He had been alone as a child and he did not want Virat to suffer that loneliness. 'My son should have brothers in case anything happens to us,' he insisted.

'Where will you keep them? On my head?' demanded his wife.

'I can build another room up here.'

'Yes, they are really concerned about your comfort. Who will give you money to build?'

'They.'

'They!' commented Asha bitterly. 'They will go on taking advantage of you, that is all that will happen.'

'You go on talking, talking, understanding nothing. It's not as though you have come from anywhere great.'

His standard argument reduced Asha to temporary silence. She knew she couldn't push him beyond a certain point, he knew that ultimately he could insult her into restraint. Still, she was his ally, and the knowledge that somebody in the house considered him a victim was balm to his soul.

His dreams were different from his wife's. He wanted to start a part-time business making Baba suits. Sets for children used little cloth and profit margins were high. If his uncles built him a shed on the barsati, he could hire a tailor, and get Asha to oversee the designs. If it did well he could even open a

106

boutique. Ready-made clothes were beginning to come into fashion, and as for the cloth, he could get it at wholesale prices from his uncles. He had already thought of a brand name: Virat Baba Suits.

Of course, all this could only happen with his uncles' consent. He ignored his own certain knowledge that business initiative had to trickle down from up. He was not trying to change anything, he declared during imaginary discussions, he was only branching out into an inoffensive sideline.

If they did object, he would demand his fair share and leave. He had to think long term for the sake of little Virat. There is a time when the joints in a joint family become visible, and as far as he was concerned there never had been a seamless merging. He spent nights restlessly tossing, arguing with the figures of his grandfather and uncles, forcing them to recognise his years of unrewarded toil.

He mentioned his plans to Asha. She was enthusiastic, yes, yes, she would supervise, the stars in his head connecting to the stars in hers. It was when he mentioned his alternative strategy that she baulked. 'I am not leaving. Where will we go? What about Virat's education?'

'Since when are you so interested in education? I have never seen you open a book.'

'So what? It is not my education that my son needs, but his own. He will be an MBA.'

'Huh. Father not even high-school pass, and son will be an MBA,' remarked Vicky cynically. 'Where do you get your ideas?'

'From all around me. You could not be high-school pass because you had to work. But Ajay is almost finished college, Vijay is in first year, Raju will go, even Nisha I am sure they will send. If girls can go to college . . .'

'Bas, bas, you are always talking. Learn to keep quiet.'

Asha kept on. 'Arre, if you have no ambition for him, I do. How can he be part of this business, with so many boys in the house?'

'There is his grandfather's shop in Bareilly.'

Asha snorted. 'Grandfather! There is not enough for you, how will there be enough for your son? I'm not going anywhere. You go if you are so keen.'

This argument drove Vicky to tackle his grandfather more forcefully than he might have otherwise dared. 'Please allow me to build on the roof. I want to make Baba suits. Give me a chance to show I too can do something. My mother would have appreciated it, she always said your grandparents love you so much, they will look after you when I have gone. Besides, I have to provide for my family.'

He chose a time when his grandfather was alone, hoping the memory of his dead daughter could be worked to good effect. Lala Banwari Lal looked troubled, his gaze wandered, he would talk to the boy's uncles, they understood the market, he himself had no experience of children's clothes, and wasn't his family being provided for?

Vicky took these comments for the bad signs they were. It was a small request, why couldn't his grandfather agree straight away? He was the head of the family, if he wouldn't help him, why would his uncles? He would be forced to live like this for the rest of his life.

It was after seven-thirty and the shop was shut. Lala Banwari Lal and his sons were sitting on the takht in front of the cash box. Vicky and the assistants had left, the shutter outside was half-down, there was only one light left on. Pyare Lal was counting money, Yashpal was making entries in a ledger. The grandfather mentioned the conversation he had had with his grandson.

'What is the matter with Vicky? Does he need his head examined?' grunted Pyare Lal, snapping elastic bands around bundles of five thousands.

'The boy wants to set up something on his own; it is natural,' said Lala Banwari Lal mildly. 'Maybe we can permit him one shed on the terrace.'

'Let him go back to Bareilly if he is not satisfied,' said Yashpal, declaring his aversion to Vicky.

Pyare Lal looked surprised. His brother was a mild man. Still, in turn he added, 'Who is he, to construct on the terrace?'

Lala Banwari Lal had a problem hearing, and he looked blank.

Pyare Lal raised his voice. 'You know how difficult it is to build anything, Baoji. It is only because his room on the barsati is not noticeable from the road that we could avoid permissions and bribes.'

'If he sets up for himself, he can make enough money to be on his own,' said the grandfather. 'That is his plan. His mother would want to see him flourishing.'

'How can he be so independent in our house? Let him go somewhere else, we are not stopping him. Who keeps their sister's child their whole life?' demanded Yashpal angrily.

'One small shed,' pleaded Banwari Lal. 'He wants to make Baba suits. Where is the harm?'

The harm was shown to him quickly. Had the love of a daughter's child made him forget the most basic principle of a successful joint family? All for one and one for all. No question of striking out on your own. Vicky could suggest making Baba suits, point out the market imperatives of branching into children's clothing, but it had to be a group venture.

Besides, there was Ajay, Vijay, and Raju to consider. Tomorrow, if one of them was dissatisfied (as was inevitable, for who is not dissatisfied?), then instead of learning to contain himself, he might, with Vicky as example, start talking of his right to set up separately. Divisions were lethal for businesses. If Vicky wanted to do something on his own, he should go back to Bareilly, but if he chose to live with them, he had to abide by family rules.

As they talked, Yashpal stared out at the street from under the half-lowered shutter. It was busy as usual. Pedestrians, rickshaws, scooters, taxis, buses, and cows picked their way around each other. Cars were double parked against the kerb, making the traffic even more congested. Every inch of the pavement was crammed with vendors. Right in front of their shop was a coconut water wallah, a juice wallah, and a bhel puri wallah. Through the years they had battled with them to keep the pavement clean so their customers wouldn't have to step through the detritus of three small concerns. The vendors, secure in the bribe paid to the local police, refused to consider tidiness in their pursuit of a livelihood. Yashpal had just today bought them a huge plastic bin as an inducement to discard peels, fruit skins, and coconut husks in a single place. He suddenly had the sense of similar debris in the shape of Vicky inside their shop. A sister's child was not a healthy thing to have living in the family. Fate had dealt them an unfortunate blow.

After trying to make their father see reason, silence followed, while both sons fiddled with their toes.

'Let me talk to Vicky,' said Pyare Lal at last. 'He won't dare try any funny business with me.'

'No, beta,' sighed Banwari Lal. 'He came to me and I will deal with him myself. I will tell him the MCD will not give us permission to build. Otherwise he might think we do not want to give him money. If he grows bitter, it will be difficult. Everybody in the house must be happy.'

Later on, the brothers agreed that age was taking its toll of their father; his concern with what Vicky might think or not think was clear proof. What did it matter whether Vicky was happy or not? They were keeping him, it would be good to remind him of that more often.

Vicky in turn resented his grandfather's placatory remarks; he knew if left to himself he would have agreed. At this moment he was intensely conscious of himself as a poor relative, with no weight to move things his way. If his grandfather was like this, what would happen to him when the old man was no longer there?

*

Asha was all anticipation. What did he say, what did he say, she demanded the minute they were alone in the barsati on the night of the great confrontation. Nothing, nothing, snapped Vicky, and so dark was his face, so surly his mien, that she made an effort to comfort instead of taunt. Never mind, there is still plenty of time, we do not know what the future holds. We must wait, be patient, maybe after Ajay-Vijay-Raju start working, and there is no room in the shop, they will want you to start something of your own.

But Vicky's frustration was so great he was driven to speak to his grandfather again. 'Baoji, I know I am a burden on you. Give me my share, and let me leave. I will open my own shop in Bareilly.'

The grandfather looked sad. By now Vicky should know that there was no question of his share. He had fed him, educated him, married him, then supported his wife and son. He should have the decency to be content. 'Beta, I will speak to your uncles,' he prevaricated. 'You are my daughter's child. You are our blood.'

But the boy/man knew that the blood lines from the female side can only whisper.

That night Vicky stared moodily at his plate on the plastic-covered tablecloth. Sona was serving the men, his wife was in the kitchen making hot chapattis. Virat had already eaten, and was sitting next to them with his homework.

'Virat did very well in his test,' said Asha brightly on her way to and from the stove. 'The teacher says he will go far.'

'That's good,' said Sona. 'I had so much trouble with his father here, you don't know. The teachers complained all the time. Kept running off to the shop.'

'*He* is very devoted to the shop. It is his whole life, working, working all the time. Being the oldest brother of course it is necessary,' commented Asha.

The men silently continued to eat.

*

Later, walking up the three flights of stairs that took them to their room on the terrace, Vicky said angrily, 'You don't have to say anything about Virat, all right? Always you are talking. Nobody is interested.'

'Why shouldn't they be interested? He is their grandson after all.'

'Grandson-shamson. We will soon be leaving, then we will see if their interest extends to visiting him.'

'Oh, where are we going? Have they agreed to give you your share?' Asha hoped her husband hadn't done anything foolish.

'I have said. Uff, this child is heavy,' Vicky groaned. He was carrying the sleeping boy, while Asha was clutching his school bag, tiffin, and water bottle.

They reached the barsati, the boy was laid on the bed where all three slept.

'What? What have you said?' Asha bent to take off the child's shoes.

'I have said I am going back to Bareilly.'

That was the trouble with her husband speaking, the man was so simple, it was as though he had a disease. How happy the whole family would be to see him go, she could just imagine.

If only she could talk on his behalf to Baoji. She sat on the bed and sighed. Life seemed so promising when she first married. She, a small-town girl, with only fairness to recommend her, had managed to catch the scion of a big business family in Delhi, or so Murli had said. The pleasure of her mother now seemed foolishness. As though catches came for people like her. She had married into the station where she belonged. It may be that she slept in a big house in Karol Bagh, that her husband was connected to a well-known trader family, but that did not make the daily realities of her existence any different. Crowded, uncomfortable, marginal, and poor – this was her life in Bareilly and this was her life here. From morning to night she was in the kitchen, chopping, cleaning, cooking meals, making drinks and snacks. She was twenty-three, and her youth would soon fade.

Still, in Delhi lay possibilities. And in this house their basic needs were taken care of. She didn't even want to know what it would be like with Vicky on his own, and no money.

'You go where you want,' she declared. 'I cannot abandon Sona Maji, it is too much for her to manage everything alone.'

'You are the one who is always complaining how uncomfortable everything is here.'

'I only want you to get your due. How will you get it if you leave? Once out of sight, out of mind. I'm not going anywhere,' she repeated, putting out Virat's school things for the next day.

Vicky ground his teeth. Why was his wife like this? First she made him feel he was not a man, then when he asserted himself like the man he was, she started objecting. Truly women were a curse. He was quite happy till he got married. He worked in his uncle's shop and his future was mercifully hazy.

With these thoughts he put on his pyjama kurta and jumped into bed. But he couldn't sleep. It was his wife's fault. Always raising issues, but never satisfied. Meddle, meddle, meddle. What comfort was there that she did not have? She dressed in the latest fashions, she had leisure enough to watch TV downstairs, she only had to care for one child, and that a bright sweet boy. She had no need to do outside work, all that was done by the men. Even cooking she did with Sona.

Since her marriage she also looked much better. She had put on weight, she had breasts he could do something with, her skin was less sallow, her now unoiled hair fell around her face before being gathered in a plait below her shoulders.

She would be nowhere without his family, nowhere.

These thoughts created so much turmoil in him that he got up, circled the bed in the dark, crept to his wife's side, and tugged at her kurta. Drowsily she opened her legs. They were used to not saying much, there was always the sleeping Virat to consider.

113

Death in the family

Lala Banwari Lal was by this time seventy-three years old. His walk was slow, his memory faltering, from time to time his head felt heavy. His sons urged him to stay at home and take it easy, but the father could no more avail himself of this solicitude than he could stop breathing. Not go to the shop, not light incense before the gods every morning, not hear the thud of bolts of cloth as they were thrown on to the display area, not hear the rustle of saris as they were unfurled before customers, not see his grandsons drape material on their left arm to demonstrate how a particular sari or suit would look, not count the money they made every evening – not to do these things was virtual death. Time enough to rest when his body gave way. The shop was the fruit of his life's labours, and old age entitled him to enjoy it just the way he pleased.

Unfortunately, the way he pleased clashed with the ideas of the younger generation. How long could duty jostle with business considerations? The sons had been trained in both, but in the grandsons the clash became explicit. First Ajay and then Vijay looked around and saw their shop as mingy compared to the lush beauties that were springing up everywhere. Shops were now masquerading as five-star hotels, with glass doors, smartly turned-out doormen, chandeliers, and marble interiors. Spotlights trained on goods in a seductive ambience and the air-conditioning was so cold it felt like the mountains. The windows were decorated with imported mannequins, allowing the customer an easy transition from imagination to reality. But the greatest change lay in what they offered. Clothes ready to wear in both Indian and Western styles were becoming popular, and there was to be no reversal of this trend.

Western clothing chains slashed their way into Indian markets, cutting wide commercial swathes. Benetton came in the late 1980s, followed by Wrangler, Levis, Calvin Klein *et al*. The Banwari Lal cloth shop needed to keep up, if not with Western styles then at least with Indian ready-made, to which women were increasingly turning.

But for Lala Banwari Lal, fabric, weaves, textures were the eternal verities; bolts of cloth, yards of sari his steadfast companions. In vain did Ajay make his father point out that this was the 1980s – the timeless appeal of the sari was timeless no more. Stitched garments may be transitory, but they were also practical, simple to look after, easy to travel in, work in, walk in, and women, first young, then old, were taking to them in droves. The salwar kameez, once considered a Punjabi garment, was becoming the vogue all over India, while the trendiest were going in for pants, jeans, tops, and T-shirts.

'Baoji,' Ajay said, simultaneously respectful and emphatic, 'all the shops in Karol Bagh are doing ready-made. We are losing our market.'

'Our customers are loyal to us, beta. If no one buys this ready-made, what will you do? Next year it will be a different fashion. Look at the sari – one size for everybody – no stitching, no tailoring, no fitting, no complaints, everything beautiful and simple.'

'We need to be market leaders, not followers.'

The old man's voice quavered. 'We are market leaders. Remember when we started printing shawls to match saris? Now everybody is copying us.'

The silence of despair followed. That was eight years ago. Who was going to confront the old man with his sense of time?

'Our bridal saris are famous all over Delhi,' went on Lala Banwari Lal.

'Yes,' said Pyare Lal, 'and Kumarsons is famous for its lehngas, which brides now prefer. The same size with a few easy alterations fits all, and there is a big profit margin in the embroidery, sequins, beads, and threadwork.'

The grandfather looked at Yashpal, and seemed to address him alone. 'If saris are out of fashion, then where does the food we eat come from? Besides, we have no space for anything else.'

Yashpal was silent. He knew Pyare Lal and Ajay were talking sense. For how long could the sari be their main selling garment? But his father was anxiously blinking, clearly not following the rationale behind the obvious arguments to their exasperation and Yashpal's distress.

'We can build a separate section,' put in Pyare Lal, worrying another bone of contention. Building involved bribes, a domain Lala Banwari Lal was reluctant to enter. Ajay picked up the thread. Did Baoji think the shops that were expanding were following the law? It was illegal to change land use, but did that stop anybody? Look, look at Bansal and Sons. They were building a third floor, which would double their floor area and multiply their profits. And observe, there were the police sitting in the shop drinking tea.

'And the MCD? How many people can you force to look the other way?' quavered the grandfather.

Who were they forcing? The MCD searched for opportunities to make money. The established rate to keep all the officers from top to bottom happy during construction was fifty thousand a month. The price was cheap for the extra space, enough room to stock both ready-made and traditional wear.

The old hand smoothed the white sheet. Before Lala Banwari Lal was the dull green Godrej box with a stainless steel handle that he used for keeping cash and change. All his life he had sat before such a box, a wooden one in Anarkalli, an old-fashioned steel one in Karol Bagh. 'After me, you can make what changes you like,' he sighed.

Yashpal frowned at his brother. They owed everything to their father. If he wanted things to remain the same, they should humour him. His brother was not only supposed to keep this in mind, but to pass this message firmly on to his sons. They were the ones applying pressure, they wanted to gallop the minute they entered the market.

For the next year an uneasy truce reigned among the Banwari men. Vijay was still in college, but Ajay had words with his father almost every day. This meant that Pyare Lal was irritable in the shop while the strain made Yashpal irritable at home.

∼

All day the Banwari Lal men nibbled something. Mid-morning snack, evening snack, feeling stressed snack, visitor snack. They worked long hours, six days a week. Their pleasures lay in discussing what to eat, in anticipation as the order was sent out, in the stimulation of the olfactory senses as the packets unfolded, in the camaraderie of sharing. They unwound over fresh, crisp kachoris with imli chutney, over chola-kulcha with sour onions and sliced green chillies, over savoury samosas and namak para, over fried potato lachchas, cashews, salty-sweet Bombay mixture. And they had to balance the hot and spicy with the sweet: laddoos, barfis, jalebis, and kulfis. In the heart of Karol Bagh, surrounded by eating places, it was mandatory they patronised the suppliers they lived and traded amongst.

It was in the shop one day that Lala Banwari Lal felt a leaden sensation up and down his right side. 'Lie down, Baoji,' was Yashpal's response – his father must be tired, it was around Diwali, and the rush was as usual very heavy.

He lay down at the back. One hour later Yashpal discovered a man whose face was contorted, whose mouth had fallen open, who could not sit up, who needed to be rushed to the hospital, and who would never be the same. A stroke had grabbed Lala Banwari Lal and refused to treat him gently.

*

The family had to deal with two casualties: Lala Banwari Lal and his wife. 'How could this happen to him?' she wailed morning, noon, and night. She cried to the photograph of the Devi, circled adamantly with fresh marigolds every morning, cried to visitors, family, to all within her range of tears. Hush, hush, they responded, enclosing her protectively, Maji so old, frail, and sickly, the shock might harm her irreparably. Hush, hush, they philosophised, it is his karma, there is nothing we can do, but be brave for his sake. Hush, hush, they encouraged, everything will be all right.

When Lala Banwari Lal was brought out of the emergency, the family shifted their positions from the ICU doors to the side of his bed in the ward. Round the clock they alternated shop, home, hospital.

Ten days later he came home, twisted and refracted. The businessman and trader had vanished, as had the head of the family.

For fifty years Yashpal had been used to his father's protective shadow. He now felt bereft and abandoned. Speechless, dependent, the state of the old man created a similar helplessness within him. He could not bear it. 'How could this happen to one so good, where is the justice in the world?' he mourned to Sona.

'He was truly noble, never gave sorrow to anybody,' she agreed. Her mind went back to her ten barren years. Ten years of insult and humiliation from his wife, while he had treated her as tenderly as his own. What a pity she hadn't been his real daughter – being married into the family demanded restraint from her side, distance from his.

Angrily she thought, why couldn't this have happened to her mother-in-law? If a stroke had to befall the family, they were well able to spare that evil-tongued crone.

Not knowing she was echoing her daughter-in-law's sentiments, the old woman herself beseeched the gods to punish her instead of her husband a thousand times a day.

*

Every morning Yashpal sponged his father. Before setting out to work he stroked his head and said to the silent, staring man that soon he would get well, soon they would go to the shop together. His customers were missing him, they kept asking, asking. Nothing was the same without him. The old man could only silently follow him with his eyes as he left.

He was an invalid, though thankfully, in the interests of dignity, he could, with assistance, still use a bathroom. A storeroom was converted into a Western toilet, and the four grandsons acquired practice in humble service to their elders by helping him there. Such levellers are the cement in family architecture.

Meanwhile his wife went on moaning, her prayer beads permanently fastened to her withered hand: 'When is he going to get better? These doctors know nothing. Take him to a vaid, a hakim, a homeopath. English medicine is very harmful, from the hospital only he has come so weak, cannot walk, cannot talk. They remove the cream from his milk, they do not put ghee on his rotis – they are starving him, how will he get strong?'

Out of pity some of the visitors tried to explain the concept of cholesterol and hardening of the arteries. But they soon gave up, as the family had long done. As she was hard of hearing, the answers had to be shouted, and by the tenth shout much of the original substance was lost.

Sona couldn't stand the thin, relentless, high-pitched voice and became unpredictably deaf. Over the years the hatred she felt towards her mother-in-law had ebbed and flowed, but now, with the preferred in-law so ill, it was in full spate.

Her antagonism fed on ancient grievances towards Sushila as well. Upstairs and isolated, that woman led a carefree life, while she was mired in every trouble of her elders, her only support the marginal Asha.

Six months later Lala Banwari Lal suffered another massive stroke and died.

The patriarch was dead, and all connected to the family came to condole. Many cloth traders and relatives near and distant gathered at the Karol Bagh house to pay their respects to a man who had embodied all the virtues of the old-fashioned bania, honest, sincere, industrious, whose love had held the entire family together through trials and disagreements. During his entire life he had made no enemies, the many tears shed for him were ample testimony to that.

The family couldn't believe he had gone so soon. He had not troubled them enough, in itself an indication that he was free from the cycle of death and rebirth, all his bad karma expiated during six months of suffering.

His wife wept ceaselessly. She had been twelve, he fifteen, when they married, and now, after sixty years, she was alone. 'Why, why,' she wailed, 'why did he have to go before me? Why did I have this misfortune? Kill me,' she begged her sons, 'kill me so I may go to him.'

They smashed the glass bangles on her wrists; her scrawny, loose-fleshed arms were now bare of colour except for two thin gold bangles. They pulled off her toe rings, they unclasped her mangla sutra, they removed all the coloured saris from her wardrobe and left the white. She insisted this be done. The whole world should recognise her for what she was, a poor old widow, as insignificant and colourless as the clothes she wore.

A month passed. The gloom in the house persisted. Rupa visited her sister every day, privately grateful that at least her Nisha was spared the constant exhibition of Maji's feelings.

'I am seriously worried about Maji,' confided Yashpal to his wife one such evening. 'Isn't there anything we can do to help her?'

'I too am worried,' repeated the wife dutifully.

'Maybe Nisha should come back here.'

Sona's hand stopped in mid-serve. 'Come back here?'

'Maji was so fond of her when she was little. She fed her,

bathed her, put her to sleep in her own bed. Now she needs somebody.'

And her daughter's tender youth was to sustain that woman's crazy age. What Sona said was, 'Remember how Nisha used to cry. That was why we sent her to Rupa's. And she does so well in her studies there.'

It was a weak attempt.

'Sonu,' reproved Yashpal, 'that was eleven years ago. The girl no longer cries, nor is there cause for her to be frightened now. She will want to help her grandmother. They were so close,' he ruminated, finishing his food and belching gently, to his wife's satisfaction.

'Ajay and Vijay can spend more time with their grand-mother.'

'They are grown men. What will Maji do with them? Now you get Nisha back,' said her husband, annoyed at having to insist so much.

That night, on the bed that had seen many wakeful moments, Sona decided to worry her wounds with thoughts of Rupa's cause. What about her? She also had claims. The child was not a rubber ball to be bounced around to whom-ever felt the need. Surely Raju was enough to keep any grandmother happy.

The daughter returns home

The next day saw Sona deeply divided. She had to bring Nisha home, but what about Rupa, and more importantly, what about Nisha's studies? At least she had one child whose performance she could boast about, even though that child was a girl who, despite the overuse of her brains, was only going to get married.

Raju had continued to do badly. He didn't show the early interest in the shop that had characterised Vicky's escape from school. All he wanted to do was play cricket and wander around with the boys of the neighbourhood. Sona tried to keep the boy separate from his cousins, she felt they encouraged him in his delinquency, but it was no use.

'Leave me, Mummy, all this talk of studies makes my life hell. What do I care if I never finish school? Vicky didn't.'

'Vicky is at least tenth-class pass. And his wife is from the gullies of Bareilly. Good girls today want at least a BA.'

'I don't want to marry,' said fourteen-year-old Raju rebelliously.

Sona sighed, stroked Raju's head, and pressed his face against her chest. 'You say that now, beta, but when she comes you will forget your mother.'

'Please, Mummy,' protested the son.

'What do you know of a mother's heart? For years I sacrificed for you.'

This oft-repeated statement had still not lost the capacity to make Raju uneasy. He struggled against his mother's soft bosom, a place he had once liked to nestle in.

'Your sister shines in school, why can't you?' continued Sona.

'It's no use. I hate studies, my brain dries up. Nisha is a girl, she has nothing better to do than sit around and read.'

Now, thought Sona, the sister might prove to be a good influence on the brother. Certainly the boy needed it: Nisha was in the eleventh, Raju in the ninth, and their board exams were coming next year.

She would have to break the news to Rupa, though. Of course they were all one family and the two houses were just a ten-minute rickshaw drive apart – one, two, three, four, five rupees away, as the years went by and prices rose.

Rupa came over as usual with Nisha that Friday. While Nisha retired with her book to the angan, Rupa, armed with her knitting, sat cross-legged with her sister on the bed.

'How is it now?' she whispered, indicating with her eyes the grief-stricken widow, stinking faintly but permanently of urine.

Sona's face twitched. 'The same,' she murmured.

'Poor Didi,' murmured Rupa back.

Soon Rupa would be the one distressed, and it would be her mother-in-law's fault, thought Sona, fresh hatred surging through well-worn tracks within her.

'*He* is very worried about his mother.'

'His mother, after all.'

'He doesn't believe she starts groaning ten times louder when he is here. Tired from the shop, he comes, missing Baoji, and then she starts. Her breathlessness, her heart, her joints, her stomach, her stools, her wind, her gripes, her gas, her pains, her blackouts – is there anything that happens to her that she does not force him to worry about? What can *he* do? Is *he* a doctor? She is sucking his life, you can see how he has aged. Only fifty, and looks a hundred. I went to the shop the other day, and a client thought I was his daughter!'

Pleasure and pain were mixed in this statement. Nobody likes having a husband mistaken for a father, though one might register the compliment to oneself.

Sona's looks were Rupa's cross and she did not respond now. A heartbeat pause before Sona continued. 'Now he has got it into his head that it will make his mother happy to have Nisha back.'

This time the pause lasted several heartbeats.

'She is yours, Didi,' said Rupa, staring hard at her knitting, willing her hands not to slow down, or the tightness in her throat to become a sob.

'Mine, yours, Roop – our daughter.'

Not really, when it came to the crunch, not really. What were an aunt's rights? Could she say, I won't give her to you, she is mine. Her husband was right, advising her not to lavish so much love on a niece-on-loan. But then her husband was a thinker, he understood the world, she was just a simple woman.

'What about her studies?' she asked now. 'Her uncle sits with her every evening. And during exam time you should see how carefully he goes through her course.'

This was an old story, and with her other troubles Sona could not give such a statement the attention it required.

'He says a good degree gives you something to fall back on, should you be forced to stand on your own two feet,' continued Rupa.

'I know Bhai Sahib is full of qualities,' said Sona impatiently, 'but if something happens, God forbid, thoo-thoo (Sona spat lightly on the floor to ward off the evil eye), she has her family, her brothers, her aunt and uncle. What is the need to blacken your face looking for a job, as though you had no one to protect you? Might as well live on the streets.'

'Times are different now, Didi. You mean to say all working women have no one to call their own?'

'I don't know,' said Sona irritably, rolling up her knitting, now an inch longer. 'We are old-fashioned people. Tradition is strong with us. So is duty.'

And in the spirit of duty Nisha was transported back to her parents' house.

Leaving two mourning people in a house that screamed her

loss. No noise, no chatter, no singing, no comfort in seeing the girl study, eat, sleep, dress, silent husband and wife with background TV. Rupa was afraid to tell her husband how she felt. His I-told-you-so would prove his prescience and her stupidity.

For now, his only comment was, 'Will the shopkeeper attend to her school work?'

'You know he doesn't do things like that. Besides, he doesn't have the time.'

'I suppose I have nothing but time. What about the case?'

'Which we are winning, thanks to you,' said Rupa hastily. 'Didn't you say he hardly ever comes to the hearings now? It's been nineteen years, how long can one fight?'

Prem Nath brooded over the injustice in the world. 'They could have waited till her eleventh class exams were over,' he said at last. 'It is an important year.'

Rupa had heard 'It is an important year' from Class I on. First the basics had to be got right, then confidence had to be built, then maintained, then prowess proved beyond a doubt. Then in middle and high school this cycle was repeated all over again.

Well, it was in Nisha's stars, rather than Raju's, to benefit from her husband's attention and perform well in exams. God knew what use an education would be to a girl from a trader family, one who was only going to marry and produce children.

After eleven years Nisha returned home to assume her place as daughter of the house, to learn the difference between weekend visits and full-time stay. Now there was less interest in her school, no pampering, and long hours expected in the kitchen.

Her mother discovered to her horror that, at sixteen, Nisha's cooking skills were negligible. Nisha discovered to her horror that her mother's idea of a daughter was one who helped her every time anybody ate.

'What can Rupa have been thinking of? I assumed she was teaching you everything she knew,' Sona grumbled. 'You take half an hour to peel ten potatoes. How will you manage in your future home?'

'Masi said there is always time to learn cooking, but only one time to study.' Nisha tried defending herself, her aunt, and her upbringing.

'That Masi of yours has ruined your head. What does a girl need with studying? Cooking will be useful her entire life.'

'Masarji agreed.'

'Of course he will agree. Works as a clerk in some government office, and uses his wife's money to pay his lawyers. Now quickly cut this ginger. Fine-fine. Like matchsticks.'

Ginger is difficult to cut. To hand a novice a knobbly piece and expect matchsticks is hardly fair. Badly scraped pencils rather than finely pared matchsticks fell from Nisha's knife.

The mother's anger rose. What was wrong with her sister, she couldn't understand. No children had produced an excess of love, and a girl who was good for nothing. 'Spoilt you, do you hear? Useless – even ginger I have to do myself. Now quickly cut up cucumbers for the salad – here, do it like this, rub the top, take out the bitter, then wash, then peel, then slice, do the same with onions, tomatoes, and green chillies.'

Nisha said nothing. Black feelings raged in her heart. Her aunt had always said when she offered to assist, 'What is there to help with when there are just three people?' (The father-in-law had died along the way.) 'Go, sit with your uncle.'

And her uncle? If her studies were really important, why had he allowed her to be sent back to her parents' place? Here nobody looked through her school diary, notebooks, or test papers. They didn't care if she failed, they only cared if she cut ginger. There was Asha always in the kitchen with her mother, laughing behind her back, cutting ginger as fine as could be.

She knew it mattered if food was not cooked properly. Her father's sense of taste was very acute. Her mother watched anxiously as he took the first bite of any dish. He was capable of frowning, saying too much asafoetida, too little turmeric, the cumin has been over-roasted. Sona would look unhappy, she hated criticism of any kind.

Her aunt and uncle visited every weekend, but Nisha said little to them. Prem Nath tried to engage her: 'How is school? The exams are coming.'

Her mother replied instead, 'After all these years of studying, the girl has learned enough to do an MA.'

Rupa knew how much her husband would make of this remark once they were home.

'Her teachers think highly of her,' said Prem Nath mildly.

'She doesn't even know how to cook,' flashed Sona angrily.

Rupa looked uneasy. 'She is a smart girl, Didi. We have cooked all our lives, where has it got us?'

'Roop, I would never have imagined you, of all people, filling the girl's head with rubbish. This is the life of a woman: to look after her home, her husband, her children, and give them food she has cooked with her own hands. Next you will be saying she should hire a servant.'

'I didn't mean that,' explained Rupa quickly.

'She is useless, absolutely useless!' Sona raised her voice. Really, her sister had no sense. She had made the supreme sacrifice of sending away her own blood for eleven years, and the woman returned a sub-standard female.

Asha sat next to them, silent and expectant. Maybe they were going to fight over Nisha. Of course Sona Maji was right. Every woman had to know how to cook. Nisha was too big for her boots; her husband had maintained this all along. She was a spoilt princess, and poor Sona Maji had to teach her everything from A to Z. Bumbling, awkward, as though her looks could make up for ineptness in the kitchen. When it came to marriage that was what counted.

'Bhenji,' interrupted Prem Nath, 'you knew how we were bringing her up. If you did not like what we were doing, I wish you had let us know earlier.'

Sona simmered down. 'It's all right, Bhai Sahib. You did your best, I know.'

Rupa guided the talk into other channels.

On their way home the couple didn't say much. 'What has happened to Sonu Didi?' Rupa tried once, but Prem Nath made a face and refused to answer. She knew he was suffering seeing Nisha so withdrawn. She wished she had resisted more when her sister took her, but she had not felt the right. Despair seemed the only option as she sat behind her husband on his scooter, her arm around a thin waist that reflected his ulcer.

'Maybe I should persuade her to send Nisha back,' tried Rupa over dinner.

'And listen to how we have not taught her cooking. No, thank you.'

'I can ask them to leave her with us till she finishes her schooling. She needs your help.'

'That's for her parents to realise.'

'That old woman must be troubling Didi. All the time complaining about her health, finding fault.'

'And Nisha is supposed to handle what your sister can't? Please, let us have no more to do with them.'

He was not serious. It was just his way. How can you have nothing to do with a sister's family? Might as well emigrate to America. But he had a point. How was Nisha going to handle all that? Perhaps they had been too protective.

～

Nisha was actually handling nothing.

Certainly not her grandmother. At night she was forced to sleep next to her, inhaling the all-pervasive urine smell; in the day her emphatic farts and loud, lingering burps repulsed her. Her mother persistently pointed out her presence to the old woman, she has come home to be with you, neglecting her studies, leaving her aunt and uncle, they miss her so so much, but still she is here.

The old woman, rheumy-eyed, thick-spectacled, slack-jawed, would pat Nisha on the head with trembling hands. 'Live for ever, bloom, be fruitful, have sons and grandsons,' she quavered, before turning her attention to her beads and the miseries of this existence.

'Your father thinks she needs to be cajoled back to life,' muttered Sona to her daughter. 'Now you are here, he must realise how hopeless that is.'

From time to time Nisha fantasised about returning to her aunt's place. They repeatedly told her this was where she was needed, this was her home, but it didn't feel comfortable. The moment she opened her books, she missed her uncle, when she sat down to eat she missed her aunt's food, when she slept she missed the quietness, when she came home from school she missed the fuss, when she worked she missed the encouragement. Her hands, altered from spotless white to nicked and burnt, reflected the change in her situation. Worst of all, no one imagined there was any lack in her life that needed to be filled.

Along with attention to her culinary skills, her mother took special care to include her daughter in all her pujas. Had she done them with her aunt? Nisha always answered yes. She was tired of her mother asking her whether she had done this or that with her aunt. It led to endless fulmination, complaint, and comparisons between her present self and some ideal daughter.

Sona was making up for negligent upbringing. Nisha needed to be grounded in the tradition that would make her a wife worth having. The art of service and domesticity should shine in her daughter so brightly that she would over-come her negative karma to be a beacon in her married home.

In the month of jesht, in the middle of summer, under a banyan tree – that is, a branch of a banyan tree stuck into a pot by Sona – the women of the family gather for puja. It is hot, the stand fan a few feet away moves the air about indifferently, the branch of the banyan tree wilts and will die in a few hours.

The gods are first bathed, fed, and prayed to. Sona, as oldest daughter-in-law, is the one who performs these rituals. Asha, Sushila, and Nisha sit around her. The grandmother watches avidly from the veranda bed.

Now for the story. Listen and like Savitri be a beacon in your married home, starts Sona, reading from the book of legends.

The Vat Savitri Katha

There was a king, Ashupati, whose childless life was bleak and sorrowful. Fervently he prayed, meticulously he fasted. A son, he implored the Devi Savitri.

The Devi appeared. 'A son is not in your fate,' she said. 'But your coming daughter will be the salvation of your family, as well as the family she marries into. You will name her after me.'

In course of time this child was born. Her eyes were long and large like shut lotuses, her skin was gold.

Savitri grew like the moon in the night sky. Words cannot describe her; it is enough to talk of her father's fear. Where would he find a bridegroom worthy of this girl?

When she attained marriageable age, he said, 'Child, people are too intimidated to ask for your hand in marriage. Go forth and find a husband.'

He sent her with beautiful clothes, jewels, and his trusted ministers into the world, where somewhere there was a husband waiting for her.

Meanwhile the sage, Narad Muni, passed by. The king

greeted him reverently. Narad Muni said, 'Oh king, you have a daughter as yet unmarried. You are not doing your duty.'

Said the king, 'As there was no one to equal her, I have sent her to choose her own husband.'

They waited. The daughter returned.

'Whom have you chosen?'

'Satyavan, who lives in the jungle.'

Narad Muni: 'Oh king, what has your daughter done? Satyavan is truthful, handsome, and full of virtues, but one year from now he will be dead.'

Ashupati said, 'She will have to choose another.'

Savitri objected, 'In my mind I already consider Satyavan my husband, for better or worse. How can I now change because he will only live a year? If such is the case, I wish in fact to be married quickly.'

Seeing Savitri's determination, the king, armed with costly gifts, set out for the jungle with his daughter. There under a tree he found the blind Dyumatsen. Touching his feet, he said, 'I wish to give my daughter, Savitri, in marriage to your son, Satyavan.'

Dyumatsen demurred. 'We live in the jungle. We have nothing to offer a princess who has been brought up in the lap of luxury.'

Ashupati insisted. 'She considers Satyavan her husband. They have to get married.'

The two were married, and Ashupati returned to his palace.

Savitri counted each day left of Satyavan's life, and trembled.

She focused on purifying her entire being through prayer and fasts. Once a month she dedicated herself to the Devi Savitri.

Three days before the year was up, she started praying. On the morning of the third day, she said to her husband, 'Do not go to the jungle.'

'I have to bring back wood, fruits, and berries.'

'Then take me with you.'

Satyavan, good son as well as husband, said, 'I am not my own master. Ask my parents.'

Savitri went to her father-in-law and, touching his feet, asked permission to accompany Satyavan to the forest.

'Beti,' said Dyumatsen, 'you have been fasting. You are weak. Go some other time.'

'I will not eat until nightfall and I am very anxious to go with my husband today.'

Savitri could not ask and be refused. She was given permission.

Savitri and Satyavan went to the forest. Savitri sat under a tree while Satyavan cut wood. As he was binding the pieces together, he suddenly said, 'Oh beautiful one, let me lie on your lap. My head is paining as though pricked by a thousand needles.'

Savitri went cold. She knew his time had come. She looked up and through her inner strength saw Yamraj, Lord of the Underworld, standing before her.

'I have come to take your husband, Savitri,' he said. 'Let him go.'

'I thought Yamraj would have many messengers to do his work,' managed Savitri. 'How is it the Lord himself has come?'

'Satyavan is no ordinary person,' replied Yamraj. 'That is why I am here to take him myself.' With his finger he drew out Satyavan's soul. Savitri looked down and saw her husband's body lifeless in her lap.

Yamraj left and, gently placing her husband's head on a grassy knoll, Savitri got up to follow. They travelled many miles. Finally Yamraj said, 'Because you are so pure you have been able to come such a long way with me, but now you must go back.'

Savitri said, 'Which way is long when I am with my husband?'

Yamraj: 'Besides Satyavan's life, ask me for any favour.'

Savitri: 'My father-in-law is blind. Grant him his eye-sight, strength, vigour, and a hundred sons.'

'Granted. Now go.'

But Savitri kept following him.

Yamraj: 'Now what do you want? With the exception of Satyavan's life, ask me anything.'

Savitri: 'Give my father-in-law's kingdom back to him, and make sure that he leads a pure, dutiful, religious life.'

Yamraj: 'Granted.'

More following.

Yamraj: 'Now?'

Savitri: 'Give my father a hundred sons, so that his dynasty will not die out.'

Yamraj : 'Done. Now go.'

She kept on, his shadow. Yamraj turned around. 'What do you want now?'

'Grant me too a hundred sons.'

'Granted.'

The following does not stop. On and on and on.

For a mortal to come so far is not seemly, the Lord wishes to shake her off. He turns around and thunders, 'Now what?'

The listeners hold their breath at the anticipated climax.

'Oh Lord, you have granted me a hundred sons. I am a pious woman. How can I have a hundred sons without my husband?'

And yes, the Lord of Death is stumped! 'Take your husband,' he finally growls. 'Return, you will find him alive.'

Savitri races back to the jungle to find her husband sit-ting up.

'Savitri, I had the strangest dream.'

Savitri smiles, listens, tells him what has happened. Satyavan cannot believe it. They return home.

To find Dyumatsen with his eyesight restored, and a

messenger coming to say that the usurper has fled the kingdom, and all is his.

Disbelief melts into an acknowledgement of this woman's power.

Sona closes the katha book with tears in her eyes. She too, like Savitri, has sacrificed for her family.

'See,' she says to her listening daughter, 'this is what you must be like.'

XII

Ajay's wedding

In her parents' house Nisha's studies began to slip, there just wasn't the atmosphere. No space was free from noise or people. Her schoolbooks were only occasionally hauled out as she sat in the veranda away from the family. From here she could see the children playing in the park, could hear their voices, could see mosquitoes buzzing about, big as flies.

In the eleventh final exams she got two compartments. She would have to repeat her Pol. Science and Economics exams in order to pass.

'Maybe she is spending too much time with Maji,' remarked Yashpal upon this news. 'The girl has a loving heart, but she shouldn't go from one extreme to another. Still, I am glad we brought her back, she is so happy here.'

'What is there in happiness? A girl has to be happy everywhere,' replied his wife tartly, knowing it was impossible to disillusion him about Maji. The man saw what he wanted to see. 'Besides, she is hopeless at cooking. Asha is ten times faster than she is. Her real education is in the kitchen.'

Meanwhile Prem Nath had to struggle mightily with himself when he heard that Nisha had got a compartment. A compartment! Nisha, of all girls – where had his teaching gone? And this just with Ajay's engagement. When he actually got married, how much she would study God only knew.

'You can go there and help her,' remarked Rupa foolishly.

Rupa's love for Nisha was the same whether she was in this house or that. But Prem Nath's affection needed the certainty of continuity. He sighed and picked up his *Bhagvad Gita*. The virtues of non-attachment were all listed there, as was the importance of doing your duty. This fine balance between

135

the two was what he had to strive for. With the practice that was about to be afforded him it might even be possible to realise in this lifetime.

Nisha for her part was not aware of these dark thoughts in her uncle's breast. She avoided him when he came to visit because she had done badly and let him down.

Raju had done as badly, but he didn't seem to be bothered. It was not fair. If she had been in this house from the beginning, she would be able to fail and still sleep at night. She had grown to like the ease of talking, listening, being together, even though her hands were as yet clumsy around the vegetables she cut during these sessions.

Ajay's marriage took place a year after his grandfather's death. The girl was from Meerut, provincial, adaptable, shy, sweet, caring, homely, devoted, and trained to put the interests of her new family above everything. Not a spoiled Delhi girl, announced Sushila with an air of personal accomplishment.

At these pronouncements Asha looked self-conscious. After all, the appellations applied to her as well.

Nisha was involved in most of the wedding preparations. 'Why couldn't they wait till the children's board exams were over?' grumbled Prem Nath often, as uncle and aunt were besieged with demands for assistance.

'Maji is so weak and frail. They want her blessings on this union.'

'You mean she shouldn't die before Ajay's marriage.'

'It will not be good to postpone it, you know that.'

'He is only twenty-one.'

Rupa did not bother to comment. For an intelligent man, it was surprising the things her husband could not see. What were boys to do with their urges if they did not marry? Once the passions of youth were calmed, he could settle down to the main things in life, family and money; it was plain as the mango juice that was drying in the sun for aam papar.

Her thoughts wandered to the clothes that would be made, to the food that would be prepared, to her own role in everything. She was indispensable to her sister, she knew that, and she looked forward to weeks of involvement in family functions.

Throughout the wedding preparations Sona paid Nisha's clothes special attention. The girl was now seventeen, it was time that clothes were engaged to do their job properly, to set off her looks, as hers had been done so many years ago at a wedding in Delhi.

'Didi is trying to get Nisha married,' commented Rupa to her husband.

The husband snorted. 'I told you her mind would not be on her studies.'

'Oh-ho, you also are not taking so much care,' said Rupa, stung into commenting on something she had observed. 'When you go there you do not even look at her. She is hurt, I can tell.'

'Why should I go on taking care? Am I a fool? Something borrowed is never yours, you should remember that.'

'A sister's child is not a borrowed thing,' said Rupa angrily. 'For your own sister's children you are ready to give your life, your money, everything.'

'I have not done less for your sister's child, Roop. In fact I have done more, nurtured her, cared for her, sweated over her, evening after evening. I would have given money too if that is what she needed,' said Prem Nath firmly. 'But I have no rights over her, nothing to counteract the mother's foolish criticism, and that too after devotion to her child for eleven years. A person can also feel used.'

Rupa said nothing. It was true, a person could feel used.

At home Asha watched the goings-on jealously. She was the only other young woman in the house, but how different was the attention that came to her, how inferior the clothes, how meagre the thin gold chain – hardly a chain at all, you could-n't even see it. All the time it was Nisha, Nisha, Nisha.

She had the comfort of complaining to her husband. 'Sona Maji is very worried about her marriage, though they say she is so pretty, there is obviously something wrong with her.'

Her husband scolded her. 'Arre, what is it to you? It will be good when Nisha marries and leaves the house. At least I won't have to hear about her every day.'

Asha, stung, retorted, 'How do you hear about her every day? Only when she is making a fool of herself in the kitchen do I say anything.'

'You are obsessed with the girl, all the time talking about her – I am sick of it,' said Vicky angrily, clearing his throat and spitting emphatically over the railing of the terrace.

'You are sick of it?'

'I, yes, I.'

'What about me? I have to keep hearing how high and mighty you think she is.'

'Only because you keep complaining about her.'

The fight continued, feeding on itself endlessly.

Sona to her husband: 'If someone from a good family likes Nisha, our worries will be over.'

The father's heart contracted. He had hardly known what it was like to live with a daughter, and soon she would go away for good.

'She is too young,' he replied.

'Nonsense,' retorted the mother. 'I was this age when you saw me.'

'That was different,' said Yashpal, his voice softening. 'An earlier time.'

'She is old enough. If someone likes her and their horo-scopes match, what is the problem?'

'There is no need to push her into responsibilities.'

The mother suppressed her irritation. When the brilliant match came along, then was the time to argue.

Ajay married, and inexplicably Nisha emerged unengaged. She had stood out like a flower, in pink, lilac, and magenta. There had been enquiries, it was true, but they were from insignificant shopkeepers – nothing really big. With their background and Nisha's looks, why should they settle for something small?

With a consideration that had not marked her life, the grand-mother was found dead in her bed a full month after the wedding.

'She could not stay in this world after Baoji died,' sighed Yashpal to his wife. 'It is testimony to her love for us that she managed to live eighteen months after he left. She had great courage, great courage.' He shook his shaven head.

His wife looked at him. He was so noble, always seeing the good in everybody. A dutiful husband, a loving son. Within a year and a half he had lost both his parents. Twice he had had his head shaved, twice gone to Haridwar to immerse ashes and bones in the Ganges.

～

The Board results were out. Raju in Class X had barely scraped through with a 45 per cent overall aggregate. As for Nisha, her uncle's training had stood her in good stead, despite his opinions. With a family wedding, she had still been able to obtain a 70 per cent in the Humanities.

This was respectable enough for her parents to distribute sweets to all and sundry. The uncle was thanked profusely for the care he had taken of his niece.

Now for the future.

Theirs was a family that believed in fate, in predestination, in the sins of your past life catching up in this, and God's firm hand over everything. There must be a reason for Nisha's 70 per cent which needed to be carefully examined.

Nisha was a mangli. A mangli, destined to marry unfortunately, destined for misery, unless a similar manglik could be found, with a similar fate and horoscope. To do this would take time, and during that time –

Perhaps an education? Not too much, just a bit. With her marks the very fancy colleges were out, but they were simple people, they wanted a simple, down-to-earth, no-nonsense girls' college, where she would not get any ideas.

The family discuss Nisha's future endlessly, parade their own experiences, and evaluate her achievement against their sense of female destiny.

'Nowadays a BA is essential,' says Sushila, who had brought this degree along with her dowry. 'She can switch to a Correspondence Course if her in-laws want her to stay at home.'

'People are suspicious of brides that are very educated. Too many ideas make it difficult to adjust,' replies Sona, resenting the slur on her own twelfth-class status.

'Education is not a bad thing,' comments Asha safely.

'These college students are just loafing the whole day,' points out Vicky. 'You want to learn something, you go to work.'

'How can girls do service?' titters his small-town wife.

'As it is, Nisha is so bad in kitchen work, she might get totally out of control in college,' says Sona anxiously.

'Seema has all a housewife's qualities, and she is a BA,' eulogises Sushila of Ajay's spouse.

Seema blushes and says nothing. She is still a new bride, and modesty lies heavy upon her.

'If anything happens in the girl's later life, she is not completely dependent,' interposes Rupa. She knows her views should be confined to her sister, who would recycle them as she thought fit. But she couldn't help herself. In this day and age there were still people wondering whether girls should get an education. And this a girl whom her husband had slaved over for years. How could they let all that go to waste?

'It would be a shame to not educate her further,' she continued in a careful, unemotional manner. 'Let her do English Honours, not too much work, reading story books.'

Her sister nudged her. It should not be said that the aunt's influence outweighed family opinions.

Nisha liked the idea of doing English Honours. She was tired of mugging dates and facts. A little relaxation would be nice.

In the end Durga Bai College was decided on. On campus, all girls, with a reputation of steady mediocrity. It would do nicely for a girl waiting to get married.

Nisha enters college

Nisha entered DBC with confidence. In school English had required little preparation. She anticipated a continuation of the same, but knew it didn't matter whether she achieved or not.

Her family's attitude to college proved sustaining. Higher studies were just a time pass, it was not as though she was going to use her education. Working was out of the question, and marriage was around the corner.

In college Nisha's best friend was Pratibha, a tall, dark, lanky girl who habitually dressed in shiny pink. She had a flat chest and hair that shone with oil. Her family was poor, a fact she compensated for by being ambitious. She had joined the NCC programme, hoping that this would lead to a government job with the police. It was her belief that an English Honours degree would look good at the interview stage, though she felt it a crying shame that such was the case. 'Why is it that Indian languages are not considered on a par with English in our own country?' she demanded passionately. 'If you haven't had an English education, what are you to do? Will they say you cannot become a police officer?'

'I don't know,' replied Nisha, for whom any prospect of work was equivalent to going to the moon. She was doing English because she was sick and tired of studying. Poor Prem Nath would not have liked to see his niece laugh off excellence so easily, and Nisha felt a pang of guilt which she stoutly ignored.

Through the corridors these two friends walked, occasionally cutting a class when they hadn't read the text – so much to read yaar, these teachers expect you to study all the time, complained Pratibha. At home Mummy doesn't keep well, and I have to get up early to make the lunch, and then when I come home, I start dinner. And on Sunday the whole family is there – where is the time, I wish they could understand.

Nisha blushed at her comparative lack of household demands. 'There is my Bhabhi,' she murmured of Asha. 'She does a lot.'

'Lucky you,' commented Pratibha. 'I have three brothers who are still unmarried.'

Nisha quickly adjusted to the rather boring atmosphere of her all-girls college. At times the only difference she felt between DBC and school was that she didn't have to wear a uniform and she could cut classes to sit with Pratibha in the canteen.

It was during the journey to the campus that Nisha really felt grown up. For the first time she was leaving Karol Bagh alone. In the mornings she caught the University Special, the bus service that catered to all the colleges, where girls and boys were not segregated, where the travellers were young (except for a few ancient teachers, who counted for nothing).

She first noticed his dark glasses and long hair. He was tall and thin, with a sallow complexion and his face was decorated with a bluish-black stubble. He took off his glasses to make sure she knew he was looking at her. She looked away, annoyed by his familiarity.

After some days he spoke. 'Where do you study?'

She didn't answer him, he might think she was welcoming his attentions.

Next day he asked again.

And the day after that.

By now she was beginning to feel silly. They were in a crowded student special after all. What harm could there be in a short, civil reply?

'DBC,' she said briefly.

A long pause. If he thought she was going to return the interest he had a hope.

He addressed his hopes himself. 'I am in KCE.'

The bus drew up to Kashmiri Gate. 'Bye,' he mumbled and jumped off.

She sought information from Pratibha. 'What is KCE?'

Pratibha looked interested. 'Khalsa College of Engineering. Why? Met someone?'

Nisha protested, 'Why are you so quick to imagine things?'

'Be careful,' cautioned Pratibha. 'Those boys are always trying to pick up girls. They are off campus and desperate.'

Nisha tossed her head. 'I am not so stupid.'

When she came home she stared at the mirror hanging over the sink in the hot, deserted angan. This was what the boy had seen when he looked at her.

Next morning Nisha dressed carefully, casting a furtive glance at the mirror when nobody was looking. How pretty was she? She was fair; her eyes, like her mother's, were light brown; her hair long and thick with copper highlights. But something was lacking. There were girls on the bus without half her looks who attracted more attention, her own included. Well, what did it matter, she thought, gathering her books and leaving the house, she was not asking anybody to look at her, she just had to go to college, do her work, come home.

In the bus every seat was taken, and working from the backs of heads, it took a while before she could locate the long hair, the slender neck, the narrow slump of shoulder.

More students got in and pushed her forwards. The bus lurched, her hand grabbed his seat to avoid falling, he looked around, reached for her heavy book-laden bag, indicating an intimacy that confused and warmed her.

She looked down, her hand still resting on the seat bar, centimetres away from his hair.

At Kashmiri Gate he got out, and with a slight gesture

offered her the seat. She slid into it, and stared ahead, clutching her belongings in her lap.

The monsoon was departing, but the days continued hot: cloudy, rainless skies alternating with stifling, muggy days. When the electricity went, the classrooms became unbearable, the level of smell casting the mind back to the interior of a crowded bus, and lingering there in a way that was most detrimental to one's studies.

Weeks passed of incessant eye contact and occasional words. There was no reason to feel shy now when the boy took her books. And no reason for Nisha to keep her body tightly away from his when they sometimes sat next to each other.

One day he mentioned that he had some work near DBC, and would get down at her stop.

They walked down the narrow pavement with its broken paving stones, their steps together, she conscious of everything about him, he looking straight ahead, a tune on his breath, the mask of dark glasses firmly in place.

They walked along, dust getting under their chappals, perspiration wetting their clothes. In this daily walk from home to bus stop to college, and back, she used an umbrella to make sure her skin didn't darken, and she took it out now.

'Hot, no?'

She nodded.

'Want a cold drink?'

She was too shy to actually agree.

'Let's go to the Coffee House, it's not far.'

There could be nothing wrong in having a cold drink with someone she had seen so often. She let herself be guided towards the Coffee House.

She returned to college feeling adventurous, daring, and modern. For the first time she had interacted socially with an unrelated male. She couldn't wait to get Pratibha to the canteen. Though when Pratibha pressed her for details it turned out nothing exciting had taken place.

Suresh had been forced to make most of the conversation. His questions, her monosyllabic replies, had been the gist of the encounter : Are you in first year? I haven't seen you before in the bus? Do you like your college? Where do you live? What do you study? What does your father do?

She had been less curious. Irritated at the lost opportunity, Pratibha opined that a new-born baby would have done better. Ah, but a new-born baby could not look, and what they had communicated through their glances was not something to convey. Quickly Nisha changed the topic. Had Pratibha got the notes she had promised her?

But Pratibha was not so easily put off. She insisted Nisha bunk the next period, a history subsidiary. More talk was needed, gaps had to be filled, silences meditated upon.

'So you like him?' demanded Pratibha sternly.

Nisha nodded, nervously swishing her chow mein around on the cracked, green-flowered plastic plate that Mr Lamba saw fit to serve his stuff on.

'What's his name?'

'Suresh.'

Pratibha tcched impatiently.

'Suresh what? You can't identify a person from his first name.'

'Kumar.'

'Kumar? He is hiding his caste?'

'Maybe he doesn't believe in caste – after all, there are lots of Kumaris in class.'

That was true. Pratibha backed down a bit. 'All right. Where is he from then? What is his family background?'

'How should I know? Am I going to marry him that I should start doing question-answer?'

'If you are going to be a modern girl you have to be thorough.'

'It's not so easy, you know.'

146

'Then it is better not to get into these things,' claimed Pratibha virtuously.

'O-ho, what am I getting into?' demanded Nisha. 'You think girl and boy can't be friends?'

'Don't get so hot,' said Pratibha in her turn. 'What does he look like?'

'Sanjay Dutt.'

Pratibha tittered. 'You like him so much, you think he looks like a film hero.'

Nisha giggled in turn. 'Arre, I am just telling you what I see. I am not asking you to believe me.'

Two weeks later Pratibha was dragged to the coffee house. The meeting was a huge success. Pratibha wore a pink satin salwar suit with a sequinned net chunni. Nisha could tell the cloth was like the lower-priced ones her father sold in his shop, and suddenly she hoped Suresh would be very nice to her friend.

He was. He found out she wanted to be an IPS officer. He teased her about how ferocious she was going to be, riding in a police van on campus putting down demonstrations. Pratibha cackled and told Nisha later he was not at all proudy like other boys she knew.

The meetings continued, but still under the guise of I have work near your college, would you like a coffee? And then came the time when she asked what work and he smiled and said you, and they both felt a milestone had been reached, enough for him to briefly touch her arm, enough for her to not pull away.

He paid her compliments that beguiled her into believing she was someone special. If Suresh thought her pretty, it was not an appearance that reflected a mother's greater beauty; if he thought her clothes nice, it was not a comment on Banwari Lal merchandising; if he thought her conversation witty, it was not the result of a relative's input into her studies. It was a heady feeling.

147

At the coffee house one day he looked long and hard at her.

'What?' asked the girl.

'Have you ever thought of cutting your hair?' he responded.

'My hair?' she repeated. This thing not her own, but family treasure, the essence of traditional beauty, oiled all her life by loving hands, first vigorously to establish growth, then lightly to keep it tidy.

'You'll look really pretty. Like Suriya. You have eyes like her.'

'I don't know,' she faltered.

'If you could, you'd look like Suriya, I'm telling you,' he insisted.

Suriya was the most popular film star of the day, and it was not easy to look like her. Nisha felt too shy to go on contradicting him, and looked on in silence while he stirred his coffee, clattering the spoon loudly against the sides of the thick, white, chipped cup. His hair wasn't oily, it fell naturally in waves against his neck, even her inexperienced eyes could see the skilful layers in it.

'Think about it.'

'My family will get very upset,' she said, falling back on a certainty. 'They will say college has spoilt you.'

Suresh understood at once what that could be like.

Meanwhile Nisha's thoughts about the way she looked intensified. It was no longer enough to have fair skin and good features. She needed to stand out. Could she cut her hair, face the storm this would create, and emerge beautiful and shining after the commotion died down?

To encourage her rebellion she thought of the girls in her class, girls with swishing, open hair, wavy, curly, blow-dried, or hanging straight, framing faces with fringes, flicks, or stray tendrils. She thought of her own, in the thick, rubber-banded plait, never falling free, ugly and unimaginative.

Strand by minuscule strand she attacked the lengths of her

plait. This was her beauty she was mutilating and her hand was unsteady. The advantage of minute snips was that though she appeared the same, in her mind her hair had begun to flap attractively around the nape of her neck.

Her meetings with Suresh became regular.

'Did you find out about his background?' demanded Pratibha.

'He is doing engineering so he can go into the family business,' said Nisha firmly, describing Suresh's prospects with a confidence that could have matched a marriage advertisement. 'They own an auto parts shop in Kashmiri Gate.'

'What's it called?'

'How can I ask? It will seem I do not trust.'

That was true. Since she could not ask, Pratibha decided she was being unduly suspicious and lapsed into the romantic. 'Oh Nisha,' she sighed, 'same background as you. Nobody can object to your marriage. What is his caste name?'

Nisha glared at her.

'Before he took to calling himself Kumar, I mean,' added Pratibha quickly.

'If he calls himself Kumar I do not want to ask. He is from a business family, same as me.'

'Oh Nisha,' sighed Pratibha again, unable to do anything else in the face of growing similarities of background, 'so lucky you are. My parents would kill me if they knew I was doing such a thing.'

Nisha tossed her head. 'I am not a fool,' she announced as she thought of the love that had driven her own parents to marry, of all the films she had seen, with myriad combinations of unequal background between boy and girl: rich-poor, Hindu-Muslim, Hindu-Christian, high class-low class, educated-uneducated. Love was the bridge over the great divide. Personal worth was all. The pure mind and the feelings of the heart.

*

149

Winter came. Nisha and Suresh could be found roaming the University lawns. One intimate afternoon he touched the little lock hanging by her ear and said, 'Come, let us go to the beauty parlour. There is one in Kamla Nagar.'

'Why?' she asked flirtatiously, 'I don't look nice?'

'Wouldn't you like to look even nicer?' he coaxed tenderly.

Now, this minute, he was forcing her to choose between an outsider and her family, modernity and custom, independence and community. Paralysis was her solution: she sat on the lawns, and refused to get up. 'Arre, you can always grow it back if there is too much trouble,' reasoned Suresh. 'Now come.' He held out his hand.

As they rode towards metamorphosis in Kamla Nagar, she felt she was entering a phase from which there was no turning back.

'Such pretty hair, so thick and wavy,' enthused the hairdresser, running her comb briskly through the dripping wet mass. 'How do you want it cut?'

'Not too short,' whispered Nisha, clearing her throat in alarm. She was on her own. Suresh, not allowed within this strictly ladies' parlour, was hanging around outside. 'Like Suriya,' she finally dared.

'Suriya has steps. How long?'

Nisha jabbed tentatively halfway down her back.

When she emerged from the beauty parlour Suresh stared and stared. Then he let out a whistle. Nisha blushed, while blow-dried waves fell around her. Before she could delight in her changed appearance, she needed to face her family.

This was not going to be easy. On the bus home she replayed their anger in all its variation, stopping short of being thrown out of the house.

It greeted her as she walked through the front door. Who gave you permission to cut your hair, suddenly you have become so independent, you decide things on your own, where did you find the money, the time, the beauty parlour, where did you find all these things?

Her hair was opened, pulled, tugged, stared at, and wept over. But at the end of it all, Sona silently consoled herself by thinking that her daughter's resemblance to Suriya might counterbalance her bad stars in the marriage market.

The academic session was coming to a close. Nisha had had a difficult year and now she felt nervous. English was so different from the undemanding course she had imagined that she had found it easier to abandon its pursuit than struggle with alien texts. By the time the teachers had done with them, even the novels were incomprehensible.

To Nisha, college had made it obvious that she did not have the skills to be a good literature student. Grammar mistakes were pointed out, and essays criticised for poor analytical content. The maximum marks she ever got were four on ten. She had never in her life been troubled by English lang and lit and she did not take kindly to it now.

'It's not your fault, it's the fault of the Indian school system,' said one teacher, looking at her crumpled face compassionately. 'To transfer from two hundred-word descriptions to cogent analysis is difficult. I do not wonder at your plight,' said Mrs Das Gupta. 'I do not wonder at your plight,' she repeated, warming to her theme by slipping into irony, 'but when you do English, language alas does count.' She smiled, twitched, and tapped her foot. Some girls tittered, others in the same situation looked uneasy. Nisha stared at the floor, flushed with humiliation.

It had all seemed so hopeless that instead of trying harder with Austen, Dickens, Plato et al she had preferred the more admiring, less stressful company of Suresh. Now that exams were around the corner she felt scared and guilty. Meeting Suresh so early in her college career had allowed her to exercise an independence that long hours away from home had given her. If only she could achieve a respectable result it would prove she could both do well and what she liked.

'I can't meet you, I have to study, I have to get a second division at least,' she told Suresh.

'Arre yaar, what does it matter? It's impossible to do badly in English.'

'That's what you think,' snapped Nisha.

'Yaar, don't get so hot.'

Nisha refused to answer her suitor. What did he know of the intricacies of literature? Indeed, she was barely cognisant of them herself.

'What is there to study in English?' repeated Suresh as they sat in the familiar, fly-buzzing darkness of the South India Coffee House in Kamla Nagar.

'Shut up,' she said, and a tear swam in her eye. If only she knew how pretty this made her look, and how moved Suresh would be to help her, she might have cried earlier. For now, he sat uncomprehending, absorbing her distress.

Two days later. Suresh in the bus – I have something really important for you – and in the coffee house Nisha watched him take out a bundle of paper wrapped in plastic.

Suresh leaned forward. 'St Stephen's tutorials. The very best. These people are first-class toppers.'

She looked bewildered. 'From where did you get them?'

'On the pavements of Daryaganj at the Sunday bazaar.'

'Tuts? They sell tuts?'

'Well, you have to know whom to approach.'

Nisha started leafing through the photocopies. In places the ink was a bit smudged, in others the handwriting wasn't clear. These tuts had obviously been through many hands and duplicated many times, but one couldn't expect perfect legibility on top of everything else. The marks at the end were six on ten, six and a half on ten, even seven on ten.

'Such marks,' she sighed.

'Written by toppers,' said Suresh with quiet pride. 'Now you can stop worrying.'

Mansfield Park, Mayor of Casterbridge, David Copperfield,

*Wuthering Heights, Mill on the Floss, Joseph Andrews, Antigone,
The Republic, The Odyssey*, the Bible, *Pot of Gold* . . . everything
in the first-year course was here.

'Thank you,' she said finally.

'Now you won't have so much tension?'

'Well, it's a lot to learn,' she said, irritated by having to be in
this position, yet grateful too that she had in her hands the
entire syllabus, in language that was undeniably grammatical.

'What is there? You're so good at studies.'

Back home, for the first time Nisha did not feel disheart-
ened as she indulged in the learning activity so familiar to
her: mugging. Mugging the Daryaganj tuts.

In the second half of April, exams. Most of the tutorial topics came, and at the end of the last paper Nisha could go
home with the confidence of a job well done.

It proved very difficult communicating with Suresh during the
holidays. Nisha lived in dread of being found out. There was
no question of meeting him, and they could only converse
through surreptitious phone calls. When she whispered into
the receiver at home, she felt those whispers reverberate
through the house till they reached her father, mother, brother,
uncle, aunt and all her cousins. This drove her to market pay-
phones, each word laced with dread that somebody would see
her. She looked forward to the opening of college eagerly.

When the results were declared in July, Nisha surprised
everybody, herself included, by getting a first division. There
was satisfaction at home, particularly from Prem Nath. All
choices justified, all expectations met. Nisha could do no less.

And in college disbelief among her teachers.

'How did that girl manage it?'

'It just shows how little you can rely on exams.'

'Well, it's our fault. We should volunteer to correct more.
Then we can set some standards.'

'How to set standards? I corrected with Daulat Rai last

year, and she said that to take grammatical mistakes into consideration was being elitist! What about the poor students in the non-campus colleges, she kept saying, why should they be penalised? So we had to pass students that we fail in our mid-terms.'

The twelve teachers of the English department looked gloomy. Nisha Lal with a first division. It didn't bear thinking of.

'That girl will become so puffed up, she will be impossible to teach. And I thought I was getting somewhere with her. She was making fewer grammar mistakes by the end of the year. Quiet girl. Eager to learn,' remarked Mrs Das Gupta.

'Her school English marks were good, if I am not mistaken.'

'Those students come with inflated notions of themselves. What kind of education do they get in school anyway? Memorising reams of facts, no writing skills, no reading interests beyond Sidney Sheldon and Danielle Steele.'

'If that.'

Flushed with the success of her marks, Nisha entered her second year. She was now nineteen and the family's attempts to find a groom were becoming serious. Her looks and intelligence were things that would balance the defect in her horoscope. Vijay upstairs was also ready to get married, and the air was thick with proposals.

Suresh hadn't done well in his exams. 'But what does it matter?' he said. 'All I have to do is pass. Then my father wants me to join the business.' How familiar and comforting this was to Nisha. In her family all the men had to do was pass too, and sometimes not even that.

Meanwhile Suresh's ardour increased.

'Arre, yaar, let's get married,' he proposed.

'Mummy Papa also did love marriage,' ventured the girlfriend uncertainly.

'Your family won't like me,' remarked Suresh gloomily at this mention of his beloved's parents.

'Why not?' asked Nisha, glancing at his handsome face, pouting red mouth, and the virile growth on his cheeks.

'I am not rich.'

'Neither are we.'

'Everybody in Karol Bagh has heard of Banwari Lal's.'

'Don't you have a shop?'

'A small one.'

'For my parents the boy's merit is the only consideration.'

'What does that mean?' asked the suitor.

Nisha was nonplussed, everybody knew what that meant. 'It might help,' she returned severely, 'if you did better in your exams.'

'You are such a boss, yaar,' said Suresh, pulling her dupatta over her eyes.

'Don't you want us to have a good future?'

'If I study, your father will accept me?'

'My father is a very kind man. He educated my aunt's son after she died, now he keeps his wife and son as well.'

'Whose?'

'Vicky's.'

'Vicky?'

'I have told you about Vicky. Lives on the roof, eats with us, watches TV with us.'

Suresh stared at Nisha. 'You don't like him?'

Nisha went absolutely still. 'Who said?'

'Look at your face in the mirror.'

'He's all right – used to trouble me a lot when I was young, then I went to my aunt's house.'

Suresh looked interested. 'Trouble you like how?'

'Always wanting me to play with him, didn't let me do my homework. It's only because of my uncle I did well in school.'

'I know how much brains you have. But tell me, how trouble you? What about the others?'

'Can I talk about my brothers all the time? Four of them in the house.'

'He has lived in your house all these years?'

The girl got angry. 'I don't want to talk about him, all right?'

The courtship continued into its second winter. Nisha, now certain of her ability to do well, began to miss even more classes. There were plenty of roadside vendors selling things to eat around the University lawns, and the pair sought entertainment there. Suresh bought Nisha green guavas, cut and sprinkled with masala, he bought her chaat of sour fruit and hot fried potatoes, he bought her bhel puri tart with lemon juice, sprinkled with chopped onions, green chillies, and fresh green coriander. Sometimes when the palate demanded variety, they took a rickshaw to Kamla Nagar to have a dosa or channa bhatura.

They also saw films. The hit that season was *Hum Aap Ke Hain Kaun,* the longest-running film after *Mother India*, the biggest box-office grosser of the decade. Family drama. Fourteen songs. Its song 'Didi, tera dewar deewana' was the number one on countdown programmes for weeks and weeks with Madhuri Dixit in a purple sari and Salman Khan aiming at her with his peashooter, invading every home that had a TV. Each time Nisha heard this tune plagiarised by devotional hymn writers and political rabble-rousers alike, she thought of Suresh, she imagined their love, and she smiled a secret, knowing sort of smile.

In the dark film hall, Suresh had whispered she was as pretty as Madhuri Dixit. In the dark film hall she could respond to the pressure of his hand. Prettiness and love went together. It was there on the screen, it was there in her own home in the shape of her mother, whose beauty had moved her father to endure family disapproval.

Suresh and Nisha went to the morning shows at Batra, near the University, frequented by college couples. Here too they saw Suriya's latest, shot in Europe and the mustard fields of the Punjab. It was entitled simply *Prem*.

Prem says it all, thought Nisha, entranced by the whole story. A daughter, although living in London, has been brought up to submit. Her marriage is arranged to the father's friend's son, living in India. As a farewell to maidenhood the girl travels to Europe, meets a boy, and falls in love. Her father's word is, however, law, and part of that law is that his daughter must marry whom he chooses. The mother understands the daughter's feelings, but as a wife she has to uphold her husband's dignity. The situation is resolved after countless threats and tears. In the end the Hindu household is intact.

Maybe it will be like that with me, thought Nisha, swept by the magic of the songs and the appeal of the story. By this time Suresh's hands were all over her, she was slumped in her seat, her head heavy with desire, her heart pulpy with longing.

During the interval, after a particularly intimate session on seats where the dividing arm between them was only a notional barrier, Suresh would breathe, 'I love you, yaar.'

Nisha looked at him, and then looked away. His eyes were so large and liquid, she felt she could drown in them. Her body felt warm and heavy, she wondered whether her father would be pleased with her choice.

Shows passed in an erotic haze. Each time Suresh went a little further. During intervals they would gaze in the foyer at Kwality ice-cream, popcorn, chips, chicken, paneer and veg patties, samosas, bread pakoras, soft drinks, tea, and coffee – an array from which Suresh tenderly asked her to choose.

Once Nisha recognised a classmate with a boy. She pretended not to see, and the girl too turned her head.

On the way back in the scooter-rickshaw, they sat close together, thighs touching. Going to the cinema became their favourite activity.

*

157

By the end of the second year, Nisha had become more adventurous in her clothing, alternating her salwar kameez with jeans and T-shirts.

Her affair with Suresh began to be commented upon.

'Look at you, so quiet,' teased her classmates. 'Come on, tell us what is happening.'

'Nothing to tell,' replied Nisha coyly.

'Sunita saw you the other day talking to a boy in the bus. Is that him? Now we know why you are missing classes.'

'Are you going to get married, yaar?'

'We'll see,' said Nisha, tossing her hair about – hair which was now regularly trimmed in steps halfway down her back at the beauty parlour, and only oiled before washing, never after.

'Do your parents know?'

'Arre, I keep telling you there is nothing to know,' preened Nisha and found she had more friends than ever before.

The Karol Bagh shop

Lala Banwari Lal's death meant that negotiations could start for the purchase of the 1500-square-foot area above the shop. The owner gave them to understand that the shop next to theirs was interested in buying it too.

The irony of fate! When Banwari Lal was alive, the owners were begging them to buy their unit for fifteen lakhs. Now his objections were no longer an obstacle, they were quoting twenty-five lakhs, 60 per cent in black, 40 per cent in white, take it or leave it. Bloodsuckers, said Pyare Lal bitterly to his brother.

'Property prices are going up, what to do?' replied Yashpal pacifically. 'Look at how much you need to buy places way out of Delhi. They keep advertising: Greenwood, Meadowvale, Hillview, Sunnyacres, I don't know what all, miles away.'

Pyare Lal stared into the middle distance. His brother's mind could meander maddeningly around trivia, while his own seldom strayed from areas fruitful to business.

He thought of his younger son, twenty-one, a college graduate, and now ready for marriage. Already the Bansals, a large furnishing store in Karol Bagh, had made enquiries. Should the Bansal dowry match the price of the flat upstairs it would be a sign that this union was meant to be.

A week later Pyare Lal said to his wife, 'You have to see a girl.'

Sushila knew her husband seldom said things without having other things in mind. She waited.

Pyare Lal poured tea into his saucer and sipped, lips puckered so his moustache did not get wet. 'A Bansal girl,' he let fall.

Sushila was at once alert. 'Which Bansal?'

'The Fancy Furnishings one.'

Sushila's mind raced. A Bansal girl! Vijay's future would be made. Such a good boy, doing whatever his elders told him to, never giving a day of trouble, he deserved the best. But to bring a Bansal girl here, with only one bathroom? Maybe they could construct more rooms on the roof. And Vicky – well, it was high time Vicky went back to Bareilly.

'How did the party come?'

'The uncle saw Vijay in the shop.'

'And?'

'They are interested.'

'And?'

'Now you have to see.'

Pyare Lal had full confidence that unless there was something drastically wrong, his wife would find the girl suitable. After Sona and Sushila had paid their visit he and his brother would start dowry negotiations.

'When things have to happen, how quickly they happen,' marvelled Yashpal over the coming month. The girl had been seen, the boy had been seen, the prices agreed upon, now the only thing left was for the young people to meet each other. Nobody foresaw any impediment. There was no reason for disliking and with their youth, similar backgrounds, education, and families' approval, every reason for liking.

At the moment of meeting, Vijay directed his gaze towards the floor. He had already declared that any choice his elders made was all right by him.

The bride's name was Rekha. She was doing a BA by Correspondence – what greater proof of her unspoiled nature, agreed the family. In addition she was attending cookery classes, specialising in Continental vegetarian. Today's girls like to indulge in fancy homemaking, said her mother. These twisted cheese straws she made, dusting them with chilli flakes, was her idea, as was decorating the eggless chocolate cake with Cadbury Gems.

As the bride's cooking initiatives were praised, her hands strayed among the bangles on her wrists. Her kurta was of a dark red satin, her bent posture emphasised the flesh that strained at the seams. Her skin was dark, her teeth were small, white and even, her lips were full. Her stature was short, but as Sushila said later, how tall is our Vijay?

The wedding was fixed for May, coinciding with the rash of weddings all over India when the good star would be in the ascendant.

It was Sushila's big moment. Her son was adding to the prestige, status, and wealth of the house. Her conversation centred around the future daughter-in-law, so sweet, so unspoiled, so loving, already concerned about her mother-in-law's health. 'Homely, just like Seema,' gushed Sushila. 'That girl never says a word.'

Nisha, listening, thought of the time, now coming soon, when she would marry. She would talk, laugh, sing, smile. There would be no need for her to be silent or demure, she was going to the home of her boyfriend (here she blushed for her own benefit). Hers would be a modern relationship. Gone were the days when women needed to be so silent. And anyway silence in itself was a subversive activity. This she had gathered from her teachers, who had spent much time explaining Fanny Price and the voices in which silence spoke.

After Vijay it would be her turn, and her boyfriend had better hurry up and do something. She didn't want her parents to embarrass themselves by promising what strictly speaking was not theirs to give – their daughter.

◆

With much fanfare the Bansal family was united with the Banwari Lal family. Months of preparation went into Vijay's wedding. Tailors and embroiderers were hired. In the angan

sewing machines whirred while swathes of expensive material lay wrapped in old saris on the charpai.

This time Sona was determined that during the wedding a
match even more advantageous than Vijay's be achieved for
Nisha. Her daughter had beauty, which the bride didn't, and
it was only appropriate that for such good looks, much
wealth be put forward, a bargain in which both would be the
winners, and happiness for ever be the result.

The wedding lasted a week. First the engagement, then the
sangeet, then the mehndi, then the all-night marriage rituals,
then the welcome home of the bride, and finally the reception. In this manner the Banwari Lal family acquired another
daughter-in-law, from the same caste, the same community,
the same locality. Everything humanly possible had been
done to ensure the success of the marriage, after that it was in
the hands of the gods.

At every function Nisha bloomed. Sona thought she had
never seen her daughter look so lovely. And true to her
expectations there were offers, offers which began with interest, then moved quickly to a demand for the horoscope. She
kept her fingers crossed.

~

With Rekha's dowry, the flat above the shop was bought, and
differences between the generations now had a fresh chance to
exhibit themselves. Ajay and Vijay wanted the fancy establish-
ment they could not have when their grandfather was alive.
Pyare Lal and Yashpal thought this was throwing away good
money. A shop was a shop – goods made it special, not extravagant decorations. 'Look at the shops around, fountains, glass
doors, soft lighting, murals, fancy show windows, with such
competition we will soon be left behind,' argued youth impetu-
ously, persistently, and finally successfully.

An architect (Ajay's friend's brother) declared that much
could be done even with such an old-fashioned structure as

theirs. Central air-conditioning a must, plaster-of-paris ceiling with frills and moulding, mirrors, a gold and glass chandelier, a tiled toilet (customers stay longer if you allow them to pee), a kitchen to store cold drinks and make tea, a stainless-steel spiral staircase at the back, a picture window out in the front, mannequins surrounded by fairy lights at night: with all this, theirs could be the best shop in Karol Bagh and his fees were thirty thousand.

Thank you very much, they would get back to him.

Yashpal and Pyare Lal had with reluctance agreed to the architect, but thirty thousand – was the man mad? It was Ajay's idea, Ajay's job now to beat him down to a reasonable figure.

Said Ajay to the architect, lower your rates and they would be his customers for life; as it is, the MCD was going to squeeze them when they started construction.

Replied the architect to Ajay, he also had to live, while he thought, yes, bribe the MCD fifty thousand per month, but refuse a designer his just wage.

As a compromise the architect suggested twenty thousand and a turn-key contract, just for them, old friends as they were.

Turn-key?

'I do the job of designer, contractor both,' explained the architect.

Ajay would get back to him, thank you very much.

Demanded the family of the world at large, did the architect think they were fools? Did he think he was doing something really useful, like getting permissions, or changing the land use? No, he just wanted to make money on the side. Twenty thousand without any turn-key business.

Pleaded Ajay with his family, 'Be reasonable. How can he change the land use? That even God can't do. Let him have his own contractor, it is not as though we are going to supervise every little thing. Any funny business, don't pay him his balance money.'

Mused Yashpal that his father would have supervised every little thing, but what was the use of teaching old ways to the young? Wasting money over architects and contractors, going in for show – but if Pyare Lal said nothing, neither would he.

Pyare Lal didn't. Both sides resentfully agreed to twenty thousand which included the building contract, and construction started. A scaffolding that covered a third of the front of the shop was erected on the pavement. All day workers climbed up and down, balancing on their heads sacks of cement, malba, boxes of tiles, bags of plaster of paris, stone, electrical conduits, mirrors, toilet, sink.

The scaffolding up and along came a policeman. He disappeared into the shop, and demanded to see the permission necessary for any change in structure. Tea was offered instead. Pyare Lal declared the policeman was his father, how could he be of service? The policeman smiled benevolently, he wished his sons well, but he was answerable to his seniors. His job was on the line.

What to do? cried the Banwari Lals. He knew how impossible it was to get permissions, even God would fail in a government office. Get this clearance and that, grease this palm and that, a whole life spent at the mercy of such people. How would they run their shop? They had children to feed and educate.

The father understood, but alas it was not up to him. He would send the Junior Engineer.

More conversation of a similar nature took place when the Junior Engineer arrived. The JE in turn was helpless, the law was the law and he was answerable to his own seniors. However, fifty thousand per month while construction was visible might ensure they looked the other way. On a meagre government salary, he too had children to feed and educate.

He left and the policeman returned the next day. His salary was even more meagre, and his children . . . The matter was settled at a few hundred per week.

With the meter ticking the speed of construction was of the essence. The architect was told he had to make sure the scaffolding was removed in one month.

This was his job, assured the architect, they were to run their business and leave the whole thing up to him.

There were now twenty labourers, working two, sometimes two and a half shifts. They slept and ate upstairs, their meals were carried up and down the scaffolding. Tea, food, tea, food, tea, food.

Pyare Lal watched the architect, his supervisor, the subcontractors, and the labour like a hawk. 'A day over a month, a day over a month, and he is fired,' he kept muttering.

His temper was not improved by the extra high bonus that the JE and the police, not to mention their own staff, demanded that Diwali. 'Congratulations! May the Banwari Lals grow and prosper, may the goddess Lakshmi shine for ever on the shop!'

But before the goddess Lakshmi could shine, the JE got transferred. What you fear is what happens. Life is going to kick you, beat you, try you. To deal with this, both stoical acceptance of what you don't have, and appreciation of what you do, are essential. Which is why, after his new start in Karol Bagh, the elder Banwari Lal had made it a business policy to be content.

'Illegal construction,' declared the latest JE.

'How is it illegal?' countered the family. 'We are just remodelling rooms for ourselves.'

'Where are your papers?'

He had them there. How could they get papers? Did they have worlds enough to spare? But he was their father. They deserved his protection, he deserved their gratitude. This relationship had been established by his predecessor.

The new Junior Engineer was not impressed.

The next day they found their shop sealed. Locks on the door and a ministry order. Once it was put on paper that they had broken the law, their shop would come under court jurisdiction, and generations of their family could kiss their lives goodbye.

Devastated, the architect, Pyare Lal, Yashpal, and Ajay spend the day running around the MCD office. Finally a meeting with the Assistant Engineer. They explain their position. Please, you must show mercy, there has been a misunderstanding, our case must not go to court. It is a question of their bread and butter, and their children's future.

The AE understood. He would do all he could to help them. The new JE was still a boy, he did not know the ways of the office.

It took two days and twenty thousand rupees to get the locks removed. They were told they were getting away dirt cheap. They knew that and were suitably thankful. If the case had gone to court, they would have had to pay countless bribes just to get their files noticed and read, and then countless more to get it heard. Years could pass. Only a fool relied on the promise of justice that the legal system held out.

The case of Rupa's husband suddenly sprang to life, proof that courts were worse than useless, and their twenty thousand well spent. Twenty years Prem Nath had fought to get that tenant out of his house, twenty years while the lawyer-tenant flourished on his paltry fifty-rupee rent and the landlord languished in poverty.

Construction continued for well over the promised one month. The architect said the delay was due to the shop being locked, during which time part of his labour had disappeared. With great bitterness Pyare Lal paid a further fifty thousand rupees to ensure continued blindness towards their illegal building for another month.

After two months a hole was punctured in the ceiling at the back of the shop. A prefabricated stainless steel spiral staircase was installed to unite the shop from the inside. Outside, after two months and a hundred and twenty thousand rupees, the scaffolding could come down and the meter stop ticking. Now only the interior of the upper floor was left to be done.

A thick polythene sheet was hung to partition off a narrow alleyway for the workers who snaked up the staircase. Round the clock they worked, laying the marble floor, building glass-cased cupboards, putting up granite counters for the salespeople. Seating took up too much space, it had to be replaced by standing, efficiency, and fatigue.

That was the modern way, none of this leisurely sitting down which allowed for old-fashioned persuasion, the unhurried display of metres of unfolding cloth, the slow creation of a buyer out of a non-buyer, the testing of sales skills amid tea and cold drinks.

Eight lakhs later the upstairs interior was ready. The architect came for his balance of five thousand, and was told to get lost. After all that trouble with the MCD, there was no way he was going to see another paisa.

The architect argued and argued, but they stood firm. As he left the cubicle he had designed for their private use, he thought it was just as well he had taken a commission from the contractor. These money-minded shopkeepers were all tight-fisted.

The Karol Bagh house

Unfortunately the gods decreed trouble in the marriage of Vijay and Rekha. The single bathroom upstairs turned into a bone of contention so big that the whole house could not contain it.

Did the new bride find it inconvenient to creep to the bathroom in the corridor after sex? Did she feel embarrassed washing her hands and brushing her teeth in full view? Did she find it awkward to knock on the latrine door when she couldn't wait for Ajay, Seema, or her in-laws to finish using it? Did the adjustment process break down when she had to confront a sink, toilet, and bathing area in separate corners of the house?

The results of what she felt were to be heard in the words that began to reverberate upstairs before spilling into the flat below.

'Why did you get me married if there is no place to even pee?' complained Vijay, who had had no problem peeing before his marriage.

Complained Sushila to Sona: 'Ajay, Seema and their child are in one room, we two in one, Vijay and Rekha in one, and in the last is the dining table, fridge, sofa, and TV, with no room to even put your leg. Big problem the bathroom, now that Rekha is expecting. She has to go – if there is someone she has to wait, then she gets cramps. Big, big problem. But downstairs it is easy, you cannot understand, only four, plus the angan and outer veranda in which to spread out.'

Sona was not receptive. 'You forget Virat and Asha, who are here the whole day,' she said coldly. There had been a time when nine people had been crammed into the downstairs four rooms, but in the spirit of family they accommodated each other. As she started on this, Sushila yawned and left. She knew each note of Sona's song, further acquaintance was not desired.

Finally Pyare Lal came to the point in a conversation with Yashpal. 'Vijay wants us to move to a bigger house. With a growing family, it is very difficult.'

Yashpal was incredulous. Marriage had turned the boy's head. He offered to explain to Vijay how it was important to tolerate, you cannot go far in life if you are always thinking of yourself, but Pyare Lal declined on his son's behalf. Sometimes there was a genuine problem, he implored his brother to see that. And if Vijay goes we will all have to follow. His mother cannot bear for him to live separately.

'One couple can come downstairs,' offered Yashpal as a solution.

'Bhai Sahib, your heart is too-too big, but now that Rekha is pregnant she needs her mother-in-law's attention, while Seema's daughter cannot even sleep without her grandmother. Separation is impossible.'

'What is the solution?' demanded Yashpal plaintively, not dreaming that Pyare Lal had one.

Pull down this house and build a modern one, a modern house that would remove the angan and give them all more floor space, with bedrooms that had attached bathrooms.

Pull down their whole house, just because of a few adjustment problems – what kind of drastic solution was this? Would he be condoning separation, or diffusing tension? Yashpal, now head of the family, was not sure. Would they be able to function with everybody's interests in mind, if they couldn't even live together? He wished his father was alive. Pyare Lal would have been forced to keep a tighter rein on Vijay.

Now the builder Pyare Lal had acquired so fortuitously through his younger son's in-laws came into the picture. Yashpal was dead against any consultation, fearing it as a first step towards major reconstruction.

'What is the harm in just talking, he is family, no question of any payment for just talking,' pointed out Pyare Lal. Besides, his brother just had to look around him to see that tearing down single dwelling units in order to construct flats was the face of the future.

Yashpal said nothing. In a joint family, compromise is of the essence, but a strong power structure meant it had to be done less often. Again he thought of his father.

Pyare Lal to his wife: 'I wish he wasn't so slow, so careful. How can you do business if you are never willing to take risks?'

To hear her husband talk like this was balm to Sushila's soul. At last he was coming into his own and asserting his particular vision. All these years, he had been held back by the cautious, careful hand of his father, mindful of his brother's good opinion, content with being subservient, content to grow at a snail's pace.

It was not his fault. He was the youngest, what could he do by himself? Now he had sons, daughters-in-law and grandchildren, now he was a patriarch in his own right.

Sushila looked into the future and saw partition. The new addition to the shop had resulted in two clear units which made division natural, as natural as day divided from night.

'He says he is going to talk to a builder,' said Yashpal to Sona that evening, 'but in fact I think discussions have already taken place.'

'Yes, let him consult, let him pay money to see a professional.'

'It is not a question of money – he is a relative of Rekha's.'

Sona was silent. Luck was living upstairs as usual.

'He will either build or move,' went on Yashpal.

'Let him move.'

'It is not so simple,' sighed Yashpal. 'He will need money for moving. Where will he get it but from the business?'

'Always you are thinking of him. Does he ever think of you?'

'He has a growing family. He says his share for himself and his two sons is three-fifths, two-fifths for me and my son.'

Sona's jaw dropped. Such greed was never seen on the face of the earth, such manipulation, such blackmail. 'One thing is to ask, another is to get,' she said grimly. 'And why two-fifths? What about Vicky? We keep him, his wife, his child, we should have at least half.'

'You know he will say sister's son. Besides, Baoji never intended Vicky to be an actual owner.'

Sona ground her teeth. She realised the Vicky wicket was weak, it would not hold under a determined onslaught.

'Anyway,' continued Yashpal, 'his sons are just married. They are full of energy, they want this and that, it must be difficult for him.'

'Why are you always seeing the other side, why can't you think of us?' wailed Sona.

'You want me to fight my brother?'

That was exactly what Sona wanted, but what could she say? The odds were against them. The upstairs family were two married sons, with one powerful set of in-laws, whereas Raju, poor boy, was only in Class XII. Let him grow up, how he would help his father, how he would demand their rights, but for now she did not think her husband was capable of winning any fight.

Next day, after work, with misery-lined face Yashpal told Sona, 'I don't think we have any choice, we will have to do as he wants, or he will leave.'

'Let him leave, what do we care?'

No answer. Kaliyug indeed, where blood eats blood, and nothing is sacrosanct.

Another tack. 'Where will they go? It is just a threat, do not listen to him.'

Yashpal remained lost in his own thoughts. Their family had changed since his father had died. Pyare Lal was tense

171

and irritable, always wanting more. Maybe there had been some sense in his father's refusal to do certain things. When he was around they never experienced such tension.

It was to Sona that Pyare Lal first brought the plans. 'I thought you should see them before anybody else, Bhabhi,' he said, stepping into her section in the middle of the day.

'I know nothing about business,' said Sona, hastily covering her head before her brother-in-law, and looking curiously at the rolled bluish sheets in his hand.

'It is not a question of business, Bhabhi, it is a question of our home. See, what all space the man is giving us. I told him to make the best, most spacious flat for my brother and Bhabhi, ours does not matter so much.'

He sat down, pulled the Sunmica table close to him, and laid the plans out.

'I do not understand these things,' repeated the Bhabhi nervously.

'Arre, I will explain. Look, you are on the first floor. Fourteen hundred square feet we are allowed, but actually he is giving us 1650. He is a clever man. Rekha's own chacha, real brother of her own father. See, with a bathroom attached to every bedroom, no inconvenience for anybody. When Raju marries there will be no problem, not like with Vijay.'

He laughed lightly. As Sona refused to join him, he continued pointing to squares on the plan. 'Here a modern kitchen with place for a fridge. No running to another room every time you want a tomato. And see, a little puja room, so you won't have to sit praying and sweating in the kitchen. On this side there is a veranda that overlooks the park. I know you like fresh air, Bhabhi, you will be able to sit outside in the evening and see all our grandchildren playing. This man has a very clever architect, one who will design beautiful ceilings with flowers in plaster of paris. There will be chandeliers in every room, the floors will be of marble, like the shop, but with Rekha's uncle all the designing will be done cheap-

cheap. I have seen a house he has decorated. If you like, I can take you and my brother?'

Sona found her voice. 'No need, Bhai Sahib, if you are happy, we are happy.' She stared at the plan and could make nothing of it. But her brother-in-law's words, poured smoothly like ghee into her ears, yes, she could make something of that. She could make herself a woman in a magazine ad for kitchen appliances.

Pyare Lal continued to unfurl his own dream. The new house would have four floors plus a basement. The builder would keep two floors and the basement, and give them two floors along with fifty lakhs cash. Ten lakhs to each family and the rest to be put into the shop. They would grow and grow.

'I don't know, Bhai Sahib,' responded Sona uncertainly. 'I don't understand these things. Your brother will decide.'

'Arre, Bhabhi, once you decide, what is there? You should be happy. I cannot bear to see my sister-in-law in discomfort.'

More avowals of love, devotion, respect, and duty followed before Pyare Lal left his dearest sister-in-law.

∼

All this while, Asha's ears were the most active part of her. She listened downstairs, she listened upstairs, and noticed that plans for them were conspicuously absent. How was it possible that in the newness they figured nowhere? In a joint family, space is carved out inch by inch, but there has to be material to work with.

'What do you think will happen?' she asked her husband as they lay bathed in sweat on the breezeless terrace. The electricity had gone, the little pedestal fan that whipped hot air about was still, its green blades, encased in a rusty metal cage, glinted in the reflected street light.

'How do I know?' replied Vicky irritably. 'Vijay and Ajay are very spoilt.'

'I suppose Rekha feels the need for a mansion like her

father's. She must think she has married beneath her, but with that dark skin what could she hope for?'

Vicky grunted. What was it to him how anyone looked? He couldn't tell if Rekha's appearance was worth more or less in the marriage market; he only knew she dressed intimidatingly and smelt like some of their clients.

Used to filling her husband's silences with chatter, Asha went on, in an effort to bolster her wavering confidence that their future was going to change for the better, though the means were as yet vague. Vicky, satisfied with a routine that revolved around shop, home, dining table, TV, and bed, never thought beyond the day. But Asha, despite the odds, still preserved shreds of that old sense of opportunity she had felt when she first got the news that she was marrying into a Delhi trader family. All these years it had hibernated, now her gaze narrowed as she watched for any slight shift in the patterns of destiny.

For ten years she had suffered on the roof, seeing neighbouring houses torn up and rebuilt to resemble miniature palaces, with stucco, reflecting glass, arches, and tiles. She had often thought that if the same was to be done to their house they would be able to live properly, but had regretfully concluded that such dislocation was inconceivable in this family. Now Rekha had come, and the inconceivable had become conceivable.

'If they build maybe we will get a flat,' she ventured.

Vicky grunted again.

'Look at that,' she gestured at the pink hotel that had recently usurped their horizon. 'Five storeys.'

'They will get caught and fined. Only three storeys is legal in Karol Bagh.'

Even Asha knew enough to laugh at the word 'legal'. 'You are too innocent for business,' she declared, stroking his arm. 'Do you think our uncles got legal permission for building on top of the shop? Sona Maji kept complaining of how much it cost to keep the MCD and police happy.'

'I don't care, what is it to do with us? Their shop, their business – I get a wage, I have no tension, I can sleep at night. Let them pay bribes, let them keep the whole police force happy, give them tea, cloth, discounts, what is it to me?'

'Oh-ho, why do you get tensed up for nothing? If they break the house, we should get a flat, that's all I am saying.'

'Yes, yes, the people who didn't let us build a room on the roof, the same people will give us a flat.'

'If they don't, where will we go?'

'Their problem. They can't throw us out.'

'We can refuse to vacate the roof. This is our home, we have rights over it.'

Vicky looked at his wife. She smiled at him. He would never have thought of establishing possession of the roof. But in this dog-eat-dog world who else was there to look after you but yourself? He had been exploited all these years, his measly return being board, lodging, and a pittance for salary. Of course, the Banwari Lal sons would get everything worth getting. The blood on that side was thick enough to cut into barfi, on his side it was a pale pink dribble through the house.

His wife had been smart enough to see this, and he gazed at her with appreciation. She deserved a reward, and he pulled her to him quietly so Virat would not get up. 'Let's see,' he whispered. 'You think too much.'

And Asha knew her words had struck home.

Vicky did some research. Yes, he did have the rights of a tenant, if he construed himself as one. But why not, what else was he? He certainly wasn't a member of the family, oh no. And people who treated their nears and dears so shabbily deserved no consideration.

It was his goodness of heart that had kept him quiet all these years, as well as respect for his grandfather. The strict code of discipline that the old man maintained meant that Vicky seldom felt discriminated against. True, he was in one uncomfortable room on the barsati, but nobody in the family had much space. Together they ate, sat around, watched TV, and if he and his wife slept on the roof – well, that had its advantages. It was private, they could sleep outside, feel the coolness of dew on their sheets, and personally witness the rising sun every morning.

Meanwhile, Sona's visions of herself as mistress of modern conveniences with vast rooms to spread out in gained clarity with every new development her brother-in-law took pains to acquaint her with. Kaliyug was no longer mentioned, instead Yashpal found himself part of his brother's meetings with the builder.

Who wanted to know their requirements.

Here there was a small hitch. Did their requirements include Vicky or not? The brothers' own division of the newly constructed block of flats was perfectly clear. They were to get the two large flats on the first and second floors, as well as fifty lakhs. The builder would get the basement and two upper floors, assuring them that the risk of exceeding the legal limit was his.

But if three families were to be accommodated, he would have to reduce the size of their flats, as well as the amount of cash he could give them. Thirty lakhs instead of fifty, and three flats of 700 square feet instead of two of 1650.

Bhai Sahib, pointed out Pyare Lal, they were breaking up their house to get more living space, not less.

In that case, suggested the builder helpfully, they could buy a barsati at cost price in another unit he was building. Twenty lakhs only.

Twenty lakhs on Vicky? Never. Rekha's uncle should not trouble himself.

They decided among themselves that now was the time for Vicky to repay his debts. The boy was beholden to them; a graceful exit would show a proper sense of obligation. They would rent him a flat somewhere in Karol Bagh so that commuting to the shop would be no problem. He would be more comfortable too – the roof did get very hot in summer.

They told him this, genially thumped his back, declared he was now a man, and ready to set up as an independent householder. Wouldn't his mother have been pleased, and Baoji, and all the dead relatives whose spirits were still protecting him.

Yes, thought Vicky, moving would please Asha; she had always wanted that they set up on their own. A mother and sister were involved.

'You,' said Asha, when he told her later, 'are so innocent – too simple to live in this world, let alone this family. You cannot even see the contempt in which your elders hold you. Would they offer such a deal to their sons?'

Vicky remained silent.

'You are no less than a son,' went on Asha. 'You work for them just the same, have the same blood, and get less in return. What do they think? That all our lives we will say yes, uncle, yes, auntie, no matter how they neglect us? We are not so stupid. If we do not look after number one, who will? Why should we settle for the uncertainty of a rented house? We are not the ones who want to leave. After all, this is our house too.'

Impatience cracked the sweetness of Asha's voice. Virat stared at his father, Vicky stared at the floor, and growled that his wife's capacity for seeing things that were not there was just amazing. From now on he was going to do exactly as he liked.

The next evening Vicky conveyed his desire to remain united with the family. Yes, of course they understood his feelings, but when families and shops grew, one had to take a dynamic view. Nisha, their own daughter, had lived apart for many years.

If they made a practice of getting rid of their children, said Vicky, that did not make it any the better.

By now the anti-Vicky feeling had reached its height. Ajay raged at him, to the family's great approval: he was a parasite, useless, good for nothing, why didn't he return to the sewers of Bareilly, but no, he was too shameless to do that, he preferred to live off the relatives who had taken him in, and were even now feeding his wife and child.

Sushila, basking in the anger of her son, announced that this was kaliyug, and who remembered what anybody did for anybody. Asha dragged Vicky upstairs.

Upstairs Vicky screamed that after a lifetime of indignity he never wanted to see their faces again. It was just a matter of time, soothed his wife, just a matter of time.

Every day his uncles talked to him, every night Asha pounded sense into his head. From lurking on the margins, Vicky moved to the centre. He felt taller, stood straighter, walked faster.

The family seethed at this centrality. For years we have treated him like our son. Brought him to Delhi, married him off, gave him work, looked after him. Was he such an ingrate that he could give them this in return?

On the contrary, Vicky declared, he was so willing to repay his debts that a lifetime at their feet was not long enough. He only wanted to serve them, in the home, in the shop, in his life.

Meanwhile, the builder was getting impatient. He had already had a fictitious plan sanctioned by the MCD, but now was the time for reality. They could make up their minds about the number of flats they needed while the demolition was going on. He had to begin, and he could not begin unless the house was empty.

Begin, begin, said the family, that would make Vicky leave.

It could also make Vicky get a stay order against construction, said the builder.

No, no, they said, going to courts and getting stay orders

was beyond Vicky's capacity. All his life he had done nothing on his own. How would he start now?

But the builder was not willing to take the risk.

In desperation they sent Rupa upstairs to find out what it would take for Vicky to leave.

Asha recognised a messenger when she saw one. She greeted Rupa warmly. They saw too little of her, even Virat kept asking.

Rupa laughed; she was getting old, it was up to them to come and see her, she hoped they would not forget her when they moved into their own place.

But, said Asha, they did not want to waste family money on a separate place, they were happy to live in a small corner of the new house.

But there would be no small corner in the new house.

Well, said Asha, with a knowledge that horrified the aunt, they could live on the topmost floor. That would only have 40 per cent ground coverage allowed as against 80 per cent on the others. They would still live in the smallest unit, as they had been doing for ten years.

No, no, she did not understand, explained Rupa, they had promised the area on the roof to the builder. She did not know the details, but the builder needed to sell those flats in order for the whole effort to be worth his while.

Asha at this stage said that they needed the hand of their elders over their heads, how else could they live?

Rupa said she had to warn them that Vijay and Ajay were talking of taking the law into their own hands. She didn't know how long the family could restrain them, especially in kaliyug, when any goonda would break a man's head for just a lakh.

A silence while Asha and Vicky absorbed this threat.

The police will be very interested to know how many by-laws the builder is breaking, the legal limit in Karol Bagh is three storeys, blustered Vicky, alarming Rupa in her turn.

What was the use of threats, intervened Asha quickly, both sides had too much to lose. Of course, had they money enough they would buy their own place and never more trouble the family. Did Rupa Masi know that in Karol Bagh a small flat cost at least twenty-five lakhs?

More chitchat before Rupa descended, each high, narrow step down accompanied by thoughts of the boy's history. How right her sister had been in hating him! He had stuck like a leech to this family, and was going to draw a bucket of blood before he left. In her opinion any price was worth getting rid of his tainted presence. But she could not see them parting with twenty-five lakhs, they were shopkeepers after all.

The family had now got Vicky's price. Both Ajay and Vijay were unanimous in wanting to hire a goonda to break Vicky's legs. Who did he think he was? They were not going to pay him one paisa, let us see how he gets anything out of us.

For Yashpal and Pyare Lal, the memory of their father, and the fact that he was related, ruled out breaking Vicky's legs – though from now on they were not going to give him either employment or salary. He had bitten the hand that fed him, let him learn this had consequences. Unfortunately, the goodness of their natures stopped short of starving him.

Asha was glad of this. Rupa's threat had unsettled Vicky, he was too simple to see it was just a tactic. Alone with the men in the shop, she wasn't sure how intimidated her husband might become, what he would be persuaded to promise away without a thought for his wife and child. In a waiting game it was imperative they wait, she explained to Vicky over and over.

A silence fell between her and Sona in the kitchen. Asha was meek, mild, and solicitous, murmuring as they worked, I don't want to leave you, Maji, you are like my mother, without your protection I am nothing. The older woman did not respond.

There were moments when Sona weakened, thinking that

the ten years she had fed Asha gave her a claim to the girl's understanding and consideration. Beti, she tried, explain things to your husband, we are not sending him away, this is what is best for everybody. But nothing changed, and Asha continued with her litany of love and longing.

Coming to terms with the idea of giving Vicky money and then negotiating the amount took many weeks. Rhetoric had to be sieved from reality, anger persuaded into compromise.

Finally ten lakhs was the price agreed upon for Vicky to get out of their house and life. He could set up shop in Delhi, go to Bareilly, to his father, or to hell for all they cared. They had been forced to part with money, for which crime there was no forgiveness.

Sona shed a few bitter tears over Asha in her kitchen. Since her marriage the girl had worked by her side. She had been careful, considerate, and economical, with the skill to use just enough of everything. Now this gem had gone, depriving her of help and companionship. She had been gravely misled as to the girl's nature and she would never forget her ungrateful wickedness as long as she lived.

Vicky took his disgraceful self, his possessions, his wife and son, and moved out. He was paid six lakhs in black and four in white by the builder – not one of his relatives could bear to actually hand him the money.

Demolition could now begin. The family moved out of the house they had inhabited for forty-five years to Hotel Palace Heights in Karol Bagh. Part of the deal was that the builder pay for their stay there.

❧

Three rooms (meals included) in Hotel Palace Heights were given over to the Banwari Lals, an arrangement that would continue till the new house was built. The rest of the family had to be farmed out. While Vijay was delighted to spend these months in his wife's home, Raju protested on being sent to his aunt Rupa's, far from action and excitement. 'Why me, why not Nisha?' he demanded, expecting Sona to act upon his distress.

Raju was now in Class XII, Commerce stream, and his mother was keen that he finish school with a decent pass. Anxious for Raju and Prem Nath to be proximate, she explained, 'Your sister did so well there,' as though the atmosphere of Rupa's house was laden with good marks.

'Send her then,' repeated Raju petulantly.

'Your father says soon she will be married, she must stay with us.'

Raju, poor boy, what could he understand of this denial of his wishes, who all his life had been so wrapped in mother love he could barely see?

So Raju left for his uncle's house, a move fraught with hope and resentment. Prem Nath cleared his throat the first day and announced conscientiously, 'I went over your sister's entire syllabus with her. Unfortunately Commerce is a foreign subject to me, but I will try my best.'

'I will manage,' said the boy sullenly. 'I have tooshun.'

Raju's tuition was with a teacher who ran afternoon classes for children who needed to be attended to personally before they understood anything.

If he opened a book, Prem Nath never saw it. What kind of tuition was this that demanded no study at home? he asked.

'We do all our practice there only,' replied the boy.

'Should I talk to your tutor? How can you study for a board year only three hours a day?'

'Let it be,' said Rupa. 'He knows what he is doing. Anything happens, you will be blamed for interfering.'

'But this is not the way to do well,' countered the uncle.

'Arre, you don't have to worry. He is a clever boy, he will manage. It's not as though he is going to do a PhD.'

Raju tittered. 'All I have to do is pass. Look at Ajay and Vijay, as though their education is helping them,' he said with a worldliness that distressed Prem Nath. He was so different from his sister, the sight of him was painful.

Meanwhile Nisha, so fondly remembered by her uncle, was also finding studying difficult. She was crammed into one small room with her parents, and even had she wanted to, there was no space to open a book, let alone write a tutorial. Gossip, eating, and sauntering around the market ruled the day at the Hotel Palace Heights.

Her second-year course was harder. There was Shakespeare, Marlowe, Jonson, Chaucer, Spenser, Milton, Donne, the Silver Poets, the Metaphysical Poets, not to mention the background associated with these writers, all beyond her interest or capacities.

Suresh was pressed into service.

'You have to get me the Stephens tuts again,' demanded his beloved. 'It's because of them I got a position, and showed my teachers who were kindly offering me Pass Course as an option if I failed.'

It was February, and the exams were only two months away. Nisha was bunking classes as usual in order to sit under a favourite tree in the University lawns and feel Suresh's hands around her waist, trying their usual stunts of wandering to forbidden places, while she focused on the peanuts she was shelling.

Suresh looked at Nisha admiringly. Since he first met her she had grown so much more beautiful. The curls in her hair were emphasised by the step cut, her arms were waxed, round, and smooth. Her little feet, peeping from black-strapped sandals, ended bewitchingly in red-painted toenails.

From time to time she wriggled casually when he got too near a breast. She was so innocent, this girl, he shuddered to think what would have happened had some unscrupulous boy befriended her.

Finally the idyll under the tree was over. 'I have to attend some classes, yaar, you don't know what will happen if I am short of attendance,' grumbled Nisha.

They arranged to meet for lunch at Kamla Nagar the next day, and get those tuts – maybe I can even hand some in as mine.

Again, those certain shops in Daryaganj yielded their wares. 'These things aren't cheap,' said Suresh, waving a bunch of tutorials under Nisha's nose.

'Are they the Stephens ones?'

'As good as. You can't get the same thing every time, you know.'

The exams came and went. Nisha's admiration for Tara, Katyayani, Agastya, and Maya knew no bounds. How well they answered questions! Unfortunately, not all the topics she mugged came up, and identifying the references to context were sometimes a problem, but still she did not anticipate any difficulty with her results. It was exhausting being a position-holder – time to give the whole thing a break.

Summer passed. A hard time for secret love. Clandestine phone calls, occasional surreptitious meetings. Living in the hotel meant surveillance was a bit lax, and Nisha got more freedom than she ordinarily would have. There was no kitchen work, and it was easier to say she had to visit a friend, see this or that film.

Raju's results were out. The reluctant learner had got 50 per cent overall aggregate. Admission to a respectable college was going to be difficult.

'How does it matter if I don't go to college?' demanded the son. 'It's not as though I have to take up some profession.'

'The boy is so wise,' marvelled the mother.

'Get a degree like your sister and brothers upstairs,' said Yashpal firmly. 'There is time enough for the shop.'

'How often have you said, Papaji, that you didn't need a college education to be a success?'

'You talk like a fool,' said the father irritably. 'You don't need a degree to make money, but you need it to be respected. Besides, marriage is more difficult with only high-school pass.'

Finally a BA by Correspondence was agreed upon.

'Will the boy take his Correspondence courses seriously? His uncle found it very difficult to make him study,' said Rupa, to her sister's annoyance, as they discussed Raju's education (or lack of).

'The boy is keen to take up his responsibilities,' retorted Sona. 'It will be good for the father to have his son working with him. Your brother-in-law is too honest, simple, and sincere. He loves his brother too-too much, and that man takes full advantage. He says decorate the shop and lakhs are spent, he says break the house and the house is broken. God knows what he will say next.'

'But you also consented,' said Rupa, thinking that in her own set-up at least you knew who your enemies were.

'That was just to keep the family together. Your brother-in-law had to hear so many complaints about space he started having chest pains. Peace of mind is more important. Peace of mind,' repeated Sona, omitting the fifty lakhs that came along with it. Some things were best kept even from a sister.

Rupa wondered what Sona's new flat would be like. Must be modern, with nice kitchen, closed cabinets instead of open shelves that gathered dust and cobwebs, attached bathrooms with unhygienic shitting, pissing, washing, bathing in one place, all granite and marble, shine and sparkle, like pictures in a magazine. But no point asking: Sona would make out that, for the sake of the family, she had agreed to accept the ugliest, most inconvenient flat of all.

Not to mention the holiday lasting months. No peeling, dicing, cutting, slicing, endless vegetables, no kneading dough, making tea, no picking over dals and rice, just sit and talk, order drinks, snacks, and knit. Nice life. Maybe when her husband won his case, they too could demolish their house and build flats. But for twenty-one years he had been getting date after date instead of hearings. For the first time she felt some irritation with her husband. Why was he of a tribe that could not get things done? Arre, if bribing was demanded, just bribe and finish. It made it possible to live your life.

Finally the new house was ready. Pundits were called and a havan performed before moving in. The function was small, they did not want to attract the evil eye.

Rupa did her best to find fault as she sat with others before the sacred fire. How hot they will feel in summer, the ceilings are so low, no open space, only a small balcony in front. Alas, she could come up with nothing else as she sat with the others on white-sheeted mattresses laid down on gleaming marble floors beneath gilded crystal chandeliers and smelt the sweet smoke floating through the empty rooms. Envy drove her thoughts again towards a future where they too could pay off the tenant, give their plot to a builder, and live in splendour. Why did her sister always have all the luck? No children, along comes a daughter; no son, along he comes; dark, inconvenient rooms, along comes a palace.

But then who in the world had a husband as difficult as hers? Even if it meant cutting off his nose to spite his face, he would refuse to reach a settlement with the tenant as had been done with Vicky. It was his religion to be blind to his own interests, and to refuse to learn from others.

She would keep her Tuesday fast even more strictly, then maybe the goddess would hear her prayers. One day she too would live in such a house, there was really no reason not to. They had fewer people to consider and a plot as big.

The room in Vijay Nagar

By now Nisha was in her third year.

'When is your family going to approach mine with a proposal?' she asked Suresh as they were sitting in one of their Kamla Nagar haunts, the light in the restaurant a murky aquamarine from the blue glass windows. Some flies buzzed around a few drops of spilt Thums Up. 'Yesterday they took me to have a fresh set of photos taken, the old ones were not good enough.'

'Naturally, you are so much more beautiful now,' said Suresh, seeming to miss the point of the photograph-taking.

'Will you be serious? It's only because I am a mangli that I am not already engaged.'

'My family is not superstitious about such things,' said Suresh hopefully.

Sometimes Nisha did wonder about Suresh's family – would her own approve of people who did not take horoscopes seriously? Did he have a horoscope at all?

'Well, if that is so, why haven't they contacted my father? Or haven't you told them about us?' asked Nisha, trying not to sound irritated. She slid her hand out of his and moved her foot away from his own.

'Arre, why are you getting so hot?' demanded Suresh, chasing the hand across the grimy, stained table.

'Many of my classmates are already engaged. They keep asking, when is it your turn, Nisha? Of course they all know about you.'

Suresh looked pleased.

'And at home they talk of this or that boy, who is manglik, who is not, it's all very tensing for me. We can break up if you are too scared to tell your parents.'

'It's not my parents, it's yours. We don't have much money, I keep telling you.'

'Haven't I told you my parents did love marriage? They are not narrow-minded.'

'Even if they do not agree to our marriage, I will never stop loving you, never. You are the princess of my dreams.'

Suresh looked into the distance. His jaw grew firm. Nisha's heart beat faster. They were walking by the sea, there was music in the background, wind was rippling through her hair, there were tears in her eyes, her full, red, moist lips trembled, white teeth flashed. Her bosom undulated conspicuously before she started talking.

SURIYA: My duty to my parents comes first. We have to break our love. I cannot go on.

HERO: Never. I will die before I allow that to happen.

SURIYA: Our union cannot be built on the ashes of their hopes.

HERO: I will find a way. Your parents will agree to our match.

SURIYA: Never. I am doomed to a life of unhappiness.

HERO: What? Are these tears? (*He holds her close and wipes them tenderly.*) Silly girl, I will see to it that there is never a tear in these eyes again.

(*Suriya looks down. He forces her chin up, she smiles, the music grows louder, the waves roll in, the water touches their feet.*)

The waiter thrust the bill on its plate of saunf and sugar between them. Suresh carefully counted out some notes. 'Do you have a fiver?' he asked. Nisha took out a fiver, and added the tip Suresh always forgot. They emerged into the heat, and took a rickshaw back to the University.

'Look,' Suresh said a few days later.

'What?'

He thrust his closed fist at her. Nisha gazed at the silver ring, the large, dark hand, the black, springy hair on the knuckle, the few threads hanging around the cuff, the steel links of the watch. She prised the fingers open. Inside was a key.

'For us,' said Suresh, closing his hand around Nisha's.

'What is it?'

'The key to a friend's room in Vijay Nagar.'

'What for?'

'So we can be alone together. It's boring only going to film halls and the University lawns.'

She knew of course what he was saying. 'I don't know,' she said shyly. 'It doesn't seem right.'

'We'll only stay as long as you like. Come, come, please come na,' he persisted, gazing at her in the way she found hard to resist, his whole heart in his eyes, reaching out, wanting her, living for her.

'How far is it?' she asked nervously, as the rickshaw wobbled towards the colonies behind the University. It was a cloudy, breezy day and women were knitting on charpais outside their houses as babies played around them. A few sabzi wallahs and fruit wallahs slowly wheeled their basket-hung, produce-laden bicycles down the lanes. Cows and dogs nosed through the garbage that lay scattered around the municipal collection points. Outside a shop a group of men sat on the pavement playing cards and smoking beedis.

'Not far,' murmured Suresh, clutching her hand.

'I wish people wouldn't stare at us,' Nisha muttered. She knew it was written all over their faces that they were going to a room in Vijay Nagar for clandestine purposes.

'Don't look at them.'

But those eyes were everywhere. The men gazed at her and divined the key in Suresh's hand, the women judged steadily over flashing needles and balls of yarn. Her own mother, chachi, masi, sitting on a charpai, knitting eternal sweaters for eternal relatives, condemned her in whispers, their eyes never on their work (which didn't need it), their eyes fixed on her.

It was a corner house in the back lane of a gully. Suresh unlatched the door into the angan without a sound. Some clothes were drying on cement banisters which led to a little room on top covered with corrugated sheets. They crept upstairs past the clothes, practically crawling behind the balustrade, the steps were so high. At the top Suresh quietly struggled with the clanking lock.

They were inside an airless, tiny room with peeling paint. On the desk a little hotplate, a small aluminium saucepan and an electric kettle were surrounded by an open packet of bread, two eggs, bananas going brown, a packet of milk powder, a bottle of tea leaves, and some sugar. On one wall a tattered flowered sheet sagged from a bit of rope stretched between two nails barely covering some shelves built into the wall. There was a mattress on the floor, with a squat stool next to it on which rested a large clay diya full of cigarette butts, a matchbox, and an empty packet of Wills Navy Cut. The bedcover had big black and red squares on it plus some holes.

Looking around her, Nisha demanded, 'Why have you brought me here? Whose room is this?'

'I told you, a friend's. The couple here take paying guests, they both work – if we see the servant we have to tip him, my friend has already worked it out.'

The friend a pimp, Nisha the tart, Suresh the buyer. Was this what his love amounted to? He edged her towards the mattress. She pushed him away.

He looked hurt. 'What's the matter? Don't you love me?'

'It's not that,' she mumbled, feeling trapped and uneasy.

'You came with me this far. Besides, I won't do anything you don't want me to.'

He put his arms around her, pulling her closer than she had ever been. His smell rose pungent, male, and musky. 'So long we have been friends, have I ever tried anything? Don't you trust me?'

'It's not that.'

'1?'

'hould wait till we are married.'

'We are waiting,' he answered. 'What else am I doing?' He took her chin in his hands. 'Life after life we have been together. No one can separate us.'

Still she looked unhappy.

'Look, we have known each other two years. Have I ever taken advantage of you? But in the Univ lawns people are always looking, it is not so nice, yaar. Don't you also feel?' he implored.

Tears came to Nisha's eyes. It was clear Suresh loved her deeply. Very slightly she nodded. She gazed at the look on his face, felt the change in his breath, heard the words that came pouring out, paeans to her beauty, her softness, her perfect skin, her divine body, more lovely than any film star's, the loveliest girl in the world, worth dying for, over and over and over, worth waiting for, always, always.

Again he tried to push her down, and this time she acquiesced. He put her feet in his lap, even her feet made him mad, he said, as he fondled them, dirty and dusty, a sign of how truly he accepted her. He began to caress her all over, and her mind divided, one part on college and parents, one part following his hypnotic touch. Then one hand snaked around the buttons of her kurta, and the muscles under her skin tightened.

'No,' she protested, pushing him away.

'Relax, I am not doing anything,' he whispered near her cheek. Slowly he inserted his hand inside. His eyes closed, and his breathing grew heavier. He gave a small moan. 'I could die for you yaar, you are my princess, my queen, for the rest of my life there is only you.'

She tried to respond in kind, but the words did not come.

Suresh was lulled enough to reach under her kurta for the tape that kept her salwar up. This time she pushed him away with all her might.

'I'm not staying,' she announced, sitting up.

'Are you angry with me? Have I done something?' he pleaded.

'Take me back.'

'What is wrong with you? Haven't we known each other a long time? Didn't you trust me enough to come with me here alone?'

He made it sound as though she had committed a crime. She turned away her head.

Here Suresh threw himself on Nisha and began to wail, 'I love you, I love you, why are you so cruel to me?'

'I love you too,' she cried, tears wetting her face, her hanky, his shoulder, as he pulled her, resisting, to him.

Eventually they left the room. Once on the road, Suresh ran back, saying he had forgotten his watch. It was just as well for Nisha's peace of mind that she did not have to see the money that passed between him and the suddenly materialised servant.

On the way back she remarked if he was so keen to do all this, why didn't he make his parents talk to her parents, let the whole thing be clear.

Yes, yes, said Suresh, all in due time, he did not understand why she kept on about the parents.

If only, thought Nisha over the subsequent months, Suresh didn't always want to go to Vijay Nagar. But he begged so hard, and was so loving when they did get there, that she was forced to agree more often than she would have liked.

She would not allow Suresh to fully undress either her or himself, there was only so far his love could carry him. 'It is just as well there is something left for when we are married,' agreed Suresh, making the best of a bad job.

On the evenings of those days she tried to avoid her parents. Her face was stamped with where she had gone and what she had done. Her skin prickled, from time to time she would scratch so hard the surface dotted with blood.

Once she showed it to Suresh. 'Look what is happening to my skin.'

'Do you think you should see a doctor?'

'I don't know,' said Nisha vaguely. 'Maybe it will go away.'

Suresh kissed the faintly darkened patch. 'I will always love you no matter what,' he declared manfully. 'I can take you to the doctor whenever you say.'

Nisha giggled – she associated doctor taking with women, not men. 'You are very silly,' she replied.

Discovery

Towards the end of Nisha's third year, her parents received a letter from the college authorities. Their daughter was short of attendance, and would not be allowed to sit for the exams.

'Why have I got this letter?' demanded her father.

'I don't know. It must be a mistake, Papaji,' quavered Nisha.

'Just like that, they are making mistakes? What does this mean, 37 per cent attendance in the whole year?'

She thought of what it meant. Sitting with Suresh in Kamla Nagar restaurants, going with Suresh to the room in Vijay Nagar, feeling needed, wanted, and loved by Suresh. She hung her head.

'Answer me.'

Nisha flinched at the unaccustomed harsh tones. 'I am sorry, Papaji,' she murmured.

'Every day you go from here, why should you be short?'

Her fear gave her a desperate explanation. 'Teachers mark you absent even if you are two seconds late, others cut attendance if you do not do your work.'

This was a poor explanation from a girl who had been a position holder in her first year.

'We will see the Principal,' said Yashpal, 'and find out exactly what has been happening.'

Nisha began to cry. 'The Principal will only say what the teachers say. Why can't you get me a medical certificate, Papaji? Many girls do that.'

'If you attend your classes, why should I spend on a medical certificate? Tomorrow your mother is going to college.'

That night Nisha could hardly sleep. She had warned Suresh that she might be short of attendance. But coming from a college where classes were hardly taken, let alone attendance, he had made light of her fears, dissipating them with the hotness of his breath.

Now she was going to be found out. When would the axe fall? It loomed before her, sharp and massive, the axe that would fall on the bad girl, the one with things to conceal.

The interview with the Principal was unsatisfactory enough for the family to take recourse to a medical certificate. With the sick leave accrued from two months' acute hepatitis Nisha would have the required attendance.

Meanwhile, at home questions, questions, questions. Why had this happened? Where did she go? What had she been doing? Had she been up to any funny business?

'Answer me,' said her mother, icy-voiced, stony-faced.

'Yes, Mummy,' said Nisha, hoping to deflect her mother's wrath with meekness.

'Have you been roaming the streets with some boy? Is that what you have been doing? That is why you cut your hair, that is why you have been coming home late, saying you have been studying in the library, lying all the time, that is why you look so happy. You have been deceiving your parents?'

'No, Mummy.'

'No, Mummy, yes, Mummy – is that all the explanation you can give?'

Nisha turned away her head, she didn't want to see her mother's face. Uncannily she had picked on the lacunae in her college life, and filled them with suspicion.

Sona raised her hand to strike her.

Yashpal caught it. 'Leave her. Our daughter is too old to be hit. Besides, I have absolute faith in our child.'

'You are too trusting, ji,' moaned the mother.

The lovers managed a hasty meeting. Suresh was told he would have to declare himself. Nisha cannot handle the situation at home, she wants everything out in the open. He will present himself in the shop, man to man.

'Don't go wearing dark glasses,' she advised, 'and you better shave. My father is a simple person.'

'I will ask the pundit what is the most auspicious day,' declared the anxious suitor. 'I want everything to be right.'

'My mother used to fast on Tuesdays in order to get children,' said Nisha. 'Go next Tuesday.'

'I hope we are as successful as your mother.'

'Don't say that. She had to wait ten years. By then we will be old.'

'I will wait for you my whole life,' announced the hero.

'I don't want to wait my whole life before I marry,' responded Nisha tartly.

Tense about the outcome of the meeting, Nisha decided to test the waters by talking to Rupa Masi.

'Masi, what do you think of love marriages?'

The aunt stared at her. 'Why do you ask?'

'Like that only.'

'They are a very bad thing. Too much adjustment. Look at your mother. She spent ten years in sacrifice before her situation improved.'

'That was because she had no children.'

'I also had no children, but I did not have to suffer like your mother, bap re.' Here Rupa shuddered.

'How come?'

How to describe the amorphous hell that had been her mother's life? 'Did you meet any boys in college?' she asked instead, misgivings raised by the interest in love marriages, and wanting to do her sister the service of revealing her daughter's confidences.

Nisha remained silent.

'You can tell me if you did,' encouraged the aunt.

'Why, Masi, will you be able to do something?'

This casual remark cast quantities of unwelcome light over the last two years. A little slower than her sister, but equally capable, Rupa too leapt to the same conclusions. The new hairstyle, the glowing looks, the forays into jeans and T-shirts, the long hours studying in the library, the shortage of attendance, the poor performance in second year compared to first – of course there was a boy in the picture.

'Who is he?' she asked valiantly.

'He's going to see Papaji in the shop on Tuesday.'

'Alone?' How could Nisha be so naive? Her heart felt heavy as she looked at the blushing girl, head down, pulling threads from her dupatta.

'How does it matter? It is him I want to marry, not his family.'

'Have you met his family? What do they do?'

'Shop owners. Like us.'

'Where?'

'Kashmiri Gate.'

'Caste?'

'I don't know.'

'He hasn't told you?'

'Of course he has. He tells me everything, but I don't have to remember, do I?'

'How long has this been going on?'

'Not long. I meet him sometimes at the Coffee House with my friends, that's all.'

'What does he do?'

'Engineering.'

Nisha's answers gave few details about the boy which could be of significance. Rupa effortlessly visualised Sona's rage, her acute sense of shame, her vanishing hope of holding her head as high as Sushila had after Vijay's marriage.

There was one thing she had to know before the storm broke and Nisha's fate overcame her. Delicately she posed the inquiry, 'Did he do anything to harm your reputation? Boys are known to take advantage of innocent girls.'

Nisha, her face on fire, her hands like ice, watched the waves that had lapped seductively around Suriya's feet receding into the distance, and mutely shook her head.

'Well, let us see what will happen. Our destiny is not in our hands,' sighed Rupa heavily.

On Tuesday Yashpal came home, and cast an angry glance at his daughter. Well, what had she expected? Congratulations that she had found her own partner? Without settling down to tea he started:

'Some boy came to see me today.'

MOTHER: Which boy?

RAJU: Has she been seeing a boy? I will break his legs.

FATHER: He says he knows you. Is this true?

NISHA: Yes, Papaji.

FATHER: He says both of you have decided to marry.

MOTHER: Hai Ram.

NISHA (*trying vainly to protect herself*): You also did the same thing, Ma.

FATHER: Beti, there is no comparison between the lives of your elders and your own. Our marriage was performed with the full blessings of your grandfather. Who is this boy? How has he turned your head so much that he tells me what you will do?

MOTHER: This girl will be our death. My child, born after ten years, tortures me like this. Thank God your grandfather is not alive. What face will I show upstairs? Vijay gets his wife from Fancy Furnishings while my daughter goes to the street for hers.

On and on, half the night, went the questions, as it became clear that Suresh and Nisha were not an item to be argued, threatened, or reasoned away.

Nisha cried, Sona cried, Yashpal cried, but the end result was the same.

The first step the family took was to ban her college-going. She was as yet publicly untarnished, they hoped to contain the damage. You can study at home, we have given one medical certificate for your convenience, Madam, now we will give another.

The easiness between her and her family evaporated. She moved like a guilty thing among them, worse than the dirt under their feet. She was not allowed upstairs. There is no need to give your Sushila Chachi an opportunity to pump you.

Raju was keenly interested. 'Tell me about this fellow,' he suggested invitingly, adding on reflection, 'He sounds like a real chutia.'

Nisha shrivelled at his calling Suresh a crude fucker – Suresh of the long hair, of the dark glasses, the three-day stubble that grazed her chin, of the delicate hands and sinuous tongue.

'Don't use such dirty language,' she said crossly. 'You know nothing about him.'

Raju stiffened. With a coldness that conferred years on him, he said, 'I know what boys like him are after.'

'If he was like that, would he want to get married?'

'Oh don't worry, we are going to talk to him all right.'

'We? Who?'

'Me and Prem Nath uncle.'

Nisha felt dull despair. They had thought of everything. An older male but not one from the immediate family, so Suresh could not imagine himself a real threat. And why was Raju going? No doubt as a learning experience, to groom him as defender of his sister's honour.

'Let me talk to him alone, please, just once. You can watch us, if you don't trust me,' pleaded Nisha.

'The time for trust is over,' said Raju. 'And if he can't even talk to us, how can he hope to marry you?'

'Who are you to decide whether I am trustworthy?' she muttered, sounding weak and defeated even to herself.

'I am only doing what Mummy Papaji want. Papaji is, as it is, finding out about him,' said Raju to his hapless sister, wriggling like a worm on the hook of her family.

*

They found out with a vengeance. They were Paswans, in class and caste so far below them that in an earlier age their son would have been murdered had he dared to raise his eyes to their girl, let alone address her. They owned a small motor workshop in Kashmiri Gate, they themselves lived in the gully above the shop. Suresh doing a BEng from DU was their hope of a better future. They were waiting for him to take over, and were quite bewildered when the Banwari Lal family accused them of conspiring to trap a young, beautiful, well-to-do girl into marriage by spoiling her name.

The family protested they didn't need to trap anyone. They had received enough offers for their son, who had asked the girl to chase after their boy? If they couldn't control their daughter, why come and threaten them?

Suresh on the other hand tried to convey to his beloved's family that he would do anything to prove that his intentions were pure. He only wanted Nisha. No dowry, no fancy wedding, he didn't even care if she was a mangli.

A Paswan telling them he didn't mind if their daughter was a mangli! Education had turned the boy's head.

Nisha, on hearing this account, was moved by his nobility.

'Who cares about caste these days? What you really want is to sell me in the market,' she sobbed with indignant emotion. 'Sell me and be done with it. What are you waiting for?'

Her mother slapped her, although the girl was too old for this to be of any use.

Night and day, day and night the issue of Nisha's marriage was canvassed. Why did she do it, couldn't she see what a prize catch she was? So pretty, and from a family rising in the world. Nisha, dear daughter, leave all thoughts of this dirty low-caste man, what can he give you compared to what we can arrange for you? Marriage into a family that will enable you and your children to live comfortably for the rest of your life. We have rejected many proposals in our search for you, the least of them better than this nobody of a man.

How could she listen to them? She had allowed Suresh to touch her in the belief they would get married. As they lay in the room in Vijay Nagar their hearts had been pure and filled with love; without the idea of marriage to Suresh she felt tainted. Anybody could accuse her of immoral behaviour.

But her family was ignorant of the issue they really had to address. They went on, he is not of our caste, our status, his family is poor, how can you stoop to his level? Look what happened to Vicky's mother, and your choice is worse than hers. At least that had Baba's blessings.

She became the injured party. Either I marry him or nobody.

'What will convince you?' they asked the stubborn wall of her back. 'Don't you realise how foolish you are being? You are throwing away your life.'

Silence met them. Silence spoke. Nothing will convince, do what you like.

All day she remained in the house, a prisoner of her deed, a prisoner of their words. She was distrusted too much to be allowed to put a foot outside. A padlock was put on the phone, only incoming calls could be received without the key.

She noticed and said nothing. She did not care what happened to her. She ate less, she spoke less, what was there to say? Have pity, said Rupa to Nisha's mother, have pity, can't you see the girl is wasting away? But the scenario was too polarised for pity to play a part.

Her exams were coming and her books flapped listlessly in her hand, the mere appearance of activity. What was the use of doing well, it made no difference in the long run, and the short run only lasted a day or two. Studies were an unimportant speck on a distant horizon; she didn't care if she lived or died. Besides, he was not there to help her with tutorials bought from the pavements of Daryaganj.

Contrary to her belief it was hard for the family to see her suffer like this. After a few covert visits to Suresh's family it was decided that if she wants to meet him, she should meet him, then she will come to her senses. Some people learn the hard way.

The meeting was arranged at four o'clock in Moti Mahal. For the first time in weeks Nisha stepped outside her house, accompanied by Raju and Prem Nath. It was the beginning of March: small opening leaves of tender pale green dotted the branches of trees around the park. She looked at them and felt hopeless, the freshness of a new beginning would never come her way. Though dressed in a starched, light-blue chikan kurta with embroidered blue and white flowers, the presence of her gaolers made her feel soiled and dirty.

'How many people coming from his side?' she asked bitterly.

'We have told him he can bring whomever he likes, we have no objections,' said her uncle, not looking at her. She had disappointed him as well. He had taught her to achieve and she had used her opportunities to run around with some boy.

'Uncle, *you* don't think I am wrong, do you? If the boy is good what harm is there?'

'You know you can't go behind everybody's back in something like this,' said the educationist, in turn disappointing his niece. 'His family should have met your family.'

'Uncle, this is the modern age.'

The uncle looked in sorrow at his niece.

'What harm is there if first we got to know each other? How can I tell him to send his family to talk to my family if I don't know him first?'

Where had the girl learned to argue, wondered Prem Nath.

'I'll tell Mummy you are talking like this,' said Raju viciously.

'Run back and tell her *right now*,' snapped Nisha. 'You think I care?'

'If we do not know what Nisha is thinking, how will we help her?' reproved the uncle, feeling the family's intransigence.

Raju scowled tyrannically, torn between contempt for his uncle and annoyance with his sister. The uncle was too soft, no wonder Nisha had turned out the way she had.

'If you have already made up your mind about Suresh, what is the point of going to meet him?' demanded Nisha suddenly. By now they had turned on to the main road.

'It is you who wanted to meet him, Madam, not us,' pointed out Raju.

'Let us see what the boy has to say. He has not been entirely open,' equivocated Prem Nath, who knew nothing of the visits to Suresh's family. 'Calling himself Kumar, so that nobody knows where he is from.'

Nisha was silent. What was the use in addressing prejudiced minds?

They hailed a scooter, haggled with the driver, persuaded him to take three passengers instead of the customary two, and roared off, the noise making further conversation impossible, to the relief of all concerned.

At Moti Mahal they were a little early. As they waited at a table for four next to the window, the waiter bustled by, plonking glasses of water before them. They ordered tea, samosas, and paneer pakoras, while Nisha began to feel sick. Why was Suresh late when it was their first opportunity to see each other after so long?

Finally there he was. He stood alone, looking blankly around the restaurant, blinded by the darkness after the glare outside. He looked more like a hero than ever: true, a little on the dark side, but tall, thin, romantic, his hair curling around the nape of his neck, his nose straight, his mouth pink and full.

Nisha stood up to attract his attention. Raju pulled her down. 'If he can't see you in an empty restaurant, he is blind,' he hissed.

Suresh waved and started towards them. He seemed ill at ease. He nodded at Raju and the uncle before glancing furtively at the girl.

She smiled at him. 'They only agreed to let me meet you in their company, Suresh. But I am glad everything is going to be made clear.'

The child has grown up, thought the uncle with a pang. He looked at Suresh, trying to see him through the girl's eyes. He had flashy good looks, but his kind of appeal would not last long. His poor niece was gazing at Suresh earnestly, feeding her starving eyes; it was clear they had been meeting more than Nisha let on. He suppressed a spasm of disgust at the implications of this.

Abruptly Suresh started, 'We cannot get married, if your family does not approve. I will be standing in the way of your happiness.'

'You are my happiness.'

'Your family doesn't think so. I cannot come between you and them.'

'What has happened, Suresh? Have they said anything to you?'

'Your friend has a great deal of sense, Nisha, more than you,' interrupted Raju, overflowing with heartiness. 'He knows you can never be happy.'

Nisha's misery by now was so great she could barely swallow. This meeting was not taking place the way she had imagined. In a dry voice she asked, 'Suresh, I haven't changed my mind, but if you have, tell me.'

The look he gave her was such a little one she barely caught it.

'After her BA, her parents are thinking of getting her married,' put in Prem Nath.

This was the time, thought Nisha, for her lover to declare his undying love. To defy prejudice and authority. To declare theirs a simple happiness that harmed no one. And when his words fell on deaf ears, they would make plans to run away. She gazed into her cup of tea and waited.

Suresh looked up, his eyes swishing like brooms around the room.

'That is good,' he said, swish, swish.

'So you understand, beta,' continued the uncle, half his attention on the belch he was about to produce, 'there must be no misunderstanding about any connection with you. She has got some mistaken notions we wish to clear up. That way everybody will know where they stand.'

There was a silence. No words were said, though many were uttered in Nisha's head as neighbouring jaws worked around samosas and paneer pakoras.

Nisha pushed her plate away with a little clatter and stared out of the window, her head turned so no one could see her tears. She wanted to run out of the restaurant, never see Suresh again, never see that lean face with its stubble, never touch the hair soft and curling against the neck, or see the white teeth framed by full lips.

Suresh cleared his throat. 'I will do whatever is best for everyone. I can have nothing to do with Nisha against her family's wishes, no matter what my personal inclinations may be.'

Raju stared at him. Suresh elaborated: 'My family feels the same.'

Nisha got up. She walked through the dining room, into the evening sun. She could hardly see where she was going. This had been a farce put up for her benefit; she was a fool not to have seen it earlier. What force, money, and threats had they used to make him behave the way he was now behaving? She would never know.

But it didn't matter. They could not have done so much if Suresh had not been willing.

Her brother was following her as she walked along the pavements, looking for a rickshaw to take her home. Her uncle, she supposed, had remained behind to complete the business with Suresh. If only her brother weren't there, she could fall and slip under the wheels of one of the many buses on Netaji Subhash Marg. Such accidents were common. Her death would be common too.

March passed, and the lead inside Nisha's heart grew heavier. They tried painting other futures in vivid colours, but she was impervious to their appeal. Her family could be as snobbish as they liked about Suresh, his caste, his class, his status; they could monitor every step she took, but in the end they could not compel her to marry. That knowledge was her only ally in the forces arrayed against her.

Once or twice she tried conveying her point of view. Their only real objection was that he was poor, and of another caste. If they did not approve, why couldn't they just let her go, her life was her own. Suresh and she were educated, they could both work. But anything she said was countered with her youth, her ignorance, her betrayal of them. These were not circumstances in which dialogue had a place.

Nisha blackmailed Rupa Masi into arranging a clandestine meeting with Suresh. At a restaurant in Karol Bagh, the aunt sat by herself at another table, pretending to read a magazine while peering at the couple. Having money was a curse, look what it did to your children. Nisha so unhappy, Suresh looking beautiful and romantic (no wonder Nisha hadn't examined the Kumar in his name, incredible though it seemed). Now he was arguing with the girl, Nisha arguing back. If her sister's family found out, they would never talk to her. She hoped her pickle business wouldn't suffer. But she was like a mother to the child, what could she do in the face of her determined misery?

Later. 'Well?' asked the aunt, partner in crime.

'I will kill myself if I can't marry him,' said Nisha dully.

'How are you going to marry him, has he offered any suggestions?' asked the aunt, a little tired of Nisha's saying she was going to kill herself over and over again. These dramatic dialogues were only effective in films; this was life.

'He is afraid of my family.'

'Sensible boy,' remarked Rupa approvingly.

'He thinks they will harm him and his parents in some way. What can they do? We don't live in some backward village where our family will massacre his family just because a boy and girl dare to love.'

Rupa knew that even in the city there were many ways to intimidate, but she wondered how far Yashpal would go down this road. She took a breath and tried explaining the facts of life to her niece again. 'That man would have been a lifelong burden. Had he been suitable, I am sure your father would have considered him.'

'Why is he not suitable? Give me one reason.'

The aunt's eyes opened wide. As far as she was aware, Nisha had been given reason after reason. 'You saw what happened to Vicky's mother.'

'Exactly. An arranged marriage.'

'So mistakes can be made. That doesn't mean they have to be repeated. And beti, this is worse, much worse.'

'It's not much worse,' shrieked the girl, beating against an intangible difference which there was no bridging over. 'Do we live in a village? If we do, why don't you just throw me down a well and be done with it?'

'Beti,' reproved the shocked aunt, 'is this any way to talk? Don't you see, if he really cared he should have asked his father to talk to yours. That is what your father did when he fell in love with your mother. He took no advantage.'

'How would I know everybody here would be so narrow-minded as to object to an innocent friendship?'

'But it led to more than friendship, didn't it?'

'I can't help that.'

'Your parents want what is best for you, beti.'

Nisha looked contemptuous. 'They know better than I do?'

'They know the world. They are not blinded by love.'

'They can't force me to marry someone I don't want to.'

From this Rupa gathered that Suresh was weak. It was Nisha's will that was pushing the whole thing.

XVIII

Nisha and Suresh

The third-year exams started in the second week of April. Nisha had never in her life been so unprepared. No sooner did she open a book than Suresh's face came before her eyes. What was she to do with that face? Her family was doing its best to erode its charm.

Had Suresh tried to trick her? Use her? And she had let him, not protesting too much, allowing her shy flesh to occasionally respond to his. The room in Vijay Nagar was embedded in her mind as her grown-up secret, now veering towards grown-up sin. Were her parents to know, they would scour the city for a well to throw her into.

What had been buried all these years in the recesses of her mind now came back to haunt her. Vicky rubbing against her, Vicky with his hand under her panties, asking her to touch it, grabbing her hand and sticking his thing into it, jerking her hand up and down, Vicky pressing himself into her while she was trying to do her homework. Suresh moaning beside her, at the height of their passion, holding her hand over him, while she, uncertainly trying to please, gripped it tentatively through his underwear as he climaxed.

Thinking of Vicky she thought of Suresh; thinking of Suresh drove her back to Vicky. If, with Suresh's arms around her, she could reveal what had happened all those years ago, she would be absolved. No matter what her cousin had done to her, he, Suresh, had touched her in love, theirs was love, nothing else.

She tried to keep her mind on love and purity, but the past intruded with all its might. It crept closer and closer to mingle with the present, till she wanted to run screaming from herself. Was there never to be relief from her thoughts? She imagined the acid used to scour toilets, yellow, evil-smelling liquid sold in old beer bottles, the strongest cleaner she knew. If only she could dip a rag in that, run it under her skin, swab her mind with it, dissolve the foul stuff so that it lost the power to affect, now and for ever.

In all the years that Vicky lived upstairs she never had to contend with his huge, terrifying figure. He grew more menacing as her nights continued more wakeful. She clung to the only pathetic reassurance that came to mind: she was technically a virgin. No one need ever know. But with every cell in her mind preoccupied with violation, what difference did virginity make?

Oh Suresh, if we could marry, these demons will vanish. You told me so many times you loved me, lifetimes together, remember? What you said in Moti Mahal only shows how good and noble you are. Don't be afraid of my family – once my exams are over we will talk to them, fight them, run away if necessary.

She spent the hours marked for sleep being dragged through the midden of her memories, ticking off the hours that would bring the dawn. Shadows reflected by the streetlights lay on the gleaming marble of the new house, heat settled slowly around her as she lay. Wistfully she thought of the angan where they had once savoured the cool night breeze and the dew that fell.

In the day she opened her books, but could make no sense of the words. She was so ill-equipped that all she was hoping for was a meagre pass. This year there would be no brilliant legacies of successful Oxford entrants to rely upon.

The fifteenth of April. The first English exam, Paper V, Eighteenth-Century Poetry and Drama. Nisha had her early morning tea, got ready, flapped through her mug books when she noticed Raju getting ready too.

'Where are you going?' she asked.

'With you.'

'Why?'

'You know as well as I do.'

'Who asked you to do this?'

'Papaji. You don't think I am accompanying you of my own accord, do you, Madam? I have exams too, you know. Now I will have to waste a morning waiting outside your college.'

They left the house at eight a.m. with the sun beginning its ferocious attack on all students travelling to exam centres. In the bus, Raju edged her towards the first empty seat he could find. She steadily ignored him, staring at the passing scenery through the broken windowpane. Then came Kashmiri Gate, Suresh's stop. Her destiny had lain here, in Suresh's tall, thin form, dark glasses, blue jeans, and long feet, dusty in their kohlapuri chappals. Surely love must find out the English Honours third-year exam timetable, and make its presence felt. If not in the bus, then perhaps at the gates of her college, only to greet her in a friendly fashion, and to hand her an innocent best of luck card. She could do with that.

Once they reached college, she surreptitiously looked for him among the group clustered around the gate, ready to brave her family's wrath for her.

But there was no one.

In the exam hall, the air was stale. The windows were shut against the hot dusty air, and the slow-moving fans creaked listlessly. The predominant smell was sweat. When the electricity went, and the fetid air collapsed in pools around the perspiring girls, the invigilators opened the windows to let the loo blast in. Nisha tried to concentrate, shutting out Suresh's absence, shutting out the faint surr-surr of desperate cheating whispers that came from behind her as soon as the invigilator's back was turned. She knew it would be enough if she could just vomit out all the ideas that had been processed during her lecture periods. In her case it wasn't much: a year of love and punishment had forced her into last-minute cramming from mug books, her memory was too occupied with other things to be of much use.

At twelve o'clock the exam finished. Chattering girls filled the corridor. Pratibha pounced on her. 'Arre, where were you all these days? I phoned you twice, but they said you were not at home. Didn't you get my messages? I thought, is she studying so hard she cannot even return a call?'

Pratibha, whom she had entertained with tales of courtship and love, whom she had felt superior to – what to tell her of her humiliation? Better to lose a friend than to venture into those treacherous waters. And wouldn't Pratibha respond with I told you so? Conscious of Raju waiting at the gate, she muttered, 'It is nothing like that,' and then escaped, almost running towards the gate, leaving the girl staring at her back.

At Rupa Masi's house, the only place she is allowed to go: 'I am going to phone him, Masi, you want me to die?'

'Your parents will kill me, beta.'

'Masi, if you don't help me, who will? What harm can there be in one little phone call? You can stay and listen.'

And the aunt had to hear her niece demeaning herself, asking the low-caste why he wasn't at the gate of her college, did he not even have friendly feelings for her?

'Well, what did he say?' she asked, as Nisha put the phone down.

'He thought if he came I would be too disturbed to do my exam.'

'I always said he was a sensible boy.'

'After the exams are over, we will talk seriously about the future. Till then I should study, and do well, as I always have. It will come in useful.'

'What, is he planning to make you support him? Very sensible, as I said.'

'Masi, if you do business, so can I.'

211

How the young misread things. Nisha must understand that women's work was allowable only in unconventional situations (no children), and that respectability demanded it be avoided as much as possible. 'Your uncle encouraged me to occupy myself, he has such a big heart he wanted to see me happy and busy.'

'Like Suresh.'

'O-ho. Who is Suresh? Here today, gone tomorrow. But you are the flesh of your parents, nobody can love you like they do.'

Nisha ignored this. 'We can both work after we marry. We are not asking anybody to support us.'

'Let us see what tomorrow brings,' temporised the aunt.

The end of Nisha's college career came two weeks later. After some stilted conversation with Pratibha, parrying her questions, she slowly walked towards the front gate. It was twelve-fifteen, the sun was pouring down in all its intensity.

'Your exams are over,' said the waiting Raju. 'Let's celebrate with a dosa at Sagar. I hear the Kamla Nagar one is good.'

Where she had gone so often with Suresh. Nisha listlessly agreed.

They walked into the air-conditioned restaurant, with its grey-streaked marble floors and glare-proof windows. Incense burned before the goddess Lakshmi, a red light bulb shone on the sandalwood garland around the photograph. They were led to a corner table.

Nisha sat lethargically in the cool, musty air. The sense of endings lay heavily upon her, depressing her into realism. Suppose love did not triumph?

In a corner she could make out a classmate with a boy. The blue-tinted light barely touched them, but had it been the blackest night she would have seen them as they leant towards each other, unobservant of the waiters, of the noise, of the other tables, their hands almost touching between the spoons and the glasses of water.

'Nisha?' broke in Raju. 'Are you all right? Why are you sitting so silent?'

Nisha looked at him wordlessly.

'You are not thinking of that chutia, are you?'

She shook her head.

'Where are those dosas?' Raju asked, suddenly angry. He gestured to the waiter. 'Bhai, is our order going to take all day? My sister is feeling sick.'

The waiter nodded sceptically and sauntered off, flicking his duster over his shoulder.

'Saala,' said Raju absentmindedly. 'Really bad service, but I suppose people come here to be left alone, like those two over there.'

So funny, thought Nisha, when she had actually been sitting here with Suresh, she hadn't thought she was that happy. They had eaten, hung around, and left. Now, every minute reminded her so vividly of him that her breath, as it slowly came and went, cut her to pieces.

Now that the exams were over there was nothing to distract the family from the main business at hand, which was the difficulty the girl had put them into, her blindness, stupidity, and suicidal desire to self-destruct. 'At least see what other boys are like, see who we choose for you, see, see, see. Nobody is forcing you, but this much you owe us.'

Their eyes were always on her, their tongues always at her. She was the sole occupant of the tower her family was laying siege to. With promises, threats, presents, kindness, reminders of obligations, with tenderness, love, and blackmail.

'Even he doesn't want to marry you,' they assured her again and again.

She did not believe them.

'He already told you so. Raju heard him, your uncle heard him, what more do you want?'

'You made him say that with bribes and threats. If I am such a catch, why would he renounce me?'

'Because he knows you will never be happy.'

But she still did not believe them.

She was only human.

So, it turned out, was Suresh.

One more meeting, please. I want to see him one more time.

How many more meetings does the child need before she accepts the situation, wondered the aunt.

But the family's love for Nisha was great.

One more meeting was arranged, with an ease she took for granted.

'I will die before I marry anyone else, don't listen to anything you hear,' she assured Suresh in Moti Mahal, Rupa Masi and her uncle sitting at a distant table.

But Suresh was not in a dying mood. He threw his desperate gaze this way and that, avoided his beloved's eyes, did not make use of this opportunity to suggest death together. Instead he mentioned his parents, hitherto inactive players.

'My family is not agreeing,' said Suresh.

'What?'

'They are saying, if your people are so against the match, it will be very bad to go through with it. It will seem we are after your money.' Suresh drew himself up as though the accusation had already been made.

'But my family says all kinds of things about you – I don't listen,' said Nisha, resentfully. Why should she plead about her love to her love? What was the point of it then?

From the corner of her eye she could see her aunt and uncle. Had they known how it would end, were they just giving her enough rope to hang herself?

'It is not good making so many people unhappy,' said Suresh. 'One day you will regret.'

'Why don't you say you have changed your mind?'

Suresh reached out his hand. Nisha kept her own clenched in her lap. 'You will always be the princess of my dreams.'

'I don't want to be in your dreams, I want us to be together. What has happened? Have they said anything to you privately?'

The boy shook his head.

'Then?'

'Leave it, Nisha, leave it,' said Suresh miserably. He called for the bill – only two teas – paid without a tip and left, leaving Nisha to the refuge of the watchful aunt and uncle.

Later, at home: 'How much money was he paid?'

Her aunt looked at her angry, contorted face and spoke gently. 'It was the family that mentioned some figure, low-class people that they are, and your parents love you so much they agreed. You should be grateful. Not everybody lets a girl off so lightly.'

After her three-year romance, gratitude towards her parents was not uppermost in Nisha's mind. 'What about him? Did they talk to him?'

'I don't know the details, but the boy must be aware.'

That her meeting with Suresh had already shown.

'How much?'

'I don't know.'

'You don't know how much I am worth?'

'You are worth the sun, the moon, and the stars. Your father would do anything to see you happy. All the time he is crying. The only daughter of the house, a girl like a flower . . .'

But Nisha had been compared to flowers too often for it to affect her much now.

Suffering paved the way for anger. Raju was right: Suresh was a chutia, a total fucker. If he loved her he had no right to decide her future on his own. She phoned him at his shop. A coarse voice asked her many questions, who was she, where was she calling from, why did she want to speak to Suresh, before reluctantly informing her that he had left town. She phoned him at home, and received the same answer.

Suresh had vanished from her life and there was nothing she could do.

Skin

Nisha's nights were now ones of restlessness. As she tossed and turned on her bed, her hands absently crept around the itchy patches on her skin. First behind her knee to explore that damp, prickly area; next to her ankle bone to soothe the greater uneasiness that lurked beneath the surface. She pulled her foot up and rubbed lightly. Rub, rub, but the skin refused to be satisfied. Harder and harder she clawed, digging her nails in deeply till the wetness under them made her stop. Next morning a scab of dried blood marked the place.

'What is that?' asked her mother as her daughter sprawled on the bed idly flipping through a film magazine.

'Don't know,' replied Nisha, looking blankly at the dried darkness. 'Must be a mosquito bite.'

'Be careful. Look, this bite became infected and left a scar.' She lifted her sari to offer Nisha her example. There, amid an expanse of plump, mottled flesh, scattered coarse black hair, and pale stretchmarks was a round, puckered mouth with a raised bar across the middle. Nisha stared with fascination at the scar, the always hidden leg, then modestly looked away.

The next lesion was in her groin. The itching in the folds of her skin was unbearable. She disappeared into the bathroom to bring herself relief, staring in puzzlement at the swollen weal. Was she sick? She tried putting on powder and cream, but the wound persisted in the integrity of its nature.

A few weeks later a lesion appeared on her stomach, making it easier for her nails to get to the troubled spot.

As her hands roamed across her body, scratching and drawing blood, word spread through the community: only daughter of the Banwari Lal Cloth Shop is ready to marry, they want a boy, now, now.

But how to attract proposals from rich, decent families, with a mangli horoscope that decrees the death of a husband, or at the very best unhappiness? In return for a large dowry, beauty, and trade connections, pundits from both sides would agree that just as there is nothing without a problem, there is nothing without a solution.

Day and night the issue was canvassed through the extended family, allowing everybody an opportunity to feel responsible for the girl's future.

The grapevine groaned under the weight of all this communication.

After three years of thinking that Suresh was her future, Nisha had to adjust to the idea of another man in his place. A better man, according to her parents. Would he be able to gauge the extent to which she had been touched?

It would reconcile her much to her future if she could open her heart to him, but how to trust someone she didn't know? It would go against her, everything around her indicated it would. Far better to keep this thing hidden.

Alternatively, suppose she were to tell her parents she didn't want to get married? There were such people in the world. But where? Nobody in her social circle, simply nobody, had not married. They were without children perhaps, widowed perhaps, but not married? Her memory could only dredge up a few teachers in her college, objects of pity, sympathy, and secret speculation.

Now a prisoner in her home, she played the part of the king in chess. She needed to be protected, as without her there could be no game. The moves concerning her were carefully planned, but she herself was powerless, quiescent, mute, and waiting.

The day came when Vijay's luck upstairs translated into

Nisha's luck downstairs. Pyare Lal brought the news that he had found a boy from Rekha's family. Should the meeting go off well, their combined pundits could work something out about the mangli aspect.

Sona cracked her knuckles around Nisha's head. 'I knew you could not look like Suriya for nothing.'

Next evening. Rupa has been called for the event. Mother and aunt hover around the girl. Thick gold bangles are put on each wrist, a heavy gold necklace adorns her neck. A Benarsi silk, with gold threadwork on the border and palla, is laid out for her to wear.

'I'll die in it,' protested Nisha, as her hidden lesions prickle in alarm.

'Once you get married you can feel hot and cold as you like,' scolded Sona.

'It's just for a while,' reassured Rupa.

'Should we put on a little foundation?' Sona worried. 'There are two pimples on her face. Never gets them, but today of all days . . .'

'Let it be. They might think that she is not naturally fair,' Rupa replied.

'People do anything to look fair,' observed Sona. 'It is not right.'

'A face like a champa flower,' said Rupa, tilting Nisha's chin up.

Nisha jerked her head away. She felt stiff and awkward, she hoped the boy would like her, so she could be over and done with the whole thing. Life would be easier and her family would be happy.

Was her appearance enough to create the desire that was going to accomplish this? This stiff, gold-covered figure, red lipstick, step-cut hair, pale face, five foot three inches tall, would this overcome the bad stars prevalent at her birth and force the man who was coming to escort her into marriage?

*

He was hardly a man, more a boy, thin, brown, shy, small-moustached, with a tendency to twitch. She was seated on a sofa, the boy in front of her, the mother next to her.

'What have you been studying, beti?' started the mother.

'I've just finished my BA,' Nisha said to the floor.

'English Honours,' added Sona.

'Which college?' continued the voice.

Rupa, standing behind her, gave her a small poke. Nisha raised her head a few millimetres. 'DBC.'

'Good college, very good college,' intoned the mother. 'Not one of these co-ed places.'

Silence fell.

Rupa sighed into the vacuum. 'Arre, it's so hard to find good girls these days. They should be educated, yet homely. Our Nisha is both. Throughout a position holder (her niece's future demanded gilding the lily) and still so simple.'

The woman looked enquiringly at the speaker, and Sona said, 'Nisha's real aunt, my real sister.'

The woman nodded and turned her attention back to Nisha.

'What do you like doing at home, beti?' she asked.

Nisha glanced sideways and saw his hand drumming against the chair, the foot in its white-toed chappal wagging like a machine. Her aunt did some more poking and prodding from the back.

Cooking was the right answer, but Nisha in a trance refused to give it. Her attention was taken by those movements: hand, foot, hand, foot, shake, shake. Rupa gave her niece a harder nudge. This time, in an exaggerated reaction, the plate Nisha was holding fell to the floor. The almond barfi and salted cashews lay scattered amongst the broken china. It was an inauspicious sign.

The woman laughed. 'These things happen,' she said soothingly. 'When one is nervous the fingers are like butter.'

'Would the young people like to go to the veranda and talk?' asked Sona's mother. Nisha had agreed this invitation could be issued.

The boy blushed, drummed, shook, and looked away. There was no need, said his mother, they were a traditional family, the son listened to his elders.

That was a positive sign, they declared after the visit was over. With a girl as beautiful as their Nisha, affection was guaranteed with just a glance. After the dowry and marriage date were finalised, the pundits would be consulted on ways to convert the inauspicious into the auspicious. They were ready to give as advised, to this temple, to that charity, to these Brahmins, to those cows, while during the ceremony the girl would be married off to a tulsi plant before the actual union with the boy.

But the stars were not going to be cheated so easily. The Banwari Lals were told that the family was conducting its own research, they needed more time.

Anxiety levels began to rise. As the days passed Pyare Lal told his brother that he had acted in good faith in suggesting Nisha's name to his daughter-in-law's family, but he could not be held responsible for their decision.

Yashpal knew his brother seldom spoke without ulterior meaning. The feelers he would almost have certainly sent out to Rekha's family had been met with rejection. But why? Could it be the girl (unlikely), the dowry (negotiable), the horoscope (resolvable)? He waited impatiently for his brother to clarify matters.

Two days later Pyare Lal said to Yashpal, they have heard rumours about the girl, and unfortunately her prettiness lent them credence. They were an old-fashioned family, they believed in old-fashioned values, and those values included absolute purity. He had assured them it was all nonsense, but they did not want to start a new life with a girl on whom there was even a shadow of a stain. What could he do, some people were suspicious just like that, this was Rekha's mother's cousin, the situation was too delicate for him to insist.

'No, no, of course not,' said Yashpal; where his daughter was concerned, there should be willingness, not coercion.

Knowing he would feel like that, continued Pyare Lal, he felt it best to let the matter drop. 'Arre, with a girl like Nisha, will there be a shortage of offers? If they are being so picky, let them go to hell.'

Sona could not take the same view. 'Are you satisfied, Madam?' she demanded. '*This* is what your roaming around has done. *This* is the way people talk. Are you pleased with our humiliation?'

Yashpal intervened. 'Pyare Lal felt they actually wanted more dowry, but since it is Rekha's family they can't be open and are using this as an excuse.'

'You will think good of everybody till the day I die,' moaned Sona.

'Leave it. If they don't want Nisha, there are other parties,' commanded Yashpal, while his daughter drearily thought that had they agreed to Suresh, they would have saved themselves many lakhs and much torture.

The hunting grounds expanded to include Meerut – Sona, Rupa, and Seema's home town. Within a month a boy was found and a day fixed for the viewing. To compound his glory, he had no sisters, only one much younger brother. The dowry was negotiable – we are only interested in the girl and an early marriage.

On a day in June when the loo blew and the windows of the new house were shut against the dust and glare, when the heat lay thick and heavy upon everything, the Meerut party eagerly made its way to Karol Bagh to view the girl. Father and son came, allowing the family to view in the heavy, overflowing bulk of the father the future of the portly son.

The suitor had plump cheeks, and a moustache that cut the fleshy pockets of his face in two and shadowed the full lips below. His brown leather chappals betrayed square, splayed feet. He wore dark-brown pants, a striped beige bush shirt with a Cross ballpoint protruding from the breast pocket. His face had a scattering of acne scars, his forehead and nose were shiny; but then in such heat all human surfaces were glazed with sweat.

Nisha glanced at him, and found his eyes did not catch and hold hers. She was a girl on whom gazes habitually glued themselves, and now this non-engagement settled at the back of her mind. Was he shy? Did he too have something to hide?

The response was immediate. The boy's side were keen, so keen that they wished the wedding to take place at the earliest. The girl was homely, the family matched their own, the union would be very auspicious.

'How do you like him?' they asked Nisha, ready to cajole, such a good match, you will be treated like a jewel in their house. Look how flexible they are about dowry, unlike others who exploit a girl for the sake of money.

Nisha tentatively remarked that there was something not quite right with him. At this her mother collapsed. Who are you to decide what is right or no? You have only had low-class bhangis to compare him with. But Nisha had spent much time in the company of a man who was attracted to her, and though she was too inexperienced to go beyond a gut feeling, she persisted with each family member that there was something wrong, hoping that despite her blackened reputation and tarnished morals, she would be heard.

Yashpal paid attention. His daughter was too precious for him to throw away on someone she was uneasy about. The enthusiasm of the other side began to look suspicious. They started doing what they should have done earlier: get in touch with people in Meerut, look for the skeletons, look for the secrets, why the need for haste, look, look.

It took only a few days for the skeleton to emerge. The prospective groom had been discovered with a boy in a compromising position, a boy who worked in his shop. The parents were insisting on immediate marriage, and he had been forced to agree.

Yashpal declared this was a sign from the Devi, Nisha's marriage could not be rushed. His daughter was not medicine for some man.

It was morning. Nisha had just finished frying the last puri for breakfast, and was sitting down to eat. As she scraped the remaining sweet mango chutney out of a bowl, her mother started lamenting.

'Did I know what troubles would be caused by my children when I fasted ten years?' she stated bitterly.

'How have I caused you trouble?' demanded Nisha, vocal with the triumph that the error in judgement had not been hers.

'She can't marry a eunuch,' said Raju reasonably.

'Why is it my fate that such a man come to our house?'

'Must be thinking in Meerut, everybody knows, let us try Delhi.'

'When a boy comes to see us, we take him in good faith. We are too innocent and trusting,' grumbled Sona.

'I don't want to be seen by all these people, why can't I do some course?' complained Nisha daringly.

'You will do the housework, Madam, just like Asha before you. All this time I have been treating you like a princess.'

'Ever since I have finished my exams, I am doing that only,' objected Nisha.

'You talk back to your mother?' shouted Sona. 'For years I have spoiled you, now get out of my sight.'

Silently Nisha got up. She cleared the dishes from the table, put the china ones in the kitchen sink and the heavy utensils on the floor for the mai to wash, returned the pickles to the cupboard, the milk, dahi, and fruit to the fridge, put the melon seeds to soak, wiped the plastic sheet on the table with a damp cloth, then pushed all the chairs in.

As she started washing the china, breathing in the sharp, clean smell of Vim, the part-time mai came in, and squatted on the floor next to the tap under the sink. Bang, bang went the pots as she scoured them with ashes and a tattered piece of coconut husk.

'How can anyone clean with only ashes? They blame me if it is not done properly,' she muttered.

Nisha mutely sprinkled some Vim on to a small steel plate and gave it to her.

The mai was in a chatty mood. 'What happened, Didi?' she asked. 'About that boy coming to see you?' she persisted, against the girl's reticence. 'He must have liked you? If you are fair, things are easy,' she sighed. She herself was black as coal.

'Nothing came of it, Rajo,' replied Nisha.

'Why nothing?'

'I don't know.'

'Dowry, must be,' was the philosophical observation. 'People today have become very greedy. With your looks and background there can be no other reason.'

Nisha let her think what she wanted. She washed the dishes quickly, occasionally scratching herself as she did so. The soap irritated her skin but in the kitchen there was no one to comment on her actions.

∽

The women of the Banwari Lal family had never been advertised for. There was always someone belonging to someone in the extended family with the essential prerequisites of caste, community, and like-mindedness. But Nisha's circumstances demanded a larger playing field. An ad was placed in the mangli section of *The Hindustan Times:*

Wanted own business, graduate, manglik boy, over 1.65, from kaiyasth community, own property, for only mangli

225

daughter, UP kaiyasth, migrated from Lahore, graduate from a prestigious woman's college, extremely fair, beautiful, homely, 1.60, 20 years. Early marriage. Horoscope a must. Send details with recent colour returnable photograph (must) to Box –, The Hindustan Times.

Sona and Rupa were going through the responses. They were all mangliks, all with an unfortunate combination of stars. 'It is very difficult to choose from just a picture,' complained Sona. 'God knows what all it is hiding.'

Nisha picked up some of the photographs. What could one tell from them? Young, moustachioed, some puffy-cheeked, mostly nondescript. But then, were Suresh to be among them, he might look the same. These faces meant nothing.

∾

The rains came. Bhutta sellers appeared on the pavements around Karol Bagh. The jamun trees that were given on contract to vendors were shaken every morning for their purple, tongue-furring fruit. There were phalsa sellers too, with small, tart, reddish-violet berries that, like the jamun, were sold in paper cones with salt and masala.

One by one the girls Nisha had known in school and college were getting married. The wedding invitations, heralds of gloom, arrived in the post, red, white, and gold reproaches, the ceremonies of sangeet, barat, wedding, vida, and reception further nails in the coffin.

Or these girls came personally, sat in the drawing room, met Sona, and rubbed salt in her wounds by airing their prizes: details of job, business, family, house, car, property, height, looks.

'Auntie, you must come. Uncle too. Mummy – Papa will be very disappointed if you don't.'

'Of course, beti, of course,' Sona would smile tightly. 'And please put some sense into the head of your friend.'

'Auntie, Nisha is so beautiful, so fair. If I can get married (giggle, giggle), so can she. In fact, in college we always thought Nisha would be the first.'

Nisha held her breath at these statements. Would they mention the unmentionable boyfriend? But thankfully they didn't, too caught up in their own futures to give Nisha's prospects more than a passing reference.

The stay was always short, for there were many houses to visit. The wedding invitation, along with a box of sweets, was left on the small centre table of the drawing room. Accusingly, it remained there for all to see and exclaim over, while Nisha's failure to live up to her future gained greater prominence.

Nisha's results were declared at the beginning of August: 48 per cent – a third division. She had not deserved more; besides, what did marks matter? The arena of competition had shifted.

Mr and Mrs Yashpal were pleased. An Honours degree from a good college, but without the distinction that might frighten forthcoming suitors.

'Now I have my degree I want to do a course,' declared Nisha.

'What obsession do you have with courses?' rebuked her mother. 'A BA degree is not enough? You want to spend your life running on the streets?'

Nisha ignored this. 'I want to study fashion designing. Lots of girls do it, why can't I? Why should I sit at home every day waiting for proposals?'

'If you had thought of your future earlier, you would not be sitting at home waiting for proposals,' snapped Sona.

'Your in-laws will not like the idea of your working,' said Raju, with conviction. 'I certainly won't let my wife work – who is going to look after the house?'

'Why can't you be mature like your brother?' demanded Sona. 'He is so sensible, while you are just a fool.'

'I don't have in-laws yet,' Nisha raised her voice.

'Chee-chee. Why do such inauspicious things come out of your mouth?' retorted her mother. 'Once you are married, and in your own home, you can do what your in-laws think fit.'

'At least till then let me do a course. Later we can see,' pleaded Nisha.

'No.'

Sona didn't add that after what had happened, Nisha would only go to an educational institution over her dead body. Who knew how many boys would ambush her on the way?

When dark-brown patches began to appear in the folds of Nisha's arms and neck, her family could no longer think of mosquitoes or prickly heat as answers to the strange things that were happening to her skin.

Instead they blamed her.

'What have you been doing to yourself?' asked Sona suspiciously.

'Nothing, I've been doing nothing.'

Sona pushed the hair from her neck and saw the darkness. She stared at her feet and saw the scabs, she pulled up her salwar and noticed the sores.

'You are not happy with the trouble you are already causing? For how long has this been going on?'

Nisha could give no coherent explanation.

When Yashpal was told of the damage, he merely said, 'If you are worried, take her to the doctor.'

'A doctor – which doctor? Who can deal with this girl?'

'Dr Gupta will tell us what to do. It must be some little irritation, these things happen in the heat.'

As her parents conferred, Nisha itched. Her skin prickled

and irritated her to such an extent that she could be aware of nothing else till she had reduced it to burning rawness. Water had begun to ooze from the sores.

'Stop it,' said her mother harshly. 'Your skin will become as black as a buffalo's, then nobody will ever marry you.'

Dr Gupta, two lanes down, family acquaintance, prescriber of all-purpose pills for reasonable charges.

That evening they sat in the waiting room, every page Sona rustled in her magazine a reproach to her daughter. That they were there was Nisha's fault of course, but it was also the mother's wretched destiny. Had she known the misery her stubborn daughter would cause her, she would not have bothered with the fasting or the praying. Fortunately there was no need for her to speak in order to make Nisha understand her feelings.

The doctor lifted the curtain that divided the room and called them in. 'I haven't seen you in a long time,' he stated briefly, before the inevitable demand for good news about the girl.

Immediately Sona started wailing. 'Dr Sahib, see what is happening to her skin. All day she itches, no matter how much I keep telling her, she goes on.'

In front of the doctor Nisha found it easier to speak. 'I don't do it on purpose. It itches so much, I can't bear it. It's like ants crawling all over me.'

Sona blinked. The doctor glanced at the mottled skin, prescribed lotions and anti-allergy pills, advised the mother to tie strips of cloth around Nisha's hands at night, and come back after a week.

Her body had been scrutinised, medicine prescribed, a return visit set up. Nisha was sick, the world had acknowledged it. But she didn't feel sick. Only dry, itchy, and restless.

For twenty years people had commented on her fairness. From the day of her birth her complexion had been protected from the sun, nurtured with uptan before every bath and in adolescence safeguarded against pimples by bitter herbs. Now it was turning against her. When the scabs dried they faded to a pale brown that stood out in patches against their pristine surroundings. She stared at herself in the mirror – her face was still untouched, but for how long?

She looked at her limbs. Sparse hair had begun to appear on her arms, stubble decorated her legs. She had always had heavy body growth. Once she entered college she often went to the neighbourhood beauty parlour to wax her skin into appearing smooth, soft, clean, and white. Suresh had loved running his hands along her legs in the little Vijay Nagar room.

And now? How could she go to the beauty parlour with these angry red blotches, which oozed under her roving, raking fingers. The parlour girls would refuse to touch her. You will infect our cloth, our knives, our waxing mixture. Go home, go home, go home.

The stubble on her legs grew to bristle, the bristle grew into rough, wiry hair, and then the wiriness became long and supple. As she itched she wondered how the scratching could peel her skin off in layers while the hair remained intact. At least one unsightliness should cancel out the other.

Her body began to haunt her dreams. She was covered with huge gaping mouths, all screaming through a jungle of thick black hair. She was a monster, coarse, dark, and hairy – she was more than a monster, she was a man.

At night Sona tore an old soft kurta into strips and twisted them around Nisha's fingers. 'You think I like doing this?' she demanded, irritated by the whole exercise.

Nisha's vulnerability meant a silent acceptance of her guilt, even before a rhetorical question.

Religiously Sona applied the cream the doctor prescribed to Nisha's sores, religiously she doled out her anti-allergy pills. Each night she patted on a mixture of katha and rose water to soothe the burning flesh.

But pieces of cloth, if scraped against the skin hard enough, are not ineffective. The patches had a life of their own, choosing to expand their territory while the girl was sleeping. In the morning, when her mother inspected her carefully, she would see fresh signs of Nisha's malady.

'Why can't you restrain yourself?' she asked in despair. 'It is in your hands.'

'Send her to me,' said Rupa.

Sona tcched in annoyance. Sometimes her sister couldn't see a problem even if it waved a hand in her face. Did she think these were poor marks her husband could fix? Or nightmares that demanded a change of place? 'What can you do? Will these scabs go away in your house? She needs constant attention. Look – look – and look –' Sona pulled up the salwar, rolled up the sleeves, lifted the hair from the neck to reveal the dark, rough skin decorated with the thin lines of powder that Nisha used to camouflage her condition.

'Maybe a change of scene –' suggested Rupa helplessly.

'The only change of scene this wretched creature will get is after her marriage. Right now she is like a small child who has no control over herself. No matter how often I tell her not to, night and day, night and day she goes on. Whoever heard of having to tie the hands of a grown girl?'

'Take her to another doctor,' said Yashpal wearily as Sona complained bitterly to her husband. They were in their bedroom on a double bed of Dunlop foam and white Sunmica, flanked by little matching bedside tables.

'But there is nothing *wrong* with her. If only she would stop itching. Sometimes I think she does it on purpose.'

'Why would anybody destroy themselves on purpose?'

'How should I know? I am just telling.'

'Don't worry, it will pass with time.'

'When?'

'It is God's will. We just have to wait,' said Yashpal, turning on his side, away from his wife, who stared at the wall, her worries pushed firmly back at her.

Why had this thing come to poison her days? Her children were of marriageable age, she had spied the end of her responsibilities. Did God have some grudge against her? She sighed. Her husband slept on. Poor man, always so tired. She stopped the second sigh. He at least should sleep.

Away in her home Rupa was also sighing.

'What's the matter?' demanded Prem Nath, unable to follow Yashpal down the paths of sleep. For him a sigh was enough to create instant and cantankerous wakefulness.

'Can't we do something for Nisha?'

Prem Nath thought bitterly of the years he had spent looking after this girl – for what? To see her idle, miserable, and eczema-ridden in her house? She had begun to wilt and darken before his eyes, but how could he help? It was an illness he did not understand.

'What can we do?' he asked harshly.

'Bring her over. She will get better here. Remember when she stopped screaming in her sleep?'

'Years ago. She was small then.'

'She is the same girl. Very sensitive. I feel they do not understand her.'

'They are her parents. If her skin gets worse, who do you think they will blame?'

So Nisha stayed where she was, in her new house, in her new bedroom, right next to her parents.

It became a family duty to stop Nisha from itching. 'Exercise self-control. The more you itch the more you will want to.'

They tried to hold her hands. She pulled them away. 'Leave me alone, I can't help it. I don't itch for my own pleasure.'

'You can. You can help it. You are not even trying. Take God's name. Say the Gayatri Mantra.'

Nobody understood. Nisha was alone in a scratchy, burning, oozing, bleeding world. Perhaps the ugliness in her was coming out. Perhaps that was what Suresh had banked on when he had felt her and made her feel him, perhaps it was this thing that had attracted Vicky.

'Don't you know what this means? About your marriage?' implored her mother, holding Nisha's hands, noticing the line of dark blood under the nails, now so usual. Nisha looked down. Her bangles tinkled, the bangles her mother made her wear after the itching spread. Two dozen on each arm, to protect the world from the sight of her scabs, clinking with sweet feminine noises, grating on Nisha's nerves. Once she had loved glass bangles, buying them eagerly, arranging them colourwise on rolled-up magazines. Now she hated them.

Months passed, months in which the family hoped that the eczema would vanish as it had come. Miraculously Nisha would get up one morning shining with pearly incandescence. Finally they had to admit that moment was not to be.

Allopathy had its limitations. They had to look further afield.

Sushila suggested a famous nature cure centre near Ajmeri Gate. Any port in a storm. There they went, Sona and Nisha, there they were offered hope. It was not going to be easy, they would have to come every morning, they would have to follow the regimen strictly, very strictly. 'In two months,' promised the doctor, 'in two months she will have a skin like a flower.'

Nisha was put on a diet of juice, fruit, and vegetables cooked without spices, oil, or salt. For two months tea, coffee, synthetic food, refined sugar, and starches were forbidden. Every morning they covered her body with a pack of herbs and mud to draw out the toxins.

'I have seen girls who emerge from this treatment looking like lotuses,' said the woman who applied the mudpack. 'They get so many offers the problem is in choosing.'

'She did have a skin like a lotus,' mourned Sona. 'Even when she was a teenager, not a pimple, not a spot. Other girls got, but Nisha – never. And now see. It is the evil eye – my daughter was too, too beautiful.'

'Yes, yes,' said the mudpack woman soothingly. 'No one knows why it happens. Some allergy . . . some disturbance in the family . . . '

'There has been no disturbance,' declared Sona.

'There has been some shock to the system,' said the mudpack lady, getting combative. 'Not everything that happens in the body has a physical cause.'

Sona sat still while Nisha fidgeted.

'Don't,' the mother reprimanded automatically. Then turning to the lady she said with dignity, 'My daughter has had no shocks whatsoever. It is the evil eye that has cursed my home.'

The nature cure centre invariably gave Sona headaches, so occasionally Rupa accompanied Nisha and found herself agreeing with the things the lady said. Illnesses did have emotional causes. Maybe the thing with Suresh . . .? The boy hadn't been that bad. Perhaps, thought the sympathetic aunt daringly, even caste and relative poverty should be overlooked sometimes. The boy and girl were educated, they were not living in some village, after all. He had seemed to love her truly, and it was Nisha's side that first suggested compensation, though that was something the girl need never know.

Eating boiled food was a strain for Nisha amid the aroma of spices and hiss of frying that pervaded her house, but she did enjoy the mudpacks. Lying on a table in the nature cure centre, her body ministered to, cooling things applied, every particle of her delighting in the heavy, wet mud.

However, two months later she was still far from resembling a lotus. Any time she missed her mudpack treatment, the itching increased. 'These doctors are just out to make money – who can spend their life going to nature cure centres? All morning it takes, and still she has not recovered.'

With improvement only partial, Rupa suggested they take Nisha to a famous homeopath right there in Karol Bagh.

They sat in the crowded waiting room, during the free consultation period, pressed close to each other. It was hot, and Nisha was perspiring. Above them, a fan suspended from the high ceiling on its long pole moved slowly. It was once a big room, and a partition made of white-painted plywood stretched halfway up. A sagging, rickety door served as the entrance to the doctor's section, scraping against the floor as patients went in and out.

'See, so many people,' remarked Rupa. 'That shows how good he is.'

'Only if he heals her will I believe he is good,' said Sona morosely.

'You have to believe, Didi.'

'I can believe day and night – but what about her? She is the one who has to believe.'

Nisha looked out of the door, on to the evening street, the hawkers, the traffic, the pollution, and suppressed a desire to itch. She knew it would drive her mother mad.

The doctor, an old Sardar retired from government service, his white beard flowing, famous for his healing skills, looked at the daughter with pity in his rheumy eyes. Then the interrogation, which Sona answered. Did the girl feel thirsty? Did she like her head covered or uncovered? Could she stand the sun on her skin? Did it burn, prickle, or get irritated when touched by sweat, food, cold air, hot air, cold fluids, hot fluids, cloth, soap, water, lotions, perfumes? Was it worse in the morning or evening? Summer, winter, or monsoon?

'Oh doctor sa'ab,' cried Sona, as the questions flowed. 'All this we do not know. It has come only now, after college. Otherwise she never had a pimple. Her brother had many, but God spared her, only to put us through this.'

'Don't worry, Mata ji,' consoled the doctor, 'everything will be all right. Once she is married this will vanish. Unmarried girls have a lot of tension.'

'But why did this happen?' asked Sona, still angry about the mudpack lady's insinuations. 'Just to avoid in future, you understand, doctor sa'ab.'

'Who can tell why the body falls sick?' asked the doctor, shaking his head, his knobbly fingers twitching a series of white pills into little packets. 'It is all in the hands of The Above. Two people exposed to the same thing – one succumbs, the other doesn't. Can you tell me the reason?'

'No, doctor sa'ab, thank you, doctor sa'ab.'

'No tea, no coffee, no fried food, no chillies, and allow half an hour's gap between doses.'

'She doesn't eat these things anyway.'

'Very good. Continue.'

'Should we stop nature cure?' Nisha and Rupa caught the hopeful note, but alas the doctor was not so sensitive.

He looked at the patient. 'Does it help you?'

The expense, the time, the inconvenience to her aunt and mother. She allowed herself only a very small nod.

'Continue then. No clash with homeopathy.'

So Nisha continued, adding the little white pills to her regimen.

When homeopathy made no appreciable difference, Rupa, always searching for effective treatments, uncovered a neighbour who suggested Tibetan medicine. The neighbour's sister's father-in-law had one side paralysed after a stroke, allopathy was no good, God only knew how many doctors they consulted, the man was so devoted to his father, all the time trying this or that. Then last year they took him to a Tibetan doctor who came down from Dharamsala to Delhi for three months every winter, and there was such a change in the neighbour's sister's father-in-law, it was like a miracle.

'No harm in trying, Didi,' said Rupa. 'It is winter now, and the doctor is here.'

'Yes,' agreed Sona dully, 'no harm in trying.'

'What is *wrong* with her?' asked Sona. The renowned old Tibetan doctor pressed down on Nisha's wrist, her eyes fixed on Nisha's face.

'She is disturbed,' replied the doctor firmly.

'Why?'

'That I do not know. But her whole system is disturbed. Do not worry, she will be all right. Come back after one month.' She then dispensed small herbal tablets, to be chewed slowly three times a day.

Bland homeopathic pills were replaced by bitter, black, pungent balls, followed by glasses of water to wash away the taste.

'For nothing you are putting me through this torture,' complained Nisha. 'All she did was feel my pulse. How does she know what is wrong with me?'

'That is the beauty of Tibetan medicine,' Rupa chided, already a convert. 'People come from far and near to see this lady. She is so good, yet she takes no money, her medicine comes from the heart. You have to give it a chance, and that too with belief, otherwise it won't work.'

'I am going to vomit if I eat more.'

'Eat as you are told,' said her mother sternly, 'and with God's grace you will be cured. Then after you are married you can do what you like.'

Each morning there was discussion over Nisha's progress, action to be taken, and results to be surveyed. Every member of the household, near or at the fringes, was ready with their advice.

'The whole world knows our shame,' said Sona to Rupa after Sushila's sister's visit. 'They all ask about Nisha. If I don't give details, they think I am withholding information. If

I do, I am broadcasting my daughter's humiliation. I wish I could go and die somewhere.'

Rupa listened patiently. This was her sister's hour of need, and the frequency of her visits increased. Her refusal to break down made her invaluable at the doctor's, at home she was a cornucopia of strength and solace.

She hid her own anguish at Nisha's condition, wondering at the heartache children could cause. Poor child. That perfect skin, that clear complexion, that resemblance to Suriya, all for nothing.

Finally, one morning Yashpal said, 'These vaids and homeopaths are doing no good. Perhaps we gave up allopathy too soon.'

'We tried Dr Gupta for months.'

'We should have gone to a skin specialist instead of resorting to a GP.'

'It is her kismet,' said Sona mournfully, 'and ours.'

'If we accept our kismet so easily,' retorted her husband, 'how will we achieve anything in life? Pyare Lal has been doing a lot of finding out. There is a very good skin doctor in South Delhi, whose son has just returned from abroad. He cured a girl in Rekha's family.'

'Is she married?' asked Sona.

'She is only five.'

'Why couldn't Nisha wait till she was married, I want to know? Then it would have been all right.'

'It is better she is our problem, than some in-laws who might be unkind to her.'

Sona had nothing to say to this.

Yashpal made the appointment with the doctor. Poor man, thought his wife, how seriously he takes his daughter's condition, has to neglect the business to get her treated. She sniffed and thought of which sari to wear.

It took three weeks to get an appointment. 'Father and son,

very well known,' said Yashpal, 'all booked.'

'These private doctors are crooks,' said Sona. 'Even when they can't cure a simple thing they take.'

'They also have to live,' said Yashpal mildly.

Three weeks later Yashpal, his wife, and Nisha were in the doctor's office in Defence Colony, waiting with many others in a small covered veranda.

Despite the appointment it took an hour for their turn to come. Perspiration gathered in the crevices of Nisha's skin, and with the dampness her skin began to burn. She and her parents were mostly silent, in Sona's lap was a file containing her unhappy history. She had lost count of the doctors she had seen, the number of times she had been examined, the number of times her story had been told and her once-perfect skin described. What did it matter what her skin once was? Now it was like this. If only her family could accept that, her life would be easier. Covertly, she started to rub her nails along her arms. Her mother frowned but the waiting room facilitated Nisha's inclination to ignore.

Finally their turn. Once again Nisha's problem was graphically described. The fairness that was, the darkness that is, the scratching, the oozing fluids, the blood, the dryness, the flakiness, the uncontrollable impulses, the concern of the whole family, the girl so young, the question of marriage.

After examining Nisha, the doctor said they were lucky, subcutaneous cortisone injections were now being used to treat this condition, and they had had very good results. In the meantime she must not go near soap and water, they were irritants. She must not cook, spices and heat were also irritants.

'But doctor, there is nothing wrong with her hands,' said Sona, horrified at this attempt to wrest a woman's occupation away from her. 'She just does a little washing and cooking, the dhobi and the mai do the heavy work.'

'Any contact with harsh detergents will aggravate,' continued the doctor, ignoring her and looking at the father. 'Her clothes must be washed separately in liquid soap and rinsed many times. Her skin is very delicate, as you can see. No washing or cooking,' he repeated.

The treatment started that very day. Tiny squirts of medicine were injected in several places in each patch. The skin swelled for a few hours, looked pink, and hurt. After the injections Nisha usually felt like throwing up, but the doctor assured the family that the reaction was psychological. 'It is quite clear she is a sensitive girl,' he said tactfully. 'Sometimes, when eczema occurs there is an emotional cause. After all, the mind and body are connected.'

His listeners nod. In the abstract this was an acceptable, non-threatening piece of information.

The doctor took out his fee book. 'Soon these patches will subside. When she looks better, she will feel better.'

At home the washing was restructured. The women had always done the personal clothing. It was their duty and their joy to precede every bath by washing for the family – scrape, scrub, beat, and wring the dirt out of the garments of their loved ones.

The washerwoman's chores increased, as did her wages. Sona stood over her making sure she rinsed the clothes in many buckets of water, making sure she did not waste the expensive liquid soap that she was forced to hand over to her.

As for the china washing, Sona now did all this herself, while Nisha lurked around guiltily. Slowly, the duties it was inconceivable for a woman not to do, became hers not to do.

XX

Raju

Ten o'clock on a weekday morning. Father and son have departed, mother and daughter are together in Sona's bedroom. Sona is shelling peas, Nisha is sitting next to her doing nothing. Her hands are idle, her spirits low.

Time has created many empty spaces in Nisha's head. Into those cavities come rumours, rumours flying about in the atmosphere of the house, borne by half-caught phrases, spread in whispers that reverberate downstairs among the adults. In a joint family it doesn't take long for information to reach a destination, desired or undesired.

Finally Nisha rouses herself.

'Mummy, I have heard –' she started.

Those few words were enough for an apprehensive shadow to fall across Sona's face. Nisha pounced on that, her voice became less tentative, her suspicions were right, she was justified in her grievances. 'Shall I tell you what I have heard?' she went on. 'And not from my own mother, but the mai – the mai, who asked me when she was going to hear good news about me, now that my brother's marriage was arranged.'

'That woman can't keep her mouth shut,' snapped Sona. 'Hears things from upstairs and comes and spreads stories downstairs. I should dismiss her.'

'Yes, why don't you?' demanded Nisha sceptically, thinking of the gossipy titbits the mai spread before her mother daily, of how the daughters-in-law upstairs barely spoke to one another, how they even cooked at separate times, how things were very difficult for Sushila, nothing compared to downstairs where values were sound and lasting.

This was one occasion when the communication system had backfired.

Now Sona barked at her daughter, 'You have nothing better to do than listen to idle talk? Besides, who is she to know anything?'

'She seems to know that Raju is getting married.'

'Don't be silly.'

'So, no need for me to go upstairs and find out what is happening?' asked Nisha as she picked empty peapods and broke them one by one.

'Don't do that, your hands will itch.'

'They won't. Who is she?'

'Can I help it if people enquire? Does that mean instant marriage?'

Peapods disintegrate under the daughter's hands. The mother continues with her shelling. 'Everybody knows a younger brother cannot get married before an older sister.'

Nisha ignores this. It is no secret how her parents have been worrying, daughter getting older by the minute, son's future blocked because of this, good matches passed over because of this.

One day a proposal comes that is so indicative of all-round advantage that they are forced to contemplate it, and as they do, the claims of the son become immediate and insistent.

'Who is she?' repeats Nisha.

'It may all come to nothing,' began Sona carefully. 'You never know. Look what happened in your case.'

'Even if it comes to nothing, I want to know.'

So Sona tells her daughter the story, prattling artlessly over the popping peas. Sushila had conveyed the interest from a richer branch of Rekha's family, showrooms in Karol Bagh and South Extension, with a dowry quoted in dreams. A good home was their only criterion. The girl had had a burn accident one Diwali when she was young, skin grafts made the scar barely noticeable – like Nisha, she did not do too much housework, but she was a very loving, caring, homely girl. She would bring a maid who could help with Nisha's work as well.

'So you have settled it?'

'You know we can settle nothing till you are married.'

But Nisha, with myriad peapods around her, could already hear the wedding band, could see her brother sitting with his bride before the marriage fire.

Unknown to Nisha, her parents were under great pressure to take this proposal seriously. As once before, the match had come through Pyare Lal, but this time it was Rekha's very own cousin, beckoning with the seductiveness of previously established ties and many lakhs as dowry.

It was during their morning walks that Pyare Lal broached the topic in earnest. As the two men, dressed identically in white kurta pyjamas falling gently over pot bellies, walked together in the coolness of dawn, rubber chappals flapping, birds chirping, Pyare Lal assured his brother that he understood his feelings, but the situation demanded judicious assessment.

Yashpal reiterated that there was no question, simply no question, of getting a younger son married before an older daughter. People would presume there was something wrong with the girl and it would ruin her chances for ever. No matter how favourable the match for the boy, her happiness could not be sacrificed.

If, responded Pyare Lal, Nisha's happiness was being sacrificed, he would rather cut off his tongue than persist. But times had changed, people were not so old-fashioned as to think there was something wrong with a girl who had not married before her brother. When she did marry, it would be to someone who would accept her as she was, not look for faults or shortcomings. In the meantime . . .

He paused. They were isolated from the interruptions so usual at home, and Pyare Lal felt the need to choose his words carefully. His brother looked ahead, breathing heavily, his emotions and the exercise combining to increase his heart rate.

First of all, said Pyare Lal, Nisha was his own daughter. He would never suggest anything that would harm her. But Raju was his own son also. With this match his future would be made. If it weren't for the accident, the girl's family would be looking much higher, they had the means. This proposal had come to them without any effort. Who knew how hard they would have to look before meeting its equivalent? Perhaps this was a sign from the gods that they should not ignore.

Secondly, the families were already related. Rekha and Pooja were like sisters. The ties between their sons would be even more firmly cemented. They could die peacefully, knowing the business they had slaved over would not be destroyed by fighting among the daughters-in-law. With wives so close it was less likely that Vijay or Raju would take their share and set up on their own; unity and partnership would take precedence over rivalry and independence.

Thirdly, with Fancy Furnishings having given two daughters to their family, business interests would be closely linked. The shop was getting too small for five men. They needed to expand, and with their combined resources it would be easier. For example, they could open a showroom that dealt in soft furnishings. Household linen, sheets, towels, bathmats, napkins: they could use the same sources that Fancy Furnishings did, they could refer to each other's shops, they would have more clout with the bank, they could keep less inventory.

Fourthly, with things as they were, Nisha would not be able to marry for some time. How long was it wise to make Raju wait? Of course younger brothers should not marry before older sisters, but circumstances provided exceptions. Suppose for the sake of argument they let this match go. Both brothers knew what the fires of youth could do. Raju unmarried, restless, at large – could Yashpal guarantee he would never look at a girl, never think himself in love, never insist on his own choice?

Silence, as Yashpal contemplated the wayward element in his son. Marriage and a new shop to stock, manage, and promote would keep him busy for years. Yashpal had to admit to a certain easiness of mind in knowing that his son was well settled, with a powerful family backing him.

'He is not like you, Bhai,' continued Pyare Lal, 'and even you, you did love marriage.'

More silence, to allow Yashpal time to reluctantly realise that there was something to be said for the scenario his brother had painted. He could sacrifice everything for the sake of his daughter, but Raju was a different matter. In the next year or so, should he happen to like some girl, Nisha might still be sidelined and the advantages of further union with Fancy Furnishings lost for nothing.

Clearly no point in that. But the idea of actually agreeing to something so obviously inimical to Nisha's interests kept him silent. From her earliest years he had imagined giving her a boy so full of qualities, both personal and worldly, that her happiness would be permanently assured. Her wedding would be the most elaborate in the family. Now Pyare Lal was urging him to postpone those visions and go ahead with Raju's marriage. How would his daughter feel with a sister-in-law younger than herself?

They were on their way home, the sun had risen, the coolness of the air was rapidly vanishing. As they turned into their lane he could see the imposing exterior of their new house, the curved balconies, the wrought-iron gates, the shining glass windows. They had risen in the world, husbanded their resources, and had three boys whose transitions into adult life had been predictable.

Was there a curse on the Banwari Lal women? He thought of his sister. Better Nisha never marry than have the miseries of Sunita's life. They must be careful, very careful.

Pyare Lal broke into his fearful thoughts. Babaji had so far been advising them about Nisha. Why didn't they consult him with all three horoscopes?

The next evening Sona and Yashpal took the horoscopes to

Babaji. They carried a box of fine pista burfi covered in delicate silver foil, while in Yashpal's pocket nestled an envelope containing five hundred and one rupees. Babaji, like his father before him, demanded no recompense for his services. Anything people gave was from their hearts in gratitude. Mere payment would have been an insult.

They squeezed into the packed drawing room of Babaji's house.

'Every time we come there are more people,' whispered Sona to her husband, pleased.

It made no difference to them. The connections between the families stretched over forty years, uniting the fathers and sons of two generations. It was natural and fitting they get preference and jump every queue.

The others watched curiously as they entered the inner sanctum, obviously favoured.

Babaji smiled benevolently at them. A small fat man with greying hair, polyester kurta pyjama, many rings, he sat cross-legged on a takht covered with a white sheet. In front of him were cane chairs and a small table. Gods and calendars decorated the walls.

'Tea?' he asked.

'We have had.'

'Cold?'

'No, please.'

Water was put before them and they could start. Quickly Yashpal outlined the situation: 'We do not want to spoil the girl's chances by marrying the boy first, but neither do we want him to go astray while waiting, and the offer seems good. Here are the horoscopes. We are in a difficult situation.'

Babaji went through the diagrams on the scrolls they proffered, two familiar, one new.

'The boy's stars are good,' he murmured. 'His marriage will open the luck in the family.'

'And Nisha?'

Some calculations were made, then Babaji looked up. 'Is the girl suffering from some illness?'

On the basis of such discernment many futures had been decided. Sona leaned forward eagerly. 'Yes, Babaji, that is why we are so worried about her marriage.' Her sari palla slipped, Babaji's eyes flickered over the long, deep cleavage framed by the red scoop of her neckline, before turning away with a frown. Sona's casual hand drew the palla back up.

'Not soon,' he remarked. 'Her marriage will be late. She is going through a bad period.'

'When will the bad period be over, Babaji?' asked Yashpal.

More calculations. 'Another three years.'

'Three years! She is twenty-two!' exclaimed Sona.

'That cannot be helped,' said Babaji firmly. 'If she marries during this period there will be trouble later.'

'How can the brother wait three years? He is almost twenty-one!'

'He, on the other hand, has no bad stars. Whatever he touches will turn to gold. Whoever he marries will be right for him.'

Yashpal felt a pang for his daughter. So pretty, so loving, so studious, only to fall prey to bad stars. Was there nothing besides the pujas they were doing that could counteract their vicious influence over her life?

Of course there was, there always was. They were not to lose heart. He looked again at Nisha's horoscope. He would choose a stone, have it set, she should wear that.

'And this girl?' Yashpal asked, indicating the third horoscope. 'Will she be good for my son? For the family?'

He would study everything and tell them. They should return in ten days.

While they waited for Babaji's verdict the family plunged into an orgy of speculation. Day and night, Yashpal–Sona, Yashpal–Pyare Lal, Sona–Rupa, Sushila–Sona.

Mostly it was assumed that Babaji would give them the go-ahead.

'It is a good family,' opined Sushila, 'not at all proudy. Rekha never says anything.'

That is not what she had heard, thought Sona to herself. In fact it was Seema, the older daughter-in-law, who never said anything, but this was not the time to delve into the distortions emanating from upstairs.

Pyare Lal suggested they consult a numerologist, but Yashpal preferred to wait. Who all could they keep running to?

Back at Babaji's ten days later. He greeted them, smiling as usual.

'Tea?' he asked.

'We have had.'

'Cold?'

'No, please.'

Water was put before them, and they could start. First Babaji slowly produced a small red satin pouch, then withdrew from it a packet of magenta tissue paper. He unwrapped it to reveal a large, glittering yellow amethyst set in gold.

'The daughter should wear this next to her skin night and day. It will counteract the bad influences.'

'Everything irritates her skin,' remarked Sona gloomily.

Yashpal shook his head at her, took the stone, admired it, then wrapped it up reverently.

'I have good news,' continued Babaji. 'The boy and girl's horoscopes are perfectly matched. This girl will be good for the family, and even Nisha's future will open after her sister-in-law comes to the house.'

Yashpal fingered the envelope he had in his pocket. Babaji was taking so much trouble, he had slipped in a thousand and one rupees this time. It was not too high a price to pay if his children's futures could really follow the trajectory he predicted.

'Keep faith, it will be all right,' said Babaji, as he gracefully accepted the envelope.

Pooja Arora was in her second year of college when Sona, Sushila, and Rupa went to meet her.

A plump, fair girl with a burn mark that trailed across the side of her face before wandering along her neck. The mother had been at pains to explain the details of her plastic surgery – superficial, it had all been superficial, Pooja was otherwise in perfect health.

Much discussion among the three women followed this meeting.

She was short, just five feet, but what will our Raju do with a tall girl, he himself is only five feet five, said Sona, echoing Sushila's two-year-old remark about Rekha.

'We want a homely girl, one who will be a sister to Nisha,' pointed out Rupa. 'Pooja will not be in a position to give herself airs, despite her background.'

What does Pooja have to give herself airs with? thought Sona with satisfaction.

Sushila remarked that skin grafts cost a lot of money, but if necessary the family should consider them for Nisha.

This was going too far. 'Nisha's skin does not look anything like Pooja's,' said Rupa quickly, while Sushila replied equally quickly she did not mean it did, only that it was obvious there were other avenues to be explored.

Raju was allowed a glimpse of the girl, though his opinion was the least important. What did the boy know of life, that he should be allowed decisions?

The would-be husband claimed he did not like her – what was that thing on her neck and cheek? It was nothing, he was assured, in time he would not notice it; besides, she was an only daughter, and did he see how fair she was? How diffident, how shy and sweet her expression?

She was also buxom, and though this was not pointed out,

Raju noticed. A wife, he was going to get a wife like his cousins upstairs, they would not be able to treat him like a child any more.

Sweets announcing the engagement were sent out in specially designed long, deep, clear plastic boxes with Raju's and Pooja's names etched in red on the lid, beneath an embossed Ganesh. Inside, dividers in baby pink and blue separated almond and pista squares.

Since Fancy Furnishings had already married once into the Banwari Lal family, the strengthening of these ties gave everybody a quiet sense of satisfaction. It was to be the cloth wedding of the season.

The forlorn misery that was Nisha's burden increased with every step made in the direction of her brother's marriage. Had her parents not been so determined to reject Suresh, she could have been revelling in attention as the groom's only real sister, instead of feeling a source of apology and justification. She wished she could disappear into some hole till the wedding was over. But the hole did not exist that could conceal a daughter of the house on such an occasion. All she wanted was to be ignored, even as she was consulted daily about clothes and jewellery, involved relentlessly in every ritual performed, and assured constantly of her luck in getting a permanent companion in her brother's wife.

All around her was nothing but wedding: the family were breathing, eating, sleeping, visiting, buying, stitching, envying, calculating, spending in its atmosphere. Relatives started pouring in, and when the house was full, they were accommodated in nearby guest houses. Some were put up by Fancy Furnishings – after all, they were family too. This side, that side. The distinguishing line had blurred.

If the bile Nisha swallowed continuously amongst these people vented in poisonous barbs from time to time, her family reacted indulgently. In her condition it was natural she be upset, and here voices lowered, and by the end of the wedding, all family members not previously privy to the details of her life could now consider them well mastered.

Nisha's skin was breaking out again, and to make sure she looked her best, it was decided to resume the mudpack treatments. Under the soothing, cooling, heavy weight of the mud slathered over her body, she felt some of the tension pressed out of her. When Raju accompanied her, though, it was harder for this to happen.

'Tell me, Raju,' remarked Nisha, as brother and sister were waiting at the nature cure centre one morning, 'now you are getting married, you must be glad that you destroyed my happiness with Suresh. Your Fancy Furnishings wife will not be related to such a goonda, no – what was the word you used? Yes, saala, chutia.'

Silence.

'Or am I misremembering?'

'Don't be silly,' he said at last. 'I only did what Mummy Papaji wanted, which was to make sure you were not taken advantage of.'

'Even if I get such a disease, and become a pariah?'

'Have you gone mad? Mummy Papaji are spending so much on your clothes, your jewellery, and you are talking like this.'

Tears filled Nisha's eyes as she gazed unblinkingly at the receptionist crammed behind her small table in one corner of the room.

With a sigh Raju put his magazine down. 'Listen, I also don't like what is happening. I always thought I would marry after you; suddenly they tell me it's my turn, the family's welfare depends on me. What choice did I have?' demanded Raju, sounding injured.

Sullen silence.

'Besides, Babaji says after I marry your fate will improve.'

'How convenient,' managed Nisha. 'I am glad you are doing your duty.'

'I am. You think I like getting married to a burnt girl? But they don't listen, not to me or to you.'

She glanced at him out of the corner of her eye. He was clothed in his engagement finery. The foot he was tapping was shod in new black Bata slip-ons. The wrist that lay across his thigh was decorated with a sleek black and gold Citizen watch, Ray Ban sunglasses were tucked into his bush shirt pocket. He radiated newness, sparkle, and complacency.

The girl may be burnt, but he didn't seem to mind too much. Everything had gone right for him from the day he was born. What had he done to deserve his fate, what had she done to deserve hers? She felt restless and suffocated; she hated every doctor and vaid she had ever seen – when had they actually helped her? She only went so her parents could think they were doing something, though the time for doing something had long past.

She got up and stepped outside. She didn't care about her treatment. She didn't care about anything.

Raju pursued her. 'Why are you always doing drama?' he demanded, grabbing her arm. Nisha shrugged him off, and strode into the crowds.

The sidewalk was as usual jammed with pavement sellers, their goods displayed on tables or hung from boards. Towards the road side, wares were spread out on dirty pieces of cloth: underwear, vests, socks, plastic dolls, knives, second-hand textbooks, cheap novels, suitcases, bags, petticoats, blouses, rubber chappals, lottery tickets, pens, pencils, stationery, magazines, scooter helmets, and key chains. Standing next to these were vendors with their trolleys hawking fruit chaat, fried potato, lemonade, water, and paan.

By the time Raju caught up, Nisha was stepping around banana, potato, apple, and cucumber peels that overflowed from a little tin can at a fruit chaat wallah's feet. The pavement was so crowded that a hand snaking across breasts or thighs was inevitable. A man brushed past Nisha, stroking the cleavage in her buttocks, his eyes elsewhere. She cringed.

When Raju turned her around to go back, she went quietly.

The Banwari Lals had agreed to wait until the bride's second-year exams were over before pressing ahead with the wedding. Throughout this time Raju was fretful and quarrelsome, he wanted a say in all the arrangements, and he complained about everything. He was the bridegroom, and as such his status was undeniable, but no bridegroom had behaved so badly.

His mother sometimes wondered whether he really liked the girl. She dared not utter her thoughts to her husband, who from time to time accused her of spoiling the boy.

'What does he know of the hardships of life? He has not had to see his shop burnt at the age of seven, nor left his country on foot, walking for miles in fear of his life, nor done all the heavy housework because his mother was pregnant and in shock, nor put in long hours in the shop helping his father. He has not done all these things so he can behave as though his wishes are the only thing in the world.'

As usual, there could be no answer to this. Instead Sona asked her son, dreading the response, 'Beta, do you not like the girl? It is a question of your future happiness. Your parents will not do anything against your will.'

Raju snorted.

His mother repeated her question. 'Do you not like the girl?' By then five hundred invitations had been printed.

'Who said anything about the girl? I do not even know her.'

'But you only refused to go out with her. We offered.'

'Nice going out it would be with ten other people coming along and staring.'

'You are too-too shy. Vijay had no problem meeting Rekha.'

'Then such a big wedding,' pouted Raju, 'so much needless show. Five days! I feel like a monkey. Why can't all that money be put in the business?'

The mother thought there was no limit to her son's innocence. 'You are such a simple boy, Raju, you have been work-ing in the shop since school, and have no idea of the world. The bride's side is arranging everything, how can we inter-fere? And then we have only one son, why should he not be married properly?'

'Huh, it's too late to change anything now,' said Raju grumpily. Sona put out her hand to stroke away his irritation, but Raju shifted from her side.

As she watched him leave the room, Sona counted the things he was getting, more than Vijay, substantially more. Part of her trembled, it was too much, but the girl had a scar, and scars had to be paid for. Pooja was bringing quantities of cash, a car, a fridge, an air-conditioner, a TV, a Godrej cup-board, a double bed with a deluxe foam mattress, a dressing table, twenty-one sets of jewellery, countless watches, saris, suit pieces, frocks, and little pant-shirts for the women, men, and children, and a honeymoon in Europe, all expenses paid.

Would they have to do the same for Nisha?

Two weeks later, courtesy of Raju, another daughter-in-law, sister-in-law, cousin-in-law is added to the house. Throughout the wedding, the guests exclaim at the bride's beauty, radiance, and sweetness, and then continue the nar-rative over Raju's handsomeness, intelligence, and genius at business.

Three carloads escort Raju and Pooja to the airport. They arrive and swell the masses already there. Durries and blan-kets are spread under sleeping people seated against the wall, flanked by stacks of luggage. Some waiting women nurse their children, some brandish foreign-looking feeding bottles, some babies have equally foreign-looking pink plastic soothers attached to stiff yellow plastic necklaces dangling from their mouths. Crowds line the glass wall of the building, peering inside.

Family clusters elbow their way towards the entrance. The going abroad one is belched forth from their midst, accosted by the stern gate man, identity card swinging importantly from his chest, demanding to see the passenger's ticket. His relatives try and stay as close as they can, they are phlegmatically, wearily, indignantly, casually, and repeatedly held back.

As the Banwari Lal-Arora group push their way to the entrance, Pooja's sobbing becomes louder, and Raju's look more harassed. Everything marks them as newly wed: her bangles, her mehndi, her jewellery, her glittery clothes, her tears, his new suit and self-conscious air, besides all the pristine luggage.

After the couple vanish, Ajay quickly buys tickets for everybody to the visitors' section. The family hasten to the authorised side of the building and frantically wave to Raju and Pooja across the barrier. Pooja looks down, Raju smiles and nods. He has checked in, he is in charge. Confidently he leads his bride closer so she can gaze at her family. Pooja's father, a big, heavy man, on seeing his daughter tries to push past the guard. In his palm is a discreetly folded hundred-rupee note. The security man sees it, blocks his way, and acts morally outraged. Legitimate people pass, the inspection of tickets and boarding passes is elaborate. During a lull, complicated signals occur and two-hundred rupee notes exchange hands. Pooja and Raju dart across the barricade. Pooja's mother cries. Pooja cries while the guard gazes on imperviously. Finally, the announcement that all passengers for BA Flight 401 to London should proceed to security. Pooja and her mother cannot bear it. The tearing-away scenes are repeated. The couple leave once again.

'There, there they are, standing in line,' chorus the family. 'Now they are closer to the gate. Closer, closer, gone.'

Sona moves to comfort Pooja's mother – 'you have gained a son' – and everybody sombrely walks to the car park.

On his honeymoon, Raju phones home for three minutes once a week. He is having a wonderful time, wishes they were there.

The night the couple are to come back, rose petals are strewn over Raju's brand new double bed, and garlands of jasmine hung on the headboard and footboard.

The flight is to land at two-fifty a.m. Everybody gets ready to go to the airport.

'I want to stay at home,' pleaded Nisha.

'Don't be silly, what'll they think?'

'They won't notice.'

'Pooja will. Husband's own real sister. Everyone will feel you are not welcoming.'

Nisha is forced to go. She stands next to Vijay and Rekha on the balcony of the arrival section, her nose pressed, like Rekha's, to the glass stained and smudged with thousands of handprints.

'There, there,' shouts Rekha. 'Pooji, Pooji.'

The couple are too far away to hear. They are absorbed in each other, holding hands. Pooja has her head covered, her wedding bangles stand out in the crowd, as wedding bangles do.

'I'll tell Mummy Papaji I have seen them.' Rekha hurries down, leaving Ajay and Nisha at the glass.

'He's put on weight,' remarks Ajay.

'Has he?' replies Nisha, gazing down.

'I could have gone abroad for my wedding,' muses Ajay, 'but I didn't like to take so much from Rekha's parents. For what? Four weeks of wandering around. Time waste. Money waste.'

Nisha is thinking her own thoughts. What was the great difference between Pooja and her? She didn't even have a scar. She too could have been at some airport with her new husband, new luggage, gold sandals, gold jewellery, wedding bangles, and covered head. She too could have been the one eagerly awaited by a family after her honeymoon.

Her attention shifts to Raju's feet. He had gone in a suit, he has come back in keds and jeans. The feet in their new white running shoes move back and forth across the terminal, she could not make out why. But his steps seem purposeful; those feet belong to a man who has visited London, travelled across Europe, and come back replete with accounts of how strange, wonderful, advanced, clean, and peculiar everything was, how he had managed to figure out things impossible for a simple Indian from Karol Bagh. Pooja will listen and smile. It was there in their feet, one pair roaming, one pair still.

At last they emerged, pushing a trolley laden with heavy suit-cases, hand baggage, and duty-free. Frantic waving, here, look here, here, look, and the dazed, expectant look on Pooja and Raju's faces turns to recognition as they rush into the arms of their loved ones.

Pooja's mother breaks down when she sees how much less noticeable her daughter's scar is after four weeks of honey-moon. The heavy garland of roses that she has been holding for two hours is put around Raju's neck. He bends and touches her feet, while Pooja bobs down towards the feet of her in-laws. The cousins grab hold of the loaded trolley and all together they move out into the dusty, oppressive heat of Delhi.

Pooja

Early on it became clear that Pooja was made of sterner stuff than her cousin Rekha. Rekha had been the first in the family to go on a honeymoon, but only for a week and only to Simla. How much metamorphosis can a week at a local hill station effect compared to a month in Europe?

The bridal couple spent all their time in their unit, their desire to be alone shamelessly palpable. Home from the shop, Raju could barely be greeted, let alone fussed over, before he disappeared into the maw of his bedroom, shutting the door softly but oh so firmly behind him. After a while Pooja emerged to make tea. Only two solitary betraying mugs on a tray, ringed with little bowls of dry fruit, spicy mixture, and biscuits.

'Isn't my son feeling well?' Sona sometimes asked, her voice trembling.

'Of course he is well, Mummy,' soothed Pooja. 'He is just tired and wants to relax.' She hastened back, leaving the mother to wonder why he couldn't relax with everyone else, as he always had. Why did it have to be private and separate? A new wife could take away in weeks what had been theirs all their life.

Sometimes the mother, asserting her rights, knocked on the unwelcoming closed door and announced to her son, lounging on the bed with Pooja, that their house had a tradition of togetherness.

'Come, come, Mummy,' Raju would respond heartily and loudly, smoothing the rumpled covers. 'Sit, sit.'

Desultory conversation followed, before Sona, propelled by the unfamiliar, claustrophobic atmosphere of the room, got up to leave.

*

'She is not behaving like a daughter-in-law,' she complained to her son. 'She spends no time with the rest of the family, no time with your sister. Look at Rekha upstairs.'

'Pooja is right. You don't like her. Why did you marry me to her, then? Was I in such a hurry?' snapped Raju before returning to his lair, leaving Sona to tearfully narrate the conversation word for bitter word to Nisha and later Rupa. Her son had become the slave of his wife, and was bent on stabbing his mother in the heart.

'He is newly married,' said Rupa thoughtfully. 'They want to be together.'

'It is not only together, it is *alone* together,' burst out Sona, thinking of the other newly married couples in the family whose desires had been decently invisible. 'I thought a girl with such a scar would be humble, grateful, make efforts, but here she is thinking too-too much of herself, and making Raju think the same.'

'Don't you see, Didi, how much fuss her family makes over her?' pointed out Rupa. 'They have indulged her because of that accident. That is why she is so different from Rekha.'

'Why is it always my fate to get the worst of everything?' wailed Sona.

Rupa and Nisha could only be silent when confronted with the workings of fate. One had to accept what was given and the faster one did that, the less one suffered.

July came. Pooja's family had requested that she be allowed to finish her education and Sona's desire to see Pooja attend her classes was by now very strong.

'When is she going to college, beta?' she asked her son.

'She's not going,' replied Raju indifferently.

'Not going! Why? She has done two years of BA, might as well finish,' said Sona, expressing a hitherto hidden enthusiasm for education.

'She says since I did Correspondence, so can she. In fact, I had to force her to even agree to that much, otherwise she is not keen on finishing. I had to really force her,' repeated Raju with a secret, ruminative smile.

His mother's hands tingled with a desire to slap him. 'When did you decide this? And without consulting your elders?' she demanded.

Raju looked weary. 'Mummy, why do you always take everything so badly? She talked to her parents, she talked to me. Now she is married, it will be difficult for her to go to college, she has to be here till I leave for the shop at ten. Besides, why should she study? It is not as though she is going to need a degree, it is only time waste,' said Raju, exhibiting the maturity that marriage had given him.

And Sona had to live with further evidence of just how good a wife Pooja was determined to be.

Pinpricks grew into wounds and festered. Pooja asked Yashpal to subscribe to another newspaper. 'Please, Papaji,' she said winningly. Her mother-in-law was nowhere in sight.

'There is this one, beti,' said her father-in-law, rustling the paper he held.

'But Papaji, he doesn't get to read it in the morning, and he likes a paper with his tea. My father and uncle each had their own.'

It was a small thing, not worth making an issue of. Yashpal nodded. The next morning, along with *The Hindustan Times,* came a copy of *The Times of India,* which Pooja quickly grabbed.

'Now a separate newspaper,' mourned Sona.

'Why do you make so much out of a little thing?' demanded her husband. 'Over one newspaper you are creating tamasha.'

'Don't you see she is taking him away from me?'

'For years you have kept him by your side, so you are finding it strange, that is all.'

'I have a mother's heart.'

'I know, but now the boy is a husband. Let him be.'

But for Sona, letting Raju be was like letting go of life.

When he came out of his room in the morning, paper read, bathed, and ready to have breakfast, she would try and feed him, but there was Pooja armed with the things he liked already cooked by her maid, ready to serve him, hover over him, careful that no one else should do the things she had been married to do.

'Tell the maid to go back,' urged Rupa. 'She gives her too much free time. Send her back, then you can at least cook for Raju, she will help you, and you will both serve him, otherwise there will be endless tension. Pooja has to adjust to the ways of this house.'

Sona was quiet. Her samdhin had pleaded about this one thing, please let Pooji keep a maid, who of course will work under your guidance only. Since her accident her father has been fearful of the girl going near fire, he has never let her work in the kitchen. Swept away by the seeming modesty of the request, the lack of trouble to herself, and the deference paid to her, Sona had graciously agreed. Now the chickens were coming home to roost.

Sometimes a car from Pooja's mother's house would arrive to pick her up and Pooja would vanish for the day. Raju brought her back in the evening, driving the car he had been given in his dowry.

At times Sona would cry, and Raju would hover over her, distraught. 'Beta, you have forgotten you have a mother, a sister, a father, all for a wife of less than six months. For this I slaved day and night, for this I sacrificed everything?'

'Mummy, no, no. Tell me what I have done? Has Pooja done anything?'

It was too intangible. Sona could only cry, while Raju looked helpless, weak, and annoyed.

Sona found that Raju looked most uneasy when she talked about Nisha. She did not hesitate to sharpen such an effective weapon at least once a day.

'Stop talking about me to him,' said Nisha, whenever she heard her mother.

'You don't know the world,' said Sona, turning on her daughter angrily. 'After us, you are your brother and sister-in-law's responsibility. It is our duty to make sure this is understood.' Even Yashpal expected the newly married pair and his daughter to make a threesome.

'Take your sister,' he said to Raju whenever the couple were getting ready to go out.

Raju remained silent, and it was left to Pooja to say, 'Of course, Papaji. We will take her. She hardly goes anywhere, poor thing, she is so shy. I will introduce her to all my friends.'

'I refuse to go with them. They don't want me,' protested Nisha to her mother.

'Don't be silly. Otherwise you will be cooped up in the house all the time. You are still young, you need to go out.'

Nisha laughed cynically.

Sona took umbrage. 'It is their duty.'

'They are younger than me. It is not their duty.'

'You are too simple. That is the real trouble. Don't you remember how fond you two used to be of each other, how he never left your side when you were young? Now a wife has come, you think all that is going to change?'

'You sent me away, how can you blame her for wanting to do the same thing?' retorted Nisha.

Sona twisted her daughter's ear.

'What did you say?'

Nisha stared at her, frightened and defiant.

'Only the truth,' she said, despite the throbbing.

Sona twisted a bit more. 'It was such a sacrifice to send you, and all you can say is we wanted to get rid of you. Let your aunt come, and I will tell her how ungrateful you are.'

Nisha didn't want her mother to say anything to her aunt. 'I'm sorry, Mummy,' she murmured. Her mother let go. Ears are hard to hold on to, and this one was now very red.

'Really, it is a curse to have children – first you, then him, then him, then you,' lamented the mother.

In the silence that followed, Nisha's fingers wandered to her head and began to dig and scrape.

Her mother snatched her hand away. How many things could she deal with? 'Just when you are getting better, you start itching again. You have learnt nothing from your experiences, nothing. You know how black your skin gets when you itch, and still you go on and on, on and on, though thousand times I tell you not to. But no matter what happens, you never listen.'

For Nisha, hating Pooja was an all-absorbing occupation. There was no conflict in this emotion, no divided loyalty, no pain besides the pain of hatred.

No single thing accounted for the loathing she felt, but everything contributed. Each arrogant breath Pooja took, each possessive gesture she made towards her husband, added to the sore in Nisha's heart. All the evil in her nature is reflected in those burn marks, thought Nisha, staring in fascination at the puckered skin. She thinks she is something. She is not, she is ugly. Ugly. But this seemed apparent only to herself.

Pooja was a snake in the house – unfortunately, a legitimate snake. She slithered towards the family from the fastness of her bedroom with its brand-new double bed and matching teak-veneer side tables. From that site of marital bliss she crept, to sit next to Nisha, call her sister, and gingerly caress the scabbed, bruised arm, pierced through with cortisone injections.

Raju didn't take part in these exchanges. He didn't have to. The shashtras declare that wife and husband are one; therefore his glance is included in her gaze.

❧

It turned out that Raju was not interested in the soft furnishing plan his uncle had so casually sketched out to his brother as a reason for the boy's marrying. He knew nothing about furnishings, his interest was in cloth. He wanted to go into Bridal. This would unite everything they sold.

'There are so many cloth shops coming up in Karol Bagh, we need a USP,' he said. 'People spend during weddings. If we cater to all their needs, they will remember the convenience, spread the word, add to our good will.'

Everybody agreed they needed to expand. But Bridal or soft furnishings? Rent in Karol Bagh or move to South Delhi?

Raju thought Bridal would be best done from the existing shop. The advantage was that they could offer every single clothing item needed for a wedding under one roof. The younger men wanted to break by-laws and build another storey, as was the tradition in Karol Bagh. Pyare Lal and Yashpal remembered the dislocation and bribe money necessary for making their shop two-storeyed and were reluctant to construct. However, other stores in Karol Bagh were expanding illegally, and the fact that the money would be provided by Raju's dowry gave his vision an edge that could never be openly acknowledged lest it offend.

It took two months to make a room on top of the shop that ran its length. All the clothing one needed for a wedding was there: saris, lehngas, cholis, odhnis, kurtas, pyjamas, churidars, achkans, heavy and light, warm and cool, male and female. In addition were the presentation sets that needed to be gifted to everybody, from grandparents to servants, with prices to suit each requirement.

Alterations were attended to by a tailor, free of charge. Measuring tape around his neck, notebook in hand, he was ready to alter a hundred things if necessary, with the promise of next-day delivery, rain or shine, sickness or accident, births or deaths, festivals or celebrations – none of those excuses so dear to tailors outside the Banwari Lal Bridal Showroom.

Every bit of stress that arose over clothes during a wedding the shop promised to reduce, promised faithfully and sincerely.

The Banwari Lal & Sons Bridal Showroom was advertised in the newspapers, on billboards around Karol Bagh, on telephone poles, and on trees.

They had never been so aggressive.

Nisha minded all this intensely. Raju was being influenced by his wife, somebody in her family had done an MBA. The Banwari Lal approach to business had always been low key. Ever since she could remember her father had liked to silently rest when he came home, slurping his tea softly from his saucer, burping gently, rubbing the sole of his foot as it lay across his leg. Now business permeated all aspects of collective conversation. Raju, Ajay, and Vijay were all shop, talk, plans, USP. As they talked, Pooja smiled contentedly at the floor.

∼

Homebound, Nisha felt more part of her mother's life. When Rupa came, Nisha joined them on the bed as they lay down after lunch, food heavy in their stomachs, dark curtains drawn across the windows. Rupa put her arms around Nisha, lying in the middle half-dozing, half-listening to the plaintive whispers that floated about her.

'Of course Madam thinks she is too great to be with us.'

It had started. It continued.

'She treats the home as though it were a hotel. The minute Raju is gone, out she goes, to her parents, to her friends. Then she phones him at the shop to pick her up. Cleverly she tells him her whole family has cinema tickets, let's go, making sure that she doesn't have to take Nisha. After that they go to a restaurant, then they come home, late, late, sometimes eleven, twelve, doesn't matter if we are waiting. A thousand times I have told the boy the sister is your responsibility, you have to look after her, but she has so many ways to make him neglect his duty.'

'I don't want to go with Pooja's family, Mummy,' mumbled Nisha, half asleep.

'Arre, even if you did, are they taking you?' retorted Sona.

Here Rupa shook her head at her sister's innocence. 'Didi, the world has changed. What did you expect? No one cares for their in-laws any more.'

'But she is so shameless. If I say anything to her, anything to her at all – and you know, Roop, how I don't like to say anything to anybody . . .'

The aunt shook her head again. 'I know, Didi, that is just your problem. Another woman would have made her cry. Instead you give her all the freedom in the world.'

'The minute I say the slightest thing, she runs and complains to Raju. Arre, a daughter-in-law has to function in her married home, or no?'

'She is too spoilt. The accident has made her feel she can do anything she likes,' commented the aunt sagaciously.

'But does that mean she should turn him against me – me, his own mother, who gave him birth from this flesh and blood?' Sona beat her chest. 'Whose milk he drank for two years – two whole years?'

Nisha stared at her mother's heavy breasts, straining through their tight casing. Her whole chest was breast, soft, warm, attention-compelling, playing hide and seek through the thin covering sari and the low-necked blouse.

'I know, Didi,' said Rupa. 'Remember our Nisha used to also drink milk when Raju was nursing as a baby. You wanted to be a baby again, han?' and here she pinched Nisha's cheek.

So, thought Nisha, staring as her mother's sari finally slipped and lost the game, they had satisfied their hungers at the same time. Their salivas had probably mixed as their mouths closed over dark nipples, their hands touched as they stroked the soft, spongy fountains.

At one time so close, now she was the cast-off. He was married, his smooth, dark skin glowing, his wife's presence adding to its lustre. And she? She was diseased, tainted, ugly. Who would look at her, marry her, give her a home, and make her theirs? To think that at one time she had been compared to Suriya! The actress's star shone on, while there was nothing left for her except this bed, this mother, this aunt. Her mind felt slow and sluggish.

'Masi, can't I help you with your business?'

An idle question, which received an idle rejection. 'Arre, with your education what will you do with pickles, messing your hands with oil and chillies? Besides, it will aggravate your skin.'

True, it might, but she needed to do something. She couldn't bear living like this.

Her mother, unable to vary the familiar refrain, said, 'When you marry you can do anything your husband permits.'

Six o'clock one morning. Summer was leaving reluctantly as usual. Pyare Lal and Yashpal were returning from their walk, when Yashpal glimpsed his daughter drooping on the park bench outside their house. Her back was hunched, in her lap her dupatta was bundled over what he guessed were jasmine flowers from a nearby bush. He gestured to his brother to go inside, opened the park gate, and sat next to her. She looked at him, he could see the wet lashes, the damp face, the reddened rims of her eyes.

He stroked her back. 'What are you doing here?'

'I wanted to be by myself.'

This alarmed him. 'Why? Has anyone said anything?'

'No. Like that only. I wanted to be alone.'

Yashpal did not know what to make of this. She showed him her hoard. 'I couldn't sleep, so I came out before the other women had a chance to strip the bush.'

He absently lifted one of the small white flowers to his nose when she slapped his hand. 'For puja, Papaji, you can't dirty it by smelling.'

'Surely you can spare one from your prayers?' he tried to joke.

A small smile. 'All right, Papaji, just one, for you.'

'Why couldn't you sleep?'

She looked away. 'Just like that.'

He stroked her back again.

She hesitated, knowing how hard her father took things, but they were alone and the hand on her back was persuasive. 'I don't know why, but sometimes I feel I will go mad sitting inside the house.'

The father's own heart grew heavy. This was exactly what he had been afraid of, a younger sister-in-law would make his daughter feel bad. According to Babaji it would be a while before the girl married.

'If only you could take me with you, Papaji,' she pleaded in a rush. 'I have seen girls working in shops. Why should it be only Ajay, Vijay and Raju? There must be something I too can do.'

Yashpal had no ready reply. Retailing was strictly men's business, talking to strangers, cajoling customers, showing them wares, negotiating with buyers, travelling – where would Nisha fit in? She was right, there were shops selling readymade in Karol Bagh that employed girls in the ladies' section, but how could the daughter of the owner stand along with them for eight long hours?

'Let me see, beti, let me think,' he said, as he pulled her by the hand to take her into the house.

All day he thought of her problem. In this matter he saw no point in consulting anybody. His brother would be neither tender nor empathetic. His wife would bemoan her fate. Rupa could only think of pickles, Sushila would suggest sewing and knitting as suitable to her condition. Perhaps when Raju had a child, her thwarted maternal longings would be able to find expression, but there might be a struggle with the mother.

What could a girl do? She wanted to leave the house, she needed a time pass that would be pleasant and easy in a place where no undesirable elements could take advantage of her.

As he was staring at the street outside, the doorman let in a neighbour, acquaintance, customer, the Principal and owner of Play-Way, two streets down from their house. With her was her daughter. Beaming, they hurried up to greet him.

'She is getting married,' announced the Principal. 'In a few weeks we will come to your house with the wedding invitations. In the meantime, we thought for Bridal this is the best place?'

'This is your shop,' said Yashpal, recognising the question as a plea for discounts. He picked up the interconnecting phone. 'Raju will look after you' – i.e. the discounts would be taken care of.

The Play-way Principal smiled.

Yashpal asked when the marriage would take place, the Principal said soon, in fact this was her daughter's last day of work. Yashpal said he didn't know beti was working; oh yes, replied the Principal, she was one of Play-Way's best teachers, the little ones were really going to miss her.

Fifteen minutes later Nisha's immediate future was decided. She would take the daughter's place at school. Every way Yashpal looked at it, this solution to Nisha's problems seemed ideal. The hours would not be long, the work undemanding. The girl was fond of children (like every girl). True, the pay was negligible (but she was not working for money and there would be neither expense nor time involved in transport). The nursery school was a five-minute walk away, and a benevolent eye would be kept on Nisha. The Principal was a neighbour, which counted for much in the give and take of life.

Yashpal discussed the matter with his family that night. 'It will be a good time pass,' he said anxiously, looking at his daughter's face.

'I do not want to be a teacher,' said Nisha sullenly. She had imagined a more exciting outside job. She knew the school her father was talking of, next lane but one, a house with a board saying Play-Way plastered on the second-storey balcony. A few desultory slides, swings, and jungle gyms were crammed together on the concrete behind the front gate. Every morning and noon, the number of rickshaws outside the place marked it as a well-attended nursery.

Yashpal tried to point out the advantages. 'Beti, it is right here. If you do not like it you can leave, but while we are doing treatment for your skin, you need to occupy yourself. Sitting at home is not good, you yourself feel.'

When she married she could leave her job, reassured Sona, which of course was understood by everybody.

'You can start next week,' went on Yashpal gently, 'the Monday after karva chauth. The Principal is a very nice, motherly lady, you will have no difficulty, give it a try, nobody is forcing you, but . . .'

It was difficult for him to go on. The women of the house had never worked. Not one. And here he was sending his beloved daughter out into the world because she did not have her own home to occupy herself with. His face crumpled.

Alarmed, Nisha quickly comforted him. 'Papaji, I will do whatever you want me to.'

'It's just a time pass, beti, just a time pass.'

'Yes, Papaji, I understand.'

❧

October 25 was Pooja's first karva chauth as a married woman.

'Now don't give her anything very fancy. Time enough for that later on,' advised Rupa.

'My Raju's wife,' said Sona, her eyes filling with tears. 'I have to give. A mother's feelings will always be the same, no matter what her child does.'

'Am I saying don't give? I'm just saying don't give too much. I know you. Left to yourself, you will part with the whole house.'

'I only hope she appreciates it.' Here tears began to fall.

'Please, Mummy, don't be like this,' said Nisha, throwing her arms around her mother's neck. 'You can take my jewellery. I don't want it.'

'Listen to your niece,' said Sona to Rupa. 'I wish everybody had a heart like hers.'

'Yes, yes. Now show what you are going to give.'

Sona got up heavily from her bed, and went to the cupboard in the corner of the room. Fiddling with the key ring at her waist, she selected the long steel Godrej key, and unlocking the doors pulled them forcefully as they shuddered away from their stuck position.

She delved beneath a pile of silk saris, took out a key knotted in one of Yashpal's handkerchiefs, and unlocked one of the two steel drawers inside. Stretching her hand to the very back, she extracted a little tin box and returned to the bed, sighing and looking sad, while Nisha and Rupa watched in silence. She gazed inside the tin for a long time, then picked out two heavy gold kadhas in an old-fashioned lattice design, set with precious stones.

'Didi, one of your wedding pairs!' exclaimed her sister.

'I know,' said Sona.

Sona's melancholy submerged the three as they held the bangles, turning them over, admiring the traditional workmanship and the fine settings of the gems.

On the evening of the karva chauth fast, Pooja wore her bridal lehnga with a gold tissue odhni covering her head. A large pearl and ruby nose ring replaced her everyday stud, and was attached to her hair by a gold chain to help support the weight. Her face was flushed red and pink with make-up.

Mehndi patterns darkened her hands, green and red glass bangles, bought by Sona, tinkled on her arms. At the beginning of each row were the thick gold kadhas her mother-in-law had presented to her.

With all the coverings her scar was invisible. Nisha felt like pulling her odhni off, shining a torch on the burnt, corrugated skin, so everybody could see its ugliness, pathetically highlighted by foundation and bridal wear.

She could feel Pooja's glance on her as they took turns bathing the little god figure in milk. She, in her turn, would be thinking she was repulsive, and she would be right. Now at least her mother should excuse her from this fast. It hadn't got her a husband, had it? Her younger brother had married before her, that is what it had got her.

When Nisha knew Suresh, the hitherto mindlessly done fast had acquired meaning. She offered him her karva chauth hunger, her discipline through the day, her prayers as she looked at the rising moon. The redness of her mehndi was a source of anxiety – was it dark enough, would her mother-in-law love her?

Now nothing made sense. Mechanically she tied eight grains of wheat in her dupatta, and listened to her mother tell the ancient story. She would begin work the following day. Her job would be the object of devotion rather than a husband.

Next morning at eight Nisha and her father walked down the two and a half lanes to Play-Way, skirting small piles of garbage on the way. Her father had brought her two new suits, one to wear on karva chauth, and one to wear on the first day of school. Yesterday she had worn the peach, today it was the turn of the lavender. The soft mul-mul flapped down the length of her arms, concealing the discoloured skin.

'I have never taught, Papaji,' remarked Nisha. 'I don't know if I can do it.'

'Principal Madam will tell you what to do, beti. They are

only small little babies and it is just for four hours. You teach them some alphabet, tell them stories, let them draw. Anyone can do this.'

The school had sixty children aged two to four; two classes, Lower Nursery, Upper Nursery, with two sections each, spanning a six-month age difference. 'At this stage even six months is very important,' explained the Principal, as they sat in her office, agreeing with everything she said.

Nisha was given the three-year-olds; being used to school, they wouldn't cry. In addition to teaching letters and numbers (it was more or less as her father had said), she had to make sure they made it to the bathroom in time, ate their tiffins, and didn't fight. In the break she stood outside and made sure nobody's fingers got pinched under the rockers, nobody fell off the slide or jungle gym, and everybody got a turn.

As the weeks progressed, Nisha found teaching gave structure to her days, the same structure that school and college had given. Although, contrary to her father's expectations, she found the four hours spent with pre-schoolers monotonous, she experienced the pleasure of being with colleagues who didn't know her problems. They didn't know she had once been as beautiful as Suriya, they didn't consider her old or unfortunate, they had no knowledge of her mangli status, and their interest in her marriage was purely academic.

In fact they found her young and charming, petted her, spoilt her, and treated her like the baby amongst them. When she complained about the students she had to tutor in the rudiments of ABC so they would pass school entrance exams, they were united in supposing her job a stop-gap measure till better things came along.

Infants

The marriage was seven months old when Raju came home
from the shop, stood at the kitchen door, and announced that
Pooja was pregnant.

Sona looked up from the floor where she was slicing green
chillies and potatoes, her sari palla disarrayed, her breasts
squashed and protruding against her knees, hair slipping
from a loosely tied knot.

Nisha was boiling a milky water mixture for tea. A baby,
there was going to be a baby in the house. She felt so angry and
upset she could barely see – other people could go on with
their lives, having babies, while all she could do was teach the
children they produced. When was her life going to begin?

'How long?' demanded the mother.

'Two months.'

'Two months and you kept it a secret? I thought so – I
thought so – she has that look on her face, and she has been
picking at her food . . .'

'We wanted to be sure, Mummy. She thought you might
mind if we did not tell you at once, but I said no, you would-
n't –'

'She thought, you thought – Uff, when did you find out?
Are you sure?' At this moment she could waste no time on
offence.

Raju smiled. 'Yes, Mummy, very sure. Today the report
came.'

'Does her mother know?'

So quickly it was clear the answer was planned, Raju said,
'Of course not. You are the first to know.'

Sona was silent for a minute. 'Beta, Pooja is very lucky. For
you I had to sacrifice ten years –'

'I know, Mummy, I know,' interrupted Raju impatiently.

Sona's lip trembled. 'I hope you never experience the pain of having a son rebuff you the minute he is married.'

'I think you should show a little consideration for Mummy,' put in Nisha.

Sona turned to scold her daughter. 'Let it be, Nisha, what do any of us matter?'

Raju left without another word.

In the following months, the fuss around the mother-to-be increased, as Pooja developed health problems. She bled, there was fear she might miscarry. She needed special care, special treatment, special love, and complete bed rest for three months. Raju, in the time-honoured tradition of the family, left the care of his wife completely to his mother. For Sona the future lay in that belly, and the desire in her eyes was blatant as she looked at Pooja. Pooja, feeling sick, weak, and frightened, looked needily back. For three months Sona did not leave her daughter-in-law's side. Pooja's mother, who visited every day, loudly praised the care her daughter was receiving. In the evening the whole family drank their tea around the pregnant woman's bed so that she would not feel needlessly excluded from family life.

Pooja was seven months pregnant before the doctor declared the baby safely anchored inside her body. Gentle exercise, pleasant surroundings, and a relaxed mind were now recommended.

'Yes, she must go out with Raju,' said Yashpal. 'This daughter-in-law of mine needs to look happier. I want to see her smile.'

Raju was sent home early to take Pooja out. It was late February – the weather still pleasant, and in all the public gardens flowers were blooming. Lodi Gardens, Budh Jayanti Park, India Gate, Nehru Park, Children's Park, Humayun's Tomb were places where couples could roam about holding hands, murmuring softly to each other.

Yashpal showed himself unaware of this aspect when he urged his daughter to accompany them. 'You also need to get out in the open air.'

To Raju, 'Take your sister.'

Pooja reacts badly to this suggestion, but she cannot contradict her father-in-law. She wants to be alone with her husband, she wants to thicken his slightly diluted attention to previous consistencies. The car is rife with tension.

Raju drives with one hand so that he can hold Pooja's hand with the other. Nisha in the back seat is not considered senior enough to warrant the restraint of passion.

'How are you feeling?' asks Nisha. Whatever the exchange, her colleagues tomorrow are going to be privy to it. They know all about wicked sisters-in-law, they will contribute their own stories. Nisha will feel she is not alone in a world peopled by relatives of dubious value.

'All right.'

'What does the doctor say?'

'Mummyji knows.'

'Tell her,' said Raju. 'She is going to be a bua soon.'

'I'm tired. You tell her.'

Nisha is not enlightened.

'Why don't you go along the next time Pooja goes to the doctor?' suggests Raju instead.

Nisha refuses to reply. She stares moodily out of the window of the car, the car Raju got in his dowry, the car that allows Pooja to act so possessively.

They are going to India Gate. The lawns are crowded, and they stroll at a leisurely pace next to sluggish pond waters. The sun sets splendidly behind Rashtrapati Bhavan, and they end their walk at an ice-cream vendor's.

' Nisha, have?' asks Raju, after Pooja has been served.

'No, I don't want.'

'Take, take,' urged Raju. 'I know you like choc-bar.' He

turns towards the vendor, while Pooja looks on with cold, cold eyes, and a mouth that twists upwards; Pooja-smile.

'No, no, really,' protests Nisha gratefully.

'Why are you forcing the poor thing? Let her be, if she doesn't want it,' comments Pooja sweetly, jabbing at her own pink and green nutty, creamy slice of ice-cream with a thin wooden spoon.

'Do you want a cassata like hers?'

'No, no, it's all right. You two go ahead.'

'Nisha, please, how can we have, and you not?'

'I'm sure it is not difficult,' says Nisha, the devil inside her totally out of control.

'To please me.'

'Arre, she doesn't want it. Why are you insisting?' snaps Pooja.

'She does want it.' He tilts Nisha's face, puts the melting bar against her lips. Sticky white syrup drips down the stick. Nisha opens her mouth. Pooja goes and sits in the car.

That evening sounds of crying came from the bedroom. 'She's tired and needs to rest,' said Raju by way of explanation as he ate dinner without his wife.

'What is all this tamasha?' said Sona. 'She must eat, or the baby will suffer. Doesn't your wife have any sense?'

'Mummy, let it be,' said Raju impatiently. 'You don't have to fuss so much.'

Sona didn't know whether to be pleased because of the criticism, or distressed because of the baby.

Raju finished, got up, took some food on a plate to the room.

'What happened?' Sona asked her daughter.

'Raju bought me an ice-cream,' said Nisha meaningfully, preparing herself for a satisfying conversation.

'Some women become like this when they are pregnant,' remarked Sona carefully. 'And your father wants peace in the house.'

'My daughter and daughter-in-law have to learn to live together,' said Yashpal. Around him conflict usually became subterranean.

'Why send me with them if a little thing is so important?' was all Nisha said. She felt betrayed. Her mother was not on her side any longer. Pooja could do anything, Raju could do anything, and she would find excuses, all for the love of her son and his baby.

The next day Pooja went to her mother's house. In the evening Raju went to get his pregnant wife back. His mother had already warned him that in pregnancy women get very moody. Pooja cried when she saw him, she was sorry she had left the way she did, she didn't want to upset Mummyji more by her tears so the best thing was to leave. She was very sorry, what must they think of her at home, but she felt unwell all the time, she couldn't bear it.

Yes, yes, said the harassed Raju, now could they go back?

Pooja twined her arms seductively around his neck, and pressed her belly firmly against his crotch. There is no escape from that belly: its contents and its owner are irrevocably his. There is no escape, and perhaps, as he felt her soft, full body clinging to him, he did not want one.

Nisha had helped her mother by hating Pooja, but now her mother had acquired an interest in the girl from which she was excluded. After the baby's birth, she supposed there would be another battle of possession, claim, and counter-claim, though even that state would not last – neither the hate nor the love was permanent. Where did that leave her? She couldn't build a life with these brittle materials. She had the school from eight-thirty to twelve-thirty, another flimsy thing. She wanted something more, more, more. The men were occupied from morning to night. She needed an equally absorbing occupation. There must be other things in the world.

*

Meanwhile, on the pregnancy front it is time for the godh bharaiye. Presents for the unborn child, presents for the new mother. The pundit hired for the occasion droned on, while Pooja sat before gods arranged on a fresh white sheet on the floor. Her belly is prominent, the puja ends with the thick folds of a new Banarsi sari draped around her shoulders. Then family lunch, which Pooja cannot attend, no, no, you lie down, lie down, you will be tired, and Nisha, take this food to her, so she can rest and eat at the same time. Go quickly, Pooja's mother is watching.

'Let her watch.'

'Do you want a tight slap?'

Nisha went.

~

Six weeks later a baby girl is born. But Pooja's karma is so good that even this did not dull her lustre: never mind, there are many years ahead, the boy to come will have a sister. And thank God she isn't a mangli. Sona promptly tied black threads around the baby's wrist and ankle, and every day put a black kaajal mark on her forehead. With so much black no evil eye would dare light on the little creature.

The letter taken out for the baby's name was 'sh'. Pooja favoured Shuchi, and coaxed the family into agreeing.

At the naming ceremony one section of the drawing room was used to display the presents, the bulk of them from Pooja's family. There were embroidered sheets and pillow-cases in pastels, soft toys, imported musical mobiles, feeding bottles, sterilising kits, a fancy foreign stroller, fancy baby carry bags, silk saris for the new mother, the new grand-mother, the new aunt, any number of baby frocks, sweaters, and underclothes. A glowing Pooja and the baby sat in front of the pundit during the long puja in the shamiana erected in the park, while the guests ate, drank, and commented on the presents, the fair skin of the new-born, and whether she most resembled Nisha as a baby (Sona's claim, backed by photographs) or Pooja (her mother's claim, also backed by photographs).

Nisha was fascinated by the baby, but since it was Pooja's, she was reticent with her affection. On weekends she watched from a distance as her mother oiled her in the sun in the veranda, while Pooja sat near by. Up and down Sona gently massaged the little limbs, bunching them then letting go, to the baby's laughter. One such occasion Nisha stretched out her hand to stroke the fine, soft, black hair. The infant's head turned towards her touch, she looked at her aunt, and opened her mouth. Nisha's heart tightened. She reached out to dip her fingers in the oil.

'I think the water is now ready, Mummy,' said Pooja at that very moment, wrapping Shuchi hastily in her towel with the attached cape. As she got up, the strings of the charpai sagged, the bowl overturned, and the remaining oil spread slowly, dripping yellow and viscous through the rope mesh on to the floor.

'Don't worry, Mummy, I'll send the ayah to clean it,' said Pooja.

Nisha stared at the retreating back, the baby's face small, white, and bobbing, the little round eyes staring over her mother's shoulder.

A few such incidents and it was apparent Pooja did not want Nisha to touch the baby.

She confronted her mother one weekend morning when her aunt was there. 'Is this true or not?'

'Try and understand. Young mothers have all kinds of fears.'

'Now I am an untouchable?'

'For you everything is drama,' snapped the mother.

'The doctor says her condition is not contagious,' observed Rupa.

'I know, but you know how new mothers are.'

'She is the child's own real aunt, in the very same house. This should not be allowed to happen.'

'Let the baby get a little older,' justified Sona. 'The girl had so many problems when she was pregnant, she is very protective.'

'Still, this is not the way to behave. You also had difficulties, you were not like this.'

Nisha could have enlightened her aunt as to Pooja's Divide and Rule policy, could have described the subtle discrimination continually exercised between herself and her mother, but she chose to cry instead. It was easier, and she could not be blamed for anything she said.

'Arre, what is this?' The aunt stroked her niece's arm, gently rubbing her hand up and down the dry skin.

'Why are you touching me? You may get infected,' hiccupped the niece.

Silence fell as Pooja appeared. 'Here, Mummy, I have to get her bottle,' she said, putting the bright-eyed bundle on to the grandmother's lap. 'I sent the ayah to buy oranges, and she is taking two hours. Never here when you want her.'

'Why does she have another ayah with so many women to help?' demanded Rupa behind Pooja's back.

'That girl needs a servant with every step she takes. Besides, this ayah massages my feet and presses my back when it hurts,' said Sona indulgently, also disappearing towards the kitchen.

'You see, Masi,' said Nisha the minute her mother was out of earshot, 'there is no place for me in this house. If it is only marriage that will get me out, then marry me off to anybody, I don't care.'

'Arre, Nishu, is this any way to talk?'

'Which prince are they waiting for? Or have I to remain here for ever?' cried Nisha. Her aunt's presence made her want to scream, shout, pull her hair, and enact the drama her mother was always disapproving of.

'Don't attract evil by speaking so badly about your future,' coaxed the aunt.

'I am fed up, Masi. I will go to an ashram and devote myself to homeless widows.'

Her aunt looked astonished. The poor girl had lost her mind.

'Don't think I am just talking. I can't stay here. Every time I see Pooja, I feel like itching. You want me to spend my whole life tearing my skin to pieces?'

'Beti, for this reason only your father made you get a job.'

'That is only four hours. What about the other twenty? Should I kill myself and make everybody happy? I am telling you, I refuse to stay here like this.'

The aunt made soothing noises, and Nisha knew her message would soon reach the whole family. She judged it would take till evening.

Dinner over, Yashpal approached his daughter. Usually after eating they all watched TV, even more mesmerising since the advent of Star. But Nisha, sequestered in the tiny veranda, refused to be part of that night's ritual.

'Why aren't you with the others?' he asked.

'I don't feel like.'

Her father sighed. Nisha looked down. From the light of the drawing room she could see his broad, brown feet in chappals.

'What is it you want, beti?' he asked.

'I want to leave this house. There is nothing for me here.'

'You know that is not possible till you marry.'

'Why? I can go to an ashram. At least there I can live with dignity and respect.'

Both of them knew Nisha was talking rubbish. There was no question of such an option, exercised by the helpless, abandoned, and destitute, yet ashrams had to be mentioned. They were her state of mind.

The father was silent. Then, 'Would you like to study further?'

Nisha fiddled with her chunni. That her father was inviting

her to study shocked her. She had not expected such hope-lessness about her future.

'No,' she replied slowly, 'I do not want to study, what has it ever got me?' Only Suresh, betrayal, pain to her family and herself.

'Are you not happy in Play-Way?'

'Papaji, I get bored looking after babies. Is this my life?'

Her father sighed again, and Nisha's heart went out to him. She didn't want to make her father unhappy, she wished she could be the daughter he deserved. 'Just send me away, Papaji,' she said again. If he could not see her, he would not grieve over her.

By now Yashpal was irritated. 'Beti, I do not want to hear these words from you again. This is your home, why are you talking as though you are an orphan?'

She had gone too far, now he was angry with her. 'Sorry, Papaji,' she murmured.

'Now come,' he went on. 'Without you it is not the same. They are watching a film. You also watch.'

Silently she went inside and for a few hours they could pretend she was part of a happy family, watching a film together.

That night a maniacal bout of itching overtook her.

'Doctor Sa'ab will be thinking there is something wrong in our house, that this goes on happening to you,' said her mother with annoyance, as she phoned the doctor for an emergency appointment the next morning.

'I don't want to go.'

'No this, and no that, do I ever hear anything else from you?' shouted Sona angrily. 'Now get ready. I will tell Raju to take us.' Though his soul belonged to his wife, his body had its duties to perform.

'Eruptions such as these can be due to stress,' the doctor said delicately after examining her.

Brusquely Raju said, 'There is no stress in our house, doctor.'

283

'Well, this has happened several times. She seems to be improving, and then she has a relapse. Injections only provide local cure. In eczema especially, mind is reflected in body.'

'Once she is married, it will be all right, doctor,' Sona burst out, the doctor's words heading towards the sore places in her heart like arrows. 'But since her sister-in-law is younger than her, she feels tense.'

Nisha looked indignant, Raju annoyed, embarrassed, and proud. His fate was markedly different from his sister's. He was the holder of house, goods, wife, and child. All on the right track.

Continued the mother of the daughter on the wrong track, 'Doctor, only you can help us with her skin. At home there is nothing wrong.'

It was the teachers' break at Play-Way. The children were resting from the exertions of the concrete playground, colouring objects that matched the alphabet in their books. Ayahs squatting against the wall kept a languid eye on them.

As they sipped their tea, one of the older teachers drew out several suits wrapped in polythene packets and distributed them. 'My sister is making,' she explained. 'See if you like.'

The others looked eager – shopping on school premises was a welcome variation in the routine.

'She makes from home,' continued Mrs Tyagi. 'She can make on order also.'

Nisha drew her suit out curiously. It was lime-green with yellow flowers embroidered down the front; similar flowers were scattered on the chunni. 'That one would look really nice on you,' enthused Mrs Tyagi.

It might look nice but it also represented half her month's salary.

'Yes,' chorused the others, 'it really would.'

'My father gets my suits from his shop,' said Nisha shyly.

'Arre, you can buy one on your own, now you are earning,'

declared Mrs Tyagi. 'She is giving at a really low price. If you buy this in the shops, you will have to pay double.'

Nisha had no idea what suits cost in the open market, never having bought one. She fingered the cloth. A synthetic mix. She looked at the flowers. Only one colour.

'Three hundred and fifty?' she queried, looking at the tag.

'For you, three hundred.'

Nisha absentmindedly fingered the suit, while disapproving of the single-colour embroidery. How much would it have cost to make? She started calculating, but there was too much she didn't know. And then her thoughts slipped from their grooves, and in an instant she saw herself the maker and seller of suits. She had the background, she had the resources, it would be far more satisfying than teaching nursery children.

Mrs Tyagi broke into her visions of the future. 'It will look very nice on you.'

'That it will,' added another.

They were all expecting her to buy. She was the daughter of a shopkeeper, she wasn't working for money, it seemed her moral duty.

'I have no money on me,' she temporised.

'Arre, that can always come later,' said Mrs Tyagi genially, wrapping up the lime-green suit in its packaging. 'My sister will be very pleased. I have told her what nice clothes you wear. If Nisha buys, I told her, then you know your suits are good.'

The other teachers relaxed. Once one suit was purchased, the pressure on them to buy was reduced.

Nisha thought of how much of her month's salary she had spent on a suit she didn't really like. She would give it to Pooja. Her mother would say, look what Nisha has bought for you, Pooji, and Pooja would simper and smile, used to the fact that everything in the house revolved around her and her baby.

That evening, in front of everybody, she handed the wrapped suit to Pooja: 'I bought it just for you, I thought the colour would suit very nicely.' Pooja took it and smiled, Sona smiled, Nisha smiled, while the men looked approving.

As she waited for an appropriate moment to speak to her father, words reiterated by her mother through childhood emerged from her subconscious. If it weren't for your father's contacts, I'd like to see your aunt do business; your father does so much to help her, she has no idea; where would your aunt be without your father; all these years, and still your father looks after her sales.

Well, she had her father too.

She waited till he had his tea, waited while he played with Shuchi, waited till dinner was over, and then called him out on to the balcony. 'I want to say something to you.'

She pulled the white plastic chairs close together, drew a breath and started. 'I want to do business, papa.'

This was not what he had expected.

'Like Rupa Masi,' she added, to make the picture in her mind match his.

'What do you want to do?'

'I want to make salwar suits.' And then in a rush came the whole story of this morning, the lime-green suit, the price, the material, the single-colour embroidery. 'I know I can do a better job, please, Papaji, please, if you could help Rupa Masi why can't you help me?'

'Rupa Masi does not have children,' said the father miserably.

'Neither do I.'

Yashpal wondered at the bends in the trajectory of his daughter's life. She sat in front of him, hands clasped, eyes alive and begging. It was possible, of course it was possible, they commissioned suits from just the kind of set-up Nisha was describing. But for his daughter to go into business herself? He shook his head.

'Pleeeeease, Papaji,' breathed Nisha, 'I'll do anything you say, please, please. If it doesn't succeed I will go back to teaching, I promise. Only give me a year.'

'A year? What are you talking? You will need at least two to establish yourself. In business you do not succeed just like that, you have to work, work, all the time, all the time,' he repeated, to convey the gravity and weightiness of business.

'Give me a chance to show you what I can do.'

The last time he had heard that note in her voice it had been about marrying Suresh. Now it was here again, and this time circumstances were such that he could listen. If she wanted to work hard all day, instead of sitting around comfortably in the house, there must be imperatives compelling her.

'Beti, let me think. I will discuss it with your uncle.'

'Papaji, if you are with me, he won't say no,' insisted Nisha. 'I want to do something of value. It will make it so much easier to . . . to . . .' Here she stopped, and looked mutely at him.

'I understand, beti, now let us go inside.'

She heard a weakening he was not yet willing to verbalise. She hugged him, and murmured in his ear, 'Thank you, Papaji.' He held her close for a moment, tilted her chin up. 'No more sadness, all right?'

'All right.'

That night thoughts pumped around Nisha's head, keeping her awake as they had so many nights, but these were thoughts with a difference. She thought of her uncle Prem Nath's contempt for traders, and the effort he had poured into her study. But shopkeepers thrived. Look at Pooja, she was what she was because she was the daughter of a shopkeeper. Despite her scar she had confidence. Even now her features were prettier than Pooja's, but it was her sister-in-law who was made much of.

She would be better than Pooja. She would not only be the daughter of a prosperous man, but be responsible for wealth herself. After all, her father's blood flowed in her, the blood of traders.

She poured her ideas into her aunt's ears the very next day.

She was going to follow in her footsteps, she needed her encouragement, her blessings, her advice.

Her aunt listened and gave no indication of the tears in her heart. Her poor, poor Nisha, forced to hew her own path in life. What kind of karma had the girl come with?

'So, Masi, what do you think?'

Rupa dried her metaphorical tears and examined her niece, looking more alive than since the Suresh days. Doesn't matter if the girl's idea had been thought of by every other house-wife over the past seven or eight years. If her pickle making could do well, then smart, intelligent, well-connected Nisha would be even more successful. She would no longer be the poor unmarried sister, not allowed to touch the baby. Indeed, she would have no time to touch this baby or any others that might come.

'What does your mother say?' she asked.

Nisha tossed her head. 'These things I decide with Papaji.'

In which case it took Rupa only a second (berating herself for being a fool) to know exactly what approach to take, and the rest of the visit was filled with making plans and suggesting ways around practical difficulties.

Yashpal too had spent much time thinking. Nisha would need a place to work from, and the only place he could think of was the basement, owned by the builder and leased to Goodlass Nerolac for storage purposes. He would have to persuade the builder to rent it to them; he would have to talk to Pyare Lal and put him in the know, otherwise objections might come from upstairs. In house matters, touchiness was the order of the day.

Pyare Lal was moved enough by the whole Nisha issue to be all reassurance. 'Bhai, where it is a question of our daugh-ter, why do you worry? It will all be all right. I will talk to the builder, he will understand.'

To his brother's relief, he became so emotional about this matter that, against his lifelong practice of never paying a single penny more than was necessary, he persuaded the builder relative to find the Goodlass Nerolac people another basement, and to arrange for them to leave before the lease was out. He even paid for the removal of the paint drums. 'She is our daughter,' he told Yashpal, when the latter remonstrated, 'this much I can do.' Thus the men settled it between themselves; for the women, more discussion was in order.

Businesswoman

Sona was not pleased at this new development in Nisha's life. 'She is going to get married, why waste time and money in all this?' A business was not like teaching, resignable when the bridegroom reached the door.

Nisha could not forgive her mother for this statement. Pooja, busy with the baby, her kingdom unthreatened, said, 'Mummyji, it is a good thing Nisha has something substantial to do. I always said she was wasted in Play-Way.'

Sushila Chachi upstairs was censorious. Why was Nisha being allowed to do business? If tomorrow her daughters-in-law upped and said they wanted to do the same, what face would she have to refuse? And what about the money? Would what she earned be her own, or go back to the family, as in the case of the sons? Had these things been thought about? Years ago, when Asha wanted to hire tailors for just such an enterprise, she had not been allowed. Was the family forgetting its values?

This criticism was conveyed indirectly, leaving Sona seething with rage, and forcing her to change her stand. She got so angry that Pooja had the pleasure of mediating, imploring Rekha to make her mother-in-law more understanding towards the plight of an unmarried daughter.

Nisha didn't care what people said or thought. She watched Goodlass Nerolac take tempo loads of their paint drums away, as her uncle supervised. He was doing this for her, and in a rush of gratitude she vowed never again to be a burden on her family.

The last tempo gone, she descended into the depths of the house with her uncle, father, brother, mother, aunt, Pooja,

Rekha, Ajay, and Vijay to inspect the place.

It was dark, with just the light from the ventilators to see by. There were holes in the ceiling where Goodlass had taken away their light fixtures, holes in the wall where they had removed their switches. 'So cheap, taking advantage of our goodness,' cursed Pyare Lal. 'I paid for their tempos, which I didn't have to, and in return they remove every light and switch they put in. This is how people prosper in business, beti, you see?'

'I see, Chacha,' said Nisha, trembling a little. Would she have had the foresight to remove light fixtures and switches from walls and ceilings? She doubted it. She said a prayer: I have to succeed, please let me succeed.

In her bag were lists of things she needed, ranging from large to small. Tailors, cutters, embroiderers, sewing machines, tables, cloth, threads, buttons, laces. Where would she get the money for all this?

That evening after dinner, Yashpal called her.

'Beti,' he started, 'business is not an easy thing.'

Nisha looked expectant.

'I will help you in the beginning, but the responsibility, profit, and loss all are yours. In teaching no matter what you do, you get your salary. This is different.'

'Six hundred rupees, Papaji!' exclaimed Nisha. 'It is like getting no money at all.'

'It is not the amount,' said Yashpal severely. 'It is the attitude. If you start making six hundred rupee losses, some here, some there, see how quickly you go under. Now I will start you off with twenty-five thousand. Let us see what you do with it.'

Nisha held her breath. Twenty-five thousand! It made her feel adult. She who had been earning six hundred a month, to be responsible for twenty-five thousand! Her father was trusting her as he would have trusted a son.

'The rent is six thousand. I will pay it the first month.'

She vowed she would return every paisa to him. As he himself pointed out, it was a question of business. Thirty days, she had thirty days in which to generate enough income to pay next month's rent.

So this panic, this excitement, this challenge, this is what businessmen lived with. She felt a great pity for all teachers.

Her father hesitated. 'One more thing. I will order twenty-five suits from you; if they are not sold within a month, you will have to take them back. And if there are any complaints about the quality, I will not repeat the order.'

Nisha looked at him. Complaints about her suits? What was he talking about? As yet unaware of the thousand things that could go wrong with orders, she felt like giving it to her father in blood that he would be satisfied with her quality. But softly, softly, cautioned her spirit, she had to go softly. She looked down, demurely said, yes, Papaji, and that night was the first to put the TV on.

Work started on the basement. Lights, fans, and switches were replaced and a partition erected. The larger space was for the tailors and their equipment, while the smaller was the display area and Nisha's office.

In the few days it took to whitewash the basement, Nisha set about hiring workers. The master tailor, the one who cut, was the first and biggest essential. On her father's suggestion one morning she patrolled the back lane of a boutique on Ajmal Khan Road along with her aunt. Rupa was quicker than she in identifying and accosting: Madam was establishing a business, she needed a Masterji and some tailors.

'How much?' demanded the man.

'Negotiable,' replied Rupa, 'but anybody who works for her will not be disappointed.' She wrote Nisha's name and address on a piece of paper, and gave him till tomorrow to appear.

By the next evening Nisha had agreed to pay five thousand a month to the Masterji, Mohseen Khan by name, who promised to bring his sidekick for three thousand the minute Madam gave the word.

She could now resign from school.

Her father suggested she call her line Nisha's Creations. He had seen many women come in with their creations, its common usage had not destroyed its artistic appeal. She ordered five hundred labels. Start small, she said to herself, but I have to pay the rent, she argued back, within three months I have to make this many suits.

From Motia Khan she procured one display rack with protective plastic covers for the suits, and two sewing machines, one for ordinary stitching at two thousand, one for embroidery at four thousand. Pointed in that direction by Mohseen Khan, she combed the bookshops of Karol Bagh for trendy design magazines, and discovered Suriya waiting for her at this stage of life as well, publisher of the monthly *Star and Style, Clothes for the Young at Heart.*

The material in her father's shop was available to her at cost price, but for threads, laces, buttons, hooks etc. she had to go to wholesale dealers in Sadar Bazaar to keep her margins low. Her mother refused to let her go to these places alone; the first time she took Raju, the second time a salesperson from the shop, the third time she went by herself without telling anyone. Her business was not to be run standing on the shoulders of others.

Every day she honed her sense of colour and design. Within a few weeks, she could sketch variations on existing patterns. Mohseen Masterji became the man in her life. His expertise covered market trends, cutting corners in business, advice as to what she needed, and where she should buy it from. He cut five suits a day, brought her three tailors, which including the embroiderer and errand boy, made her the employer of six.

She learned to be meticulous in keeping track of every expense. What did it cost to make one suit? Salaries (the easiest part), rent, sewing machines and their depreciation, tea, cloth, hangers, plastic covers, scooter fares, threads, laces, hooks, scissors etc. etc. – nothing was too small to take into account.

Every time the electricity went, her production went down; she had to invest in an inverter. Another ten thousand to recover.

Sometimes she marvelled over the nature of business, so demanding of care, attention, and thought. No wonder the men in the family were incapable of brooding for days on the troubles at home. Now for her too the same indifference, her spirits instead rose and fell with the levels of her profit.

❧

When she was out buying, Nisha had to use Sona to supervise in the basement, see what the tailors needed, check the embroidery samples, test the fastness of colours, keep an eye on the boy as he ran to and from the dyers.

Despite the activity, Sona found the basement depressing. It was damp, seepage stained the fresh paint, and it had a musty smell. Yet Nisha needed her help to control these tailors. There was a limit to how much tea they could drink, how early they could pack up and go home.

The first time Nisha left her mother in charge, she came back to find her bursting with accomplishment. She had shown them. Masterji had actually lain down after lunch, was Nisha paying him to rest?

Masterji showed his displeasure by not coming for two whole days. 'Mummy, what have you done?' wailed Nisha. 'Even if he sleeps he never cuts less than five suits a day. I promised Gyan's twenty by day after, if he doesn't come, my reputation will be spoilt. Do you know how competitive the market is?'

Mummy was offended. 'Don't ask me to help if you are going to find fault. These people know how to take advantage of a young girl.'

There was no point saying anything. Nisha had to send the tailor Nasir to his house before Masterji unbent enough to come.

The next time Nisha left her mother in charge the same thing happened. This time it was the boy, who objected so much to being accused of making money with the threads that he quit. A boy was not like a Masterji, but it was irritating to have to find another, irritating to have to give her workers tips so they would ignore what Sona said.

There was another alternative lurking in the house. Shuchi was now in Play-Way, and her mother was relatively free. The delicate balance between sister-in-law and sister meant nothing was said in the open.

Pooja moved carefully. All her friends loved Nisha's Creations, thought it remarkable that in a year she should be making suits as nice as the ones at Deepson's and how fortunate they were to be getting one-third off when they bought from her.

Nisha looked pleasant and non-committal at the same time.

Raju picked up the thread. 'They love your suits, Nishu.'

Nisha smiled accommodatingly. She didn't mind supplying Pooja's wide circle of acquaintance, but she was doing them a favour, they were saving on the store's mark-up, for her it made no difference. She made this clear by saying, 'Gyan's was asking me just the other day whether I could increase the number to a hundred a month. I said I don't know. Family comes first, but I have to see to the outside market as well.'

A few days later Pooja offered more directly. 'I could help you in any way you like,' she said, looking longingly at the magazines Nisha had just bought.

Nisha was divided. She was sure that Pooja would prove a more effective helper than her mother, but she was not her blood. Once she asked her, she could not unask her, and

Pooja might prove as destructive in the basement as she had to her peace of mind earlier.

Meanwhile the marriage mill went on. On Nisha's birthday the family pundit came to deliver his predictions for the year. He unrolled the little chart tied with red thread and assured the anxious parents that this was the year Nisha was definitely going to get married. Shanni had moved from its house, the malevolent influences on her life were weakening.

Babaji was visited along with sweets and five hundred and one rupees in an envelope. She needed a new stone, he said, the old one had done its work and was no longer needed.

'What about her marriage?'

'Soon,' said Babaji. 'She will make a good marriage but it cannot be hurried.'

To lighten the sorrow the thought of her marriage caused him, Yashpal turned his thoughts to his daughter's business, where lay uncomplicated pride and pleasure. In a gruelling, competitive sphere she had proved herself with nothing beyond a small loan and a few initial introductions to big shops. Within a year she had increased the number of her tailors, invested in an inverter, and an ari machine for zardozi. A wooden frame, enabling sequins and beadwork, was now permanently installed in the basement with the craftsman specialising in this sleeping under it in the night.

She had repaid half the twenty-five thousand loan. With your blessings, Papaji, you will get the other half by next year, she laughed, almost recapturing the liveliness that had been hers in college. His daughter was growing, not in the way he had anticipated, but growing. Sometimes it occurred to him that she was more intelligent, methodical, and independent than Raju. Still, it was his duty to see that she married. Her fulfillment lay there, no matter how successful her business was.

*

Nisha had begun to respond to the issue of her marriage as a woman of a world she was not prepared to leave. She would only consent to a match with a family who let her work.

Sona objected: working was all right as a time pass, but if she started making such conditions, who would take her? Families wanted a daughter-in-law, wife, and mother; husbands were not looking for businesswomen. They might as well not waste their money on advertisements, if she was going to be so difficult.

'If she wants to work, she should be allowed to,' Yashpal said stubbornly. 'My first duty is to her, not to her future family. Otherwise, the karma on our heads will be too much. Too-too much.'

'Has the love of your daughter made you mad? You have a strange idea of karma. Her in-laws will not thank you.'

Yashpal was silent. He could not express his ideas and he ignored his wife's barbs. But nobody who was privy to Nisha's account books could call her Creations a mere time pass.

Meeting

At last the searching narrowed down to a widower in his early thirties, just right for a twenty-six-year-old. No issue, reassured Sona, only child, lives with mother in Daryaganj, a manglik like you, no dowry, sole interest is in a steady, homely girl. Triumphantly she produced a picture. See, here he is.

Nisha looked but could make out nothing. Pictures lied. Her own certainly did.

'What happened to the first wife?'

'Died.'

'How?'

'Accident.'

'What kind?'

'Something on the road.'

'Oh.'

'When they come he wants to see you alone.'

This made her afraid. She was no longer what she was. For the last five years she had watched her skin darken and her future grow ugly. Her mind darted down the sewers of her past, weaving through Vijay Nagar and the threatening places of her old house. What would he find when he looked at her?

'Why? Raju didn't meet Pooja alone.'

'Arre, Raju was a child, he knew nothing. This man is thirty-four, he has been married, he has certain ideas. What is the harm? We will be in the next room.'

'Why does he want to see me?' persisted Nisha. 'I don't want to see him. You have chosen, it is enough.'

Sona beamed at the proper feelings of her daughter. 'Of course there is no need, but he is very particular. But mind, you don't say much,' she added.

At that moment Nisha's skin began to prickle. She could not bear the sensation, and surreptitiously dug her nails through the thin material of her kurta and raked them across her skin.

Next morning the vigilant Sona noticed fresh weals on the inside folds of her daughter's elbows. 'Do you do this on purpose?' she asked harshly. 'The minute we mention somebody is coming to see you, you itch. I don't see you scratching when you are talking to your tailors. Is that the class of men you prefer?'

Nisha stared at her mother in hatred. What a low mind she had. She wanted to get rid of her, get rid of them all. 'What do you know about what I prefer?' she demanded.

Yes, let the father go on indulging her; make her so independent she can talk back, thought Sona angrily.

Nisha spent the day in the basement with her tailors. Staring at her designs, discussing them with Mohseen Bhai, the tumult in her mind died down. One thing was certain, no matter who she married she was going to come here every single day. She too had something to say to the groom.

'They will meet in Raju's room,' Yashpal declared. 'The door will stay open, beti, don't worry, we are near, you won't feel odd.'

How could she not feel odd, when she had no idea of what he was looking for? She wanted no expectations, no hostile gaze, no turning away because her appearance hurt his eyes.

They would cover her up when he came to see her, that she knew, but could they cover her up in the married home? And what about cooking? For the first time she appreciated the concern that had made Pooja's parents insist on a maid for their daughter. Would her parents insist too?

'Papaji.'

Love and anxiety in his gaze, met by love and anxiety in her own. She would do anything for her father, anything. But she wanted to avoid humiliation.

'Does he know about me?'

The father sighed. 'We have told him. Babaji also advised.'

'That is why he wants to see me, to see how bad it is?'

'Beti, you get nervous for nothing. It is not so bad, hardly noticeable.'

What could she say in the face of such blindness?

The father continued with his own preoccupations. 'He wants no dowry, he feels a dread of doing anything similar to the first time. But we are giving, you are our only daughter, it is your right.'

'Papaji, I do not want.'

'Don't talk like a fool,' scolded Yashpal. 'It is our custom. We have taken with our daughters-in-law, we will give with our daughter.' And without her asking, he added, 'We have also spoken to them about a maid. If your mother-in-law wants, she will stay there; if not, we will pay for her to come and go every day. We have told them you need help in the kitchen. It was Pooja's family who showed us how to do these things.'

Pooja was put in charge of the drawing room. On the morning of the meeting she and Raju went to the wholesale flower market near Hanuman Mandir and chose red and pink roses to match the maroon velvet sofas of the drawing room. These were now tightly bunched in brass vases in two corners of the room.

Sona had spent the day preparing kachoris, green chutney, dahi bhallas, and halwa. The china tea things were taken out, her stress dissipated in harassing the maid. It was a tense and hopefully auspicious occasion, a manglik coming to see a mangli, after a prolonged bad period in the lives of both.

'Now for the sake of your poor mother, do not itch,' said Sona in the bedroom, taking out the sari Nisha was going to wear, the matching long-sleeved blouse, and two dozen glass bangles. 'And remember there is no need to say too much.'

'If I am going to marry him, I should be able to say what I like.'

'Later, not now.'

'The horoscopes match, Didi,' said Rupa quickly, getting the make-up ready. 'It is good if they get to know each other. This time everything will be all right. They have agreed to the maid, they are trying to be accommodating.' She carefully applied foundation to Nisha's face. 'See how nice it smells. Shall I put perfume?'

'Arre, Roop, she will itch with perfume. They are coming to look at her, not smell her.'

The aunt looked at Nisha's face critically, tilting it to the light.

'All right?' she asked the mother, who was standing by with the sari.

'Little more, perhaps. If we can match the hands it will be good.'

Nisha's hands; still fair, unblemished. Long white fingers with the nails painted a pale pink. Two gold rings on each hand, with stones to bring out the colour. As for necklace and earrings, the thin sari material simultaneously revealed and concealed.

Meeting.

The man cleared his throat. Nisha kept her eyes down. She was concentrating on not itching. Her two dozen bangles tinkled emphatically whenever she moved. She twisted the four rings on her fingers, her flickering glance resting on the man's stomach spilling over the belt, straining the buttons of his shirt.

Why does he want to see me, will he say he doesn't like me, is that why he doesn't say anything? Nisha directed these thoughts towards the hem of her sari.

He cleared his throat again. She looked up briefly, took in the black moustache over full lips, took in his round, perspiring face, the cheeks that imitated the bulge of his stomach, the red-brown skin. His hair was streaked with grey, his watch clasped a dark and hairy wrist.

'You know I have been married before?' he asked eventually.

Nisha nodded.

'I asked to meet you because I think people should know each other first.'

She nodded again.

'First time I was twenty-one. Only son. We lost my father early, my mother needed someone.'

More nods.

'She was seventeen. When we could not have children, my mother blamed her. They were alone in the house together, and she was very young . . .'

Was this man telling her his wife was murdered, or had committed suicide, that the story of the accident was a fabrication – what was he really saying?

She shifted her gaze from her sari to the floor between his squarely placed feet, allowed herself to take in the tightly held knees. Maybe he was tense too. It had not crossed her mind that others could be scarred in the marriage market. And a man at that.

'Won't you say something?'

'What happened?'

His face twisted.

'You don't have to tell,' she added nervously.

He looked up; no, he had to, it was her right. A bus hit the rickshaw she was in, it was evening, she had gone to the market to buy vegetables and was on her way home. She was only twenty-three.

She heard the protective note in his narrative and was reminded of her father. Maybe at last the planets that had reigned over her life were bidding their long-held position goodbye.

'Is there anything you wish to ask me?' enquired the man in the space of Nisha's thoughts.

It felt odd to be giving conditions as though everything was settled, but maybe this was how it was done. 'I work,' she offered.

'I know.'

'I would like to continue.'

'They told me,' he said heavily.

Was that all he was going to say? She was disappointed.

The man shifted his weight about and looked at her. 'How long have you been doing this business?'

'Two years.'

'Two years.' More pause, more thought. 'You must have worked very hard.'

Again he reminded her of her father. 'Yes,' she said, 'it is called Nisha's Creations.'

'Lots of women are doing ready made. I see small boutiques operating from houses all over Daryaganj.'

'I cannot give it up,' she confided. This was the only thing she could visualise in any marriage, that she had to come to the basement every day.

'Let us say, you come here till I have found room for you nearer home.'

She blushed, then felt suspicious. Were his words genuine or false?

'One last thing,' he now said. 'I want registry. You do not mind?'

The many family weddings stretching down the years, bringing brides into the house, taking daughters away, had all been traditional. Not to have one of those. No ceremonies where she would be the centre of attention, of laughter, jokes, and teasing, no dressing-up or jewellery, no red and white bridal dots across her forehead, curving under her eyes, no arrival of the barat, no groom on horseback, no wedding fire, no sisters hiding the bridegroom's shoes and taking as much money as they could to give them back, no vida, no tears, no photographers, no wedding album – nothing. She had not realised how much she expected these things in her future.

The man looked up and read her face. 'You do not like the idea?' he asked.

'It seems strange.'

303

'At thirty-four, I feel too old for fuss.'

She nodded briefly. Perhaps she had never been destined for a traditional wedding. What was important was the life after the ceremony, not the day itself.

They were looking at each other now. It seemed possible to ask a personal question. 'What was she like, your first wife? Was she pretty?'

He looked at her. His face relaxed, he almost smiled. 'She was not chosen for her looks,' he replied.

Nisha felt comforted.

'I have to marry and we are not interested in such things. My mother needs someone in the house.'

Nisha nodded. She didn't question the world's need to marry, it had been dinned into her head since birth.

They sat like that for a minute, then he got up and indicated they should join the others.

In the drawing room Nisha shrank as his mother turned her attention towards her.

'Where have you studied, beti?' she asked, holding Nisha's face up by the chin.

Nisha did not reply. This stock question came as a shock after the intimacies inside. The woman kept looking at her.

'Answer her, Nisha, answer your mother-in-law, do not be shy,' chorused the family.

The woman let her go and looked carefully at her son. Assessing glances crossed the room.

Shuchi toddled towards the kachoris and began to crumble them in her fists. Pooja giggled, and snatched her up.

'So naughty these children are,' said Sona to the man's mother.

'Children should be naughty, otherwise where is the fun?' commented the mother in turn.

Now that they were practically related, the atmosphere lightened, and in that spirit they talked of this, that, and left.

*

Immediately the family crowded around Nisha. What had he said? Did he like her? What did she say to him, how was it? Quick, they wanted to know, how was it?

Nisha was not sure. Overwrought, she began to cry.

'My Nisha,' said Sona, answering Nisha's tears with her own, 'you are going to be a bride.' She cracked her knuckles around her daughter's head.

Pooja hung around her, Rekha ran to get the cup of tea she had not been able to drink during the meeting. They had to wait to hear from the party, though with the mother telling Sona as they left that the girl was good, Nisha's marriage, it seemed, was settled. Guilt and sorrow were packing their bags, soon it would be time to say goodbye.

Now that things had been arranged Nisha allowed herself to show some curiosity.

'What is his name?' she asked her aunt when she visited the next day.

Rupa Masi giggled. 'Such a simple girl. Doesn't even know that.'

Nisha frowned. She did not like being called simple, for a businesswoman it was tantamount to losing money.

'Arvind. His name is Arvind,' said her aunt.

'What kind of shop?'

'Upholstery.'

What were the connections of an upholsterer, could he help her to more retail outlets? But all she said was, 'He is fat.'

'Arre, Nishu,' said Rupa, looking at her in surprise. 'You know, sitting in the shop whole day, must be used to eating fried food. He is thirty-four after all, what can you expect? And he is just a little fat, it is not like you to be so fussy.'

Suresh's body came to Nisha's mind. Jeans around straight hips, the flat, yellow-brown belly with the line of hair going down, the small round buttocks which she tentatively touched when she could bear her feelings no longer.

Maybe Suresh looked like the man now. Raju had changed

after all, his own belly beginning to strain his buttons, his gold watch beginning to sit on a larger, thicker wrist.

'If he is fat, you can feed him food with less ghee, what is there?' her aunt's voice was going on. 'He is the homely type, you can tell. Very hard working, looking after his mother, wanting no dowry as this is his second marriage, no smoking, drinking, really he has all the qualities. And they do not live far from here, you will be able to see your mother-father, look how often Pooja goes home.'

'I am coming here every day for my tailors,' reiterated Nisha.

'We will see,' said Rupa Masi indulgently. 'Your family has to come first.'

She didn't tell her aunt he had mentioned finding a place for her workshop. It made her feel shy; besides, she did not know if she could trust him.

At that point Sona entered the room and discussion of the boy and the match started all over again.

'The mother looked very old,' observed Rupa.

'It is good. She won't live long,' remarked Sona. 'Then Nisha will be sole mistress of the house.'

'Uff, Didi, why are you talking of death on the eve of Nisha's marriage?' laughed Rupa at what must have been the thought in the minds of many, though to utter it were inauspicious.

'My duty is done, and now I can die in peace, Roop,' said Sona, incandescent with relief.

Relatives were informed about the match along with the registry qualification. 'Simple wedding. They are very keen on a simple wedding,' was the accompanying explanation.

Disbelief hung in the air. This was pushing simplicity to absurd extremes.

Voices lowered. Talk of the first wife, the groom's sensibilities, he wants everything different, both are manglik, it is better not to attract the evil eye with too much show.

The whispers went on. In the middle of his grief at losing his wife, there was ugly bickering with the first one's in-laws, who had been most unreasonable in their blame and greed. They wanted the girl's dowry back. Arvind returned the jewellery, but the money had been spent on the shop, they had been married for six years. Only low-class families behaved like that.

Pooja's parents, Rekha's parents, the Yashpals and Pyare Lals all had much to do with each other. The medium of material called to them, binding them, weaving them, dyeing them in the same colours, dressing them in the same fabric. Now Nisha was the warp to be woven into the weft of a cloth-owning family in Daryaganj, but in her case she was bringing her own fabric, her own tailors, her own business. How would it be with her, for whom nothing had been as it should?

Nisha's wedding

After many years the girl was doing as expected. Nisha was their precious daughter, and they were going to give with a generous hand, irrespective of the boy asking or not. It was her right, and their duty. The days passed, shopping expeditions increased.

By this time Nisha was having all her clothes stitched from the workshop, as well as every new suit worn in the family. For the informal wedding occasions, the younger women wanted her to make trendy clothes; for the formal, only saris would do. They came to her basement, she showed them magazines and samples, offered variations in shades, embroidery, laces, and materials. Various cousins commented frequently on the great convenience of having a boutique at home, recounting nightmares during previous weddings. Now endless trips to harassed, absconding, recalcitrant, cheating tailors were avoided, all thanks to the bride.

Nisha had to hire two more workers to cope with her personal and professional demands. She now had six tailors who churned out nine suits daily. And since she was getting married, she could even take Pooja's help. She needed it and she no longer had to be wary of power struggles at home. 'Pooji, make sure the seams are turned properly, Pooji, check that the laces the boy gets matches the old ones, Pooji, test the fastness of the embroidery thread, last time the colour ran, Pooji, send the boy to the dyers, they promised to give the material today.'

Pooja was more than willing. She even asked Nisha to show her how she priced the suits – 'for when you are not here, Didi.'

Pricing was the heart of the business. Every night when Nisha sat down to do it, the different strands of her work came together. According to a formula her father had worked out, she calculated first her base costs, rent and electricity, then payments to staff, then money spent on material and accessories, then transport expenses. Once this was done she added the 50 per cent that made up the wholesale prices she charged her retailers. Every figure attached to a suit proved she was a businesswoman, making profits, and she hugged this precious feeling to her heart. No matter who helped her, the final act of control had to be in her hands.

She left the delicate matter of family billing to her mother. Sona grew adroit at urging relatives to go to Gyan's or Deepson's, see Nisha's label, compare the prices there, and then decide whether they were getting a good deal or no.

'Do you like it, beti?' asked Yashpal, bringing home her wedding sari from the shop.

Nisha looked at the gold mangoes and peacocks on the dark pink palla. Pooja and Rekha had got married in heavy brocade lehngas, with sheer gold tissue odhnis, crusted over with gold and silver embroidery. A registry wedding did not encourage this kind of finery.

'Let's see how it looks on you,' continued Yashpal, drawing out the crackling tissue paper inserted into the folds and draping it around Nisha.

Sona joined them on the bed with the tea tray. 'So beautiful,' she remarked, 'shows off her colour.'

'It is fine, Papaji,' said Nisha, turning her attention back to the sketches she had brought upstairs. 'I am sure he does not care what I wear.'

Yashpal found himself wishing his daughter's wedding day over so she could quickly get down to enjoying the home every woman needed.

The day before the wedding the sangeet cum mehndi ceremony took place. Just a few people, Sona averred, as fifty female relatives assembled to apply henna, choose bangles, and beat a dholak while singing loud and tuneless songs. At their centre sat Nisha in her new salwar suit, hands and feet outstretched. Two women crouched over her, painstakingly applying the bridal mehndi. If it turns out dark, her mother-in-law will love her, giggled the cousins.

All night Nisha slept with her mehndi on. She slept badly, the mehndi flaking on to the sheet, getting into her face and hair as she tossed and turned. As the sky grew lighter, she could hear the twittering of waking birds outside. Finally when the darkness had turned bluish grey she got up, and went into the kitchen. It was four-thirty on her wedding morning and she wanted to be alone before the others got up.

She lit the gas, carefully added tea leaves, milk, and sugar to one cup of water, and waited for it to boil. Her hands were sticky from the sugar-lemon mixture that had been smeared on to deepen the colour. She rinsed them and peered at her palms. Now she had a face to put to the word mother-in-law.

The intricate, lace-like patterns were an intense brown, the skin between the lines lightly stained with orange. It had been years since she had applied mehndi, though she had loved it as a child.

Holding her mug of tea, Nisha sat in the veranda, observing the growing brightness that illuminated the dust-coated leaves of the scraggy trees that bordered the park.

In a few hours she would be married. She wished she could see beyond the ceremony, but she couldn't. His family was just him and his mother. Such luck, her relatives had exclaimed, comes only once in seven lifetimes.

She thought of her sari. Maybe Arvind would notice it after all.

She thought of her eczema. She hoped she would not itch during the function, she hoped that all the recent cortisone injections had done their work. They were going to cover her face and neck with foundation, her sleeves would hide most of her arms.

They had an eleven o'clock appointment with the registrar at Tees Hazari. In the evening there would be the reception at the Sartaj Hotel, followed by a free bridal night.

And there, in the bridal suite, he would see her body, see those patches. That was on the surface, what about the rest? Would he find her lacking in some virginal essence? He, who was a widower, and she, who was so scarred and scared?

After tonight, the worst would be over. The seeing done, the shocks of physical realities absorbed. Then she could focus on being a good wife, daughter-in-law, maybe mother, along with the business she clung to so doggedly in her mind. Had she been younger she would not have been faced with giving up anything; now what she had created was the most real thing in her life.

By ten-thirty the family, in four cars, are on their way to the lower courts. Ring Road is as usual jam-packed with traffic and the lights are not working. At each intersection policemen exercise despotic power over converging roads. With calculating eyes, they survey the lengthening line of cars that pour forth from the city. The bride sits in a car and sweats, no doubt the groom is doing the same on some other part of the road.

Finally, at ISBT they turn off towards Tees Hazari. 'We are nearly there,' whispers Sona to her daughter. Nearly there, nearly there.

Everybody stares at Nisha as she steps from the car. All the locals, the hangers-on, the typewriters-wallahs in sheds and shacks, touts waiting for those in need of lawyers, notary publics, or stamp-paper – all stare at the bride, so conspicuous in her pink sari with the gold peacocks. With her head down, Nisha follows her father inside. The corridors are dirty, the walls smeared with betel-juice stains. Masses jostle together, united by legal wrangles.

They take several wrong turns trying to find the place for registered marriages. They march up and down flights of narrow stairs – Nisha, Sona, Rupa, Pooja, Shuchi, Rekha (plus child), Seema (plus her two), Raju, Vijay, Ajay, Yashpal, Pyare Lal, Prem Nath.

They find the groom and are made to wait in three different rooms. Finally they collect in front of a magistrate in the nicest room of all, airy, high above the clusters of desperate humanity. Here Arvind and Nisha sign their names in several places. Pooja takes out a box from her heavy leather hand-bag and unwraps the paper covering to reveal fat white squares of cashew barfi. She firmly holds a piece out to Arvind. 'Now you are married,' she says laughing, 'you should be the first to sweeten the mouth of your bride.' As Nisha shyly accepts this love token, everyone, magistrate included, watches with approval.

From the court they drive straight to the Sartaj Hotel in Karol Bagh. The family mill around the check-in counter, complete the formalities, then pack into the lift to escort the newly-weds up.

The bridal suite is on the top floor. In the centre is a big double bed, strewn with a few rose petals, on the coffee table is a bowl of fruit, with a little white card inscribed 'With Compliments from the Management'.

Family members crowd in, deposit the suitcases, relax on the bed, while children run from bathroom to room to corridor to room, shouting and screaming. Raju switches the TV on and off to check whether it is working. Those who have to use the toilet do so, splashing water liberally around the sink. Sona whispers to her daughter that Pooja, Rekha, and Seema will come early to help her get ready for the reception, they will bring her jewellery with them. Half an hour later they leave. Nisha and Arvind are alone for the second time.

They are seated opposite each other.

'Would you like to eat something?' he asks, clearing his throat. She wonders whether there is something wrong with his throat the way he keeps clearing it.

She looks down and shakes her head.

'Something to drink? Limca?'

More negatives.

'Tea?'

She recalls herself to herself. Activity is necessary to lighten the silence between them. A waiter would come, tea would be poured, milk and sugar added, spoons rattled. 'All right,' she agrees.

Arvind can now busy himself with phoning and ordering, and Nisha can feel free to move. She unlocks her suitcase.

'Go and change,' advises Arvind. 'You must not be very comfortable.'

She takes out one of the salwar suits she had made. It is a deep pink organza, heavily embroidered, with sequins scattered across a chunni in two shades of pink, edged with a broad gold band.

'Nisha's Creations,' she offers, holding it out to him.

He turns it about. 'Yours?'

She nods.

'Are these the ones you supply?'

Again she nods.

'Where all?'

'Gyan's, Deepson's, Ahuja and Sons in Karol Bagh.' (She never mentions the steady supply to Banwari Lal and Sons – people might assume she is incapable of making it on her own.) 'Later I want to branch out to Connaught Place.'

He looks startled. 'I had no idea your business was so large.'

She informs him that during the wedding preparations she made nine suits a day. She cannot keep the pride from her voice.

He says nothing.

Does he mind? 'Doing this I found some peace, and now I cannot stop.' Her explanation brings tears she cannot help.

He sighs, 'Work is good when the mind is disturbed.'

She gets up from the floor, gently tugs her salwar suit out of Arvind's lap, and disappears into the bathroom.

The tea comes, along with paneer pakoras and a plate of biscuits. She pours the tea, he hands her a pakora sprinkled with black salt and chillies. She eats it. It tastes good, he hands her another. She feels looked after, and wonders whether this is an aspect of marriage that will continue or fade.

They eat pakoras and drink tea. Arvind says, 'You rest, I will have a bath.'

She smiles but remains sitting till he locks the bathroom door, only then does it seem safe to lie down. After a few tense minutes she drifts into a doze, so tired is she; after all, she has been up since four-thirty. Some time later the bed sags, he too has lain down, she remains as still as stone. But it is all right, he turns on his side, and in a while she can hear gentle snores. Reassured, she drifts back to sleep.

Two hours later Pooja and her daughter arrive to take her to the hotel beauty parlour for the free bridal make-up and hairdo.

'How do you like our sister?' asks Pooja coyly, her eyes flickering over the slightly rumpled surface of the bed.

Arvind smiles but vouchsafes no opinion on this delicate matter.

Nisha blushes. What can the poor man say?

'Now you must be on your own, we are taking her to the parlour.'

'Leave her with me,' says Arvind, pointing to Shuchi.

Shuchi clings to her mother's Nisha Created suit, and refuses to be coaxed away.

'So naughty at home, so shy outside,' explains Pooja.

'Are you her sister?' they ask Pooja at the beauty parlour. They have many brides coming in and are democratically curious about all.

'No, sister-in-law.'

'Such a pretty smile she has.' This they can say safely. Eczema hasn't touched her teeth.

'Yes,' agrees Pooja, baring her own lips in the mirror.

'Do you want a body wax?' they ask. 'Very popular with brides. Leaves the body smooth as silk.'

'No,' replies Nisha reddening, thinking of the marks on her body and the roughened texture of her skin.

They go over her face with a magnifying glass, thread the few stray hairs on her upper lip, tweeze her eyebrows. They give her a facial, while Pooja has a pedicure, and Shuchi has nail polish put on her hands and feet.

'Relax, relax,' exhorts the small Chinese woman, gently massaging Nisha's face, neck, and shoulders, going into routine patter: what kind of marriage, love or arranged, what kind of job, business or service, what kind of household, joint or separate?

A mudpack (the one Nisha prefers) is applied, cotton pads put on her eyes, and the overhead light turned off. As she lies there Nisha thinks of all the treatment she has undergone at the Nature Cure Centre. Would she still need to go there? Mudpacks and she are old familiars.

Finally the make-up. First the foundation, a thick uniform white, then the cheeks coloured a definite, unambiguous pink, with a touch of rouge on the forehead and chin. The mouth is painted bright red, the eyes lined in black, a faint purple eye shadow applied, and her whole face given a light silver dusting.

'Isn't she looking beautiful?' they enthuse, as they pull her hair into an elaborate arrangement that has ringlets brushing her neck and shoulders.

Finally, when Nisha's face is finished, Pooja opens the suitcase in which Nisha's mother-in-law has put the clothes she is to wear for the reception. Out comes a lehnga. Nisha gazes wordlessly at this auspicious sign. It is not the most elaborate she has seen, but she likes the colour, a pearly pink with a gauzy silver dupatta, and silver embroidery. As she slips on the heavy skirt, the beauty-parlour women exclaim, so beautiful, such good taste, and Nisha feels a sense of personal accomplishment.

She is ready. The three of them take the lift upstairs to wait for Rekha and Seema to come with the jewellery.

At the far end of the hall the bride and groom are seated on two high carved wooden chairs on a dais covered with a green carpet. The bride wears four thick necklaces: gold with enamel work, gold with the nine precious stones, gold filigree, and gold embedded with pearls and rubies. Pearls and rubies dangle from her ears. The matching bangles of each necklace are on her wrists, along with a dozen ordinary gold bangles for everyday use.

The guests come to the dais one by one and press presents, mostly envelopes of money, into the couple's hands, envelopes which are passed on to Pooja, standing behind them with a little bag. The women admire Nisha's mehndi and incidentally examine her ornaments. They finger her necklaces, ask which ones are hers, which ones her in-laws have given her. They look satisfied as they delve into these secrets.

As each guest comes up, the photographer takes pictures.

After two hours plates laden with food are thrust at the married couple. Nisha picks at hers, Arvind eats heartily.

'Aren't you eating?' he asks, turning to her.

'I'm not hungry.'

'Arre, is this any way to treat your wife? Feed her, feed her, nah,' laughs a cousin's daughter, a fourteen-year-old girl versed in marriage ritual. 'Don't be so shy.' She arrests the groom's hand travelling towards his mouth, pushes Nisha's face towards it, saying to the bride, 'Now you are married Didi, you won't get anywhere being shy.' Nisha's mouth closes on the morsel, her teeth graze his fingers, and there was contact, sanctioned contact.

In the bridal suite, Nisha's family has augmented the flower arrangements of the hotel. Rose petals are strewn everywhere, strings of jasmine and lily of the valley hang on the footboard of the bed. The wedding presents have been taken to the house in Daryaganj.

The bride can hear her husband in the bathroom gargling and spitting. He comes out, sighs, belches, and scratches his belly. He sits down on the edge of the bed, unwraps the hotel paper from the glass, pours himself some water. Nisha sits on the edge of the bed, ill at ease, not sure what to do with her eyes. He turns to her, points to the other paper-wrapped glass on the tray, asks, 'Want some?'

She shakes her head. All power of even drinking water is removed from her. As he drinks she can see his bared teeth through the bottom of the glass. She remains still – each move, it seems, he must direct – and now he gestures to the bathroom.

'Would you like to use?'

She picks up her things and locks the door behind her, to spend a long despairing minute staring at a white, pink, unfamiliar face in a mirror uncompromisingly surrounded by light bulbs. Slowly she bends her head to wash the mask off.

She can't help it, Suresh comes to her mind, and how different it had been. With Suresh the initial alarm at his touch had been mixed with excitement, longing, pleasure. Now it is dread hoping for gentleness, with love not even a guest on the horizon.

When she comes out, in a pink, lace-beribboned nightgown, he is lying on one side of the bed, hands folded on his chest. She can see the brown of his skin through the thin cotton of his kurta. He does not embarrass her by his gaze, merely gestures to her side of the bed. She gets in, he puts off the light, inspiring gratitude. Street lights filter through the curtains, she can make out his shape across from her. He doesn't say anything. Were they just going to sleep? Her chest tightens, she is perspiring despite the air-conditioning. The smell of flowers is strong in the room, the sheets are crisp, draped cool and light about them.

317

'Are you all right?'

'Yes.'

'You are not tired? You did not eat very much.'

'I was nervous.'

'You must not be nervous,' he murmurs.

Her heart expands. Obliquely she refers to her skin. 'You may not like me.'

'You are my wife,' he answers, venturing beneath the material. 'There is no question of not liking.'

'I have waited so long for this,' she tells him at the first tentative touch of his mouth on her face.

He does not respond directly, she wilts a bit – perhaps he has not been waiting, it is only she. His weight shifts on top of her, her arms are around his back, his knees push her legs apart, and it is over.

They lie there, arms across each other, simulating an intimacy which their bodies express with more confidence than their thoughts. Half an hour and her husband's snores draw some of the tension out of her. He is sleeping. She is alone. She relaxes and slowly turns on her side. Her feet twitch against the stiffness of the sheets, the hum of the air-conditioner continues as the steady background noise to her first married night.

The next morning Nisha is escorted to her new home by a carload of relatives belonging to her husband. At the threshold she puts first one foot then the other into a tray laden with rice, wheat, and cloth, and with those feet she enters the house, bringing food, clothing, and prosperity to her married home. Some older women sing in the background, the mother-in-law sobs. Nisha is led to her, she takes her by the hand, crying, crying all the time, while it is whispered that Ammaji feels too much, but such is her nature.

Ammaji now places her before a framed black-and-white photograph surrounded by a garland of sandalwood flowers. The group sighs. The mother-in-law laments brokenly, 'Your father-in-law. Pay your respects.' Nisha bows her head and raises her folded palms. An aunt thrusts the girl down towards her mother-in-law's feet. Obediently she bends and touches the feet she has touched countless times in the last few days. The mother-in-law pats her head. 'Blessings upon his son's wife, and their sons,' she sighs, tears in her voice. 'Come, come,' says her sister's daughter. 'Now your daughter-in-law has come into the house you must not be sad. Everything is going to change.'

Nisha is seated on the bed, barfi pushed into her mouth, to sweeten your married life, now and for ever.

'Your mother-in-law insisted on giving up this room,' a cousin whispers in her ear. 'They both slept here after . . . you know, the accident. We were so worried about Ammaji, thank god Bhaiyya agreed to marry at last. There will be someone in the home at least.'

'Arvind put tube lights everywhere when he got engaged. Thanks to you we have modern lighting – before, it was so dark,' reveals another cousin.

Nisha, still a bride, can barely look up, let alone notice tube lights.

For lunch the whole group descends the narrow stairs to go to the newest South Indian restaurant in Daryaganj. Dosas, idlis, vadas, uttapmas later, the family take rickshaws back, distribute themselves through the house, on the marital bed, on Ammaji's bed, on the sofa, on chittais on the floor, and gossip, chat, drift off to sleep. At four-thirty they get up for tea and pakoras, served with the help of the new maid, and then, towards evening, replete and satisfied, a good job done, Arvind married, the new bride settled, they slowly disperse.

The couple are left alone for the second night. Nisha notices Ammaji's bed in the covered veranda just outside their bedroom and declares her discomfort.

'I do not feel nice about her sleeping out there,' she says.

'What to do, there is no other place,' he sighs.

They get into bed. She wonders if he will do it again. She does not have to wonder long. Ten minutes later he has done it and this time they lie awake a little longer before he starts snoring. Embarrassed, she speculates if the mother outside has heard anything, and it is only much later that she can bring herself to use the bathroom.

After breakfast the next day, the bride's brothers come to escort her back home. Raju, Vijay, and Ajay laugh and joke with Arvind, call him their Jijaji. Nisha feels odd hearing him addressed thus. Sister's husband.

At home everyone crowds around her. How was it? Were they nice to her? What was the mother-in-law like? What was the house like? What had they done after they left the hotel? What were the other relatives like? How many were they? Did they comment on her clothes? Did she tell them she was wearing a Nisha Created suit? Were there any pictures of the first wife in the house?

She hardly knows the answers to so many questions. As at the engagement she resorts to tears, tears they understand and expect.

Then they enquire, 'Happy? Are you happy?'

She now knows when brides are asked if they are happy that the sexual aspect of the marriage is being delicately investigated. Had a bride ever shook her head and said no, she was not happy, she wonders.

Briefly she nods, then gets up. 'I must see my tailors. Two days and I am sure they have slackened.'

'Arre, now you are married, you don't have to be so serious,' counter the family, slightly shocked.

But how can she explain? Of course she has to be serious, even more than before. Orders will not wait because she is married.

Nisha was home two weeks. The husband phoned once a day. With her family listening to every word, she answered his questions: how was she feeling, how were Mummy, Papaji, everything all right? She asked the same of him: how was he, Ammaji, and the shop, was he eating well, had the maid settled down, was she doing whatever Ammaji wanted her to? She waited for him to ask about her business, but he didn't, and she did not bring it up.

She had a talk with her parents. She was not going to sacrifice her work to her marriage, she was not sure how clearly they had conveyed this to her in-laws. Had they stipulated she had to visit her workshop every day?

'Beti,' replied her father, 'we made enough demands. The maid for one, we were very firm you do no washing, no cooking, especially in the heat. We mentioned your work, we said you wanted to continue; they showed themselves willing to accommodate, how could one ask for more?'

Nisha tried not to feel cheated at what she suspected was insufficient emphasis on this aspect. She now repeated, if she did not get the necessary support, she would hire someone. The mother looked scandalised, wasn't she helping already?

When her husband arrived to take her back, Nisha could feel her increased status in the respectful goodbyes.

'My mother was very keen you come home,' Arvind said shyly in the car. 'Kept saying where is my bahu?'

Nisha could not respond. She felt she was leaving a part of herself behind, and this time there was no coming back. At the thought of Mohseen Bhai and Nisha's Creations, tears came to her eyes.

'We will visit Mummy Papaji often, very often,' soothed her new husband.

XXVI

A new home

The house in which Nisha now found herself was very different from the homes she had known. In Karol Bagh, the little park they faced had offered trees, birdsong, a few scraggy flowering shrubs, and a semblance of openness. The noise and chaos of the main market, three lanes away, did not penetrate their world. All its commotion came from within.

Her new home was above her husband's shop. Its entrance was from the back gully, dumping place for rubbish. The paving was rutted and uneven, the foot slipped between the debris of eternal construction, loose brick, piles of sand, bajri, and puddles of stagnant water. Down the gully, rows of doors led to identical steep, narrow staircases that darkened as they rose higher. At the top a narrow entrance let into a small angan, bordered with plastic ropes stretched across for clothes to dry. The household bathed, peed, shat, cooked in cubby-holes on opposite ends of the angan; the eating was done in an alcove adjacent to the kitchen. On the left of the entrance were two large, old-fashioned, high-ceilinged rooms, one to sit in, one to sleep in. Beyond them lay a covered veranda with a bed-cum-divan.

'Now you are home,' said Arvind as they climbed the stairs, he carrying her suitcase, she following on gold high heels.

Home.

Nisha first touched her mother-in-law's feet, then moved into the kitchen to see how the maid was managing. She was now a daughter-in-law, she had to anticipate responsibility, not wait for her lack of involvement to be pointed out.

That night as Nisha served dinner, moving from kitchen to alcove in two steps, taking, bringing, fussing, anticipating, her mother-in-law kept up a steady patter: 'Now he is married, how much more life there is, everybody kept saying, Arvind must marry, the old mother must have someone to look after her, it is not right the place is so empty, son is busy in the shop, someone should be there to see, notice, care, and where are the children going to come from?' Myriad relatives were quoted, all of whom had said the same thing year in and year out. Their words eddied gently around them, while Arvind went on eating and did not look up.

He did not need to. He now had a substitute, one who was getting acquainted with what was expected of her, one who was uneasily wondering if this was compatible with her own longings. She looked to her husband, but the silent man was digging into his teeth with a toothpick, and did not seem to realise that a response was required.

After dinner, she got her mother-in-law the glass of hot milk she said she always drank before bed. As she was reheating it – 'soon you will know exactly how I like it' – she wondered if it had been like this for her mother and her aunts. Definitely not for Pooja, but then Pooja had Raju behind her. That made things different.

In the next few days Nisha figured out what comprising half the female population in the house entailed. Her mother-in-law claimed her attention morning, noon, and night, in the kitchen, in the bedroom, in drawing rooms, theirs and others, as visitor and visitee. She received and gave attention, care, concern, and food, with little time left over for anything else.

Ten days later Nisha decided to take the plunge. Neither Arvind nor his mother had enquired after the health of her business, it was clear she could not depend on them to preserve its well-being. As Arvind got dressed in the morning, she said, 'I will be going to Karol Bagh today, I can't do everything on the phone, I will be back by lunchtime.'

'Just tell Amma,' he said.

Nisha stood still. He had not dealt with his mother. It was

going to be left to her. Though her parents had laid down her working as a condition for marriage, she could see the conditions melting into nothing before her eyes.

Besides, she herself saw the difficulties of leaving her mother-in-law, duty towards whom had been bred into her blood and bone.

She tried to sound firm. 'I have to go. Remember my parents also said.' She stopped as she heard the independent ring of her words, and hastened into conciliation, 'For a short time, two or three hours.'

'Yes, yes, tell Amma and go.'

'Can't you inform her? As it is, I am worried she might feel bad.'

'Then why are you going?'

'Please tell her, nah.' She needed him to make it easy, couldn't he see that? 'I thought you liked what I did,' desperation allowed her to accuse.

'I do.'

'Then why don't you say something to her? From me she will misunderstand.'

'She won't. She really wants you, I have never seen her so affectionate,' he faltered, and Nisha could not go on. So the mother-in-law hadn't been like this with the first wife, was she trying to make up now – was it guilt, and if it was, did it mean her Creations had to pay the price?

The mother called, his breakfast was ready, and Arvind lovingly approached his morning cool salty lassi, crisp fried-potato parantha, and sour mango pickle.

Arvind did tell his mother and she responded by silence and withdrawal. Still Nisha went, but without the support that would have made her comfortable and secure. She saw every inch of the way to Karol Bagh covered with fragments of her broken future. Working was not going to be easy. She had better initiate Pooja into the pricing she so wanted.

Back at home she took long breaths in the dampness of the

basement to stamp that fragile, threatened essence on her mind. She stood at the two shining steel racks and ran her hands along the plastic-covered suits. She looked into the account book, and saw how neatly Pooja had kept all the expenses, here and there was her mother's hand. She had not intended to run a family business when she started Nisha's Creations, but now the relatives had seeped in, and she could not be there to plug the leaks.

Her body again decided her fate. Within a month of her marriage she missed a period. A couple of weeks more and she was toying with her breakfast, morning nausea added to the queasy feeling at dinnertime.

She only had to do this once before her mother-in-law announced cryptically, 'Beti, tomorrow you have an appointment at Dr Mehra's in the evening.' Nisha gazed at the folds her pink nightie made over her flat stomach and blushed. In one area of her life at least she had performed as expected.

The pregnancy test was positive. The doctor was encouraging. Normal healthy foetus, seven weeks, due date 6 January, iron, vitamin, and calcium supplements to be taken, normal activities to be followed, none of this eating for two business, exercise a must.

Next morning her mother-in-law produced the almonds that were going to be part of her daily diet for the next year.

It turned out that the mother-in-law was very insistent about rest. 'You must not get tired,' she said, hovering around Nisha anxiously. 'No going here and there. It is a big strain, something might happen, then you will regret it for the rest of your life.'

Nisha talked to her husband. 'I have to go to Karol Bagh. You know I do. Even the doctor said I should lead a normal life.'

Arvind put his hand on hers for a brief encounter. 'Amma gets very worried. She has waited so long, it is natural.'

'I know, but I will suffocate if I have to stay here the whole time. The mind also needs to be active.'

He did talk to his mother, but in the case of pregnancy his mother was not willing to budge: what do you know, you are a man, we have to be careful, very careful.

She talked to her parents. 'They are not letting me come.'

It was a question of someone else's child, what could her parents do? Should anything happen they would be the ones blamed and this was not a risk they could take.

Even Rupa Masi, businesswoman, sided with them. 'You have your whole life ahead of you – what is there? It is out of love that she says all this, you are a very lucky girl. Some families do not let their daughters-in-law stop working the entire pregnancy.'

'I would rather work,' said Nisha sullenly.

'Nishu, it is a question of attitude. Are you determined to be unhappy? Should anything happen, you will be the first to cry. What is making suits compared to a baby? Suits will always be there, you think the market is running away?'

'Pooja is running away with my business.'

'You are the clever one, you can always start again. There is a time and a place for everything. Now is the time for you to have children and enjoy them. If your mind is always somewhere else, you will be irritable. If you do too many things, you will be exhausted and create tension.'

'I told everybody I wanted to keep on working,' cried Nisha into the wilderness, 'and nobody is letting me.' Tears began to fall. They were bad for the baby. A compromise was reached.

It was arranged that Mohseen Khan would visit her every day, while Pooja manned the home front. 'Don't worry, Didi, everything will be all right, I am here, nah?'

However, Mohseen Bhai did not like commuting between Daryaganj and Karol Bagh. He demanded seven hundred rupees a month extra for transport costs. 'Mohseen Bhai,'

Nisha cajoled as she tried to negotiate him down to four hundred, 'this is just for a few months. I cannot afford so much. Please bear with me.'

But Mohseen was busy with his own complaints. It was not easy working for Nisha's Creations, so much interference from so many different people, the tailors also didn't like it. With the per suit incentive Nisha had started they were all affected when demand fell. They had their families to think of.

Nisha could negotiate no more, she had no choice. But seven hundred extra in overheads meant she had to price her suits that much higher. And to top it all Mohseen Khan was now permanently dissatisfied.

In frustration she turned on her husband. He didn't really notice her unless she made a fuss.

'How will I retain my clients if I do not provide them with suits?' she wailed softly, rocking back and forth. 'Before the wedding I was making two hundred and seventy, now even a hundred is difficult.' Managing her affairs now seemed a hopeless dream. Sitting in Daryaganj, she wasn't able to look after a business in Karol Bagh, let alone sustain its growth.

Arvind looked concerned. 'Don't you have someone to help you?'

'Pooja.'

'Then?'

'But it's mine, not hers. My sales are falling.'

'Arre, there is always ebb and flow in business. It grew, it will grow again. Right now you have to rest. Amma is worried about your health.'

'And only I am worried about my business. You don't care.'

'I do, I do. The day you are ready, we will hire a workshop for you here. But let the baby come. See, even with not travelling, you are always tired.'

'I am not.'

'Then why are you crying? Amma won't like it.'

Amma, Amma, always Amma. What about him? Though he was kind to her, she never felt any intimacy beyond fleeting moments in the dark. Did he like her at all? Was it her skin? Was the first one beautiful? She was sure she was.

That night she dreamt of Suresh. Suresh of the red mouth, unshaven look, gold chain, and hirsute chest, lean, slender, with liquid, loving eyes. He was lying on a sea of lotuses, mutely gazing at her. She couldn't go to him, there was too much water in between, she could only look at his face and feel her loss. His features blurred, he grew larger, threatening, he was on the roof, he was chasing her, she woke terrified.

It was just a dream, she told herself, I am all right. I am all right. She stroked her husband's back, he turned and took her in his arms.

Maybe feeling sad is part of life, whatever you get you are not happy. She had the respect of her husband, yet she was dreaming of Suresh. Her skin itched less now, but still she longed and was dissatisfied.

Every morning she threw up. The nausea lessened in the afternoon, only to come back at night. Even one small roti had to be forced down.

Despite all this, her husband was distant. The fuss made over her came from her mother-in-law. Once when the old woman was near she wondered out loud, lying tiredly on the bed, staring at damp marks on the ceiling, whether this was a child he wanted. And for the next hour the mother expounded on her son's character. He is always like that, nothing he shares, even his business worries he keeps to himself, I tell him what do you have a family for, but he doesn't listen, and ever since that happened, it has been worse, he has gone so inside himself, when his son comes he will be different, really he is too-too good. As she talked, Nisha remembered it was the mother who had been wanting him to marry, and if that was the way it was, what was she doing on this bed?

*

Arvind had returned home, taken off his shirt, and Nisha could smell the stale odour of his sweat. There had been no electricity for much of that day, and in the shop, the generator could not take the load of air-conditioners.

Now his skin glowed with a sallow, yellowish sheen, his eyes were red and weary. It must have been a hard day, she thought sympathetically.

'Should I get your tea here? Do you want to lie down?'

He turned towards her. 'Have you had yours?'

'I was waiting for you.' Had he forgotten she waited for him every day?

He nodded. 'No, I'm not so tired. Bring it to where Amma is sitting.'

Amma, again Amma, never any thought for her. Never how have you been, is your back paining, has the baby started kicking yet? Anger began to tremble below her considerate exchanges. Why did he have to marry if he was to treat his wife to indifferent looks, she thought, sweeping aside the tenderness he showed at night. She wanted something in the day as well. Not this preoccupation, not this looking through, not this ignoring of their coming child. If he felt so little for her, she should go home to her tailors, why enact this farce here? Mohseen Bhai would love it, though no doubt he would refuse to let go of his transportation allowance.

She said nothing for the moment, going to the kitchen to make tea. When she returned, her husband was sitting silently with his mother. She could sense the bond between them.

She thought of how Pooja's presence had weakened the link between her mother and brother, and wondered miserably at her fate. Restlessly she served them, restlessly she walked between the kitchen and the veranda.

That night, when her husband made his move towards her, she kept her back turned. She was operating on instinct now, and instinct told her he would not take his hand away.

'What is it?' he asked.

'You don't love me,' she replied. 'Why did you marry me?'

They were on delicate ground. The word love had not been used between them. She was shy, he was a widower. But now that she was going to be a mother, she could be more assertive.

'You are being silly,' he replied. 'Can you complain of mistreatment?'

'If you are never going to talk or share things with me, why don't you take me back to my mother's house? You have done your duty, married and made me pregnant. When the baby is born you can collect it.'

'Why are you talking such rubbish?'

But this was a question Nisha could not answer. 'You are not interested,' she repeated, turning her back on him. She heard him sighing, but she heard nothing else.

She lay awake, no doubt he did too, but her own misery was too large for her to pay attention to anything else. Her feelings settled themselves into the back of her neck, at the base of her head, where it embraced her shoulders, and shot little tentacles into her hair.

She was careful to keep still. The fact that her head was hurting was startling. All that was wrong with her life had so far flowed to the surface of her skin.

The next day she refused to get up.

'What is the matter?' asked her husband.

As though he cared. 'Nothing,' she said, face to the wall.

'Should I call Amma?'

'I don't want Ammaji.'

'What do you want then?'

She had never allowed herself to look at her wants. Whether it was love, importance, attention, it was all going to be denied.

'Nothing.'

He stood there irresolute. 'Come, get up,' he said, stretching his hand towards her. Through her half-closed eyes she saw his brown hand, flat, hard palm, the edge of his white kurta crumpled from the night.

The throbbing pain at the base of her head made it easy to resist. 'My head is hurting. I can't get up.'

'Do you need to go to a doctor?'

'It is all right.'

Again the hesitation. Finally she heard him go to the bathroom. She waited for him to say something after he got ready. He stood next to her. Through her lashes she could see the crease in his brown trousers, the socks on his feet (he would not wear his shoes till he was in the outer room of the house), the gold watch her parents had given him on his wrist, his fingers drumming against his side.

'Do you want anything to eat?'

She shook her head slightly.

'Is it still hurting?'

To this she gave no reply. What did he think, she was doing this for fun?

The morning passed. Arvind must have said something to his mother because she was not disturbed. All day in bed and the house felt different. She put her hand under her nightie, and rested it on her stomach. She could feel the swell. Slowly she caressed herself, and the baby inside her. Her agitation ebbed. Whatever will happen, will happen, she thought. She had grown up listening to this fatalism, now she felt its consoling power. Whatever has to happen, will happen. She could not control events, she could not demand love. This had already been made clear, but now she was willing to accept it.

Next day was Sunday, the day the Daryaganj market closed. Her husband was free.

'Let's go out,' he suggested.

Nisha was silent.

'All right?'

'Who all?'

'Just you and me.'

'Ammaji might mind.'

'Nobody will mind. Now come on. We can have lunch at Connaught Place, wherever you feel like. Do you feel like anything?'

'Chaat. I really want chaat – fried potato chaat, with lots of lemon, gol gappa, and dahi paapri. Ice-cream, I want sour orange ice-cream.'

He smiled at her. 'You're like a child.'

A day of roaming around Connaught Place. It wasn't the things they bought so much as his hand under her elbow, her face turned towards him, the concern in his voice when he asked if she was tired, the buying of ice-cream cones from Nirulas, the being together, them two. No wonder Pooja minded so much when I came with her and Raju to India Gate, thought Nisha, that moment of being an unwelcome third, now lost in the mists of time, wondering how she could have been hurt by so small and natural a thing.

And Nisha's Creations? Slowly, slowly it left her hands.

One day, to her surprise, Raju came to see her. Was something wrong? No, no, nothing. They made small talk, but how small can talk be? After many silences Raju mentioned the boutique.

'Pooja has been managing nicely,' he commented.

'I started it – once you start a thing it is not so difficult to continue,' replied Nisha smartly.

'Of course, Didi, it is all because of you,' agreed Raju hastily.

'It is not easy doing business,' interjected her mother-in-law.

'After the baby it will be even more difficult, don't you think?' continued the brother chattily.

Nisha refused to be drawn into this useless conversation. 'Do you want some more tea and pakoras?' she asked.

'Arre, why are you asking?' demanded the mother-in-law. 'Give, give.'

Nisha disappeared again into the kitchen to tell the maid to fry more pakoras and make another cup of tea. She knew how much Pooja fed her brother when he came home.

'Jijaji not home yet?' asked Raju, delicately slurping at his cup.

'He has to work very hard,' sighed the mother. 'Too-too hard. Nobody to help him.'

Nisha waited. Why had Raju really come? 'Everything all right at home?' she repeated, to give him a lead.

'Yes, everything is all right.'

'Tell Pooja that soon I will take the business back. *He* was just saying we could move it here.'

'Yes, yes, plenty of place here,' lied the mother.

'And Ammaji is willing to help,' lied Nisha.

Raju drank his tea and went home.

Ultimately it was Rupa Masi who was deputed to make the delicate suggestion that Pooja thought it time she take over everything, the responsibilities, the liabilities, the interest, the good will, the profits, the sense of occupation, everything. Only because of Nisha's circumstances, otherwise what was there? She wouldn't even offer.

Nisha ignored the latter part of the speech. 'Is this what everybody wants?' she demanded bitterly.

'Your father will not allow Pooja to take over unless you are happy about it.'

'Without Papaji, they would not do even this much, I know.'

'Well, he is insisting. So, beti, unless you agree nothing will happen.'

Nisha was silent. She didn't tell her aunt of the immediate relief she felt as she heard the proposal. Just to let it all go and sleep, sleep, sleep. To not think of fashion, the latest designs, laces, fabrics, colour schemes, embroidery patterns, to not co-ordinate dyers, tailors, arri workers, to not have to try and placate Masterji, to concentrate on what was happening inside her body.

'You know, beti, you can always restart a business. You have shown a flair for it. But this time with your baby, this will not come again.' Rupa Masi choked and further words failed her.

'You talk to your husband, see if he won't agree with me,' she finally said as she left.

Arvind did agree with Rupa Masi, as Nisha had known he would. 'Let your sister-in-law have it, you can always start something again. We will hire a place near here, so it will not be difficult for you. Close to the shop, I can also keep an eye on the workers.'

He did care, there would be a future. But not at the moment. Why was she clutching on so? After so much time away it didn't even feel completely hers. 'All right,' she sighed, 'let it go.'

She stipulated that Pooja could not use the name Nisha's Creations. That good will, that reputation was not transferable. One day she would resurrect it, one day it would be there, waiting for her.

By the time the next batch of suits were ready, they were labelled Pooja's Creations with an alacrity that suggested the labels had been ordered before Nisha was even asked.

The months passed. At seven months, the gode bharaiye, the presents from Nisha's parents' house for the new child.

'Beti, we will not display anything,' said her mother-in-law. 'Why attract the evil eye?'

By now the proprietary note in her voice had become so customary that Nisha took it for granted. Her concerns were her family's concerns. There was safety and security in that.

From time to time she asked her husband, 'Suppose the baby is a girl?'

'It doesn't matter, whatever it is, is God's gift.'

Nisha could only suppose this attitude sprang from years of suspecting he might never be a father. She had not realised how lucky it would turn out to be, marrying an issueless widower.

She asked her mother-in-law.

'The child should be healthy, that is all,' she replied. 'If it is a girl she will be ghar-ki-Lakshmi.'

Nisha knew that part of that Lakshmi would come from gifts her family would give, but still she felt reassured. She looked down at her belly. The skin was stretched, the eczema scars looked lighter. She hardly itched any more, and never to draw blood.

Night and day the baby kicked. What force there is in the child, she wondered, it had to be a boy, a girl could not be so vigorous.

This was something every relative unanimously concurred in. 'It is a boy,' said Amma confidently. 'Look, all the weight is in the front, it is a boy.'

'It is a boy,' said her mother. 'You are always eating sweet sweet things. Pooja ate so much sour, I knew she was carrying a girl. I don't know why she is taking so long to conceive again. Raju says she is still young, but they may have to try two, three times for a boy, they should start now.'

Nisha didn't say that Pooja's Creations was probably occupying the space of a baby. Strange how distant she felt from it. Her workshop was a dream away; with the baby kicking inside her, she felt no regret, no sadness, only faint nostalgia mediated through the immensity of her belly.

The monsoon receded, the days grew less muggy, winter touched the air, but still Nisha felt hot all the time, each night she tossed and turned trying to find a position that was comfortable. 'I'm so tired yet I can't sleep,' she moaned in order to wake her husband. 'Oh when will this baby come? I can't eat either, there is a sour feeling at the back of my throat.'

Arvind looked anxious. 'Shall I call Amma?' he asked, driving her to fury.

'What can she do? Let her sleep in peace – go join her if you like.'

'What rubbish you talk,' he commented.

'No – go.'

He sighed, and stroked her belly. She liked the feel of his hand on the tight, hard, dry skin. 'Patience,' he murmured, 'patience. It is almost time.'

She lay there in the dark, her back hurting, feeling the motions of his hand ceasing slowly and his heavy breaths deepening into snores.

During the last trimester, Dr Mehra informed the mother-in-law that Nisha was carrying twins. Twins!

The mother-in-law's joy knew no bounds. 'The day I saw you I knew you would be good for my son. Truly we are blessed, after so long.' Tears ran down her cheeks in the taxi.

And Arvind, how would he react?

That night he stroked her belly without her having to resort to tears. 'My father would have been pleased,' he murmured. 'He loved children.'

'Perhaps I have twins because he is being incarnated in our child. They say parents and children have bonds that never break,' Nisha whispered back.

'Maybe,' he sighed. 'You have made Amma very happy.'

'And you?' she asked sharply.

Without a pause, without the silence that used to mark every emotional exchange, he replied, 'Me too.'

'If they are both girls?'

'Even then. They will bring prosperity into the house, enough to pay for their dowries. And the boy to come will have two sisters, he will not be lonely.'

Ten months after Nisha's marriage, twins were born. One girl, one boy. Her duty was over – God had been kind, however hard it was to believe.

Forty days later, during the naming ceremony, Nisha sat in

front of the havan, and through the smoke gazed at her tiny babies. Their colour was the way hers had been before blemishes had come upon her life. The mother-in-law sitting next to her held the fragile boy in her lap. Just like his grandfather, she murmured as she caressed his cheek, a statement she made every day, to the approval of all. The more robust girl lay balanced on her mother's knees, eyes shut, cradle cap stuck to her scalp. Nisha clutched her daughter tightly to her breast. Her milk began to spurt and stain her blouse. She quickly adjusted her palla and looked up. Surrounding her were friends, relatives, husband, babies. All mine, she thought, all mine.

Acknowledgements

In my research I was helped by Uma Arora of Karol Bagh, the Walia household on Ramjas Road, Nidhi Dalmia, Vimla Kapur, Vijay Kapur, Anita Kapur, Anil Kapur and Prem Shankar Sehgal.

Ira Singh as usual had to read the manuscript with indefatigable patience many many times. Anuradha Marwah offered invaluable advice on both style and content. Ashok Chopra verified facts painstakingly. For the third time Julian Loose brought a sensitive understanding to my writing. I am grateful he is my editor.